*for Katie*

# BEFORE HE
# FINDS HER

MICHAEL KARDOS is the author of the award-winning story collection, *One Last Good Time* and the novel *The Three-Day Affair*. He currently co-directs the creative writing program at Mississippi State University.

Also by Michael Kardos

*The Three-Day Affair*

*One Last Good Time: Stories*

*The Art and Craft of Fiction: A Writer's Guide*

# MICHAEL KARDOS

# BEFORE HE FINDS HER

A Mysterious Press
book for Head of Zeus

First published in 2015 by Mysterious Press,
an imprint of Grove/Atlantic, New York.

This edition first published in the UK in 2015 by Head of Zeus Ltd.

9 7 5 3 1 2 4 6 8

A CIP catalogue record for this book is available from the British Library.

ISBN (HB): 9781784082482
ISBN (TPB): 9781784082499
ISBN (E): 9781784082475

Printed and bound in Germany by GGP Media GmbH, Pössneck

Head of Zeus Ltd,
Clerkenwell House,
45-47 Clerkenwell Green,
London, EC1R 0HT

WWW.HEADOFZEUS.COM

*It was the truths that made the people grotesques . . . It was his notion that the moment one of the people took one of the truths to himself, called it his truth, and tried to live his life by it, he became a grotesque and the truth he embraced became a falsehood.*
—Sherwood Anderson, *Winesburg, Ohio*


*It's the end of the world as we know it (and I feel fine).*
—R.E.M.

# PART ONE

# 1

## My White Whale, Set Free

*September 22, 2006 * by Arthur Goodale * in Uncategorized*

Three weeks since my last entry, and I don't know if I'll be writing again any time soon. So please forgive me for today's lack of brevity.

Anyone who's followed this blog for any amount of time knows the premium I place on honesty and candor. So here's my disclosure: I'm writing today from a hospital bed in the critical care unit at Monmouth Regional Hospital. Last Sunday—all day, apparently—I was suffering from congestive heart failure. But who knew? Look, I'm a smoker and always have been. (Readers of this blog know all about my failed attempts to quit). For years, decades, I've awaited the numb

3

left arm, tightening in the chest, those unambiguous precursors to a fast demise, or at least a stagger to the telephone before collapsing, maybe bringing down the living room curtains on top of me. Something dramatic. But mild back pain?

I had spent most of that day bent over the garden, pulling weeds and tying a few droopy tomato vines to their stakes in the hopes of keeping my plants productive until the first hard frost. Why wouldn't my back be aching? In the past, my cure was always three Advil and a couple of James Bond flicks on the TV while I lounged on the recliner. So that's how I treated my symptoms this time—with international intrigue and soothing British accents. And a couple of vodka martinis.

When Tuesday afternoon rolled around and the pain was no better, I called my doc. He said come in. I came in. Now I'm here in the hospital, where I'm told I might not leave.

Maybe if I had swallowed a couple of aspirin instead of those Advil, the attending cardiologist tells me. Maybe if I had driven straight to the hospital or dialed 911 instead of waiting two days. But why would I have done any of those things? That's not what you do when you're an old fool with a back sore from overdoing it in the vegetable garden. You don't dial 911. You watch television. You take a nap.

Who will pick my last tomatoes?

I'll stop being macabre. You deserve better than that. And there *are* some of you—both here in New Jersey and beyond. Last month this blog had 2,300 views, about 75 per day. I can hardly

4

imagine 75 people being interested in my musings, but you're real, my readers, and apparently you're from all across the country and as far away as Vietnam and Australia. I'm constantly amazed. Such a contrast from my newspaper days, with its ceaseless and frantic scramble to increase paid circulation— that is, before we became a free paper in order to focus on ad revenue, and before we gave *that* scheme up and sold out to Kingswood Holdings, Inc.

So, my 75 loyal followers, please know that I'm deeply grateful to you for reading my postings these past three years and for sticking with me through my frequent meanderings and digressions. Despite my abiding respect for the strict conventions of newspaper writing, I've come to derive deep satisfaction and enjoyment from maintaining this blog, where word limits don't matter, where impartiality is besides the point, and where I may freely indulge in conjecture, parentheticals, and serial commas.

For obvious reasons, I hope this won't be my last post. But if it is, it is. I'm 81, a ripe age by any measure. I suppose that no age ever feels old enough, but with my daily cigarettes (a habit I picked up almost *seventy* years ago) and, with the exception of my own tomatoes, the takeout-menu-diet of a lifelong bachelor, I know I'm lucky to have made it this far. I don't regret never marrying or having children. If I had met the right woman and passed up the opportunity to spend my life with her, I'd feel different. Maybe it was the long hours on the job, or maybe it was my comically long nose. Regardless of the cause of my lived-alone life, the fortuitous effect is that my departure, when it happens, will be met with the sadness of quite a few, but the genuine grief of none.

Was I married to my work? This cliché might be true. If so, I ask that you don't pity the relationship. It was a strong marriage. I have loved being a newspaperman—publisher and editor and, above all, reporter. I can recall no better feeling than those moments when I was in thrall to a story that finally snapped together—the facts, and my particular way of telling them. Better than striking oil, I tell you.

What a shame that this time-honored industry is rapidly vanishing and becoming overrun by ideologues and illiterates. Our democracy requires better. But this is a problem for younger minds than mine to solve.

The title of today's post alludes, of course, to the unattainable object of Captain Ahab's obsession. This morning, a young male nurse entered my hospital room to check my vitals and the wounds in my chest and leg. (I had bypass graft surgery on Wednesday morning.) I asked this nurse what day it was, and he said, Friday, September 22. I told him that today was the fifteen-year anniversary of the Miller killings.

"The what?" he asked.

I was taken aback, though I shouldn't have been. The young man would have been a child when the murders took place. Still, Silver Bay is a peaceful town, even today, and the crime had been a major story in the news for weeks. I told him so.

"I guess maybe it sounds a little familiar," he said, having the sense to be kind to his loony, dying patients.

Faithful readers of this blog know that the Miller case is my white whale. In all the years I have lived in this town, there have been only five homicides. One man dialed 911 himself within hours and turned himself in. Three times, the men (they were all men) were booked within a couple of weeks and pled guilty to lighten their sentences. Ramsey Miller is the only accused who got away.

I lived—live—just one neighborhood away from where the Millers once did, and I was on the scene that morning only minutes after hearing the blaring of the first-response vehicles. I drove my car the few blocks to Blossom Drive and witnessed the aftermath of a terrible event, one that I've never fully been able to get past.

It shook us all. A couple of days after, I remember ordering my cup of coffee and plate of eggs at the Good Times Diner, same as every morning, and the waitress (Tracy Strickland, who always wore a "kiss my bass" pin on her waitress uniform) sat in the booth across from me, placed her elbows on the table, cupped her head in her hands, and wept. She was about Allison's age. I didn't pry. But you see, Silver Bay is a small community, and Allison Miller was the sort of woman you couldn't help admiring, and Meg was a girl just shy of three who deserved to grow up.

A couple of months earlier, while shopping in the Pathmark one afternoon, I happened to find myself in the same aisle as Allison and Meg. Allison, pushing a full shopping cart, was following her daughter, who was running in my direction and calling out the colors of the floor tiles. Finding herself beside me, Meg tugged the leg of my slacks, and commanded: "Pick me up!"

I hadn't held a small child for many years, maybe even decades—not since my niece and nephew were small.

"Up!" the girl repeated.

"You'd better do it," her mother said.

I lifted the girl—she was amazingly light—and for thirty seconds, maybe a minute, I held her, breathing in the smell of baby shampoo, while her mother hastily pulled items from the shelf and placed them into her cart. Meg seemed content to be held, watching her mother.

"Thank you, Arthur," Allison said, taking back her daughter and flashing a smile.

We had introduced ourselves not long before, while waiting together at the dentist's office. I hadn't expected Allison to remember my name or who I was, and now I didn't know what to say. Despite the countless interviews I've conducted, I've never been much good at small talk—especially with someone who was, even when harried in the supermarket, a knockout. So I nodded, maybe mumbled something. She coaxed her daughter back to sitting in the shopping cart and rounded the end of the aisle. I finished my shopping and paid. When I went outside, Allison was loading bags into her car. Meg was in the cart, kicking her legs. I considered strolling over and saying something neighborly. But it was late afternoon, and the sun was making this pretty image of the two of them—mother and daughter—and I decided not to ruin the tableau.

8

I never saw either of them again.

From time to time, when it seemed appropriate, I have posted pertinent public documents about the case, notable media coverage, and my own musings (here, here, here, and here, and less articulately in perhaps a dozen other posts). If you are a new reader of this blog (unfortunate timing, if so), here is a brief summary:

On Sunday afternoon and evening of September 22, 1991, the Miller family hosted an outdoor block party. As many as fifty people were in attendance over the course of several hours. The party ended around 9 p.m. Sometime later that night, after the guests were gone, an inebriated Ramsey brutally murdered his wife, Allison. (I won't rehash those details; the curious can read about it here.) The next day, authorities found her body in the backyard and began a search for Ramsey and their young daughter. Two witnesses placed Ramsey at the Silver Bay Boatyard the night before, around 10 p.m., and one of them saw him board his motorboat carrying a bundle the size and shape of a small child. Neither Ramsey nor Meg was ever seen again. The boat was never found. The prevailing theory—the correct one, in my view—is that Ramsey took the boat out to sea and threw his daughter overboard, either alive or already dead.

Because of the condition of Allison Miller's body when it was found, the time of death can only be estimated, and some experts disagree on which came first, the murder or the boat ride. The order matters when trying to create a chain of causality. Had Ramsey planned to commit both murders? Or did one horrible deed make the other, after it was committed, seem unavoidable?

(Writing this, I feel nauseated all over again. Apparently it's possible to feel ill on top of already being critically ill.)

I don't believe the case will ever be solved. Scratch that. As far as I'm concerned, the case was solved long ago: Ramsey committed two murders and fled. So what I mean is, I don't believe there will ever be sufficient answers that might get to the heart of what happened, and why. Nor do I believe that Ramsey's whereabouts, assuming he's still alive, will ever be known—especially now that Detective Esposito, who worked the case diligently and always had the good grace to return my phone calls, has retired to South Carolina, where the weather is better and the golf plentiful. He has earned his retirement, and I suspect he's making the most of it. Unlike the bitter and lonely protagonists of many detective novels, Danny always planned to spend his golden years on the fairways with his lovely wife, Susan. He knows better than to waste his time on a sad, frustrating, and hopelessly cold case.

It really is the strangest case.

If there was a motive, no one could ever uncover it. The family had no history of violence. Ramsey was, as far as anyone knew, a devoted husband and father. His run-ins with the law were long behind him. There isn't even a satisfactory explanation for the party that preceded the murders. Most news reports claim it was to celebrate Ramsey's 35th birthday, but that wasn't for another week. Others claim it was simply a block party—but the neighborhood never had one before, and the Millers apparently footed the whole bill. Was the party yet another part of Ramsey's elaborate plot? And then there's the mysterious fact of Ramsey's big rig, which he inexplicably sold the Friday before the murders. The truck was his livelihood. Why would he sell it?

Some in the community hold on to the hope that after Allison's murder, the little girl was kidnapped by her father and spared. That maybe she's still alive somewhere. I understand why people would choose to believe that, preferring to avoid thinking the unthinkable. But I've never believed in fantasies and refuse to start now. The man who just murdered his wife did not then motor out to sea to go stargazing with his young daughter before disappearing with her. It didn't happen that way.

The unthinkable is what happened.

Can I prove it? Not without the little girl's body, which is never going to be found. You can't dredge an ocean. But everything about this case has felt like dredging an ocean. Violent as it was, the crime was small-town. Ramsey Miller was no mastermind. Why did he do it? How did he vanish? The not-knowing has kept me awake for more nights than I care to recall. Only recently have I begun to admit to myself that the absence of proof is, in this case, a permanent condition—or at least a condition that will outlive me.

It helps to remind myself that supplying proof is the problem for a district attorney or maybe a newspaperman, and I haven't been a newspaperman for years. I'm simply a blogger and an old man who, approaching his own big sleep, feels done with all the hedging and the caveats and deigns to tell the plain truth.

So here it is: 15 years ago on this day there was a party, two murders, and a boat ride. Other than that, I know not one damn thing and never will.

My doctors are demanding that I rest, not type. I need to focus on my health, but they're asking me the sort of questions that lead me to conclude that "my health" is a euphemism for "my death." Which means that the time has come for me to close the laptop and bequeath my white whale to some younger, cleverer sea captain.

Bon Voyage,
Arthur Goodale

P.S. Please forgive me for disabling the "comments" feature on this particular post. Should these be my last written words, I'd prefer they not be followed by off-topic political sniping.

*Posted by Old Man with Typewriter at 9/22/2006 2:23 PM | Comments are disabled.*

# 2

September 22, 2006

Melanie Denison—for that was her name now—had ruined breakfast.

Otherwise, it was an ideal fall morning. There was no better time of year in Fredonia, West Virginia, everything still growing and sweet smelling, one last push before the first hard frost.

Her uncle Wayne stood by the window overlooking the back-yard garden, where tomatoes and peppers clung to worn stalks. "You know I love you," he said, turning to face her, "but what you're doing . . ."

Most mornings, one of them would say grace and then they would eat together as a family. Then Melanie would clean the dishes, Kendra would shower and dress for work, and Wayne would go outside to weed or cut the grass or spray dirt off the trailer's vinyl siding with his power washer—anything to be outdoors for a few minutes before driving to the Lube & More in Monroeville to work underneath cars for eight hours.

"You really don't have to worry," Melanie said. "I'm being careful."

"I don't doubt that, honey," he said. "But you have to see it's still dangerous."

Maybe. But the fact was, she was nearly eighteen. And the family's rules, in place for so long, were becoming harder than ever to abide.

*You go straight to school. When school is done, you come straight home.*

In high school, she could understand. But last Tuesday she'd stayed on campus at the community college to get lunch with some fellow freshmen. A couple of days later, she'd driven alone to the JC Penney in Reynoldsville to find jeans that fit her better. She actually had to convince herself that these weren't major transgressions.

"It's just that a *newspaper*, of all things," her aunt said.

Melanie didn't like keeping secrets from them. She had told them about joining the staff of the college paper as a way of testing the waters: see how they react, then decide what else they could know.

Well, they were flunking the test royally. Melanie set the glasses of juice on the table and asked her aunt, "What do you mean, 'of all things'?"

But she knew. She was a seasoned pro at imagining how her father might find her even after all these years.

Her aunt and uncle? Also pros.

"Does the paper have a website?" Uncle Wayne asked.

"I don't think so," Melanie said—though of course it did.

"Still," he said, "your picture could end up on the Internet."

It all sounded so paranoid, it was easy to forget that her aunt and uncle hadn't chosen to live like this, hidden away in a remote hamlet in West Virginia. But the U.S. Marshals had determined that this was best place for them all to "relocate," which meant to hide. Which was why, at seventeen, Melanie had never been to a city, had never stayed in a hotel or traveled farther than Glendale for its music and hot-air ballooning festival. She'd never ridden in an airplane or seen the ocean. Never met a famous person. She had hiked in the Allegheny Mountains but had never eaten sushi or a fresh bagel. She had twice seen tornados funneling in the distance but had never attended a dance or a football game.

Whenever she felt herself becoming too critical of her aunt and uncle, she would wait until she was alone in the house, open her uncle's desk drawer, and read through the horrible letters from the U.S. Marshal's office that he kept hidden there—letters she'd first come across innocently enough years earlier while rummaging for a pencil. The letters were horrible because they were uniformly brief, never more than a paragraph or two, and because they said nothing. Or, rather, they said the same thing again and again, which was the same as saying nothing. Ramsey Miller continued to elude the authorities; the authorities continued to fear for Melanie's safety. The letters were horrible, too, because they were crisp and clean and on nice paper (she pictured a tidy but bustling office where the employees joked with one another and talked about football games and their plans for the weekend), and they were horrible because of their consistently optimistic tone, despite there never being any real cause for optimism. She would return the letters to the manila file in the bottom desk drawer and remind herself not to depend on some hero in a police uniform ever coming to their rescue. Not after fifteen years. No, the only heroes were her aunt and uncle and the sacrifices they had made to keep her safe. But that didn't make it easy.

At least they were okay to be around. In winter, they played board games. They played cards. In spring, Melanie helped Wayne turn over the soil and plant the seedlings. Kendra bought cheap paperbacks from the CVS, and at sunup the two of them would carry their juice or coffee and whatever books they were reading out back, where they'd sit in adjacent chaise lounges, their privacy protected by the high hedges that surrounded their property, and by the woods beyond. Maybe once a month, as a treat, they ate at Lucky's Grill—always a weeknight at 4:30 p.m., when the place was mostly empty.

Her aunt homeschooled her through the eleventh grade, at which point Kendra admitted that she'd reached her limit as a teacher. So, frightened but excited by the idea of being away from 9 Notress Pass for seven hours each day, the next fall Melanie stepped onto the groaning yellow school bus each morning and afternoon, sitting either alone or next to Rudy, an autistic boy who pressed his nose against the window and said nothing. She didn't join any extracurricular activities. Didn't attend games. She went to school, ate alone in the cafeteria, and came home.

Still, that uneventful high school year had been a morsel of freedom, and now she found herself wanting more. After all, she couldn't stay shut inside the trailer forever, could she? If she were to die of natural causes at the age of ninety-five, having never seen or done a single thing, what kind of victory would that be?

Many of Melanie's high school classmates were bound for West Virginia University. They wore Mountaineer T-shirts and talked about how "we" were doing in various sports, as if they were already gone. Melanie made one weak attempt to convince her aunt and uncle that being one of 25,000 students would make her inconspicuous. She let herself fantasize a little about living in a dorm, going to football games, meeting boys. Making friends.

That TV show *Friends* had been on her whole life, it seemed, and she was always amazed by the smugness with which those six New Yorkers lazed in a coffee shop and took their banter-filled friendships and their freedom totally for granted. She let herself wonder if maybe college would be like that.

But college to her aunt and uncle meant student directories, ID cards, a wide-open campus where anyone could find her, follow her, do terrible things. In the end, they compromised. She could attend— part time—Mountain Community College, twenty miles up the road. She'd live at home and take a course or two at a time. Wayne would find her a used car and teach her to drive it. To help pay her way, she'd look for part-time work somewhere in Fredonia.

She accepted their best and only offer. If she couldn't be a Mountaineer, then she would be a Fighting Soybean.

"I don't understand your sudden interest in journalism, anyway," Wayne said, pulling himself away from the window. He uncapped a can of Folgers and spooned heaping tablespoons of grounds into the filter. He poured water into the machine and turned it on.

"It isn't sudden," she said. "I just think it's interesting."

"Well, sure it's *interesting*—but I still say it's a risk."

"Oh, everything's a risk, Uncle Wayne." She was suddenly queasy from the smell.

"That's right," Kendra said. "Everything is." She came over to Melanie and took her hand. "Baby, what's going on?"

"See? Exactly—I'm not a baby. And you both still think I am."

"You could never become a journalist," her uncle said. "You know that, right? Not until he's caught."

"He'll never get caught, and you know it." The words were out of her mouth before she could stop them.

"*Melanie.*" Kendra could always convey sympathy and admonishment in a single word.

"I'm sorry, Uncle Wayne." Melanie sighed. "It's just that I'm an adult. If I want to take a risk, it's really my decision." But that sounded ungrateful. "Come on, it isn't that big a risk when you think about it. And anyway, Ramsey Miller could be in Antarctica right now. He could be dead."

"He isn't dead, Mel."

"Yeah, but he could be."

Uncle Wayne shook his head. "I don't think so."

She was about to keep arguing over her father's hypothetical demise, ask how Wayne could be so positive he was still a threat, when suddenly her neck hairs tingled and she had her answer. She was sure of it.

There was a new letter. One that actually said something.

But she couldn't ask about it, since she wasn't supposed to know about the letters in the first place. And worst of all, as of about a year ago, Wayne no longer kept them in his desk.

The dripping coffee smelled so rancid that Melanie wanted to flee the house for air—except even the trees smelled sour to her these days. Feeling less confident, she said, "It's just a stupid college newspaper that probably nobody ever reads anyway. I don't see why you have to freak out." But she knew it was easy for her to talk a big game about taking risks when she had others devoting their own lives to her survival.

Her aunt and uncle glanced at each other. "Honey," Wayne said gently, "I love you dearly. But if you honestly think we're just freaking out for the heck of it, it only proves you need to think it through some more."

Underneath the table lay a rust-colored rug. She could make out the discolored blotch where as a flu-ridden child she'd vomited. She remembered that illness more than any other, lying on the sofa and watching game shows and soap operas for a week. Sipping ginger ale, nibbling on Saltines, throwing up into a trash can. Her aunt laying cool rags on her forehead, holding her, taking her temperature. Being there for her. Always being there.

Outside, the change of seasons caused migrating birds to sit invisibly in trees and caw at obscene decibels. Soon the leaves would change. But nothing ever changed inside these walls. Her aunt and uncle had furnished the hastily rented trailer with only two criteria: expediency and thrift—hence the Goodwill furniture, Walmart bookshelves, discount rug remnants. They assumed that their time here would be temporary. Once their initial panic had melted into a lasting, dull fear, they saw no reason (and had no money) to furnish the place a second time.

But it wasn't only the furnishings. The three of them—how they were around one another; the countless ways they'd arranged their lives so as not to be overtaken by their deepest dreads . . . a whole life could pass this way.

"It's always going to be like this, isn't it?" Melanie said. She wasn't feeling argumentative anymore. Rather, she was seeing the truth about her future, maybe for the first time. "No matter how old I am, or how old you are, or how long it's been. Nothing will ever change, will it?"

"When he's caught . . . ," Wayne began. At one time he must have said these words with conviction. Now they sounded perfunctory. Their life in Fredonia was all she knew and, more and more, all her aunt and uncle knew, too. The three of them hardly ever referred to the past at all, let alone to the "he" at the center of it. "When he's caught . . . ," Wayne began again. But he didn't seem able to finish the sentence, because it would have been pure fiction.

As if coming to the same realization, he frowned and poured himself a mug of black coffee. He set it on the kitchen table and steam rose into the air. Melanie willed herself not to gag.

"In other words, never," she said, her hand moving instinctively to her belly. She wanted to rub it, soothe it. The past couple of weeks, she'd been doing that in class, in bed, in the car. But she wasn't going to give up this secret—not yet—and so she lowered her hand again.

"When he's caught," her uncle said.

Midafternoon, Melanie was still feeling upset by the morning's argument with her aunt and uncle when, in her required math class, the instructor got to talking about fractals, mathematical designs that repeated at every scale. "Like how a head of broccoli has those florets," he explained, "each one containing self-similar smaller florets, which in turn contain even smaller ones." He was projecting images from his laptop onto the whiteboard behind him. "Or how the shoreline has the same basic windy shape whether you're standing on the beach and looking at a few yards of it, or if you're up in a satellite looking down at the whole coastline." He spoke slowly, with an air of strained mystery, as if he were a sorcerer and not a middle-aged community college instructor who wore the same blue blazer to each class session.

The fractals made for beautiful images, equations made visual and color-enhanced, and then an idea struck Melanie with such devastating force that her palms started to sweat.

"That's me," she muttered under her breath, staring at the projected image. "I'm a fractal."

"I beg your pardon?" The instructor stared at her. Melanie never spoke up in class, and the humming of the projector drowned out her voice. "Miss Denison, did you say something?"

She kept looking at the geometric shape, amazed because it was so obvious and true. She hid in her small house, hidden on a deserted road, itself hidden in a small town in a remote part of West Virginia. The same at every scale, her hiding, and so total it felt like a mathematical certainty.

"I'm sorry," she said to the instructor. She was calling attention to herself in the worst way—a way that wouldn't soon be forgotten. The weird, quiet girl was finally saying something. A few students chuckled nervously. "I just . . ." She looked around at the twenty or so other students and thought about this baby growing inside of her, how this smaller scale of herself would end up deeply hidden, too, layer under layer under layer.

This she couldn't allow.

"I have to . . ." She made fists of her clammy hands. She wouldn't have been able to finish her sentence even if she'd had the words. She stood and rushed out of the room, down the hallway, and into the bathroom, where she vomited into a toilet. She knelt on the floor until the queasiness subsided, went over to the sink, and splashed cold water on her face. She stood over the sink, rubbing her belly and taking controlled breaths, until she felt steady enough to drive back to Fredonia and wait for Phillip.

She sat on the concrete front steps of his rental house, feeling the breeze on her face and laundering time.

For the last couple of years, she had been reading old Nancy Drew and Hardy Boys mysteries in bed at night. She knew the books were for children, but she found them comforting to read at bedtime. The sleuths were always being bound and gagged, but they came out of every situation unharmed, and the criminal was always apprehended.

In one of the Hardy Boys books, a pawnshop accepted stolen money and then over-reported its sales. Money laundering, they called it. This is what I do, Melanie had immediately thought— only with time instead of money. The two hours of homework she told her aunt and uncle she was doing in her bedroom rarely took more than an hour. With the other hour, she paged through whichever copy of *People* happened to be stowed under her mattress. More recently, her job at the office supply store in town never demanded those extra hours that Wayne and Kendra believed she was putting in.

A trip to or from the college was the easiest way of all to launder time. From the start, she'd lied about her class schedule in order to give herself a full hour on either side of the day, two hours that belonged solely to her.

She didn't like deceiving her aunt and uncle, but they'd think it was a huge risk for her simply to be sitting here on this quiet street where no one ever walked (too hilly, no sidewalks) and where drivers, the few that passed by, had better things to do than take notice of her.

She wasn't the sort of person people noticed, anyway. A girl in Melanie's freshman composition class, Raquel something, was tall and blonde with huge blue eyes, and looked like she belonged on the red carpet. She carried herself with remarkably casual poise. *I'm happy to,* she'd say to their instructor whenever he asked her to pass out an assignment. *How was your weekend?* she'd ask whoever was sitting next to her. She chatted with people as if their presence made her day special.

Melanie didn't look like Raquel, and she didn't know how to act like Raquel.

And yet here Melanie was, and not Raquel.

It was 3:15. She didn't mind waiting, watching the cars pass. Her own home sat at the end of a long driveway on an unpaved road that cut through the woods. For a number of years, long before Melanie ever lived there, the road was nameless. Over time, a large, hand-painted No TRESPASSING sign that somebody had stuck into the ground where the road began suffered enough weather damage that those final three letters became too faded to read. First the neighbors, then others in town, and finally the U.S. Postal Service began referring to their road as Notress Pass.

Other than that sign and the story behind it, nothing was remotely notable about the road where she lived, which was the whole point. There were a dozen homes, about half of them trailers. On any given day, fewer than ten cars might rumble by. Now, sitting on Phillip's stoop, she imagined she was behind the wheel of each car that passed, on her way to somewhere. It didn't need to be somewhere amazing. Just somewhere else. She thought about Dorothy, singing about wanting to go somewhere over the rainbow. It'd been on TV again the other night, that stupid movie. Why on earth would Dorothy want to go home at the end? She's a hero, she has friends, everything is in beautiful color. What a tragedy, returning to Kansas.

The high school let out at 2:30. Unless there was a faculty meeting, Phillip was usually home by three. He wasn't expecting her today, though, and it wasn't until 3:40 that he came walking along up the hill, carrying a stuffed-full paper shopping bag. He owned a thousand-year-old Mazda hatchback, but it had broken down twice on his drive to West Virginia last year, and the brakes made an awful metal-on-metal scrape. He preferred to leave it in the carport, which meant lugging his groceries a half mile from the store.

Seeing Melanie, he smiled and set the bag down on the ground.

"A sight for sore eyes," he said. "An absolute vision."

The temperature had spiked since this morning, the humidity returning. Phillip still had on his coat and tie. His face glistened as if he had the flu.

She got up from the stoop and went over to him.

"Don't," he said. "I'm disgusting."

She moved in for an embrace. Phillip's heart thudded against her, and she imagined that she, and not the walk in the heat, had caused it. They separated, and she picked up the grocery bag while Phillip fished in his pocket for his keys and opened the door.

When they went inside, no cold blast of air greeted them—just some noisy overhead fans pushing around the oppressive air.

"What're you doing here?" he asked. "Your face is flushed—let me get you some water."

She was hot suddenly, and woozy. In Phillip's bedroom window was an old air-conditioning unit, but it only half worked and it blocked out the room's natural light. So she sat down on the sofa. The house was a one-bedroom shotgun shack, smaller than a single-wide, tidy, and decorated not so differently from her own home: everything bought cheaply or used.

He set the groceries on the kitchen table, filled up a glass of water, and handed it to her. She took a long swallow despite the taste and passed the cup back to him. He downed the rest.

"Your water tastes rusty," she said.

"Really?" He looked into the empty glass.

If only she had that girl Raquel's ability to put people at ease. But Melanie never had anyone to practice on. She knew it had to be frustrating for Phillip, trying to get close to someone who seemed capable of bluntness and secrecy and nothing in-between.

"I've been meaning to buy a filter," he said.

"Why don't you sit down." She patted the sofa beside her, but he was eyeing the grocery bag. "What's wrong?"

"Nothing," he said. "It's just . . . I don't want this stuff to spoil."

She knew what it was like when every dollar counted, each egg or ounce of milk something to take seriously. Her family had more money now that Kendra was freed up from tutoring Melanie and could work at the dollar store. But they'd never be a name-brand family. "Put everything away first. I'm sorry."

"Oh, don't be—just hang out for two seconds. Can I get you something else? Juice? Glass of wine?"

"No, nothing, thank you."

24

He stowed ground beef and yogurt and milk in the refrigerator
—the other stuff he left in the bag—and sat on the sofa beside her.

"I've never seen you move so fast," she said.

"I don't like to keep my women waiting."

"How many do you have?"

He smiled. "Dozens."

"I have something serious to tell you."

"Oh." He sat up a little straighter. "Okay."

She couldn't just say it, could she, with no preamble? Melanie placed a hand on Phillip's knee and forced herself to look
him in the eyes. "You're a really . . ." and to her horror, the
word that sprang to mind came straight out of a Hardy Boys
novel. *Swell.*

*Swell?*

She couldn't say that, of course, so she tried harder. ". . . a
really great guy. What I mean is, I care about you."

He pulled his gaze away and bit his lip. He looked absolutely
distressed. "You're breaking up with me."

"What?"

"That's what you're doing."

"It is?"

He looked at her again. "It isn't?"

Somewhere, Raquel was shaking her head in disgust. "Why
would I break up with you?"

"*I* don't know," he said. "Listen, Melanie, are you or aren't you
breaking up with me?"

"I'm not breaking up with you."

His body visibly relaxed. "Good. I'm really glad."

To launder time without arousing suspicion, you had to choose
small increments. But this was going nowhere, and soon her aunt
would come home from work, find her missing, and freak out. So
okay, forget Raquel and her comforting chatter.

"When I was two and a half," Melanie blurted out, "my father killed my mother and would've killed me, too, but I got away but so did he."

For several seconds, the only sound was the pulsing of the ceiling fan. Phillip watched her face, as if gauging how to react.

"Is this a joke?" he finally said, but with gentleness in his voice. He knew it wasn't. She'd been secretive with him from the start, evasive to the point of bizarre. Why he'd put up with her this long, she had no idea.

"I've never told anyone before," she said, looking down at her lap.

He took her hand. "Oh, Melanie," he said. "Oh, dear God."

This wasn't the secret she'd come here to tell. But Phillip needed to know that the woman carrying his baby was putting them all at risk. And when he led her toward the bedroom, saying, "Let's cool down," she said yes. She had already laundered enough time this afternoon, and, especially after the morning's disagreement with her aunt and uncle, she knew she ought to be getting home. But looking at Phillip looking at her, she realized that she was sick and tired of laundering time, and that she was desperate, instead, to spend it.

When they went into his bedroom and he said, "Do you think you can tell me more? Can you tell me everything?" she said yes again. And when he said, "You know you can trust me, don't you?" she willed herself to say yes one more time—the brief hesitation not a matter of distrust but rather disbelief.

*This is real*, she told herself. *This is happening. I am doing this. I am not alone.*

# 3

September 19, 1991

Ramsey Miller had been awake for thirty-two hours when he stopped his truck for the hitchhiker.

Usually he preferred solitude. Maybe some local FM station (music, never talk radio—the beauty was in getting away from talk); maybe just the engine's hum and his own thoughts, while the forests and fields and mountains slid past. Not that he objected in principle to helping a stranger move from Point A to Point B. But strangers always felt the need to talk—about nothing or, worse, about *something*. Life lessons, road wisdom . . . whatever foolishness they were urgent for you to hear. As if they were doing you the favor. And when they weren't trying to impress you, they were stinking up the upholstery with cigarette ash or worse. After the first year of driving his big rig, Ramsey swore off hitchhikers entirely.

In the six years since, he'd made only two exceptions. First one hardly counted: no older than thirteen or fourteen, walking along the narrow shoulder of the eastbound side of I-80 at sunrise, middle of nowhere, PA, thumb in the air while sheets of rain pummeled her. From fifty yards off, she could've been a kid. Wasn't till she was in the cab and shivering that Ramsey decided she was *slightly* older than that.

"I'm going to New York," she said through chattering teeth, arms wrapped around herself.

No luggage, no umbrella. Soaked hair and clothes. After she was settled in with the heater blasting, Ramsey radioed ahead and deposited her at the nearest exit, where a couple of cops were waiting to get to the bottom of that particular tragedy.

The second hitchhiker was female, too, but older—probably older than Ramsey. Her hair was graying and chopped real short, but she wasn't bad looking—she was someone you might take up space with in a bar near closing time and think, *Sure, okay.* This was back a few years, when Allie was early in her pregnancy and the two of them got to arguing sometimes about nothing. The argument had occurred just as he was leaving for eleven days on the road.

About ninety minutes later—too soon for the road's gentle rhythms to ease his temper—he saw the woman thumbing a ride on the Jersey Turnpike, a handful of miles north of the Delaware Memorial Bridge.

He slowed to a stop, waited for her to come over, and said hop in. A couple of hours later, past the DC beltway, she was hopping out again. It was Saturday, and all they'd done was listen to part of a Top-40 countdown. She'd been an ideal passenger: quiet, nonsmoking. He took an exit to refuel and let her off, stopping at the edge of a flat of asphalt away from the fuel pumps and the other trucks. She got her backpack from the floor by her feet and said, "I sincerely appreciate the lift."

"You do, huh?" Ramsey said. "Then how about a kiss?"

"No, I don't think so," she said, hand on the door. It was locked.

Ramsey didn't especially want to kiss her, but the embers of his argument with Allie still burned, and he had the vague sense that he was owed something by somebody. "What are you, a dyke or something?"

"I'd like to get out now." The woman was glancing back and forth between Ramsey and her side window, her hand still on the door.

He waited long enough—six, seven seconds—before pressing the power unlock. "Yeah, okay."

He watched her leave the truck and walk quickly toward the safety of others, his self-loathing already cresting like a wave.

*That ain't you anymore,* he repeated to himself later that afternoon, seated at the end of a neon-lit bar just off the interstate that stank of piss and sawdust. He pounded shots of well whiskey and thought about how in the past he'd been responsible for all kinds of meanness. His heart had, at times, been black, and he knew he was a lucky SOB to have escaped his teenage years—and, let's be honest, his twenties—without crossing that invisible line you can't ever uncross. But all that was in the past. He'd worked so fucking hard to become a changed man. A family man, and soon to be a father.

*That ain't you anymore.*

Afternoon bled to evening. He drank hard and woke up puking his guts out in his truck in the Walmart lot, no memory of the half-mile walk from his seat at the bar. He wasted half the next day washing his bedding in some laundromat and scrubbing the fabric in his cab until the stench was gone and the stains faded, reaffirming with each wipe of the rag his vow never again to stop for hitchhikers.

Now, this third and last time, he was doing it for his own safety. Company policy and federal laws were already being violated—he was fudging the log book and was way over the eighty-two-hour limit—but these were no longer concerns. All that mattered was getting home by Friday afternoon.

He had been seriously revved all week, content only with his foot on the gas, and had logged as many miles in seven days as another trucker might in ten or eleven. Jersey to Memphis to Kansas City to Phoenix. He was due home, 2,500 miles away, in three days, but all his life he'd wanted to see how the real Grand Canyon matched up against the pictures he'd seen. So he took the extra day and drove north, trusting his juices to keep flowing at the same rate they had been, until he was home again safe and sound.

A miscalculation.

Now it was Thursday night. An hour earlier, the sun had dipped below the tree line behind him, and with 1,100 miles still to go, every part of him was sagging and slowing. It dawned on him that his body, being a body, needed sleep.

A few years back, he'd have gone pharmaceutical. Now he cycled through the lawful tricks—air conditioner full blast, heavy metal station roaring, face slaps, extra large Diet Coke, fast food fries—and they all helped push him through Missouri to the Illinois border. But that left fourteen hours, more or less. And while the truck's fuel tank might've been full, Ramsey himself was out of gas—besides which, his time spent at the Grand Canyon had left him feeling magnanimous. So when the truck's headlights fell on the man thumbing a ride on the shoulder of I-70, Ramsey put on the brakes.

"You're a kind soul," the man said over the engine's idle. He looked as if hitchhiking were his chosen profession: all-weather jacket, thick shock of gray hippie hair tied into a ponytail, huge backpack.

Ramsey waited while the man climbed aboard, stuffed his backpack by his feet, and strapped on the safety belt.

"This ain't your first ride in a rig," Ramsey said.

"Brother, you got that right." The man shuffled in the seat, trying to find a suitable position. "All I ask is that you deposit me a little further along this road than I was when you met me."

"Can do," Ramsey said. "But I got a favor to ask."

"Shoot."

"I'll be honest with you—I don't ever pick nobody up these days. But I'm dog tired, and I need help staying awake so I can get home."

"Sorry, friend—but I been clean for over a decade."

Ramsey shook his head. "I mean talking. Conversation—so I don't nod off."

"Well, that I can do." He adjusted the seatbelt. "Where's home at?"

"Jersey shore. North of Asbury Park."

"Bruce Springsteen."

"Yup."

The man nodded. "You regular tired, or coming down off speed?"

"I ain't coming down off nothing," Ramsey said. "But I wouldn't call it regular tired, neither."

They were far enough now from St. Louis that the sky was no longer tinted orange from all the lights. Traffic had thinned somewhat, and the outlines of woods lining the highway faded in the encroaching dark. Soon Ramsey could stop worrying about the deer. He knew to plow on through—a deer won't damage your cab too bad—but the road was dominated by fools who jerked their cars from lane to lane and slammed on their brakes to avoid twigs and jackrabbits and imaginary things, never noticing the semi in the next lane. So he was always glad when the deer hour ended and dusk darkened to actual night.

"How long you been on the road?" the man asked.

"Six days, 4,200 miles," Ramsey said.

The man let out a low whistle, either impressed or skeptical. "But no speed?"

"Sober as a judge."

"No wonder you're tired."

Ramsey sighed. "No wonder I am."

"You overdue for a break?"

"Like I said, gotta get home."

They watched the windshield a moment, and then the man said, "Looks like I just may be your fairy godmother."

"Now how's that?" Ramsey asked.

The man shimmied a little in his seat and pulled his wallet from the back of his blue jeans. "You aren't in the habit of giving lifts," the man said, "and I'm not in the habit of offering this particular piece of assistance." He removed something from his wallet and held it up for Ramsey to glance at. A driver's license.

"I can't read it in the dark."

"Well, it says Class A."

"I'll be damned," Ramsey said.

"Quit driving in eighty-six—flatbed for five years, dry van for ten. Name's Ed Hewitt."

"Glad to know you, Ed," Ramsey said.

They went another half mile before Ed asked, "Am I being too subtle?"

"Come again?"

"You're fading, man—I'm offering to drive for a spell so you can recharge."

Ramsey looked over at Ed. "You aren't serious."

"I most certainly am."

"I never heard of a hitcher driving the truck," Ramsey said. "That'd be a first."

"I imagine it would—but I been in lots of trucks, and you look more beat than fellows coming down hard. You sure you aren't . . ."

"I told you, I don't do that," Ramsey said. "Not since the kid was born."

Ed nodded. "Well, the way I see it, if we help each other out these next few hours, it'll raise the odds that we're both alive when the sun comes up."

The idea was absurd. Yet over these last few months, Ramsey had learned to trust the universe rather than his own limited understanding of it. And when fate drops a hippie with a Class A commercial driver's license into your cab, the best course of action might well be to switch seats and catch a few hours of overdue dreams—especially with so much to do these next couple of days.

So he slowed the truck again and stopped it in the shoulder, and once the two men had exchanged seats, Ramsey gave Ed a brief tutorial. But the guy didn't need one. He wasn't bullshitting. He worked the clutch like he'd never retired.

*Maybe you are my fairy godmother,* Ramsey thought as Ed accelerated to the speed of traffic. "She's gonna shimmy some—I'm carrying balloon freight."

"Got it."

"And it's windy out there."

"I know," said Ed. "I was walking in it."

"And remember, you get stopped for anything, it's bigger trouble than either of us needs."

"But no bigger than dying," Ed said, "which is what I see happening if we let you stay behind the wheel much longer."

"Fair enough," Ramsey said, reclining way, way back.

He dreamed again of flying. This time, a gentle summer breeze carried him high over the ocean like a lone gull dipping in and out of the clouds. Not since he was a kid had his dreams been so vivid and wondrous. He swooped down over walls of baitfish moving in unison and shimmering in the sunlight. Bluefish and bonita glided through the water alongside flashier, supersaturated fish that his dream transplanted from the Caribbean. He could smell the brine. Closer to the shoreline, jagged hills of orange and red coral jutted up from the ocean floor. If he were to dive under the surface, he knew he'd be able to breathe underwater. But he stayed in the air, where the sun warmed his skin.

When he opened his eyes again, he didn't know where he was. His truck, the highway. A millisecond of panic—*asleep behind the wheel!*—until he noticed that he wasn't behind the wheel. He looked over to his left, and the rest fell into place.

In front of him, the truck's headlights cut into dark empty lanes. The canopy of stars overhead revealed no sign of morning. The dashboard clock showed 5:12.

"You could've woke me any time," Ramsey said, rubbing his eyes.

"No need to interrupt a peaceful ride."

"Whereabouts are we?"

"We went through Columbus about forty minutes back."

"What'd you do at the weigh stations?"

"Pretended they didn't exist."

Ramsey massaged his neck, unstiffening it. "We're making good time."

"Not bad. Though I sure could use a pit stop about now."

"Next rest area, I'll buy you breakfast. You earned it."

"Can do."

Ramsey yawned and shut his eyes again, feeling the engine's hum, the road beneath him, the soft push of air past the windows. When they exited the highway a while later, the blackness around them had become infused with hints of blue and gray. The border between tree and sky was starting to become visible.

*Today.* Ramsey's heart rate quickened at the thought. *Today, it begins.*

After sleeping all those hours, the remainder of the drive was nothing. Ramsey reached the Toys"R"Us distribution center in Wayne, New Jersey, by 9:30. It was a frequent stop, and he trusted the dock supervisor to have him in and out. Sure enough the unload moved, easy paperwork, and by noon he was pulling into the Monmouth Truck Lot.

The office was a narrow trailer up on cinder blocks. Inside, the walls were wood paneled, the floor linoleum. Same as when he'd bought his truck five years earlier. Probably the same as twenty years before that. On the grassy lot itself, trailers and cabs sat like vast tombstones surrounded by swaths of reedy weeds. Nothing about the place hinted at a successful business, but Bob Parkins, the owner, knew more about trucks than anyone Ramsey had ever met. Ramsey had bought his sleeper cab and trailer here on a tip from his fleet manager after two years of driving a company truck. Hard to say whether the move from employee to dedicated owner-operator was worth it, but the tip on where to purchase had been sound. Ramsey came away with a dependable truck at a fair price. Since then, he returned whenever his rig needed servicing beyond what he himself could do.

A counter split the trailer down the middle. Behind it were a couple of desks with papers piled everywhere, Bob's filing system. In a corner of the trailer, on the customer side, was an upended milk crate, and on it sat a coffeemaker, a stack of Styrofoam cups, and a container of powdered creamer.

"Help you?"

The guy behind the counter was some kid with a faded blue collared shirt and stupid-looking spiky hair.

"Where's Bob at?" Ramsey asked.

"Took the afternoon off," the kid said.

"You gotta be . . . " He felt the heat climb and took a breath. "Bob said he'd be in till three today. I talked to him from the road, coupla days ago. I made sure."

The kid shrugged. "Weather got good, and he hasn't had a day off in forever. He went fishing."

"What do you mean, 'weather got good'?"

The kid nodded toward the window. "You know—sunny. Warm."

There was a time before Ramsey started driving when he considered buying a fishing boat and chartering it out. The risks ended up being too great—bad weather, red tides, polluted water, expensive insurance—but you didn't need to be sea smart to know that today was no fishing day. "Wind's blowing hard out of the northeast. There's gotta be four- to six-foot seas out there."

The kid shrugged again. "I wouldn't know about it."

"You don't fish?"

"Nah, never did."

"Your old man never took you?"

"My old man's a piece of shit."

Ramsey sized the kid up some more. Shirt too large in the shoulders and neck. Probably a hand-me-down from the piece-of-shit himself.

"So Bob ain't coming back today?" Ramsey said it more to himself than to the kid. He was counting on Bob being here, making everything nice and easy.

"That's what taking the afternoon off means."

"You being smart with me?" When the kid's eyes narrowed, Ramsey backed off. The kid's name was Frank, according to the tag on his chest. He couldn't be older than twenty or twenty-one, and he had a lousy old man and a crappy haircut and God only knew what else. "Forget it. Listen, Frank. Bob sold me my truck five years ago. I need to sell it."

Frank looked out the window again. "The Kenworth?"

"The very one."

"What year is it?"

"Seventy-four."

"How many miles?"

"Million two."

"You bought it with how many?"

"About five hundred thousand."

He nodded. "Runs good?"

"Real good."

"You trading in for a newer one?"

"Nope."

"Then why do you want to sell?"

"That's my business."

The kid looked unsure whether to be courteous or a brat. He wasn't a bad-looking kid if you ignored the oversized shirt and that spiky haircut of his. But girls his age probably liked his hair that way. And he had an okay job, which was more than Ramsey had at his age.

"Bob'll be in tomorrow at seven," Frank said. "He can—"

"No, I need to sell it now."

"I can't just buy your truck, man."

"Name's Ramsey, son."

"Bob'll want to run diagnostics on it, test drive it—"

"I want fifteen thousand for the whole thing. Cab and trailer."

The kid looked confused. Ramsey suspected it wasn't a new look. "If it runs like you say, it's worth three times that."

"I don't want three times that."

"Well, like I said, Bob'll be in first thing tomorrow."

"Tomorrow's no good."

The kid looked at Ramsey like he was drowning. He hadn't learned yet that sometimes you just needed to do a thing. Like how Ramsey had left that fellow, Ed, at the rest stop earlier that morning. Ramsey was grateful to him for driving all those miles, but it was important to be alone for the last leg of his last drive in his truck. That's how he always imagined it. So when the two of them went into the rest stop for breakfast, Ramsey handed Ed a twenty and said to order something for the two of them. *I forgot something in my truck*, he said, and that was that.

"Tell you what," Ramsey said now. "Is Ralph over in the shop?"

"He and Andy, yeah."

"Give Ralphie a call. He knows me. He knows I shoot straight."

"He ain't sales."

"I *know* he ain't sales—just get him on the phone for me."

Frank looked relieved, having something to do. He pressed some buttons on the phone. Seconds later: ". . . and he says he's got to sell it *today*." He held the receiver to his ear, then said, "Yeah, okay," and handed the receiver to Ramsey.

"What the hell you doing?" Ralph said over the phone.

"I'm selling you my truck is what I'm doing," Ramsey said.

"You gotta let me look it over," he said. "Leave it here, come back tomorrow. We'll get you hooked up. Bob'll give you a fair price."

"It's got to be now, Ralph. Fifteen thousand in cash. You know I take care of my truck. You know it's a steal."

"Ain't my call—boss is *fishing*, man."

"Oh, he ain't catching nothing. Do him a favor. You know I'm on the up-and-up."

Ralph wheezed into the phone and said, "Put Frankie back on the phone."

Ramsey handed back the receiver.

"You sure about that?" the kid said. "But you ain't—" He grimaced. "All right, man, I'm just saying. Yeah, okay." He hung up the phone. "Looks like you got yourself a deal."

"That's good to hear," Ramsey said. "I appreciate you calling up Ralph like that." He nodded in the direction of the shop. "He lay into you a little bit there?"

"If shit goes down, it's on him, not me."

"Trust me," Ramsey said, "the truck's good." He glanced out the window. "Wind's gonna calm down over the weekend. That's when you want to be out in the ocean, not today. Saturday will be ideal. Sunday, too."

"Like I said, I don't fish."

"No, I suppose you don't," Ramsey said. "Well, find some other way to enjoy your weekend. You got a girl?"

The kid actually smiled. He had alarmingly bad teeth. "Yeah."

"Treat her right. Show her a good time."

"I always do." He leered some.

"Nah, I don't mean that. I mean buy her something nice, take her out, cause you never know."

"Never know what?"

Ramsey didn't want to start freaking the kid out. He needed that truck sold. "I'm just talking. Title's in the cab—I'll go get it."

"Yeah, okay." Kid still looked a little puzzled. "I'll start on the paperwork. There's a lot of it."

Ramsey checked the clock on the wall. "Think you can have me out of here in a half hour?"

"You're selling your truck," Frank said. "You got someplace more important to be?"

"Yeah, I do," Ramsey said. "I got band practice."

He returned to his truck for the title and a last look around. Before coming to the Monmouth Truck Lot, he'd cleaned the trailer, scrubbing his own existence away. Ramsey always kept the cab neat—but there was the bedding, tape collection, towels, sleeping bag, old fleeces, survival kit, road atlas, fire extinguisher, alarm clock, laundry detergent, rolls of toilet paper, paper towels. The cab was like the smallest apartment he'd ever lived in, and by far the most comfortable. He'd spent well over a thousand nights in it. So it wasn't a truck he was selling, but a second home. Or maybe a first home.

Too many truckers were slobs, their cabs ankle deep in dirty clothes, fast food wrappers, soda cans, cigarette butts, old tubs of chew, spit cans, piss bottles, porno mags, balled-up paper towels full of snot or cum, petrified French fries . . . you name it. *That's your home, man,* he'd reminded a rookie driver some years back who'd been generous with his pill supply. *You gotta smell that when you drive and when you sleep.* Ramsey was hardly some blowhard always handing out free advice, but he had an instinct for when a kid could land either way, and he considered it his duty to tip him in the right direction if he thought it might make a difference.

And the truth was, a cab was a decent place if you let it be. More than decent. That's what Ramsey had discovered early on, then taken for granted but rediscovered these past few months. Rolling along some hot highway on the way from who-cares to doesn't-matter, the temperature just right, the music just right, you have your own kingdom.

But that was over now. He opened the storage compartment between the seats, where he kept the few items of special importance: couple of photos of Allie and Meg, a notebook where he sometimes jotted down stuff that occurred to him on the road, a song lyric, whatever. A few mementos collected over the years: small cow skull whittled by a dude in Amarillo; necklace of green Mardi Gras beads; smooth blue stone that he found one silent, foggy dawn on a beach in Trinidad, California; pinecone from

Colorado, where on a whim one windy summer afternoon he pulled to the side of the road at the wide point of a pass cutting through the Rockies and ate his lunch at a picnic table. All of it, he put into the black trash bag.

He picked up his copy of *The Orbital Axis*, its cover creased and spine worn, and nearly decided to keep it before changing his mind. From moving apartment to apartment over the years, he'd gotten into the habit of keeping a thing only as long as it was useful. The book had led him to sell the truck. Well, here he was, selling it. He added the book to the black trash bag, which he spun around a few times and knotted at the top.

The cab looked and smelled fresh, but it wasn't his kingdom any longer. Before hooking up with Allie, he'd moved apartments all the time, eviction coming about as frequently as a head cold. He'd forgotten all about that sad feeling of leaving a place, knowing you'll never smell that particular smell ever again. Even a place you don't like. Even if you only lived there for three or four months before getting chased away by some prick landlord. It had to do with mortality. Leave a place, and you've finished a chapter, moved closer to the end.

Now, keys in pocket, title of ownership in one hand, trash bag in the other, he gave the truck one last look and shut the door.

He didn't need to come by fifteen thousand dollars this way. He wasn't poor. There was money in savings, enough or close to it. But symbolic actions mattered. Filling out a withdrawal slip at the bank didn't mean squat, whereas selling your truck showed commitment. Finality. He'd promised Allie back in June that he wouldn't sell, and he'd kept his word. He kept working right through today. She'd been right, as she almost always was. Working was the best thing. He lifted the trash bag higher and tossed it onto a pile of other trash bags inside the green dumpster behind the sales office.

But now he was done with work. Time to cash out. And this, he knew, walking into the sales office again carrying the title of ownership, was the proper way to do it.

The kid was no wiz at simple math and kept hitting the wrong buttons on his calculator. Nearly an hour passed before Ramsey's business with Frank was done. But okay, the title was signed over, the keys placed on the counter. In Frank's shirt pocket were two hundred-dollar bills, courtesy of Ramsey.

*(Two hundred bucks? What for?)*

*(For helping me out today, Frank.)*

*(Jesus.)*

*(Like I said, do something nice for your girl.)*

In Ramsey's front pants pocket were the other 147 hundred-dollar bills and five twenties. One of the twenties was for the taxi ride back to Boater's World, where his car was parked. For years, the store manager let him park his truck there when he wasn't on the road, and his car there when he was. After driving the truck, the Volkswagen always felt to Ramsey like a toy.

At 1:45 p.m. he arrived at the Methodist church and walked through the side door labeled "Kid Care." He wished his daughter's day care wasn't at a church. But Allie had done the research and said this place had the best reputation.

"I'm here for Meg Miller," he said to the woman sitting in a black swivel chair. "Didn't see no one in the Ladybug Room." He knew this woman by sight and found her distasteful.

That was why—the scowl. On her desk were stacks of paper, a typewriter, and a huge white mug with lipstick smears on the brim. She held up an index finger as if the form she was reading were vitally important before looking up. "Mrs. Miller said you wouldn't be here until three."

"Well, I'm here at two."

The woman sighed. "They're in the Little Gym. Do you know where that is?"

He didn't.

She braced her palms against the desk to help herself stand up.

"Let me ask you something," Ramsey said, following her into the hallway. "Is Meg the best kid you ever had here?"

Along the walls, between classrooms, were hooks with names above them. On the hooks hung jackets and knapsacks.

"She's a well-behaved child."

"And sweet, too," he said.

"Yes," the woman conceded, "she is."

"Goddamn right she is." Ramsey smiled, watching the woman flinch.

Meg: three months shy of three years. Preferred running to walking. Hair, wavy with funny-as-hell cowlicks when she woke up in the morning. Best laugh in the whole fucking world. Loved the color orange. Amazing with numbers and letters, except for the tricky patch between U and X.

She spotted Ramsey in the entrance to the gym and came running, all teeth and flailing arms, shouting, "It's Daddy!" over and over. She was never shy around him, even when he came home from a long haul. He knew to give Allie credit for all the photographs of them—of him—stuck on the refrigerator, in albums, the daily reminders of Daddy while he was away, no different from what military spouses did. There was no bigger dread than your kid not knowing who you were.

Ramsey stepped into the gym. "Hey, baby," he said. He'd seen other dads glance around self-consciously when their kids delivered a blast of full-on affection. Men were always glancing around. That was their problem.

When Meg reached him, he rocketed her into the air and swung her around a couple of times. He kissed her cheek, she honked his nose, he carried her outside to the parking lot, and they were on their way.

Or they would've been if he could secure the car seat's straps around Meg's shoulders. When he took too long, she started to fuss. He tried to remember the words to some kid's song, any song at all. "Oh, I love trash," he sang. "Anything trashy or smashy or grungy—"

"I want Daddy to sing Barney!" she shouted, still squirming, the one arm that'd been secured now free again. The tears were real.

Not liking Barney and not knowing what he (she? it?) sang, he ignored the request. "Come on, Meg." he said. "Baby, let me just—"

Not a chance.

By the time she was secured in the seat—crying, miserable—Ramsey's whole face was sweating. He started the car and turned up the radio, which helped. Thank you, John Cougar Mellencamp. He told Meg they were going to the playground, and her face brightened at once, and he cursed himself for not thinking to mention that *before* trying to put her in the car seat.

The afternoon's itinerary was simple: playground, home, band practice. All week, Ramsey had looked forward to this hour alone with the kid. Back when Meg was a baby and couldn't sit up or play with toys or do hardly anything, time spent alone with her slowed practically to a stop. But now she did everything: ran, threw a football (usually into the shrubs, but still), climbed on him like a monkey. And whenever he returned from being away, she was ready with new words and fresh techniques for getting him to obey her.

In the park was a shallow pond where kids threw balled-up bread to the turtles. He had forgotten to bring bread, but Meg was happy dropping woodchips and pebbles into the water. Then she ran over to the playground and tried the slides. Ramsey sat on the green metal bench at one of the picnic tables bordering the play area and watched. On this sunny afternoon, he found himself wanting time to slow just as it was picking up speed. His daughter was the result of Allie and himself, but she was neither of them. She was becoming herself, entirely.

When he looked at his watch, more than a half hour had passed. "Okay, Meg," he said, "time to go."

"No, Daddy!" she called, and raced toward the twisty yellow slide.

Another man was coming his way with two kids, boy and a girl, both a little older than Meg. The man's hands were stuffed into the pockets of his khaki pants. He had on a loosened tie and sports coat. Seeing Ramsey, the man saluted. Nothing in the world was more depressing than other men at a playground, with their sad salutes and their "Mr. Mom" remarks and that look on their faces of having been snookered—like they'd thought they were headed to a Jets game with their buddies but somehow ended up here.

"We're about to leave," Ramsey said to this other man. "You have yourself a good weekend."

The man shot Ramsey with an imaginary pistol and called over to his boy, Tino, to leave the baseball cap ON like he'd been told a thousand times.

"They're all deaf at this age," the man said to Ramsey, heading over to where his kid had flung his cap to the ground.

Ramsey was working on a plan to leave the playground without tears when Meg ran over to him, took his hand, and said, "Want to go home." There was no figuring her out.

They were halfway to the car when, out of nowhere, she looked up at him and said, "Meg feed the turtles."

45

"We did, baby," Ramsey said. "We already—"

"Meg feed turtles now!" She yanked her hand away and repeated the demand, hysteria entering her voice.

So they walked over to the bridge and threw more woodchips into the water, until Meg said, "Want to see Mommy." She walked cheerfully to the car and, amazingly, climbed into the seat without a fuss.

When they arrived home, Eric's pickup and Paul's El Camino were both facing the wrong way on the street. The pickup's body was caked in dried mud. The El Camino was rusted and dented, with a black trash bag duct-taped into place where a rear window should have been. Ramsey imagined the neighbors looking out their front windows and shaking their heads.

He and Allie had moved to the Sandy Oaks neighborhood from across town back when they decided that Allie would go off the pill. The people living here worked in offices with secretaries of their own. If asked, they'd call themselves "comfortable," which was horseshit. In the scheme of things, they were rich. *He* was rich. Anyone who didn't go to bed fretting about money and wake up fretting about it all over again? Rich. And damn lucky to be living someplace where you were never woken up at 3 a.m. to drunken obscenities shouted down the street, to police sirens, to glass shattering in the road.

More than three years since they'd moved in, and whenever he drove up to his home he still felt, for an instant, as if he were visiting someone else—someone wealthy and temperate and respectable. Then he reminded himself that he had all those qualities now, more or less, and had worked damn hard for them.

"Down, Daddy!"

Meg insisted on walking to the door rather than be carried. On the way, she petted a hedge, got down on her hands and knees to examine an ant, and asked Ramsey repeatedly where the sorties (stories? shores?) were. The closer they got to the house, the more Ramsey could hear the low tones of the bass guitar. He felt it in his chest, vibrations like the engine in his truck before putting it into gear and driving off someplace. But he wasn't going any-where, not anymore.

"Can you feel that?" he asked.

Meg knocked on the red front door. "Home."

"That's right, sweetie pie." He stroked her hair. "We're home."

# 4

September 22, 2006

Uncle Wayne and Aunt Kendra had never hidden from Melanie the fact that they were raising her because her mother and father could not. When she was five, they explained that her mother had died and her father had gone far away but that they, Kendra and Wayne, loved her very much and thought of her as their own daughter. This was one of her earliest memories, and what she remembered most clearly about it was that to stop her from crying, they had all climbed into bed and watched *The Little Mermaid*, her favorite movie, on videotape, and shared a large bowl of buttery popcorn.

When she was ten, they explained that a very dangerous man had ended her mother's life and unfortunately had not yet been caught. He was still dangerous, which was why their lives had to be so private. Two years later, they explained that her father had been that man—something that by then Melanie had already suspected.

She sat beside Phillip now on his neatly made bed, the air conditioner straining to cool the room, and told him the essence of what she'd learned over the years: how her name used to be Meg Miller, and how when she was a little girl her father had thrown a big party and then, later that night, strangled her mother and dumped her body into the backyard fire pit. She told him about how she herself was believed to be dead, too, and how Wayne and Kendra were able to get her away, and how the U.S. Marshals, working with local law enforcement in two states, had successfully hidden her but utterly failed to apprehend her father.

"But he knows you're alive," Phillip finally said after several seconds of saying nothing.

"Of course," Melanie said.

"Then why is it a secret?"

"If everyone else thinks I'm already dead," she explained, "then we never have to worry about reporters or TV people or anyone trying to find me. No one can ever help my father, even accidentally." Phillip was rubbing her hand with his thumb. "Anyway, it wasn't my decision, and it had to get made really fast. And no one ever thought it would take this long to find him."

"Are you still afraid of your father?" he asked.

"I'm terrified of him," she said. "He's a madman."

"Can I ask why you're telling me about it now?"

She decided not to mention the fractals. But come on—had he not noticed her larger breasts, her clearer skin? Did he not find it strange that suddenly she was saying *No, thanks* whenever he offered her a glass of wine? Why was she telling him now? Because it isn't just me anymore, she wanted to say. But she needed to know how he would take the news of her strange past before going further. "I've wanted to tell you for a while," she said, "but I didn't want to scare you away. Is this going to scare you away?"

His arm was around her now. "Of course it won't," he said. "But . . . " He frowned.

"What?"

"It's just that all of this happened so long ago. And you have a new identity, and obviously look a lot different from when you were a little kid." He shrugged. "What makes you think your father's still looking for you, anyway?"

She could have told him about the letters, hard evidence that Ramsey Miller was still out there causing trouble. She could have mentioned the feeling she would get sometimes that someone was out there watching her. She would catch something in her periphery, turn her head, and see nothing. But the chill would linger. Even out in her own yard, in bright daylight, sometimes she'd gaze into the hedges and swear she saw movement. But this was bogeyman stuff, more than likely, so she decided to answer Phillip's question another way.

"When my father dragged my mother into the fire, they think she was still alive. He choked her and left her to burn." She watched his eyes, hoping he would understand. "What I mean is, I don't get to be optimistic."

Phillip said nothing for a moment. Maybe he was imagining the murder scene, the charred flesh. "I wonder if it's time for someone other than your aunt and uncle to look out for you," he said. "They can't do it forever—and I'm not afraid."

"You're not, huh?"

"Not really. Nope." He chanced a smile. "Which is weird, because I'm actually afraid of a lot of stuff."

"Yeah? Like what?"

"Oh, you name it. Flying. Heights."

"That's the same thing."

"Not to me," he said. "Also, tornadoes."

"You don't live in a trailer," she said. "We had a couple of close calls when I was a kid."

"And I'm afraid of having to use CPR on somebody at school and then doing it wrong. And being crushed in an avalanche."

"Is that everything?"

She thought he might say yes. Instead: "Rabies."

"Like getting bitten by a bat?"

"Sure—a raccoon, a bat . . ."

"But you're not afraid of a murderer?"

"No—just everything else." He shrugged. "Maybe it's because you mean more to me than bats or airplanes or whatever." His smile was more confident. "You look very pretty right now."

He kissed her mouth, her throat. She placed a hand on his arm. "Seriously, Phillip—I have to know if this is all too much for you."

"Seriously, Melanie—it isn't."

"Don't answer so fast," she said. "I want you to really think about it."

"*It isn't.*" He looked into her eyes. "I can handle anything."

She bit her lip. "How about one more surprise. Can you handle that?"

The box of condoms said 96% effective. But 96 percent effective, it turned out, was a world away from 100 percent, and now she was in her tenth week. Before telling Phillip, the only two people who knew were herself and the doctor at the college health center, who had confirmed those drug-store pregnancy tests with yet another test, then handed her several pamphlets ("Your Guide to a Healthy Pregnancy"; "Breastfeeding with Success"; "Labor, Delivery, and Postpartum Care"), all of which she skimmed late that first night before stowing them in the back of her closet behind a box of old clothes.

She'd been careful and responsible, yet the result was no different from that girl in high school last year whom Melanie had actually overheard saying, *We thought God would keep me from getting pregnant.* And her options—either an abortion or the prospect of introducing a baby into her hidden, fearful home—were too awful to think about. So for a few weeks, she didn't. She went to class. She went to work. She read her Hardy Boys and Nancy Drew mysteries. The pamphlets stayed stowed.

Which was why she felt glad, in a way, that her instructor had shown the class those fractals this afternoon. They made her see that she didn't want to stay hidden at every scale any longer, and didn't want her child to be hidden at all. And those two desires intertwined. If not for the child, there'd be no reason to stop being who she'd always been—the fearful, hidden girl.

When she actually said the words "I'm pregnant" to Phillip, at first the color drained from his face, his own version of morning sickness. "I intend to have the baby and raise it," she said. "Just so you know."

He said all the right things. He'd be there for her. He'd support her. He went so far as to say that he was "excited about this," which she didn't believe but appreciated hearing. Before long, his face regained its color. And gradually the two conversations—her past, their present—melded into one.

She knew he found their relationship odd. How could he not? They almost never went out in public other than for coffee or soda at the gas station or, a couple of times, for a very early dinner at the McDonald's on the highway. She let him assume it was their age difference that made them reclusive, the fact that he was a teacher at the high school where she'd just graduated.

As she'd become more comfortable around him, she began to imply that there was more to the story. She'd wanted to tell him about it but saw Phillip's invitation for her to reveal herself, to trust him, as coming from an earnest young man who viewed the universe as fundamentally benign. It wasn't him she distrusted but rather his optimism.

But things were different now, and he had a right to know everything. So everything is what she told him. And as she shared her secrets with this person of her choosing, each disclosure lightened her, made her feel less alone. It was like nothing she'd ever felt before. Phillip held her long after she was done talking.

By then it was early evening. She knew she should call her aunt and uncle. She didn't want them to worry. But there would be no reasoning with them. She imagined telling them the truth: *I'm at my boyfriend's house. He's twenty-three.* They'd demand she come home right away. And she could actually see herself obeying them, allowing herself to be yanked right back to the house on Notress Pass.

So maybe she did want them to worry, a little. Maybe that's what they needed to finally begin to understand that she wasn't a kid anymore. All she knew for sure was that she needed to prolong this moment with Phillip through dinner and beyond, and whether that was despite the potential repercussions with her aunt and uncle or because she wanted there to be repercussions, she wasn't sure.

She stayed. She didn't call home, and she slept in Phillip's warm bed, and early Saturday morning, with the birds noisy outside but the room still dark, she awoke beside him feeling a little surprised that he wasn't already long gone, having driven his Mazda as far as it would go or thumbed a ride back to Connecticut. Content, she fell back to sleep. When she woke up again it was to the sound of Phillip in the kitchen putting away last night's dishes, whistling a few notes of something soft and tuneless—and these ordinary sounds filled her with gratitude and wonder. This was the permanent rupture, she could feel it, separating every day in her past from every day in her future.

The air conditioner blocked her view through the window, but she didn't hear rain. No rain meant that their plan for today was on—a plan, made hastily before falling asleep last night, that to Melanie had seemed monumentally reckless. Yet she'd agreed to it.

The carnival at the Baptist church opened at eleven. There would be games and rides and food sold out of carts. The two of them would go there and spend the afternoon together like regular people.

So many bodies, and she was moving toward them. The excitement she felt last night at the thought of going to the carnival with Phillip had faded over breakfast, faded more on the walk over. She'd been able to compress her fear into the smallest nugget. But stepping onto the church grounds, her body stiffened. It would be easy to release his hand, turn around, walk away. Rush home and apologize to Kendra and Wayne for being an ungrateful niece.

She willed herself on.

As they walked toward the center of the grounds, stepping around muddy patches, Melanie kept an eye out for anyone she might recognize. What if someone spoke to her? She walked head down, avoiding eye contact and talking only in quiet, clipped sentences that were lost among the carnival sounds. "Pardon me?" Phillip kept asking. Finally, he stopped walking and put his hands on her shoulders. "Melanie—no one cares that we're here."

She chose to believe him and tried to enjoy herself, taking in the scene: kids riding the Zipper and shrieking; clusters of people huddled at the game booths; smoke from the food carts rising into the sky; couples everywhere strolling arm in arm or hand in hand. She took Phillip's hand again and let herself be guided through the grounds.

When she first smelled the smoked meat, corn dogs, caramel popcorn, she awaited the nausea, but it was just the opposite

—she found herself wanting all of it, right now. And the creaking of the rides' moving parts, the shouting coming from the game booths, the hum of generators beneath a curtain of calliope music, it hit her all at once, a sharp hunger. *Look at what I've missed*, she thought. Then she shook it off. She hadn't missed everything. She was here, right now, living this.

She stopped walking on the trampled grass and looked around, slapping one finger into her palm, then two fingers, then three.

"What are you counting?" Phillip asked.

"I'm making a mental list of the things I've never done before."

"What've you got so far?"

"Funnel cake," she said.

He whistled. "What else?"

"Ferris wheel."

"Is that a good idea?"

"How do you mean?" When he placed his hand gently on her belly, she said, "Oh, look how slowly it's turning." They watched until the ride stopped, and a couple of young children—seven or eight years old—stepped out of a car. At its highest point, the cars swayed gently in the breeze. "I can definitely do that," she said.

"Well, count me out."

"Why? I thought we could . . ." She grinned. "Oh, right. Heights. I forgot."

"It's a common fear," he pointed out.

She patted his hand. "You're a delicate flower. Oh, and I've never played one of those games where you try to win stuff."

So they tried to win stuff: ring-toss, then a booth where Phillip's plastic racehorse, moved forward with a squirt gun, finished a close second. The winner, a boy of eleven or twelve who himself looked like a horse, with a broad nose and hair down to his neck, pumped his fist into the air and reached out to the game attendant for his prize, a stuffed-animal horse, which the boy looked proud to receive until it occurred to him that he was a twelve-year-old boy holding a stuffed animal. He handed the horse to a smaller girl beside him, who hugged it to her chest.

Melanie was watching the girl pet her new horse, combing back its mane, when she heard: "Mr. Connor! Miss Denison!"

Melanie dropped Phillip's hand and spun around. Her twelfth-grade English teacher, Mrs. Henderson, beamed at them. "Why, just look at you!" She was flanked by her two daughters.

"Hello, ma'am," Melanie said.

"You know, Bethany was just asking me if I'd run into any of my students here, and I said to her, well, we'll just have to wait and see. Isn't that what I said?"

"Yes," said her older daughter, who was six.

"No, *I* said it," said her three-year-old sister.

"You *didn't*," Bethany said.

"And now here you are," Mrs. Henderson said, "looking beautiful as always. So what have you been doing with yourself?"

"I'm taking classes at Mountain Community," Melanie said. Saying it made her realize how proud she was of this small achievement.

"Oh, I'm glad to hear that," Mrs. Henderson said. "I thought you'd decided against college."

"My parents and I talked it over." She always referred to Kendra and Wayne as her parents. "Aunt" and "Uncle" would invite questions.

"Parents do know best sometimes," she said, and raised an eyebrow. "Now on to more pressing matters: Phillip, why didn't you tell me that you and Melanie were an item?"

"We like keeping our business to ourselves," he said.

It wasn't particularly scandalous, the two of them. He was never her teacher. Their age difference was only six years—five, come December. He'd graduated from the University of Connecticut and come down here as part of the Teach for America program. Had she seen him in the high school hallways? Sure. But they didn't formally meet until after she'd already graduated, and she was working in the office supply store and he'd come in one day as a customer.

"Oh, how silly!" Mrs. Henderson said. "Secrets don't stay secrets for long in Fredonia. Well, you picked yourself a good one. Melanie didn't have much to say in class, but she's as smart as— Caitlin, please don't do that. *Caitlin.* You'll get muddy." She took her younger daughter's hand and helped her to stand up again before refocusing her attention on Melanie and Phillip. "Young love is a wonderful thing!" she announced, and then fake-whispered to Melanie: "You watch out for his big city ways."

Melanie forced a smile.

"We were about to head over to the Ferris wheel," Phillip said.

"Of course. You two have yourself a good time." She winked at Phillip. "See you bright and early on Monday, young man."

He smiled back. When they'd walked away, he said, "That woman is an idiot."

"She was always nice to me."

"Let me ask you something—did you learn anything from her?"

A good point. Melanie was better educated in the progression of Caitlin's toilet training than in *Hamlet* or *To Kill a Mockingbird.* "Well . . ."

"And she treats me like a child. You know she's only twenty-six?"

That seemed impossible. "So tell me," she said, "what exactly are those big city ways I've been warned about?"

He stopped walking. "Come over again tonight, and I'll show you."

Her face got warm. "I'm going to ride the Ferris wheel now."

It was almost 1 p.m., cooler than yesterday, a lovely day to be out. As she waited in line, she plucked a dandelion out of the grass and tucked it behind her ear. The ride attendant put her alone in a pale-green car, lowered the lap bar until it was snug, and said, "Bon voyage." A few seconds later, she was rising into the air and swaying softly. The ride didn't go very high, but at the top was a view of the streets of her town, the houses and lawns and cars. Below were the fairgrounds, clumps of people waiting for rides and food. She went up and around, down, up again. The car moved slowly, and the sensation in her belly wasn't unpleasant. She lost sight of Phillip. Scanning the ground for him, she noticed a group of young kids waving at whichever car was at the top of the loop. Next time she reached the top, she waved back, and then, scanning the crowd again for Phillip she noticed an older man watching her. His gaze stayed on her as she came down to the bottom of the ride, and as she climbed again he raised a large camera to his face and held it there.

"Hey!" she shouted, but he was already walking quickly away, melting into the crowd.

When her car descended again—how many loops would this ride make?—she shouted to the ride attendant, "I need to get off the ride!" but he either didn't hear or didn't care, and there she went up again, and down again. "Please!" she shouted the next time, her eyes filling with tears. She considered leaping off, but this was a crazy thought, and anyway she was stuck underneath the lap bar. When the attendant had lowered the bar, his fingers had grazed her thighs. Was it an accident? A cheap feel? In the span of seconds, the whole place had turned sinister.

On the next loop she spotted Phillip again—he had moved off to the side, near where she'd be exiting—and she shouted, "Stop the ride!" just as it began to slow. The attendant started letting people out of the cars beneath her, but the process was maddening: one car, then another, then another. Finally, hers. She ran down the ramp and nearly collided into Phillip.

"Did you see that man?" she asked.

"Who?"

She grabbed Phillip's arm and tugged him in the direction the man had gone. "He was watching me. He took my picture. We have to find him." As they ran, she described him: thin, older, gray facial hair, faded blue jeans. They move in and around the crowd, which had swelled from just a few minutes earlier. There were too many people. They'd never find him. He was already gone.

Then, remarkably, there he was: over by the game where you threw Wiffle balls into colored cups to win prizes. His camera was out again.

"Why did you take my picture?" Melanie asked, breathless.

The man turned to face her. "I did?" He studied her face. "Oh—the Ferris wheel." He stuck out his hand. "Manny Simpson, *Mason City Democrat*."

"You work for the newspaper?"

"Of course." He nodded to his camera. "I'm taking pictures for tomorrow's paper."

She was momentarily relieved. Who had she thought this man was? She'd been reading too many Hardy Boys novels. But her relief lasted only a moment. "You can't put my picture in the paper."

"You looked lovely up there—so happy. And with that flower in your hair . . ."

She reached up to where she had put the dandelion behind her ear, but it must have fallen out during her rush across the carnival grounds. "You can't use it."

"She doesn't like being photographed," Phillip said.

"I'm taking hundreds of photos, and the paper will probably only use two or three, so it's highly unlikely—"

"You can't, though," Melanie said. "You have to promise."

"All right. I'll make a note of it. No lovely girl on the Ferris wheel." He smiled and turned away.

Still feeling uneasy, and no longer hungry, Melanie said to Phillip, "I want to leave."

"Are you sure?"

She didn't want to disappoint him. This was supposed to be their day out. Their day together. "I'm sure," she said.

They walked away from the carnival, back toward Phillip's house, neither of them talking. Finally, he said, "What about my own camera. I'm just curious. Would you ever let me take a picture of you?"

She thought about it. "No."

"Don't you trust me?"

"It isn't a matter of trust."

"I don't understand."

"If I didn't want you to photograph me naked, would you understand that? Even if you never planned to share the photo with anyone else?"

"Sure," he said.

"Then just think of me as naked all the time." She didn't like her own response—too flippant for the occasion—and she stopped walking. "Okay, I don't like having to say this, but I will. I need you to protect me. Not like a policeman or a parent. I'm not a helpless child. But I'm also not some typical college freshman. I spend every minute of every day looking over my shoulder. It isn't a joke."

"I get that," he said, rubbing her arm. "It's just that it was all so long ago—"

His touch felt good, but she needed him to understand. "You've been dealing with this for less than a day. I've been dealing with it for fifteen years." The sun had moved out from behind some clouds and was heating up the ground. Before long, the day would probably be as oppressive as yesterday. They started walking again. "Forget it," she said. "We can talk about it some other time."

"All right." He put his arm around her. "But I can handle it. I really can."

These were reassuring words that raised her spirits until about three seconds after he'd said them, when a squirrel dropped out of the tree under which they were passing. It had either misjudged a jump or slipped, and came whooshing out of the branches and plopped down onto the road just a few feet in front of them.

Melanie heard: *Slap, slap, slap, slap, slap, slap.*

The squirrel froze, momentarily stunned, before finding its bearings and darting away from the road toward the curb and scurrying up the nearest tree.

Melanie looked left. Phillip was no longer beside her. She turned around. He was at least twenty feet back, looking sheepish in his flip-flops, which had broadcasted his hasty retreat.

"What the hell was that about?" she asked.

"It startled me."

"You ran away from a squirrel?"

He walked back to her. "It could have been rabid."

She started walking quickly ahead without him, this man whose quirky fears were suddenly not remotely endearing. Maybe she'd been drawn to him because he was so different from her aunt and uncle. But if they were smothering her, this was no antidote. An antidote like this would get her killed.

"I need to go home," she said. "I need to not see you right now."

"Melanie—"

"Let's just walk."

62

The carnival sounds faded. Soon there were only their footfalls and the cars going by, and the birds and, yes, squirrels mocking them from the trees. When they reached Phillip's house, they went inside and Melanie collected her backpack and returned to the front door.

"I'm sorry," Phillip said.

She wouldn't look at him, wouldn't talk to him. She wasn't intentionally giving him the silent treatment, but she felt nauseous and sweaty and exhausted. She descended the concrete steps and returned to her car.

There was only one way to deal with the storm she was walking into. By the time she'd made it back to Notress Pass and driven up the pebbly driveway and put the car into park, her aunt and uncle were already rushing out of the trailer.

"I'm fine," Melanie said, shutting the car door behind her. "I spent the night with the man I've been seeing. But things between us didn't work out. I'm very tired and need to rest. We can talk about anything you want, I promise—but later. I'm very, very sorry for worrying you, and I love you both very much." She walked between them, her face hot with humiliation, and was quickly past, up the stairs, into the trailer, into her bedroom, shutting the door and locking it behind her.

Her aunt and uncle, to their tremendous credit, didn't come knocking.

An hour later, she'd emerged from her bedroom and was lying on the living room sofa, feet resting on her aunt's lap. Her uncle sat in a chair opposite them. "I thought there might be a future with him," Melanie said, "but I was wrong. That's really all there is to it. I'm sorry to have worried you—I know that was awful of me."

She'd expected plenty of yelling when she returned home. Wayne and Kendra weren't people who yelled, but Melanie had never stayed out all night. There was no rule forbidding it, because such a transgression was unthinkable.

Yet there had been no yelling, no tirades when she came out of her room—only concerned embraces and as much patience as she could possibly hope for. They were wonderful from time to time, she had to admit.

"Who is this man?" her uncle asked.

Melanie shook her head. "It doesn't matter. It's over."

"When did you meet him?" her aunt asked.

"Did he hurt you?" her uncle asked.

"No, nothing like that. He's a decent guy. It just didn't work out."

Her aunt and uncle exchanged glances. "You told him, didn't you?" Wayne said. Melanie briefly considered lying, but her hesitation told them everything.

"So what happened?" Kendra asked. "He couldn't handle it?"

"Something like that," Melanie said.

Her aunt, eyes wet, reached out and took Melanie's hand. "That's why you have us. We'll protect you—always, always, always."

# 5

September 20, 1991

Before that amazing and utterly accidental late-morning moment seven years back when Allison Anne Pembroke stepped out of the elevator and into the third floor of Monmouth Regional Hospital, Ramsey's entire life had added up to nothing, $0 + 0 + 0 = 0$, the equation of a loser whose existence was as aimless as it was pointless. Flash forward a year, and the two of them were still together, and not just together but a whole new equation with a sum far greater than anything he'd ever imagined himself contributing to. In quiet moments he'd fall into the habit of asking himself the obvious.

*What if we hadn't met? What then?*

He'd imagine the alternatives when falling asleep at night, and on interstates, and while fueling up. The scenes he imagined always led to the same conclusion: He'd be dead. Beer bottle to the head, knife to the gut, maybe a high-speed chase. Or he would've woken up one gray day and said *enough already* and used his belt to rig up a nice noose. Or something less dramatic—illness, since Lord knows he didn't take care of himself when he was on his own. Surely he'd have died as he had lived: angry and alone, underwhelmed and underwhelming, unwilling to give of himself to another or see the beauty in anything or anybody. He'd have left the world a little worse off than he had found it. That would have been his legacy. His tombstone would have read, *Here lies another shithead.*

Before meeting Allie, he had never been in love or close to it. When he would stop to dwell on the matter as a teenager and young man, this lack of love gnawed at him, so he tried to convince himself that he didn't give a shit. He had honed this particular skill, not giving a shit, over many years, which served him well much of the time but also made him take risks he knew he shouldn't. The cars he stole, for instance. You ought to feel a thrill, revving somebody else's engine and peeling away from the curb. Going through their glove box, looking under the visors. But there was no thrill in it. What he stole, he stole to pay rent and buy food. The fights he got into brought him no satisfaction, either—not when a fight almost always meant a night in some drunk tank that reeked of every human excretion. And it wasn't as if his fights were ever about anything noble. Nobody was defending anyone's honor. Typically it was about nothing at all. You get drunk, you get mad, shit happens. It was sad, this life of his, like a mushroom pushing out of the ground after a hard rain, random and poisonous. He actually tried out this metaphor on his friend Eric while lying in the hospital seven years back, hopped up on painkillers. Eric was trying to cheer him up with dirty jokes, but Eric was too religious for the jokes to be dirty enough, and there was no cheering up Ramsey that day, anyway. He had mangled his leg out of his own stupidity, he'd just been canned from the only good job he'd ever had, and he'd been given a summons for taking a drunken swing at a cop.

*A mushroom?* Eric had said. *What you are is a fool.*

He was absolutely right. And yet a day later, Allie stepped out of the elevator and into Ramsey's life.

He didn't deserve her—especially not then, when anything redeeming about him was hidden under a thick shell of defensiveness, evasion, and straight-up aggression cultivated over many years. But they got together, he and Allie, and they stayed together. She taught him what love meant, how it was the truth that made all other truths possible. She came along at the exact right moment and saved his life in every way that a life could be saved. So for her, he did that singular thing that human beings almost never did no matter how much they might want to, and never, ever for another person.

For her, he changed.

The door swung open as he was reaching with the key. The surprises revealed themselves gradually. The late-afternoon light always made her face lovely, for instance, but today her beauty staggered him.

And when he stepped into the house, he was struck by its tidiness. The housekeeper came on Wednesdays, letting herself in and out, but by Friday, especially when Allie was alone all week with the kid, the place would revert to its natural state. Not today.

He followed Meg inside. "The house looks great," he told Allie. "So do you." It immediately occurred to him he should have reversed the order of compliments.

"You didn't tell me they were coming over," Allie said.

"I didn't? The guys? Sure, I did."

"No."

Of course they needed to rehearse, with the gig on Sunday. But maybe he hadn't told her. When she bent down to kiss Meg on the head, saying, "Hi, sweetie," Ramsey saw that underneath Allie's Monmouth College sweatshirt was a lacy red bra. The panties would match, he was sure of it. Allie used to keep two sets of underclothes, one for when Ramsey was on the road and another for when he was home. He only ever saw the shapeless, faded garments in the laundry hamper, until after the baby was born, at which point dutifully separated laundry became an extravagance, and the only pertinent question became whether something was clean enough.

These small surprises—tidy house, sexy underwear—were like Easter eggs for him to find. A lit candle somewhere filled the house with the smell of fall. A Sam Cooke CD was playing, though the sounds coming from the garage drowned it out.

Meg ran through the house toward the kitchen. Watching their daughter together somehow reset their reunion. "It's good to see you," Allie said. She placed a hand on his arm and kissed his lips. "Thanks for getting her today."

"Happy to," he said. Allie could have gotten Meg from day care herself—she often came home from work early on Fridays—but before leaving town last week Ramsey had said he would do it. He had developed, over the years, this technique for proving his own decency to himself—making small promises that he could fulfill. This time the promise had come from the basic need to spend a little time alone with Meg before the weekend's bustle of activity.

Six, seven years ago he would come home from a week away, and within minutes he and Allie would fall into bed. But Allie was still trying, the Easter eggs proved it, and Ramsey knew he ought to try, too. His face needed a shave, his hair a trim. He didn't like wearing sunglasses, and over the years his squinting had etched permanent gouges in his face. He should've exercised more. He was thin, always had been, but that wasn't the same as being fit. Not like when he was younger and could drink a twelve-pack and spend the whole next day in the sun doing some rich guy's yard work.

In the kitchen, Meg was peeling magnetic letters off the refrigerator and dropping them on to the floor. "I was thinking we could get pizza for the guys," Ramsey said. "From the good place."

"How long do you think rehearsal will go?"

"Don't know—but I'll make sure we turn everything down at eight." Meg's bedtime.

"Because I was hoping you and I could have some time tonight."

Already the plastic letters were everywhere. Now Meg was over by the toy barn. When she threw a plastic pig across the room, Allie said, "Sweetie, don't throw the animals," and Meg pursed her lips and slammed a cow onto the ground.

"Are you little mad?" Ramsey asked her, and cursed himself for forgetting to use this surefire trick back at the park.

"*Big* mad," she answered, already smiling, her anger allayed by their inside joke.

Ramsey winked at Meg and said to Allie, "The thing is, this isn't some ordinary jam session. We got a gig coming up."

"You do?" Feigned astonishment. "Why, I had no idea."

Okay, he deserved that. He'd been yammering on about the gig for weeks. But Allie only knew the half of it. There hadn't been time during these last few days of reflection and near-constant driving to tell her that the plan had expanded. And they had to be finished rehearsing by ten tonight because of the town's noise ordinance. When they'd first moved to Sandy Oaks, a cop had broken up a weeknight jam at 8:30 p.m. Someone in the neighborhood had called the cops on them anonymously, rather than just knocking on the door like a normal human being and asking Ramsey if they could turn it down a notch or two. Welcome to the neighborhood.

"I want us to be great, is all," he said, getting a six-pack from the refrigerator and setting it on the counter.

Laid out on the kitchen table were 3 x 5 index cards, with more cards in a plastic box. Allie had a computer in her office at work, but she preferred the index cards, which she carried with her when she traveled from doctor's office to doctor's office, wearing tight business skirts and being outgoing and drumming up demand for whatever new drug her company decided that these doctors' patients' bones or blood or organs couldn't do without. Fridays, she confirmed the next week's appointments. It wasn't lost on Ramsey that at different points in their lives, they both worked as drug pushers—he as a sixteen-year-old pot dealer, she as a grown woman shilling expensive pharmaceuticals for a megacorporation. But he kept this observation to himself.

Allie handed Meg her *Little Mermaid* cup of water. "You guys will be playing for family," she said to Ramsey. "They'll be proud no matter how you sound."

"Yeah, about that." Just then, the bass amp got a lot louder. The last thing they needed was a cop breaking up their rehearsal before it got started.

"About what?" Allie asked.

But Ramsey was heading upstairs to the guest room for his guitar case. "About *what*?" she called after him. Seconds later, he was back. He kissed Allie's neck, bent down and kissed the top of Meg's head.

"I'll tell you later," he said. When Allie's eyes narrowed, he added, "Don't worry—it's good. Like a surprise. Killer bra, by the way."

He grabbed the six-pack with his free hand and headed to the garage. As soon as he'd opened the door separating the laundry room from the garage, a beer can was arcing toward him, and he had to drop the six-pack on the ground (it was either that or the guitar) to catch it. Ramsey opened the can, took a swallow, and looked around.

"I had a dream last night," he said, closing the door behind him. "I could fly, and breathe underwater." He set the guitar case on the ground and snapped it open. "I could do anything. I think that dream was about this gig." He looked up at the guys. "It's going to be like that on Sunday. Like flying. And breathing underwater."

"Amen," said Eric.

"Preach to us, brother Ramsey!" called Paul from behind his drum kit. Eric, sensing sacrilege, shot his younger brother a look.

Ramsey wiped down the fretboard with a rag and lifted the guitar out of its case.

"You have no idea," he said, "how good it is to see you assholes."

Ramsey gladly parked his car outside, in the driveway, to make room for the drumset, microphone stands, speakers on tripods, a jumble of patch cords and speaker cables snaking across the ground. The four-channel P.A. sat on a scratched-up coffee table that Ramsey had claimed from someone else's curb back when he needed to furnish his first apartment on the cheap. Tacked to the drywall were a half dozen rock-star posters and twice as many classic album covers. In the corner of the garage stood a spare refrigerator/freezer, left by the house's former owner.

They had a name, Ramsey and Paul and Eric and Wayne. They called themselves Rusted Wheels, but they weren't a real band. Real bands played out. The point of Rusted Wheels was always exactly this—to jam in Ramsey's garage. They met up every couple of weeks, depending on Ramsey's driving schedule, and in all that time, since before Allie was pregnant, there had never been talk of playing in public. There had never been a need. Playing a gig, they all knew—or at least suspected—meant hauling gear and negotiating payment with dickhead bar owners and hustling for people to show up, and that all seemed a lot like work, which was the opposite of why they came together to play.

How many teenagers jammed in similar garages? Plenty—but teenagers appreciated nothing. You had to be over thirty and over-burdened. You needed battle scars to prove you'd earned the right to a few hours of amplified jams and words sung with feeling and reverb.

"Wayne called me earlier," Paul said. "He can't make it tonight."

Case in point: Wayne was under thirty. When you're young and still have all your hair, apparently the rules of band practice don't apply.

"He's not coming at all?" Eric asked.

Paul gave a *Hey, not my problem* shrug.

"What's he got that's so important?" Ramsey asked.

"He's performing brain surgery." Paul drank from his beer. "He didn't say, I didn't ask. Probably a date." He belched. "You remember those, don't you?"

"I just want to do these songs right on Sunday," Ramsey said. "I want us to be good."

"I got sad news for you, pal." Eric grinned. "We ain't good."

"Well, it ain't Sunday yet, either." But Eric was right. Only Wayne had any real talent. Paul was especially weak on the drums. His tempos defied all logic. But he had problems of his own—handicapped son, wife who'd gone inpatient a couple of times for depression. He worked as an EMT, so it wasn't as if he could veg out on the job. He was a good man who needed Rusted Wheels at least as much as any of them.

Ramsey removed several sheets of paper from the back pocket of his jeans. He had composed the set list in his head while driving through New Mexico and written up four copies at a truck stop in Amarillo.

"This is a lot of music," Paul said, scanning the list.

There were eighteen songs, many of them already part of the Rusted Wheels repertoire, plus three or four that they'd tried in the past and found too hard. "Some neighbors might be coming," Ramsey said. "I want it to be a real show."

They'd slogged through a third of the list when, at 7:30, Allie came into the garage carrying pizza boxes. At eight Ramsey made them play quieter, but at nine they were still going strong. At a couple of minutes before ten, they settled on an ending to "Magic Carpet Ride," called it quits, and made plans to meet up again the following afternoon.

By then the garage felt superheated, three bodies working hard. Eric was slick with sweat. Paul had stripped down to his undershirt. Ramsey felt the urge to say something before they dispersed. "I can't thank you men enough. This gig, your dedication. Your friendship." He forced himself to look at Eric and Paul, rather than down at the concrete floor or across the garage at the ladders hanging on the wall. "It means more to me than you could know." And with no one knowing what to say next, Ramsey decided to cut them all a break. "Okay, fuckheads, see you tomorrow."

Eric snapped open a can of Diet Coke. "So spill it, partner. What's going on?"

"How do you mean?"

"Come on—the marathon rehearsal, your rousing speech . . ."

Paul had left. Ramsey was changing his guitar strings. The instrument was damn fine, better than he deserved—a Telecaster with a sunburst finish, Allie's gift to him for his thirtieth birthday. That guitar replaced the piece-of-shit knockoff-of-a-knockoff that followed him from lousy apartment to lousy apartment over the years.

New strings brought out the Telecaster's full depth, but Ramsey knew better than to change them right before the gig. They'd go flat every two seconds, and he wasn't a good enough musician to make corrections on the fly. He wasn't good enough to tune his new strings while holding a conversation, either, so he laid the guitar back in its case. "I want to tell you a true story," he said, "about something I did three days ago."

Eric's eyes widened. After all these years, he was still protective of Ramsey. He still felt responsible. "I hope it's nothing bad."

"No, you idiot. I went and saw the Grand Canyon." Ramsey tossed a few empties into an open trash can. The beer was really for Paul and Wayne. Eric was in A.A., and Ramsey drank exactly one beer each rehearsal to prove to himself that he could stop after one. "Ever seen it?"

"The Grand Canyon? Of course."

"I don't mean in pictures."

"Then no, I haven't seen it. Been too busy."

"Well, I been busy, too. But I was in Phoenix on Tuesday and my load-in got done early, and I said to myself it was time to see something I always wanted to see. Something I always heard you've never seen till you see it in person. So I drove through the desert, and when I got there I parked my truck and I saw it."

It felt familiar, telling Eric about something he did or some-place he went, though with a crucial difference. Early on in their friendship, Ramsey's stories were usually confessions: The time he got drunk and beat up some prick outside the Pink Pony. The time he got canned for insubordination. He would confess, and Eric would listen and offer a few words to remind Ramsey that we weren't simply the sum total of our mean-spirited actions.

"So how was it?" Eric asked.

Off and on these past couple of days, heading east, Ramsey considered how he might describe the indescribable. "It was big.

And silent." He frowned. "Damn. I can't do it. There's no words, you know?" There was only a feeling born of an expanse so wide that standing on the rim was like leaning over the surface of an empty planet. At the same time, he liked knowing it wasn't some other planet but just dumb old America. And he liked knowing that he was experiencing the same stunned hush, the same loss for words, that other men had experienced for as long as there had been people to stand there and look. No, he couldn't describe to Eric what he could barely describe to himself, about feeling small and unimportant, but in the best sense. *You don't matter as much as you think you do*, the canyon told him, *so lighten up.* To get that feeling, to grasp the wisdom written on the immense canyon walls, you had to be there yourself. Otherwise, you sounded like the sort of hitchhiker Ramsey despised, blathering on and saying nothing.

"I got high that day," he said. So maybe this was a confession after all, he realized.

"Weed?" Eric asked.

"Amazing weed."

"Maybe not the best idea," Eric said.

"Maybe no, maybe yes," Ramsey said. "What happened was, I got this idea into my head to climb down into the canyon a ways. There was a trail. It looked sort of steep, but what the hell."

"Sure. Worst that happens is you fall a few thousand feet to your death."

"Exactly. So about a half hour down the trail I can smell it. A minute later, I come across a couple of kids, guy and a girl, on a big flat rock soaking up the sun."

"Hanky panky?"

Eric was thirty-nine, only five years older than Ramsey, but sometimes he sounded like a whole other generation. "No, they weren't screwing or nothing. They were just sitting there, smoking and talking and looking out at everything. It was already a lot hotter there than up on the rim. It felt like July all of a sudden. They had a jug of water and they offered me some, and then they offered me the joint they were smoking, and I surprised myself by taking both. These kids, they were smart. In college. We talked." Ramsey tried to recall the conversation. With a good conversation, though, where you're just having it and connecting with other people, do you ever remember *how* it got good? "You got to understand the degree of beauty there," he said. "It was late afternoon, and the sky was this dark shade of blue you don't ever see in New Jersey. The light kept changing. Every few minutes it was like a whole new landscape. A sight like that makes you open up. I told them things I haven't even told *you*, and you're my best friend."

"Shut up," Eric said, and looked away.

"Well, you are. It shouldn't embarrass you to hear it."

"I ain't embarrassed." But Eric was still looking over at the Jimi Hendrix poster.

"Yeah, you are. See, there's your problem. You're a hell of a guy but you'll never admit it."

Eric looked back at Ramsey. "So what'd you tell them at the Grand Canyon?"

Ramsey smiled. "I told them the truth."

"Care to elaborate?"

It occurred to Ramsey that maybe Allie had confided in Eric. She was the only person he'd ever told about the orbital axis. If she told Eric, it would be a betrayal, but a minor one, done out of her love and concern. She knew that Eric held sway with Ramsey, and for good reason. Were it not for him, Ramsey would still be some angry shitbag drifting from job to job, some legal, some not— except, now he'd be a thirty-four-year-old shitbag, which was a lot less forgivable than being an eighteen- or a twenty-year-old one.

"It means," Ramsey said, "that I told them they better take in all this beauty while they can, cause it won't be here forever."

"You told them the Grand Canyon won't be here forever?"

"Nothing will. Not me or you or this garage or the Grand Canyon, neither."

"Ramsey Miller, philosopher."

"Bust my balls if you want, but those kids taught me something. I offered them a few dollars for the weed I'd smoked, but they wouldn't take it. The guy, after college he plans to join the Peace Corps. He said the key to life is magnanimity. Can you beat that? His word. It means generous."

"I know what it means."

Ramsey doubted this but let it go. "He says if you have magnanimity, it comes back to you twofold. Sure enough, we'd just started back up the trail. It was steep and not an easy climb—you know that means something, coming from me—and the girl he's with, she steps funny on a rock and twists her ankle, bad. I'll tell you, once the sun goes down it gets real cold in the desert. This time of year, it goes below freezing. So they'd of been in real trouble. They didn't have provisions or nothing. Just that one jug of water, and we'd already finished most of it off."

"But they had you."

Ramsey smiled, remembering. "Me and the boy took our time, making sure every step was in the right place. We got his friend up to the rim, safe and sound."

"The Lord had a plan for you that day."

That wasn't Ramsey's point at all, but he stopped himself from correcting his friend. "Afterward, when I was driving, I kept thinking about those two. I shouldn't call them kids, because they weren't kids. But I kept thinking about them, and about magnanimity. And that's when I realized we're doing this gig all wrong.

It shouldn't be just for us—our families and whatnot. We need to invite everyone."

"Who's 'everyone'?"

"Everyone in the neighborhood."

"You hate everyone in the neighborhood," Eric said.

"That's my point—we need to come together. Listen, I know there's people who don't think much of me, and for a long time I didn't care. Or I did, but it was easier to pretend I didn't. But that ain't how I want it anymore."

"And you think a party will fix everything?"

"Ain't a matter of fixing things—it's about doing what's right. I want people coming to my house, eating my food and drinking my beer and listening to Rusted Wheels. I want their kids trampling my lawn."

Eric glanced at the door separating the garage from the rest of the house. "Ramsey, I have to ask. How much does Allie know about this plan of yours?"

"Haven't had time to fill her in yet on all the details."

"You might want to get around to that. I doubt her ideal Sunday includes hosting all your snooty neighbors."

"*I'm* hosting," Ramsey said. "She can sit back and drink margaritas. Point is, this is no time for selfishness or hard feelings or any of that bullshit."

"What do you mean, 'no time'?" Eric asked.

Yeah, Ramsey thought. Allie told him. Definitely.

On a freezing January afternoon, Ramsey had sat her down and explained the orbital axis to his wife, what it meant, and she made him swear to keep it between them. Frankly, he didn't care who knew, but he gave her his word and kept it, because he loved her, honored her, and obeyed her, just as he'd promised six years earlier. Anyway, she had a point. There were some things that people would rather stay ignorant about.

Take those kids in the Grand Canyon. During their truth session, before the shadows got too deep and they all started back up the trail, Ramsey had swept his arms across the magnificent vista and said, *You know, God's going-out-of-business sale is coming sooner than you think.* He chose to say it that way for their benefit—clever, a little humorous to lighten the impact—but when the kids started trading glances, he backed off right away, laughing at himself and blaming the weed. He told them about a time when he had been high and decided it would be a good idea to climb the utility pole by his apartment, and then it started to thunder and lightning, and he got so scared that he froze way up there like a cat in a tree, and the power company had to come and rescue him in one of their bucket trucks. It hadn't been a funny experience at the time, and he'd been drunk, not high, but he told it the way he did because he admired and respected these two kids and wanted them to like him. That was before they all began their ascent and the girl sprained her ankle and Ramsey got to show them what kind of man he could be, what kind of man he was.

"My friend, there's no time for bullshit," Ramsey said to Eric now, "because that's not how a magnanimous person behaves."

In the family room, Allie was facing the TV—a drama, from the serious, argumentative voices. "Eric's leaving," Ramsey said as he led his friend to the front door.

"Good night, Allie," Eric said to the back of Allie's head.

"Mhmm," she replied without turning around.

"She feels my judgment," Eric said once he and Ramsey were alone outside. His voice was just above a whisper. "I shouldn't be judging anyone. That's the Lord's job, not mine."

Ramsey always felt uncomfortable when Eric talked as if he were in church or at an A.A. meeting. "Nah," he said. "She's just really into her show."

Once Eric was gone, Ramsey went inside and sat at the kitchen table, bit into a slice of leftover pizza, and began writing his to-do list. The pizza was cool and hard, but he *tasted* it. It was that way with everything now: land and sky drenched in color. The band's music reverberating in his gut with richer resonance. The felt-tip pen dragged across paper and a car whooshed by out front. In the family room, the music on the TV swelled toward a dramatic crescendo. In the laundry room, the dryer thudded rhythmically: *b-b-duh, b-b-duh.* The dryer caused the recessed kitchen lights to pulse as if transmitting a code he was this close to cracking. He was paying attention, noticing everything. Some people—scientists, maybe, or detectives—must live this way constantly, attuned to every crumb of sensory data. He might have imagined the experience exhausting, but it was the opposite. He felt the world offering up its treasures. The least he could do was receive them.

He should go to Allie. He would. But first, the list. Thirty-four years old, and he'd never thrown a party before. How much food do you buy? How much beer? Where do you find a pony for pony rides?

He looked up. Allie came over and stood behind him, a hand on each of his shoulders. She pressed down with her thumbs. She'd been loosening his shoulders this way for seven years, ever since he returned from his first week on the road. *My shoulders are killing me, Allie,* he'd said, and she came to him and knew exactly what to do. She worked her thumbs now, pressing hard. Ramsey let out a sigh.

"You schedule a band practice for the minute you come home," she said. "Now you're hiding in here."

"I'm making a to-do list."

"Unless I'm on that list," she said, still rubbing, "I'm not interested." Dark outside, but the curtains were open, and in the window's reflection Ramsey saw the two of them. The tableau looked intimate, yet all the details were in shadow. "It's a joke, Ramsey. We can still joke, can't we?"

"How do you mean?"

"Come on."

"What?"

She let out a breath, almost like a laugh. "You've been gone twenty-six of the last thirty days."

"I have a job."

The rubbing stopped, though her hands continued to rest on his shoulders. "You haven't had a schedule like that for years. I can only conclude that you can't stand being here, with us."

"No, Al—you know that's not true."

"And Eric—what the hell is *his* problem?"

"What do you mean?"

"He's creeping me out lately. The way he looks at me—he's acting weird. You're all acting weird." She sighed. "Even when you're here, it's like you're not here."

"I'm here now," Ramsey said. "I really am."

"Then let's go to bed."

"Soon," Ramsey said. "The thing is, I'm inviting some extra people to the gig, and I want to be sure there's enough activities and food—"

"What extra people? Who are you inviting?"

He shrugged. "The neighbors."

"*Which* neighbors?"

"Well—all of them."

Her hands on his shoulders curled into fists. "Because of your orbital axis."

"It isn't mine, Allie."

She sighed. "Can I ask why you plan to invite the neighbors?"

"I want to bring people together."

"You want that? Come to bed."

81

"Soon," he said.

"You'll come to *our* bed soon? Is that what you're telling me?"

When he didn't answer right away, she said, "Goddammit," and walked away from him, toward the sink. Ramsey turned around to look at her directly. She had on her plaid pajamas. From behind, she could have been any age, anyone. A stranger. She poured a glass of water, drank it down.

Ramsey brushed his teeth in the upstairs hall bathroom while one of the songs from tonight's rehearsal ran through his head. He couldn't help agreeing with Mick Jagger. Satisfaction was fucking elusive.

The house was quiet. He imagined Allie in their bedroom, on the other side of the closed door, waiting for him, reading by the light of her bedside table.

Unless she'd given up on him. That was a possibility, too.

He rinsed, wiped his face. Checked himself in the mirror. There was no good mirror in the truck, and after a long haul his own face always surprised him a little. His hair had gray in it now. The lines in his face were deepening. He looked every bit of his thirty-four years. He wanted to go to Allie, longed to. It wasn't that he preferred the trundle bed in the guest room. But the trundle was hard, like the mattress in his truck, and that was the only place he slept soundly anymore. In fact, he slept better parked at a truck stop—even with the drunken shouting, middle-of-the-night Jake brakes, and lot lizards knocking door-to-door—than he did in his quiet bedroom with Allie.

He was no fool, though. Tonight he needed to be with her. Allie had looked beautiful earlier, sun-kissed in the doorway. The small, gradual surprises this afternoon were all enticements for him to share their bed tonight. As husband and wife. As lovers. It had been too long. He knew this.

He got as far as their bedroom door and hesitated.

*Magruder.*

He tried to push the name from his mind. It was impractical, thinking about that man now, with Allie. Best to put it away once and for all. *Your wife is in there waiting for you,* he thought. *Go to her.* If he could be magnanimous to his neighbors, to strangers, then surely he could be that and more to his wife.

Husband and wife. Lovers. He took a breath, held it, breathed out.

*I love you, Allie. I married you and I would marry you again and I will marry you a thousand times over, from now to as long as we both shall live.*

He gently pushed open the bedroom door. The overhead light was dimmed, the candle on her bedside table lit. Seeing him, Allie smiled.

"Well, hello there," she said, and closed her book.

# 6

September 24, 2006

The rules at 9 Notress Pass arose as they became necessary. An early rule: Do not reveal your home address. Later, when Internet access became available, there was never any discussion about getting it. Wayne and Kendra knew nothing of IP addresses. They simply didn't want their name and address in a database unless there was no choice. Sometimes, like with the electric company, there was no choice. But any time there was, they chose no: no cable TV, no Internet, no newspaper delivery.

No library card.

That was the first time Melanie remembered breaking one of the family's rules. Every so often, Kendra brought her to the library, where for an hour they'd sit together quietly and read before going to McDonald's for lunch. Sometimes Melanie would read a book, other times one of the celebrity magazines. Sometimes she'd pretend to read but really she'd be watching others in the library—mothers reading to small children, the librarians gossiping behind the book-return counter. McDonald's was an even better place to watch people. Truckers on their way to Charleston (Columbus? Chicago?) smothered their food with ketchup and mustard, and chubby kids cried for soda refills, and teenagers a little older than Melanie punched the cash registers and barked commands to one another to keep everything running smoothly.

One afternoon when she was fifteen, Melanie convinced her aunt to drop her at the library before running her errands, rather than leaving her at home or taking her along.

At the library, Melanie examined the "newly received" shelf, looking at the covers of novels until one caught her eye. It had a picture of a girl about Melanie's own age standing on a balcony and looking out over a city. The city wasn't in America—she could tell from the way the buildings looked: very old, colorful, and built into a hillside. The novel was titled *The Cobbler's Sister*, and from the inside flap, Melanie learned that the city was Salamanca, Spain.

She was sitting by the window, reading the opening pages, which had wonderfully descriptive sentences that wound around like the narrow streets of Salamanca, when a number of younger kids stomped into the library. The middle school must have just let out. The kids' pent-up energy, released all at once, made reading impossible, so Melanie closed the book and began to page through a magazine. Practically the whole issue was devoted to the wedding between Jessica Simpson and Nick Lachey. Ordinarily, she'd be enthralled. An eleven-carat diamond headband was attached to the bride's veil. But that day, she wished she could keep reading the novel. Her aunt would be returning soon. So she went up to the counter, determined to get her own library card. Taped to the counter was a note:

To obtain a library card you must present either a driver's
license or a piece of mail addressed to you showing that you
reside in the town of Fredonia. No exceptions. Thank you.

The only mail that she could remember coming to her house,
rather than the P.O. box, was the phone bill. Maybe she could
steal the envelope from the kitchen trash the next time it came.
But when would she next be left alone here at the library? It could
be weeks, maybe longer.

"May I help you?" asked one of the librarians.

If there were a house nearby, she'd have dug through strangers' trash to find an envelope and said to the librarian, *Yes, this is
me*. But there were no houses on this block, just a barbershop and
a dollar store and a Baptist church.

"No, ma'am," she said, and returned to her seat by the window, furious. She tried to free her mind of Salamanca, its 800-year-
old cathedrals, its olive trees. Jessica Simpson and Nick Lachey
had been serenaded by a twenty-five-member gospel choir. The
reception hall had been decorated with 30,000 roses.

By the time her aunt picked her up, Melanie vowed that the
next time she was allowed to visit the library alone, she would
leave with her own library card and as many novels as she could
cram into her backpack without her aunt noticing.

Eight months later, she did just that.

The books she borrowed, she read late into the night and hid in
her closet or under the bed. The library was a way to escape
Notress Pass, and the books they contained allowed her to escape
it further.

Tonight, however, Melanie had come to the library not to borrow books but rather for its Wi-Fi. Behind the building, in the dim
shadows cast by an orange streetlight some hundred yards in the

distance, she crouched against the library's brick exterior wall, holding the laptop computer that Phillip had lent her two months earlier. PROPERTY OF FREDONIA REGIONAL HIGH SCHOOL read the label stuck to its side.

There was so much to see and learn online, and not just about celebrities. If the library books were her glimpse at the larger world, the Wi-Fi Internet connection was freedom writ large. Whenever she snuck out her bedroom window and walked here at night, she sat on the ground and read as fast as possible, no agenda, just clicking links and typing words and phrases into search engines and exploring the wider world though the computer screen. Once her initial thirst was quenched, she visited a few particular websites: the online edition of the *Silver Bay News*. The *Star-Ledger*. The *Asbury Park Press*. There were others, too, but those were the papers that had published the fullest coverage of her mother's death and the failed hunt for her father. Her aunt and uncle had only ever told Melanie the barest facts of the crime. Beyond that, they never spoke about the place where Melanie had lived for the first thirty-three months of her life. From the newspaper archives, she began to fill in the gaps.

How strange it always was to see that name—Meg Miller—in print, to read about her own alleged demise. *Death by drowning.* Reading those words always made her throat constrict and chest tighten as if she really were being held underwater. Then again, everything in those articles made her lightheaded and nauseous, a feeling not unlike morning sickness.

One reporter in particular wrote about the crime over a period of years for the *Silver Bay News*, with articles appearing on the first anniversary, the fifth, the tenth. One night, Melanie had searched online for the reporter's name—Arthur Goodale—and learned that he'd retired from the paper but kept up a news blog. Sometimes he would write about the "Miller killings," and these posts always struck her as surprising and sort of wonderful. To know that somebody still thought from time to time about her mother, and about her, too, made her feel less alone. She hoped that he might write about her mother this week, with another anniversary coming and going—the fifteenth.

She didn't expect to read that Arthur Goodale was dying.

His heart had given out, and now he might never leave his hospital bed or write another word. This connection to her past, tenuous as it was, would soon be severed. She herself had no memories at all of Silver Bay. She tried over the years to see her mother's face, the walls of her nursery, the kitchen where she must have sat in a high chair and eaten meals. Anything. But not a single image remained.

She shut the laptop computer, stood, brushed the dirt off her blue jeans, and began to walk toward the woods, toward home. Why hadn't she told her aunt and uncle this afternoon that she was pregnant? Was it embarrassment, believing that she and Phillip would . . . what, get married? Live happily ever after? And live where? In Fredonia? In Connecticut, near his family? She had let herself believe that Phillip Connor might be the key to a fresh start, but she should have seen that for the fantasy it was. She never should have let herself get carried away. It was depressing and dangerous.

Anyway, none of that mattered. Phillip probably thought she was crazy by now, and her aunt and uncle would find out about the baby soon enough.

The night sky was brighter than usual, the moon nearly full. She crossed a couple of streets and entered a larger section of woods that would have her home in fifteen minutes. Had she driven to the library, the car's engine would almost certainly have woken Kendra, who was a light sleeper, and these excursions were too important to jeopardize. Plus, Melanie liked the woods at night. She'd never been afraid of them, and consequently she knew them well. Or maybe it was because she knew them well that she wasn't afraid.

Yet tonight she wasn't enjoying the walk. Despite herself, she kept thinking about Phillip, leaving him at his front door looking hurt and confused. Had she broken up with him? Even she didn't know. So he ran away from a squirrel. So what? And then she started thinking about that poor journalist in New Jersey dying alone, eighty-one years old and totally off base about the case that had haunted him for years.

"Surprise!" she said aloud. "Meg Miller is alive!"

A twig snapped.

Someone was in the woods with her.

She looked around and saw no one. Her imagination? Other than the occasional deer, the only animals out here were small—squirrels, possum—and they kept to themselves.

She found the woods comforting, she reminded herself, not spooky. Whatever hormones had turned her favorite smells putrid were playing games with her brain's fear center. Or something. Her pace quickened, and she tried to move quieter, and then she started thinking about killers and rapists on the loose, behind every tree.

Her breathing quickened. *I'm losing the woods*, she thought. *They were mine, and now they won't be anymore.*

Before her semester began, her aunt and uncle had given her a cell phone with prepaid minutes, but she'd used up all the minutes long ago, talking to Phillip. Still—if she'd had minutes left, would she have called him now? She hoped not. These were her woods. She willed herself to slow down, relax—*no one is here; no one is here.* Yet by the time she saw the abandoned tractor, the landmark telling her she was just a few hundred yards from Notress Pass, her sweat had turned cold and her pulse throbbed in her neck. The air was still. The only sounds were her quiet footfalls and her heavy breaths. As she passed the tractor, she could swear she saw a shadow glide across it, and she let out a gasp and started sprinting. She squeezed through the tight gap in the hedges, discovered long ago, onto her own property. Her aunt and uncle must not see her leaving or returning, or else there would go her freedom. Still, she half hoped that one of them would spot her darting across the lawn. At this moment she yearned for their safety, yearned for them to take away her freedom. It didn't matter that the woods had been hers. They were gone now. She climbed through her bedroom window, closed and locked it, and slipped soundlessly into bed, not even removing her shoes.

She fell asleep but was awakened by images of hundreds of snapping turtles crawling over one another to get at her—a recurring nightmare since childhood. She awoke several more times, sweating, then freezing, then sweating again. During one of the sweating spells, she removed her shoes and clothes. During the next freezing spell, she found her pajamas in the dark and put them on.

The next time she awakened was to the hard wrap of knuckles on her bedroom door.

"Yeah?" she groaned.

"Get up." Her uncle's voice, uncharacteristically stern.

The room was getting light. She looked at the clock: 7 a.m. Her alarm would go off in fifteen minutes. So why the urgency? She sat up in bed a moment, trying to shake off sleep, and left her room wearing her pajamas and slippers. Her aunt was seated at the kitchen table. Her uncle stood beside her, leaning over the morning paper.

"Come over here," he said without looking up.

She knew without having to look. But she looked anyway.

"He promised not to use it," Melanie said. "I made him promise."

The photographer must have had a powerful zoom lens. She could see individual freckles, each petal on the dandelion.

"People can't be trusted, Melanie," her aunt said.

There were three photographs in a row. Hers was in the middle. To her left, two small children with wide grins, attacking a tall cone of cotton candy. To her right, an older man wearing a gold-and-blue West Virginia T-shirt, giving the camera a thumbs-up. Behind him, the Zipper ride in motion, a blur of purple and green.

A single caption described all three pictures: *Local Fredonia residents enjoying the First Baptist Church's Carnival for Christ.*

Her uncle shut the paper and began to pace the small kitchen.

"I never gave him my name," Melanie said. Still. There was her photo, large and clear, placing her right in Fredonia. And the *Mason City Democrat* published an online version. Did her aunt and uncle know? Probably not, but *she* knew. Her image was now online. Permanently.

"So is this your definition of being careful?" Uncle Wayne put his hands up to his head and massaged his temples. He sighed. "I want you to come to work with me. Learn the trade."

"What—you mean fixing cars?"

"It's been good for this family. You're left alone to do your work—"

"Uncle Wayne, I'm in college."

"Well, your aunt and I don't think you should be. It's causing a lot of problems."

"College has nothing to do with it."

He glanced over at his wife. "We'll talk about it tonight, Mel. You have class today, don't you?"

"Yes."

"Then go to class. But I want you to consider something. You're seventeen and still alive. That isn't luck."

"I know, Uncle Wayne," she said.

Her uncle made the coffee. She endured the smell and poured the juice. They sat together at the table.

*Thank you, Lord, for providing us with this food that will nourish and sustain us,* said Aunt Kendra.

*Amen,* they all said.

After Wayne left for work, Kendra walked out of the kitchen and, a minute later, returned again carrying a manila folder.

"You're right, you know," she said to Melanie, who remained at the table. "You aren't a kid any longer." She placed the folder on the table in front of Melanie. "I'm going to take a shower. I think you should take a look at these." She squeezed Melanie once on the shoulder and walked toward the bedroom.

When Melanie heard the water come on, she opened the folder. The newest letter was right on top of the small stack, dated just a little over a month earlier.

It was worse than she'd imagined.

United States Department of Justice

U.S. Marshals Service

Investigative Operations Division

VIA NEXT-DAY EXPRESS MAIL

August 18, 2006

Wayne Denison
P.O. Box 31
Fredonia, WV 26844

Mr. Denison:

Pursuant to our phone conversation of this afternoon: Ramsey Miller is confirmed to have been in Morgantown, West Virginia, on the afternoon of August 14.

His fingerprints were taken off the handle of a switchblade after an incident near the University of West Virginia campus. By the time police arrived, Mr. Miller had fled the scene, and his whereabouts at this time are once again unknown. The fingerprint match, which came through this morning, was conclusive.

Be assured that we have no reason to believe that Mr. Miller knows of your location. Still, Morgantown's proximity to Fredonia is obviously troubling. We are in touch with law enforcement in Fredonia as well as with W.V. Highway Patrol and the Marshal in Charleston, but we are also asking your family to be especially alert and vigilant. Vary your routines, including your routes to and from your home. Report anything unusual to local law enforcement and do not hesitate to contact my office at any time.

We will be in touch as soon as we know more.

Sincerely,

Avery Lewis
U.S. Marshal
U.S. Courthouse
50 Walnut Street
Newark, NJ 07102
201-555-1108

She reread the letter, which must have arrived the same week that Melanie had started classes at Mountain Community College. Yet her aunt and uncle had said nothing, nor had

94

they done anything to stop her from starting school. So she'd been wrong about them. They could actually show remarkable restraint.

She scanned the rest of the letters, which were stacked in reverse chronological order. There were eight total, most of which she'd read before.

. . . to your recent inquiry as to the present status of the case that pertains to your ward of court: We continue to receive tips as to the whereabouts of Ramsey Miller. We are actively pursuing these tips and will inform you right away of . . .

. . . will be retiring from the U.S. Marshals Service at the end of this calendar year. Going forward, U.S. Marshal Avery Lewis will be the lead investigator . . .

. . . but has again eluded local law enforcement. Fingerprint evidence corroborates the eyewitness account, which placed Mr. Miller outside his former home early in the morning. Unfortunately, the eyewitness did not report the information for several hours because . . .

. . . hope to have positive news for you before long. In the meantime, I trust that you are all adjusting to your new environment. If you ever . . .

Eight letters in fifteen years. Together, they told a sad story of botched opportunities and administrative detachment, and it seemed pretty clear that within the walls of the U.S. courthouse in Newark, New Jersey, the successful capture of Ramsey Miller had never been anyone's top priority.

"We do the best we can, Mel," her aunt said when she came back into the kitchen dressed for work, her hair blown dry. By then Melanie had returned the letters to the folder and was staring across the kitchen at the clock above the sink. "I hope you know that." Kendra took the folder back and left the kitchen with it.

When she came through the kitchen again to leave for work, Melanie said, "I'm sorry."

"Oh, don't be sorry, honey." Her aunt came over and knelt down to Melanie's level. "Just be careful."

Melanie didn't get up until her aunt had left the house. Then she began to straighten up the kitchen. She was about to throw away the newspaper, but instead folded it into quarters so that her photograph remained visible. She returned to her bedroom and looked at it some more. Her mother had died at twenty-eight. In the photo that many of the papers ran when covering the murder, her mother might only have been a few years older than Melanie was now. She was standing on a beach, wearing a gray sweatshirt and squinting a little in the sunlight. Behind her was the ocean. One hand was on her head, trying to keep her hair from blowing everywhere. Only one in a hundred women, maybe one in a thousand, could look that glamorous trying simply to keep her hair from knotting up.

From this and other photographs of her mother that she'd found online, Melanie concluded that although she resembled her mother, the resemblance was limited to component parts—angular chins, brown eyes, small noses—rather than cumulative effect. Her mother's beauty, alas, had not been passed down, though on the best of days, with the humidity low and her acne in remission, Melanie sometimes felt a little pretty.

She got dressed, and removed her textbooks and notebooks from her backpack and stowed them in the closet. Then, rethinking, she retrieved one of the notebooks—a journalist should always have paper handy—and put it into her backpack again, along with the newspaper and some clothes: bras, underwear, a couple of shirts and skirts, and another pair of jeans. She got her toothbrush, toothpaste, razor, and hairbrush from the bathroom and put them in, and carried the backpack, purse, and laptop computer from her bedroom into the kitchen. She returned to her bedroom for another pair of shoes.

After getting her driver's license, she'd briefly driven a loner from Uncle Wayne's garage, a boat-sized Chevy Caprice, until her uncle had bought her a Ford Escort with nearly 200,000 miles on it. But the radio wasn't bad and Wayne made sure the engine and tires were in perfect working order. Before leaving town, Melanie would stop at the gas station to buy a road atlas and to top off the tank and get a hot cup of tea for the long drive north, to the one place where she was forbidden.

*I'm breaking every rule.*

The thought should have brought her no thrill. It did, though. It brought a small thrill. Though she'd never driven farther than the college, she always enjoyed being behind the wheel, her body settled into the seat, her mind drifting, imagining.

This was no field trip, though. No adventure. She reminded herself that she was about to visit a terrible place where her father committed murder and her mother burned.

But Arthur Goodale was alive—for now—and she needed to see him while there was still time to find out everything he knew about her mother's murder. And then she would do what everyone else had failed to—find her father before he found her. Then she and her baby would live without fear.

Before going to the car, she tore a blank page from the notebook and found a pen in her bag.

She wrote:

*Dear Aunt Kendra and Uncle Wayne,*
*I'll be back in a few days. Please, please don't worry. I promise I'm*
*okay.*
*Love,*

She hesitated. Melanie? Meg? Finally, she decided on "M." She left the note on the kitchen table, beside the salt and pepper shakers.

Then she was on her way.

# 7

September 21, 1991

In a day, the world would end dramatically. But right now it was just another dreary Saturday morning in New Jersey, the sky a misty and monochrome gray as Ramsey walked from his car to the Kinko's.

At 6:30 a.m. the copy shop was empty except for a young man behind the counter sitting cross-legged on a table and eating a banana. One more large bite before coming over to Ramsey, who set his coffee cup on the counter, removed the hand-drawn invitation from his pocket, and unfolded it.

"I need a hundred fifty of these," Ramsey said, sliding it across the countertop. "But typed up all nice."

The young man was already thick in the jowls and starting to sag. He looked at the paper and said nothing until he'd swallowed the gob of banana. "I can set you up on one of the computers over there." He nodded toward the far wall.

"No, I don't use those," Ramsey said.

"It's simple."

"Simple enough for you to do it for me?" The three twenties were already out of Ramsey's wallet and on the counter.

Sixty bucks sounded all right with Danny Chester, Customer Associate, and twenty minutes later Ramsey was leaving with 150 invitations—large, eye-catching typeface on bright blue paper. Danny had thrown in an image of a kid's teeter-totter in the top right corner, maybe hoping for a tip.

Task one was complete with ninety percent of America still in bed.

Main Street Music didn't open until ten, leaving Ramsey with time to stop by the Shark Fin Marina, not far from his present location. Before long he was approaching the marshes on his left and the Shark Fin Inlet on his right. Despite two decades having passed, everything looked the same, and he wondered now why he'd never thought to pay a visit here before, considering it was a rare place from his youth that held warm memories.

He drove toward the boatyard—the road unpaved gravel, still—where at this time of year about half the boats were in the water and half were dry-docked. The smell of burning diesel always reminded him of the boatyard, but it hadn't occurred to him before now how much the rows of dry-docked boats resembled trucks at a yard or a loading dock, and how his love of these boats—many of them thirty-five or forty feet or more—might have fed his attraction to the big rig, which was like a yacht on wheels, its cab a marvel of efficient interior space, pushed along by a massive diesel engine.

Ramsey parked his car in one of the visitor spaces by the docks and inhaled the sweet, rotting smell of the inlet. The water this morning looked glassy, with just a single charter boat creeping at no-wake speed toward the bridge that led out to the ocean. This time of year the water remained warm but the wind could whip.

With summer gone, only a few boats were needed to satisfy the demands of the most ardent fisherman. Ramsey was too far away to read the boat's name. A seagull hovered over the stern, but the boat wasn't weighed down yet with fish. The gull swooped up and, cawing, veered off toward the ocean.

Ramsey walked over pebbles to the boatyard, trying to identify any of the half dozen men he passed. Some of them looked younger than he was. When an older man with a clipboard stepped out of the office, Ramsey approached him and asked whether his father's old boss, Bruno, still worked there.

"Bruno Crawford?" The man sniffed up a bunch of snot and grimaced. "Afraid he died eight, ten years back."

Ramsey nodded. "I used to come here as a kid. My old man worked here, and Bruno was always good to him."

"Bruno was before my time, but I only ever heard good things." He held out his hand. "Donny Mazza. I manage the yard."

"Ramsey Miller."

"Glad to know you, Ramsey. You a boater?"

"Not really," he said. "I keep a thirteen-foot Boston Whaler on a floating dock in Silver Bay."

"That's just the boat you want for tooling around the bay."

"It is," Ramsey said. "Wish I had more time to take it out."

"Don't we all?" Donny looked around at the boats, the water. "The boat owner's curse—we're all too busy." He smiled at Ramsey. "Now what can I do you for?"

"I was in the area, is all," Ramsey said, "and thought I'd drop by and kick around a few old memories."

"Been a long time?"

Ramsey did the math. "Twenty-four years."

"Well, it's good to have you back," Donny said. "Tell you what. You relax, take in those memories, and let me know if you need anything. We got a full pot of coffee in the office."

"Nah, I don't plan to linger," Ramsey said. "I was hoping Bruno might still be around—I'm having a party tomorrow and wanted to invite him."

"I'm awfully sorry to be the one to rain on that parade," Donny said. "Dino's still here, though."

"Who?"

"Little fellow with the one bad eye? He goes back longer than anyone. Not sure if he goes back twenty-four years."

A few names came to mind: Bert. Chuck. He tried to recall Dino and conjured up a small, trim man in the same greasy clothes they all wore, but maybe that was only his imagination working. "Say, Donny, you don't by any chance want to come to a block party tomorrow in Silver Bay? There'll be plenty of food, and my band's gonna play a set or two. You'd like it."

"Wish I could—but tomorrow I'm working all day."

"Then come by after."

"Can't." The shift in Donny's smile was almost imperceptible. When he said, "Thanks, though," his voice dropped a few decibels.

*Crazy fuck.* That's what Donny Mazza was thinking.

"I ain't crazy," Ramsey said.

"Never said you were, friend." The smile looked false now, frozen.

"Yeah, but you thought it." Ramsey felt his heart rate quicken, the blood rush to his hands and feet. He demanded—commanded—that he stop this, pronto. He wasn't twenty anymore, and he wasn't drunk, and this was no hole-in-the-wall bar. He took a breath. Softened his face. "I'm playing around." He didn't dare lay a friendly hand on the other man's shoulder. It would be taken the wrong way. Instead, he forced a smile of his own. "You're a good sport."

He shouldn't have come. The past was nothing but a fish straight out of the ocean—slippery, and never as pretty as you think. Without another word, he returned to his car, every step of the way feeling the shame of Donny Mazza's stare.

He rumbled back along the gravel road, retreating hastily from his past to the safety of his to-do list.

He walked every street in the Sandy Oaks development, placing an invitation into each mailbox, and tried to figure out why he'd been willing to beat the hell out of some dipshit boatyard manager who did nothing to deserve it. How was it, he wondered, that he was still a breath away from that sort of madness? After all these years, had he really changed so little?

Then again, he hadn't gone through with it. He'd walked away. Surely that said something. But not much. And he wondered what miniscule difference—a slight change in inflection, a single extra utterance—might have led to a different outcome. As a kid he'd heard his father at the boatyard once talking with another man about how the United States and the Soviet Union had nearly blown up the earth over missiles in Cuba. The war never happened, but it just as easily could have. That's what stayed with Ramsey for years afterward: The fact that the world had survived didn't mean that anyone had behaved well or wouldn't push everything over the brink the next time around.

He could save time by driving from mailbox to mailbox, but he wanted to press his feet to the asphalt in this neighborhood of families. By now Allie knew many of their fellow owners of half-acre plots of soft sod and border shrubs and close proximity to the better primary school. To Ramsey, the people were basically interchangeable; they certainly didn't give two shits about him. But like he said to Eric, the point of this party was to treat them like lifelong chums.

Even David Magruder, whose mailbox was crooked and loose on its stand. Ramsey had never spoken to the man but knew what he looked like from TV—long face, balding, big teeth. Yet he exuded utter confidence when he told you what was "on tap for the weekend." A TV weatherman must be the only job in the world with no penalty for being wrong half the time.

Ramsey briefly considered skipping this house. But no. If Ramsey was serious about being magnanimous, then he *must* invite Magruder. He slid an invitation into the mailbox.

Three more streets. Then he'd turn to the other tasks on his list—sound equipment rental, ball pit rental, materials to buy for the stage, kegs to reserve, fire pit to dig, food to buy and prepare . . . the list was long, and he looked forward to doing all of it.

Seventeen hours later, he was still checking off items, though he'd accomplished a hell of a lot for one day. Even figured out the pony situation. (As simple as looking in the yellow pages under Party/ Children.) The woman promised a healthy and gentle Rocky Mountain pony as well as a trained Great Dane to lead the pony around.

The afternoon's rehearsal went smoother with Wayne there. His excuse for having gone AWOL the night before was lame— "girl trouble." Even after three years of living in Jersey, there were still flare-ups with this girl Kendra back in West Virginia who'd stayed stuck on him. *Cut the cord and find yourself a Jersey girl!* Ramsey had wanted to say on any number of occasions. But he knew that love was a messy thing, and he wasn't going to get on the kid's case today—not after Wayne had convinced his manager at the music store not only to rent Ramsey a P.A. but to run it during the gig.

Wayne was basically a decent kid trying to figure shit out, same as anyone. It hadn't taken him long, a couple of years earlier, for him to barf out his story the day Ramsey came into the music store for strings: raised in foster care in West Virginia, ditched the on-again/off-again girlfriend (or tried to, anyway), and left home at seventeen on a Greyhound bus the moment he'd scraped together two hundred bucks, nothing but a knapsack of clothes, his acoustic, and a vague notion that seeing the ocean might be a good thing.

"Actually, it was my foster dad's guitar," Wayne had said. "I figured he owed me."

Ramsey smiled. "I take it your family wasn't *The Waltons*."

He thought maybe the kid wouldn't get the reference, but Wayne shook his head and said, "Man, you wouldn't believe me if I told you."

Ramsey wasn't about to get into a pissing contest over who had the crappiest boyhood, so he let it go.

In the couple of years since, Ramsey sometimes broached the topic of Wayne learning a trade and making a real living. The kid always brushed him off, which was fine—he was young with no obligations—but Ramsey couldn't help trying to steer him in the right direction, like Eric had done for Ramsey. One thing Ramsey had come to believe, you had to pay it forward. Otherwise, the planet was fucked. Of course, a young man alone in the world wasn't going to seek out guidance. Not the right sort of guidance, anyhow. So you had to reach out, show him you gave a damn by overpaying him to clean your truck or change the oil and filters, and while he's there with the hood up, you teach him a thing or two about the engine.

Asking him to join the band, though—that was no simple generosity. Not with Wayne's fancy chords and clean solos. Truth was, Wayne was too good for Rusted Wheels, but evidently the camaraderie, or at least the free beer, meant enough for him to keep showing up most of the time.

Their rehearsal today ended around five, and despite all he still had to do, Ramsey took Allie and Meg out to their favorite restaurant overlooking the bay. Meg behaved herself, scribbling on the paper place mat with crayons given to her by their waitress and chattering to herself. Allie and Ramsey watched Meg, watched the bay, and spoke little, but the restaurant was festive enough from other people's conversations that their silence didn't announce itself.

Now, at 1:30 a.m., Ramsey carried the trays of hamburger patties out to the garage refrigerator. He drove to the 24-hour Exxon station for another twenty-pound bag of ice.

He wouldn't try to sleep tonight.

Last night hadn't gone well. Allie clicked off her light and they kissed and he tried to imagine that it was long ago with the jagged scar still fresh on his thigh. Allie had just moved into his apartment over the laundromat with the dryer-exhaust smell and the squeaking bed that made them laugh. But none of it would stay fixed in his mind.

They fumbled awhile in the dark, he and Allie, until he slid her hand away and said, *Babe, I'm sorry.* He explained that his back hurt from all those hours on the road. He went to the kitchen for a heat pack, and when he returned he told Allie he was going to try the trundle bed for a while, see if the hard mattress might help.

When he returned home tonight from the gas station with the bag of ice, rather than go upstairs he wiped down the kitchen counters and scrubbed the downstairs bathroom, because that was the one the guests would be using. At 4 a.m. he sat in the living room with his guitar and a pair of headphones, closed his eyes, and started to run through some of the songs in the set. He soon abandoned those for his all-time favorites. Zeppelin, the Stones, the Allman Brothers, Skynyrd, Hendrix, the Who, the Doors, the Dead. It was nothing less than the soundtrack to his whole life he was strumming, everything electric and tinged with blue.

He felt his breathing slow and his muscles relax, similar to how his body responded to being on the road these past few months. When he was behind the wheel, all the human struggles—wives and husbands, rich and poor—faded away, leaving only the soothing sounds of a well-tuned engine and wide tires rolling over a hot highway.

He'd always enjoyed driving, but since learning about the orbital axis his life in that truck had come to feel important, like he and the truck were a drop of the earth's blood moving along a wide vein to deliver vital nutrients. Didn't matter if it was pallets of Campbell's soup or Huffy bikes or Gap jeans. He and the rig, he sensed, were part of a system larger than himself, much larger than the company he worked for. Used to work for. These past couple of months, he found himself requesting longer hauls from the fleet manager. He hadn't been a true over-the-road driver since buying his own truck. The company treated him well, and for years he had it good—fairly regular stops, no-touch freight, usually stayed east of the Mississippi. Nearly always home for his mandatory thirty-four-off.

But when he started requesting longer hauls and more territory, the fleet manager was more than happy to oblige—isn't often an experienced driver requests *less* predictable routes—and sometime in the past few weeks Ramsey had started getting creative with the log book. Started driving for sixteen, seventeen hours, watching the road the way an NFL quarterback watches the field—hyperalert and able to see everything before it happens. Wet roads and wind gusts and weavers and tailgaters and narrow lanes and deer and none of it raised his pulse. And all this without a single illegal substance. The brief naps in his berth felt like the most restful sleep of his life.

No question, the orbital axis was having an effect on him. As the days and weeks passed and July became August and then

September, Ramsey had begun to feel an electrical charge in the air all the time, as if a thunderstorm were always imminent, even under a blue sky. And yet he knew that this charge wasn't electricity at all, but rather the tug of galactic forces beginning to nudge everything into place, including him.

He was glad he hadn't sold the truck back in June. That'd been his first instinct.

"What would you do instead?" Allie asked when he ran the idea by her.

"Why would I need to do anything?" he replied. With no reason to make money anymore, he could stay at home. He could jam with Rusted Wheels and hang out with the kid. And his presence in town would keep Magruder away, without anyone ever having to bring it up or admit to a damn thing. Ramsey could pretend like he never knew—he would give her that gift—and he and Allie could face the end together, man and wife.

But she wanted him to keep working. And—there was no denying this—the road was tugging at him, hard.

Now, as he played the guitar through headphones in his silent house, he allowed himself to consider his own childhood, all those regrets, and yet he could chart exactly how his rough start had led to Allie, and how their love had led him to a respectable job, to their home in a good neighborhood, and, of course, to Meg. He imagined their daughter all grown up. He saw her as a school principal, doling out punishments to kids like Ramsey. He couldn't help smiling at the thought.

It was sad, of course, that the future he imagined would never come to pass, but not overly sad. The orbital axis gave him perspective. Made him see that we were all just small animals on a small planet in a huge universe, not cold but impersonal. Matter-of-fact. A planet forms and then it dies, end of story. And the closer the end came, the more Ramsey felt resigned to it, the way in a movie, when the screen goes black and you know the credits are about to roll, you become resigned to the ending even if it isn't the ending you might have chosen.

At 6:15 a.m., a time when fishermen and truckers readied their vessels, Ramsey removed his headphones, laid the guitar on the sofa, and went upstairs. First he entered Meg's bedroom, a risky maneuver because if she woke up now, with the birds already chirping outside, she would be up for the day. He stood over her crib. Recently, she'd started sleeping with a thin pillow. But she never wanted any stuffed animals in there or even a blanket, preferring instead to face each night alone. She was asleep on her stomach, her face toward the wall, and Ramsey watched her body's gentle rise and fall. He could easily watch her for the next hour, but he pulled himself away, slipping back into the hallway and toward the master bedroom.

He'd told Allie that he would be up late, not to wait up, but it looked as if she had waited—for a while, anyway: The candle on the bedside table was burned down to the base. The TV remote lay on the bed not far from her hand. Twenty-eight years old, and she still slept on her belly, same as the kid, a fist curled under her chin.

Standing over her—she was so, so pretty—he wanted to wake her, to lie wordlessly beside her at the beginning of their last day together. But the curtains were open, and the light would wake her soon enough. How incredible, he thought, moving toward the window and looking out above the rooftops across the way, that this morning looked exactly like every other. There was no way to see those eight other planets dragging themselves mind-lessly into position. But they were. He could already feel it, the inevitability.

He considered frying up some eggs and serving Allie breakfast in bed. He did that sometimes on her birthday and on their anniversary. She was going to die tonight. They all were. That was an unfortunate given, a scientific certainty, but in the meantime he could bring her eggs. Then he changed his mind. Let her sleep. Anyway, his remaining tasks wouldn't take care of themselves: propane to buy at the grocery store, and horseshoes. He still needed to pick up the kegs from the liquor store. And Eric would be here soon to help him build the backyard stage.

The list seemed to grow even as it shrank, but he'd get it all done. The party would be a success, and the band would play better than it ever had, and because of Ramsey Miller the overall goodwill on the planet would have been increased by some small but measurable amount. And when the gig was done—the last chord played, the amps silenced—he would clutch his family tight, and knowing he'd led a fuller life than he ever could have imagined, he would welcome the earth's own spectacular finale.

# 8

September 25, 2006

For ten glorious miles, the road trip was as Melanie imagined: windows down, adrenaline pumping, radio remarkably static-free as she wound around hills and through forest, crisp morning air mixing with the smell of mint tea steaming in the cup holder. If there was a better feeling than being behind the wheel, chugging along an open road on a sunny morning, she couldn't imagine what it would be. For ten miles her troubles were forgotten even as she was driving toward them.

But as she approached the county line, she rounded a sharp curve and became the next in an eternal line of cars with their brake lights on. A full minute at a dead stop. Then she began creeping along so slowly that she might as well have been walking to New Jersey. When the radio station began to crackle, she shut it off, and in the stillness there was time to consider where she was going and why, and to think about how easy it would be to turn the car around, to find Phillip and tell him that, yes, squirrels were damn scary creatures, and let's just hunker down in your bedroom and never leave.

But what would that solve? She'd still be living in hiding, in fear.

Yes, but you'd still be living, she thought.

*Trouble ain't nothin to fear—it'll find you there, it'll find you here.*

A lyric from one of the songs her uncle played on his acoustic guitar. Maybe once or twice a year, he fetched it from the back of his bedroom closet and wiped off the strings with a rag and messed around with a few songs. When he did, it was always music from a long time ago. Bands Melanie knew by name, but not bands she knew. They were from before her aunt and uncle's time, too, but Wayne explained to Melanie that he was an old soul. Melanie figured she must be an old soul, too, because she liked the songs he played, and the way he played them—as if he went someplace deep into the songs and was inviting Melanie and Kendra to go there with him. For a man who played so rarely, he was really good—anyone could see that. There was this guy who played the guitar on the quad sometimes at college, and his fingers strained to make the chords and his voice strained to sing the melody. Her uncle's hands were always relaxed, and his voice found the melody the way water finds the low ground. And although he sang other people's words, the words themselves mattered less than the feeling behind them. But he had to be in the right mood. And even then, after twenty or thirty minutes of song, the guitar went back into its case, which went back into the closet for another long hibernation.

After nearly an hour on the road, the two eastbound lanes merged into one. An enormous pine tree had fallen across the road and taken down a power line with it. One at a time, cars from both directions crept onto the grass along the eastbound shoulder and squeezed by the mess.

Some three hours later, she approached Baltimore. By then she'd eaten all the snacks she had with her, the tea was long gone, she was desperate to pee, and her driving leg was throbbing. Her reward, after a quick restroom break and more fuel for herself and the car, was several hours of white-knuckled driving on I-95. She couldn't get over how wide the highway was and how many vehicles traveled on it, and how fast everyone was going, and how recklessly: cars darting between lanes, eighteen-wheelers cutting her off, motorcycles roaring past, weaving as if they weren't particularly interested in remaining alive. There were a million radio stations to choose from, but she couldn't imagine listening to music while navigating this sort of highway. She clutched the wheel, kept her foot on the gas and her eyes on the road ahead, reminding herself not to become distracted by all the billboards and all the cars entering and exiting the highway, by the approaching Philadelphia skyline, by the stretches of oil refineries and power plants, all soot and smokestacks that looked as if they belonged in a movie about the end of the world.

The Rand McNally road atlas took her as far as Monmouth County, New Jersey, Exit 105 on the Garden State Parkway. By the time she rolled down the window to pay the toll collector, she felt exhausted from the trip. After a few miles of car dealerships and strip malls and impatient drivers, the speed limit dropped—to thirty-five, then twenty-five—and traffic thinned. Sidewalks and trees lined the road.

When she passed the WELCOME TO SILVER BAY sign, she half expected the town to look familiar, though of course it didn't. Shore Dry Cleaning was on her left. Luigi's Pizza was on her right. Had she ever eaten there? Was it even around back then? She passed a couple of brick office buildings, a number of homes, then a two-block stretch of shops and restaurants before coming upon a yellow hotel on her left called the Sandpiper. One hotel seemed as good as another, so she parked her car in the lot and went inside.

"I need a room to sleep in, please," she said to the man behind the counter. He was older, at least sixty.

"Two queens or a king?" he asked.

His question sounded surreal, until she figured out he meant the beds.

"Oh, it's just me," she said, and immediately regretted saying this. Kind faces could be deceiving. People did horrible things. She considered telling him that someone might be joining her later.

"I'll need to see a credit card for incidentals," he said. When she frowned at him, he added, "In case you order a movie, or make any long-distance calls."

She had planned to sign the guest registry under a false name, like the people were always doing in Hardy Boys novels. Nobody in Silver Bay would know the name Melanie Denison, but she didn't want there to be any way to trace her having come here.

"No, that won't be necessary," she said. "I'll be paying with cash."

"I understand," the man said, "but it's our policy."

She bit her lip and dug into her wallet for her debit card and handed it to the man, who swiped it and told her that her room was down the hallway on the first floor. He handed her a plastic room key and her debit card—but not before taking a good long look at it.

"Enjoy your stay, Ms. Denison. There's a pool out back." He shrugged. "It's a little grimy." His face brightened again. "If you need anything, be sure to ask."

She already had a question. "Where can I get a map of town?"

He knelt down and reappeared with a photocopy of a hand-drawn map. He pointed to the star and said, "We're right here." He tapped his finger against the solid blotch running along the right side of the map, labeled ATLANTIC OCEAN. "If you ever get lost," he said, "just head east."

From the diner two blocks away, she ordered a cheeseburger and French fries to go. She ate in her room with the TV on, changing channels. The Yankees and the Devil Rays were scoreless in the first inning. *Casablanca* was just beginning. The Skipper hit Gilligan with his hat. This was how you stir-fried pork. A man in a suit told three other men in suits that the antiwar rallies on Wednesday would lead to real change. Race cars roared around a track. The number of channels boggled the mind.

The sky outside her window began to lose its daytime blue. The sun would set soon, and she was tempted to stay in her room and see exactly how many channels there were. Maybe even watch a movie on HBO. But there was one thing she had to do before the day was out. And according to her map it would be easy to find: zero turns.

After a couple of miles of driving east along the edges of suburban neighborhoods, the landscape became watery. She crossed several small bridges over marshes, then was back on solid land for another mile or so until the houses became older and larger, and the road abruptly ended. In front of her, a boardwalk ran north to south.

She got out of her car, stepped onto the boardwalk, and was struck as if by a physical force by the ocean's enormity, by the sun's fierce reflection off the water that rose and dipped everywhere, white peaks spilling over themselves all the way to the horizon. No photograph or TV show she'd seen had ever gotten it right. To call the ocean "blue" or "green," to name a single color, was like defining a living, breathing human being with a single adjective. To call the air "salty" was to ignore all the other smells, the muskier, living ones that, remarkably, didn't bother her at all—whether it was fish or seaweed or critters dying in their shells.

A few people, maybe a dozen, were walking along the boardwalk, looking straight ahead, and Melanie wondered how they could not all be staring east. How could their knees not be weak?

She walked north along the boardwalk a few dozen yards until a gap allowed her to descend to the sand. There, some reptilian part of her brain knew what to do: She kicked off her shoes and socks, cuffed her pants to mid-calf, and walked across the cool sand toward the water. Back at the hotel the air was calm, but here a strong breeze whipped and snapped her hair, which she brushed away from her face with her hand. She wondered if this could be the same spot where the photograph of her mother was taken.

Away from the boardwalk, she was alone. The only sounds were the waves, the wind, and the gulls.

Where water met sand, the ground became rockier and full of black shells and seaweed. She stepped more carefully, bent down, and cupped water in her hands. Tasted the salt, swooshed it around her mouth before spitting it out. When another wave pushed water past her and up over her ankles, she held her ground and her feet got sucked into the wet sand. The sensation was surprising, even a little frightening. And although the shoreline might have looked the same at every scale, she didn't feel like a fractal any longer, having removed herself from the old pattern. The waves, the gulls, the salt air all went a long way toward erasing any lingering doubt about having come here.

Behind her, the sun dropped over a thin band of clouds, turning the sky astonishing shades of pink and red and orange. She couldn't care less. Sunsets put on their gaudy show everywhere. Not this, though: waves smashing onto the shore, and beyond it the water rising and falling and colliding into itself, and still farther the wide, endless stretch to that thin, perfect line where sky and earth meet.

Her lack of planning was its own strategy. Planning ahead would mean imagining all the potential pitfalls—just the sort of thing that could have her packing her car and returning to Fredonia. So the next day, instead of calling ahead to the hospital, fretting over whether Arthur Goodale was allowed visitors (or, she hesitated to think, whether or not he was even alive), she simply showed up at Monmouth Regional Hospital and hoped for the best.

She dressed like she imagined a journalist would: skirt, blouse, more makeup than she felt comfortable wearing. Hair pinned up. She ditched the backpack and carried a spiral notebook, its first three pages containing the questions she'd written last night and this morning. She stuck a pencil behind her ear.

Her hands were clammy, but she felt refreshed from a surprisingly good night's sleep and energized by the fact that she had actually done it, had traveled here on her own to New Jersey, to this hospital. The place was vast and sprawling, nothing like the clinic back home. Yet somewhere within these walls, Arthur Goodale was waiting to talk with her. He just didn't know it yet.

She parked the car and followed the signs for the main entrance. Inside, she scanned the signs on the wall for the critical care unit, then rode the elevator to the second floor. Two women in white coats stood behind a high desk labeled NURSES STATION. Seeing Melanie, one of them smiled. Melanie approached the desk. "I'm here to see Arthur Goodale," she said to the smiling nurse. "Is he still here?"

The nurse asked, "Are you family?"

"Me? No."

"May I ask your relationship with Mr. Goodale?"

"Actually, we've never met." When the nurse squinted at her, she added, "I'm a reporter."

"With . . ."

"The *Star-Ledger*." The biggest paper in the area.

"We try to restrict visitors in the unit to family and close friends." She exchanged a glance with the other nurse. "I'll have to ask the patient if he's willing to see you. Assuming he's awake. May I ask your name?"

"Alice Adams," she said. "Would you please tell him it's about the Ramsey Miller case?" She hadn't said her father's name aloud more than a dozen times in her life.

"One moment." The nurse walked down the hall and entered a room on the left. Seconds later, she was back in the hallway—remarkably, waving Melanie over. "He's all yours."

The door was already open, so Melanie stepped into the room and was struck by Arthur Goodale's compromised state: shirtless, thin blanket pulled halfway up his chest. Several monitoring devices ran underneath the blanket. His left hand was connected to an IV. His face had several days of white stubble, the hair on his head was white and wispy, uncombed, and his pale blue eyes were set within a dense web of wrinkled skin, with dark bags underneath. Were their situations reversed, she wouldn't be accepting visitors.

"I'll admit, you've piqued my interest." The strength of Goodale's voice surprised her. "Who are you again?"

"Alice Adams."

"I'd shake your hand, but I'm attached to too many machines," he said. "A horror show, getting old. Though I'm told it beats the alternative. Please, hand me my glasses." They were on the bedside table. She did as asked, and he fumbled a bit sliding the glasses into place. "Much better." He smiled. "Take a seat."

Melanie moved the room's lone chair away from the wall and sat.

"So how can I help you?" he asked.

"I've read your blog," she said.

Apparently, this was the right thing to say, because his eyes lit up a little. "Is that so?"

"I only started recently, but I went back and read everything about the Miller case. And everything you wrote about it in the *Silver Bay News*."

"Going back how far?"

"Everything."

He attempted a whistle, but it was all breath and no tone. "It's a fascinating case."

Fascinating wasn't the word she'd choose. "It's terrible, what happened."

"It was. But I think it's finally becoming ancient history. I had a nurse in here the other day—a local—who knew nothing about it." He cleared his throat. "So what's your interest in the case?"

How, she wondered, had this already become his interview? "I work for the *Star-Ledger*."

"Crime beat?"

"Sir?"

He blinked a couple of times. "How long have you been writing for the paper?"

"About a year."

He scratched the stubble on his cheek. "You're not from New Jersey."

"No, sir—I grew up in a small town in North Carolina." She opened her notebook. "Mr. Goodale—"

"You can call me Arthur."

No way could she do that. She wasn't brought up that way. Now she'd have to call him nothing. "From what I can tell, you know more about the case than anyone."

"Well, the police obviously know more than I do."

"Do you think?"

"The police? I should hope so."

"Even now that the lead detective has retired?"

"Well, the file's still there."

She nodded. She dreaded going anywhere near the police station, but knew she probably couldn't avoid it if she wanted all the facts. "I plan to look at that," she said.

"At what—the file?" Goodale's eyes narrowed. "The investigation is technically still open."

His point escaped her. "So . . ."

"So with an open case, the police won't let you see a thing." He gazed out the window. The view was of a brick wall, another wing of the hospital. He looked back toward Melanie. "You can imagine that a hospital is a fairly depressing and extremely boring place to be. And I've never been a TV watcher." He sighed. "So I hate to do this, because it's refreshing to have a visitor, and a pretty one at that—but you're either the worst journalist I've ever met or you're lying to me about being one."

"Pardon me?"

"You're very polite—and I can tell that's genuine. Ingrained. Your parents raised you right, and I mean no condescension in that." He licked his lips. "But what is this? If you're simply interested in the Miller case, you've come to the right place. I'm happy to chat about it—I hardly ever get to, anymore. But you don't have to pretend to be a journalist."

"I'm not pretending, sir."

He smiled. "Ronny Andrews is an old friend of mine. I know the kind of reporters he hires and the sort of assignments he— you don't know who that is, do you?" Another smile. She was starting to seriously dislike that smile. "Ronny Andrews edits the news desk at the *Ledger*. He'd be your boss."

This was all a game to him.

"May I ask why you don't think I'm—"

"A pencil behind the ear? Come on. And you display no knowledge whatsoever about how journalists get their information." He paused. "Also, you look fifteen years old."

"I'm way older than that."

"Anyone who says 'way older' isn't way older."

"Well, I am." *What am I doing?* She ordered herself to quit arguing with the one person who could help her, who also happened to be in critical care.

"Then how about this: You haven't asked me how I'm feeling."

"Sir?"

"Even a reporter who's all business would ask me that. And we've already determined that you're ingratiatingly polite." She made a mental note to look that word up. "So I can only conclude that for whatever reason, you're pretending to be reporter when in fact you're something else."

Plan A was to pose as a reporter for the *Star-Ledger*. Plan B didn't exist. "How are you feeling today?" she asked.

"Tired and uncomfortable. But thanks for asking." His smile had softened, or maybe she just chose to see it that way.

"You're welcome, Mr. Goodale," she said.

"Call me Arthur."

She forced this much-older man's first name from her throat. "*Arthur* . . . I want to know everything there is to know about the Miller case."

"Now *that* I believe," he said. "It's what I want, too. I've wanted it for fifteen years. But I'm a journalist who spent much of his adult life in this town. What's your reason?"

His voice, his eyes—they betrayed the rest of his body, this hospital room. He wasn't a frail man. *He knows who I am*, she thought for an instant—though of course he couldn't.

"You're a really good interviewer," she said.

"Thank you, Alice. That's flattering. And I'm thrilled that you've read my blog. I really am. But I'm frankly not thrilled at all with the way you come in here and start telling me lies. So how about we start again. Who are you? And what's your real interest in this case?"

She respected his investigatory instincts, but he was driving her mad. For her, this was life and death. For him, it was an entertaining break from soap operas and his view of the brick wall.

She summoned all her courage. "Mr. Goodale, would you really like to know who I am?" she asked, lowering her voice to add drama.

"I truly would." His voice had lost its tinge of superiority, become plainer—the voice of an unassuming journalist seeking a source's trust.

"Can you keep a secret?" she asked.

"Yes, Alice," he said. "I really can."

She held his gaze as long as she dared. "Well, so can I."

She stood, turned her back on him, and walked toward the door. She was halfway into the hallway when he uttered a single word that meant nothing to her.

She stepped back into the room. "Sorry?"

"Magruder," he repeated. When she didn't respond, he said, "David Magruder."

Alice frowned. "The TV guy?" She pictured the square jaw and cleft chin, the thick salt-and-pepper hair, the dramatic interviews with storm survivors, criminals, antiwar activists—and quite often of late the spouses and children of soldiers who were overseas.

"Fifteen years ago," Arthur said, "he was only a local weather-man. Listen, this is probably nothing, but—" He sighed. "Did you mean it when you said you can keep a secret? Or was that just a clever exit line?"

She remained just inside the doorway. "Both, I guess."

"Fair enough," he said. "Shut that door, please. Don't go. I don't want you to go." She shut the door. "Now take a seat again. Please." She sat and waited. Finally, he said, "I'm going to tell you something that I haven't written about."

"I thought that was the point of your blog," she said. "You can write whatever you want."

"No, not everything. I'm not going to slander a man like David Magruder, even on the blog. That'd be asking for a lawsuit."

"I'm not a real journalist," she admitted, sensing that a bit of truth might go a long way.

"You aren't going to stick a needle into me," he said. "That's enough for me."

"What if I spill your secret?"

"You won't." He shrugged. "Or you will—what do I care? I'll probably be dead in a week."

She smiled at his attempt at gallows humor, opened her note-book, and removed the pencil from behind her ear.

It wasn't much, what he told her. Before David Magruder started on his path to fame and fortune (a path, Arthur made a point of saying, that included cosmetic surgery and a hair trans-plant), he was a weatherman on the local TV news. He happened to live just down the street from the Millers. And of the few dozen people who attended the block party, he was one of them.

"Sounds like he was just being a neighbor," Melanie said. Yet she had trouble imagining David Magruder as being anyone's neighbor, or having come from anywhere other than the TV, already fully formed and photogenic and wearing perfectly fitted suits.

"Exactly," Arthur said. "But that's what makes it strange. Magruder wasn't a neighborly man. I knew him then—not well, but well enough to tell you that he was already too big for this town. In his eyes, anyway. So I've never understood why he attended a party thrown by some trucker he probably didn't even know."

Maybe it was relevant, Melanie thought, or maybe Magruder had simply found himself with a little free time that day. Maybe he liked hamburgers. "Is that everything?" she asked.

Arthur shook his head. "In the days after the crime, the police questioned everyone who attended the party. Which is what you'd expect. But Magruder—he was questioned more than once."

"How do you know?"

"Alice, I've lived here my whole life. I have friends on the force."

She couldn't imagine anyone being friends with a policeman, but she took him at his word. "What did they ask him?"

"I don't know," he said. "But the police must have thought—for a while, anyway—that he knew something or saw something, or maybe had information that might help them find Ramsey." Something started buzzing, and Arthur became distracted for a moment before realizing that the sound was coming from the hallway and not one of the machines in his room. "I really don't know. But my attempt to speak with him about the crime is what ended our acquaintanceship, and he's refused to speak with me ever since."

"What do you think he might have known?"

Arthur still seemed distracted, glancing around the room, up at the blank TV mounted to the wall, then back at Melanie. Finally, the buzzing in the hallway stopped and he visibly relaxed.

"If you came here looking for answers, I'm afraid I don't have any. Everything you read on my blog and in my articles? That's it. It's all I know, except for what I just told you. I know it doesn't amount to much. But if you're set on investigating what happened on the night of September 22, 1991, there are worse places to start than with David Magruder."

"Except that he won't talk to a journalist about it."

"Then it's a good thing you aren't one." Yes, his smile was definitely irritating, but she would try to get used to it. "I think I can help you, Alice. But if you find out anything, you have to tell me, okay? It's really boring in here." He frowned. "And this case. It's important to me."

She nodded. "It's important to me, too."

# 9

Melanie took a deep breath, let it out, and entered the dim marble lobby, which was empty except for a security guard in the far corner, sitting behind a desk. As she approached, the man glanced up at her. She told him she had a 3:00 appointment with David Magruder.

"ID, please." He barely looked up from the newspaper spread across the desk. When she didn't respond, he said, "Driver's license? Passport?"

Yesterday, she'd given a false name to Magruder's assistant. "I don't have my license with me," she said. "I took the train in from New Jersey."

He looked up from the paper. "What's your name?"

"Alice Adams." The more she said this name, the faker it sounded. "Mr. Magruder is expecting me. His assistant never said anything about—"

"Hold on." He picked up the phone receiver and dialed a few buttons. "Yeah, a young woman—Ms. Adams—says she has an appointment with Mr. Magruder." A long moment passed before he said, "Okay. I'll send her up." He hung up the phone. "Sign here. Eighteenth floor. I need to look in your bag."

On the eighteenth floor, the elevator doors opened directly into a reception area with carpeted hallways extending in both directions. Hanging on the wall behind the reception desk were enlarged photographs of David Magruder and the name of his current TV show, *Magruder Reveals*. Melanie had watched it a couple of times. Everyone was always shouting and crying and reconciling, and the music in the background told you how to feel.

A stunning woman with long black hair and a black dress sat behind a small wooden desk. She was quietly telling someone on the other end of the telephone line that "some people are just bastards, and you can't let the bastards stand in your way. You just need to . . . Hold on." She lowered the phone. "Yes?"

"I'm Alice Adams," Melanie said. "I have a three o'clock appointment with Mr. Magruder."

The woman looked Melanie up and down and uncapped her hand from the phone receiver. "I'll call you back," she said, hung up, and dialed an extension. "Mr. Magruder," she said, her voice sultry and full of promises, "I have an Alice Adams here who says she's waiting to see you." She picked a speck of nonexistent lint off her shoulder. "All right, I'll tell her. Thank you." She hung up the phone and said nothing for five seconds, ten. She was studying her fingernails.

"Is Mr. Magruder—"

"Yeah, I know. He's coming." She looked up from her nails. "Where are you from, anyway?"

"North Carolina," Melanie said.

"Yeah, your accent is crazy thick," the woman said in her crazy thick New York accent, and then, thankfully, the man Melanie recognized from TV and the photos overhead came rushing around the corner.

Arthur Goodale had told her to forget about posing as a pro. *You're a college student working on a project, spotlighting Magruder and his amazing career. You're completely enamored with him.* She'd laid it on thick with his assistant, embarrassingly so, but the approach had worked.

"Alice?" Magruder came up to her now, arm extended, beaming at her as if she were the celebrity. "I'm David. I'm so glad to meet you." His handshake was firm, his palm dry, just as she knew it would be. "Come on," he said, "let's go back to my office where we can chat." She began following him. "Did you have an easy trip?"

She decided not to mention her battle with the NJ Transit ticket machine, or being overwhelmed by Penn Station and the crush of people with their briefcases and their scowls, or, emerging onto 34th Street, being stunned by the searing daylight and mammoth buildings and wide sidewalks and the crowds everywhere she looked, moving fast, fast.

"Yes, sir," she said, and smiled.

"Good. Jeremy told me you're majoring in broadcast journalism. Hard road, changing landscape—but if you keep your eyes and ears open and your nose clean, then you'll . . ." They passed a few offices where on the other side of the glass young men and women sat at cubicles and stared at their computer monitors. Everyone was on the phone.

David Magruder had on a dark blue suit with subtle pinstripes and freshly polished black shoes. On TV, he was a good-looking middle-aged man with terrific hair and a pleasing voice. In person she wouldn't call him handsome, exactly. The parts were all there: cleft chin, blue eyes, that perfect head of hair, but the parts didn't quite fit together. It was as if he'd been ordered a la carte.

He had stopped in front of a double door with a TAPING IN PROGRESS sign attached to it. "They're doing promo spots right now," he said. "Otherwise, I'd give you the full tour. Come on, let's go to my office."

At the end of the hallway, he opened the door and waved her in. His office looked about the size of Melanie's home on Notress Pass. One corner was nothing but floor-to-ceiling windows, overlooking a large portion of Manhattan. Magruder strolled over and scanned the skyline as if it had been erected this morning just for him.

"I do well," he said. "But nothing was ever handed to me."

When he was done looking out his window, he turned around, smiled at Melanie, and told her to take a seat. The sofa was leather, soft, and probably cost more than all of her family's furniture put together. Above the sofa were photographs of Magruder shaking hands with President Bush, and another with him shaking hands with President Clinton. Both settings looked like the Oval Office. That seemed to be the recurring theme—Magruder with incredibly famous people, most of whom even Melanie recognized: Madonna, Tom Cruise, Michael Jordan. Angelina Jolie. Hillary Clinton. Magruder flashed the same smile in all of them: friendly, slightly crooked, with his teeth showing a little. A smile divorced from an actual expression.

He sat down on a leather chair at the head of the coffee table, which looked like a slab of petrified wood. He crossed his legs. The crease in his pants was sharp enough to cut steak.

"We produce a show a week, which airs on Wednesday night. Thursday we're off, and then on Friday morning we start all over again."

"That sounds really intense," Melanie said.

"Maybe. Though I have to tell you, Alice, after years of daily TV and having to chase every unfolding story and be everywhere at once, it feels like a walk in the park. I can plan my shows ahead of time, get the interviews I want."

Now that Melanie had a better look, she noticed that Magruder's face had the same orange cast as some of the girls at college who hit the tanning salon too often. Not sure what to say next, she took Arthur's advice and paid a compliment. "Your office is amazing," she said.

"Thank you. This whole floor is mine," he said. "The network wanted me to rent space in their building, but I said fuck no. Pardon the bravado, but it's the truth. I refused to have them looking over my shoulder." He shrugged. "What're they gonna do, Alice? Last week, I got a twelve-share with those marines, guy and a gal who got nailed by an IED and fell in love in rehab. We broadcast part of the wedding, their first dance . . . did you happen to catch it?"

"I'm sorry," she said, "but I missed it."

"Well, you'd have been weeping. Trust me, it was very beautiful." He smiled again, but the smile quickly vanished into an expression of genuine concern. "I have no manners."

"Sir?"

"Would you like coffee? Tea?"

"No, thank you."

"I'd offer something stronger, but I probably shouldn't, ha ha. But if you want it, it's here. But we probably shouldn't."

"If you have any water."

"Sure, we can rustle that up." He picked up the receiver of the phone on the coffee table and dialed an extension. "Please bring Ms. Adams a glass of water. No, nothing for me." He hung up. "You're southern."

"North Carolina," Melanie said.

He nodded. "It's a sexy accent, and it suits you—you're quite lovely—but you'll want to lose it or you'll be relegated to the small markets. This isn't a come-on, by the way, just some free advice. Back when I was doing weather, I used to sound like a real hick. Point is, I lost the accent. Point is, I beat out *60 Minutes* last week. Ratings talk. Everything else walks." He slapped his lap twice, as if encouraging a small, obedient dog to jump up and be petted. "So—your class. Tell me about it."

"It's called Introduction to Mass Media," she said.

"What school?"

Last night she'd gone online to prepare for this question. "Gaston College."

"Never heard of it." Exactly why she'd chosen it. "Go on."

"Well, one of our assignments is to interview someone in TV or radio. I thought I'd have to find someone back home, but when I found myself in New Jersey for a cousin's wedding and realized I'd be this close to New York . . . anyway, I'm like your biggest fan."

Arthur Goodale had insisted she say that.

"So instead of interviewing some local yokel, you came to me. That's ambitious. I like that. And I always try to make time for the next generation of media moguls." His smile was reassuring. "So what do you want to know?"

She unzipped her backpack, removed her notebook and pen, and scanned the list of handwritten questions. She decided to begin with a question about past shows he worked on, but almost at once he stopped her. "You can learn all that on Wikipedia. Lesson number one: Don't waste your interview's time. What is it you really want to know?"

She looked at the list again. He'd just invalidated eleven of her fifteen questions. If only she were subtle and clever and able to improvise, able to chat. All she could do was skip to question twelve on the list. "You're single with no children, isn't that right?"

"It is," he said, a little uncomfortably. "But again, that's something—"

"Why do you still live in Silver Bay?"

He frowned. "I don't talk about my home life." He must have realized that sounded curt, because he added, "I'm sure you understand why a public figure might want to keep his private life private."

This was a serious blow—her plan, such as there was one, was to get him talking about Silver Bay and then, acting naïve, bring up the crime. How do you develop a rapport?

"My school assignment," she said, "is to get to know my subject. His life as well as his work. That's why I asked about Silver Bay."

"Trust me," he said, "my work is a lot more interesting than my life." He shifted in his seat.

Five, maybe seven seconds of silence. Her armpits felt sweaty. Feeling out of options, she shut the notebook and braced herself. "When you lived in the Sandy Oaks neighborhood," she said, "how well did you know Allison and Ramsey Miller?"

"I beg your pardon?" He leaned back in his seat and got a good look at her. "Were you not just listening to me?"

"In nineteen ninety-one—"

"What the hell kind of a question is that? I'm not discussing that."

"I only wondered if you knew them. Because you lived in—"

"I know where I lived, sweetheart." No smile now. "I don't talk about that. You don't ask about that. Do we have an understanding?"

Her heart pounded. "Yes, sir."

"I didn't know either of them. Not even a little. Okay?"

"Okay," she said. He was lying, though. Why would he lie?

"Damn right, okay."

Just then, a young woman barged in carrying a tray. "Here you go," she sing-songed. On the tray sat a single glass of ice water.

Melanie and Magruder watched as she set the glass in front of Melanie, on a ceramic coaster. She smiled. "Anything else?"

"No," Magruder said.

"I didn't know if you wanted lemon or not," she said, "so—"

"We're fine," Magruder said.

"All right," the woman said, her smile faltering and then reaffirming itself. Then she left.

"I'm really sorry," Melanie said when the woman was gone, doing her best to sound apologetic and reasonable. She meant it, too. She didn't want to be burning this bridge already, when there was no other in sight. "I promise, I didn't mean to upset you."

"You? You can't upset me." She looked down at the table, accepting his condescension. He took a breath, laid his hands down on his lap atop those perfect creases. "Why don't you try telling me the truth. Why are you really here? Who are you?" When she didn't immediately answer, he asked, "What college did you say you're going to?"

"Gaston College."

"We'll see about that. Because *this* . . ." He motioned to her clothes. "The college students I know would've dressed up for an interview." At Arthur's advice, she had dressed like a "typical student": simple blouse, worn blue jeans. Sneakers. Hair in a ponytail held together with a black elastic. Subtle lipstick and a touch of eyeliner—an amount that Phillip always mistook for no makeup at all. "If I find out you're with the *Enquirer* or some other—"

"I promise, I'm a college student," she said.

"You promise." He laughed. "No, you're a liar. I can spot a liar every time." He glanced around his office at all those photographs, as if refueling. Then he massaged his temples. When he spoke again, his voice was softer. "All right, Alice. I'll tell you what

I know." He leaned in closer. "I know two things: I know you're going to leave through the door you came in. And I know it's going to happen right now."

"Sir?"

"You heard me."

Her vision began to get swimmy, and she fought to control herself. "Mr. Magruder—"

He reclined in his seat and folded his arms. "I'm waiting for my two things to come true, dear."

"I can ask other questions." She looked down at her notebook, the useless list. "What is it like to inform so many millions—"

"Let me make it plainer." His voice had hardened. "Get the fuck out of my office."

She stood up, placed her notebook back into her backpack. She felt Magruder's stare as she walked to the door. She felt it all the way down the hall to the elevator—which took an eternity to arrive.

"Don't keep pressing the button," the receptionist said. "It doesn't make it come any faster."

After hurrying past the security guard and leaving the lobby, she walked a full two blocks before realizing she was going in the wrong direction, then backtracked the twenty blocks to Penn Station. Her feet throbbed, and she felt lightheaded and nauseous from not eating—she'd been too nervous to eat for most of the day—and all she wanted was to lose herself in the train terminal at rush hour, where thousands of people would cocoon her in anonymity.

When she got there, she saw from the list of departures that the next Coast Line wasn't for 30 minutes, and braving the coffee smell, she stood in line to buy three donuts and a bottle of orange juice. She moved away from the counter so that she would no longer smell the coffee, sat against the terminal wall, and bit into the first donut. It was the most incredible thing she'd ever tasted. All around her, throngs weaved past one another. If everybody who lived in Fredonia was put inside this railroad station, it probably wouldn't be this crowded, but at the moment she felt reassured by all those people, to be just one among them, an anonymous grain of sand on the beach.

She filled her stomach and was ignored by everyone. She'd botched the interview badly, probably left West Virginia for nothing—but at least she was in Penn Station, this subterranean place of human voices and music and track announcements. It was wonderful and safe. A paradise. A womb. She could stay here forever.

She drank some juice, wiped her lips with a napkin. As she was deciding which donut to eat next, a tall man in a yellowed tank top and camouflage pants ran past. He was middle age at least, his hair ratty and gray, but he had ropy arms. He'd barely passed her when a heavy uniformed policeman caught up and tackled him to the hard floor. Then an even more massive officer jumped on top of the man, who was already down, and his face mashed into the ground. This second officer lay across him, covering him with his body, while the first officer yanked the man's arms behind him and snapped handcuffs around his wrists. By this time the man was howling wordlessly, like an animal badly hurt, and the first officer was telling him to shut up, shut up right now, as people nearby stopped what they were doing and edged closer, and a few started taking pictures with their cell phones, and one man in a business suit said to another man in a business suit, "Fucking New York," and when Melanie saw the small pool of blood on the ground near the man's head, the donut she'd just eaten felt like a stone in her gut.

Afraid to stand because her legs might not support her, she squeezed her eyes shut, covered her ears, and started reciting the names of Nancy Drew characters as if it were a litany: *Carson, Nancy's father. Eloise, Nancy's aunt. George, the tomboy; Bess, George's plump cousin; Ned Nickerson, Nancy's boyfriend; Hannah, the housekeeper. . . .*

# PART TWO

# 10

1965

His was a love story, though the love came later. First came all the climbing.

As a young boy, on nights when his father and mother put too much beer or vodka into themselves and got to screaming and hurling picture frames containing happier times, Ramsey would scurry up the black oak behind the apartment building, perch in a nook, and sway with the highest branches. Eighty feet up, his breathing eased. He'd sit up there for two or three hours before becoming so drowsy that he feared falling in his sleep or so butt-sore that he had no choice but to climb down again and face the loud and unkind earth.

Yet the earth wasn't always unkind. Saturday afternoons, his mother sometimes took him ice-skating. He kept to the perimeter, hand on rail, but enjoyed the friction of his blades on the ice.

He liked watching his mother, an expert skater. A single warm-up loop and she was drifting toward the center, where she might slide backward, spin, even leap into the air. While the strange truck smoothed the ice, Ramsey and his mother would put quarters into a vending machine near the skate-rental counter, and a paper cup would drop down and begin to fill. They passed the salty chicken broth back and forth. It gave them the warmth they needed for another hour on the ice.

And sometimes he went with his father to the Shark Fin boatyard, where Ramsey would watch his old man climb inside churning engine rooms as large as bedrooms. His father might explain a thing or two about whatever he was working on. Sometimes he took advantage of Ramsey's smaller size and asked him to squeeze into a space. More often, he let Ramsey explore the docks and climb aboard the dry-docked yachts. The other men in the boatyard trusted Ramsey not to drown or fall or break anything. They always took the time to shake his hand, not because they cared about him but because they respected his father. Ramsey liked these men's faces, red and deeply lined from the wind and sun, and he liked their generous laughs and the black coffee they drank out of Styrofoam cups, and how their clothes were always stained with grease from a hard day's work. He liked knowing that his father was one of these men.

When the workday was over, the two of them would share a Dr Pepper at the end of the dock overlooking the bay. Standing there, the sun warming the backs of their necks, his father would look out at the charter boats returning with their day's catch, a cloud of seagulls hovering over the decks.

*I got my mind set on a thirty-eight-foot Sea Ray*, he'd say. Or: *I got my mind set on a forty-six-foot Viking*. Or maybe that day his mind would be set on some other yacht, as if he had all the money in the world to spend and all the time in the world to contemplate his purchase.

It would be years before Ramsey started to sort out just how much of his parents' troubles came from life's usual slop of suffering—money troubles, boredom, graceless aging—and how much was due to the particularly poor alchemy of two people with hard tempers and short fuses. More and more, anything could set their ferocity into motion: something quoted from a newspaper, someone's car in the wrong parking space, a comment, a glance, or nothing at all. Ramsey would sit rigidly on the sofa or on his bedroom floor and wait for it to start. He could always sense it in the atmosphere, the way animals know a storm is coming. And when one parent's remark begat a louder response, and when the profanity started, and certainly by the time the first coaster or mug or TV remote got slammed down onto a coffee table or hurled against a wall, Ramsey would be long gone, already halfway up his tree. His parents never stopped him or called his name. When he came home again, they never asked him where he'd been. Then again, the flecks of dirt and crumbles of tree bark on his clothes and in his hair surely gave him away.

One fall night a week before his ninth birthday, Ramsey was hiding in his tree and imagining, as he often did, how it might be to live alone in a log cabin in the mountains, maybe by some lake, where at night all you heard were crickets and coyotes, and where there were a zillion stars overhead. He'd been learning constellations at school and was naming them to himself when a patrol car pulled silently up to the apartment building, its flashing lights blotting out the stars and brightening the branches around him like a multicolored strobe. He felt cold, sitting up there without moving, but seeing the patrol car made him start to sweat. One of his parents, he figured, had finally gone and killed the other. Neither had resorted to physical violence before, unless you counted the sliver of glass lodged in the meaty part of his mother's hand, just below the thumb, from when she'd slammed down and shattered a mug. But their rage had grown worse in recent months, and now anything seemed possible.

But no: His parents were still shouting at each other. The wind that night came from the west, carrying their voices all the way up the tree.

The officer knocked. The shouting halted.

A short while later, the officer emerged from the apartment, shook his head once as if clearing it of muck, walked to his car, and sat in it for several minutes with the headlights off. Like the officer, Ramsey sat and waited for the fighting to resume. When the officer finally drove away, Ramsey counted to five hundred before climbing down again.

"You probably saw what happened here tonight," his father said to him, sitting at the foot of Ramsey's bed an hour later. It was a school night. Ramsey already dreaded having to wake up in a few hours. He watched the fish decals stuck to the walls. During the day they looked happy, but at night, lit by the dim lamp on his dresser, they were shadowy and sinister. But because they'd always been there, he never thought of asking that they be taken down.

"The police came," Ramsey said.

"They came because some nosy neighbor felt he had to get involved." His father found one of Ramsey's feet under the covers and began rubbing it in both of his hands. "But it's true, your mother and I are no good at keeping our mouths shut. We're going to try fixing that."

Ever since Ramsey could remember, his father's coarse thumb on the soles of his feet calmed him. It never tickled. "I don't like it when you fight," Ramsey said.

"Of course you don't. I don't like it, either. That's why your mother and I are going to fix it."

"You promise?" In daylight he never would have dared ask his father to promise anything. But the dark bedroom made it hard to see his father's face and therefore easier to push.

The rubbing stopped. "Listen to me, son. You don't know yet what it's like to be in love. How sometimes it makes you crazy."

"You're in love with Mom?"

His father laughed. "Indeed, I am. Most of the time, anyway."

He'd never tell his father this, but Ramsey was in love, too. With Rachel Beaner. But there was no possibility that what he felt, looking over at Rachel in the next row of desks, had anything in common with what his father might have felt, looking at his mother. And besides, Ramsey knew that if he and Rachel ever married, he'd love her *all* of the time. And he'd never raise his voice to her, not ever.

"Then why won't you promise?"

"Jesus, Ram . . ." From the kitchen came sounds of dishes being rinsed, then clanking together as they were placed in the drying rack. More than once, his father and mother had fought over not owning a dishwasher. Ramsey couldn't remember, now, which side either of them was on. Or maybe they'd switched sides. "Yeah, okay, kid," his father said. "I promise."

They shook on it in the dark. And for six days, his father kept his promise. His mother maintained her own civility, too, despite not having promised anything. And on the seventh night, a Sunday, the night before Ramsey's birthday, his father and mother went out for a drive, and only his father came home.

The rain had fallen steadily that day—not violently, but nice—and Ramsey's mother and father had sat together on the sofa, reading parts of the paper aloud, something they hadn't done for some time. His mother's feet were up on his father's lap. Ramsey lay on the rust-colored carpet reading the comics and listening to the rain on the roof.

After supper, his parents went out on a few errands, his father's wink—so fast, Ramsey had nearly missed it—leading Ramsey to believe that birthday presents were involved. They left him at home in front of the TV with a glass of soda and a bowl of pretzels. His mother said something to the effect of "We'll be back in an hour"—but who knew, exactly? By then, Ramsey was fully engrossed in *Lassie*. When the rain began to fall heavier on the roof, he got off the sofa and turned up the volume. Sunday was a good night for TV. He watched *Walt Disney's Wonderful World of Color*, then *Branded*. By then he should've been in bed. *Bonanza* was on next and when no one returned by the end, he watched *Candid Camera* and then *What's My Line?*, which his parents sometimes talked about but never let him stay up for. By then he knew something was wrong, and when the building's superintendent led in two policemen, and Ben Cramer's father went over to the TV and shut it off, Ramsey—whose arms by now were shaking and legs were shaking and mouth was dry despite all the soda—looked up and, not knowing what to say, said, "Hey, I was watching that!"

"Tell me," Ramsey said.

Outside. Recess. The day after the funeral.

"You sure you want to hear this?" Larry Ackerman's father was a cop, which meant that Larry heard the sort of rumors that could be trusted. His parents had no clue that the air-conditioning vent in their bedroom broadcasted all their conversations.

"*Tell me.*"

Larry glanced over at Ben Cramer as if he were Ramsey's keeper. Maybe for the moment, he was. Ramsey had stayed with Ben's family in the days leading up to the funeral, and had only returned to the apartment yesterday. Today was his first day back at school, and Ben's parents must have asked him to stick close—that, or Ben was as loyal a friend as a nine-year-old could ever hope to have.

Ben nodded.

"All right," Larry said, softly, and sat down on the freshly mown grass. The other two sat so they made a tight circle. They were at the edge of school property, fifty yards from the playground and all the other kids and lunch monitors. *I have information you'll want to hear*, Larry had said, first thing that morning in the hallway. But they were in different classes in the fourth grade, and Ramsey had to wait for three long hours.

Sitting here now, near the chain-link fence separating school property from a narrow creek that ran through much of town, Ramsey knew that to Larry this was all a game, like trading ghost stories. But if Larry knew the truth, then Ramsey wanted to hear it. All he knew for a fact was that his mother was dead. Yesterday he'd stood over her casket and looked at her face. Everyone had said, *You don't have to*, but he did have to. Neither his father nor anyone else had said one word to explain what had happened, other than *car accident*. Ramsey knew not to ask his father for details—like how his mother could have been killed when his father didn't seem to have a scratch on him.

"Your father and mother were fighting," Larry said now.

"He didn't kill her." Ramsey had considered and rejected the possibility so many times in the last week that the words came automatically. Anyway, if that was what had happened, then his father would be in jail right now, not back at the apartment.

"Let me finish," Larry said. His voice softened again to ghost-story decibels. "They were fighting in the car, and your father got really mad and made your mom get out."

"Out where?"

"Out of the car. He kicked her out in the rain and drove away. And then—" Larry looked back toward the school. A handful of kids were playing kickball, and he watched as a girl kicked a slow roller toward the pitcher and ran to first base. The pitcher threw the ball at the girl but missed, and she was safe.

"And then what?" Ramsey asked.

For the first time, it must have occurred to Larry that this wasn't a ghost story he was repeating. He watched the kickball field a moment longer before looking down at the grass. "She got hit."

"What do you mean?" Ben asked.

"It was dark and raining," Larry said. "The truck driver didn't see her."

"A *truck*?" Ramsey said. He knew he'd never be able to stop imagining the thud of his mother's body against the truck, the sight of her in the air, turning, the sound of her hitting the ground. His mother.

"A pickup," Larry said. "The driver was going around a curve, and it was really dark and the rain was heavy. He wasn't speeding or nothing." The next thing he said, he must have overheard word-for-word through the air vent. "A damn tragedy, is what it is." Even his register dropped so he sounded like his father. He looked up at Ramsey and reverted to his own voice. "She's in heaven now."

"That's true," Ben added.

Ramsey tried so hard to believe them that tears came to his eyes, but he knew his friends were fools. He had long observed how other kids spoke about their dead grandparents and great-grandparents as if being dead meant dancing with angels and eating supper with God. But the truth was, when you're dead, you're dead. His father had said so a long time ago, after a stray dog they'd kept for a couple of weeks had died of distemper. It wasn't pretty, but it made sense. When a dog was dead, it was dead, and the same was true for people.

"Why do you suppose your father did that?" Ben asked. "Why would he kick her out like that?"

"I don't know," Ramsey said, looking out past the fence and the creek and into the thicket of woods. Who knew why anyone did anything? But then the answer came to him. "I think he was trying to keep a promise."

A week after the funeral, his father returned to work at the Shark Fin boatyard. That Saturday, Ramsey went along. It could have been any other Saturday, except that when the workday was done and they stood at the end of the dock, Ramsey felt the urge to talk about his mother. He wasn't sure what he wanted either of them to say. He would have liked his father to say something comforting for Ramsey's sake even if neither of them believed it. Like how his mother was in heaven. At least a dozen times, Ramsey almost asked the question—*is Mom in heaven now?*—and each time he caught himself. When he finally got a sound to leave his lips, it was more of a squeak than a word.

"How's that?" his father asked.

"So is your mind set on a forty-two-foot Sea Ray?" Ramsey asked.

His father shook his head. "No, son. It sure isn't."

Ramsey knew he was right not to ask if his mother was in heaven. He kept looking out at the boats and the gulls and the water. At one point he felt the gentle weight of his father's hand on the back of his neck, and he told himself that this was enough.

Maybe his father was thinking about yachts, redemption, or nothing at all—but he wasn't thinking about his work, given the injuries he started sustaining. First there came the minor accidents— mashed fingers, concussion, twisted ankle—and then the major one. A sailboat boom swung around and walloped his father in the back, throwing him off the dry-docked boat and down onto the concrete.

This was less than six months after Ramsey's mother died, and it seemed to be the injury his old man had been waiting for. Now he spent his days kicked back in the recliner, watching TV, the remote control resting on his ever-expending belly. At some point in the afternoon he would replace the remote with a vodka on the rocks. A woman named Gina, who rang the register at the 7-Eleven where his father bought his smokes, started coming over to the apartment. She came with snacks from work and sometimes went grocery shopping for them. Ramsey couldn't understand where the money came from, with his old man not working. He didn't know about disability payments. All he knew was that when Gina worked the morning shift, she'd come over at 2:30 and she and Ramsey's father would start their drinking and their shouting, a return to the fighting his parents used to engage in. If Gina worked the evening shift, it all started earlier.

Twelve years old. He came home from school to an apartment that had been either burglarized or tornado-ravaged from the inside.

"Dad?"

Drawers pulled from shelves and overturned, cabinets emptied, stacks of unopened mail swept off the kitchen table. Books littered the floor. Every object in the house, it seemed, was strewn and tossed and disregarded.

"Dad?" He considered running to the phone to dial 911 or banging on a neighbor's door for help. But then his father emerged from the bedroom, limping as always from his bad back, muttering to himself, a look of anger and horror on his flushed face. His eyes glassy. Drunk, drunk, drunk.

"What's going on?" Ramsey asked.

"Have you seen my wedding ring?" his father asked.

He hadn't.

"It's got to be here." His father knelt down on the floor in front of the sofa, an action that resulted in his cursing at whatever pain flared or sliced through him. He rummaged through a desk drawer that'd already been rummaged through.

"Where's Gina?" Ramsey asked, because he knew that something was making his father act this way.

His father looked up from the carpet. "Gina has left us, son! She is, and I quote, *moving on and improving herself*." He ran his hands under the sofa, then under the cushions. All he found were crumbs. He turned around so that his back was against the sofa. "Fucking whore," he muttered, burying his face in his hands.

Ramsey had no idea what to do, so he just sat there and watched his old man come apart. After a minute or so, his father moved his hands away from his face. His eyes were redder than ever. "I loved your mother," he pled to his son. "I loved her so much."

Ramsey nodded. "Okay."

"You don't understand. You're only a kid. There's no way I can explain it to you. I just loved her."

"What did she look like?" Ramsey asked.

"What?" his father said. "What are you talking about?"

"Mom—what did she look like?"

"Don't ask me a question like that," his father said. "You remember."

"I don't," Ramsey said. "I want to, but I don't. What did she look like?"

"I said don't ask me that."

"Sorry."

His father tried to take a deep breath, but it caught somewhere in his gut and became a whimper. He looked around at the trashed apartment. "What the hell am I gonna do?" he said. "Will you just answer me that?"

"I . . ."

"Shut up before you embarrass yourself, Ramsey," his father said.

The black oak looked dead for months, its remaining leaves brown and crusty, before some guys got around to taking a chain saw to it. One late October morning, when the leaves of all the other trees were in full color, a cherry picker raised one of the men up, and he started chain-sawing through the lower, thicker limbs, then the higher, thinner ones, all of Ramsey's hiding spots dropping to the ground one after another. Though he couldn't remember the last time he'd hidden in the tree, he still thought of it as his. He sat on a chair in the kitchen and watched through the window as the men shed layers of clothes over the long morning, calling out to one another, working the cherry picker, branches falling every minute or two, until only the trunk was left standing like a totem pole that someone had forgotten to carve. Then they cut that down, too. By noon the men had chopped the branches into pieces, fed them into a wood chipper, sectioned the trunks and loaded the pieces on to their truck, and were gone, leaving only a low stump and the cherry picker's muddy tracks mashed into the grass.

Ramsey was fourteen. He wore his hair longish and shaggy and had developed a habit of squinting even in shade. He was a short, lean kid with a voice pitched too high for menace. When the men left, he went outside to where the tree had stood only a few hours earlier. The stump was covered in sawdust. He brushed the dust away to reveal the tree's age: so many rings, so much survival. He looked around, hoping to see a new hiding place in case he ever needed one. The roof? The storage garage? Or maybe the tree coming down was a sign. He considered this possibility all afternoon and tested it that night. When his old man came into the kitchen for a refill, Ramsey headed him off, removing a beer can from the refrigerator and opening it. He began to pour the contents down the sink.

"Hey, stop that!" his father shouted. "What the hell you doing?"

Ramsey considered calling his father by his first name—*I'll do whatever I want, Frank*, or *This ain't your concern, Frank*—but decided it was better, older, not to pay his father any notice at all. When the last trickle was in the drain, Ramsey dropped the empty can into the trash and calmly explained to his father that he would no longer allow alcohol in their home.

"You got to be joking," his father said.

"Do I look like I'm joking?"

"You look like a kid who's upset because your fucking tree came down." He whistled once. "God almighty, what a baby."

"Hey—"

"Don't *hey* me. You should be thanking me for getting the rental office off their asses before that tree crushed us in our sleep."

His father, hands on hips, met Ramsey's gaze, and Ramsey felt the tears well up. "You should've asked me first." He meant to sound tough, but he heard the quaver in his own voice.

"Oh, yeah?" His father stared him down. "And who the hell are you?"

His father was a master at mutating a fight so that the fight itself became the issue. He'd had years to perfect the art, but Ramsey was only an amateur and no words came.

"I think you'd better answer me, son."

"You shut up!" Ramsey finally shouted, and socked his father in the nose.

In the past, his father had occasionally shoved Ramsey into the wall or the refrigerator but never struck him with a fist. And

Ramsey had never done anything remotely like this to his old man or anyone else. The punch connected because it contained the element of surprise: It surprised them both. And all the blood was another surprise, which made up for the fact that what he'd said to his father was so damn stupid. *You shut up?* He knew he'd have to change the story when he told it later to Ben. That was where he decided to go, Ben's house, until things cooled down.

He knew better than to take time to pack a change of clothes, a toothbrush, or a coat. He left the house with his father standing in the kitchen, dripping blood onto the linoleum.

*Who the hell am I?* Ramsey said aloud, walking through neighborhoods and past shops that were closed for the night. *I'm your goddamn son, that's who.*

He wanted to hate his father but wasn't up to it. It was sad, seeing him there in the kitchen, looking hurt in every way, without even Gina there to help. Still, Ramsey felt himself waking up on that walk across town, and was glad for it. That punch had opened something in him that he didn't think he'd be closing any time soon. He imagined and reimagined the scene back at the apartment—his father's insolence, the blood. He shivered from the cold and the excitement. Cars whooshed by on Second Avenue in both directions, but otherwise it was a cool, quiet night with the smell in the air of burning leaves. Ramsey's left hand, his punching hand, tingled but didn't hurt at all. Just the opposite. It felt warm and ready. It practically glowed in the dark. He made a fist, unclenched it, and made it again, having absolutely no inkling that his solo walk across town on this night, so crisp and shimmering with promise, was to be the highlight of his next ten years.

*I'm the one who settles the score*, he said in a movie star's deep drawl.

*I'm your worst nightmare.*

154

# 11

POLICE ARREST RECORD
RAMSEY JEFFREY MILLER

JURISDICTION DESC: MONMOUTH COUNTY CLERK
OFFENDER ID: 33204
DOB: 09/29/1956
RACE: WHITE
SEX: MALE
HEIGHT (FT): 5' 8"
WEIGHT (LBS): 148
HAIR COLOR: BROWN
EYE COLOR: BROWN
ALIASES: NOT KNOWN

CHARGE #1
CHARGE ID: 555009321

STATUTE: 2C:17-3 STATUTE DESC: CRIMINAL MISCHIEF
CHARGE: CRIMINAL MISCHIEF, 4TH DEGREE –
DISORDERLY PERSONS
    VANDALISM
CHARGE CLASS: CLASS 1 MISDEMEANOR
CHARGE DATE: 07/16/75
AGE WHEN ARRESTED: 19
DISPOSITION: GUILTY
SENTENCE: FINE, COMMUNITY SERVICE
NOTES: SUBJECT FOUND VISIBLY IMPAIRED IN PARKING
LOT OF BIG AL LIQUORS. PARKING LOT LIGHTS WERE
SMASHED. HE ADMITTED TO DRINKING "TOO MANY
TO COUNT" AT HOME AND BECOMING ANGRY WHEN
THE STORE'S NIGHT MANAGER REFUSED TO SELL HIM
ALCOHOL BECAUSE HE WAS VISIBLY INTOXICATED. HE
ADMITTED TO SMASHING THE LIGHTS WITH ROCKS
AND ATTEMPTED TO DEMONSTRATE BUT ALL THE
LIGHTS WERE ALREADY SMASHED. WHEN ASKED HIS
NAME THE SUBJECT SAID NEIL ARMSTRONG.
IDENTIFICATION CARRIED BY THE SUBJECT PROVED
OTHERWISE.

CHARGE #2
CHARGE ID: 555010301
STATUTE: 2C:17-3 STATUTE DESC: CRIMINAL MISCHIEF
CHARGE: CRIMINAL MISCHIEF, 4TH DEGREE –
DISORDERLY PERSONS
    VANDALISM
CHARGE CLASS: CLASS 1 MISDEMEANOR
CHARGE DATE: 02/11/76
AGE WHEN ARRESTED: 20
DISPOSITION: GUILTY

SENTENCE: FINE, PROBATION
NOTES: SUSPECT INVOLVED IN AN ALTERCATION AT
STUFF YER FACE RESTAURANT WHERE HE WAS
EMPLOYED AS KITCHEN STAFF. MANAGER CALLED THE
POLICE AND ACCUSED THE SUSPECT, FOLLOWING A
REPRIMAND FOR FAILING TO WASH DISHES
APPROPRIATELY, OF PLACING THE MANAGER'S HAT,
LEATHER GLOVES, AND HAIR PIECE INTO THE DEEP
FRYER. WHEN CONFRONTED BY POLICE THAT
AFTERNOON AT HIS HOME, SUSPECT CONFIRMED THE
MANAGER'S STORY.

CHARGE #3
CHARGE ID: 555019986
STATUTE: 2C:12-1 STATUTE DESC: ASSAULT
CHARGE CLASS: CLASS 1 MISDEMEANOR
CHARGE DATE: 9/4/76
AGE WHEN ARRESTED: 20
DISPOSITION: GUILTY
SENTENCE: FINE, PROBATION
NOTES: SUSPECT INVOLVED IN AN ALTERCATION
WITH A NEIGHBOR IN HIS APARTMENT BUILDING
AFTER NEIGHBOR ASKED SUSPECT TO TURN DOWN
THE MUSIC IN HIS APARTMENT. A THIRD NEIGHBOR
CALLED THE POLICE AFTER THE FIGHT BEGAN. BOTH
MEN ADMITTED TO HAVING CONSUMED ALCOHOL.
BOTH WERE TREATED ON THE SCENE BY PARAMEDICS
FOR MINOR CUTS AND BRUISES AND REFUSED
FURTHER MEDICAL ASSISTANCE.

CHARGE #4
CHARGE ID: 555018100

STATUTE: 2C:17-3 STATUTE DESC: CRIMINAL MISCHIEF
CHARGE: CRIMINAL MISCHIEF, 3RD DEGREE –
DISORDERLY PERSONS,
    POSESSION (MARIJUANA, 50G OR LESS) – RESISTING
    ARREST (NO WEAPON)
CHARGE CLASS: CLASS 1 MISDEMEANOR
CHARGE DATE: 06/04/78
AGE WHEN ARRESTED: 22
DISPOSITION: GUILTY
SENTENCE: FINE, JAIL, PROBATION
NOTES: SUSPECT REFUSED TO LEAVE THE PREMISES
OF A HOUSE WHERE HE WAS EMPLOYED TO MOW AND
EDGE THE LAWN. SUSPECT SPOTTED BY HOMEOWNER
IN WOODS BEHIND HOUSE. HOMEOWNER
APPROACHED SUSPECT AND NOTICED HE WAS
SMOKING A MARIJUANA CIGARETTE. WHEN HE TOLD
SUSPECT TO LEAVE THE PREMISES, SUSPECT REFUSED.
WHEN POLICE ARRIVED ON THE SCENE, SUSPECT SAID
THAT HE HAD BROKEN UP WITH HIS GIRLFRIEND THE
PRIOR EVENING AND "THOUGHT HE WOULD CHILL
OUT HERE." WHEN OFFICER ATTEMPTED TO ARREST
SUSPECT, SUSPECT CLIMBED NEARBY TREE.
ADDITIONAL OFFICERS AND A FIRE TRUCK CAME TO
THE SCENE AND THREATENED THE SUSPECT WITH A
HIGH-POWERED WATER HOSE. SUSPECT CLIMBED
DOWN WITHOUT FURTHER INCIDENT.

CHARGE #5
CHARGE ID: 555019867
STATUTE: 2C:12-1 STATUTE DESC: ASSAULT
CHARGE: ASSAULT
CHARGE CLASS: CLASS 1 MISDEMEANOR

CHARGE DATE: 10/2/79
AGE WHEN ARRESTED: 23
DISPOSITION: GUILTY
SENTENCE: FINE, PROBATION
NOTES: POLICE WERE CALLED TO THE CORNER
TAVERN BECAUSE OF AN ALTERCATION. BOTH
SUSPECTS WERE TREATED ON THE SCENE AND
ARRESTED WITHOUT INCIDENT.

CHARGE #6
CHARGE ID: 555117394
STATUTES: 2C:12-1 STATUTE DESC: ASSAULT
 2C:17-3 STATUTE DESC: CRIMINAL MISCHIEF
CHARGES: ASSAULT, CRIMINAL MISCHIEF 2ND DEGREE
CHARGE CLASS: CLASS 1 MISDEMEANOR
CHARGE DATE: 08/15/81
AGE WHEN ARRESTED: 25
DISPOSITION: GUILTY
SENTENCE: FINE, JAIL, PROBATION
NOTES: SUSPECT WAS DELIVERED A PACKAGE FROM
UPS. HE THEN FOLLOWED THE UPS DRIVER TO HIS
TRUCK AND WITH A KEY CREATED AN APPROX 4 FOOT
GOUGE ALONG THE SIDE OF THE TRUCK. WHEN
ASKED TO STOP, SUSPECT TOLD THE UPS DRIVER
THAT IF HE SAID ANOTHER WORD HIS TRUCK
WOULDN'T BE THE ONLY THING CUT. WHEN POLICE
ARRIVED, SUSPECT SAID HE DID IT BECAUSE WHEN
THE FRONT DOOR WAS OPEN, THE UPS DRIVER MADE
A REPEATED MOTION WITH HIS TONGUE IN THE
DIRECTION OF SUSPECT'S GIRLFRIEND THAT SUSPECT
FOUND OFFENSIVE AND INAPPROPRIATE. WHEN
QUESTIONED, THE UPS DRIVER SAID HE DID NOT DO

THIS, AND THAT ANY LIP SMACKING WAS DUE TO
EXTREMELY CHAPPED LIPS. (HE PRODUCED A TUBE OF
BLISTEX FROM HIS PANTS POCKET.) THE GIRLFRIEND
WHEN QUESTIONED STATED THAT THE SUSPECT
"WAS ALWAYS ACTING LIKE AN IDIOT" AND THAT SHE
HAD TAKEN NO NOTICE OF THE UPS DRIVER.

CHARGE #7
    CHARGE ID: 555332344
    STATUTE: 2C:12-1 STATUTE DESC: ASSAULT
    CHARGE: ASSAULT
    CHARGE CLASS: CLASS 1 MISDEMEANOR
    CHARGE DATE: 08/08/83
    AGE WHEN ARRESTED: 27
    DISPOSITION: GUILTY
    SENTENCE: FINE, JAIL, PROBATION
    NOTES: AFTER BEING EVICTED FROM APARTMENT
FOR FAILURE TO PAY RENT, THE SUSPECT
CONFRONTED LANDORD IN THE PARKING LOT AND
SHOVED HIM AGAINST THE BUILDING'S BRICK
EXTERIOR, CAUSING BRUISING TO THE LANDLORD'S
SIDE AND SHOULDER. LANDLORD PHONED POLICE
AND SUSPECT WAS LOCATED LATER THAT DAY IN
MUGSHOTS BAR AND WAS ARRESTED WITHOUT
INCIDENT.

Absent from the police arrest record: Ramsey's first disorderly persons arrest, later expunged, for which he spent the night of his sixteenth birthday in the drunk tank. And of course all those actions that weren't crimes but that were nonetheless reckless and unwise: rude comments to teachers, fights in the hallway, a host of foolish behavior that led to detention, suspensions, and threats of expulsion.

Nor does his arrest record mention the Porsche, keys left on the seat, that he swiped one night from the parking lot of the Trattoria, took for a joyride, smashed, and abandoned. Or the weed he sold to a few discreet classmates and later to those same individuals once they'd graduated. Or the time he drove a truck of stolen electronics from one warehouse to another, or the time he kept watch outside a house while some other guys broke in through the back door and took whatever they could cram into a couple of canvas bags.

And there was the time—the only time—that he accepted money from one guy to beat up another guy. He was never told, nor did he want to know, what beef the one guy had with the other. He knew only that he was risking a felony but that it would be the easiest 300 bucks he'd ever earn, since the fight didn't have to be fair. This was fall 1983, not long after he'd spent three days in county jail for shoving his asshole landlord. If caught now, he'd be looking at a lot longer than three days. So he was careful. After learning the guy's routine, he waited outside his building one weekday morning at sunrise. The man descended his front stoop and yawned audibly before heading into the alleyway to the parking lot. One unsuspecting shove from behind and into the brick wall, a few hard punches, a few harder kicks once he was down on the sidewalk, and it was over.

That final kick to the jaw, though. It felt a little too much like scratching a deep itch, and it scared him. He replayed the beating in his mind once he was back home—his new home, across from the plasma donation center, the shittiest apartment God ever created. He lay in bed with the lights off and shades drawn and studied the cracks in the ceiling. Before that day, the only time he'd beaten someone while sober was that single lucky punch that had busted his old man's nose a decade earlier. Since then, Ramsey hadn't grown all that many inches, but he'd gotten much stronger. And the feeling of his hard shoe torquing toward that man's face . . . it was nothing at all like the spontaneous bar fights of his past, fueled by beer and momentary rage. This was a darker, smoother feeling, one he could imagine needing to revisit. He felt disgusted with himself, nothing new, but for the first time he felt afraid of himself, too.

With no food in the apartment, hunger eventually drove him outside. But when he passed the sub shop on the corner he kept walking, because walking felt better than eating. He briefly considered walking all the way to the police station and turning himself in, but his feet pulled him eastward, toward the ocean. It was mid-September, a dry day with the sky a deep blue interrupted only by the white half-moon. A generation or two earlier, you might have still called this town a resort, but not anymore. Now it was just a town that happened to sit next to an ocean.

The road ended where the beach began. At first, still a block away, he saw water brilliantly alit with sunlight, the beginning of three thousand miles of shining sea. But as his eyes adjusted and he crossed Ocean Avenue, he was hit with the truth: plastic containers, crushed cans, overturned shopping carts and postal bins and waves of junk shoved ashore by the incoming tide. Worse this year than the last, worse than ever, and it wasn't lost on Ramsey that he felt drawn to the place where all that trash ended up. Every damn year, he thought, was one earth's revolution closer to the end of his life, and so far his life had amounted to a heap of garbage. There was no point to any of it. He was broke, friendless, estranged from the old man, unable to hold down a job, and his only reason for staying in this town was that moving would cost money. That, and the half dozen steady marijuana customers who gave him a fighting chance at paying whatever landlord had been too lazy to do something as simple as a proper credit check.

One of Ramsey's customers had only one arm and wore a permanent smirk. He had the bad luck of being born a year earlier than Ramsey and got sent to Vietnam. Now he worked pest control, spraying other people's homes with poison. Even that guy could keep it together. Ramsey stood on the boardwalk, looking down at the ruined beach and added self-pity to his list of faults. He turned around and got irked by the guy who seemed to be looking at him.

He crossed Ocean Avenue again and approached the base of the telephone pole so the other man had to crane his neck and look straight down. "How's that job?" Ramsey called up to the man, who looked too thick in the middle for a guy in that line of work.

"You yanking my chain?" The man looked at least a decade older than Ramsey, though that might've been because of his face, which was weathered from the sun like the faces of the men his father had once worked with.

"Fuck you," Ramsey said. "I'm just asking."

"Then here's your answer: It's a better job than you'll ever have."

"Tell me something I don't know," Ramsey said.

"Oh, so now you want my pity?"

"Man, I don't want your nothing. But if I ever wanted it, believe me I'd just take it and it would be mine."

The man watched Ramsey for a second. "I don't know what that means," he said.

Neither did Ramsey.

To his amazement, they both laughed. Ramsey couldn't remember the last time he let himself do that.

"Listen, man," Ramsey said, working to rid his voice of aggression. "I'm asking is that good work, being up in those poles like that?"

"You need a job? Is that what you're saying?"

"Yeah."

"Then stop by the GSE office on 36. Ask for Dennis. Tell him Eric Pace sent you."

"Why?" Ramsey asked.

"*Why?* You just said you're out of work."

"No—I mean, why would you do that for me?"

Eric shook his head. "Man, I thought you didn't want my pity. Make up your mind."

"Yeah, okay," Ramsey said. "Maybe I'll go over there in the morning."

"Or don't—it's all the same to me." The man went back to screwing or unscrewing a metal box near the top of the pole.

"Hey!" Ramsey called up. Eric stopped working and looked down again. "You never said if it's a good job or not."

Eric paused to consider the question. "It can be. It all depends."

"Depends on what?"

"On whether you can climb."

Four weeks later, and Ramsey was an eager grunt at the start of a four-year apprenticeship to become a journeyman lineman. Training expenses and supplies would come out of his paycheck, but the pay was good and for the first time he'd have medical benefits. He knew he'd been handed a gift he didn't deserve, and he told himself not to fuck it up. During the classroom part of his training—daylong sessions on electrical theory and equipment and safety—he did his best not to squirm or fall asleep. He applied for his CDL permit, and the company started training him to drive a truck. At night, he studied hard so he would pass the motor vehicle exam on his first try.

Eric Pace, the guy he'd met up on the pole, volunteered to be Ramsey's first mentor. Other than being a Jesus nut—A.A. had done it to him some years earlier—Eric was a regular guy with uncommon generosity. It drove Ramsey a little mad that his training would literally be "from the ground up," and that out on the job site, his day-to-day was entirely earthbound: work site setup and breakdown, loading and unloading trucks, digging trenches for lines and holes for power poles. But he told himself to be patient for once.

He wasn't someone who ordinarily quit things cold turkey, especially things he was good at like drinking and asshole-being, but because it all meant a lot to him—the job, his friendship with Eric—he found it not so hard, really, to keep those baser tendencies in check. And on the third Friday of his training, two very good things happened: He passed his CDL exam and he picked up his first paycheck. Obviously, it was time to celebrate. He decided on Chuck's Main Street Tavern, because it was only a few blocks from his apartment and a DUI would be a real screw right now.

When 2 a.m. rolled around and Chuck kicked out the last stragglers, Ramsey stepped out onto the sidewalk feeling happy, which almost never happened leaving a bar, and invincible, which always did. The storefronts on his street were all closed, the windows dark in most of the apartments above them. A few Christmas lights drooped under windows, a few wreaths hung on doorways. And though the night felt too warm and sticky for early December, the weather didn't stop Ramsey, as he ambled along the sidewalk, from singing a booming, belch-punctuated rendition of "Jingle Bells."

Across the street from his apartment building, he sized up a power pole that he'd never really noticed before—simple three-phase subtransmission pole (forty-five-footer, from the looks of it) with a streetlight attached and an extra line to the nearest building.

He thought: *Yes. Yes, I will.*

Because it was bullshit, when he really considered it, how after three weeks he hadn't even been allowed near the *practice* poles behind the main office. He removed his coat and laid it on the ground at the base of the pole. He didn't have his spikes on him, of course (spikes that the company made him buy to the tune of ninety-five dollars), but by squeezing his legs around the pole, he was able to start creeping upward. In fact, climbing a utility pole, even without the spikes, wasn't very hard at all—though he was pretty toasted, and by the time he was halfway up the pole he was sweating and sucking wind. His heart thudded. His hands felt raw and were cut with splinters. But he kept climbing—squeezing his legs, pulling with his arms—because he was on a mission. He belonged to that special class of climbers, those who felt more free up here than on the ground. It was total bullshit that he was only allowed to dig ditches and wash the fucking trucks.

He knew from his training and from common sense that you could get fried too close to the power lines, but the lines were still five or six feet above his head, which seemed far away until lightning slashed the sky and the lines above his head hissed in response. Seconds later another slash, closer this time (since when was there lightning in December?), and in his surprise Ramsey slipped an inch or two and felt a sharp pain in the meaty part of his left hand, where a large splinter of wood must have gotten lodged. Shit, he thought. He looked up again at the wires, then down again, and got a little queasy. Bed-spins. He hated bed-spins even when he was in bed.

He eased the pressure between his legs so his weight would carry him down the pole a few inches, but his left hand was nearly useless, and he almost fell. His legs squeezed the pole again. More lightning crackled, and the power lines started humming and hissing again, and thunder rolled across the sky, and these facts came to mind: Linemen on the poles always wore rubber gloves and insulating gear. Apprentice linemen were forbidden from working on live-wire poles until after an entire *year* of training.

The insanity of what he was doing came into sharper focus.

"Help!" he called. "Help! Anyone!"

He was calling out to God and to the cats that roamed his street, because there sure didn't seem to be any people around. Everyone was probably watching him from behind their darkened windows. He should just climb down. But the ground was spinning hard now, and his hand . . . *shit*. He didn't like what the nosy neighbors were probably thinking about him right now, but he'd forgive every last one of them if only somebody would pick up the damn phone and call for help.

The wind howled, and every flash of lightning made him brace for a taste of those 765,000 volts. His legs trembled, and the sweat on his body had turned cold. Then the rain started in—hard—because of course it did.

When flashing lights finally rounded the corner and came his way, for the first time in his life Ramsey felt grateful for the sight of a patrol car. But when the officer approached the pole and shouted up to him about a bucket truck that'd arrive in short order *courtesy of the electric company*, Ramsey shouted, "Fuck that!" and tried once more to scramble down on his own power. Damn, the hand hurt. But pain was only pain, and he gritted his teeth and lowered himself a foot, two, three. The hissing above him lessened, and he focused all his attention on this one thing, getting himself to the ground before the truck came.

Now his left leg was bleeding. What the hell? It only stung a little—what had he even cut it on? Probably a nail sticking out of the pole. The leg hurt less than his hand. But damn. Blood was definitely dripping down the one side. His pant leg was sticky. The worst part was, he couldn't lower himself anymore. The cut leg didn't allow it. If he were ten, twelve feet in the air, he'd have let go and taken his chances with a fall. But he was still close to thirty feet up.

"I cut my leg!" he shouted down to the officer. "I think it's bad." His whole body was shaking.

"Can you hang on? The truck will be here any second."

"How about a fucking ladder?"

"Just hang on." While they waited, the officer tried to keep Ramsey calm. "I'm Officer Ogden," he said. "You're going to be okay. We'll just wait a—"

"*Bob* Ogden?" Ramsey said.

"Yes, sir," the officer replied.

Bob Ogden was a year younger than Ramsey. They'd gone through school together, and now he was a cop with a cop's uniform and a cop's car, and Ramsey was trapped like a shivering cat in a tree, too stupid to know its own ass from third base.

Ramsey said, "You were a pussy in high school."

"How about we just wait for the truck," Officer Ogden said.

It was the only time Ramsey would ever stand in the bucket.

When he was finally on solid ground again, his legs were shaking so hard that he could barely stay upright. But that didn't stop him, the second that Bob Ogden came over, from taking a swing at the officer. Ramsey ended up in the road, splayed on his back, with Officer Ogden standing over him and shaking his head—because he, being sober, already knew what was still hazy to Ramsey: that by morning, Ramsey would be facing a court date, no job, and a line of staples in his thigh.

The next day, thunderstorms gave way to a hard, steady rain. Ramsey's roommate slept. On the muted TV, race cars looped stupidly around some track. Beneath the heavy disinfectant smell in the room, Ramsey detected traces of a thousand diseases. Hospitals always made him feel sick. Yet the doctors reminded him that it could've been much worse (electrocution, broken spine), and he knew he was damn lucky to be lying there, medicated on a soft bed. The pills, the pills, thank God for the pills, which insulated him from the sharpest pain and the bleakness that would otherwise be devouring him. His former self would've already been scheming ways to steal some of those pills for later use or profit. His current self was simply grateful that they were in his system.

Climbing was all he ever did well, and now they'd taken that away from him. The "they" in his thoughts were hazy and constantly changing: his supervisor at the electric company, Officer Ogden, his father, Gina, his teachers, karma, his own stupidity. He'd never climb again. His leg was a disaster, and apparently so was his constitution. He'd been terrified up there. Lightning and thunder had never bothered him when he was a boy in a tree. It thunders, you climb down. No big deal. You don't clutch on for dear life and make a spectacle of yourself. Jesus.

There wasn't even anyone to pity him. Eric had visited briefly, called him a fool, laid a hand on his shoulder, and left for work. His roommate, a teenager who'd been beaten to a pulp, was useless as a distraction, what with his jaw wired shut.

Late afternoon, a big female nurse with a man's haircut shoved him out of bed and made him walk down the hallway. *Up, up, let's go, just to the water fountain, just to the EXIT sign, just to the elevator and back, just to the far wall, just, just, just.* The two of them left Ramsey's room, and he limped past the nurse's station. When they got near the elevator, it opened. Its sole occupant stepped out, carrying a vase of flowers.

This was his future wife.

She was startlingly pretty, alarmingly so—with the sort of face you only ever saw when part of what you saw came from your own imagination: You're in a bar when you've had a few but before you've had too many, when the jukebox is playing the right song and the lighting is dim and cigarette-fogged. You know that what you see isn't real, that everything will change in daylight.

Well, it was daytime, and the only music came from some idiot doctor down the hall whistling to himself. Yet her green eyes were real, her smooth skin was real, every last thing.

When she smiled, Ramsey knew. That fast. He'd fallen for pretty faces before—who hasn't?—but one thing those pills did was filter out the noise and let you perceive the essence of things. He could practically see the light within her—not purity, exactly, or innocence, but an essential goodness that her lived experience hadn't quashed.

"What took you so long?" Ramsey asked.

She played along, looking at her watch. "I'm only three minutes late—I didn't think you'd mind."

She had on a white top and blue skirt, well tailored. Business attire, he supposed. Professional but snug-fitting. He was glad he had on the sweatpants that Eric brought him, rather than the paper gown. Glad he'd brushed his teeth. Glad he happened to look his best when he was a little scraggly with a day or two of razor stubble—something he'd been told by some girl once and chose to believe now.

What Ramsey did next was positively absurd, nothing he'd ever do in a bar at 1 a.m., let alone in a hospital corridor beside his overbearing nurse. He said, "I'm just glad you made it," and doffed—doffed!—an imaginary hat. She'd obviously come to visit a sick friend or relative, making the next thing out of his mouth utterly inappropriate. "And how thoughtful of you to bring me those."

She looked at the flowers, then back at Ramsey. "Just be sure to change the water every day," she said. A small card was attached to the bouquet. She plucked it off and handed him the vase.

"Wait . . . what?"

"These aren't cheap, either," she said. "There are gardenias and lilies . . ." She squinted. "What am I saying? You're a man, you don't care. Trust me, though—they aren't cheap." She looked over at the nurse. "Will you make sure he changes the water every day? Otherwise, he won't do it."

It was nice to see his nurse speechless. She nodded.

"Excellent!" she said to the nurse. To Ramsey she said, "Well, take care now," and pressed the elevator button. The doors opened, and she was gone.

The next day, she was back.

He'd spent hours thinking about her, the pills that worked miracles on a leg doing nothing to dull the ache of knowing he'd failed to get her name before those elevator doors closed. In the dark overnight hours, the error had grown enormous and irrevocable.

But here she was again, his only visitor since yesterday afternoon, when a policeman came by with a court summons. Three light-knuckled knocks on the door, the same knock of faux respect perfected by the attending physicians before they entered with whatever grim news they couldn't wait to dump on you. But it was neither cop nor doctor. Today she had on blue jeans and a long-sleeve T-shirt. Less makeup. She looked even lovelier. It was a word—lovely—he'd never considered in his life, yet it was the only word that fit.

He felt embarrassed. In the hallway, standing face to face, he could pretend he wasn't an invalid. Now he lay in bed, same clothes on as yesterday, a frail patient with his mute roommate looking on. He hadn't showered since the day before coming to the hospital. He propped himself into a sitting position, stifling a grimace of pain, and made a show of examining the new bouquet she'd brought, which was significantly larger than yesterday's.

"Those are nice," he said. "I like the . . ."

"You have no idea what any of these are."

Taped to the vase was a cream-colored card with neat cursive writing:

> *To Ramsey Miller.*
> *Feel better soon!*
> *Your friend, Allie*

"So me and you are friends now?"

"Don't believe everything you read," she said, smiling.

He nodded. "That one there's a purple rose."

"The purple part's right—it's an iris."

"Huh. Looks like a rose."

"Not really."

"How do you know my name?" he asked.

"The nurse's station," she said.

He looked up at her. "Are you rich or something? These flowers cost a lot."

"They seemed to make you happy yesterday. That's what flowers do—so I figured, what the hell?" She noticed yesterday's bouquet sitting on the table beside his bed. "They look good there."

"Who were they for?"

She shrugged. "I don't know. Someone. Don't worry, she got her delivery later."

"You just lost me."

"Well, I brought up another vase later." She squinted, as if trying to figure out what she was missing, and smiled. "Of course—why would you know? I run the flower shop downstairs."

"Ah." Ramsey motioned to his two bouquets. "So you aren't exactly paying for these."

"Are you kidding? On my salary?"

"Won't you get in trouble?"

She smiled. "I manage a small flower shop for a very large chain. I think there's like a thousand stores. No one cares if a few flowers get donated to a worthy cause." He must have flinched, because she said, "What's wrong?"

He couldn't bear to tell her that *a worthy cause* was the best compliment he'd ever been paid. So he said, "It's just . . . I got to be honest. I'm gonna be here another few days. And I'm sort of getting used to the sight of fresh flowers."

Her outfit yesterday, he learned later that day when she ate her bagged lunch in his room, was because of a job interview. She was a college senior, business major, with an eye on the pharmaceutical industry—specifically the corridor of companies between Princeton and New Brunswick: Merck, Johnson & Johnson, all the biggies.

She sat in the chair beside his bed, one leg underneath her, sipping from a sweating cup of Diet Coke.

"You can't imagine," she said. "They hire you right out of college, no experience, and you can pay back your student loans so fast." When she named the starting salary, Ramsey was pretty sure she had it wrong.

"What would you actually do?" he asked.

"Drug rep."

"Yeah, okay, but what would you *do*?"

She shrugged. "Meet with doctors and their office staff, talk about the drugs your company makes, give them free samples and other swag." He didn't want to admit that he'd never heard the word *swag*. She must've read confusion in his face, because she added, "You know—coffee mugs, pens, stuff like that."

Ramsey nodded. "And that makes them buy your drugs?"

"I guess," she said.

"So what about the flower shop?"

"That's just getting me through college. The pay is terrible, but it's super easy. And there usually isn't much to do, so while I'm there I can study."

"And hang out with creepy older men."

"You aren't that much older."

"I thought you might say I wasn't creepy."

She raised an eyebrow. "Well, are you?"

He actually had to think about it. "No."

She watched the TV a minute. Downhill skiing. No one crashed. "So what happened to your leg?"

Telling her about the leg meant telling her about his job at the utility company, and how proud he'd been to pass his CDL exam on the first try, and how the best and freest days of his life were gone, gone, gone before he'd even had a chance to climb a single pole for real.

"You'll find another job," she said, as if the whole mess of his life could be capped like a pen. "An even better one."

"I will, huh?"

"Of course. You're a take-charge kind of person. Like me."

He laughed. "Did you not hear everything I just told you?"

"Sure, but that was the story of your past. It ended with you here, in the hospital, talking to me. Now it's your present."

"You're saying that today is the first day of the rest of my life?"

Her face reddened. "I know that sounds cheesy, but it's true."

He wanted to believe that he could emerge from the hospital as if from a cocoon, transformed from anything he'd ever known or been. And of the many reasons why he began to fall so quickly in love with Allie, one of them was because he yearned to become worthy of her too-generous assessment of him. And in that way, she was already correct—in falling for her, he was taking charge of his life.

"Hey, do me a favor?" Ramsey asked, and looked over at his roommate. "Bring that guy some flowers tomorrow. I'll pay for it—the kid hasn't had a single visitor." His roommate looked over and waved, then looked back at the TV.

"Okay," she said, and whispered: "Can he really not talk at all?"

"Nope," Ramsey said.

"Bummer. Yeah, I'll bring him something." She stood up. "Well, I know where to find you."

The next day, the roommate got his flowers. Ramsey's came with helium balloons.

The day after that, both roommates were discharged. It was Allie's day off, but she'd already given Ramsey her telephone number.

The roommate was being kicked out first, so Ramsey said, "See you, man," and strolled around the hospital for a while so the kid could pack his things and leave in peace. That was what the nurses wanted, anyway—for Ramsey to walk walk walk. So he went the length of the hallway, then the hallway above and the one below. When he returned, his leg was throbbing a little. His roommate had left a slip of paper on Ramsey's pillow.

*Topaz Trucking*, it read in neat letters. Below it, a phone number.

> *Bobby Landry is my uncle. He's a training manager there. (I noticed your bad leg isn't your driving leg.) Is your CDL Class A? That would help.*
> *Take care,*
> *Vic*
> *P.S. Don't tell Bobby where you met me.*
> *P.P.S. Don't blow it with the flower girl.*

To his own astonishment, Ramsey didn't blow it. The vow he made to change his life was no transitory side effect of the good meds. It was real and lasting, and every bit as solemn as the vow that Eric had made years earlier to quit drinking and thank Jesus for every last thing. In fact, first on Ramsey's own agenda was to deal with his booze situation. He was reasonably sure he wasn't an alcoholic, but he knew he had to cut way back. Eric still put a dollar into a shoe box every day that went by without him taking a drink. Ramsey tried a ritual that suited him better: one drink whenever he drank, and no more. If that didn't work, he'd try something else.

He dialed up Topaz Trucking, met with the mute kid's uncle, and a week later enrolled in the company's training program.

At home, he followed his doctors' orders to the letter, stretching the leg and cleaning the wound meticulously. And while he was in the spirit of cleaning, he bought a new vacuum and a mop and some Windex. He bought a napkin holder for the kitchen table. He bought a kitchen table for the napkin holder.

He also began making lists. He listed things to do each morning: forty sit-ups; fifteen push-ups; walk to the ocean and back, followed by fifteen minutes of leg stretches; wash any dishes/pots/pans in the sink; read the front page of the newspaper; learn a new word from the dictionary.

He listed current skills and skills he'd like to acquire. He listed short-term goals (pay all bills on time; stay sober for three months; learn some more chords on the crappy electric guitar that was gathering dust in his closet), and he listed things he felt grateful for (living this long; meeting Eric; having health insurance when he got injured; meeting Allie).

Meeting Allie. Of course she was the reason he did any of this, why he awoke each morning with energy and optimism rather than festering in his dark bedroom all day and letting his leg harden into a permanent, painful handicap. Each day brought the possibility that he'd see her. She might come over after her shift with takeout, and maybe she'd stretch out on his sofa and study for one of her classes. Or maybe they'd watch something dumb on TV. Or maybe they'd go into his bedroom, and she'd be gentle with his injured leg and less gentle everywhere else.

Like Ramsey, she was alone in the world. When she was a freshman at Monmouth College on a soccer scholarship, she told her evangelical parents about dating one of her teammates, and that was pretty much that. Within the year, her mother and father had sold their home in Freehold and moved to the Florida panhandle, where the weather was warmer and the people more God-fearing. Allie was told, explicitly, that she wasn't welcome in their new home.

"The funny thing," she said, telling Ramsey the story in his apartment one night, "is that Amanda and I were only together that one semester. Turns out, I like guys."

"Glad to hear it," he said. "But that was it with your parents? You never patched things up?"

"We talked a few times on the phone. My father agreed to let me back into their lives if I agreed to fly down there on my own dime and stand in front of their congregation and admit to my sin and pledge that I'd stay pure until marriage."

Ramsey smirked. "I hate to break the news to you, babe, but you ain't so pure."

She hit him with a sofa cushion. "If I needed their money, I might've said whatever stupid thing they wanted me to. But they were broke, and I was paying all my own bills. So I didn't see the point."

"People sure are different," he said to her.

"Yeah, they were always intense, but it got a lot worse over the years."

"No," Ramsey said. "I mean . . ." He was thinking about the difference between Allie and himself: how his own response to his family's dissolution was to become a degenerate, while hers was to play varsity soccer, earn a 3.5 GPA, and manage a flower shop. He shook his head. "Never mind."

She started spending the night—once, then twice, then a few nights a week. They'd just about gotten into a regular routine when Ramsey's training period ended. It figured that he'd be hitting the road just when he finally had a reason to stay in town. Yet when he factored out the utility company, which had canned him for good the day after his late-night climb, he wasn't qualified for anything that paid more than minimum. And working for Topaz Trucking was a great deal. The company was paying for his training, and there was a guaranteed job at the end with a salary even better than he had been making not climbing telephone poles. And for the second time in his life, Ramsey had a job he could actually stand—one with a future, too, provided he didn't do anything stupid again, like slicing up his driving leg.

As a rookie, he went over-the-road, meaning anywhere and everywhere. But unlike a lot of truckers gone for three, four weeks at a time, he had it pretty easy. Home every two weeks for four days.

Those were good days.

He was home for Allie's college graduation and cooked dinner from a recipe in the Sunday paper. He was leaving the next morning. After the dishes were washed and the two of them were on his sofa with *Led Zeppelin IV* playing on the stereo, he took Allie's hand and said—casually, but with his heart pounding—"So if we got married, would you be okay with that?"

Fifteen days later they landed at McCarran International Airport and were in Vegas fewer than six hours before a grinning minister at the Xanadu Drive-Thru Wedding Chapel declared them man and wife. Flower bouquet, boutonnière, five-by-seven photo, marriage license: eighty-seven dollars, plus tax. Back in their motel room, they propped the photo up on the dresser, and Ramsey couldn't stop looking at it. He'd never seen that expression on his own face before. One of the words he'd learned recently from the dictionary was *effervescence*, and that was close, but the more accurate word was a lot simpler. *Joy*.

# 12

By 1991, six years later, Allie was a senior sales rep whose boss was grooming her for management, and Ramsey was doing damn fine, too. He'd built up enough goodwill at Topaz that they started keeping him east of the Mississippi, usually seven days away rather than fourteen. He and Allie remained man and wife, remained in love, the love having become more nuanced, perhaps—less desperate, but more dependable, a love as essential to each of them as their blood and bone, inseparable from the life they had created together, the child they had created.

Which was why Ramsey's phone call with Eric on the morning of June 10 completely blindsided him.

The argument that morning between Ramsey and Allie had been over Meg's day care. Meg was two and a half, and her December birthday made her one of the oldest in the Ladybug group. Allie thought she should move up to the Grasshoppers, where she'd be one of the youngest. Let her learn from the older kids, Allie said. Let her be challenged. Ramsey thought: She comes home happy every day. Why rock the boat? Besides, she was challenged enough, navigating a dozen other kids and two teachers every day. She'd be challenged her whole life, same as everyone. Why rush it?

They didn't shout at each other, Ramsey and Allie. That was never their way. And this fight that Ramsey and Allie were having, it was about nothing. Meg would be fine in either group. Ramsey knew this. But he also knew that Allie was being short-tempered with him lately, as if any view he held was the wrong one. From time to time she brought work-stress home, especially at the end of the quarter when there were reports to complete, but her stress had always shown itself as an unspecified moodiness, a cloud that settled over the house for a couple of days before lifting again. This was different. Her impatience seemed directed specifically toward him.

So when she said for the fifth or maybe the thousandth time that she wanted Meg to be *challenged*, that it was important she be *challenged*, Ramsey said, "For Christ's sake, Allie, it's fucking day care, not NFL training camp."

He didn't intend to sound mean or rude—okay, rude maybe— but people hear what they want to hear. And her dismissive reply—"Oh, fuck you, Ramsey"—felt worse than if she'd hit him. In all their years together, neither of them had ever said that to the other, even kidding around. And because he was hurt and stunned, he left angry later that morning on a weeklong haul without so much as a good-bye. Last time he'd done that was three years earlier, and it had ended with him frightening that poor hitchhiker in his cab and then nearly drinking himself to death.

Driving the familiar roads that began most of his trips, he felt awful about the fight and how he'd left. She had looked especially attractive this morning. The outfit she had on, and her hair, curled with the iron she used . . . whatever it was, Ramsey would have preferred to part for the week with a proper good-bye in the bedroom, rather than fighting about day care in the kitchen. And now he was alone in his truck, heading away, and Allie was alone in the house, and although they'd talk on the phone tonight or maybe tomorrow, the hurt wouldn't fully resolve until he returned, which was too long.

He didn't like driving agitated, never had, so he blasted the radio. It helped some—music always chilled him out, kept him from stewing in his juices. Near the Jersey / Pennsylvania border a couple of hours later, a song came on by one of the new Seattle bands. He could take or leave what he'd heard so far from these bands whose music sounded like heavy metal on downers. That was why he had on the classic rock station, songs he knew and loved, but somehow this one track had made it into the rotation. It wasn't classic, not yet, but something about it grabbed him. The lyrics were half indiscernible, half impenetrable. Nirvana, the DJ said the band was called. The song sounded nothing like any nirvana Ramsey might imagine, but that was okay. The energy and the anguish were real.

Ramsey took the next exit to find a gas station with a pay phone and call Eric, who was spending his hard-earned, week-long vacation renovating his kitchen—ripping out linoleum, putting in tile, installing new cabinetry. When Eric answered, Ramsey informed him that he'd just heard a new song that they must learn right away, and if he *hadn't* heard it yet, then he'd better put down the trowel or tile or grout or whatever and get his ass over to the radio, pronto, and request—

"Hold it a minute," Eric said. "I need to tell you something." But then he didn't say anything else.

"You still there?" Ramsey asked.

"Yeah, I'm here. I hate to . . ." He paused again. "Ah, shit—but you have a right to know."

Ramsey wasn't sure why all his muscles had suddenly tensed. Then it occurred to him that until that moment, he had never heard Eric utter a single vulgar word.

"What is it?" Ramsey asked.

"I went to pick up my amp from your house earlier." Of course. With his fast exit this morning, Ramsey had forgotten to tell Allie that Eric would be dropping by. "So I was driving down your street. And I saw something."

"Well, don't draw it out, man. What'd you see?"

"Yeah, okay." He heard Eric take a breath. "It was Allie, standing in the driveway with a guy. I'm pretty sure it was David Magruder—you know who he is?"

"The weatherman? Yeah, he lives down the street from us."

"He does? Oh. Okay. It was him, then, for sure. Well, the thing is, they were standing in your driveway, by the front door. And . . . Ramsey, he had his arms around her."

"No," Ramsey said. "You got it wrong. They don't even know each other." But did they? How would Ramsey know? With him gone half the time, he couldn't be sure. Except, Allie would have mentioned Magruder at some point. Unless she didn't want Ramsey to know.

"It was him," Eric said. "I know what he looks like."

"Then there's an explanation." Ramsey's mind worked to come up with one. Sprained ankle, one leaning on the other? "Trust me, I'm sure—"

"And they were kissing," Eric said quickly.

The phone receiver became a heavy weight in Ramsey's hand. He lowered his voice. "Like a real kiss?"

Eric's silence made everything worse. He could tell that his friend was thinking hard about his words, something that friends shouldn't have to do. "You don't want the answer to that," he said.

"I fucking do," Ramsey said.

Eric cleared his throat. "What can I tell you, man? They were kissing. He had his hand . . ."

"Where?"

"Doesn't matter. On her rear end, okay?" Another throat-clear. "I didn't want to tell you. I was praying on it when you called."

"Did they see you?"

"No, I doubt it. I was driving toward the house, and when I saw what I saw, I just kept going. It all happened fast, a couple of seconds. Anyway, they were still kissing when I drove past. They weren't looking anywhere else."

"Man."

"Listen, I'm real sorry. I didn't want to tell you. But I figure that God must have put me in my truck and made me bear witness so I could be the one to break the news. So I had to tell you, you know?"

All around Ramsey, cars were fueling up. A man in overalls returned to his pickup from the gas-station store carrying a cup of coffee. A hundred yards away, vehicles rushed across the highway overpass in a steady hum. An absolutely ordinary Monday morning on the road in the middle of nowhere, U.S.A.

"Sure, man," Ramsey said, barely aware of Eric's words anymore, or his own. "Sure you did."

His call with Eric must have ended, and Ramsey must have climbed back into his truck, shut the door, and started the ignition, but he couldn't remember doing any of it. Couldn't remember leaving the gas station or pulling back onto the highway or shutting off the radio, but he must have done those things as well.

185

He continued west toward Pittsburgh. Without music, his thoughts drifted and focused, drifted and focused. He replayed the morning—something extra in the way Allie had put herself together, the way (he now remembered) she wouldn't quite meet his eye—and he replayed all the times lately when she'd been short-tempered with him or exasperated and he couldn't figure out why, almost as if she wanted to be mad at him. His thoughts drifted further back to times when they would be pushing Meg along in her stroller and Allie would exchange nods or smiles with neighbors who walked or drove past, many of them men. He visualized Magruder's house—split-level, gray, just a few hundred yards from their own—and how Allie never once mentioned that she knew him. That seemed more damning than anything. Other neighbors, she mentioned: the retired couple who lived across the street, the boy at the end of the block who was bald from chemo, the veterinarian with the Great Dane puppies that Meg played with. But Magruder? Not one fucking word.

A truth began to emerge like a person walking toward him through thick fog—invisible, invisible, then startlingly clear.

She'd done this once before, cheated on Ramsey, though she refused to see it that way. When they first started spending time together, she was still seeing some college boy. She never mentioned him until the day she told Ramsey that it was over.

*What's his name?* Ramsey had asked.

*It doesn't matter what his name is*, she said. *What matters is that I ended it. I chose you.*

He'd believed her. It hurt, though, knowing she'd continued seeing this college boy while things with Ramsey were heating up. (Not "seeing him," Ramsey told himself now. No sugarcoating, big guy: "fucking him.") He'd been alarmed at the time, how she had it in her to lead two lives without him ever having a clue. But by then he was already in love with her. And like she said, what mattered was that she'd ended it with the other guy. Anyway, the two of them were having this conversation in a fairly expensive restaurant, celebrating three months of whatever it was they were. And the fact was, she *had* chosen him. That was what mattered, he told himself at the time.

He wondered, now, how long it'd been going on with Magruder, how long the life he thought he was leading wasn't his life at all. Weeks? Months? Or much longer? And he wondered if over the last few years there had been *other* other men. He tried to remember all the men on his block, every last leering accountant and dentist, every shithead with a business suit and a neatly mulched yard. But they all blended together. And soon enough, those other men stopped mattering—they were merely interchangeable parts—and he began to see Allie more clearly than he'd ever seen her before.

He must have been driving, but the universe was collapsing in on itself, obliterating time and distance, and now he was a boy in a tree and now his mother was turning in the air and now his father was bleeding in the kitchen and now he was smelling piss in a drunk tank and now he was lying in bed in one dark apartment and now in another and now, and now, and amid this barrage of memories, all the rage he had worked tirelessly over the years to rid himself of came rushing back as if through a busted levee. He was driving toward Pittsburgh, past farms and over hills and through valleys, but what he saw was Allie as she'd first appeared from inside the hospital elevator, blue skirt, vase of flowers in her hand, and then he saw her standing outside his house kissing David Magruder, and then their hands were all over each other, and she and Magruder were in bed, clothes on the floor, and he was inside of her, thrusting, and she was looking into his eyes.

Ramsey didn't touch the truck's radio dial. He wanted the silence, the thoughts to keep coming, wanted to experience in its fullness the fact that the single truth he had lived by every day since first meeting Allie in that hospital corridor, the truth that made all truths possible, was a lie. And the worst part was, he should have known it. Should have seen that his life these last seven years had been too good to be true—the wife, the kid, the house, the two-car garage, the job, the band, and on and on. But now, alone in his cab with no distractions, he saw the past seven years for what they were: a big sham. *That* was the only truth. He should have known.

The land rose as he bypassed Wheeling and crossed the Ohio River. He passed a weigh station without stopping, and then the land flattened again to ten million acres of corn stalks and soybean crop. He saw none of it. As his big rig rolled at a steady seventy-five miles per hour toward Columbus, his anger continued to build and crash down on him in waves—strong, then stronger still—again and again and again, a rage so distilled and devastating, it was almost like bliss.

He pulled into the Buckeye Travel Center around 5:30 p.m. for diesel and a leak. Got out of his truck and blinked several times in the late-afternoon haze. Once more he became aware of his surroundings. After fueling up, he entered the facility and went through the shop toward the fast food. Ordered a sub and looked around for a place to sit. Half the dining area was roped off for construction. He didn't want to return to his cab yet, though. The travel center was already doing him some good, forcing him to move in a world of other people. He knew he easily could've driven off the road, earlier—from inattentiveness or from a decisive yank on the steering wheel. Jump an overpass and create one of those video-game fireballs.

When a man left his table near the windows, Ramsey claimed it. At the adjacent table, a man wearing a Pennzoil cap sat hunched over a book spread open on the table. The pages were all marked up. Bible, Ramsey figured. Many truckers passed their time that way—all well and good until they found one another, and suddenly you're stuck listening to a group of impassioned truckers quoting—probably misquoting—chapter and verse and tossing their discoveries around as if the truck stop were their personal church.

When the man turned the page, Ramsey saw it wasn't the Bible, not unless there was a new version with charts and graphs. The young man wore a button-down shirt and brown pants. He was sort of short and thin like Ramsey, but not muscular. Clean-shaven but with terrible acne. His glasses were wire-rim, the lenses round and professorial. The Pennzoil cap might have been a red herring—he was probably a student, not a trucker. Ramsey unwrapped his sub, and as he chewed he kept glancing over. Eventually, he took a sip of soda and said, "So you in school or something?"

The man looked up from his reading. "Me?" He shook his head. "No, I drive for Safari."

"They got a good reputation."

"Can't complain," the man said.

"The way your book is marked up," Ramsey said, "I had you pegged for a Bible thumper. Then I saw the graphs and whatnot."

"Student wasn't a bad guess." He licked his lips. "I went two semesters at Humboldt County College. Was gonna be an oceanographer. I always had a knack for science." Although the man looked younger than Ramsey, his smile was already full of nostalgia. "But life gets in the way sometimes."

"Brother, I hear you there," Ramsey said.

The man shrugged. "What I found, you don't have to be in school to be a student." He patted his book twice for evidence.

"So what's that, an oceanography book?" Ramsey surprised himself, engaging with this other man, shooting the shit today of all days. But he'd been so deep inside himself, it came as a relief to talk to someone who didn't know him from Adam.

"There's oceanography in here," the man said, pulling his chair a little closer to Ramsey, "but a lot more than that." He licked his lips again. "See, there are these two scientists—one's an astronomer and the other's a geologist. They're two of the leading scientists in their fields, and . . . well, you know how when the moon is full, the tides get extra big?"

"Of course," Ramsey said, and went on to tell the man about having grown up at the shore—how on moon tides, boats in Shark Fin Inlet were always getting grounded on sand bars.

"So you know that the moon affects the earth's gravitational pull—it's literally sucking the water up and pushing it back down again." The man touched the bridge of his glasses. "And when a planet—Jupiter or Mars or any of them—when it lines up with the earth and the moon, the tides get even bigger. That's called a planetary conjunction. Doesn't happen too often. But it's nothing compared to what's going to happen on September 22 of this year, when they *all* line up."

"All nine planets?"

"Plus the moon." His eyes widened. "That's called a superconjunction. It's never happened before—not like this, anyhow."

"So the tides should get pretty wild," Ramsey said.

"The tides?" That smile again. "Brother, you won't be thinking about the tides." He licked his lips some more.

Ramsey looked down at the book. "And it's all in there?"

"Everything you want to know—or maybe everything you don't want to know. But I choose knowledge over ignorance."

"Mind if I take a look?"

The man gave Ramsey a once-over and looked down at his book. "Tell you what. I was planning on showering before getting back on the road. You want, you can have it till I'm ready."

"To be honest," Ramsey said, "I wasn't much enjoying my drive today. I don't mind putting it off a while longer."

The man shut the book and handed it over. The cover was entirely black except for the title, which was printed in large yellow capital letters—*THE ORBITAL AXIS*—and the two authors with Ph.D. after their names.

"Have at it," the man said, and went off to the showers.

It was a day for hearing hard truths. And this scholar/trucker/whoever-he-was—he was right: The tides weren't the half of it. The book wasn't long, under two hundred pages, but each paragraph was jammed with ideas, with long sentences in a small typeface. From the introduction alone, Ramsey knew that he wouldn't be able to understand most of the science, and the charts were largely impenetrable, but the broader picture nonetheless soon began to emerge: There had never been a superconjunction as pure and complete as the one coming in September, and it was going to affect more than just the oceans. The tectonic plates, Mother Nature's concrete slabs lying beneath the continents, were going to buckle and snap and cause unprecedented numbers of earthquakes and tidal waves. But most important, the gravitational effect of all those lined-up planets would be cataclysmic. As in, for a brief period—several hours, maybe as long as half a day—there would barely be any gravity. As in, kiss your ass good-bye.

There was far more to *The Orbital Axis* than Ramsey could absorb in thirty minutes. So when a half hour came and went, then thirty-five minutes, and the man hadn't returned from his shower, Ramsey took his absence as a sign. He got up from the table with the book and returned to his truck. He didn't feel much like driving and went only as far as the next rest area, where he used the bathroom and brushed his teeth. Back in the cab, he stripped down to his boxer shorts, and though it wasn't even 8 p.m. he got into bed. He examined the book as if it were an exotic rock or seashell, turning it over in his hands, touching the surfaces. He opened the book and thumbed through it. Pages were dog-eared, much was underlined, and there were scribbles in the margins. He turned back to the introduction and began to read, unhurried this time, doing his best to understand, trying to free his mind of everything but the words and the sentences in front of him, working to be the best unschooled student that he could be.

Whenever his mind started drifting back to Allie, to the affair that could easily gut him like a fish, he forced his attention back to the book, the book. And the more he read—there went 11 p.m, there went midnight—the more relieved he felt by the notion that he, Ramsey Miller, wouldn't have to do one damn thing about his awful predicament. On the night of September 22, in a little under three months, God would take his own tools out of the garage, sharpen them up, and set everything right.

Only, not God. The cosmos. The universe itself.

The apologies came a day later. So easy. She apologized for her words, he for leaving in a huff. They talked twice more that week, quick conversations from rest stops, and over the course of several days, his anger evaporated into the ether, just as the trees and rivers and beasts would all do in three months' time. After the trip's last drop-off, he deadheaded back to the Boaters World lot feeling purified, exchanged the truck for his Volkswagen, and drove home. Kissed his wife, his daughter.

"How was your week?" he asked Allie that night over dinner. Her week was fine.

"Eventful?" he asked.

No, she said, not especially. How was his week?

"Remarkable," he said, and took a bite of chicken. Sipped his beer. "I'll tell you about it after Meg goes to bed." And he did. He sat her down and told her about meeting up with the other trucker and reading his book and what it all added up to. He didn't tell her that the book was still in his truck, didn't want her reading it, taking on the role of debunker. He wasn't looking for a debate or a confrontation. He told her because she was his wife. And despite what she'd done to him, to them, she had the right to know that her time on this planet was more limited than she might think. She could do whatever she wanted with the information. As for him, he was thinking of selling his truck. Why did he need it anymore? he asked her. What was the purpose of working to earn money? Also (and this he didn't mention), Ramsey's presence at home should be enough to keep Magruder's hands off his wife.

Maybe for the same reason, Allie told him he ought to keep working. Then she suggested he see a shrink.

"I ain't crazy, honey," Ramsey said, and yawned. "What I am is dog tired." He'd logged 800 miles that day.

So they went to bed with the matter unresolved, and to Ramsey's surprise the resolution happened of its own accord. Hours of sleeplessness, despite his exhaustion, led to brief spells of frantic, sweaty dreams of cars and houses, trees, entire forests hurling upward toward the sky. By sunrise, the road was already pulling him back, the tug so strong it startled him. Since Meg's birth, he was usually home for sixty hours between hauls, but he found himself making up some story about an urgent delivery, an important customer, and he was packing hastily and kissing his family and racing back to Boaters World. Shifting that diesel engine into gear was like surfacing from the bottom of a pool after holding your breath ten seconds too long.

He drove more and more, missing Allie and Meg with every mile—but he'd been a trucker enough years now that he'd long since massaged that familiar ache into a softer longing. Anyway, it felt good to long for them, because longing was the opposite of rage.

Before long, he was rarely driving fewer than seventeen hours in a twenty-four-hour period. The law called what he was doing an "egregious violation," but nothing about it felt egregious. He cut back his coffee intake to almost nothing. He'd always slept best in his cab, but his sleep now—each night nothing more than an extended nap—was the most restful and dreamless of his life. He was rarely back in Jersey for more than a day, day and a half, before leaving the house again for Boaters World and his pre-trip inspection. And rarely out of arm's reach was the beat-up copy of *The Orbital Axis*, his reassurance that he wouldn't have to deal with Allie's affair—because he didn't trust himself to deal with it well.

He read the book cover to cover several more times, adding his own notes in the margins, his own underlining. Without trying, he memorized passages. He developed a habit of looking up at the sky, especially on remote stretches late at night when everything was dark and star-filled. And as the days turned into weeks and June became July and then August, Ramsey could swear he felt an electrical charge in the air all the time, as if a thunderstorm were always imminent, even when there were no clouds. And yet he knew that the charge wasn't electrical at all, but rather the tug of galactic forces beginning to nudge everything into place, including him.

In Phoenix on the morning of September 17, he was about ready to start home again with his load of bicycles bound for Toys"R"Us when he saw, hanging in the warehouse bathroom, a framed photograph of the Grand Canyon. Like every photo he'd ever seen of it since being a boy, it didn't even look like Earth.

"How far am I from the Grand Canyon?" he asked the dock supervisor when she handed him the forms to sign.

She squinted at him as if she couldn't fathom a single reason to visit that pile of rocks. "Maybe three hours?"

It would set him back at least half a day, and he was already on a tight schedule. But it was now or never, and three hours didn't seem so far to drive. New Jersey didn't seem so far.

Hell, on the energy currently pumping through his veins, he could easily drive to Mars and back.

# PART THREE

# 13

September 28, 2006

Melanie sat beside Arthur Goodale in his bed in the critical care unit of Monmouth Regional Hospital and waited for his laughter to subside. It was a deep laugh that revealed a mouth full of yellow smoker's teeth and finished with a cough that sent him grasping for the cup of water bedside.

Melanie had just told him, reluctantly, about her disastrous meeting the previous afternoon with David Magruder.

"You, my young friend," he said, when the coughing had subsided, "are a truly awful interviewer."

"It was bad," Melanie said. She didn't like being amusing to him.

"Bad?" Another laugh. "Your *second question* was about Ramsey Miller?"

"He said he didn't want to be bothered with the routine stuff."

"Sure, but . . ." He shook his head. "Listen, moxie is one thing, but oh, boy. Your interviewing technique . . ."

"I get it," she said. "I'm horrible at this, and I blew our only chance."

"Now, wait a minute—who said it was our only chance?" He looked out the window. Still nothing but a brick wall. "No, it probably was." He sighed. "Well, your options were limited from the start. You could probably try tracking down Eric Pace."

"I think I know that name," she said. Probably from one of the news articles she'd read online.

"He was a close friend of Ramsey's," Arthur said. Melanie must have given him a terrified look, because he smiled. "Relax— I interviewed him years ago. He's totally harmless." She found this hard to believe, but she needed to be willing to talk with any- one who might know something useful. "Not that he ever gave me anything useful, either. But you never know."

"How can I find him?"

"He used to work for Garden State Electric, in their equipment warehouse. It shouldn't be too hard to find out if he's still in the area."

She nodded. She would do it. She would steel herself and meet the totally harmless Eric Pace, who just happened to have been friends with a murderer. "Who should I be this time?" She wasn't feeling ready for the return of Eager Young Coed.

He smiled. "I'd go with the *Star Ledger* cover."

"I thought I'm not a believable journalist."

"Oh, you aren't. Not to me, anyway, but I am a journalist. He won't know the difference. Just remember to *ease into* the conversation."

She thanked Arthur for his help, but when she went to stand up to leave he reached for her arm. "Come on, Alice—what's your interest in all this?"

And why not just tell him? Funny, she'd expected the pressure in her chest to tighten here in the town where the crime had occurred. Yet Ramsey Miller had last been spotted in Morgantown, not here. And in fact, away from West Virginia and the daily reminders that her whole life was constructed around a single secret, she found it easier to imagine that her secret didn't matter or even exist. She was staying in a hotel. She had seen the ocean. She had traveled alone to New York City, had been one anonymous soul among millions. How could she be of any consequence to anybody? But she knew better.

"Sorry," she said, "but I can't."

"You can't, huh? So you want my help, but you won't be honest with me?" His expression was parental. He wanted her to feel guilty. "Do you know what I think, Alice? I think you're selfish."

"No, I'm really not," Melanie said, heading for the door. "I'm not even doing this for me."

Sometimes you catch a break. The woman behind the counter at GSE made one phone call and told her that Eric Pace supervised the utility warehouse across town. She wrote the number and address on a slip of paper. When she called the number from a gas station pay phone, Eric said she should come by at 4 p.m.

It was one o'clock now. So she returned to her car and drove toward the star she'd drawn on her map, the place that'd been pulling and repelling her since coming to town.

232 Blossom Drive was a white, two-story wooden house with a steep roof and columns in the front. On the front stoop, several flowerpots framed the red door. The flowers were in bloom, bright blues and yellows.

It all looked extremely ordinary, yet sitting in the car, pulled up to the curb across the street from the house, she felt her hands shaking. For several minutes she didn't get out of the car. She watched the house and imagined, and the imagining nearly made her drive away. But she made herself step out of the car and onto this quiet street with mature trees and well-tended lawns. She couldn't just stand there and stare, however, so she walked along the street—there were no sidewalks—until it ended in a T. One of the houses on this other street had belonged to David Magruder, but she didn't know which. They were all nice houses, much larger than the trailer she lived in. Some of the houses had basketball hoops in the driveways. A couple of them had bicycles or tricycles out front. She walked back along Blossom Drive, this time on the even side of the street, and when she reached 232, she stopped again. It was one of the few houses with a privacy fence bordering the backyard. You couldn't see out. You couldn't see in.

She walked up the side yard to the fence, where there was a gate. By moving the gate a little she was able to peek through a gap by the hinges and see—a backyard. More lawn. More shrubs. A few large oak trees near the back fence. A cluster of smaller, scragglier trees. In a spot away from the trees, a chaise lounge. A soccer ball. It didn't make sense. How could this place—

"Can I help you?"

A woman in faded blue jeans with a bandana in her hair and a baby on her hip was standing near the house and looking at her.

"Sorry." Melanie immediately backed away from the fence. "No, ma'am. I didn't mean to pry."

The woman watched her—not angrily, just curious and maybe a little concerned.

"I'm sorry," Melanie repeated, quickly walking to her car. She started the engine and drove toward the T, where she made a U-turn and left the neighborhood.

"Been a long time since anyone asked me about my friend Ramsey," said Eric Pace, after Melanie had identified herself as

Alice Adams, crime beat reporter for the *Star Ledger*. He was an obese man sitting in an armless wooden chair, behind a metal desk. On the desk were several wire bins filled with forms.

"You still think of him as your friend?" After slinking away from the house on Blossom Drive, Melanie had treated herself to a bacon cheeseburger from the diner, cable TV, and an hour-long nap. She'd driven to the utility company feeling restored and eager to talk with Eric, but uneasy, too, about meeting the man who knew her father as someone other than the subject of a lurid news story.

"I still think of him," he said, "and that counts for something." He was in his fifties, maybe older, wearing a collared shirt with the company's name on the breast. Tired eyes. Except for an oval-shaped patch of raw skin on one cheek, his face was so pale it looked translucent. It was hard to imagine he had once worked outdoors. "So has there really been a development in the case?"

"We got a tip the police are renewing their search for Ramsey Miller." She didn't like lying to the man, but otherwise there'd be no plausible reason for her to have sought him out.

"Well, no cops have been here to see me. Not for years. So what do you think—some new evidence turn up?"

"I think someone might have seen him somewhere and reported it."

His index finger scratched the pink patch on his face. "Saw him where?"

She reminded herself of Arthur's advice to ease into things. "I'm only speculating. I really don't know." She took a breath. "So how are you, sir?"

He seemed to study her a moment. "Me? Look around." Flickering fluorescent lights, vast warehouse, rows of equipment stacked on pallets, no windows anywhere, the only sound a distant forklift. "My ex passed on five years ago," he said. "My brother, a year after that. My sons are grown and gone. They couldn't get away fast enough." He coughed. "They have their own lives. I leave them alone. I come here, and I think about drinking, and when I leave I go to my A.A. meetings, and on Sundays I pray in church. That's how I am."

She was relieved, at least, that he was talking to her about his life. Unlike David Magruder, Eric didn't seem like he was going to toss her out on the street. "You and Ramsey Miller worked together."

"I wish he could've stayed with it," he said. "Before my knees gave out, I used to get a great deal of satisfaction from being a lineman. It was interesting work. Challenging. It was good for me, and good for Ramsey, too, for the short time he did it."

"What was good about it?" she asked.

He squinted as if trying to see the answer somewhere far across the warehouse. "I liked knowing I was bringing light into people's homes. And I liked training the apprentices." He looked around. "Now I sit on my butt and check boxes on forms, make guys sign their name on pickup and delivery. Sign here, here. Initial here." He took a long breath. "It's bull, Alice—but if you live long enough you're gonna get sick, and the union benefits are worth their weight in gold." Although there wasn't another soul around, he lowered his voice. "When the ex got sick, I remarried her just so she'd have the benefits."

"You and your ex-wife stayed close?"

Eric smiled. "She hated me. You can't blame her. When we got married, I was a lousy drunk. When we split, I was a lousier one. But we stayed in touch because of the boys."

Melanie wasn't sure how they'd gotten to talking about Eric's wife. This was what happened when you eased into a conversation.

"How long did Ramsey Miller work here?"

"For the power company? Just a few weeks."

"Why'd he stop?"

Eric paused before answering, as if choosing his words carefully. "He hurt his leg on a climb."

He seemed to have no more to say on the subject, so Melanie asked, "Do you have any guess as to why he threw the party at his house on the night of the murder?"

"You stay on point, don't you?" His smile was friendly enough, but tired. Who could blame him? This place would sap the energy out of anyone. "No guesswork needed," he said. "But I'm not gonna tell you."

"Why not?"

"I won't make him sound crazier than the press has already made him out to be."

"Mr. Pace, he *was* crazy."

Eric shook his head. "He lost his way. He believed something with all his might, and when it didn't come to pass . . . well, we all know what happened. But he loved his wife and daughter."

"No, he didn't." Realizing that she sounded personally affronted, she added, "How could he have?"

"Ramsey Miller battled to be a good man. He just lost the battle. And I get it. I lost more than my share."

"You never killed anyone."

Eric looked into her eyes, and she felt reprimanded for her flip comment. "I found the lord Jesus Christ and put my faith in him before it was too late."

"Are you saying that religion would have stopped him from doing what he did?"

"I'm saying he insisted on walking alone, and nobody can do that. But it's too easy, calling him a monster, or crazy. He was neither."

"What did he believe with all his might?"

Eric shifted in his chair. "Forget I said that. Ramsey was hardly the first man to worship a false prophet."

"Sir?"

He scratched his face again. "He spent too much time alone. His job as a trucker demanded it, but it wasn't good for him. He got to thinking in ways that worked against him. I tried to help, but I should've tried harder."

"What could you have done?"

"Now there's the sixty-four-thousand-dollar question. All I know for sure is that I should've been my brother's keeper, like the good book says. Only I wasn't. All that time in church and I failed the most basic test. On the night when my friend was crying out for help, I wasn't listening." He bit his lip. "I sat in that God-forsaken bar, and then he . . ." His breath had a wheeze to it. "Well, that's my cross to bear."

"What bar?" Her eyes were adjusting to the dim lighting, but the warehouse smelled of mildew and rust. What a horrible place to spend every day.

"It really doesn't matter," he said.

"It does to me. Please."

He watched her a moment. "When we all left Ramsey's house that night, the guys and I went for a drink. Me and Paul and Wayne. At the old Jackrabbits—"

"Wayne?"

"Wayne and Ramsey played guitar. I played bass. My brother played drums."

She knew she shouldn't be so surprised—her uncle had been friends with her father, and he played guitar. But Uncle Wayne never talked about that night, and she knew better than to ask.

"The bar was less than a mile from the house," Eric was saying. "It wasn't very late, and I don't drink. It would've been easy for me to check up on them. We even discussed it, the guys and me. But

Wayne and Paul were already three sheets to the wind, and I was dog tired, and Paul started saying that the best thing we could do was give Ramsey and Allie time to cool off. I let myself be convinced. We paid our tabs and went home. But I was sober, and I should've known better. I should've checked on them."

"You aren't to blame, Mr. Pace." As soon as it was out of her mouth, she realized it probably wasn't a very journalistic thing to say.

More face scratching. "That's kind of you," he said. "But the fact is, Ramsey was having a time of it, and I knew it, and I was his friend. I should've gone. If I had gone back to that house, I think maybe I could've stopped it."

Melanie felt suddenly woozy. What if Eric—or Uncle Wayne or Paul—*had* dropped by? Might that have changed everything? Would her mother be alive today? Would her father be someone who'd merely gone through a rough period in his life, rather than becoming a murderer on the run, or—worse—on the hunt?

"For a long time after," he was saying, "I was certain that the whole reason I became an alcoholic was so that years later, on one particular September night, I'd be guaranteed to be stone sober and would be my brother's keeper and save a couple of lives." He sighed. "I'm a humbler servant these days. I'm less certain about what the Lord wants out of me, and I'm less certain He wants me introducing other people to His word. May I ask if you're a believer?"

"Mr. Pace, I don't think my beliefs are relevant." She wondered if it was really Eric's knees that had relegated him to the warehouse, or if maybe he had been preaching a little too fervently to the apprentices.

He smiled. "No, I suppose not. But I do know that the Lord forgives us for our sins, and if He can do that, then we should be able to forgive ourselves. So that's what I've been trying to do all these years. Forgive myself."

Melanie nodded. Although the two of them were alone in this warehouse with the workday ending, she couldn't help feeling safe around Eric, and sympathetic toward him. She knew how it felt to be stuck inside a place for years on end, wondering *what if, what if.*

"Where do you think Ramsey Miller might be now?" she asked.

Eric closed his eyes for a couple of seconds, and Melanie found herself looking at the irritation on his cheek and wondering if the rawness made him scratch or if the scratching had caused the rawness. When he opened his eyes again, he said, "For a long time I would dream about him coming to me. I dreamed I convinced him to turn himself in and accept man's punishment and God's judgment." He shrugged. "He could be anywhere. He could be dead."

"Do you really think?"

"No, not really. Ramsey's a survivor." His smile widened to reveal a missing tooth. "The man's too stubborn to die."

She arrived back at the Sandpiper Hotel with a sandwich and a Coke, feeling ready for a meal, more cable TV, and an early night's sleep. Thirty minutes in that twilight of a warehouse had worn her down. No wonder Eric had accepted her invitation to talk. And unless he was lying, he believed he knew why her father had thrown his party. It couldn't just be a birthday celebration, could it? But what then? Tomorrow, she'd see whether Arthur thought it might be important, or just some habitual teaser that led nowhere.

Walking toward the hotel lobby, she gave only passing notice to the black Lincoln Town Car parked in the fire lane. When she heard the name "Ms. Adams?" being called out the car window, the name she'd invented didn't register at first.

Then the driver's door opened and a man stepped out. "Excuse me." Melanie stopped walking. "Are you Alice Adams?"

The man was dressed in dark blue jeans and a gray blazer. Black shoes with a fresh polish. He was very tall and his hair looked mussed in a purposeful way.

"Yes, sir," she said.

The man nodded, as if he knew all along. "David Magruder wants you at his home."

# 14

It took all the nerve she could summon to get into that car. She had no clue how Magruder had found out where she was staying or why he might seek her out after the way he'd chased her away the day before. *Remember why you've come all this way*, she kept telling herself, looking out the tinted window as the car rolled away from the hotel. *You're here for answers. You're here to be brave.*

They drove toward the ocean, went over several marshes, then turned onto a winding road where on either side the homes became larger. After some more driving she saw the bay through the trees and knew they had to be close. She'd never seen anything like it—homes that could be museums, each landscaped with its own small forest, it seemed, hand-tapered so that every branch of every tree hung just so. Some of the houses were obstructed from the road by hedges or trees or fences, so that you only caught them in glimpses—and in addition to being awestruck by these estates, Melanie couldn't help feeling bewildered by these people for whom privacy was merely an aesthetic choice.

Magruder's house was almost completely hidden, first by a row of hedges and, behind it, a wrought-iron fence. From the road, only the roof of the house was visible, set far back on the property. The driver pressed a button on his remote device clipped to the sun visor, and twin gates slowly opened.

"Here we are," he said—his first words the entire trip—and pulled into the pebbled driveway.

Inside the gate, the driveway curved around a grove of trees and then cut like a moat through several acres of lawn toward the stone house. When the car approached the house, she could see clear through one of the downstairs rooms to the dock out back, a sailboat tied up there, the wide expanse of the bay.

Somehow the driver was out of the car and opening her door before she could even grab the handle. Once she'd exited the car, he shut the door behind her and dialed his cell phone.

"We're out front, David," the man said, and put the phone into the inside pocket of his blazer.

She looked up at the driver and said, "Thank you," as if this had been her idea all along.

"Don't mention it," he said.

Before they reached the front steps, the door opened and David Magruder stepped outside wearing black pants and a maroon cashmere sweater with the sleeves pushed up. He was all smiles, a replication of his greeting the day before. "Welcome, welcome," he said, rubbing his hands together. "Thanks for getting her, Bill."

The man nodded. "My pleasure," he said, and returned to the car.

When the two were inside the house, Magruder said, "You look very pretty today." Maybe he meant it to be nice, or ice-breaking, but considering how he had behaved in his office the day before, the compliment came off as super creepy. And either he didn't know it, which made him dense, or he did know it, which was worse. Regardless, she was feeling extremely aware of the fact that the two of them were alone in the house.

"This is a big house," she said.

He laughed. "I suppose it's a little much for a bachelor pad." The room they were in—the one she saw from outside—could comfortably seat thirty. "But you can't beat the view."

No, you couldn't. Beyond the house, beyond the dock and the sailboat, Silver Bay shimmered. Across the water, maybe a half mile away, another line of mansions mirrored those on this side of the water. Toward the north, the bay opened up so wide she couldn't see the other side.

"Listen," he said, "I want to apologize for yesterday. The way I treated you was . . . well, it's unforgiveable. There were problems with the show we were working on. My anger had nothing to do with you."

Almost certainly a lie, but at least they were talking.

"It's all right, Mr. Magruder," she said.

"You're in my home. Please—I'm begging you to call me David." She nodded. "All right, David."

"Good. And it's definitely not all right," he said.

*What's going on?* she wanted to ask. *Why am I here?* But she'd learned her lesson about getting to the point too fast. "Is that the ocean over there?"

"That's New York Harbor," he said. "From the roof deck you can see the Manhattan skyline." He took her hand. The gesture was too intimate, and she almost pulled away but relented. "Come on—I want to show you my office."

His office was out back. The yard was private and absolutely serene, the only noise coming from the engine of a distant motorboat. They passed the pool, with its own pool house (*It's really a guesthouse*, he explained. *I didn't ask for it, but it came with the property*) and they passed the garage (*I was going to have Bill pick you up in the Ferrari, but then I thought you might be more comfortable in the Town Car*) and they passed a clover-shaped pond (*Would you believe the osprey have been swooping down and stealing my koi!*), and finally they entered a smaller structure, built beside the dock, that made her feel as if she were on a yacht, everything wooden and polished and uncluttered. There was a sitting room and office adjacent to a full kitchen and what looked like a fully stocked bar. On the walls hung various medals, plaques, and framed letters both typed and handwritten.

"In the main house," he said, "the walls are full of original artwork. George Rodrigue, William Baziotes . . . would you believe I recently acquired a Warhol? But *here*"—he motioned to the wall—"is where I keep what really matters. Gifts from soldiers, students, husbands, wives . . . ordinary folks whose lives I've helped in some way over the years. They mean a lot more to me than my Emmys."

He was showing off, but only when he opened a half-empty bottle of Scotch and poured himself a not-small glass did it occur to her that he might also be drunk, or at least on his way. Other than on TV, she'd never seen a drunk person before. Wayne and Kendra rarely drank alcohol. Being drunk was less obvious than she would have thought—or maybe Magruder was a subtler drunk than most.

"What's your poison?" he asked, and smiled.

"No, thank you—I'm okay," she said.

"I know you're okay," he said, "but I want you to be comfortable."

He couldn't keep still. A tap of the foot. A slight bite of the lip when he thought she wasn't watching. It reminded her of Phillip, screwing up the courage to kiss her that first time.

"Did you know that presidents vacationed here, once?" he asked. "In Silver Bay, I mean. Woodrow Wilson, Teddy Roosevelt. And movie stars: Jayne Mansfield, Buster Keaton. A train used to run right up to the bay. The boardwalk—have you seen it?"

She said that she had.

"It's nothing, now," he said. "But at one time it was jam-packed with the rich and famous. You wouldn't know it, but there's history in these five square miles." Another sip from his drink. "It's a lot quieter now, but that's how I like it. Silver Bay is my antidote to the New York office. I don't know if I could face the insanity every day without a serene place to come home to." He smiled. "And that, by the way, is my answer to you from yesterday—why I still live in Silver Bay." Another sip. "You should sit at the desk for a minute." The wooden desk had nothing on it and was right up against a floor-to-ceiling window overlooking the bay. She sat down and placed her hands on the desk's cool, smooth surface. "So what do you think?"

When seated, she couldn't see the dock—only the water. "It's like being on a ship," she said, though she'd never been on a ship.

"That's because it's how I designed it. See across the water? That pinkish house?"

It was one of the largest on the bay. "Yes."

"That's my ex-wife's house. I know—it's all very Gatsby. But she bought it after the divorce, and *I* wasn't going to be the one to move."

Melanie had no idea what he was talking about. And before she could stop herself, she made a mental apology to Arthur and asked, "Why am I here?"

"Why, indeed." David looked out over the water. "You're here because I treated you badly yesterday and wanted to make up for it."

"That's nice of you," she said. "But you don't have to ingratiate—"

"Also, I was hoping you might answer something for me."

Ah. "I can try."

"I'm really glad to hear you say that," he said, finishing the drink and setting the glass down on the desktop. Looking out at the water, he said almost offhandedly, "Who are you?"

"What do you mean?" She kept her breathing steady. "You already know. I'm Alice Adams."

He sighed. "You're a lovely young woman—beautiful, in fact—but you'll notice that I haven't called you Alice since you've arrived. That's because there is no Alice Adams enrolled at Gaston College. Which makes sense, given that your name is Melanie Denison." Hearing her name said aloud gave her body a physical jolt. "Except, there's no Melanie Denison enrolled at Gaston College, either. So I was hoping you'd be willing to explain that for me."

"No," she said, all of her muscles tightening. "I'm not willing to."

He took a long breath and looked at her. "You need to understand that I do this for a living. Even if the Sandpiper Hotel hadn't given us your real name, we'd have found it out. I have a very capable staff. Compared to the kind of investigatory research we do every day, this is nothing." When she didn't respond, he said, "Look, Melanie, if you're working for one of the rags, that's your business. I'll even keep it a secret." She continued to stare out the window. "I'm not angry about yesterday, anymore. Honest." He gave her a smile that was probably meant to seem reassuring, but she couldn't help thinking that the person he was reassuring was himself. "In fact"—he reached out and took her hand—"I'd like to become better acquainted."

If she were better at this—if she were Nancy Drew—she would pull her hand away and fearlessly continue her line of questioning from the day before. She'd get what she came for. Instead, she quietly said, "I should go. This isn't a good idea."

Magruder's eyes widened. At first, she thought he had become angry, but no. There was fear in his eyes, or something like it. He couldn't stop looking at her. At last, he said, "Let down your hair."

"I beg your pardon?"

"Your hair. I'll have Bill return you to your hotel in just a minute. I swear it. But do this for me first."

She felt very alone in this man's bachelor pad. "Mr. Magruder, I don't know what you think I'm here for, but—"

"I'm not making a pass at you. But please." His voice was suddenly desperate. "Put your hair down, and I'll answer whatever questions you came to New York to ask me."

And with that promise, she found herself removing the clip from her hair. She hadn't cut it in a while—it was about the longest it'd ever been. Tied up all day, it would look scraggly, so she ran her fingers through it a few times before facing him head on.

He squinted a little in the early evening light, and the way he studied her face felt both clinical and tender. And just as it occurred to her why he might have made his request, and why he was now looking at her so intently, his eyes watered and he said, "Oh, my God." He opened his mouth as if to say more—once, then again—before going to pour himself another drink, larger this time.

He dropped into one of the leather chairs, took a swallow, and set the glass down. "I didn't actually think . . . I mean, it crossed my mind, but . . ." He closed his eyes. And when he opened them again and confirmed that Melanie wasn't a mirage but an actual young woman in his office, he smiled and said, "You aren't the spitting image of your mother, but you come damn close."

# 15

They sat together on the sofa, watching the sun dip behind his ex-wife's neighbors' homes across the bay. Melanie held a glass of water while David Magruder went through most of a bottle of champagne. "You sure you don't want any?" he said. "I mean, if Meg Miller being alive isn't cause for celebration, I don't know what is."

The man could put away a lot of alcohol. He was clearly practiced at it.

"Water is fine," she said, the ice cubes knocking together in her glass surely giving her fear away. He knew. Him. A journalist. An untrustworthy journalist. A volatile journalist with money and power. It couldn't be worse.

"What about food—are you hungry? We could rustle something up in the main house."

Her stomach was growling. For the baby, she had to get on a better eating schedule. But how do you eat when you're nauseous all the time? "Maybe if you have some crackers or something."

"Crackers?" He laughed. "Sure, we can rustle up some crackers." But he didn't get up. He still seemed stunned. "Look at you—Meg Miller. God damn." He shook his head. "Meg Miller, alive and well."

"I go by Melanie," she said.

"Sure, okay. Melanie." He smiled at her. Now that he knew her secret, he couldn't stop smiling. "Where've you been all this time?"

She shrugged. "Hiding."

"You lost me."

"From my father. So he can't find me."

His smile disappeared. "You've been hiding since nineteen ninety-one?"

"That's right."

"Oh, Jesus."

"And I know your job is to expose stuff, but you have to keep this secret. You have to. Please. The only reason I'm alive today is that everyone thinks I'm not."

"Your accent—do you really live in North Carolina?"

She shook her head. "Please. I'm not going to tell you, and I'm begging you not to try to find out. I need your help." She had sought David out because of the unlikely possibility that he'd have something useful to say about the night of the murder. But when she thought about how easily he had investigated her without her knowing, a new idea started to take shape. "I need you to help me find my father."

"Darling, your father had a fifteen-year head start. The police have gotten nowhere. I'm not sure what you think I can do."

"You said you do this for a living."

"I'm a TV journalist, not a bounty hunter."

"But you can try, can't you?"

The yard had darkened a shade, and he squinted out the window, as if Ramsey Miller might be standing on the dock, waving at them.

"I can try."

He insisted on taking her back to her hotel, but she insisted on being the one behind the wheel.

"I've been drinking for enough years to know when I can and can't drive," he said.

"Either I drive or I'm calling a cab."

He shrugged. "It's a nice night—we'll take one of the convertibles."

"How many cars do you own?" she asked.

"Six," he said. Then: "Seven. I forgot about the new one. Can you drive a manual transmission?"

"No," she said.

"Then so much for the Alfa Romeo." He grinned. "Come on, we'll take the Corvette."

They went out to the massive garage, where seven shiny cars were parked in a line. The yellow Corvette was in the center. After David pulled the car's top down, they got in, and she backed out of the garage, scared to death of hitting something, and went around the circular driveway to the road.

She turned left and accelerated, the engine revving beautifully, and headed back to town, passing the large estates, and then the road curved around so that it ran along the bay, which looked smooth as glass underneath a sky that was fading from purple to black. She hadn't ever ridden in a convertible before, let alone driven one, and she decided on the spot that of all the things missing from her life, this one ranked high.

"You remember your way around?" David asked from the passenger seat.

"Only from the past few days. I have no memories of this town," she said. "I wish I did. I wish I could remember my mother. I try all the time."

At the light, she turned away from the bay and headed west on Main Street.

"Let me tell you something. She's worth remembering."

"So you weren't strangers."

"No," he said. "We were close. I loved your mother."

"What do you mean?"

"What do I mean? I mean we were good friends. She was a wonderful person. I think I'm actually pretty drunk."

"Were you ever more than friends?" Melanie was glad that it was dark and she had a reason to keep her eyes straight ahead.

"No," he said. "Never. Turn right here."

"Why?"

"Just do it—I want to show you something."

The turn sent her in the direction of her parents' old neighborhood. She'd seen enough of that for one day. But then he had her make another turn, and another, onto a road that was new to her.

"Pull into that parking lot," he said. There were no other cars. "Drive to the end there and park. You need to see this."

David got out, and she followed. Though it was dark out now, she could see that they were in a park, a pretty spot with mature trees and a playground ahead and a pond off to the left. At the edge of the playground were a few picnic tables. David climbed up and sat on one of the tables.

"So is it familiar?" he asked.

"No. Should it be?"

"This is where you used to play."

"Really?" She tried to imagine herself as a toddler, sliding down those same slides. Swinging on those same swings. She climbed up on the table and sat beside David.

"There used to be a taller slide over there with several twists. It was your favorite. And that rubbery surface is new. Back then there were woodchips, I'm pretty sure. Same swings, I think. Though sometimes you just liked chasing the birds."

"Why do you know this park so well?" she asked.

"I used to meet your mother here when she came with you," he said. "With your father away so often, I think she appreciated the adult company." Melanie knew from the articles she'd read that her father was a trucker. "We would talk."

"What would you talk about?"

"Oh, I don't remember now. Our jobs, our lives, politics, the weather . . . whatever was on our minds, I guess. You'd throw crusts of bread to the turtles in that pond." He smiled. "That was the only way to lure you away from the playground and back to the car—the promise of feeding the turtles."

*I used to play here. I used to feed the turtles. This was my home.*

Melanie climbed off the table and went over to the swings. There were bucket swings for babies and another set for older kids. She sat in one of the larger swings, lifted her legs, and glided back and forth a few times before lowering her shoes and dragging to a stop.

"Thanks for taking me here," she said, going back over to him. "Sometimes I feel like I don't have a past. So . . . thanks."

"You're welcome," he said. He reached out and clasped her shoulder, then moved his hand away. The gesture brought unexpected tears to her eyes. She turned to face the pond.

They stayed like that a minute—him sitting on the table, her standing beside it—their eyes adjusting to the dark. A gentle breeze moved the leaves in the nearby trees.

"Back at the house," Melanie said, looking at him again, "you told me I could ask you whatever I wanted."

"Okay—I might have said that."

"You did."

He nodded. "All right."

"After the murder, why did the police talk with you several times?"

"Who told you that?"

Melanie held firm. "You said you'd answer my questions."

A bullfrog honked from the pond. "You're being tough," he said. "That's a good journalistic instinct. I used to be a tough journalist, you know. Pretty legit. I have those instincts. But I like having money, too. Sometimes it's a trade-off. God damn, I make a lot of money." He shook his head. "I'm just so glad you're alive. You have no idea how mind-blowing this is."

She returned the smile. "The police . . ."

"Right. Okay. My mistake was that I was honest to them up front about being friends with your mother. And also . . ." He shrugged. "I had a shit alibi for the time of the murder."

"What was it?"

"It was that I didn't have one."

"You mean they thought—"

"No, they didn't think anything. This wasn't a whodunit, you know? But the police like tidiness—people verifying other people's stories. And God forbid if anyone is ever alone. I was married then—bad idea, by the way. I highly recommend never doing that. But I was married and my wife was in New York that night. Anyway, these local yokel cops were looking for the same thing you're looking for now: something that might help them find your father. Well, I didn't know anything. I barely knew the man. But you know how it is. I'm a public figure, and there are people in this world who make a lot of money running with nonexistent stories about public figures. Which is why I don't ever talk about that time in my life, or about knowing your mother. I was very fond of her, and what happened was horrible, and I don't like being reminded of it."

"You didn't say 'fond.' You said you loved her."

The bullfrogs were louder now, and the crickets. It reminded her a little of West Virginia, the woods teeming with life.

"She was a beautiful, complicated woman," he said.

"And you loved her."

"Yes," he said. "I loved her very much."

David Magruder had interviewed movie stars and astronauts and every living president. Yet it felt less strange than she would have imagined, driving a drunk celebrity around in his fancy convertible.

"I wish I'd brought a six-pack," he said from the passenger seat, his eyes closed. Though her hotel was only a couple of miles from the park, by the time she arrived David was fast asleep.

She pulled the car into a parking space and shut off the engine. She nudged his arm, rousing him.

"You need to call your driver," she said.

"He isn't on twenty-four-hour call, Melanie."

"Then a cab."

"I'm a grown man," he said, and yawned.

"Well, there's no way you're driving yourself home," she said.

"Of course I am." He sounded wounded. "I've been my driving—" He tried again. "I've been driving since dinosaurs roamed the earth."

Her room had two beds, but no way. "There's a sofa in the hotel lobby," she said. "You can sleep there for a couple of hours."

He looked at her and smiled. "Your concern for me is wildly endearing. Tell you what—leave me here. The seat reclines way back. I'll just rest awhile."

"I guess," she said.

"She guesses!" He grinned drunkenly. And when she handed over the keys, he leaned forward and kissed her cheek. "Absolutely amazing," he said, reclined his seat, and shut his eyes.

"You'll probably want to put the top up," she said softly. When he didn't answer, she said, "Good night, David," and shut her door, leaving him there to sleep in the Sandpiper parking lot. She did it reluctantly, suspecting that the minute she entered the hotel, the Corvette's fancy engine would roar to life. Which was exactly what happened.

# 16

September 22, 1991

After standing over his sleeping wife for a serene minute, Ramsey left their bedroom and went downstairs. His hands needed something to do, so he put on his coat and work gloves, went outside, and began carrying the sheets of plywood and two-by-fours from the garage to the backyard. It was still more night than morning outside, and cold—but the work encouraged a sweat. When he'd finished moving all the wood, he went inside again to wait for Eric.

The tap came only a couple of minutes later. The two men shook hands. Ramsey would've offered Eric coffee, but his friend was already carrying a cup from 7-Eleven, so they cut through the house and went out back.

" 'Preciate your help," Ramsey said. "I know it's cold out here."

"Cold nothing. We're a band, aren't we?" Eric said. "Band needs a stage."

One good thing about the cold, everyone's windows would be shut. Ramsey didn't want the neighbors moaning about the pounding of nails on a Sunday morning. Not that this would take long. The plans were so simple, Ramsey barely needed to explain them to Eric: six pallets supported by thirty-six-inch sections of two-by-fours, which the hardware store had precut yesterday. They'd finish in time for Eric to get to church.

Ramsey offered up his work gloves, but Eric declined and blew into his cupped hands. The ground was wet, so they knelt down on one sheet of plywood while working on another. Each man started on a pallet, working apart, not talking for a spell, the rhythmic hammering like a drumbeat to a song you can't quite remember. Just as Ramsey expected, a project like this was what he needed. It was good to build something. After a few minutes, Eric broke the rhythm, saying, "So Wayne tells me you're cracking up."

Ramsey looked up from his work. "What's that now?"

Eric set down his hammer. "The end of the world, Ramsey?" He said it disappointed, the head shake implied. His father had used the same tone when Ramsey was young and his rap sheet still in its infancy. *Shoplifting, Ramsey? Vandalism, Ramsey?*

Ramsey had never intended to tell Eric, whose clay brain religion had baked hard, but now he knew anyway. Which explained why he'd agreed so readily to get up in the dark and come over here. He'd decided to be a one-man intervention.

"I know it to be true." Ramsey shrugged. "That's all there is to it, my friend."

"Ramsey—"

"I *know* it." He said it final like, and made a point of returning to the two-by-four he was hammering into place. The morning was getting lighter, beginning to feel like today and not yesterday.

"So you know the world is ending, but you don't bother mentioning it to me?"

"Didn't see the point," Ramsey said.

"You told Wayne."

"Yeah, I told Wayne, but I hadn't planned to." Outside the music store yesterday afternoon, after arranging the P.A. rental, Wayne was smoking a cigarette and moaning to Ramsey about how he'd barely gone surfing all summer. So Ramsey told him he'd better get to it on Sunday morning, and he told him why—not too much detail, just the *Reader's Digest* version.

"So why'd you tell Wayne and not me?"

Ramsey stopped working again. "I'll bet you never knew that Wayne grew up in some shitty orphanage till he was ten. Or that when he was eleven, his foster dad broke his arm for fighting at school. Cracked it right over the kitchen table."

Eric said nothing for a few seconds. "I'm sorry to hear that, but what's your point?"

"My point is, Wayne's had it rough. And he hasn't had one damn person in his whole life to look up to, and for some crazy reason he looks up to me. He confides in me. So I was returning the favor."

"Well, you shoulda confided in me, too."

"Oh, come on, man, don't look all hurt—I knew you'd think I'd gone loony. Or worse, you'd believe me and start to freak out about your standing with Jesus."

"Strange, how I don't remember reading about this in the newspaper."

"Make fun if you want," Ramsey said, "but it's no joke."

"So what's your source?"

Ramsey remembered everything about that late-afternoon: the roped-off seating, the other trucker, the way time had seemed to stop. "Saw it in writing a couple months back. In a science book." Eric still had that parental look on his face. "I read it cover to cover. Trust me—it adds up."

"You're no scientist," Eric said.

In a tree near the back fence, a couple of squirrels sounded like an old couple bickering. When they quieted down, Ramsey said, "Let me ask you something. Do you believe in God?"

"What?"

"Come on—do you or don't you?"

"You know I do," Eric said.

"But you ain't a priest or a prophet or nothing, are you?"

"It's different." He set his hammer down and drank some coffee. "My belief is about putting trust in Jesus Christ. It's about having faith in the Holy Spirit."

Ramsey tried to imagine a time before Eric's conversion, when he was just another drunk, one more fuck-up in over his head.

"So on a scale of one to ten," Ramsey said, "how much do you believe in Jesus and God and all that?"

"Don't ask me that," Eric said. "It's crass, putting it on a scale."

"So you won't do it?"

Eric sighed. "Whatever, Ramsey. Ten. All right? I believe it a ten."

Ramsey lowered his voice. "You can knock that number down a peg or two if you want." He smiled. "No one's listening but me and the squirrels, and we won't tell."

"I don't need to lower my number." Eric glanced up at the sky. "And there's always someone listening."

"Ah, so you're only saying 'ten' out of fear. That's messed up."

"You got it wrong."

"Then you're hedging, so just in case Jesus *is* real you don't end up on his bad side."

"Ramsey, it's a ten, okay? You asked me, and I gave you my answer. I have complete faith in our Lord and Savior Jesus Christ."

"All right, all right," Ramsey said, hands raised in defense. "You don't need to get all nutty about it. So your faith is a ten. And so is mine. You wouldn't know it, because I always said the concept of God was a bunch of—" Seeing Eric's eyes narrow, he softened his words. "I've never been a believer."

"That I know," Eric said.

They started working again, and Ramsey knew what was coming and waited for it. He'd forgive Eric, because his friend was an addict. Eric used to be addicted to booze, and now he was addicted to God.

"Maybe this is the right time for you to reconsider your own relationship with Jesus," Eric said after a long-enough pause that not saying it must have felt like ignoring the world's worst itch.

Ramsey smiled. He knew people. "Nah, it's too late for me." He said it to lighten the mood, self-deprecate a little. But when it came to Eric and God, there was no mood lightening. "What I'm saying is, I already know all about faith. In fact, I have more of it in my little finger than most people have in their whole body, even religious kooks."

"Hey . . ."

"I only mean that without faith I'd be dead by now."

Eric said, "I've always respected how you pulled yourself up, with God's help."

"God nothing, man—*you* pulled me up. And Allie did, too. That's what I'm talking about: For twenty-seven years I never had faith about one damn thing in my life, and then out of the blue I decide to put my faith in some douchebag stranger hanging from a utility pole who's giving me lip—I decide *that* guy's gonna save me . . . and he does! You. You fucking did." Eric cringed from the double blow of a compliment and an obscenity, but Ramsey could think of no other way to make his point. "And when I'm in dire straits again, some college girl enters my hospital corridor, and I take one look at her and somehow I know with complete certainty that lightning's gonna strike me a second time and now *she's* gonna save me. And she does. But it's more than that. She keeps on saving me every day since, twenty-four/seven/three sixty-five—just like I knew she would."

"Does all this by any chance have to do with—" Eric took a breath. "With what I *saw* a few months back?"

Since their phone call back in June, Ramsey and Eric hadn't ever talked about what had taken place in the Millers' driveway.

"We were never supposed to meet," Ramsey said. "The damn flowers weren't for me. But okay, we meet and I say to myself— *put your faith in her.* And believe me, I've had enough hours alone in my truck to consider the matter from every angle. And now the end is almost here."

"So you say."

"Listen—up till now, in my whole entire life I've only ever known two things for sure: that I needed to put my faith in you and in Allie. Almost every other decision I ever made was a bad one, but not those. And that's because it wasn't ever a decision. It was a feeling— I just knew. And now here's this third thing that I know even stronger than the other two put together. Ten times stronger." He shook his head. "I can't explain it, but I don't need to."

"I still say we'd have heard about it on the news."

"Not if the government doesn't want to alarm everybody and there's nothing they can do about it. Then they'd keep quiet so there's no mass panic. It's like if a thousand nuclear warheads were about to obliterate the U.S. They'd keep it to themselves. Nobody ever fucking tells the truth."

"Ramsey—"

"No, I get it. You think I'm wrong. But the fact is, my faith is better than yours, because there's science to back it up."

"So where exactly is this science book? You keeping it to yourself, or can I have a look?"

"I don't have it any longer," Ramsey said.

That parental look again.

"For what it's worth," Ramsey said, "I never once asked you what makes you so sure about Jesus and Mary and all the rest."

"You want to see my book?"

"No."

Eric looked at the plywood scattered around them. "I'm willing to put up a grand says you're wrong."

Ramsey smiled. "Nice bet. If I'm right, you don't need to pay up."

"I only ever make smart bets."

"Except on me, you mean," Ramsey said.

"Yeah, you were always my long shot." Eric tried a smile of his own but it didn't stick. "Listen, man, we're gonna play this gig, and then we'll all go to sleep tonight and wake up tomorrow and it'll just be another Monday. And when that happens . . . it's not going to *disappoint* you somehow, is it?"

But how does one answer a hypothetical about an impossibility? And anyway, the answer was really none of Eric's business.

"Of course not," Ramsey said. And that was the end of it. They went back to aligning boards and pounding nails as the sky lightened around them. And when their stage was built and Eric had left, Ramsey went to the garage for his shovel. Might as well get the hard work done while he was already sweaty.

He found a spot away from any large trees and their hard underground roots, and not too close to the stage, and began to dig up the grass in a large circle. He dug the hole about a foot deep with a diameter of four or five feet—a large fire pit—and deposited the soil in the small wooded area at the rear of the fenced-in property. The job only took a half hour, and the result was simple, but a fire pit doesn't need to be complicated. It's just a shallow hole. Some bricks, stacked in pairs, would make an ideal ring around the pit. He'd buy those later this morning at the Home

Depot. As for firewood, that dying dogwood along the back fence no longer needed to be anyone's eyesore.

"Daddy pancakes!"

Meg stood on the back deck. She had on her yellow footie pajamas. "Hi, sweetheart," Ramsey said. "Does Meg want some Daddy pancakes?"

Allie came up behind Meg. "She's telling you that she just *ate* Daddy pancakes." Daddy pancakes were in the shape of Mickey Mouse's head. For a reason only understandable to a toddler, she refused to touch them unless Ramsey manned the spatula.

"I thought only Daddy can make Daddy pancakes," he said to Allie.

His wife shrugged. "The times they are a-changin'."

This stung more than it ought to have. "I'll be in real soon, I promise. I'm just getting some things set out here."

"All right," Allie said. "Come on in, sweetie." She guided Meg back into the house and closed the sliding door.

Ramsey returned to the garage and exchanged the shovel for an axe so he could cut down and section the dogwood. The chain saw would be faster, but a Sandy Oaks resident knows better than to fire up a chain saw on a Sunday morning.

# 17

David Magruder's front yard had the expertly tended look of someone who farmed out his lawn care. The grass was thriving, with no brown patches. The shrubs running along the front of the house were perfect orbs set in cypress mulch that smelled and looked freshly laid despite it being fall.

The house itself, white with green shutters, looked recently painted. The roof was free of leaves and pine needles, as were the gutters. Ramsey had noticed that the property looked, always, primed and ready, as if a realtor could plant a FOR SALE sign in the yard at a moment's notice. Ramsey appreciated tidiness, but Magruder's property was so immaculate it suggested a flaw in the man's character—not so much arrogance as secrecy.

The Sunday paper lay at the base of the driveway, the single haphazard item on the property. Ramsey picked it up, and as he walked toward Magruder's front door he slid the elastic band from around the paper, unfolded it, and glanced at the front page.

*Health Effects of Chernobyl Disaster*
*a Long-Term Matter*

He scanned the first paragraph. In addition to all the radiation sickness and cancers that had cropped up in the last five years, geneticists were now estimating that other maladies might not show up for fifty years or more.

Ramsey refolded the paper and slid the band around it again. It was a little early still to be knocking on someone's door, but there was a lot to do, and he didn't want to miss his chance to catch the weatherman at home.

He rang the bell. A full minute passed before Magruder answered in bare feet, wearing blue jeans and a white T-shirt. He looked different from on TV. Up close, he was smaller and paler—a skinny guy with a weak chin and a concave chest.

"I'm Ramsey Miller," Ramsey said.

"I know," Magruder said.

"I'm hosting a party later today."

"So I've heard."

"That right? Who from?"

"From my mailbox. I got an invitation. Some kind of block party, isn't it?"

Ramsey forced a smile. "That's why I'm here. I'm inviting you to come."

"You inviting everybody?"

"That's the idea of a block party. Everybody's welcome."

"No, I mean are you inviting everyone personally, like this?"

Of all the items on his to-do list, Ramsey had looked forward to this the least. But if he intended to walk the walk—to be magnanimous, or, to use a phrase that Eric and his pal Jesus might prefer, *turn the other cheek*—then he had no choice but to face

Magruder and invite him to his home. "I wanted you to know that you're welcome in my yard."

"Why wouldn't I be?"

Ramsey held Magruder's gaze, letting the weatherman know that his belligerence was noted but wouldn't faze him. "No reason at all." He handed the man his newspaper. "Fact is, I'd be honored if you came to my house. That's all I'm here to say."

Magruder unfolded the paper and glanced down at it.

"Chernobyl back in the news, huh? What a fucking mess."

"So are you gonna come?"

Magruder tossed the paper into his foyer but then had nothing to do with his hands any longer and clasped them together awkwardly. "Ramsey, we've never said a word to each other before now. What's going on here? Why are you so interested in what I do?"

Motherfucker.

In the past, Ramsey might have taken the bait, gotten into some pissing contest. But any pleasure he once took in someone else's insolence, that pure surge of heat, was long gone, and he made himself grin. "Lighten up, Magruder." He reached out and patted the weatherman on the shoulder. "It's just a party. My band's gonna play." And to show his neighbor that he'd made peace with the universe and everyone in it, he added, "I'm sure Allie would love to see you."

The weatherman eyed him a moment, and Ramsey waited to see if Magruder would deny knowing her. But he just looked out past Ramsey at the bright autumn day unfolding—or maybe he was looking in the direction of his lover's house. "What time does your party start?"

"Five," Ramsey said, and then he gave the sky a long look. "You know, you predicted rain for today."

"It still might."

"I don't know—seems to me like it's gonna be a nice one."

Magruder shrugged. "It's the weather. Sometimes I get it wrong."

After that, it was easy. A handful of errands—kegs of beer, ice, the fire pit bricks, a cooler large enough to keep the meat close to the grill—and then he waited at home for others to arrive and set up their own areas of expertise: the sound guy, the petting-zoo woman, the ball-pit guy, everyone jockeying for space in a yard that seemed large until everyone needed parts of it.

Then came the waiting to see who would arrive. And to Ramsey's relief, at a little after five the first neighbors began to show. Ramsey lit the grill, tapped the kegs, and greeted everyone with hearty handshakes and an invitation to eat, drink, and be merry.

At a little before six, beer in hand, Ramsey glanced up at the sky: no signs or celestial winks yet, just late-afternoon sunlight and a deep blue expanse that revealed nothing but the presence of secrets.

"Check," Eric said.

They were on stage. Nothing fancy, but it got them and their gear off the ground and would add some legitimacy to the gig.

Eric said "check" a few more times into the microphone, and then their second-rate soundman was calling up at them, "Hang on a sec!" No juice. Thirty feet in front of the stage, connected to them by a thick snake of cables, Joe Tisdale, assistant manager of Main Street Music, squatted down on his haunches in front of the sound console, turning knobs, pressing buttons, scratching his head as if he had hair there, trying to figure out what was preventing any sound from coming through the main speakers. He was no professional soundman but claimed to understand his gear well enough to set it up and run it. And anyway, Ramsey's three-hundred-dollar tip, up front, promised to make him a quick study.

Behind the drum set, Paul crossed his arms and uncrossed them and then crossed them again. He hunched his shoulders as if the temperature had just plummeted. He'd never been on a stage before.

"You guys have to chill out," Ramsey said. "It's rock and roll."

"I'm chill, man," Paul said.

He wasn't. Paul's tempos were bad enough as it was. Ramsey could hardly imagine the musical crimes that Paul would commit soon if he didn't chill out.

"Get yourself a beer," Ramsey said. That's what Wayne was doing. That's what he wished Eric were doing, too, instead of noodling on his bass guitar, which was plugged into its own amplifier and therefore immune to their soundman's incompetence. Eric was playing the main riff to Led Zeppelin's "Ramble On," which he shouldn't have been doing because it gave the song away. It was unprofessional.

"You're ruining the surprise, man," Ramsey said.

"I'm warming up."

"Well, warm up to something else."

Eric shrugged and started playing some funk riff with lots of slapping and popping, except he didn't have anywhere near the technique for slapping and popping, and it sounded as if a small rodent were caught in the strings.

He was just being nervous, fidgety. And Ramsey had to admit, he was nervous, too. The feeling took him back to his wedding day: suit and tie, spiffy shoes, fear of standing in the wrong place or saying the wrong thing. He was glad that the rent-a-preacher at the Xanadu had kept everything simple. When prompted, Ramsey had said "I will," even though he'd hoped to say "I do" like he'd always seen in movies and on TV.

He looked over now at his wife. She sat with Meg across the yard on a spread-out blanket on the grass amid books and toys. He felt the urge to go to them, send everyone else home, but the urge passed. The reason for this party went beyond proving his own magnanimity and touched on his growing understanding of the connectedness of all people, all living organisms. Each of us was irrelevant in the grander scheme, but our irrelevance was worth celebrating because it was ours and it was temporary.

Still, this wasn't the block party of his imagination. There were fewer people than he'd hoped, only around thirty, not enough to generate the kind of crowd sounds that signaled a party in full swing. For better or worse, though, this was as grand a celebration as Ramsey could summon. It would have to do.

Anyway, his preparations weren't for naught. A half dozen children jumped around the ball pit. A guy and gal, younger than he and Allie, adorned their burgers with sliced tomatoes and onions. The pony was proving to be popular: a small line had formed, mothers and small children, and even the children in line seemed happy enough watching the animal being led around the backyard's perimeter by the Great Dane and, next to the dog, a pretty young woman wearing a yellow sundress.

No one was using the badminton set or the horseshoes, a shame, though a middle-age couple had started rolling the bocce balls. Three older men huddled together along the side fence. Two held loaded-up plates of food, the third a beer. He caught Ramsey's eye and gave him a long-distance toast. Ramsey drank from his own beer, his third of the afternoon, and remembered a long-forgotten truism, how the third beer was always the best. Even today, with plenty of reasons to be anxious, the third beer flowed through him like warm syrup. The challenge was to maintain the sublime quality of the third beer's high when it invariably faded and the only solution was a fourth beer.

He was breaking his one-beer rule, obviously. But after today he'd no longer drink beer or play music or do any other thing. So temperance seemed a little beside the point—even if some part of him suspected that temperance when it no longer mattered was exactly the point. Okay. But facts were facts: In his backyard sat two kegs of beer and, from the looks of his neighbors, not enough drinkers.

A sharp crackling erupted from the speakers—either progress or the opposite of progress. Then an awful, wailing feedback caused everyone in the yard to cover their ears, until a few seconds later the screeching stopped and everyone's hands tentatively lowered again.

"All righty," said the soundman, crouched behind his gear with only his head poking up like a turtle's. "Let's try this again."

The microphones worked now, loud and clear, just as David Magruder came through the fence door and into the backyard. Ramsey was feeling warm now, looser, three cups of syrup loose, plus he had his bandmates with him on stage to back him up. He watched Magruder look around for a familiar face, nod to the bocce couple, glance at his watch, and finally head over to where Allie and Meg sat on the blanket. He crouched down to them.

"Check," said Eric, his voice now crisp through the speakers.

Ramsey stepped up to his own microphone, his mouth already full of the things he wanted to say to Magruder—loud and clear through the P.A. for everyone to hear, things he would have a hard time holding back were he on his fourth beer and not his third.

"Check," he said, watching his family, breathing them in, storing them up—the high five that Meg gave Magruder, the smile that Allie flashed, a smile that Ramsey hadn't seen in ages, a smile that was a promise—a smile that said: *I will.*

"Check one," Ramsey said. "Check two."

# 18

From her spot on the blanket with her daughter, Allison Miller watched the stage and did her best not to look terrified and torn apart—like a woman whose life wasn't one big sham.

After the band's stupid *check ones* and *check twos*, Ramsey thanked everyone for coming—*from the bottom of my heart*, he actually said, as if this random group of parents, motivated by the simple, desperate desire to occupy their kids on a Sunday afternoon, were his lifelong chums. Then he said an extra thanks to Allie.

"This performance is dedicated to the woman who's always been there for me. My beautiful, faithful wife, Allie. I love you, baby."

Allie matched his smile with her own and replied from her blanket, "I love you, too."

It wasn't so hard—like saying a password when you no longer remembered what it unlocked. So she had little trouble attesting to loving her husband in front of these people. With one notable exception, none of them could be called a friend. Since meeting Ramsey, she had systematically lost touch with everyone: parents, friends, all those people whom the self-help books would call a "support system." No one was at fault. When you're a spouse, you're with your spouse. Add a full-time career, and your energies go there, too. Then you become a mother—a job that devours absolutely everything—and it's little wonder that everyone outside your world's tight nucleus eventually floats away.

Then your husband throws himself an end-of-the-world party.

When she considered it (which she had, constantly, these past three months), she was actually glad that Ramsey had confided in her about his coming apocalypse. There was no dismissing an admission like that, no more pretending everything was okay, that the Millers were just another reasonably happy middle-class family in the neighborhood. No more telling herself that if she only tried a little harder, put on a happier face, cooked healthier meals, straightened the house better, stopped resenting Ramsey for being away when he was merely doing his job, then everything would be hunky-dory. Before his confession, Allie would rationalize her unhappiness in myriad ways. Each day, she'd cycle through them, and what they all had in common was that Allie had herself convinced that she could somehow make it better. If only she were a little more self-reliant, a little more fun, more grateful . . . if only she were a little *more*, then everything would fall into place.

For a long time, years, she'd told herself that if she tried hard enough, she could love her husband the way she once had. *God, I loved him*, she would say to herself aloud. To a twenty-one-year-old college student pissed off with her mother and father, Ramsey was Tom Cruise and Matt Dillon and Bruce Springsteen all rolled into one. He was hot and sharp and smarter than he let on, and he fucking *got* her. He had a scar on his body and a scar inside, too, one that he revealed to her and her alone. His bare apartment with the secondhand furniture, that shiny toaster he was so proud of. She would push down the TOAST button and then she'd go down on Ramsey, try to get him to come before the toast popped up. Her idea. They were creative in that apartment, the two of them. His ideas usually came at night. He'd kiss her neck till it bruised, graze her thigh with his razor stubble and goose bumps would appear. He'd light candles. Nothing was sexier than a tough guy lighting candles, because it meant the toughness didn't reach all the way to the core.

If only we could've stayed that age forever, she would tell herself alone at night, wistful, looking at her face in the mirror. If only she could stay twenty-one, he twenty-eight—the age when they got together, each of them yearning for someone to see their own potential, astonished that they'd found each other. They'd be happy and in love forever, the two of them against the world, *I will I will I will*, till death do they part.

Since June, she'd been rethinking all of this. And by now it seemed little more than romantic drivel, especially since she'd never been honest with Ramsey. For one thing, her parents had offered to pay for her flight to Florida. And when she got there, if she'd patently refused to repent in front of their new congregation, what, really, would they have done? Nothing. Not when push came to shove. Her father and mother were devout and infuriating but not evil the way she'd portrayed them to Ramsey. But now too many years had gone by, and her talk of being estranged from them had come to pass, all so that a hot guy would find her intriguing.

In fact, when she was being the most honest with herself—now, for instance, watching Ramsey and his friends jump around with their instruments on their homemade stage like teenagers trying to impress the neighborhood girls—she wondered if there had ever been that strong a connection between the two of them. Maybe their respective desperations, with their unrelated causes, had simply come into alignment long enough for desperation itself to become its own form of romantic momentum, pushing them forward like a wave through courtship and marriage and pregnancy before receding again.

Which was why Ramsey's confession back in June was as useful as it was alarming. Had he not revealed himself to be fucking delusional, their marriage might have lumbered on forever—Allie looking into the mirror each night and convincing herself that there was no problem, not really, and if there was, then it was her fault. Before his confession, leaving Ramsey had never seriously crossed her mind. As long as no one hit anyone or screamed all the time, there were always more reasons to stay together than to split: because of the child, because you don't want your parents to think they were right all along, because of inertia, because of denial.

Now, at least, denial was out of the picture.

As the band played its first song, a too-fast rendition of "Honkytonk Woman," she clapped Meg's hands with her own, presenting to her neighbors the image of an adoring wife sitting on a blanket under the late-day sun, enjoying her husband's music. She wasn't in denial. She was pretending. But she saw everything now for what it was: The music, shit. This day, shit. Her marriage, shit.

"David," she said. He couldn't hear her over the music. "David!" He turned to face her. He was standing alone, not far from the blanket, wearing his pressed blue jeans and NY Giants T-shirt that was too large on him, holding a beer, looking as uncomfortable as a freshman at a homecoming dance. When he crouched down to hear her, she said, "You didn't have to do this."

246

"Are you kidding? It's a party," he said. "Anyway, I love these guys." When she raised an eyebrow at him, he grinned. "I own all their albums."

She smiled. "Well, thank you."

He stood up again, making some distance between them. Awkwardly, he tapped his foot and watched the stage. A good man.

She hadn't ever mentioned David around Ramsey, because you do things like that for your spouse. You make their life a little easier. Ramsey was jealous at heart—she'd always known that—and he wouldn't understand why Allie might have a friendship with a man who wasn't her husband. Especially with a man who was on TV. A man who was going places. Anyway, she hadn't set out to deceive Ramsey. For a long time, she and David weren't friends, only neighbors. But Allie was fairly compulsive about walking Meg around the block after dinner, and David was one of those slow-and-steady joggers, and when they passed on the street, they would smile and sometimes say hello—

*Can't you do something about all this wind?*

*I don't make the weather. I only predict it.*

—and gradually they began to chat, and over time the chats became longer and more substantive . . . and by the time they were what might possibly be called friends, it was too late to say anything to Ramsey. He would think she'd been hiding something all along.

But over the last half year or so, she and David had become closer. Their relationship was like none she'd ever had before—it was wonderful, frankly—even if from time to time she found herself wondering, *What if?*

The first time they made plans to meet up for breakfast at a diner, rather than waiting for their walking/running schedules to coincide, Allie felt her face become hot as she said, "I want to be clear with you that I have no romantic intentions."

He laughed at her formality, but when he spoke his voice became serious. "First of all, you know I'm also married. Second of all, TV people are horrible. I work in an terrible industry, and I don't make friends at work. I miss having friends. I think we can be friends. I think we already are."

"I think we are, too," Allie said.

"Anyway," he said, "I don't think you're all that good-looking."

He could make this joke because she was obviously beautiful and he was obviously not. Still, he cringed until her own expression let him know that his joke had been received okay.

She hadn't realized how much she'd been needing a friend until she had one. Where before there was nobody, now there was somebody with whom, for instance, she could talk about her job. Such a simple thing. Yet Ramsey seemed to think that her job selling pharmaceuticals consisted of dolling herself up and shaking her ass like a cocktail waitress. Whenever she'd get into the details, he'd smile as if he knew the real story. But David understood how it was to work in a competitive environment, having to look your best and act professional at all times. He was actually interested in the complexities of her career: how she had to be a veritable chameleon in dealing with the various physicians and nurses and office administrators, an expert in persuasion one minute, an expert in fibromyalgia the next.

She found herself, over time, letting her guard down in a way she never could with Ramsey—about how hard and frustrating the daily grind was when working full time and raising a child more-or-less singlehandedly. Or how sometimes the thought of spending her life married to a trucker, living in this quiet neighborhood, nothing ever changing, was enough to make her want to run naked through the street.

And he would tell her that, yes, parenting must be frustrating at times, but look at Meg: a happy kid, thriving, well adjusted. Or when David had no words of wisdom, then that was okay, too. Sometimes the unburdening was enough. And David unburdened himself, too, talking about being picked on as a kid, and how his too-thin body still embarrassed him. His balding head, his weak chin. How his wife, a Wharton MBA and news producer in New York, still intimidated the hell out of him after two years of marriage.

Not that she and David saw each other all the time—sometimes three times in a week, other times not at all for two or three weeks at a stretch. But now, even when the TV news came on, a simple weather report was like a friend speaking directly to her. *Any lingering rain will be moving out to sea overnight. And tomorrow? Well, I think you're in for a treat.*

She was so lost in thought, she didn't notice that the band had stopped playing and that her husband was speaking into the microphone again. The word "weatherman" snapped her back to the yard.

". . . our resident celebrity over there"—he was pointing at David—"said it would rain today. Rain, rain, rain, he said. But look!" He looked up at the sky. "Barely a cloud. Soft air. A perfect day for a block party." He forced an easy laugh. "A weatherman must be the only job in the world where you get paid for being wrong half the time. Ain't that right, Magruder?" Another laugh, but the sound was tinged with meanness. Ramsey's face was red and pinched. "But I'm honored you came. Welcome, welcome— glad you found the time to slum it a little." Ramsey toasted him with his beer. How many was that?

That's when Allie realized: drunk.

In all their years together, she'd never seen him with more than one drink in him.

She looked up at David, who was looking back at her. He shrugged. "I think I'll go now," he said.

"This is . . . wait here, Meg." She deposited her daughter on the blanket beside her and stood up. "This is absurd." People were watching her, watching the two of them. "David, you don't have to—"

"It's fine," he said. "Really. I'm just going to go." He set the half-empty cup of beer on the grass, gave the briefest of waves/ smiles to the small crowd gathered in the yard, walked to the side fence, and let himself out.

On stage, the band watched him leave. From across the yard, Allie saw the change come over Ramsey's face, as if he'd put on a mask, or maybe taken one off. She watched him, and he glared back at her with an expression she'd never seen on him before. There was no word for it other than *hate*, and it took her breath away.

As he held her gaze for two or three interminable seconds, she realized that at some level, she'd convinced herself that her husband was a faker—that all his end-of-the-world talk was some weird play for attention, a midlife crisis, maybe, or a more manly way to be depressed than curling up in bed. Until this moment, she wasn't aware of the extent to which she'd convinced herself these past three months that Ramsey's behavior was ultimately rooted in immaturity, rather than in something far scarier.

He finally broke their gaze and, his face relaxing again to a smile, he turned around to the band. "Okay, fellas," he said, "let's hit it." Paul clicked his sticks four times, and they launched into the Ramones' "I Wanna Be Sedated."

Sedation sounded like a damn good idea right now, and she poured herself a beer. Then she and Meg got food and returned to the blanket. She'd felt bad earlier about not circulating more, playing the hostess or at least the host's wife. But fuck the neighbors, she was thinking now. She owed them nothing. She and Meg would have their own picnic right here, the blanket their own island, their entire world. Allie knew now. Even when she thought she was no longer in denial, she still had been. But not any longer. This was real. This party: real. Her husband, on stage, losing it? Real. She didn't know what she was going to do about it, but she could no longer do nothing.

Meg wouldn't try the hamburger but loved the potato salad and especially the pickle, which made her pucker.

"That's a funny face," Allie said.

"Then laugh, Mommy."

It wasn't easy convincing Meg to leave the party and come inside to get ready for bed, and Allie was in no shape emotionally to deal with a full-on tantrum or to summon the energy that went into preventing one. For a while, there'd been a strategy. Allie had found it in some parenting book several months back, when the tantrums had become unbearable—frightening, really—and Allie and Ramsey were desperate for guidance. The idea was to teach your kid the words for their emotions, get them to say it at the moment they were feeling angry, sad, whatever. A kid who could name her emotions, according to the book, was halfway there.

Meg herself had turned it into a game. One morning at breakfast, she smiled at Allie, who said, "Are you happy?" And Meg said, "Little happy." Then she widened the grin and said, "Big happy!"

They'd practiced that morning over their frozen waffles, mother and father and daughter: They made sad faces—"little sad"—and really, really sad faces—"big sad." Ramsey asked Meg what "little mad" looked like, and Meg scrunched her face into a scowl. Then, unprompted, she whacked the tabletop with her open palm and shouted, delighted, "Big mad!"

They played this game at random times in the day. And sure enough, before long Meg's tantrums started becoming less frequent and less violent. When she'd start to show signs of a meltdown, Allie or Ramsey would ask, "Are you mad right now?" and even if Meg admitted to being "big mad," the naming itself, the awareness, nearly always had the effect of letting some steam out of the pressure cooker.

Ramsey seemed to take special pride in this particular act of parenting. But as with everything else, the solution was only temporary, and Meg's temper these days was as unpredictable as ever. Thankfully, though, after several high fives with strangers, a trip to the stage between songs, where she insisted on precisely three hugs with Daddy, and a fruitless search for the moon, Meg finally looked up at her mother and asked the magic question—"Where are the stories?"—which required the proper answer—"On your bookshelf"—which meant that Meg would now deign to be led up the porch steps toward the back door and into the house.

Allie welcomed the routine activities of Meg's approaching bedtime. It was already past 7:30, so she skipped the bath, but she gave her daughter's face a good scrubbing with a washcloth, helped her brush her teeth, and changed her diaper. A flash of guilt jabbed Allie. She should have started the toilet training by now. There was a girl Meg's age down the street who . . . But this was a project that Allie needed to gear up for, and . . . Okay, she promised herself. Next week.

Pajamas on, stuffed animals properly arranged in the crib (Shouldn't Meg be sleeping in a real bed by now? Another guilt-jab), stand-up fan turned on for white noise. The fan somewhat drowned out the music in the backyard. With any luck, all the excitement would tire Meg out. A last sip of water (from an actual cup—at least Meg no longer relied on sippy cups), and then mother and daughter sat side by side on the wide rocker and read two books. Then one more.

Sure enough, with the last book, Meg was leaning her head against Allie, her eyes heavy. When the book was done, Allie stood up with Meg in her arms and, as always, quietly narrated the day. *We played with puzzles, we watched the beginning of* The Little Mermaid, *we ate special cheese with apples for lunch, we played at the park, we rode around the block in our stroller, we played in the yard, we had a picnic and listened to Daddy's band play music. We had a good day, my beautiful girl. And now it's time for bed.*

Allie shut off the bedroom light. Then one last kiss, and—*sweet dreams, baby*—she gently lowered Meg into the crib. Meg immediately rolled onto her side, a good sign, and didn't make a peep as Allie eased the door shut, keeping the knob turned so that when it latched, there would be no click.

Most nights, Allison would sit in the hallway outside Meg's door and listen to her daughter talk to herself for five or ten minutes before dropping off to sleep. It was one of Allie's favorite times of the day, listening to her daughter's intricate monologue of stories real and imagined, sometimes with bits of songs mixed in.

Tonight, the only sound was the fan's gentle hush, so she walked down the hallway to her own bedroom and lay down fully clothed on the bedspread. Her body instantly relaxed, and she felt her eyelids getting heavy. Then she noticed that everything had become quiet. For a moment she thought that she'd been asleep for hours and that the party had ended. She looked over at the clock—8:20 p.m. She'd slept for only a few minutes. The band must have gone on its set break.

She lay there for another minute, then rose, used the bathroom, splashed water on her face, and went back downstairs and outside to the yard. Fewer than twenty people remained. A few of them were sitting with their cups of beer on the grass around the fire pit, which now blazed, sending smoke across the yard. The smell sent her back to being a young girl, camping with her parents and members of the church. She'd loved the woods, loved cooking hot dogs and s'mores over the fire, but she knew that sooner or later the marshmallows and chocolate would be put away and her parents and their friends would begin their stern talk of Satan's treachery. There would be hours of prayer and public repentance. Yet even that she found herself missing, at this moment.

She collected a few abandoned cups from the grass, a few plates and napkins, and put them into the trash bag by the grill. No one seemed to notice her. Ramsey stood with Eric near the stage, talking and periodically glancing upward. Now that the sun had set, the sky was quickly darkening to purple.

She had to leave him. The hows and whens could be sorted out later, but theirs was not a marriage with a future. When she awoke from her brief sleep, she did so with a clear picture of how this would all play out. Ramsey would wake up tomorrow, shocked that his superconjunction was all a bunch of nonsense. He'd find some excuse to get back on the road sooner rather than later. While he was gone, Allie would get down to logistics: hire a lawyer, find a place where she and Meg could stay if Ramsey refused to move out of the house . . . whatever the details were, she'd tend to them. It would be hard, but her life with Ramsey on the road all the time had only been half a marriage anyway. How could they not grow apart when their home was merely Ramsey's mailing address? When he didn't know the names of any of Allie's coworkers or what Meg had tried eating for the first time or some new thing that she'd said? When he had no clue what it meant to work a full day and then be on all night with a baby, a toddler, day after day after day? When he didn't understand what her promotion to Assistant Director of Sales, Mid-Atlantic Region meant to her because he hadn't bothered to ask? Or that maybe she didn't necessarily want to have sex with him the minute he came home from a week on the road, because she was exhausted from having been a single parent all week and needed some time to reconnect with Ramsey, to remind herself that this was her husband and not just some acquaintance with a key to the front door.

Not that *that* had been an issue lately. Since June, in a relationship in which any emotional or intellectual connection had long since dissolved, the last vestige of their nominal marriage—the occasional late-night screw—had vanished as well. But that wasn't a reason to stay. It was a reason to go.

*Superconjunction.* Give me a break.

Yes—when he was off on his next cross-country haul, she'd end the sham.

And while she was at it, she'd end a second sham, too.

# 19

If Allie needed confirmation that her decision was the right one, she didn't have to wait long. Just a few minutes later, the band returned to the stage, and Ramsey walked up to the microphone.

"I want to thank you all again for taking the time to be here on this beautiful and important evening." Another glance up at the sky. "The beautiful part I think is clear enough. But why 'important,' you ask?"

Good lord, she thought. She knew what was coming, because she'd heard the same lecture back in June.

"No, Ramsey." She came forward, right up to the front of the stage, cutting him off. He looked down at her, and she lowered her voice so that only he could hear. "Nobody wants to hear that. They came for a party. For good music. That's what they're here for."

Chastising while also placating—something she did with Meg. But Ramsey wasn't a toddler, and come tomorrow he would have to carry on with his life. Even if Allie were to leave him, he'd still have a daughter and a job. So it was important that he keep it together, or at least keep up the appearance of keeping it together—for his own sake, and also for hers. She could do without the Miller house being a topic of juicy neighborhood gossip.

Ramsey seemed to weigh her words. "Allie, these people have a right—"

"No, they don't." Because he was standing a few feet above her, the closest approximation to an intimate gesture she could manage was to lay a hand on his shoe. "And what does it matter, really? You wanted to throw a party to make everyone happy, right? Then do that." She kept her voice barely above a whisper. "Play your music. Make them happy—don't freak them out."

He looked up at the sky for longer this time, but not for dramatic effect, Allie could tell. Out of concern. She couldn't tell, however, if the concern was because of what he believed was going to happen or because it wasn't happening yet.

He stepped back to the microphone.

"In simple terms," he said, glancing again at the sky, "the real show tonight won't be coming from the stage."

She rushed across the yard, headed for the side gate and the freedom beyond, her eyes blurry with tears.

"Now, we can't do a thing to prevent it," she heard as the gate clanked shut behind her. "But that's okay."

She stood on David Magruder's front stoop, wishing she had a mirror to see how awful she looked. Maybe better not to know. Her eyes burned from crying and from the fire pit smoke.

The music in her backyard had started up again on her walk over, so Ramsey couldn't have spoken for long. Long enough, though. Jesus. She rang the doorbell and waited. An outdoor light came on, and then the door opened, and seeing David in his T-shirt and those starched jeans, an expression of immediate concern on his face, made her well up all over again. She stepped into his house and embraced him, fighting the urge to full-out bawl. She clung to him tightly, breathing in his scent, feeling grateful to him for simply letting this moment linger while mosquitos and moths and humid air rushed into the house. When she released her grip, he took a half step back, looked her over, and said, "Tough day?"

Her response was a half laugh, half sob, and a split-second decision to end the second sham first. She moved forward again, into him, and kissed David on the mouth. Unlike their kiss of twelve weeks earlier, this one was for real, close and lingering, and when they separated again, the look of surprise in David's eyes was comical and lovely.

"I think you'd better come in," he said, looking somewhat dazed.

He shut the front door and turned on a hallway light. Despite how close they'd become, she'd never set foot inside David's house before. His wife wouldn't be home tonight. Allie knew that. She was counting on it. When David and Jessica married, she maintained her Greenwich Village apartment, where she stayed when she worked late at the network. Every Sunday night she slept there to get an early jump on the week.

Allie knew this and many other things about David's life because they were close. They were confidantes. Everything, really, but lovers. She knew, for instance, that he'd been second-guessing his marriage almost since the wedding. *She isn't a warm person*, he once told Allie. *Not like you are.*

He'd been a little drunk the morning he said it, but being drunk didn't make you lie—if anything, it encouraged truth-telling.

They met for breakfast sometimes, when Allie had a gap between dropping Meg at day care and her first appointment with a physician's office. Jessica was usually out of the house at dawn to get to Manhattan, and Allie was pretty sure that David's wife knew as little about these breakfasts as Ramsey did. But that was David's concern, not hers. And anyway, there was nothing to hide.

On that morning, Allie had argued with Ramsey over which level of day care to put Meg into. He wanted her to stay in the younger group, the Ladybugs, but for no good reason, and this tiff—it was hardly more than that—made her seethe. He wasn't home enough to have the right to weigh in. He was dealing in abstractions about *what's best*, while she was dealing with their daughter. Anyway, at one point she said, *Fuck you, Ramsey*—something she'd never said to him before. There were worse offenses between husbands and wives, she knew, but they had both grown up in hostile households, and civility was something they had long ago promised each other. She was immediately sorry, but Ramsey's response—to get up from the table and leave for a week without so much as a good-bye—refueled her fury, which battled her guilt to the point where no way could she meet with that dermatology group in Wall Township at 9 a.m. No way could she put on a tight business suit and act bubbly and informative while overstating benefit A and downplaying side-effect B. Their new, hot product was an "exciting new treatment" for psoriasis called D-Derma. In the trunk of Allie's car were D-Derma mugs, pens, and mouse pads. On none of this swag did it mention that the cream could, in some instances, cause liver damage.

No, the dermatologists could wait. She canceled her appointment, phoned David, and made breakfast plans.

Something in her voice (even she could hear it) made him add, "I'll pick you up." In the past, they always drove separately, despite living in the same neighborhood.

On the ride to the diner, she told him about her argument with

Ramsey. The moment they were seated at the diner, David ordered two Bloody Marys. When their food arrived, Allie backed off ordering a second drink—the first was potent enough, and there were afternoon appointments to be awake for. But David ordered another.

"This breakfast is actually a celebration," he said.

"It is?"

"Indeed." Then he told her his good news: He'd been promoted at the station. Now, in addition to weather, he'd be reporting select news stories on air.

"David!" She smiled. One of his hands was resting on the table. Instinctively, she reached across and took it in hers. "That's amazing."

Though trained as a meteorologist, he'd always wanted to do more than report the weather. He saw himself, someday, somehow, anchoring or producing one of the New York network newscasts.

"I wouldn't call it *amazing*," he said, grinning.

"You know it is," she said, and ordered a second drink for herself.

After breakfast, he drove her home, and she honestly didn't think anything of it when he said, "I'll walk you to the door." They were both a little tipsy. And how they got on to the topic of David's wife, she couldn't remember. But that was when David made his comment about Allie being a warm person. Which made her smile, because at the moment he said it, with the start of summer evident in the growing shrubs and trees and grass all around them, the azaleas blooming pink, the yellow coreopsis, the potted petunias and zinnias framing the front door, she *felt* like a warm person, and then David put his hands on her shoulders as if he were steadying himself.

*He's going to kiss me.*

261

She knew it immediately. But when it came, it was a kiss at war with itself, coming only after resting his forehead against her own for what seemed like an eternity. In fact, the head-touching was almost more intimate than the kiss itself. He put his lips to hers and repositioned his arms around her back, and she felt one of his hands dip a little lower, and none of it lasted more than a few seconds.

A drunk kiss—she'd been the giver and receiver of them before and felt no need to pull away. She wasn't even particularly annoyed at David. He'd kissed her because of her warmth. Because they were both tipsy. Because his promotion was making him feel invincible, and because they had become close, these past few months.

He wasn't much to look at. He was married. She was married. This was going nowhere. So she let herself be flattered and amused, and she decided that David's transgression was a forgivable offense. And just as she knew would happen, the moment that the kiss was over, his face got red and he made an "oops" expression, and with a pat on his cheek and a single line—"Not the best idea, probably"—she dispelled the moment's potential severity with a rejection that was its own flirtation. She did it effortlessly, like tossing dust that happened to be magical into the air.

And because David's friendship was important to her, she made sure to call him the next day and invite him to walk around the block, which gave him a chance to apologize, and gave her a chance to assure him that it was no big deal, honestly—the matter was already forgotten—and allowed for the situation to be put to bed before it ever became a situation at all.

But she knew. He desired her.

She followed him now into the living room. His home, like his yard, was tidy and uncluttered, the sofas all leather, the tables all sharp angles—a home with no children. A peaceful home, which she was making less so with her presence. On the coffee table lay two Sunday newspapers, neatly aligned, and several books.

"Do you have anything to drink?" she asked. "I could really use—"

He put up a hand, silencing her, and went over to the bar (in the corner, with a sink, something she'd never seen in a living room other than on TV), poured her a small glass of Scotch, and delivered it. The first sip was like a full-body massage, and she sank a little deeper into the couch.

He poured himself a drink and, to her disappointment, sat across the coffee table from her. But his smile was warm. "So it seems that you, too, have fled the event of the century."

From inside David's house, she could hear traces of music coming from her backyard. In a quiet suburb, sound traveled at night. "I can't do it any longer," she said. "My marriage is over. It's been over for so long." Lying alone at night, she came up with various metaphors, all having to do with movement: ships adrift, birds flying in two directions, or one flying and the other staying still, which, given enough time, still created a chasm. But she spared David the metaphors. "Ramsey and I—we have nothing. Not any longer. Please"—she patted the sofa beside her—"sit here. I need you right here."

David rose, moved around the coffee table, and sat beside Allie. She placed a hand on his knee and looked at him. "You and I are good for each other, aren't we?"

"We are," he said, and hearing this, she released a breath she wasn't even aware of holding. "I'm grateful for what we have."

"You are, huh?" She said it with a sideways glance. She knew what she was doing. The flirtation and the Scotch made her face hot. It'd been a while, this feeling. She missed it. He wasn't much to look at, but he was a good man, and he was intelligent and going places. And their connection wasn't some long-ago remembrance that might not ever have been real. It was happening now, in Allie's adult life, with its experience and its complications, its logistics and uncertainties. An adult connection. It could be love.

She moved her hand up the leg of his pants, just slightly.

"Allie."

She moved her hand up a little more.

He placed his hand on top of hers, stopping its movement. "Allie—listen. This can't happen."

But he was wrong. It could and should. This past year proved it. His kiss proved it. Their easy conversations and their candor and his obvious attraction to her proved it. She wanted to explain all this to him, but when she spoke she was horrified to hear that her voice sounded drunken and pleading and shrill. "*Why not?*"

"It's complicated," he said.

"No, it isn't. Nothing is simpler." Her words came faster. "I'm getting a divorce. And I know you aren't in love with Jessica, not really. So you can get a divorce, too. You don't even have kids. It isn't complicated at all."

"Allie, I can't leave Jess."

She refused to be fazed by his use of his wife's nickname. "You deserve to be happy. So do I. Do you know what a superconjunction is?"

He frowned. "You mean the planetary alignment thing?"

"Ramsey thinks the one tonight is going to end the world."

He raised an eyebrow. "Yeah, that won't happen."

"He's delusional," Allie said. "I can't live with it any longer."

"Then you shouldn't. You deserve better."

"You need to leave Jessica, too."

He sighed. "You don't understand."

"Then explain it to me."

264

He released her hand, stood up, and went to pour himself another drink, leaving Allie to endure the distant but relentless
thumping of drums and bass coming from her backyard. David
didn't speak again until he was back on the sofa beside Allie,
though not as close as before. "There's a spot opening up on ABC
news. New York network. *Jessica's* network. They've narrowed
their search to two people, and I'm one of them." He nodded as
he spoke. "She's opened this amazing door for me, and I'm *this
close*." He must have seen the tears in Allie's eyes, because his
voice raised in pitch, became a little more desperate. "Allie, this is
it—the chance you wait your whole career for. God knows I've
paid my dues for so long, and now Jessica's opening doors that
. . . well, these are doors that open maybe once in a career. It's all
I've ever wanted."

She let the words sink in. "Do you love her?"

He looked away. "It's complicated."

"You fucking coward."

"*Allie* . . ."

"Do you love me?" He didn't answer. "Coward."

She ran her hands roughly through her hair, pulling at the
roots.

"I'm not a coward, Allie," he said.

"Yes, you fucking are. When you use people to get ahead and
ignore the chance to be with your soul mate? What do you think
it makes you?"

"We aren't soul mates, Allie. You're only saying that now because . . ." He shook his head. "Look, we're two people who meet
for breakfast a few times a month. I keep you company sometimes when you're alone with Meg, because—"

"Because I'm so desperate, is that it?"

"No. But I do think you're lonely."

*I don't want to hear this*, she thought. He was twisting what the two of them had. Making himself feel better. He was being cold because that was easier than dealing with the truth.

"We're neighbors," he concluded, and the words were like a knife.

"We're a lot more than that, and you know it," she seethed. But were they? She considered, in horror, that maybe she had it all wrong. What she saw as friendship, as intimacy, maybe he saw as nothing more than a charity case. And now she was here, and her daughter was alone back in the house with no adults to hear her if she was crying for something.

Allie thought that nothing David could say could possibly be worse than what he'd already said. "Listen, Al, I'm not going to leave my wife. That just can't happen." He took a breath. "But if you have . . . what's the right way to say this?—*needs* that aren't being met . . ." He looked away. "We'd have to be very discreet."

It took a moment for his words to make sense. When they did, she shot up from the couch and rushed to the door, sobbing.

"Okay, forget I ever said it. I'm sorry. Allie? Come on, Allie. Come back."

But she was already out the door.

The Sandy Oaks section of town was almost completely residential, though one bar, Jackrabbits, was only a couple of blocks away. It probably predated the neighborhood itself. It had a decent jukebox, and when she and Ramsey first moved into the house, they went there sometimes for a beer and a few games of pool. She considered going there now, she could walk it, but her head was already swimmy from the beer and the Scotch, and she didn't want anyone, even in a dark bar, seeing her like this. So with nowhere to go, she went home, walking the too-bright streets of her neighborhood. So many damn light posts. Safety, safety. How about a little darkness at night? Why must a person always be on display?

At least the music had stopped, though she wasn't sure why. When she crested the small hill on her street, her own house became visible. Two police cars were parked out front.

She quickened her pace, and by the time she reached her driveway she was breathing heavier. She went around to the side yard and through the gate in the privacy fence.

A dozen or so guests lingered. The fire pit coughed up smoke, and picked-over food sat out on tables. Near the stage, the band huddled with two police officers. When she approached, Ramsey glanced up at her and, taking little notice, continued talking to the officers. "What does ten p.m. even mean if we can't play till ten p.m.? I mean, you tell me." She could tell she'd walked into a conversation that'd been going on like this awhile.

"Can't allow it," the officer said. "Not with the complaints we've gotten."

"Who's complaining?" Ramsey asked. "Everyone was *here*. It's for them."

"What about two more songs?" Eric asked, looking at his watch. "We'll be done by nine thirty."

"Two songs, nothing," Ramsey said. "I know the ordinance, and it's ten p.m."

"Can't allow it," the larger officer said. "This is a quiet—"

"Yeah, a quiet neighborhood. I get it," Ramsey said. "That doesn't change the goddamn ordinance."

"*Sir* . . ."

"Oh, don't 'sir' me."

"*Ramsey*," Allie said, before either of the officers had a chance to reply, before this escalated further.

"Why, yes, Allie, what is it?" He spoke slowly, his tone mocking and loud, intended for all to hear. "Has my wife returned from one last roll in the hay with the great weatherman to offer us her words of wisdom?"

"*What?*" She glanced around. "How dare you . . . that's not what I . . ."

He leaned in closer and fake-whispered: "So how was his lightning rod?"

She glared at him. "You fucking—"

"Cool it, Ramsey!" Paul moved between the couple, the first responder springing to action. "Whatever's going on, you need to calm it down."

The air was oppressive. Allie's head spun. She thought she might become sick.

"Your friend is right," said the officer. "You need to calm it way down. Because I'll haul you in for drunk and disorderly. I'll be glad to do it. So take a deep breath and count to ten. Because this party's over. And you can either be cool about it, or you can come with us. And I'm this close to making that decision for you. Am I being clear?"

"Officer," Eric began, but his younger brother laid a hand on his shoulder, silencing him.

"Yeah," Ramsey said through gritted teeth. "You're clear."

"That's right—I am." The officer stood almost a head taller than Ramsey and stared him down another few seconds. "I know it's been a while since you've seen the inside of our drunk tank, Mr. Miller. But I promise it's ready and waiting."

Ramsey's face took on a wounded look. "Man, why'd you have to go and say that?"

The officer's expression stayed rock hard. "Why? Because I've been a police officer long enough to know that some things never change."

"That's not true," Ramsey muttered under his breath, like a child protesting to himself on the way to the principal's office.

"We won't have to come back here, will we?" asked the officer.

Ramsey shook his head, still looking deflated. "Nah. It's like you said. The party's over."

Halfway to the gate, the younger, shorter officer turned around. "Since you're so concerned about ordinances, you should know your fire pit's too large and too close to the trees. We could ticket you for that."

They left, shutting the gate behind them.

"I want you all out of here," Allie said, loud enough for everyone in the yard to hear. "Get out of here this second."

"There's all this gear," Paul said apologetically. "It all has to be—"

"Fine. Pack up your gear and leave."

"Allie," said Eric, who stood beside Ramsey, "maybe the three of us should—"

"I really don't want to hear it, Eric. I want you and everyone else gone." She walked toward the house. "You, too, Ramsey," she said without bothering to turn around.

# 20

September 28, 2006

Such a strange mix of assertiveness and nervousness, Melanie thought while fishing through her purse for change in the Sandpiper's lobby. All of David's fake charm masking his actual charm. And such a large and lonely house. Or maybe she was merely detecting her own loneliness now that the evening's excitement was over.

She perused the vending machine's sad offerings and wondered if she could have a pizza delivered to her room.

She missed Aunt Kendra's garlic cheese toast. She missed Uncle Wayne's Western omelets, which usually ended up being scrambled eggs after the flip had failed. It'd been three days since leaving home. She missed Phillip. How comforting, that lone night spent in his bed. Alone in her hotel room with the too-large bed and the smell of industrial cleaning products, it was easy to feel lost and hopeless.

She was exhausted, and pizza would take too long, so she settled for a bag of corn chips and a Snickers bar.

Back in her room, she opened the chips, which were stale. It felt like a personal insult. She dropped the bag into the trash can, and before allowing herself any time for second-guessing, she picked up the phone in her room and dialed Phillip's cell. She didn't know if he'd pick up, seeing the unfamiliar number, but he did.

"It's me," she said nervously. "Melanie." He might not want to talk to her, she now realized. She'd walked out on him, hadn't she?

"Melanie—where are you? Are you all right?"

"Yes, of course. I'm fine," she said, because now she was.

She told him the truth: She'd returned to Silver Bay to find her father. She refused to live in hiding any longer, and she absolutely refused to raise a child in hiding.

She told some half-truths: She was gathering leads, making progress.

She told an outright lie: No, I don't want you coming here. I want to do this alone.

They talked for thirty minutes—about what? She had no idea. The point was to hear his voice, bridge the distance. Before hanging up, she demanded that he keep her whereabouts a secret, and after a brief debate (*Your aunt and uncle, Melanie. They must be going crazy*) he relented.

She had lied and half-lied to Phillip, but she couldn't lie to herself, and when she hung up the phone (both of them having said *I miss you* but lacking the guts to say any more) she felt lonelier than before. What was she actually accomplishing, being here? David had agreed to help find her father, but what did that mean, exactly? How would he go about it? And how assertively, given how little he wanted to be reminded of the past?

But these were tomorrow's problems. She still hadn't eaten. She should have ordered the damn pizza. She ate the Snickers bar, brushed her teeth, and went to sleep.

She'd forgotten to draw the hotel room's heavy shades before going to bed and woke up at 6:30 a.m. to soft natural light and the awareness that her anxieties had eased overnight. Phillip had been relieved, even happy, to hear from her. And David knowing her secret, even that felt okay. Pretty good, actually. Melanie felt lighter. Someone else just knowing she was alive made her feel more alive. Not only someone else—a man with connections. A man who could get things done, if he had a mind to.

Anyway, there was no choice now but to trust him.

Her plan for the morning was to visit Arthur, see about Eric's statement that he knew why her father had thrown the party. Maybe look into why Eric no longer worked outdoors as a lineman—whether it was his health or his proselytizing or some-thing else. Also, she wanted to learn what Arthur knew about the Monmouth Truck Lot. That was where her father had sold his truck just two days before the murder. She found that fact especially chilling. No one had been able to make a connection between the truck sale on Friday and the murder on Sunday, but surely it meant that he knew he wouldn't be returning to work. She wanted to see if anyone from the truck lot was still around. If they remembered her father. After a good night's sleep, she was feeling more optimistic. She was feeling more sleuth-y. More Nancy Drew-y.

But before any of that, before Arthur or the truck lot, she'd have an actual breakfast. She wanted bacon and eggs. (Why all the bacon suddenly? she wondered. Pregnancy was weird.) And if they had them, grits. A tall glass of orange juice. And she was will-ing to brave the smell of coffee to get it.

And that's what was on her mind—bacon, eggs—when she walked out of her room a few minutes after 7 a.m. and pulled the door closed. It had just clicked shut when she felt herself being grabbed from behind and mashed against the door, hard enough for her head to thud loudly and for the wind to get knocked out of her.

*"Not a fucking word,"* came a man's voice behind her, low and breathy.

Her wrists were suddenly clamped in his hands, and his body—it was definitely a he—pressed against her from behind, crushing her against the door, against the sharp doorknob. She couldn't move and didn't dare to, couldn't see anything besides the white door in front of her.

She tried to catch her breath but could only gasp.

"Drop all this." So softly, his voice, lips grazing her ear. "Go away and never come back—or you're so fucking dead." He pressed her even harder into the door—forcing a grunt from her. "Now count to fifty before turning around. And *don't* rush it."

She felt her wrists being released. The weight against her body removed. She wanted to drop down to the carpet but willed her legs to keep supporting her. She heard the man running toward the end of the building, toward the exit.

Pain in her stomach, from the doorknob.

Bruised, for sure. She wasn't counting to fifty. She was thinking: *My baby.* And as the man neared the exit, she turned her head. She had to. It might be the only time she ever saw her father.

There wasn't much to see. Long gray coat with the collar turned up and a baseball cap. From behind, he could have been any tall man at all who kept his black shoes freshly polished.

In the hotel bathroom's mirror, shirt lifted, she was horrified by the wide purple bruise from the doorknob. She touched several spots on her side and abdomen, wincing.

Then she was in her car, driving fast.

Then she was in the elevator, then hurrying to Arthur Goodale's room, a nurse she didn't recognize trailing her, saying, "You can't just . . . excuse me, you have to let me . . ."

His door was open, and she barged in. The room was empty.

When she spun around, the nurse was right behind her.

"Where is he?" Melanie heard the panic in her own voice. She already knew the answer. "Where's Arthur?"

"Miss, are you all right?" The nurse went to take Melanie's arm, but Melanie yanked it away.

"Tell me where he is!" But she knew.

"Let's just calm down a minute. Catch your breath, and tell me who you are."

"I'm Arthur's friend," Melanie said, "and I want to know where the hell he is."

The nurse sighed and pursed her narrow lips, as if Melanie's directness were the problem.

"Downstairs," the nurse said.

"No," Melanie said. "I'm not going anywhere until—"

"Mr. Goodale is downstairs. He didn't need to be in critical care any longer. You can check with the front desk for his room number. But your head is contused—what happened?"

"You mean he's okay?"

"Mr. Goodale? Yeah, he's okay."

And then Melanie ignored some words the nurse had to say about her needing medical attention. She hurried back to the elevator, which couldn't arrive fast enough.

More concern in the face of the woman working the hospital front desk, but she gave Melanie Arthur's room and instructions for finding it. Melanie rushed down the hallway, nearly slipping once. The door to Arthur's door was partly open. She rushed in

275

and, seeing him there, felt such relief that she wanted to throw her arms around him.

"Alice!" He looked up from a magazine and smiled as if they were old friends reunited. Then: "My God, what happened?"

Seeing his face and hearing the worry in his voice made her start to cry. The room was larger than the one upstairs, or maybe it only looked that way because there was less equipment filling it up. Outside the window was blue sky, rather than a brick wall, but the sunlight streaming into the room felt oppressive and blinding. She spotted the chair near his bed and slumped into it.

"Alice," he said, "your head . . ."

Why was everyone carrying on about her head? In the hotel mirror, she'd looked nowhere but her stomach. Why in the world would she look anywhere but her stomach? She touched her forehead now and winced at the sting and by the size of the lump. The room started to spin around her. She gripped the chair's arms for support.

"Alice?"

Her heart raced. The room spun harder: the window, the walls, the ceiling, the bed. She sought and found Arthur's eyes, and stayed locked on them.

"Alice, please—"

The churning in her gut frightened her—it wasn't morning sickness, she felt sure of it—and she remained focused on Arthur's blue eyes as she blurted out, "David Magruder's driver attacked me, and my baby might be dead, and my boyfriend doesn't know about any of it, and I miss my aunt and uncle, and I want to go home, and I'm Meg Miller."

She had never enjoyed food as much as she was enjoying the sandwich that had been delivered on a green plastic tray, placed on a table that rolled right up to her hospital bed. Chicken salad, fresh romaine lettuce, slices of summer tomato, not too much mayonnaise, soft potato bread.

"You need to eat better," the doctor told Melanie when all the scans and tests were done, and she had heard a sampling of Melanie's meals over the past week. The doctor, a middle-aged woman wearing green scrubs, no-nonsense glasses, and a stethoscope around her neck like a scarf, sat on a stool beside Melanie's raised hospital bed while Melanie felt vaguely annoyed at the doctor for pestering her with questions when there was this amazing sandwich to be eaten. "I'm talking about actual meals, not junk from vending machines. The way you've been eating, you easily could have ended up here even if you hadn't been attacked."

"Yes, ma'am," Melanie said, and took another bite.

"Before you're discharged, we'll give you some pamphlets about nutrition for pregnant women."

"But the baby is okay?"

"Yes—but you have to take care of yourself. Just because you're young doesn't mean you're invincible." She kept looking at Melanie for a moment, letting the words settle. "Speaking of which, a police officer will be coming by your room shortly."

She imagined her statement: *I got shoved up against a door by a man who might have been David Magruder's driver.* It would lead to nothing and only make her presence in this town more public. The police have never been helpful, she reminded herself.

"I don't want to talk to any police."

The doctor sighed. "Why not take a few minutes to think about it."

"I don't need a few minutes."

The doctor shook her head. "This is very frustrating—it happens too often."

"Ma'am?"

"A young woman gets beaten up and feels she has to defend her attacker. Especially when it's a boyfriend or a—"

"It wasn't my boyfriend."

"Are you sure about that?"

"My boyfriend is a gentleman."

The doctor nodded. "You can refuse to make a statement to the officer if you must. But then I'd like a social worker to speak with you before you're discharged."

"Why?"

"She can give you important information about available resources: counseling, prenatal guidance . . ." She lowered her voice. "Safe houses."

"What's that?"

"Places where women can go and live for a while to get away from . . . whoever it is they fear." The doctor eyed Melanie as if they both understood. "The woman can feel safe, knowing she can't be found. It's all very tightly run—even I don't know where the safe houses are located." The doctor smiled as if Melanie would find the idea of disappearing relieving, even wonderful.

Why is the answer always to hide the girl? she wondered.

"On second thought," Melanie said, "I'll talk to the cop."

Don't be afraid, said the doctor before leaving her—but she was afraid, and insisted she meet with the police officer in Arthur's room.

Poor Arthur. *I'm Meg Miller*, she had said to him, exploding his fifteen-year certainty. And all he could do was buzz for a nurse to rush Melanie away to the ER. Then two hours of tests and scans to see if the bruise to her stomach might have caused any damage to the fetus (unlikely) and to see if she had a concussion (she did, though it was minor). They took her blood to check for some other stuff the nurse had rattled off—and all the while, Arthur waited, because he had no choice.

So now she would speak with an officer, but Arthur would get to hear it all.

The officer was a stocky man with thick arms and almost no neck. She imagined he could be tough if he had to. They formed a triangle—she and Officer Bauer on chairs, and Arthur in his bed, raised almost to a sitting position. Sometime in the past two hours, he had put on a blue golf shirt and combed his white hair.

"I want to be sure I have this right," said the officer, after Melanie had laid out the basic and amazing facts of her whereabouts these past fifteen years. "You're telling me that you're Meg Miller, daughter of Ramsey and Allison."

The officer had made her nervous at first, but that word the doctor had used—*safe house*—had made her stomach burn. She was through with hiding. She wanted the opposite of hiding.

"Yes, sir."

"And that since 1991 you've been living in West Virginia with your aunt and uncle."

"Yes."

"As part of the witness protection program."

"Yes, sir."

"My, my," Arthur murmured, and the officer shot him a look. "Sorry."

"And now you've come back to Silver Bay to try and find your father," the officer said.

"That's right."

Officer Bauer jotted a few notes into his notebook. "Why?"

"I'm pregnant," she said, "and I don't want my baby to grow up afraid."

The officer glanced down at Melanie's body, then back at her face. "Tell me what happened this morning."

So she told him about leaving the hotel room, getting slammed up against the door, the breathy voice in her ear, the man's fast exit.

"Do you know who it was?" he asked.

"At first I assumed it was my father. But I'm pretty sure it was David Magruder's driver."

"Wait—David Magruder?"

"Yes."

"How do you two know each other?"

"We only met twice. I thought he might know something about my mother's murder."

He frowned. "And what makes you think David Magruder's driver is the one who attacked you?"

"He told me not to look at him, but when he was leaving the hotel I looked anyway. His black shoes were shiny. I think he wore the same pair as the man who drove me to David's house yesterday."

"Do you know the man's name?"

"No."

"Do you remember the kind of car he drove?"

"A black Lincoln Town Car. But I think David owns it."

"How are you so sure about the make of the car?"

"I notice cars. My uncle works on them for a living. And I like them."

"You don't by any chance remember the plate number?"

"No. But—I think his name was Bob. I think David called him that. No—*Bill*. That's what he called him."

"Did you get a last name?"

"No."

"Did you see the Town Car today at any point?"

"No—only yesterday."

"And are the shoes the only reason you think it was this man?"

"He was tall."

"How tall?"

"Like maybe six two?"

"And besides his shiny black shoes, what else was he wearing?"

She told him about the coat, the cap. How she couldn't see his face because of the upturned collar.

"And why do you think this man would have assaulted you?"

"I think David made him."

"Why would—" He shook his head. "Let's back up a little. You said you went to Mr. Magruder's house yesterday."

"Yes."

"Why?"

"Well, I tried to interview him on Wednesday—"

"Interview him? What for?"

"I thought he might"—she looked over at Arthur—"I thought he might tell me something useful about the day my mother died. Something that might help me find my father."

"Why did you think that David Magruder would know anything about the death of Allison Miller?"

She didn't want to get Arthur in trouble. "I just thought he might."

"It was my suggestion," Arthur said from the bed. "I'd told her about Magruder's multiple interviews with the police following the murders. Sorry—the murder."

Officer Bauer watched him a moment. "So did anything come of the interview?"

"No. He acted really rude and then made me leave."

"Why did he make you leave?"

"He didn't want me asking about his past."

"So if he was so rude to you on Wednesday, why would you get into the car with his driver on Thursday?"

Good question. She tried to remember. Her head throbbed, and she knew her thinking wasn't as clear as it should be.

"David summoned me to his house," she said.

"Summoned? Why would he do that?"

It was either his tone or her deeply ingrained distrust of the police, but she thought she heard doubt in his voice and didn't like it.
He wasn't so young. He'd probably forgotten how his uniform
made a person feel guilty and afraid. She tried to answer accurately.
"I think he felt bad about how he treated me the day before."

"So he wasn't rude, when you went to his home?"

"No. He was nice. He even promised to help me find my father."

"You mean he knew who you really were?"

"He sort of figured it out. But then he must have changed his
mind about helping me and made his driver . . . do this." She remembered what David had said about his driver the night before.
*He isn't on twenty-four-hour call, Melanie.*

"The man who attacked you—he also told you to leave town?"

"Yes, sir."

"And it's your belief that this message, this threat, came from
David Magruder?"

"Yes, I do."

"Why would he want you to leave town?"

"He told me he had no alibi for the time of my mother's
murder."

"David Magruder told you that." The officer raised an eyebrow.

"Officer?"

Officer Bauer turned to face Arthur.

"Please remember," Arthur said, "that you're speaking to a
traumatized young woman who's doing her best to answer your
questions."

The officer kept his gaze on Arthur a beat too long, but when
he spoke again to Melanie his voice was gentler. "Ms. Denison,
why do you think Mr. Magruder would tell you that?"

"I think he was so surprised to see me alive that he started spilling his guts. Also, I'm pretty sure he was drunk."

"Why do you think that?"

"He drank most of a bottle of champagne while I was there. And some Scotch, I think."

"So are you suggesting that he had you assaulted because he regretted telling you about lacking an alibi for the night of your mother's murder?"

"I guess so, sir. And he told me he knew my mother really well, which is something he'd lied to the police about."

The officer made a face like a bug had just flown into his eye. "That's—surprising, frankly. We'll have to go back to the file on that. Are you sure you have it right? That Mr. Magruder said he had lied to the police about his relationship with Allison Miller?"

"Yes, sir. I'm positive."

The officer clicked the stop button on his tape recorder. "I know you've been through a lot already, but I'll need you to speak with a detective."

"*Why?*" Her voice sounded panicky even to herself. A cop, now detectives . . . she wasn't supposed to be in this town—ever. Those were the terms. Why was she doing this to herself? To her aunt and uncle? "I don't want to talk to more people."

"Ms. Miller—"

"Denison, please," she said.

"Ms. Denison, someone obviously doesn't want you in this town, digging up the past. He's pissed off enough to hurt you, maybe worse, and whether it's David Magruder or someone else, a detective can move fast on this. I can't. My part ends here. I file the report, and the detective takes it from there. So please—will you talk to her?"

And maybe because of the "her" at the end of his sentence, and maybe because Arthur didn't indicate that she shouldn't, she reluctantly said okay, she'd speak with the detective.

The officer was barely out the door before Arthur Goodale, finally privy to it all, began silently to weep.

# 21

In a town with little crime, the law moves fast when it must. A nurse led Melanie downstairs for a few more tests, a little more poking and prodding, and then into a small room outfitted with a hospital bed and a chair, a TV mounted from the ceiling, and two paintings of birds hanging crookedly on one wall. A woman standing in the room identified herself as Detective Isaacson. She waited while the nurse helped Melanie into the bed and then left the room, shutting the door behind her.

The detective was tiny and fit, like she could probably run a marathon today and another one tomorrow. Except for her hands, which gave away her age, she could have been in college. Her skin looked flawless, but that made it hard to read her face.

"Ms. Denison," she said after shutting the door, "you told Officer Bauer that you're actually Meg Miller. Is that right?"

"Yes, ma'am," Melanie said.

The detective watched her a moment. "It's an astounding statement. That case—that was my rookie year. I remember it really well. So if you're telling the truth, if Meg Miller is alive . . ."

"She is. I am."

"But you go by Melanie?"

"Yes, ma'am."

The detective nodded. "So where've you been, Melanie?"

She repeated for the detective where she'd been all these years, and how she was nearly eighteen now and pregnant, and how she'd driven north because she was tired of being hidden and afraid. She repeated the events of that morning, but it all felt like so much wasted time, going over the same story again.

When she'd finished, the detective spent another minute writing notes into a small spiral notebook. "May I sit down?" she asked.

"Yes, ma'am."

The detective pulled the chair close and sat. "Tell me a little more about being in the witness protection program. How did that come about?"

Her instincts still said *Don't talk. Not a word.* But she had already said more words than she could ever take back.

"The night my mother was killed, everyone was afraid that my father would kill me, too, so the witness protection people hid me away. And my Aunt Kendra and Uncle Wayne agreed to go with me and raise me."

"And they took you to West Virginia?"

"Yes, ma'am."

"What town?"

Melanie hesitated. Then: "Fredonia."

"Why there?"

"It's where they're from. Not that town, exactly. But nearby, in West Virginia."

The detective wrote down a few notes. "And that's where you still live?"

"Yes, ma'am."

"And who did you say arranged all this?"

"The U.S. Marshals. And a local judge."

"Do you know the name of the judge?"

"No, ma'am."

"But it was a judge from here in Silver Bay?"

"I think so. But it was definitely a judge and the U.S. Marshals. They did it in the middle of the night and no one else knew about it."

Detective Isaacson was looking over Melanie's shoulder, deep in thought. She put the pen down. "I have a problem with this."

And suddenly the small, plain room, the two chairs—it all felt like a trap. "What do you mean?"

"Were you ever involved in criminal activity?"

"No, of course not."

"Were your aunt or uncle."

"No, ma'am."

"Because that's how witness protection works. It's for people who have been involved in criminal activity. So they'll be safe to testify in court."

"Then they made an exception for me."

The detective shook her head. "And they never relocate people to somewhere they once lived. It's always somewhere brand-new." She tilted her head. "You're sure it was witness protection and not some other program, maybe?"

"Yes. I'm sure."

"Not the FBI? Some other organization?"

Melanie was getting angry with the detective for doubting her. "Yes—I'm sure." Why was *she* suddenly under fire? What had she done wrong?

"Tell me about your aunt and uncle. How are they related to you?"

"Ma'am?"

Every question felt like a trap. The detective's small stature—even that felt like a ploy to gain Melanie's trust.

"You said 'aunt and uncle.' Which side of the family are they on?"

"Uncle Wayne was friends with my father. Aunt Kendra . . . I'm not sure. They've been married a long time."

"So they aren't blood relatives?"

"No, ma'am."

The detective gave her a long, hard look. "I'm told you need to stay here a while, make sure you're stable enough to go home. In the meantime, I need to get in touch with the U.S. Marshals. Tell me something—are there any gaps in your past, or in your aunt and uncle's, that they don't talk about?"

*Rule: We do not discuss the past.*

Melanie didn't answer.

"All right," said Detective Isaacson. "We'll get to the bottom of it. Tell you what. I'm going to see about having a conversation with David Magruder's driver. But I'll be in touch soon." She smiled. "Did Officer Bauer give you his card?"

"Yes."

"Well, don't use it. You need anything, you call me." She handed Melanie a card with her name and phone number.

As soon as the detective was out the door, a nurse came into the room wheeling in a blood pressure machine. After checking Melanie's blood pressure, she said, "We'll keep you here a couple more hours for observation. You can sleep unless you're feeling nauseous. Are you feeling nauseous?"

"A little." But whether it was from the assault, the interviews, or the baby, she couldn't say.

"Then you should try to stay awake," the nurse said.

Beside her, on a small table, was a telephone. "Does this phone make long-distance calls?" Melanie asked.

"You have to dial nine first." The nurse turned on the TV and left.

Melanie called Phillip's cell. He would be at school now, probably lunchtime.

"I'm sorry," she said when he answered on the second ring. "I thought I could do this alone, but I can't." She told him she was in the hospital, and why. She told him she needed him there with her. "Do you think you can come here soon?"

"I can come there now," he said.

"I'm so, so sorry," she said.

"For what?"

*For being such a child*, she thought. "I miss you," she said.

"I love you, too, Melanie."

She didn't think she wanted to watch TV, but she was wrong. Leonardo DiCaprio and Kate Winslet were on the screen looking beautiful in the sunlight, and she allowed herself a much-needed break from everything other than that amazing, unsinkable ship.

Three hours later, Detective Isaacson was back and escorting Melanie from the hospital. Melanie had been advised not to drive for the rest of the day, so the detective would be taking her back to her hotel. In the hospital lobby, Melanie said, "If you don't mind, I'd like to stop in there."

The flower shop just off the hospital's main entrance was cool and fragrant—peaceful. She ordered a vase of fresh flowers to be delivered to Arthur's room. She signed the note, "Your friend, Melanie."

"Are you hungry?" the detective asked once she'd left the shop.

Melanie nodded. "Extremely."

"Me, too. Let's eat."

While she drove, Detective Isaacson talked about herself, how she was the youngest of six children—runt of the litter, she called herself. How she was the first in her family to go into law enforcement. Her stories sounded prepackaged—like she'd used this exact same small talk to try to bond with previous victims—but Melanie felt grateful not to be asked any more questions.

They went to the diner by Melanie's hotel—she was beginning to feel like a regular—and Melanie followed her doctor's advice and ordered an actual meal: cheeseburger (no bacon—the thought of bacon suddenly nauseated her), French fries, side salad. While they waited for their food, Detective Isaacson's small talk began to worry Melanie. There was no way the detective would spend this kind of time with her unless she had something meaningful to say. "I got the address of David Magruder's driver and hope to speak with him later this afternoon," she said. But that didn't warrant this kind of personal service, did it? "Mr. Magruder is in New York today, working, but I'll pay him a visit at his home later, depending on what his driver has to say."

"Okay," Melanie said, sensing more.

But the detective waited until the food had come and Melanie's burger was nearly finished before saying, "I need to tell you something."

And Melanie knew she wouldn't be eating any more of her lunch.

"My chief," said the detective. "He spoke with the U.S. Marshal in Newark, and *he* made some more calls." It was 3:30 in the afternoon, and the diner was nearly empty. Still, she kept her voice quiet and steady, watching Melanie closely. "After you and I spoke, I got the strong sense that your aunt and uncle have withheld the details of their protection from you. Maybe for your sake, or maybe for theirs. Because like I said, the witness protection program is just that—it's for *witnesses* who have committed a crime but are exonerated in exchange for testifying. The program doesn't just . . . well, the point is, I was wrong, but I was on the right track." She lowered her voice still further. "We think your aunt and uncle have been lying to you, Melanie. The U.S. Marshals Service—they have no knowledge of you, or of your aunt and uncle."

"I'm not lying to you."

She nodded. "I know. You told me what you believed to be true, what your aunt and uncle told you was true. But what I'm saying is, we think they made it all up." And in case there was any misunderstanding: "I don't understand why yet, but I think that on the night of September 22, 1991, you were kidnapped."

# 22

September 22, 1991

All the party guests were gone.

Ramsey was helping the soundman wrap cables. The repetitive motion was good for him. He snuck peeks at Allie, who sat on the back porch steps. Anger coursed through her like blood, he could tell. He would wait to speak with her until they had both calmed a little. When she stood up and slipped back inside the house, he didn't follow her. Soon—but not now.

The guys said little to one another as they packed their gear. A few words about which songs had gone best, which chords and lyrics they'd screwed up. Before long, the soundman's cables were looped, his microphone stands folded, and his sound console back in its crate. The guys helped him load the speakers. They all shook hands. No one would look Ramsey in the eye.

Why does everything always have to end badly? Ramsey wondered. Those cops had treated him as if he were still some young punk. All his years of good behavior had amounted to nothing. *Some things don't change*, the officer had said.

"We're headed to Jackrabbits for a drink," Eric said to him. "You should come along."

Come along to watch Eric sip club soda while everyone avoided Ramsey's gaze some more and the jukebox blasted the Cure and Depeche Mode and every other whiny pop crap?

"No," Ramsey said. "I'm gonna stay here."

Paul frowned. "I think you should do what your wife says and clear out for a while."

"She didn't mean it."

"I think she did," Wayne said.

So now fucking *Wayne* was weighing in? "Well, it's my house, too," Ramsey replied, but his words sounded petulant even to himself, so he tried again. "I just want to talk to her," he said to the three of them. "And then if she really wants me gone, I'll go." The fire pit crackled as a piece of wood shifted and settled. "Heck, I'll even meet up with you guys and endure that horrible fucking jukebox."

Allie must have been watching from inside the darkened living room, because the moment that the other men had left and Ramsey was alone, the door to the back porch slid open and she stepped outside. She looked smaller, shrunken, as if she'd been sick and lost weight. She sat on the top porch step and wrapped her arms around her knees. Ramsey glanced up at the sky and went over to her. He sat down on the lowest step. Looked up at the sky again. As a boy he had known the constellations, but even then the light-filled Jersey sky never let you see many stars. Over the years, he'd forgotten nearly every mythical man and beast who lorded over the earth. He remembered the Big Dipper. *Ursa*

*Major*. Tonight it was half hidden behind the trees. Cassiopeia was overhead. The other stars were just nameless points on a map. But when the earth was no more, those stars would remain in the sky, unfazed.

Not a word from Allie, who just sat there, breathing deeply.

"Some party," he said, and attempted a weak smile.

She sat up. "What the hell's the matter with you, huh? I mean, you can't keep this up."

"Keep what up?" he said, and she screamed in frustration, high and piercing and long.

"Hey!" he said.

"What—are you worried about the neighbors? You're a little late for that." She shook her head. "And forget about *me*—you have a daughter. If you cared about her even a little, you wouldn't be antagonizing the police, practically begging them to arrest you."

"I *do* care—"

"No. All you care about is your superconjunction, which you have to know isn't real and is nothing and is a fucking joke."

He looked up at the sky. "Al—"

"No, you're going to listen to me now. You're on the road too much. You get these ideas in your head, and there's no one around to tell you you're wrong. Well, I'm telling you now. You're wrong. You're so fucking wrong about everything." She was crying. "I want a divorce."

"How could you sleep with that man?"

"Oh, my God—didn't you just hear me? I'm leaving you."

The words he heard, of course, but they didn't square with the facts. They were married, he and Allie. "You're my wife."

"No—I don't love you anymore." She might as well be taking an axe to him. "Maybe I once did, but I don't now."

He looked at his wife. "You have no right, saying that. Not when you're having the affair."

*"I'm not having an affair!* For God's sake, get it through your head—you're so . . . David and I are . . . nothing. We're nothing. We're less than nothing."

He heard Eric's words in his head as clearly as the day he'd said them.

*They were still kissing when I drove past.*
A real kiss?
*You don't want the answer to that.*

"I don't believe you," Ramsey said. He couldn't unsee the image of their kiss, or the images he created in the kiss's aftermath, images perfected after three months of seeing them. "You're lying to me."

She stared at him. "Well, then to hell with you." She opened the sliding door, rushed inside, and slammed the door home.

Ramsey sat there a minute on the step. "You're a liar, Allie," he said to the used-up yard with all its trash.

He wanted to go inside. His anger and sense of injustice were such that he wanted to continue this, escalate it. He wanted to lose control. He wanted to break through.

*That ain't you anymore,* he told himself under his breath, but the words rang false. He said them again anyway, and then a third time, but he wasn't able to convince himself.

*I could hurt you,* he said.

And these words shimmered with truth.

He went out the side gate to his car and pressed the automatic door opener for the garage. In the garage, he got the empty five-gallon gas can and returned to his car. He started the engine and backed out of the driveway. He'd had more to drink tonight than he had in many years, but not nearly enough. He could still see straight. Could still drive. Could still think—which was why he had to escape from here, fast, before he let his thinking go too far and he acted on those thoughts. He passed Jackrabbits and headed east. Stopped at the Sunoco station that was attached to a mart and liquor store. Filled the gas can, put it back into the trunk, then went into the mart and bought a fifth of Jack Daniel's. Returned to the car and drove toward the bay.

This town, this town. Thirty-four years, and what? One store became another, a diner went out of business and a month later opened under a new name. Same flooding every few years when a nor'easter came through—houses damaged, houses repaired. Same yellow school buses. Same schools. Same firehouse. Everything a little faded, a little dingier after three decades—but not fundamentally any different.

Some things don't change.

The road took him over marshes toward the bay, which at night was dark in the middle but shimmering along the edges from the streetlights and porch lights. He passed two marinas, then followed the road as it curved into a quieter area of larger, spread-out homes with views across the bay. This was a part of town he never visited when he was younger, where the real money was. It was dark enough here to miss the entrance to the boat-yard's narrow lot, but Ramsey made the turn—a little too fast—and crunched along the gravel. Some of the boats were dry-docked for the season, but many were still in their slips. Beyond the hedges and trees stood houses to either side.

Ramsey only ever took his motorboat into the bay three or four times a summer. But when he'd bought the boat from the yard's manager five years earlier, the man had quoted Ramsey a next-to-nothing docking fee (the *Sea Nymph* was only twelve feet long), and he hadn't upped the fee since.

The boat was the epitome of simple—aluminum, flat bottom—and ideal for puttering around the bay on the occasional summer morning to fish for fluke. For an hour or two he'd float with the tide and jig his rod and feel the morning air on his skin. Whatever fish he caught he'd take home and cook. If he caught nothing, the outing was no worse.

Tonight the tide was high, the ramp down to the floating dock not steep at all, which made carrying the gas can easier. The bay was absolutely still tonight, but Ramsey knew he wasn't sober, so he stepped carefully into the boat, cradling the gas can and then, once in the boat, setting it down gently at his feet. He opened the cap on the outboard and poured some gas in until it seemed like enough. Capped the engine, capped the gas can. The eight-horsepower engine started on the first pull—a rarity, as if it'd been waiting for him. He untied the line from the clamps at port and starboard, dropped them onto the dock, and idled into the bay. His boat was so small it left no wake, so once he was twenty or thirty yards away from the dock he turned the throttle, and the outboard motor's pitch raised (an almost comical whine compared to the truck's 560-horsepower engine), and the boat moved slowly but steadily away from the lights and into the mouth of the bay.

This was not a boat made for the ocean. But tonight it cut through the calm water like a blade, and with all these houses and condos in sight even from the middle of the bay, he couldn't find the solitude he sought. So he motored out toward the tip of Coral Hook, and even there, a place where the ocean meeting bay usually created strong currents, his small boat glided on. There was an outgoing tide, helping him along, and in no time at all (thirty minutes? forty-five?) he was around the tip of the hook, with the Verrazano Bridge and New York skyline to his north, the ocean to the east and south. He headed southeast, where ahead of him was more water, more water, then glorious nothing, where he would have a front-row seat to the end of all things. In the storage compartment underneath the seat was a flashlight, he was pretty sure, but the whole point was to escape the light. If another boat slammed into him, then so be it. The odds were slim.

He opened the bottle of whiskey and drank. The air was still warm and humid, unusually so, with barely any sea breeze at all. For a while he kept checking the sky, but eventually he stopped doing that and simply piloted his boat. Kept heading southeast, steady and true, and tried to free his mind of everything but the small engine's hum. The shoreline was always in sight but receding. The New York City skyline faded to a brownish-orange smear over the northernmost part of the sky.

For maybe another hour he puttered along. By then, Ramsey's eyes were fully adjusted to the dark, and when he took another drink and leaned back in his seat, he almost got knocked out by what he saw.

Stars everywhere. So many more than he ever could have imagined as a boy sitting high in a tree. Even when he used to imagine mountaintops, he never imagined this: so many stars, they ruined constellations. So bright they were screaming. He couldn't have been more than five or six miles offshore. Unbelievable, that his whole life he was so close to this view and never knew it. He cut the engine. The only sounds were his own breathing and water lapping the side of the boat. Finally a breeze kicked up, warm and comforting.

He slid down to the floor of the boat and lay back, resting his head against the plank seat. He drank some more, capped the bottle, and cradled it under an arm. Looked up at the unobstructed heavens.

Other than the moment when he saw Allie stepping out of the hospital elevator for the first time, this night sky was the most beautiful sight of his life.

"My marriage is ending," he said aloud.

The wide, white-gray splotch running across the sky. That was the Milky Way. He was seeing the entire galaxy from his small boat.

"My marriage is ending, but the world is not ending."

To his ear, the sentence was a paradox. Black was white. High was low. So he tried again. "My marriage, and not the world, is ending."

The boat softly drifted. There was more fuel in the gas can. He could douse the boat with the spare fuel and set it alight. One last grand gesture. But at the moment, grand gestures had lost their appeal. He thought about having sold his truck for a song, and let out a sad laugh. Only one of many problems for tomorrow.

There would be a tomorrow. He had believed in the superconjunction, just as he had believed that he was nothing without Allie, who had saved his life. But maybe everything he believed, he believed a little too hard.

Some things don't change.

But I did, Ramsey thought.

He knew he was right, and that the cop back at the house was jaded and wrong. Yet he understood how the cop could have made that mistake, understood how fucking tempting it was to cling to easy beliefs and call them truths.

He never should have thrown the party. Never should have stormed out on Allie back in June. Never should have spent so many days and nights away from her and from Meg, who wasn't even remotely a baby anymore, and who seemed, tragically, to be replaced by someone new every time he went away and came home again. God damn, he wished he knew his kid better. His list of never-should-haves was long, and his head, full of whiskey, wasn't up to reviewing all of it. But he knew that even if Allie were to leave him, even if she didn't love him anymore, there would be a tomorrow.

I will never, ever hurt you, Allie.

He added this vow to the one he made seven years earlier. They were vows he'd keep even if they divorced. He would honor her and obey her and protect her and love her till death do they part.

He imagined his wife kissing David Magruder. His hand on her ass.

"But I'm big mad at you, Allie!" he shouted into the darkness, and choked out a pitiful laugh. "I'm big, big mad!"

To the west, over land, a flash of heat lightning punctuated his words.

He lay back and drank some more. Looked up at the canopy of stars and silently mourned the end of this part of his life as the boat drifted and rocked and drifted.

# 23

September 29, 2006

Detective Isaacson received a call on her cell. She didn't say what it was about. "I'll be right there," she said into the phone, and then offered to drive Melanie the couple of blocks back to her hotel.

Melanie didn't want to spend a minute longer in the company of Detective Isaacson. "No, I'd rather walk," she said.

After the detective left, Melanie remained in the booth and picked absently at her French fries. She had been attacked almost ten hours ago. Since then she'd been scanned, poked and prodded, stuck with needles, interrogated. Her injuries had been photographed for evidence. And now this detective was asking her to accept that her whole life was a lie.

Melanie found herself resenting Detective Isaacson—no, hating her—for laying all this on her. She had known the detective for less than a day. She had known Wayne and Kendra for fifteen years. It was too much, too fast. She sat in the booth a while longer and then walked numbly from the diner to her hotel. She felt tired but didn't want to be alone in her hotel room, and her legs carried her toward the beach. It wasn't a terribly long walk—she had driven it in only a few minutes—but she got winded easily these days, so she took it slowly.

*We do not discuss the past.*

She'd convinced herself that the reason was so simple, the pain and memory of loss, the sadness that threatened, always, to bubble over. We don't discuss the past because that's our way of dealing with the past. It's how we cope with the present.

But what about Melanie's lack of curiosity over so many years? What accounted for her easy acceptance of her aunt and uncle's explanations? She had wondered about her mother, but never about herself. What if, at some deep level, she knew that if she ever probed too much into the puzzle of exactly how she and Wayne and Kendra had ended up hidden together in that remote West Virginia town, the pieces might not fit together so well? What if she knew she lacked the stomach for the truth? Might she not have been complicit, all these years, in her own ignorance— contributing right along with her aunt and uncle to the myth-making? Ramsey Miller, bogeyman, always about to get her. A terrible way to live—but far better than the possibility that you were being raised by your kidnappers.

But what about the letters from the U.S. Marshal's office? Forged, she supposed. But if the detective was right about her aunt and uncle, then of course there was the most basic question of all: Why had they done it?

Her walk was on its way to becoming a substantial hike when she reached the ocean block. She hadn't noticed the first time she'd been here that the houses were in states of decay. Hadn't paid much attention to the trash on the boardwalk and the beach. Still, seeing the ocean made her wish she'd been seeing it all her life. She wished she'd grown up here. How dare her aunt and uncle convince her that Silver Bay was someplace to fear? She sat on a bench and watched the waves, putting off the return walk as long as possible. When the wind suddenly shifted, cooling the air, she told herself to get a move on.

The walk home left her sweaty and short of breath. She finally crossed the parking lot and was close to the hotel when she heard: "We sacrificed *everything* to keep you safe, and this is how you repay us?"

She turned toward the voice and scrambled to make sense of what she saw: her uncle leaning against the cement ledge near the front entrance.

"How did you—"

"You know you shouldn't be here," he said, and lowered his voice. "My god, Melanie, the one place on this earth you can't be." He squinted in the sunlight. "What happened to your head?"

"I got beat up. It doesn't matter. How'd you find me?" But she knew.

"Of course it matters. You look—"

"Tell me how."

"The young man you've been seeing had the decency to—"

"He had no right." Melanie was already backing away. "And I have nothing to say to you." She rushed away from him, into the hotel lobby.

He followed her inside before the automatic doors slid closed. Followed her right out the back sliding doors to the swimming area, which was deserted and consisted of several dirty chaise lounges around a small pool filled with murky water. Melanie sat on one of the chairs and put her head in her hands. Wayne sat on the lounge chair nearest her.

"Who hurt you?" he asked.

"I don't know," she said. "I just got mugged, is all."

"Figures—this place is a fucking nightmare." His voice was harsh but whisper-quiet. "We were scared to death. I'm very angry with you."

"I told you in my note not to worry."

"Well, we did worry. We worried a lot. We thought *he'd* gotten to you."

"Oh, stop it already!" She glared at him.

"Stop what?"

That damn detective. Melanie didn't want to believe her. "Stop lying to me."

"Honey, I'm not—"

"You kidnapped me, Uncle Wayne."

"What? No. Keep it down. What are you talking about?"

"The witness protection program—I know you made it up."

"That's not true. Why would you think—"

"The police checked it all out. They spoke with the U.S. Marshals. It's just not true."

"The police? You went to the—" He shook his head. "Honey, the police are idiots. You know that. They obviously made a mistake. It's been a long time and the files get . . ." He took a breath. "You shouldn't be talking to law enforcement. You shouldn't be here. It's too risky. We're not even allowed here. It's like I always said . . ." She remained quiet, watching his mouth form words that were increasingly losing any meaning. "It's like I said—we have to . . ."

With every fumbling word from her uncle's mouth, Melanie became more certain. He had taken her and lied to her about it, inventing the sort of lies that made her afraid, lies that kept her within the tight perimeter of their trailer. "Why?" she said. "Why would you do that?"

He watched the pool for a few seconds. Large leaves floated in the water. "Growing up without parents, Melanie . . . the Hope Home for Children—you can't imagine. The beatings, the daily humiliations . . . it didn't matter how well you behaved." He was looking at the leaves in the pool but seeing into his past. "The noise that never stopped—the crying and screaming and moaning. Older kids hurting the younger ones at night with rocks, with handmade knives. The smell of sickness. The stink of it. Vomit and piss and shit." He looked at Melanie now. "At night I'd lie in bed and pray to die in my sleep. And then one day the place closed, and the people that took me—I knew it had to be better. But it wasn't. She locked us in closets with no lights. She put out her cigarettes on my arms. And *him*. He was worse." She had never seen tears in his eyes before. "No way was I going to let you live that way."

"This is crazy," she said. "I don't want to hear this."

"You're the one who came here for answers, Melanie. So now you're going to get them." He took a breath. "The night your mother died, me and Eric and Paul—we went to a bar near the house, but we were worried about her. None of us grew up protected like you did. We had all seen the sort of things that people did to people. And Ramsey—your father—he was acting crazy that day. The look in his eyes—we'd all seen it before in other men. So when we left the bar, I drove back to check on them."

"Eric Pace told me you were drunk and drove straight home."

"You talked to Eric?" His eyes widened. "Well, sure, Mel— that's what I told him. I had to keep the truth from *everyone*, even him. To keep you safe. Damn, Melanie, you know I don't like talking about this . . ." He took a breath. "So we all left the bar together and got in our cars, but then I went back into the bar and had one more drink. I was afraid, you know? I didn't want to go, didn't want to face Ramsey. But I felt like I had to. So I stayed and drank one more beer, and then I got in my car and went over there. It was so much worse than I ever thought . . ." He swallowed. "I saw her in the fire, Mel. And I knew that Ramsey would go to prison, probably forever, and you'd become a ward of the state. I'll admit, it all happened fast. I was practically a kid myself and didn't have time to think any of it through. It was instinct, you know?" He looked distraught, remembering back. "I knew I had to keep you. I'd take care of you. Raise you in a good home. Give you what I never had. And when I found out that Ramsey was on the loose, it only proved I'd made the right decision to protect you. I knew that's why I was put on this earth."

"And Aunt Kendra—she knew all this?"

"She knew we could all be a family," Wayne said. "She knew we could have a peaceful home where we look out for one another, which is all she's ever wanted."

"That's not what I'm asking."

"Then no—she doesn't know everything. She thinks everything is legal. I did her that favor."

Of course: the letters. They were never meant for Melanie.

Every meal together as a family. Every night, going to bed and believing you knew the raw data of your own existence.

"My whole life, you've lied to me," Melanie said. "Everything's a lie."

"No—that's not true." His eyes were begging her. "Your aunt loves you. And so do I. We're a family."

"Don't say that."

"You know we are."

She wanted to get up and plunge into the water, cleanse herself of everything she was hearing. But even the pool was dirty.

Her skull throbbed. "I need to take some Tylenol." She got up and walked toward her room. She let Wayne follow her. In the room, she took two pills and lay on the covers of her bed while Wayne paced the small carpeted area.

"Forget what I said about working in the garage," he said. "You can pick up where you left off at the college. Take any course you want." More pacing. "If you want to be on that newspaper . . . well, I guess that's okay, too."

The school newspaper? Did he not understand anything she was saying?

When he tore open the complimentary packet of coffee grounds, Melanie's stomach seized. "Please don't make coffee." He frowned at her. "My headache is making everything smell bad." He shrugged and dropped the opened packet into the trash.

"You're almost eighteen," he said, taking a seat at the table by the window. "I know we have to start treating you like an adult. I mean, I get that," he said. "But we can make it work. Everything's on the table."

Nothing was simple. Wayne had lied to her for years, but not about sacrificing everything for her safety. And she felt safer around him, still—even now, protected in a way that was familiar and seductive. She could almost chalk this whole trip up to some failed Nancy Drew sleuthing, the stunt of an impulsive teenager, and head home to Fredonia. But she also understood exactly why she felt so tempted: As long as she was with her aunt and uncle, she'd never have to be responsible for herself or anybody else.

"No," she said. "I'm never going back there."

"Honey—"

"I can't live this way anymore. I won't. I'm going to find my father."

"You won't find him," he said. "Not if the police and F.B.I. can't."

"Well, I'm trying, anyway. You might as well go home. Phillip's on his way—he'll take care of me."

"Him? I find that hard to believe," Wayne said, and they both watched through the window as a police cruiser pulled into the lot.

"That's probably for me," she said. "Because of this." She touched her forehead.

"Melanie, this is a bad place."

"Okay. But I should go out there. I doubt either one of us of wants an officer coming to the room."

When she got out of bed, he reached out and touched her arm. "You never should have come to Silver Bay," he said.

She wondered if she would ever feel his touch again. "Go home, Uncle Wayne." And in case he needed to hear it: "Don't worry—I'm not going to turn you in."

It was Officer Bauer, who'd come to take Melanie to the station.

"Why?" she asked.

"Detective Isaacson wants you there."

"Why?"

"I suppose she wants to talk to you."

"Can I make a call first?" Melanie asked.

"Can it wait until we get there?"

"Not really."

She had to borrow the officer's cell phone. Phillip picked right up.

"I'm in Trenton!" he announced as brightly as if he had just entered Emerald City.

She was furious at Phillip for telling Wayne where she'd gone, but there was nothing she could say with the officer standing right there. All she could tell him was to meet her at the Silver Bay police station, not the hotel. She handed the phone back to the officer, who pocketed it and opened the back door for Melanie. "Watch your head," he said.

For nearly an hour, Melanie sat on the hard wooden bench in the station's cramped lobby, her headache not helped any by the fluorescent lights buzzing overhead. Only a few people came and went, taking no notice of her. At some point she heard rain on the roof. Finally, Detective Isaacson hurried into the room from somewhere within the station's depths. "Sorry to keep you waiting," she said, "but if we didn't pick you up at the hotel, there'd be no other way to reach you." She shook Melanie's hand. "You might think about getting a cell phone. Thanks for coming. Coffee?"

"No."

"All right. Let's go somewhere we can talk."

Melanie's body tensed. Every time they talked, Melanie learned something she didn't want to know. The alternative was to choose not-knowing over knowing, and that option was starting to have its appeal. Nonetheless, she followed the detective down a narrow corridor with an uneven floor. On the wood-paneled walls hung framed photographs of police academy graduating classes—trim officers with proud postures and eyes that seemed to follow her accusingly.

The detective led her to a small room with a desk and a few mismatched chairs. She shut the door and motioned for Melanie to sit. The detective sat beside her and opened the file folder. "I had your statements from this morning transcribed off the tape. I'd like you to read them and let me know if you have any corrections. Then sign them."

Melanie glanced at the papers; it was odd seeing her own words in print.

"You were right, by the way, about the man who assaulted you. Bill Suddoth has had trouble with the law before. Misdemeanors: a couple of drunk and disorderlies. He was very cooperative with me when I went to his apartment this afternoon and told him I was investigating an assault committed by a man of exactly his size, wearing the same shoes he was currently wearing. And you were also right about his shoes. I kind of wish he'd polish mine.

Anyway, he immediately blamed Magruder, said his boss wanted you dead and threatened to fire him unless he took care of it."

Melanie looked up from the papers she was holding. Despite her bruises and aches, she had trouble believing this. "David wanted to kill me?"

"That's what Bill Suddoth claims. He also claims he decided all on his own to convince you to leave town—you know, talk to you instead of doing something a lot worse. He claims he never meant to hurt you." Detective Isaacson held Melanie's gaze. "I think it's complete bullshit."

"Which part?"

"All of it. Magruder, with all his money and connections, would never rely on a man like Bill Suddoth to commit a murder for him. He'd pay top dollar for a professional hit man. So here's what I think. I think that driving Magruder's fancy cars is the best job Bill Suddoth has ever had, and he'd do a lot to keep it. Not murder, but a lot. Now, if Magruder was surprised to see you alive yesterday—I think you even used the word 'happy'— then I doubt very much he'd want you dead today. But after sobering up last night he must have become very anxious about something, and decided it was best if you left town and never came back."

"Anxious about what?"

"Well, we don't know for sure. But I'm going to try like hell to find out when I interview him. That's why I want to make sure your statement is totally accurate."

"When are you going to interview him?"

"Now."

"You mean he's *here*?"

"Yes, but he doesn't know he's a person of interest. We told him we've arrested Bill Suddoth for an assault, made it sound like an open-and-shut case. The moment he feels threatened, he's going to demand his lawyer. So I figure we have one good shot at catching him off guard."

Melanie glanced at her statement. All the facts were there, but something didn't add up. "You're doing all this—messing with a famous person—because his driver shoved me?"

The detective sighed. "David Magruder committed a serious crime today, orchestrating your assault, and he did it stupidly, getting Bill Suddoth involved. Why do you think he would take a risk like that?"

"I guess he panicked," Melanie said.

"Exactly. And why did he panic? Because of you." Then the detective did the most surprising thing. She took Melanie's hand. "Honey, I think it's possible—actually, more than possible—that David Magruder is responsible for your mother's death."

"My father killed my mother," Melanie said automatically, pulling her hand away. It was true because it had to be true. It was the one true thing left.

"Melanie, I went back and read the file from 1991. You were right. Magruder had no alibi for the time of the murder. And he lied to us on tape about having a relationship with the victim."

"So what?"

"So in my opinion, the police went far too easy on him back in ninety-one. The lead investigator at the time, Esposito—our careers overlapped by a few years. He was a sweet man who threw great holiday parties. But as a detective?" She shook her head. "All I'm saying is, the fact that he interviewed Magruder more than once is actually pretty astonishing. But he never would have pursued Magruder as a suspect. Not without hard evidence screaming at him. Not when Magruder was already a local celebrity who denied knowing the victim, and especially not with an obvious suspect in your father, whom a dozen people had witnessed acting angry and unbalanced—unhinged—on the night of the murder."

"He's the obvious suspect because he did it," Melanie said. Needing this to be true, she repeated it like a mantra. "My father killed my mother."

"Honey—"

"Please don't call me that." After a full day of being bossed around by doctors and cops, everyone believing they knew best, it felt good, even pleasurable, to stand up to the detective. "I'm not a child. And no matter what David might have done, or why he did it, I know that my father killed my mother. I know it." She stood up.

"Melanie, I agree that your father's disappearance is a mystery. But not everyone who vanishes is a murderer. And I think it's possible that David Magruder killed your mother and fled, and sometime later that night or early the next morning Wayne Denison came upon the crime scene, panicked, and took you away where he thought you'd be safe."

"That's not right."

"It makes sense, your uncle jumping to the same conclusion as everybody else. He thought he was protecting you from your father. I mean, it was a reasonable thought to have. But holding you for all those years." She exhaled. "I can't begin to imagine."

Melanie had been working hard this afternoon to hate her uncle—*he isn't even your uncle!* she kept reminding herself—but she couldn't make herself do it. "He wasn't 'holding me,' detective. He was raising me. He did what he thought he had to."

"But he *didn't* have to. He never should have taken the matter into his own hands." The detective softened her voice. "We'll be coordinating with authorities in West Virginia to pick up Mr. and Mrs. Denison. I hope you understand we have no choice."

Melanie's legs were weak. She sat back down. In her head, she was trying out a new sentence: *David Magruder killed my mother.*

"Given all of this," Detective Isaacson said, "I'd like you to remain at the station while I interview Mr. Magruder. Like I said, I'll have one shot at this before he sees what we're up to and he starts spreading his money around on lawyers, at which point he'll become a far more difficult suspect. So in case he says something I need to verify, or that contradicts something you've said, I need to be able to ask you right away. He'll never know you're here."

*My father did not kill my mother.*

"We don't have nearly enough evidence for a murder charge yet," Isaacson was saying. "I'm hoping this interview will let me start building a case."

Evidence. Building a case. Meaningless words. My father killed my mother. My father did not kill my mother. Her vision became swirly. She wasn't listening to the detective. She was thinking about every mysterious sound she'd ever heard over the years, all the times she felt as if she were being watched or followed. None of it was real. The tens of thousands of hours fearing that the smallest mistake would mean her death. Being terrified that her father was always just beyond the hedges, always around the next corner.

"Melanie?"

Her attention returned to the police station, to this detective who in a single day had shaken every belief she'd ever had. It wasn't the detective's fault, yet Melanie knew she would never forgive her.

"I want to hear all of it," Melanie said.

"Hear what—the interview? No, I'm afraid I can't do that."

But Melanie was done enduring everyone else's explanations and theories and justifications. She was done learning about everything after the fact. If Magruder was guilty, she wanted to hear it firsthand. If he wasn't, she wanted to hear that, too, from his own lips.

"Sure, you can," Melanie said. "Through one of those one-way mirrors or whatever."

"We don't have any of those."

"Then a microphone. Or a video camera. You've got to have some way of—"

"We use a webcam—but Melanie, I'm afraid the answer is no. We have a way of doing things to preserve the integrity of the evidence."

"Is that so?" Melanie was infuriated by her own powerlessness, and she felt the childish urge to hit something. "Then I'm leaving."

"Melanie . . ."

"I take back my whole story. I won't sign this." She shut the file folder and slammed it on the table. "My father killed my mother. You can't change that. And my boyfriend will be coming soon, and as soon as he gets here I want to go."

"We simply can't do what you're asking," the detective said, struggling not very successfully to control her own frustration. "I wish I could."

"You wish you could?"

"Of course I do."

Melanie looked right into the detective's eyes and said, "I fell down the stairs. I hit my head at the bottom of it. And my stomach."

"Melanie, don't do this."

"It was stupid of me," she continued, "but that's what happened. I fell down the stairs and that's the last thing I'll ever say about it, and I refuse to sign this statement. I don't know why I ever said those lies. Probably because of the concussion. But you can charge me with stuff if you want—for wasting your time or telling lies or whatever. But I want to make a new statement that I fell down the stairs. I'll swear to it and sign it."

In the ensuing silence, the detective looked at the closed file folder, and Melanie could see her weighing the risks.

"You can watch one of the computer terminals." The detective sounded displeased, but she was saying the right words. "Officer Bauer will sit with you. But I'm telling you now, you can't utter one word about what you hear to anyone. You could jeopardize your own case. You could jeopardize your mother's. Am I being clear?"

Melanie was so stunned, having gotten what she'd demanded, that all she could do was nod.

# 24

If David Magruder had been taken to a formal interview room—which was as inviting as a jail cell and meant to arouse a person's anxiety—he would have known instantly that he was under suspicion, and that Detective Isaacson's request that he "help them deal quietly with a delicate situation regarding his employee" was at best a half-truth. This was why, Officer Bauer explained to Melanie, the detective had arranged to speak with Magruder in the station's "swing room"—typically the site of brief officer meetings and coffee breaks.

There were two vending machines, soda and snacks, humming against one wall, and four chairs surrounding a circular table on which sat a small vase of plastic flowers. There was also a small webcam, its lens one-sixteenth of an inch in diameter and nearly invisible, taped to the top of the door frame, recording everything in the room. A cork board was attached to the wall, and pinned to it were newspaper comic strips of police officers. Magruder, wearing a suit with the tie loosened, sat beside a uniformed officer, chatting. At one point, the officer laid a hand on David's arm and they both smiled about something. Either the setup was having the intended effect or Magruder faked being relaxed amazingly well, especially for a man who'd just worked a long day after drinking too much the night before.

"This won't work," Melanie said to Officer Bauer, suddenly certain of it. Bauer sat in a creaky chair in front of the monitor. Melanie sat beside him. Watching David on the monitor was like watching him on TV, where he was in total control, always. "David does interviews for a living," she said. "He's a master at this."

Bauer raised the volume on the monitor. "So is the detective," he said.

Together they watched Detective Isaacson enter the swing room and shake Magruder's hand. She was intentionally short of breath and acting distracted, sitting down and flipping through a file folder.

"Thanks again for coming in, Mr. Magruder," she said.

"You can call me David."

She smiled. "I will, David." She turned to the other officer. "We're all good here. Thanks for keeping David company."

He smiled, and shook Magruder's hand. "A real pleasure, sir. I like your show."

Magruder nodded.

When the officer left, he swung the door casually behind him so that it closed most, but not all, of the way. Nobody was being held here against his will. It was all strictly voluntary, a matter of mutual respect.

Detective Isaacson sat on the chair beside Magruder. "Like I said in the car, you have no idea how helpful this is, wrapping everything up quickly. I'm afraid that Bill Suddoth—" She frowned. "Do you want coffee? Soda? Anything? I should've asked."

"Nothing, please." He crossed his legs.

"All right." Another friendly smile. "But if you change your mind. So Bill Suddoth assaulted a young woman this morning. I told you that in the car. Forgive me. Anyway, she got pretty banged up—bruises, contusions, concussion."

"I'm very sorry to hear that."

"Thank you. Well, fortunately, she—Alice Adams is her name—she was able to identify Mr. Suddoth shortly after the attack. When I spoke with her this morning, she could only figure that Mr. Suddoth must have become obsessed with her yesterday while driving her around. She said she'd found him a little odd at the time. I think she used the word creepy. And this morning—well, like I said, he beat her up. We don't believe it was an attempted sexual assault, but we're looking into the possibility."

"That's terrible."

"Have you ever known Mr. Suddoth to be unstable?"

"I wouldn't hire someone who I thought—"

"No, of course not. I'm not suggesting you could have known he might do something like this. But he has a prior record."

"He does?"

"No felonies, but he's no boy scout, either. I'm sure you didn't know that when you hired him."

"No. Absolutely not."

"In the future, you can always check with us." Detective Isaacson got out her wallet and removed a business card. Slid it across the table. "Check with me—I'll personally run the search." She smiled. "One of the benefits of living in a small town."

"Thank you." Magruder glanced at the card and put it in his shirt pocket.

"Oh, I'm happy to. We're living in really litigious times, and you want to be extremely careful."

Magruder nodded. "You know, I hadn't thought of it until just now, but Bill has been acting somewhat erratic. In fact—"

"Just so I have my notes correct, Bill Suddoth drove Ms. Adams to your house last evening around what time?"

David Magruder looked momentarily bothered. He wasn't used to being cut off. Then: "I'd say around six o'clock."

She jotted it down in her notes. "Okay, and Ms. Adams said that she'd come over to interview you for a school assignment. That you'd talked for a while, and that you dropped her off later that night at her hotel. So it was during the initial drive to your house that Mr. Suddoth must have become obsessed with her. Would you say that's the only time he'd have been with her? I'm just trying to get the chronology right."

"That sounds right," he said, and leaned forward. "Just out of curiousity—what did he say about all this? Or is that confidential?"

The detective let out a laugh. "Bill Suddoth knows he could be facing jail time, so I don't take anything he says very seriously." She coughed into a closed fist. "Pardon me. Can you think of any other reason why he might have wanted to hurt her, other than some kind of sexual obsession? Could she have said something to him to make him angry?"

"I really have no idea. But I doubt it. He's just a driver."

Detective Isaacson nodded. "I honestly think this is a pretty straightforward case of a young, attractive girl being in the wrong place at the wrong time." She smiled knowingly.

"What is it?" Magruder asked.

"Nothing, it's just—well, you asked what Mr. Suddoth said. Would you believe he said *you* put him up to it?"

"What?" Magruder uncrossed his legs and sat up straight. "Why the hell would he—"

"Because Bill Suddoth is basically a thug in nice shoes, and he did a bad thing, and now he's trying to blame the bigger fish because he has a prior record and is worried about jail time." She shrugged. "Like I said, I don't take him too seriously. Anyway, you shouldn't let it worry you—it's what guys like him always say. Would you believe he said you ordered him to kill her, and that he decided to warn her instead to leave town?"

"My god!"

"I know—welcome to the police force. We deal with guys like him all the time. 'The president made me do it.' 'The pope made me do it.'"

Magruder risked a tentative smile. "'Jesus and Buddha conspired . . .'"

"Exactly!" Detective Isaacson returned the smile. "Tell me something. What *did* you and Ms. Adams talk about at your home?"

A nearly imperceptible tightening of his face. "Well, like you said. She interviewed me. About my job and my life."

"I never said she interviewed you."

He tilted his head. "Yeah, you did."

"I said she went to your house in order to interview you. According to her, you quickly identified her as Meg Miller, presumed to be dead. Needless to say, that trumped a school interview, am I right?"

Through the computer monitor, Melanie watched Magruder's body stiffen. For maybe ten seconds—an eternity—nothing got said. Magruder glanced around, as if for the first time realizing where he was.

"I'm not following," he said.

"It's okay," the detective said. "I know she asked you to keep her identity a secret. That's why I'm letting you know that *I* know. She told us, too. It's remarkable that she's been alive all these years, isn't it?"

He nodded. "Yes. It absolutely is."

"Amazing coincidence, though, wouldn't you say?" said the detective.

Melanie could tell that David didn't want to take the bait. But he couldn't not. "What coincidence?"

"Well, think about it: A woman is murdered, and her daughter disappears. Fifteen years later, the daughter returns to town and within a couple of days gets violently assaulted herself. I mean, that family has some really bad luck."

"I hadn't thought about it like that," Magruder said.

"Because there's no way those two things could be connected, is there?"

Magruder stared at the detective for a few seconds. Then he smiled broadly, his excellent white teeth gleaming. "Detective Isaacson, what is this?"

"What is what?"

He shook his head. "You're interrogating me, aren't you? *This*"—he motioned toward the vending machines, the partly opened door—"this is all show."

"Absolutely not. I'm completely confident that Mr. Suddoth is at fault here. That's why he's the one who's under arrest. But he insisted it came from you—"

"Which it didn't—"

"Which it didn't. Obviously. But Melanie—that's what Meg likes being called these days, though I guess you know that—anyway, Melanie says that when she was assaulted this morning, Suddoth told her to, quote, 'leave town.'"

"Okay . . ."

"Well, that's a strange thing for him to come up with on his own, isn't it? I mean, why would someone obsessed with a girl order her to leave town?"

Magruder sighed deeply. "I haven't a clue. He's obviously a nut. Obviously, I never should have hired him."

The detective waved the statement away. "Oh, we all make mistakes. Live and learn, right? But okay. I'm sure that when this is all said and done, Bill Suddoth will be charged and either plead guilty or be found guilty. But what—and this is just a hypothetical —but what if you did want Melanie to leave town? Why would that be?"

"Detective, I *don't* want—"

"I know—that's why I said it's a hypothetical. Just let me finish. Why would he want Melanie Denison to leave town? I asked myself. And then I remembered—actually, I didn't remember. I checked the file—but okay. I checked the file and saw that you didn't have an alibi for the time of Allison Miller's murder—"

"Stop." David Magruder had his palm out like he was directing traffic. "We're done here."

"Please, Mr. Magruder," said the detective. "I'm not accusing you of anything. I'm trying to help you."

"Now detective, you know that's a load of—"

"I really am. Hear me out. I'm seeing this through the eyes of a thousand newspapers and TV stations—if they were to learn a couple of simple facts. Now, I don't want to give Bill Suddoth's story credence, because I don't want you to become fodder for . . . well, for journalists. You know how they can be." When Magruder said nothing, she continued. "It just seems a little weird to me that Bill Suddoth's story—that he told her to leave town—actually matches what the victim herself told us." She paused again. "Is it possible that maybe you asked Bill Suddoth to *talk* to Ms. Denison? That maybe you told him specifically *not* to hurt her, but just to make this helpful suggestion that she was better off somewhere other than Silver Bay?"

"What you're saying is all very ridiculous, detective. Still, I'll have my lawyer present before this goes any further."

"Mr. Magruder, of course you can have your lawyer here. Of course you know that anything you say can be used against you in a court of law. But you aren't under arrest or even a suspect. What

I'm doing is just trying to wrap this up fast, get you out of here before anyone in the media knows you're here. See, if I knew that you had directed your driver to politely ask Ms. Denison to return to wherever it was she came from, for whatever reason you might have had—that's not my business—and if *he*—all on his own—took things too far and became physical, then I should have all I need. It would explain why he talked to her about her leaving town. And her injuries certainly prove that he took things too far. We could get this wrapped up and no one will ever have to know you were here. Because it's certainly no crime for you simply to ask your employee to *speak* with Ms. Denison. So is that maybe what happened?" When he didn't answer, she added, "Because otherwise, I'm going to have to look into the ridiculous claim that you ordered Ms. Denison to be killed, and I really don't want to start investigating the wild claims of unreliable thugs. Especially when it threatens to put a man like yourself in the spotlight—in the news, online—where it will undoubtedly damage your career. That isn't right."

"And I don't want to start investigating a corrupt and incompetent small-town police department. But I will if I have to, and I have more resources than you do."

"You don't have any evidence of that, Mr. Magruder."

"And neither do you," he said.

"I have the sworn testimony of the victim and the accused," she said calmly, "plus the business card of every journalist who's ever shaken my hand over the past seventeen years. We both know this is a juicy news story, Mr. Magruder. It's your call."

Magruder stared down the detective for maybe five seconds—five seconds of fast calculations and cost-benefits and, quite possibly, an awakening to the notion that his invincibility was neither inevitable nor everlasting—and then he broke eye contact and his posture sagged. He looked down at the table until he had collected himself somewhat. "I made him promise to treat her nicely—I *specifically* told him not to hurt her or even threaten her. Just to speak to her nicely. I'd have talked to her myself, but I had to get to New York early this morning."

"See? That's what I figured." The detective sounded almost cheerful as she wrote a few fast notes in her pad. "So help me to understand just one more thing, will you?"

"I'll try," Magruder said. He still sounded extremely wary. He was in uncharted waters, and he knew it, and he knew that the detective knew it.

"You were happy to learn that Ms. Denison—who you once knew as Meg Miller—was alive, is that fair to say?"

"Of course. I was very glad to learn that her father had spared her life."

"That's what I'd assume. So then why did you want her out of town so quickly?"

"Why did I . . ." He bit his lip. "Well, I didn't really want her to—"

"You did. I mean, you just admitted to that."

"*Detective.*"

He took a breath as if he were going to chastise her, and the detective even gave him time to put his words together. But when no words came, the detective said, "Mr. Magruder, did you kill Allison Miller back in 1991?"

"What!" He snapped bolt upright in his chair.

"Because I think you did," she continued. "She was a beautiful woman, and you were in love with her."

"What are you—"

"And on the night of September 22, 1991, when everyone had left the Miller house, you went there, and she rejected you, and so you killed her."

"That's a lie!"

"You strangled her and threw her into the fire pit and let Ramsey Miller take the blame. But it was you."

"I want my lawyer here right now!"

"Fine. I'll get you a phone," the detective said. "But know that I'm seconds away from reaching for those business cards. Every slimy journalist—their numbers are all in a drawer. And I know you understand exactly what will happen to your career when the world learns that David Magruder is suspected of killing Allison Miller and now, fifteen years later, of trying to murder her daughter."

"I didn't—"

"And this will drag on a long time. I personally guarantee it. We'll start tonight with a warrant to search your home. A dozen police cars will park out front with their lights flashing. It won't take long for the news helicopters to start circling. And I'll take as much time as I need to build my case, and eventually I'll have enough evidence for a homicide charge. By then, the David Magruder brand will be long defunct."

"Why are you doing this?" David looked wounded, a child unfairly punished by his teacher.

"Because you murdered a woman," Detective Isaacson said. "And now the daughter returns, and it makes you have to remember —it makes you feel that woman's throat in your hands all over again. It makes you smell her burning flesh."

"Stop it."

"You killed Allison Miller, Mr. Magruder. Admit it."

"I didn't," Magruder said. "I swear it."

"You swear it?" The detective lowered her voice. "Did you order Bill Suddoth to assault and threaten Melanie Denison?" When he didn't answer, she said, "Either you tell me the whole truth about this morning or else the world finds out in the next hour that you're the prime suspect in the murder of Allison Miller." She lowered her voice. "That's how it has to be. If you admit to ordering the assault, we're probably talking probation and a fine. If you didn't murder Allison Miller, then tell me the complete truth about the assault. Prove to me you can say something truthful. Now. Not later."

"I only asked Bill to convince her to leave town."

"What—specifically—did you ask him to do?"

"I didn't say," he said. "I didn't say, 'hurt her.' I didn't even tell him to threaten her. I left it vague."

She nodded. "But you knew he might not be very diplomatic."

"Yeah. I guess I knew that."

"Because you knew he had a criminal record."

David looked at the detective. His shrug was barely detectable.

"So you were lying when you said you didn't know about that." When he didn't respond, she asked, "Why did you want her to leave town so badly, David?"

Silence.

"What were you so worried about that you were willing to jeopardize your precious career over it? And why in the world would you put your fate in the hands of a man like Bill Suddoth?"

More silence.

"You panicked, I get that. But why?" The detective waited a long moment before apparently reaching her limit with David's irritating silence. "I'm giving you ten seconds," she said. "Then I'm out the door and you'll have your lawyer and I'll have your face on the ten o'clock news on every TV in America."

She stared him down, and Melanie was certain that more than ten seconds passed. When David finally spoke, his voice was soft, almost meek. "Can I tell you something off the record?"

"*Off the record?*" She shook her head as if in pity and closed her file folder. She stood up. "I'm a cop, pal, not a journalist."

She was almost to the door when he said, "What if I saw a crime happen and didn't report it? How bad is that?"

Detective Isaacson closed the door all the way and returned to her seat at the table. "How about you start talking and we let the D.A. decide."

# 25

Barely able to breathe, eyes glued to the small computer monitor, Melanie listened to David Magruder tell the detective about the night of September 22, 1991, when a distraught Allison Miller came to his house, suggesting that they leave their spouses and give their friendship a chance to become something more. How he'd rejected her—rudely, cruelly—because his wife was about to give him a shot at the big time. He spoke slowly, his tone flat, and Melanie recognized his frequent pauses as attempts to control himself and fight back waves of emotion and probably nausea.

Allison Miller left his house. He called after her, but she kept walking home. An hour or so later, he was sitting on his front stoop, brooding, when Ramsey Miller's car drove by on its way out of the neighborhood. At that time, David decided to walk over to the Millers' house.

"She'd been so angry," he said to the police station wall. "I never saw her like that before. I wasn't going to change my decision, but I had been a bastard and I wanted to apologize."

He went around back—for all he knew, the party was still going on—but everything was dark outside and quiet, lit only by the smoldering fire pit. The gate was ajar, and through it he saw movement near the rear of the property. When his eyes began to adjust, he spotted Allie, kissing someone.

"My first thought was that she and her husband had made up, and I'd been mistaken about it being Ramsey's car. But . . . no. It wasn't right."

"What wasn't right?" asked the detective—gently nudging him along but otherwise staying out of the way.

"How they moved." He was looking beyond her, describing his past as if watching a movie. "Their bodies. It wasn't an embrace. It was something else."

"Did you witness the murder of Allison Miller, Mr. Magruder?" But he wasn't listening to her. He was seeing into the past, fifteen years. "Mr. Magruder?"

"Yes," he said.

"You did nothing to intervene?"

"I got there too late to stop it."

"Are you sure? Was she already dead when you arrived?"

"No, just that . . . it was too late. I knew I couldn't have . . ."

"All right. You did nothing afterward, either. You could have called the police at any time."

"I was afraid."

"Afraid of what, David?" When he didn't answer, she said, "Do you mean physically afraid?"

"Yes," he said. Then: "No."

"Which is it?"

"I know how people are," he said. "If it got out that I was at the scene of a murder, it would've been too much."

"Too much? I don't understand?"

He kept looking at the wall. "It would've been too much. They'd have chosen the other guy."

"What other guy?"

"It was down to the two of us—me and another guy, some former jock out of California. One of us was going to get the job. It was the New York market. I had to get it. That was the only thing that mattered. It was never going to come around again."

"And that's what you were thinking about while you watched your friend get murdered? It's the New York market?" When he didn't answer, she said, "So then what did you do?"

"I went home."

"What did you do when you got home?"

"*Planet of the Apes* was on TV. I watched it."

"Mr. Magruder, who killed Allison Miller?"

He squeezed his eyes shut as if zooming in on the picture in his mind, then opened them again. "That's just it—it was hard to see in the backyard, and my night vision was never any good. But Ramsey Miller, he was a smallish man. The man in the backyard with Allie, he was big."

"Do you mean obese?"

It was Eric, Melanie thought. Eric returned to the house and—

"No," Magruder said, "not that kind of big. Tall, I guess. Broad. You know. Big."

"Who do you think it was?" the detective asked.

Melanie's teeth chattered. Her hands trembled.

"I'm not positive," Magruder said, "but I think it was one of the musicians on stage. The young one on guitar."

# 26

September 22, 1991

Allison paced the house, muttering to herself. Oscillating between humiliation and self-righteousness.

*If you have needs that aren't being met.*

How dare he. Balding weatherman for a two-bit local station. Well, she'd been dead wrong about him. God, and she would have done anything for him—stripped right there in his living room, screwed him on his leather sofa, on the carpet. She was his. All he had to do was admit what he felt. Admit the connection between them. That it all meant something. So either she'd been wrong about the connection or wrong when she thought he might have a little courage.

But all that was over now, leaving her with a marriage that was also over. Her whole body hurt, thinking about it. Better not to.

She went to the kitchen for trash bags, stepped outside to the backyard, and began picking things up—paper plates, balled-up napkins, plastic ware—from the grass, the tables, the porch railing, the bushes. People were slobs. She emptied beer from plastic cups into the grass and threw the cups away. Same with the soda cans.

She took her time. At one point she poured herself a beer from the keg, drank it a little too fast, and threw the empty cup into the trash. The yard was quiet at last. Peaceful. The air was warm with a gentle breeze. The only light came through the kitchen window. She kept cleaning up. Twice, she almost stepped in pony shit, but otherwise she was glad to be outside. She felt exhausted, worn through, but knew she wouldn't be able to fall asleep, and cleaning gave her something to do.

In the fire pit, a few last chunks of wood smoldered. She would have to throw dirt over it before going in for the night.

She was carrying a full trash bag across the yard toward the garage when she heard: "Hi, there." She started and turned toward the side gate.

Wayne was tall, over six feet, but the way he stood—hands in his pockets, bad posture—he looked smaller. And embarrassed, as if he'd caught her doing something shameful.

"What'd you forget?" she asked, more rudely than she meant. Not his fault that he was good enough on the guitar that shitty musicians latched on to him.

"Ma'am?" He glanced around, like maybe she knew something he didn't. "No—I just came by to see . . ."—he made a pained expression—". . . how things are."

"*Things*? Things couldn't be better."

"Oh, that's good," he said. "Where's Ramsey at?" He looked around, as if Ramsey might've been hiding behind a tree.

"Your guess is as good as mine."

"Oh." He picked up a plastic cup in the grass that she'd missed. She opened the bag, and he tossed it in. "Need some help?"

"Actually, I could use some help moving these chairs." Before the party, Ramsey had carried rented folding chairs into the yard as well as several chairs from inside the house. Together, Wayne and Allie moved them all into the garage. Wayne carried four at a time. When they were done, back in the yard, Allie looked around. "One more favor?"

"Sure thing, Mrs. Miller."

"Will you cut the Mrs. Miller shit and just call me Allie?"

He said nothing. Too dark to see his face turn red.

"All this extra wood," she said, nodding toward the fire pit. "You mind helping me move it all back to the tree line? If we don't do it now, I know it'll still be here in a year."

"Okay, Allie," he said.

Several trips back and forth between the pit and the back edge of the yard, where the tall trees were.

"You're not much of a talker, are you?" Allie asked him after their fifth or sixth trip.

Wayne shrugged. "I don't always know what to say."

"Since when has that stopped anyone from talking?" she asked.

He smiled. No—definitely not a talker.

It was sweet, him checking up on her, but Wayne obviously wasn't the brains behind this particular operation. "So why didn't Eric come himself?" she asked.

He stacked some of the wood so it wasn't so haphazard. "Him and me and Paul were over at Jackrabbits, and I said I'd do it. I don't know. I guess I'm trying to be better."

She looked at him in the dark. "Better at what?"

He seemed to consider the question. "Just better. Like what Ramsey did."

"What are you talking about?"

337

"Used to be, he was a sonofabitch, the way he tells it. But he made himself better. Got himself a nice house and a family. He got you." Wayne shrugged. "I want what he has."

In the dark, she couldn't see where his own gaze fell. "Well, it was a decent thing to do," she said, "coming by. And you can assure all interested parties that I'm fine." Then she told herself to drop the phoniness. "Really, Wayne." She forced a smile. "I'm okay."

Wayne picked up another load of wood, and in the rear of the yard he dumped the logs onto the stack.

"You know, I skipped rehearsal on Friday because of you," he said.

"What do you mean?"

"I get nervous when I'm here. I think about you, and . . ." He paused, as if choosing his words carefully. "You're in my heart, Allie." He coughed. "That sounded so dumb. Listen, can I ask you something?"

*You're in my heart.* Her whole life, men had said things like that to her. And Wayne was right—it *was* dumb. But it was she who'd invited talk. And undoubtedly, this day had been strange for him, too—between Ramsey yammering on about the apocalypse and the police showing up and then him having to return to the house to make sure Ramsey hadn't beaten Allie senseless or drunk himself into a coma.

"All right, Wayne," she said. "What do you want to know?"

He sniffed once and nodded toward the stage. "What song do you think we played best?"

She laughed. "I thought they all sounded pretty good," she said.

"For real? Do you think?"

Typical man—why settle for one compliment when you can hear it repeated?

"I think you're a guitarist with a future," she said, and he looked away, embarrassed. "I think you've got big things ahead of you." She stepped closer, slowly—she had his attention now. He was youthful and very handsome, and *Just do it, Allie, for God's sake*, she said to herself, and put her arms around him.

The sensation of holding on to him nearly took her breath away. Wayne was not only tall, he was deceptively muscular in the shoulders and back, a surfer's body, and holding him was a wonderful, thrilling experience. He smelled like the outdoors, and he was boyish—not a kid, but a young man, and, yes, he reminded her a little of how it was with Ramsey when they were both so much younger and everything was full of possibility. She hugged him tightly, and it felt like exactly the right thing to do.

So did kissing him. She searched for his face in the dark and found this beautiful, youthful mouth, and he might've been naïve but he wasn't without experience, she discovered, because he kissed her back forcefully and without shame, his one hand on her cheek, her neck, then his arms around her back, a hand on her ass. She pressed into him, and he pressed back hard enough that she was pushed backward a step into one of the big oak trees, which provided support for her shaky legs. He lowered his head and bit her neck, and a soft moan escaped her.

Wayne stopped cold.

"This ain't right," he said.

"What? No—" Her face was hot. Her whole body. "Keep going." She stepped forward to kiss him again.

He stepped back.

"Wayne." Her breathing was labored. "Listen to me." Her eyes had adjusted to the dark by now, and she focused on his face. "This night has torn me apart. I can't handle another rejection right now. Can you understand that?"

Conveniently, he was back to being wordless.

"Listen," she said, "I guarantee I need you more than he does."

He backed up more. "I'm sorry, Mrs. Miller."

That's when she shoved him with all her might. He barely flinched.

"*Mrs. Miller!*" he said—same words, different tone.

The fucking nerve of this one. Innocent only when convenient.

"I said don't call me that!" She went to shove him again, but he was ready and blocked her hands. And she knew it was just him being nervous, but he smirked and laughed a little, and Allie could have killed him for it. She tried to punch him—anywhere: face, side, gut—but he was far too strong to be bothered and easily held his ground, and now with tears of shame her fury mounted, because it was so clear that she could neither hurt nor move him.

The longer her rage lasted, the more pitiful it became, until finally Wayne pushed her away. To him, it must have felt like nothing at all—flicking away a bug—but the shove sent her backward, off balance, knocking the back of her head into the hard trunk of the oak tree.

For a moment she was stunned. She worked to stay on her feet and make sense of what had just happened.

"Mrs. Miller, I didn't mean to."

She felt the back of her head: already, a large lump. "You son of a—" She blinked. Something wasn't right with her vision. The outlines of everything were off. She felt frightened, but less of Wayne than of what she realized Ramsey would do when he came home and found her injured. "Ramsey's going to kill you."

"No, he isn't," Wayne said. "Don't say that to me."

"So help me God, he is." This wasn't a threat, so much as fact. Despite everything that had happened tonight, she knew that Ramsey would protect her, always—and with as little nuance as he did everything else. Her fists had inspired no fear, but her words, her words . . . "He's going to make you pay."

"Shut up, Mrs. Miller. I mean it."

Despite her blurry vision, she saw the change come over him, his own terror mounting, then mutating. Hardening.

"Now, Wayne, you get out of—"

The second shove happened completely outside of time. One moment the two of them were standing several feet apart, and the next she was on her knees at the base of the tree. She wanted to move a hand to her head again, but for some reason she couldn't. The only sound was a low, low hum, as if the earth itself were shifting and cracking beneath her. Something was badly wrong. Wrecked. She tried to stand but couldn't. She would have cried out, screamed, wailed, but her voice was already beyond reach.

Wayne came toward her again, crouching low, and like before his hands moved toward her face, and like before his hands were on her throat, and like before their bodies were pressed so closely together they could have been dancing or making love.

# 27

September 29, 2006

Melanie was pleading with Officer Bauer to get Detective Isaac-son. She struggled to catch a breath while the officer left the room and pried the detective away from David Magruder. The moment the detective entered the office, Melanie blurted out, "He's talk-ing about my uncle Wayne. He was here at the hotel."

"Wayne is in Silver Bay?"

"I should have said something." Her whole body was shaking. "But I didn't know—" *The young one on guitar.* Magruder's words were blackening out everything else. "I thought—"

"Okay, try to relax." The detective put a hand on Melanie's arm. "What kind of car does he drive?"

"A black Ford Escort."

"Plate number?"

"I don't know."

"Did he go into your hotel room?"

She nodded. "That's where he was when I left to come here."

"What room number?"

She gave the number and handed her room key to the detective, who hurried away. But Melanie knew there was no need to rush. Wayne was long gone. She had left him at the hotel almost three hours earlier and practically dared him to run. By now, he'd be halfway across Pennsylvania. Or in Maryland. Or Connecticut. New York. Delaware. For someone whose whole life was centered around hiding, a three-hour head start was an eternity.

In the video monitor, David Magruder sat perfectly still in his chair, hunched over the table, head in hands.

Officer Bauer, perhaps feeling the need to fill the silence, began talking about procedure: "Officers will head to the hotel," he was saying. "If the suspect is still there, hopefully he'll surrender peacefully. Usually, people do. If he's not there, they'll put out a bulletin with the information about his car. More than likely, highway patrol will spot him heading back to West Virginia. Especially if he doesn't know he's being—"

"I need a bathroom," Melanie said. The image that Magruder had painted in her mind of Wayne strangling her mother overtook everything. "I'm going to throw up."

Officer Bauer led her quickly down the hallway, toward the station lobby. "I'll wait out here," he said, and Melanie barely made it into the stall before vomiting. She sat on the bathroom floor until the nausea subsided. Her throat screamed, and her headache had returned full force. When she felt steady enough on her feet, she went to the sink and splashed cold water on her face and cried and splashed more water. When she left the bathroom, the officer was waiting for her, and from the lobby she heard her name being called.

Phillip looked bedraggled and anxious. "What's going on?" he asked. "Are you okay?"

She was so completely not okay that she went to him and for a full minute all she could do was keep holding on, unable to speak. When she finally found her voice, she disregarded Detective Isaacson's directive to say nothing by saying everything.

No one seemed to care. One of the officers, a young woman, offered Melanie a bottle of water and joined the chorus of reassurance. The truth was finally out, everyone was telling her (word traveling quickly around the station), and Melanie could take solace in the knowledge that she was finally safe, finally free, and that the guilty would soon be brought to justice.

So well meaning, all of them, and so naïve.

Wayne had murdered her mother and let her father take the blame, and his disturbed version of atonement, apparently, was to kidnap Melanie and raise her. Yes, the truth was finally out, but where was the solace in a truth like that? And the worst part, she thought, sitting beside Phillip now on the wooden bench in the lobby and looking out the windows at the dark street, is that it had worked. All these years, Melanie had grown up feeling indebted to her mother's killer. All these years, she had felt loved, and she had felt love.

"Where's my father?" she said to Phillip.

"I don't know," he said.

"If he didn't . . ." She choked back a sob. "Where has he *been* all this time?"

He put an arm around her. "I don't know."

They sat there together saying little else, while across town a team of officers surrounded, then entered her hotel room. And when they finally radioed in, Officer Bauer knelt down and told Melanie what she already knew.

"Don't worry, though—we'll find him," he added, his words sounding so scripted that Melanie could only shake her head.

In the meantime, she wasn't allowed to return to her hotel room. Everything there was now evidence. "We can check you into another hotel," Officer Bauer said. "We aren't expecting it to be long, but I'm sure you could use some rest."

If she weren't exhausted and hurt in every way, she would have laughed at the officer's optimism.

Officer Bauer called ahead and reserved a room for Melanie and Phillip at the oceanfront Atlantic Hotel. After giving them directions, he wrote down Phillip's cell number and promised to be in touch the moment there was any word.

"And you should feel free to call the station anytime," he told the two of them.

"Okay," Melanie said.

"And check in with either me or Detective Isaacson in the morning, regardless."

What the hell for? Melanie thought. Despite everything that had happened and everything she had learned, her mother's killer was out there, same as before. Nothing had changed. Or rather, it was so much worse now. Ramsey Miller at least had the courtesy of being a bogeyman. But Uncle Wayne had handcrafted a puppet theater for her, a birthday present when she'd turned six, with shiny gold curtains that opened and closed when you pulled a string. He made the puppets himself, too, out of foam and felt and yarn—a pig and a frog. He watched her endless performances. When she asked, he would play the frog. Or the pig. His pig voice made her laugh. For some reason it had a British accent. Later, for other presents in other years, he added to the menagerie. A horse. A wolf.

"Melanie? Will you do that?"

"Sorry?" Melanie asked.

"Will you call one of us in the morning?"

"Oh," she said. "Sure. Whatever."

346

\* \* \*

The police station sat on a lonely side street between a tire store and a plasma donation center. Everything was closed at this hour, and only a handful of cars were parked along the curb.

Melanie walked beside Phillip toward his car, her arms crossed for warmth. It had stopped raining but remained dreary. The sidewalk and street were wet. They had passed the tire store when Melanie's peripheral vision caught movement near one of the parked cars—someone coming their way. By the time she turned around, Wayne had a hand on her arm and was saying, "Come on—let's go."

She yanked herself free. "Get away from me!"

"Mr. Denison." Phillip approached Wayne. "Leave her alone."

"You?" Wayne dismissed him with a head shake. "Melanie, I waited for you, but there's no time now. Please—you have to trust me."

When he reached out to take her arm again she tried to pull away, but his grip was firm. Phillip grabbed her body and got her away from Wayne, and then stood in front of her, creating a barrier, protecting her body with his own.

"Now listen, don't you come one step—" Phillip started to say, but he never finished the sentence, because Wayne smashed his face with a lightning-fast punch and he stumbled backward into Melanie.

A second punch caught Phillip in the gut when he was already teetering, and then he was thrown to the ground—where he was headed, anyway. He hit the wet pavement with a thud and curled into himself.

"Damn it, we don't have time for this," Wayne said, and motioned to his car. "Now *please*, honey, let's go—we have to get out of this town."

Melanie was on her haunches, a hand on Phillip's face, trying

347

to get a look at him without taking her eyes off Wayne, whose face was full of anguish. He should have been long gone by now, and she couldn't understand why he would have stayed behind. How could he think she'd go with him? Of course—he had no idea that Melanie knew the whole truth. And where the hell were the cops? For God's sake, the station was *right there.*

"If you scream," Wayne said, reading her mind, "I swear to God I'll bust his head in."

"I know you will," she said, terrified but enraged, too. Because that's what he did. He killed the people who loved her. *"Murderer."*

"What?" He shook his head. "No. No—don't say that. It's not—"

"Someone saw you."

He froze for a moment. "You don't know anything about it. Who? Who said he—"

"David Magruder. He saw you in the backyard, choking her. He saw you kill her."

"You're gonna believe *that* guy?" A police siren wailed in the distance, someone else's tragedy. "No, your mind's been poisoned, honey—it's this goddamn town."

"No. It's you. You did it." She wasn't even trying to make him believe her. She was saying it because it was true. And yet she wanted him to deny it again. The longer he denied it, the longer a tiny part of her could deny it, too.

"It was . . . I was just a kid." His gaze shifted, and it seemed to Melanie that he was no longer seeing her or this street. "I never meant to."

Hearing Wayne's admission made all the breath escape her body as if she'd been the one he'd stomach-punched.

"You killed my mother," she said, unsteadily, trying out the words. They seemed to bring Wayne back to the present, to this cold wet night.

"I gave you a home," he said. "I raised you right."

"You didn't."

"Of course I did!" He looked deeply hurt. He must have been repeating that refrain to himself for years. *I'm giving her a home. I'm raising her right.* Maybe that was how he slept at night. "I loved you like—"

"Don't you use that word."

"It's true. And look at you now—so beautiful and smart."

"I fucking hate you," Melanie said.

"You don't. Don't say that."

Phillip let out a groan. When Melanie glanced down at him, he said, "I think I'm okay." But he wasn't. Blood pooled under him.

"Come with me," Wayne said. "You know you're not staying here with him." Wayne could have left town the minute she got into that police car back at the hotel. He must have known that the longer he stayed, the greater the risk. By now he could have been hundreds of miles away. Yet he had stayed for her. Did he really expect her to go home with him again? Return to Fredonia? Live under his roof? Or did he think the two of them would escape into the night, find some new place to disappear? It was terrifying to think he might be that deluded, but even scarier was the possibility that he didn't know *what* he wanted from her, just that he had to have her because she'd always been his.

"I'm staying with Phillip," she said.

He shook his head sadly. "Oh, Mel—this isn't the good-bye I wanted." For an instant she felt positive he was about to reach for her throat, do to her what he'd done to her mother. Instead, he backed up a step toward his car. "You're going to let me go, and when I'm gone you're going to help your boyfriend get to his car. You'll leave with him. You'll both leave town tonight and won't come back. Not ever. You'll do that for me, Melanie."

"I won't do anything for you." Another glance toward the front of the police station, where absolutely no fucking officers were coming or going.

"Don't be a brat, Melanie," he said, voice rising. Then it softened again. "If the cops find out from you that I stuck around, I'll still get away. You know I will. You know I can hide. But I'll come looking for you both."

"You love me, but you would—" He caught her eye, and she stopped talking because she could see that yes, he did, and yes, he would. She shivered.

"This isn't hard," he said. "If you ever loved me even a little, you'll let me drive away. Let me go, and you're free. It's the freedom you always wanted." Three more steps toward his car. "Now promise you'll let me go."

She held his gaze for a couple of long seconds.

"Go," she said.

"*Melanie*," Phillip said.

"Good girl," Wayne said. Five more steps. He'd almost reached the car. "Melanie?"

"What."

"Tell me you love me."

She almost screamed right then, and biting her lower lip hard enough to draw blood probably saved Phillip's life. She gritted her teeth and, still looking at Wayne, forced the words out. "I love you, Uncle Wayne," she said.

For an instant, his face softened.

Then he got into his car. It started right up. His cars always did.

She watched him drive away, and then she was alone with Phillip on the wet street.

"Can I leave you here a minute?" she asked.

"Melanie, how could you let him—"

"It'll only be a minute. Is that okay?"

A raspy breath. "Where do you think I'm gonna go?"

In the station, she hurried through the lobby, past the dispatcher, and shouted for help. When Officer Bauer appeared, she said, "Wayne was just out front, and he drove away in a tan Honda Accord with New Jersey plates—BZM-18A. He turned left on the far side of that bar. And Phillip is hurt outside. He needs help, and something to stop the bleeding—a rag or paper towels. I'll be out there with him."

She said it all with the calm efficiency of a pro. And then she left the station.

When she woke up, the room was dark but a door was cracked open to a lit hallway. Then she remembered. Hospital. She lay on a narrow folding cot beside Phillip's bed. Half his face was bandaged. The one exposed eye was shut. She listened for his breathing, and when she heard it she reached out and found his hand under his sheet and gently squeezed. No response. So he was either asleep or heavily sedated. Those two punches had done a job on him, the doctor told her. Broken eye socket. Ruptured spleen.

It had taken the police just minutes to spot Wayne's car and arrest him. So in that way, Wayne had been right—for the first time, she was free. Yet lying there in the dark, with all the strength she'd demonstrated in the police station now gone, all the adrenaline depleted, she felt sad and guilty and overwhelmed—homesick, but with no home to root the emotion to. She held on to Phillip's hand, and that made it better, though it wasn't enough. Maybe someday it would be. But right now she was seventeen years old and she wanted her mother. And for the first time, she wanted her father, too.

# 28

September 23, 1991

Ramsey Miller awoke in panic, heart racing: *I fell asleep while driving!*

But no. The boom he'd heard—felt—was no head-on collision, but thunder. The deep sway was no deadly truck roll at 80 m.p.h., but a wave moving his boat. And boats were made to roll.

As he assessed his actual situation—*on my boat, in the ocean*—another wave blasted the boat, sending it rolling again. Lightning splintered overhead like shards of a giant windshield, giving Ramsey a couple of seconds to take in the whipping ocean, to notice the absence of stars, and to understand the magnitude of the storm that had moved in while he slept. Understanding came just seconds before the rain began—almost as if his understanding had caused the rain to start.

The fucking weatherman. Though still shaking off sleep, Ramsey could see the comedy in it: The fucking weatherman had it right all along.

The narrow band of man-made light—land—was clear enough to the east, but he had no idea how far his boat might have drifted. He wasn't even sure how long he'd been asleep, though the sharp pain in his neck from lying against the seat suggested hours, not minutes. He didn't like the idea of being in a metal boat during a storm, but that fact was nonnegotiable, so he put electrocution out of his mind and leaned over the engine to pull the starter. Not easy, given the boat's swaying, but on the third try the little engine revved to life.

The rain fell in torrents, carried by gale-force winds. Lightning and thunder intensified into the sort of storm that made you say "Holy shit" even from inside your house. But the waves were his concern. The flat-bottom boat wasn't made for this. He'd turn into the waves if he could tell where they were coming from, but they seemed to come from everywhere. So he headed east, toward shore. Too far away to recognize any landmarks, but he'd deal with his position once he got closer. The main thing was to get moving.

The wave that knocked him overboard came out of nowhere, a huge roller that sent the boat onto its side. Ramsey hit the water and forced his head to the surface so he'd keep sight of the dark boat in the dark water. At first he couldn't spot it. Then, as he rose on a wave, he saw it bobbing in the water fifteen feet away: to the west, he thought, but couldn't be sure. The fall into the ocean had sent him spinning, and with only his head above water now, he could no longer see the shoreline. He could see nothing at all except the wave in front of him.

He swam toward the boat, but when he rose again he was dismayed to see that the boat's position had shifted. He should swim east, to shore. But which way was east? He had a sense. Yet he *might* be able to catch the boat, which, without his hand on the throttle, seemed to move in a wide arc. If he swam toward where the boat might end up—

Another wave pounded him, and when he surfaced he could no longer find the boat. He turned in a circle. Which way was east? His waterlogged clothes pulled at him. He tried to kick off his shoes but ended up with another mouthful of water and a frantic race back to the surface. He needed to find east. The boat would keep moving but the shore would not. Swim to shore. Which way was the shore?

Ramsey was a strong swimmer. The water wasn't cold. The storm would let up.

Another wave knocked him under. Which way was up?

He surfaced again but no air came, only a hack, and more rain, and he vomited something sour, and when his mouth dipped below the surface again, that's when the first full intake of seawater came, and that's when the first full moment of understanding came.

And although he was drowning horribly in the pitch dark, surrounded by nothing and no one, anyone watching would have been proud to know Ramsey Miller, who did not give up.

# 29

## Alive and Wrong

*December 26, 2006 * by Arthur Goodale * in Uncategorized*

"That's how we know we're alive: we're wrong."

So wrote the novelist Philip Roth in his Pulitzer Prize–winning novel *American Pastoral*, which I read when it was published a decade ago. I remember that sentence striking me as surprising and provocative when I first read it, and over the years it has stuck with me. But only recently have I come to appreciate its insight. We spend our lives trying to understand the hearts of those around us and the actions those hearts inspire, and we get it wrong, wrong, wrong.

Because let me say this now: I was wrong about everything.

I knew—absolutely *knew*—that Ramsey Miller had killed his wife.

I knew that Meg Miller was dead.

I knew that the Miller case, my self-declared white whale, would remain open, at least during my lifetime.

And on a more personal note: I knew, twelve weeks ago, that I was dying, my bad habits finally overtaking my acceptable genetics.

Every bit of it, wrong.

As you've probably noticed, this is the first post since my macabre musings of September 22. I'd have thought that recent events would motivate me to write a flurry of posts about the Miller case as well as my own road to recovery. Not so. (Wrong again, self!) In fact, I haven't felt the urge to write at all. More to the point—after this entry, I plan to abandon the blog altogether. If I decide to resume it someday, then so be it. But I don't think I will, now that the blog's purpose has been fulfilled.

For three years I believed I was casting my private musings into a vast and swirling world, when in fact I was reaching out to Meg.

I just didn't know it.

Nonetheless, my blog did attract 75 of you along the way, and I owe you some facts:

1. I did not die. : )

(Until this very moment, I have never in my life used an emoticon. Let that, my loyal readers, tell you something about the vicissitudes of old age.)

More precisely, if I was dying that weekend in September, I'm not dying anymore. The doctors demanded that I change my lifestyle, and that's what I've done. You should see me eating oatmeal. You should see me eating fish. Also, after two-thirds of a century, I finally quit cigarettes back in October. Cold turkey. Boy, has that been a horror show. I've become an irritable SOB—but an SOB who walks the boardwalk five mornings a week and who no longer becomes winded climbing the stairs.

2. Wayne Denison pled guilty to the second-degree murder of Allison Miller and the first-degree kidnapping of Meg Miller.

Details from his confession can be found in any number of newspaper accounts. But a friend on the Silver Bay police force who shall remain anonymous did me the favor of showing me the actual document. After killing Allison Miller, Wayne Denison evidently abducted young Meg and drove her straight to West Virginia, where he convinced his girlfriend to look after her, and returned immediately—that same night—to New Jersey in order to feign surprise around plenty of witnesses when Allison's body was found the next morning.

Quite a different story from what he told police fifteen years ago—that he left Jackrabbits bar at 10:45 and drove straight home to his apartment. His earlier story was corroborated by his downstairs neighbor, who swore he saw Wayne entering the apartment—an alibi that we now know was purchased for the price of three marijuana cigarettes. In the days leading up to Allison's funeral, Wayne dropped hints at work that he'd become disillusioned—after all, Ramsey, a man he'd looked up to, had apparently murdered his own family in cold blood. When Wayne quit his job and left town shortly after Allie's funeral, nobody thought much of it. He returned to West Virginia, reunited with Kendra and Meg, and the three of them disappeared together, this new family that would remain in hiding for the next fifteen years.

In exchange for his guilty plea, Wayne was spared a first-degree murder charge. He is now serving forty years with no chance of parole in the U.S. penitentiary in Allenwood, PA. Kendra Denison claimed that she had been duped by Wayne all these years into believing that she was lawfully protecting Meg (who has grown up using the name Melanie). Prosecutors found Kendra's story hard to believe but reduced the charge to second-degree kidnapping in exchange for testifying against her husband. She was sentenced to ten years in a federal correctional institution. She is currently serving her term in Cumberland, MD, and will be eligible for parole in five years.

3. Regarding the many news stories praising David Magruder's investigative prowess as instrumental in cracking the long-cold case and leading the police to the proper suspect, I have only this to say: Don't believe everything you read.

4. Ramsey Miller's whereabouts remain unknown.

Yesterday, I ate Christmas dinner with Melanie and Phillip Connor. Like every time Melanie has invited me into their home, I felt uncomfortable and intrusive on the drive over, until the moment their front door opened and I realized there was nowhere I'd rather be. This time there was another guest as well, Eric Pace, whom I failed to recognize from our few conversations years earlier. He was physically larger than I'd remembered, yet somehow diminished. We had nothing in common save our mutual affection for our hosts, but that was enough.

Eric hadn't yet seen Phillip's scar, a fact that Phillip remedied by lifting up his shirt at the dinner table and recounting what happened on the sidewalk outside the police station on the night of September 29. He used phrases like *My body was her shield* and *In a fair fight, I'd have*. . . . Having now heard the story on a few separate occasions, I will note only that Phillip's role in the narrative seems to increase in drama and heroism with each telling.

"Your face was highly effective against his fist," Melanie added.

Good for them, I found myself thinking, for tinting a tragic moment with comedy in the retelling so they can move beyond it.

It would be impossible for me to gush properly about the Connors or for me to enumerate all the reasons why I tear up so easily in their presence—especially now that Melanie is well into her pregnancy and visibly showing. Suffice it to say that I ate too much last night, stayed too late, and went to bed feeling immensely grateful and lucky.

After sleeping late this morning, something I rarely do anymore, I awoke with that line from Roth's novel in my head and went to my bookshelf to discover that it's actually part of a much longer passage that includes the following:

*That's how we know we're alive: we're wrong. Maybe the best thing would be to forget being right or wrong about people and just go along for the ride. But if you can do that—well, lucky you.*

I'd like to say that from now on I'll live my life that way—content with being along for the ride. Trouble is, I've had an entire lifetime to practice being wrong. I don't know if I can stop this late in the game. So let me close out this post, and this blog, by saying the following:

Melanie Connor—formerly Melanie Denison, formerly Meg Miller—rose from the dead, sought me out, and became my friend. That will always be one of the great joys of my life.

About that, I know I'm not wrong.

*Posted by Old Man with Typewriter at 12/26/2006 5:42 PM | Comments are enabled.*

# 30

June 17, 2009

Eight a.m. and already a scorcher. Soon the slides will all be too hot to ride.

Melanie sits on the park bench while her daughter climbs and slides, climbs and slides, and monologues a nonstop jumble of songs and stories that Melanie can only half follow.

The two of them are alone in the park. All the other young children in town are either later sleepers or their mothers are less desperate than Melanie to start burning off excess energy.

Phillip is at the high school administering final exams to restless seniors. If the weather holds, the three of them might head to the beach in the afternoon.

"One more, sweetie," Melanie calls to Brianna, who turned three in April. They named her Brianna—Brianna Allison Connor —because the name is trendy and other girls have it. Melanie wants her daughter to have many things in common with other children.

"Two more!" Brianna shouts back.

In not so long, Brianna will have a sister, or brother. Melanie peed on the stick this morning, and plans to tell Phillip tonight after Brianna goes to bed. If Melanie can hold on to the secret that long. She's out of practice keeping secrets.

"Okay—two more," Melanie says. "And then we'll feed the turtles."

There are newer, better parks in town, but this one has Turtle Pond. Melanie always enjoys coming here with her daughter, knowing that she used to come here with her mother. And with her father, who is out there somewhere.

After Wayne and Kendra were arrested and briefly made national news, Melanie kept waiting for her father to return. She would scan the faces of men she saw in town, hoping for that flicker of recognition. At night she dreamt that she was still living with Wayne and Kendra in Fredonia, imprisoned in their trailer, and Ramsey would find her there and set her free.

Her home phone number was listed. Her address was listed. Her information was there for the taking. He could have found her if he wanted. But as the weeks and months passed and the media moved on to other stories, Melanie began to accept that her father had chosen to remain hidden. He had been a fugitive for fifteen years, and it must have been agonizing for him, knowing he was innocent but that everyone had already convicted him. By now he must have started a new life somewhere and decided that, all things considered, the best choice was to keep living it.

Still, Melanie wishes he'd return. There will always be a light on for him. But that's his decision.

She has decisions to make, too. She is enrolled part time at the community college but is still too many credits away from graduating. Her major—journalism—is a dying field, she's coming to find. Or at least it's shifting too quickly for her academic courses to adjust. Lately, she's been thinking of something completely different: enrolling in the police academy. At first it was only a fleeting thought, but she's warming to the idea. When she floated it to Phillip a couple of months ago, he shrugged and said, "Well, you're tough enough."

She agrees with him—she *is* tough, but not tough enough to join the force while she's pregnant or has a newborn. She can wait a couple of years, she supposes.

"Okay, kiddo," she says to Brianna. "Last one."

"Then the turtles!"

"That's right."

Silver Bay is hers now. She hasn't returned to Fredonia and knows she never will. She visited Kendra, once, in prison in Maryland early on in her sentence. There were things Melanie wanted to know.

*I was so young,* Kendra said into the phone receiver on the opposite side of the thick glass divider, *and I loved him so much. He kept me safe when we were in foster care and made sure I didn't get it too bad. When he left for New Jersey, I fell apart. I spent two months crying. Three years, he was away—I saw him a few times, but he seemed older. He was tougher. Then he came back all of a sudden. And he needed me so badly.*

Kendra sobbed into the telephone the whole time she spoke.

*But all those years,* Melanie said. *My whole life—you were never suspicious?*

*He had those letters from the Marshal's office. And why would I doubt him? Why would I try to wreck our family?*

Almost immediately, Melanie realized it was foolish to have driven the three hours expecting an honest look into Kendra's heart when Kendra herself was unwilling to look there. A full minute passed without either of them saying anything.

Melanie tried again: *But how could you never even wonder?*

Anger flashed in Kendra's eyes. *I could ask you the same thing,* she said. Then she began to weep again.

The visit was scheduled to last a half hour, but after twenty awkward minutes, Melanie stood up to leave, and Kendra said, pleadingly, *When are you going to visit me again? You have to tell me when.* Her eyes were shot through with red. Melanie left the prison knowing little more than she knew before coming, and with no better sense of in what proportion to feel hatred or pity for the woman who had raised her.

It doesn't matter, Melanie told herself then and has continued to remind herself. I'm home now. This is my home.

The beach, the bay, the roads, the neighborhoods, the shops and restaurants. The schools and cemeteries. At some point this week she'll visit the cemetery off Cedar Lane, where her mother is buried and where Melanie does her best thinking. Should she try to become a police officer? she'll ask her mother. Then she'll ask Arthur Good-ale, who is buried there, too. She'll leave flowers by both graves. She tries to make a point of doing that regularly, though she often goes too long between visits. With a young child, everything is hard.

How hard it must have been for her mother, she often thinks, with her father away so much of the time. Phillip goes to Atlantic City for the New Jersey teachers' convention just two nights each fall, and she always dreads it.

But it must have been hard for her father, too, being away, knowing he was missing all those small moments that transform a child every day, it seems. She wishes that Ramsey could meet his granddaughter, get to know her. But if he were going to reach out, he'd have done it by now. She knows that. She also knows that her father might not be alive. Yet she chooses to believe Eric's assessment. Since her return to Silver Bay, Eric has introduced her to a side of her father that was unavailable in any newspaper, the side of him that explained why he once had friends and a wife who loved him and a daughter who did, too. So she chooses to believe, as Eric does, that Ramsey Miller is too stubborn to die, and is still out there somewhere.

Of the several scenarios that she imagines for her father—he has a new, adoring family; he works as a mechanic in the mountains, maybe Colorado; he drives a big rig under an alias—here is what she always comes back to.

Somewhere outside of the United States, maybe in Panama or Costa Rica, a quiet man with a slight limp rents out his small fishing boat for day trips. He has a kind face and is the most mild-mannered man anyone has ever met, and although he's only in his fifties, he seems much older. He never misses a day of work unless the ocean is very rough. Each night, he returns home to his cabin in the woods, away from everyone and everything. He pours himself a single drink, looks up at the stars, and thinks about his wife and daughter with nothing but fondness and light.

To Melanie's surprise, after going down the slide one more time, Brianna comes right over and takes her hand.

"Did you remember the bread?" Brianna asks. (Three weeks ago, Melanie forgot the bread, an oversight that caused a full-on tantrum.)

Melanie removes the zip-lock bag from her purse. "Right here."

Brianna drops Melanie's hand and runs toward the footbridge, stopping at the center. Melanie follows her, and when they're together on the wooden bridge they both look over the railing.

"There's one!" Brianna says. A small turtle is sunning on a branch sticking out of the shallow water. Moments later, a second turtle swims their way. The turtles know. For years, decades, people have been feeding them from this footbridge. Now, all you have to do is stand on the bridge and the turtles begin to gather.

Melanie removes the slice of bread from the zip-lock bag and hands it to Brianna, saying, "Remember—small pieces."

Brianna breaks off a corner and tosses it over the railing and into the water.

The second turtle swims closer, jerks its head forward, and grabs the bread. Brianna breaks off a few more pieces and throws them into the water as more turtles gather. As always, the turtles multiply, until there are fifteen, twenty, thirty, of every size. The largest are probably forty pounds and almost certainly swam this pond before Melanie was born.

By now the turtles are churning up the water only a few feet below. It's a little unnerving, all those prehistoric creatures jockeying for bits of stale bread, furiously snapping and climbing over one another. But Brianna isn't afraid.

She feeds the turtles one small piece of bread at a time. And when a third of the slice is left, the massive head of one of the largest, oldest snapping turtles rises above the surface.

"Look, Brianna!" Melanie points. "Over there."

There are probably only three or four turtles this large and old in the whole pond. They're so heavy that usually only their heads rise out of the murk. But something about the sunlight this morning, the early hour, makes more of the shell visible—faded green and splotched with moss. The animal is easily sixty pounds and as many years old.

"Look at it!" Brianna beams. She knows this is a rare sight. All the locals know it.

"Why don't you give him the whole piece," Melanie says.

"*All* of it?" asks Brianna.

Melanie nods. So Brianna holds what remains of the bread over the railing—tentatively, with beautiful anticipation—before letting it fall down to the water. A perfect drop, it lands inches from the turtle's head, which shoots forward and back again like a cobra's strike, the bread vanishing in its jaws, and then the old animal drops beneath the surface and is gone.

# Acknowledgments

I couldn't imagine a better team than agent Jody Kahn and editor Otto Penzler; I am incredibly grateful to them and routinely amazed. My sincere thanks to those who read the novel in manuscript form and helped to make it better: Catherine Pierce (a.k.a. Katie), Felice Kardos, Michael Piafsky, Christopher Coake, and Sarah Reeder. Thanks to Captain Ron Albence (Ret.) and Sergeant Laura Hines Roberson for their help with police procedure, and to Julie Kardos, Stephen Kardos, and Tracey McKinnon for guiding me through hospital logistics. Any mistakes are mine, though any mistakes will invariably be dismissed with a coy smile and an utterance about artistic license. I am thankful for the marvelous support and camaraderie of the faculty, students, and administrators at Mississippi State University. Thanks to Carl Pierce for his immense generosity in allowing his town of Rehoboth, Delaware—where much of this book was written—to become ours, and thanks to John and Judy Rioux for my table at Gallery Espresso. Finally, one more thanks to Katie, whom I couldn't have done this without and wouldn't have wanted to.

# THE THREE IMPOSSIBLES

By the time she hit her teens, **Susie Bower** had lived in 8 houses and attended 7 schools. This theme continued in her working life: she's been a teacher, a tour-guide, a typist, a workshop facilitator, a PA and a painter. She formerly wrote and directed TV programmes for children at the BBC and Channel 4, for which she won a BAFTA Award, and she currently writes audio scripts. *School for Nobodies*, her debut novel, is also available from Pushkin Children's. Susie lives in Bristol.

# THE THREE IMPOSSIBLES

## SUSIE BOWER

PUSHKIN CHILDREN'S

Pushkin Press
71–75 Shelton Street
London WC2H 9JQ

*The Three Impossibles* was first published by Pushkin Press in 2021

1 3 5 7 9 8 6 4 2

ISBN 13: 978-1-78269-292-8

Epigraph from Michael Rosen originally appeared in the *Guardian* on
28 June 2020. Reprinted with kind permission of the author.

Designed and typeset by Tetragon, London

Printed and bound by CPI Group (UK) Ltd, Croydon, CR0 4YY

www.pushkinpress.com

*For Jamie*
*with love*

'"Be curious" is the best advice I've ever been given. It came from my dad. He also said: "Be bold". I think that was quite useful.'

—MICHAEL ROSEN

'It always seems impossible until it's done.'

—NELSON MANDELA

# HAPPY CURSE DAY

**B**ONGHHHHHH...

The tolling of the bell echoes round the stone walls of my bedroom in the castle. It will ring twenty-four times, like it does on this day, every year. Once for each hour of Curse Day.

It's the twenty-first of December, the winter solstice. The darkest, shortest day, when you wake in the dark, and the dark creeps up on you in the middle of the afternoon and clings to you all night.

Also, it's my eleventh birthday.

Shivering, I throw back the thin blanket and, sitting on the edge of my bed, grope in the dark for the stub of candle on the rickety chair. With icy fingers, I strike a match. Nothing happens for a moment, then a blue-yellow flame creeps along the wick, opening up the room like a book, with its empty walls and curtainless window. My comfy old trousers and holey jumper aren't on the chair where I dropped them last night. Foggy must have come in while I was asleep and hung them in the cupboard. She never knocks, which is why I hide things. (I've hidden the book

9

I'm reading—*Volcanoes*—under my bed.) But at least my slippers are where I left them.

I creak open the cupboard door.

All my clothes are gone.

'Foggy!' I yell. 'FOGGY!!!'

The sound of the bell tolling is the only reply.

I grab the blanket from my bed and wrap it tightly round my shoulders. Then I pad to the castle window and scratch at the frost on the glass with my fingernail, clearing a patch big enough to see out.

Icicles hang from the lintel in cold spears. Last night I sat shivering at the window for two whole hours, watching and waiting for the exact, magic moment when the dripping water would turn into ice. But Foggy came in *right* before it happened and groused at me for not being asleep. I told her I had an Enquiring Mind and she sniffed, muttering that curiosity killed cats.

*BONGHHHHHH...*

Below my window, the castle courtyard glistens with frost. And beyond that, the path—which runs right round the inside of the Great Wall—lies in deep shadow. Father built the Wall, thirty feet high, around our town to protect us from the Outside. Set into the Wall is the Gate—closed, the way it always is. A flag hangs at half-mast from the flagpole, like it does every Curse Day. Beyond the grounds of the castle, the cobbled streets of the little town of Galena are silent and empty, shrouded in darkness, and the low buildings hunch against the cold. No one's supposed to leave their house on Curse Day.

Further along the path, just beyond the Gate, a small stone building is built against the Great Wall. That's the forge, its single window glowing from the furnace inside. A lantern hangs from a metal hook; its dim, glimmering light falls over the rickety wooden platform outside the forge. The light shines down on the executioner's block, with its gleaming axe.

A mountain of a man, wearing only a vest and trousers, stands on the platform: his huge black arms strain at the bell rope, his breath sends smoke into the air and dreadlocks start from his head like electric shocks. The bell is bronze, half the size of Smith himself, and made by his father.

I rap hard on the window, though Smith is much too far away to hear. But somehow he turns, raises one arm with a black armband, and gives a Happy-Birthday-Mim sort of wave. A flicker of warmth tickles my heart. Sam Smith's my best friend—my *only* friend—in the world.

The cold from the stone floor has seeped through the soles of my slippers, so I jump up and down a few times to get the life back in my feet. Then the door flies open and in marches Foggy, carrying a pair of shoes and a long black dress.

'Was that *you*, Miss Jemima, yelling in that coarse manner? On this day, of all days? And *what* are those feet doing, stamping about in such an uncouth way?'

Every Curse Day, Foggy gets gloomier and tighter-lipped and snarkier, and the dank cloud she always seems to carry round with her becomes even chillier and clammier. For the thousandth time, I wish I had a proper mother,

11

instead of a Foggy. But my real mother died on Curse Day, on the day I was born, and Foggy took over; first as nanny, then as governess. And I might just as well be an orphan, since Father spends most of his time shut away in his rooms.

'*Mim*,' I correct her, like I always do. I hate being called 'Miss Jemima'. 'And I'm stamping my feet to keep warm. Where are my clothes?'

Foggy glares at me through her thick spectacles. She looks even more like a crow than usual today. Everyone wears a black armband on Curse Day, only Foggy wears black all over, from the moth-eaten muffler around her neck right down to her thick black stockings and her black scuffed boots. She's exactly the same height as me, which means I get a close-up of her red nose and the drop of water hanging from it. Will that turn into an icicle too? She gives a sharp sniff, and it leaps back inside her nostril, probably grateful to get out of the cold.

'Look sharp, Miss Jemima. Wash the sleep out of your eyes. And brush that bird's nest hair!'

Foggy throws the dress onto the bed. It's shiny and thin-looking, nothing like my usual patched-up, comfy things.

'What's that? Where are *my* clothes?'

Foggy scrapes her hair behind her ears and pulls a spotted handkerchief from her sleeve. She blows her nose with a mighty honk, then she pulls off her misted-up spectacles and fixes me with a watery eye.

'Today is your eleventh birthday, Miss Jemima.'

'I *know* that,' I mutter. 'Only no one else seems to.'

Foggy ignores this. She ignores pretty much *everything* I say.

'His Majesty'—her eyes go all dreamy and gooey like they always do when she mentions Father—'wishes to see you.'

'Father? Why?' Father never usually sees me. Sometimes I wonder if it's because I remind him of my dead mother.

'Apparently he has a special gift for you.' Foggy sniffs again, as if gifts are something to be suspicious of.

'A gift? For my birthday?' My heart gives a little jump, and my feet do too. 'What is it? Is it... could it be...?' I hardly dare say the words 'telescope' or 'globe of the world'.

'The sooner you're washed and respectable,' snaps Foggy, 'the sooner you'll find out.'

The water in the basin is iced over. I use my toothbrush to break it. Taking a deep breath, I plunge in my hands and wet my face as quickly as I can, drying it with the threadbare towel which hangs on a hook beside the basin. Then I dip my toothbrush in the water and shove it into my mouth. My teeth jump and throb like it's an ice cube, which it nearly is.

'Get a move on, Miss Jemima, and get dressed.'

'*Mim.*' I turn to the dress lying on my lumpy pillow and pick it up. It's cold too, and thin, made of black silk.

'Why have I got to wear this? Is it because of seeing Father? Or because of Curse Day?'

'Please stop calling it Curse Day and give it its proper title.' Foggy's lips tighten into a thin line. 'The Day of the Catastrophic Curse. And you ask too many questions, Miss Jemima. Try to show some restraint, on this of all days.'

'It's not my fault there are so many secrets.'

Foggy glares at me. 'That's *enough*, Miss Jemima.'

Living in a castle of secrets is like playing a game of hide-and-seek that never ends: you know the person you're seeking is near, maybe even close enough to touch, but you can't ever find them. You glimpse pale shapes, or catch the whisper of a voice, but if you reach out to touch them, they're gone.

I know that my mother died on the day that I was born, on Curse Day. But I don't know how she died, or why. That's the first secret.

After that, Father built the Great Wall right around Galena—a Wall so high I've never seen over it. People say that beyond the Wall live the Outsiders, but who they are and why Father shut them out is another secret.

One day I shall find out. I wasn't born with an Enquiring Mind for nothing. I've asked and asked, but grown-ups are full of cunning ways to avoid telling you what you want to know. Father does it by locking himself away. Foggy does it by ignoring my questions or telling me off. Even Smith, who I tell everything to, won't give me the answers to these secrets.

I slip the black dress over my head. It slithers over my skin like an icy waterfall and spreads out, way past my toes, over the floor. I poke my arms into the sleeves. They are long and tight to my elbows, then they flare out like trumpets and cover my hands. The back of the dress gapes open and I grope about behind me, searching for a zip. There are rows and rows of buttons and hooks instead. I fumble at them.

'Will you *never* learn dexterity?' Foggy wrenches the material out of my hands and begins to do up the buttons. I can hardly breathe. 'We have no time to waste. His Majesty must not be kept waiting.' The higher she fastens, the less room there seems to be for *me* in the dress.

'It's too small,' I tell her.

'The dress is not too small,' Foggy snaps, buttoning, hooking and squeezing. 'You are too *big*.'

'I don't see how,' I mutter. 'There's never enough to eat.'

'Impertinent child!' Foggy sniffs and a cold drip lands on the back of my neck. 'His Majesty has fed and clothed you for eleven long years. Under extremely difficult circumstances.'

'Since Curse Day? I mean, the Day of the Catastrophic Curse?' I try to roll up the trumpet sleeves, but they unroll immediately. 'Foggy, what exactly happened on—'

'*Miss Fogarty*, if you please!' Foggy hands me the pair of shoes. 'Put these on.'

The dress is so long I can't see my toes. I hoist it up, then push my feet into the shoes. For the first time in my life, I'm wearing high heels. I stand up—and nearly topple over. Everything is wrong and off balance. My chest is squashed against my backbone, my hands are smothered by the trumpet sleeves and my toes feel like they're diving head first at the floor. No wonder grown-ups look so miserable, even when it isn't Curse Day, if they have to wear clothes like this! I can't wait to get the meeting with Father over, and go back to my own comfy, scruffy clothes.

**BONGHHHHHH...**

That must be twenty-four bells. Soon, Smith will go back into the heat of his forge and busy himself with the bellows and the furnace.

'Here.' Foggy hands me a black armband, and I shove it up my arm.

As the echoes of the final bell settle into the castle walls, there's a strange, ominous silence, as if the castle's waiting for something to happen.

On Curse Day, that something isn't likely to be good.

# THE FIRST DAY OF THE
# REST OF YOUR LIFE

'Enter.'

Father's thin, finicky voice calls from inside the throne room. Foggy pats her hair, sniffs, straightens her skirts and pushes me inside ahead of her. I almost trip in the high-heeled shoes and grab at Foggy's muffler to steady myself. She gives a strangled yelp and tugs it free.

Of all the buildings in Galena, our castle is the coldest and the emptiest. Most of its rooms are shabby and cold, with crumbling plaster, leaky windows, white squares on the walls where paintings once hung, and empty spaces on the bare flagstones, where grand furniture used to stand. But the throne room is warm. Logs crackle in a fireplace big enough for half a dozen people to sit inside it. Jewel-coloured carpets lie soft on the floor.

The first thing I look for is the painting, just to make sure it's still here. The paint's cracked and faded. It shows the ocean, with a ship sailing on it. I've never seen the ocean in real life, but I know it's right outside the Great

Wall because I hear it roaring and crashing when I'm lying in bed.

'Stop dreaming, Miss Jemima!' Foggy gives me another shove. I stumble up the long, crimson rug which leads from the doorway to the dull, grey throne.

There sits Father. All around him hang mirrors. Their frames, like the throne, are dull grey. Each has a candle flickering beneath it, so that there seem to be dozens of him. He, too, wears a sombre black armband, but his silk waistcoat shines like the sun, embroidered with exotic birds and flowers. He studies a letter written in crimson ink, all the while twirling his white-blond moustache into curly points. Beside him, on a bow-legged table, is a parcel wrapped in black crêpe paper.

Foggy clears her throat.

'Your Majesty...' She puts on an extra posh voice when she speaks to Father. 'Your daughter, Jemima.' Just as if she's introducing me to him for the very first time! She drops into a deep curtsy, her ancient black boots squeaking.

Father folds the letter evenly in two and lays it down so that its edges line up with the edges of the table. Then he looks up. His cold grey eyes widen in surprise at the sight of my dress.

'Jemima,' he says. 'Is that *you*?'

I nod, trying not to breathe out. I'm sure if I do the buttons will ping off in all directions and I'll burst out of the dress.

'Come.' Father beckons me with a manicured finger, ignoring Foggy, like he always does. She backs away, still bent in a curtsy, until she almost disappears into a black curtain at the back of the room. Foggy gazes at Father through her misty spectacles with a hungry expression, as if he's a juicy tomato.

I hoist up my skirt and totter towards the throne. Now there are dozens of reflections of *me* in the mirrors: small and dark with too-high heels and a too-tight dress. I don't look like Mim any more. And I don't look like my tall, blond father either. I must take after my dead mother, who I've never seen. Foggy says Father locked away all the pictures of her after she died.

He stares at me for a long time without saying anything. Then, as if reluctant to squeeze the word out, he says: 'Jemima.'

'Yes, Father?'

'I am disappointed in you.'

'But why, Father? I haven't done—'

'Sssst!' He clicks his fingers. 'Fogarty informs me that you have become wild and undisciplined. That your speech is slovenly and common. That you ask too many questions and do not think before you speak. That you spend your time hanging around the forge with Samuel Smith, stinking of smoke and daubed in soot—or else lying in the library with your head in a book.'

'But I'm learning, Father! Smith teaches me about black-smithing and metals and making things. And books teach me about volcanoes and xylophones and... and woodpeckers and vegetables. Books fill up my head with ideas—'

'Books don't fill stomachs,' says Father coldly. 'Or purses.'

'So very true, Your Majesty,' sniffs a voice from the curtain at the back of the room. Father glances at Foggy, as if noticing her for the first time.

'You may leave, Fogarty.'

Foggy hesitates, clearly longing to stay.

'Now!' Father slams his fist down on the table. The parcel shakes, and Foggy's shoes squeak out of the room. The door creaks shut behind her.

Father turns back to me.

'Eleven years ago,' he glances at his black armband, 'your poor mother, the Queen, perished on the day of your birth. Since then I have laboured to restore the fortunes of this castle, and to protect Galena from the threats of the Outside. I cannot be expected to oversee your education as well. I trusted Fogarty to tutor you, to teach you to be a daughter who would one day be a credit to me. Clearly, Fogarty has failed.'

His eyes flicker towards the letter on the table.

'It is your eleventh birthday. And I intend to remedy Fogarty's neglect. Today, Jemima, is the first day of the rest of your life.'

I consider this idea. 'But that's true of *every* day, isn't it, Father? Every day is the first day of—'

'Sssssst!' he snaps. 'Your tongue runs away with you. Show some respect before your king!'

He picks up the parcel. My fingers itch to take it, to tear open the paper and discover what's inside.

'You are growing up, Jemima. It is time to put childish ways behind you and follow your destiny.'

'My destiny?'

'What is inside this parcel,' Father turns it over and over in his white hands, 'will change your life for ever. Take it and unwrap it.'

He hands me the parcel, and I almost drop it, it's so heavy. My heart thrums in my chest. With shaking fingers, I tear the black crêpe paper away.

In my hands lies a circle of dull, greenish-grey metal with spikes on it.

'Oh.' I try not to show how disappointed I am. When you've been waiting for a present from your father your whole life and the one you finally receive turns out to be so different from what you hoped for, how do you keep your mouth from turning down and tears from pricking at your eyes? But I do my best.

'Kneel, Jemima.'

I lift my dress and shuffle down to kneel on the red carpet. Father takes the object from my hands. He lifts it high into the air, muttering words I don't understand, and then lowers it onto my head. It lies heavy over my eyebrows. Now my head feels squashed, as well as my chest and my tummy and my toes.

'Arise, Princess Jemima,' says Father.

Foggy leaps back as I jerk open the throne room door and hobble into the corridor. Her long face is flushed. She must have been eavesdropping. Then she notices the crown on my head.

'Your Royal Highness.' She bends in an awkward curtsy.

'Stoppit, Foggy,' I say. 'My name is *Mim*.'

'Yes, Your Royal Highness.'

'C'mon!' I lift my skirt and set off along the corridor towards my room. 'I want to get back into my proper clothes.'

But Foggy hurries past me and stands in front of me, barring the way.

'Oh no, Your Royal Highness.'

'What?'

'*These* are your clothes from now on.'

I stare at her.

'As His Majesty told you. Today is the first day of the rest of your life—your life as a princess.'

My mouth is suddenly dry. I open it, and all that comes out is a croak. I lick my lips. 'I don't understand—'

'One day you will be Queen. What sort of a queen wears patched trousers and old shoes? What sort of a queen associates with blacksmiths, daubed with soot and grime? What sort of a queen has her nose always stuck in a book, and a mouthful of idle questions? From now on, you will dress as a princess and wear your crown to remind you of your future.'

'You, you mean I've got to wear these... all the time?'

'Correct, Your Royal Highness.'

I stare at her. 'You can't make me!'

'Impudence!' Foggy sniffs. 'Your father can.'

I turn and hobble away, as best I can in the shoes and the dress.

'And exactly *where* do you think you're going, Your Royal Highness?'

'Out!' I shout.

Foggy lunges forward and grabs my arm.

'That is strictly forbidden, on the Day of the Catastrophic Curse.'

'Who cares about Curse Day?' I shake off her hand and stumble towards the door.

If this is the first day of the rest of my life, is there *anything* left to look forward to?

# IN THE FORGE

**T**here's only one place to go.

I hobble along the corridor to a circular hall. It has three doors: one to the library; one down to the old dungeons; and the front door of the castle, with seven steps leading to the courtyard. I pull this one open, slip through and slam it shut on Foggy's whingeing. Then I teeter and slide down the slippery steps in my high-heeled shoes. At the bottom, I look back at the castle, with its grand entrance and small arched windows. The throne-room window is empty so I tuck the long dress into my knickers, pull off the heavy crown and the horrible shoes and, clutching them in my icy fingers, run diagonally across the courtyard.

Luckily, there's no one to stare, because of Curse Day, but the cold flagstone floors of the castle are nothing compared with the frosty cobbles under my bare feet. The wind tears at the thin dress and my breath mists about my face like smoke. I grit my teeth and run on, along the path beside the Great Wall. I hurry past the Gate, up towards the forge.

'STOP! Who goes there?'

The sentry, high on the Great Wall, holds a loudspeaker to his mouth, a grey shadow against the dim sky. Father orders a pair of sentries to patrol the top of the Wall, turn and turn-about, and it's their job to open and close the Gate.

'It's me—Mim.'

The light from a flaming torch flickers down over the Wall.

'Miss Jemima?' The sentry's voice echoes through the loudspeaker. 'Didn't recognize you in that get-up.'

I nod and walk on, but the voice booms out again.

'Miss! Why are you out here on the Day of the Catastrophic Curse?'

'I-I have to see Smith.' I cross my fingers behind my back. 'Father sent me.'

'All right, miss,' the sentry grunts.

Even though the forge is only a few yards further on, my feet are numb by the time I race up the steps to the wooden platform. My eyes squirm away from the executioner's block, with its stained, neck-shaped hole and the gleaming axe. Even though I know the block hasn't been used since the first Curse Day, it seems to crouch on the platform, waiting for its next victim.

I untuck the dress from my knickers and bang on the door of the forge. It opens with a rush of hot air, and a massive figure wearing a heavy apron and thick leather gloves stares down at me. Smith's eyes are black as coal and his skin is smoke-dark. His mouth splits in a grin and his voice—as deep as if he'd found it at the bottom of a mineshaft—booms out.

'Mim, bonny girl! Happy Birthday!'

I'm lifted right off my feet and swung round. The tang of soot and sweat and hot, sweet tea makes my nose twitch. Smith always smells of home.

'What brings you here, Mim?' Smith's beetly brows push together in a frown. 'You know you aren't allowed out today.'

'I-I had to see you, Smith.' Suddenly I'm shivering.

'You're cold as a polar bear! Come in, get warm.'

The forge is a single room, its walls blackened with soot and hung with metal tools. There's a workbench, a mattress with a rough blanket, and a tall cupboard where Smith keeps his food and washing things; but mostly the room's full of the furnace—a huge brick fireplace where a heap of coals glows ruby red, and flames crackle and spit.

Smith sets me down beside a large pair of leather bellows. I drop the shoes and the crown onto the stone floor and stretch out my icy fingers to warm them.

'What's this?' Smith stares at the crown.

'Oh, Smith!' Hot tears prick my eyes and I wipe at them with the back of my hand. 'Foggy took away my real clothes and made me wear these—and Father says I've got to... to grow up and face my destiny—and I've got to wear that crown—for the rest of my whole life!'

Smith says nothing.

'And... and he says I spend too much time with *you*!'

Smith's eyes are glued to the crown. I stamp my foot.

'If Father stops me seeing you, I swear I'll—well, I'll run away to the Outside!'

Smith tears off his gloves and stretches out one of his huge hands. But instead of comforting me, he bends down and picks up the crown, as if it's as light as a dandelion clock. Then, he lifts it to his lips.

'What're you doing?'

Smith shakes his great head. A tear streaks down his smoky cheek.

'What is it? What's the matter?' Smith never cries.

'I last saw this crown eleven years ago.' He cradles the crown as if it was a baby. 'It were the last thing Dad made, before he—' He swallows.

I reach out and pat his shoulder. Curse Day must be extra hard for Smith. I was a newborn baby and never knew my mother. But Smith was sixteen when his dad died, so it must have been sixteen times harder for Smith to lose him. He blinks hard, then places the crown carefully on the workbench. He pulls a large, sooty handkerchief from the pocket of his apron and blows his nose like a trumpet.

'No point visiting the past. Nobody lives there.' He clears his throat and forces a shadow of a smile. 'And it's your birthday. I've something for you, Mim.'

He bends to open a drawer in the workbench and pulls out a small bundle wrapped in faded blue cloth.

'What is it? Is it a present?' Smith's never given me a present before. No one's allowed to be happy or celebrate on Curse Day, which is why it's the worst day *ever* to have your birthday.

'Open it and find out.'

I take the bundle. It's warm from the furnace. I almost don't want to open it, just in case it turns out to be as disappointing as Father's present. But this is Smith, the one person in all the world who understands me.

Slowly, I unwrap the blue cloth.

# SECRETS

**A** little brooch gleams in the light from the furnace. It lies in my palm, its three metal letters the colour of flames.

MIM

'For me?'

My voice is all croaky. Smith is the only person who calls me Mim.

Smith nods gruffly. 'Happy Birthday, Mim.'

I run my fingers over my name. 'It's beautiful. Like it's been made out of fire.'

'Near enough. Made from pure gold.'

'Gold? What's that?'

Smith bends over the brooch, and the glow from it seems to light up his face. 'Gold's the most precious of all metals. This were the only piece left, after...'

'After what?'

Smith suddenly seems very interested in a daddy-long-legs which is heading over the workbench towards the furnace. He captures it, cupping it in his huge hands, carries it to the window and sets it free.

I pin the brooch to the front of my dress. It feels warm against my heart.

'Wait till I show Foggy! This'll remind her to call me Mim, not Jemima.'

'Ah.' Smith scratches his nose.

'What?'

'You can't show folk. If your father or Miss Fogarty were to see it, there'd be a ton of trouble.'

'But why?'

Smith looks away. 'I told you, gold's a precious metal. Your father would likely want to sell it.'

I unpin the brooch and put it carefully into my pocket. 'There. Now it's my secret brooch. No one will ever know.'

'Good,' says Smith. 'And you'd best be off. You'll catch it if Miss Fogarty finds you here. And I've work to do.'

He turns his back to me, pulls on his gloves and, using a pair of metal tongs, draws something out of the furnace and lays it on the workbench, white-hot. Then he picks up an enormous hammer and begins striking it. The clanging echoes round the forge.

I go over to see. A chain, each link at least two inches thick, coils over the bench like a metal snake. At one end of it—the end Smith's hitting—is a ring, as big as a dog collar.

'What are you making?'

Smith pauses and frowns. 'Goodbye, Mim.'

'Why won't you answer my questions?'

'You ask too many.'

'That's because questions need answers—just like people need friends.'

Smith's eyebrows beetle again. But I go on anyway.

'See, Smith, questions without answers get lonely. And they sort of swirl around inside you and hurt your tummy.'

'Enough of your blethering, Mim!'

'It's my birthday, Smith!' I say. 'Just one little answer?'

He sighs. 'What is it you want to know?'

'Tell me about the crown. How do you know it's the one your father made?'

Smith puts down his hammer, picks up the crown from the workbench and turns it upside down.

'Here, see?'

On the rim, flickering in the light of the furnace, is stamped a single S.

'That's Dad's special mark. His Majesty ordered Dad to make it for his firstborn child—that was you, Mim—in the weeks before you were born. Dad worked on it day and night. It were made from the purest gold.'

'Gold?' I pull out my brooch and compare it with the dull grey-green crown. 'But it *isn't* made of gold.'

'No.' Smith's face looks weary and sad. 'Not any more.'

'You mean, it changed?'

Smith doesn't reply for a while. Then he says: 'It changed into lead on the Day of the Catastrophic Curse.'

'What's lead?'

'The heaviest of all metals. Hardest to change. Poisonous, too.'

'But why—'

'Enough, Mim.' Smith picks up the hammer again. 'I've answered your question. Now, take yourself off.'

He raises the hammer to strike at the chain again, his broad back like a big closed door. I step forward and grab his arm. His eyes flash with anger.

'That's dangerous, Mim. Never, *never* step between a man and his work.'

But the questions are piling up inside me. They tumble out of my mouth.

'Why are there so many secrets? Whenever I ask about Curse Day, people ignore me or tell me to shut up or to go away. If I'm growing up, like Father and Foggy keep telling me I am, then I'm old enough to know the truth. Why did the crown turn to lead? Why did my mother die, and your father too? Why are we so poor? It seems like everything went wrong on Curse Day. Is it because I was born on that day? Is it all my fault?'

Smith bends down and takes me by the shoulders.

'It's not your fault, Mim. None of it.'

'Then whose fault is it?'

There's a bang on the door of the forge. Smith strides to open it. A blast of icy air swirls in, along with Foggy. Wrapped in her long grey billowing cloak, she looks like a gloomy, damp cloud. She glares at me.

'I might have known I'd find you in here. And on the Day of the Catastrophic Curse, too! When you know full well that your father has ordered that no one should leave their house.'

'Why are *you* disobeying him, then?' I can't help being cheeky. Foggy is such a wet blanket.

'Impertinence!' Foggy's cheeks flush with anger. 'And Samuel Smith, you should be ashamed of yourself, allowing her to run around barefoot in a forge!'

'Yes, ma'am.' Smith gives me a wink, which Fogarty doesn't miss.

'Be very careful, Samuel Smith. His Majesty sees you as a bad influence on Miss Jem—Her Royal Highness.' She turns back to me. 'Put on your shoes immediately. And what have you done with your crown?'

Smith silently hands it to me.

'And on other matters, Samuel,' Foggy continues. 'His Majesty wishes you to finish the—' she glances at me and lowers her voice—'the *work* as quickly as possible.'

'That chain?' I say. 'With the ring on it?'

Foggy gives me a look. 'One more question from you, and I will wash out your mouth with soap. Now, come!'

'See you later, Smith.' I slip my hand into my pocket and feel the hidden brooch there. Its glow seems to warm my fingers.

'See you, Mim.'

'That's Her Royal Highness to *you*, Samuel Smith!' And Foggy pushes me out of the forge.

That night in bed, hundreds of thoughts run round and round in my head, even when I tell them to stop and let me go to sleep. I toss and turn and shiver. There are so many questions to be answered, so many secrets to be uncovered.

*What really happened on Curse Day?*

*Why did the golden crown turn into lead?*

*Why do we have so little money?*

Outside, in the darkness beyond the castle, the wind whistles round the Great Wall, and the ocean hushes and whispers. Maybe the answers are outside, beyond the Gate. Maybe the most important secret of all is:

*Who—or what—lives on the Outside?*

Maybe if I solve that secret, I'll find the answers to all the others.

My fingers cradle my birthday brooch, its golden warmth like a hug.

I *will* find out, in spite of Foggy and Father. I'll show them that questions don't have to be lonely.

Somehow, whatever it takes, I'll find each one its answer.

# THE LIBRARY

I lie on my back on the library floor, gazing up at the sky and breathing in the musty smell of books. You know how some places just smell interesting? The library has the most interesting smell in the whole castle.

The flagstones are hard and cold, so I've slipped *Volcanoes* between me and them. The library is a tower with circular walls which get narrower and narrower towards the top. The walls are lined with bookshelves, round-and-round, and up-and-up. It's like being inside a wrong-way-up telescope. At the very top is a circle of windows and a glass roof.

No one except me comes here. Father and Foggy aren't interested in dusty old books. And these books are *extremely* dusty, because no one ever cleans the library, so cobwebs hang all over the place and hairy spiders run over the stone floor and scurry into the dark spaces behind the books. When my eyes get tired from reading, I lie down like this and gaze up through the glass roof, at the Outside. The clouds drift in soft patterns; sometimes cotton-wool white, sometimes pink as Foggy's nose, sometimes sheep-grey. At night, the moon changes from a thin sliver of light to a great round cheese and the stars glitter like tiny holes in black velvet. Sometimes gulls coast over, blown about by the wind, screaming and mewing their stories about the ocean. On stormy days, the ocean sucks and crashes. I've read *Waves: The Story of the Ocean*. What would it be like to actually see it?

The stone floor is just *too* cold, even though I'm lying on *Volcanoes*. I jump up and rub my bottom. The lead crown and the high-heeled shoes lie in a pile in the corner, where I dropped them when I came in. I slip *Volcanoes* back into its place on the shelves, in between *Vitamins* and *Voyages*.

I've almost worked my way through the books on the bottom shelves. The shelving is arranged in alphabetical order, with the As at the very top, near the ceiling; the Ms in the middle; and the Xs, Ys and Zs at the bottom. If I stand on tiptoe, I can *just* reach the Vs. So I know a bit about things beginning with V—Violins and Ventriloquists and Volcanoes—and a lot about Wolves and Windmills, Yachting and Yodelling, and almost everything about Zoology and Zebras and the Zodiac. If only Smith was allowed into the castle, he could reach the higher-up books and get them down for me. But he says the likes of him don't belong here.

I s'pose there's one good thing about growing up: one day I'll be tall enough to reach the books about Stars and Skeletons and Taxidermy and Trees.

I reach up and pull out *Voyages*—and then almost drop it. Outside the library door, a strange sound approaches: a rattling and a dragging, a puffing and a sighing. My eyes flick to *Vampires* and then move down to *Zombies Through The Centuries*.

*Don't be daft, Mim.*

Vampires and Zombies don't exist. More likely it's Foggy moving furniture in the corridor. The sound comes nearer and nearer, so I quickly tuck *Voyages* under my arm, pick up the crown and shoes, and duck into my hiding place, which is a small cupboard by the door. Inside is an ancient bucket and a mop and a pile of grey dusters. There's only just room enough for me and the book and the crown and the shoes, and the air smells of must and dust and damp and beetles.

I'm just in time. The library door creaks open, and the rattling and dragging and puffing and sighing is right outside my cupboard. What's Foggy up to? If only there was a keyhole to peep through! I press my ear against the cupboard door and listen as hard as I can.

A sort of screech, like something heavy being scraped across the floor.

More rattling.

The sound of heavy breathing.

Footsteps creaking upwards.

A hammering and a banging, coming from high above.

After what seems like for ever, footsteps creaking down... until they're right outside my cupboard.

I can't help what happens next. The cupboard's full of dust, and dust gets up noses. I pinch my nose as hard as I can, but I can't... stop...

SNEEZING!

There's a long silence, full of question marks.

And then the cupboard door is flung open.

It isn't Foggy.

Or a Zombie, or a Vampire.

'Smith!' I gasp.

'Mim!' Smith seems just as shocked as me.

Behind him stands the tallest ladder. The top of it reaches to the As, and to the windows. But that's not all. An enormous metal hook has been set into the centre of the glass roof. And hanging from the hook is the thick metal chain I saw in the forge, with another hook hanging from the end of it.

'What's that for? And what are *you* doing in the castle?'

'King's orders.' Smith taps his nose. 'Top secret.'

'Oh, c'mon, Smith. *Tell* me!'

But Smith's eyebrows draw together and he shakes his great head.

'Best get on.' He picks up his hammer and a box of screws, and walks over to the ladder.

'Wait!'

Smith's eyebrows leap like frogs. 'What now, Mim?'

'Smith, let me go up the ladder!'

'Impossible.' He grasps it in his huge hands.

'Please, Smith—*please*! It's my only chance to reach the books at the top. Oh, *please*, Smith. Let me?'

Smith glances up at the ladder, then back at me.

'I don't know, Mim. What if you fell?'

'You could hold the ladder steady. I'll be really careful, I promise.'

Smith frowns. 'What would Miss Fogarty say?'

I make my face long and gloomy, push pretend spectacles up my nose and give a loud, wet sniff. 'Samuel Smith!' I do my best Foggy impression. 'How *dare* you allow Miss Jemima up that ladder!'

Smith grins. Then—

'SAMUEL SMITH!' Foggy stands in the doorway, glowering. 'Get on with your work. And as for you, Your Royal Highness—'

'I'm *not*!' I glance at my kicked-off shoes. 'I'm not even high!'

*But I would've been high up the ladder, if you hadn't barged in.*

'Put those shoes back on. RIGHT NOW!'

Reluctantly, I push my feet into the shoes and cram the crown over my eyebrows.

Foggy grabs one of my trumpet sleeves and hauls me towards the door. 'The library is out of bounds.'

'Since when?'

'Since right now. Smith has work to do here. And ladders and children do *not* go together.'

She pushes me out of the door.

# THE CLIMB

I can't sleep. I can't stop thinking about the ladder, and Smith, and the chain hanging from the ceiling. More secrets! It all feels unfairer and unfairer, and I'm boiling up inside. Thanks to Foggy poking her nose in, there's no chance of climbing the ladder to the high-up books. When you've got an Enquiring Mind, you *have* to read, and now Foggy's banned me from the library, I won't be able to read at all.

I won't just lie here. What if... what if I sneak to the library now, in the dark? The ladder might still be there. Then I could climb up, up to the highest shelves. I could pull out books on Acids and Albatrosses and Anteaters and Acrobatics. I could hide them in the cupboard there, under the dusters, so I could read them whenever I wanted to.

I throw back my blanket, shivering as my feet land on the icy floor. The trumpet-sleeved dress and the lead crown lie in an angry heap on the chair. The high-heeled shoes sprawl on the floor by my bed, where I kicked them.

'I'm not wearing *you*,' I hiss at them. 'I'll go as I am, in slippers and pyjamas.'

I tiptoe to the door, open it and listen. The castle is silent. All I have to do is get past Foggy's door without waking her. She usually goes to bed early, and often takes a sleeping potion, so by now she should be safely asleep. She's probably dreaming about Father—*yuck!*—with a soppy grin on her face.

Holding my breath, I feel my way along the corridor.

Only Foggy isn't asleep. She's moving around her room, muttering. I duck back inside my bedroom, leaving the door open a crack. I'm just in time—Foggy's door opens and she comes out, wrapped in her billowing grey cloak, her head covered by the hood, carrying a lantern. The light flickers over her body. She looks strangely plump. But Foggy is thin as a stick. She must be hiding something under her cloak.

She sniffs and looks left and right, still muttering under her breath. What's she up to?

Foggy's boots squeak along the corridor. As she disappears through the door to the circular hall, I slip out to follow her. I can hear her fumbling with a door. Which of the three doors is she opening? The front door of the castle creaks closed.

I count to ten, then follow. I needn't get close, so long as I keep the light of her lantern in sight. The castle courtyard is empty and the cobbles glisten in the light of a half moon. A sliver of light wavers along the path towards the Gate. Keeping to the shadow of the Great Wall, I slip after it.

At the Gate, Foggy stops.

'Who goes there?' It's the sentry, high up on the Wall.

'Miss Fogarty, on the orders of His Majesty,' Foggy whispers hoarsely, lifting the lantern to her face. 'Open the Gate.'

'Yes, miss.' The sentry turns the winch and slowly, slowly, the Gate creaks open, just enough for Foggy to slip through, then creaks shut.

Where's Foggy going? No one's allowed in or out of the Gate without special permission. And what is she hiding under her cloak? Has she stolen something? If only I could follow her. Except there's no way the sentry would let me.

But with Foggy out of the way, I can go to the library, just as I planned. I can climb the ladder. I can get as many books as I want. And maybe, just maybe, I can look out of the windows at the very top. Maybe I'll be able to see the Outside for the very first time.

The moon hangs high above the library windows, sending silvery light over the topmost books and casting the bottom of the room into the darkest shadow.

The ladder's still there, leaning against the highest shelf. The rungs seem to go up for ever.

What if I get halfway up and the ladder sways? There'll be no Smith to hold it steady. I could fall from a great height and get smashed to smithereens on the stone floor. My fingers creep to my pyjama pocket and find my golden brooch.

*You'll keep me safe, won't you?*

But what if Foggy comes back while I'm up the ladder? I pull out ten of the thickest books from the lowest shelf

42

and pile them right under the door handle, so it won't open. Then I take a deep breath, grab the ladder with both hands and begin to climb.

I've only climbed up ten rungs when I discover something.

I don't like heights.

The rungs of the ladder cut into the soles of my slippers. At every step, the ladder judders and sways.

*Keep climbing, very slowly,* I tell myself. *And don't look down.*

As a distraction, I fix my eyes on the bookshelves, and whisper the titles of the books as I climb:

'*Umbrellas...*

*Unicorns...*

*Tribes...*

*Time...*

*Tigers...*

*Aardvarks...*'

Aardvarks?!? That doesn't belong with the Ts. My fingers itch to pull it out and put it in its proper place on the very top shelf. But now that I'm actually up here, letting go of the ladder isn't so easy, even with one hand. I climb slowly on.

'*Taxidermy...*

*Tapdancing...*

*Seas and oceans...*

*Sculpture...*

*Royalty...*

*Rabbits...*'

This is taking *ages*. I *so* want to read every one of these books. Can I somehow pull each one out, one by one, and drop it? But what if they splat to pieces on the stone floor? Books are like friends and I wouldn't do that to a friend.

'*Fish...*

*Fairies...*

*Detectives...*

*Dancing...*'

Now I'm right beside the bottom end of Smith's chain, which is hanging from the hook in the ceiling. Whatever is it for? And why is Smith being so secretive about it?

'*Battles...*

*Bacteria...*

*Babies...*'

Almost there. Four more rungs and I'll be at the top, where the windows are. Where the Outside is.

'*Arithmetic...*

*Angels...*

*The Three Impossibles...*'

Another book in totally the wrong place! Someone must have swapped it with *Aardvarks* by mistake. But that's not the only odd thing about it. Its title—*The Three Impossibles*—glows gold, like my brooch.

It must be the moonlight shining on the title, lighting up the words. But as I watch, a bank of cloud drifts over the moon, and everything goes dark.

And when I look back at the book, *the title's still glowing*.

I have to get it. I grip the ladder with one hand and try not to breathe. As I pull the book from the shelf, a ginormous spider scuttles out and abseils down its web—and the book sort of jumps out into my hand. It's heavy, and very dusty.

44

I can't climb the ladder *and* hold the book. Wedging the book between me and the ladder, I undo the top button of my pyjamas—trying not to think about the spider and the dust—and slip it down inside. It seems almost to throb against my chest, like a second heart. Then I climb up the last four rungs. I'm level, at last, with the circle of windows. For the first time in my life, I can see the Outside.

# ATTACK

**A**ll my life I've lived in the castle, surrounded by the Great Wall. I've always longed to find out what's outside. My heart thuds, my breathing stops and my knuckles gleam white in the moonlight. I've read *World: Our Living Planet* from cover to cover, but reading about something and seeing it in real life are two different things.

The moon hangs above the Great Wall. In the distance, across the land to the right, a jagged black rock towers, its top disappeared in heavy cloud. This must be a mountain, or even a volcano. It says in *Volcanoes* that they can be thousands of feet high. I tear my eyes away from it to see the rest.

Right outside the Gate, something lies flat and pale and gleaming.

*Sand.*

And foaming over the edge of the sand is a grey-and-silver mass of water that stretches as far as I can see, darker and darker, until it meets the sky. The water has swellings in it that tower up, bigger and bigger, as they near the sand, and sort of curl over and crash in a flurry of white froth. Then the water sucks back, leaving wet, glittering sand before it swells up again. It's as if the ocean's breathing in and out.

There's something else. Is it a star, hanging low in the sky? No, it's too close to be a star. It seems to be only a short distance from the shore. Its light winks on... and off... and on again. I screw up my eyes to make it out. It's a tall, thin white tower in the ocean, and the light winks from the top of it.

And there's another light. Something small floats on the ocean, tossed up and down by the waves, between the tower and the sand.

*A boat*—moving steadily towards the shore. Someone's sitting in it, but it's too dark and far away for me to see who it is.

Then the birds come.

At first, they're dark shadows skimming over the ocean. There must be fifty or more of them, flying in convoy, so close that their wings almost touch. Have you ever seen a murmuration? When hundreds of starlings fly like a black cloud, making wind-patterns in the sky? Only these are no starlings. Even at a distance, they are far, far bigger. Almost human size. The birds streak towards the library like dark arrows and fly right over the glass roof, their wings blocking out the moon. One of them breaks away from the group—as if it's searching for something—and swoops down over my head. I catch sight of a thin, black face, a beak-like nose. A pair of dark eyes stares into mine. The creature dive-bombs the glass with an unearthly hiss.

I duck—it seems as if it might shatter the glass—and the ladder swings away from the shelves. My tummy turns inside out with fear. For an endless moment I grip the swinging ladder and squeeze my eyes shut, my legs turned to jelly. Then, miraculously, the ladder rights itself and settles back against the shelves. When I finally dare to look up at the glass, the creatures have disappeared.

My heart pounds against the solid lump of the book inside my pyjama top. The ladder trembles with the shaking of my legs. And then a moving light at the edge of the ocean catches my eye.

The boat has reached the shoreline. A small figure climbs out and pulls it up onto the sand. Lifting out the light—which must be a lantern—the figure hurries up the sand towards the Gate. High on the Great Wall, the sentry turns the winch and the Gate slowly opens. The figure, its grey cloak billowing, slips inside.

*Foggy—she's back.*

I must have taken *ages* climbing the ladder and reading all the book titles. That's the trouble with having an Enquiring Mind—you have to think about *everything*. I scramble down the ladder, my slippers sliding on the rungs. I slither down the last few and land on the floor on my knees. Then I stumble across to the door and reach for the handle. It won't open.

*The books!*

I bundle them back onto the shelf. Then I jerk open the library door and race along the corridor to my room. I leap into bed, clutching the book to my chest and tugging the thin blanket over my head, just as Foggy's footsteps squeak towards her room.

The footsteps stop, as if Foggy's listening. Then they come closer and closer until they're right outside my room. The door creaks open. I squeeze my eyes tight shut and try to make my breathing even, but it's hard because of all the scrambling and the running. The book digs into my ribs.

'Your Royal Highness?'

Foggy's voice sounds suspicious. Did she see me coming out of the library? Her old boots squeak over to my bed and pause for a moment. Then she gives a sniff and her footsteps squeak away.

I wait for a long time, counting in my head to two hundred, just in case. Then, I sit up in bed, light my candle, unbutton my pyjama top and pull out the book.

There's no need for the candle. The book glows like the embers in Smith's furnace, lighting up my hands and face. And it's warm. There are no pictures on the cover, only the words:

*THE THREE IMPOSSIBLES*

And underneath them:

*A Book of Alchemy*

I've never seen the word 'alchemy' before. Could it be some kind of chemistry book? There's one way to find out.

I pull and tug, but it's as if the book's pages are stuck together with glue. I hold it sideways-on and peer at them. They look real enough. I turn the book upside down and back to front, but whichever way I try, I can't make it open.

I sigh. All that scary climbing, for this: a strange, fake book that I can't even open. No wonder it's called *The Three Impossibles*.

I push the book under my bed, but when I blow out my candle, its glow creeps across the floor. I jump out of bed, grab my trumpet-sleeved dress, wrap it around the book and push it as far under the bed as I can. Then I get back in and pull the scratchy blanket around me. My dreams are full of oceans and towers and boats, and hissing, attacking birds.

# A VERY IMPORTANT VISITOR

**I** wake early next morning, wondering if I dreamt it all—seeing Foggy sneaking off to the Outside, climbing the ladder in the library and finding the book, seeing the mountain and the ocean, the bird-creatures dive-bombing the library window. There's only one way to find out. I jump out of bed and peer underneath it.

A dim glow meets my eyes. The book is just where I left it last night, bundled in my dress. So it *did* all happen! Quickly, I pull it out and unwrap it. Its golden gleam warms my hands, and its title—*The Three Impossibles*—almost seems to dance. Maybe I imagined that it was glued shut. After all, what's the point of a book that won't open? It's like asking somebody a really important question which they refuse to answer. So I try again. But the pages stay sealed.

My dress is creased and cobwebby and smutty from being under my bed—I don't think anyone ever cleans there—so I brush it down as best I can, which only makes it more streaky and grubby, before I pull it on. I can't do up the buttons without Foggy's help, so the back gapes open and gives me goosebumps.

Footsteps squeak along the corridor.

I run to the cupboard and shove the book right to the very back, behind a couple of old pillows. Not a minute too soon. Foggy bursts through the door without knocking, like she always does.

She glares at me.

'You're a disgrace. A complete disgrace. *What* have you been doing in that dress? It's *filthy*. This is what comes of running off to Samuel Smith's forge at all hours and grubbing around his furnace. I'm ashamed of you, Jemima!'

At least when she's angry she forgets to call me 'Your Royal Highness', though 'Jemima' isn't much better.

'Sorry, Foggy.' I turn around so she can do up my buttons.

'*Miss Fogarty!* I've a good mind to leave you like this until you learn to fasten your dress for yourself. We can't afford you a maid, and I'm certainly not going to perform that role for the next ten years!'

When Foggy has finished grumbling and buttoning, she grabs a hairbrush and begins to scrape it through my tangled curls.

'Ouch!'

'Stop wriggling, and stand still.'

At last she finishes, and plonks the crown down over my head.

Then she gives an extra-watery sniff and says: 'There will be no lessons today.'

I hide my grin. You might be thinking that someone with an Enquiring Mind would enjoy lessons. If so, you've never had a lesson with Foggy. Think of the most bored you've ever been: so bored your eyes droop; so bored your head's as heavy as lead; so bored your ears buzz, like they're refusing to let in another... single... word. That's what Foggy's lessons are like. She drones on and on about subjects like economics and politics and mathematics and I'm supposed to write down what she says and never ask any questions. She gives me maps and charts to colour in, only she never actually explains what they are maps and charts *of*—and if I ask, she raps my knuckles with a ruler. I learn far more from Smith, who teaches me about blacksmithing. And the difference is that we don't just talk about it, we *do* it.

I set off for the door.

'Where do you think you're going?' growls Foggy.

'To Smith's. I want to see what he's—'

'Not so fast, young lady! We have work to do.'

'Work? But you just said—'

Foggy's nose has turned very pink. It does this when she's really, really annoyed or upset. 'We have a visitor arriving.'

'A visitor? Who is it?'

This is exciting. No one ever comes to stay in the castle. Father's far too stingy to feed guests.

Foggy glowers. 'His Majesty has ordered the guest suite to be prepared. You are to help me with it.'

'What guest suite?'

'The rooms in the cellar.' Foggy flicks her fingers at the floor.

'The old dungeons?'

She nods. 'Unfortunately, His Majesty did not see fit to ask my opinion. Had he done so, I would have told him that the castle dungeons are no place for a visitor. They are damp and filthy and quite unfit for human habitation.'

'But who? Who's coming?'

'Never you mind.' Foggy avoids my eyes.

'Do you actually know who it is?'

Her nose flushes bright red. So Father hasn't told her. Foggy sticks her crimson nose in the air, jerks her head at me to follow her and stalks out of the room.

At the top of the stone steps that lead down to the dungeons, the smell of fresh paint hits my nose. If I was alone, I'd slide down the banister, landing in a heap at the bottom. But with Foggy watching me like a hawk, I have to hobble down the steps in my high-heeled shoes, clutching the banister for dear life.

But for once I don't care about my shoes, or even the crown. A visitor from the Outside is thrilling! Who are they? What will they look like? How long will they stay? Maybe I can ask them about the Outside. Maybe... maybe they'll even take me there!

The door to the dungeons is made of thick wood studded with nails, with a metal grille in it so the guards can spy on the prisoners inside. There are no guards now, just like there are no executions. Last time I visited the dungeons, they were dark and damp and musty-smelling, piled with broken furniture and other rubbish that couldn't be sold.

Foggy pulls out a rusty key from her pocket and jiggles it in the lock. At last, the door creaks open. I gasp.

Whatever I'd expected, it wasn't this.

# RED, CRIMSON, SCARLET

**E**verything in the dungeon is painted red: the walls, the floor, the ceiling—even the iron bars over the window. It's like walking into blood. Foggy stares too, her mouth open. Then she sees me looking and pulls herself together.

'We are to make these rooms comfortable for our visitor. Wait here, while I fetch the necessary things.'

As soon as Foggy's squeaked off, I hurry into the next room.

An enormous four-poster bed with a scarlet headboard and heavy ruby curtains stands in the middle of it. Red-framed mirrors—which must have come from Father's rooms—reflect me in my grubby dress and crown and heels. There's a red wardrobe in the crimson dressing-room. In the bathroom, even the toilet is painted red, and the bath—an old-fashioned claw-footed one—gleams scarlet, with red taps.

I go back to the bedroom. Foggy's standing there with a face like a raincloud, almost disappeared behind a huge pile of sheets and towels.

'Take these towels and put them in the bathroom.'

'But they're not red.'

'We've neither the time nor the money to dye them.' Foggy dumps the sheets on the four-poster bed. 'When you've done that, you can help me make up the bed.'

The sheets were once white but now they're a sort of pale grey, and there are bobbly bits where Foggy's darned up all the holes. We each take one end of a sheet and spread it over the massive four-poster. Then I look at the bare walls.

'What about pictures?' I suggest. 'It's all very... red, and a few pictures would make it prettier.'

Foggy snorts. 'When did you last see a picture in this castle?'

'There's the one in the throne room. And I sort of remember lots of pictures when I was little. Where've they all gone?'

'Sold.' Foggy sniffs.

'What, all of them? Was it something to do with Curse—I mean, the Day of the Catastrophic Curse?'

Foggy shakes a pillow and gives me a look as if she'd like to shake me too.

'And what about all the other stuff? The statues and the jewellery? Have they been sold too?'

But I've asked these questions over and over, and Foggy never answers. She kneels at the hearth, her black skirt billowing around her, making up a fire with bits of coal and wood. Her billowing skirt reminds me how I saw her last night, hurrying out of the Gate with something hidden under her cloak.

'Fog—I mean, Miss Fogarty?'

'What?'

'Have you ever seen the Outside?'

Foggy stops, her fingers black with coal dust, then starts screwing up balls of paper and poking them under the coal.

'The Outside is forbidden. You know that.'

My mouth opens to ask why she's avoiding my question, then I stop myself. If Foggy wants to keep her visit to the Outside a secret, there must be a good reason for it.

'I don't see why it's forbidden.'

Foggy strikes a match and holds it to the grate. 'The Outside is dangerous. Why else do you think your father built the Great Wall around Galena? Why else does a sentry keep watch at every hour?'

'Have you ever seen an Outsider?'

Foggy presses her lips together in a thin, cross line. 'I may have. And I wouldn't recommend it.'

'I saw—' I press my mouth shut. Why does my tongue run away with me when I get excited?

'You saw what?'

'I think I saw a... a sort of bird-creature. Maybe.'

There's a silence. Then, to my surprise, Foggy stands up and beckons me to sit on the four-poster bed, beside her.

'Very well, Jemima,' she says. 'You are old enough to know.'

She sniffs and pushes up her spectacles. My feet tap with impatience.

'The Outsiders,' she says at last, 'are wicked, evil beings. There are the creatures of the air—led by the King of the Wings. A savage, through and through.'

These must have been the creatures that dive-bombed the library. 'Are they the only Outsiders? Are there others?'

'There are creatures of the ocean. Half fish, half human.' Foggy suddenly turns and looks right into my eyes. 'They are known as the Mers.'

'Like mermaids? And mermen?' I read about them in *Wrecks and Wreckaging*.

'Mermaids?' Foggy sniffs. 'Murderers, more like.'

'Murderers? Who do they kill?'

'Anyone foolish enough to sail on the ocean.' Foggy tosses her head. '*Their* ocean, they think it is.'

'How do they kill them?'

'By singing.' She pulls out her handkerchief and blows her nose loudly.

'Singing?' Foggy must be making this up, just to scare me. *She* was in a boat last night, on the ocean. Why didn't these Mers kill her?

'They sing to sailors and hypnotize them,' Foggy replies, 'so they can't steer their ships. The ships are wrecked on the rocks and the sailors drown. Then the Mers steal their treasures.' She lowers her voice to a hoarse whisper. 'And the Wings swoop down and pick the flesh from the sailors' bones.'

I shiver. Is that what the Wings would've done to me last night, if they'd come through the glass? But I must find out more.

'Do any humans live on the Outside?'

Foggy busies herself with tugging my curls into place. I let her—anything to keep her talking. 'The merchants, and travellers from distant lands.'

'How do they stay safe?'

'Bribery,' says Foggy shortly.

'What do you mean?'

'They bribe the Outsiders with precious objects in order to gain safe passage.'

Is this what Foggy herself has been doing? Has she been smuggling things out of the castle under her cloak, so she can bribe the Outsiders to let her pass safely? Is that why there are so many spaces on the walls where paintings once hung? Is that why all the sculptures and jewellery have disappeared from the castle?

Foggy suddenly turns and grabs me by the shoulders, her eyes boring into mine.

'Listen to me, Your Royal Highness. Never—*never*—venture into the Outside. Not if you value your life.'

Then she lets me go and stands up.

'Now, make yourself scarce. I've work to do in the kitchen.'

'When is the visitor arriving?' I ask her.

'At noon, I believe. And stay out of the way!'

I nod, crossing my fingers behind my back. Only an hour to go before the visitor arrives—and no way am I going to miss it!

# THE ARRIVAL

As soon as Foggy disappears into the kitchen, I race to my bedroom and pull open the cupboard door for my coat. A faint glow creeps out from behind the old pillows. The alchemy book's still where I hid it. But there's no time to think about that now. I put on my moth-eaten coat and totter out into the castle courtyard. Cotton-wool snowflakes whirl around me, blown by an icy wind, and settle in drifts on the cobbles. I whirl with them—or try to. My new shoes skid in the snow and the crown keeps falling over my nose. I put out my tongue and let a snowflake land on it, tasting the Outside.

Word must have got round in Galena that a visitor's coming because people are gathering at the Gate. Just in case Foggy decides to come looking for me, I push my way into the thick of the crowd. Several people bow and mutter, 'Your Royal Highness'.

'I'm *not*!' I growl. But they just keep bowing and scraping. So I pull off my crown and hide it under my coat. And then something happens that makes them stop looking at me.

From outside the Gate comes the eerie sound of a horn—a long, high, mournful note. The crowd falls silent. There's no 'Who goes there?' from the sentry. Father must have given him orders to let the visitor straight in. Up on the Great Wall, he turns the winch, and slowly the Gate creaks open.

Even standing on tiptoe, I can't see over the heads of the people in front of me, so I elbow my way to the front of the crowd.

'Walk on!'

A red carriage, pulled by roan horses wearing red plumes on their heads, moves slowly through the Gate. It's being driven by a puny man in a scarlet cloak, his nose and lips blue with cold. A large horn lies on the seat beside him.

I crane my neck to see inside the carriage, but crimson curtains are drawn over the windows. The horses toss their heads, whinnying, as their hooves clop over the snowy cobbles. Behind the carriage come two red-painted carts covered in tarpaulins, each drawn by a burly man on horseback. The crowd moves with the carriages towards the castle courtyard.

Outside the entrance, the little man shouts 'Whoah!' and the horses stop. He puts the horn to his lips and blows, and the same haunting note echoes round the Great Wall. Then, the castle door opens and Father appears, looking even more dashing than usual, his moustache waxed into twirly points.

The driver jumps down and opens the carriage door with

a flourish, and a figure in a long red cloak, its face hidden under a hood, steps from the carriage and hurries up the steps. Father bows and escorts the figure inside.

The other two drivers—hulking men with shaven heads and tattoos on their arms—pull off the tarpaulins from the carts. Underneath are piled red trunks and lacquered red boxes. One by one, the three men lug them into the castle. Soon, the carts are almost empty. The three drivers gather in a huddle around a large humped object draped in red silk, muttering and whispering. I creep forward to listen.

'Well, *I* ain't doin' it this time!' says one. 'It's your turn, Jase.'

'No chance,' says the other. 'Not after wot it did to me last time.'

'We can't leave it 'ere, boys.' This is the puny one. 'We'll 'ave to risk it.'

'Jokin', ain't you, chief? Look at *this*.' The man pulls up his sleeve and reveals a huge black bruise.

'You was lucky.' The other waves his hand, wrapped in a handkerchief. 'It nearly killed me!' He peels back the handkerchief. Drops of blood drip from an angry wound onto the white snow.

The humped object rocks from side to side. A hissing sound, like a thousand snakes, makes the drivers step back, their faces pale.

'Morning, gentlemen.'

Smith, wearing his usual vest and trousers in spite of the cold, towers over the men, even the two hulking ones. Beside him, they look like minnows around a whale.

"Oo are you?' asks the puny man.

Smith holds out a massive hand. 'Sam Smith, blacksmith. And you are?'

The puny man's hand disappears inside Smith's. 'Hercules.' He waves at the other men. 'An' this 'ere's Jason, and that's Atlas.'

The two men nod at Smith.

'Can I assist you gentlemen?' Smith offers.

The three men stare at Smith's vast muscled body, then glance at one another. Hercules nudges the others, then turns back to Smith.

'Can yer lift this 'ere cage?'

Smith walks up to the rocking object. 'Reckon so.'

'By yourself?'

Smith doesn't reply. Instead, he grabs it, his muscles straining, and hefts it from the cart. A terrible sound comes from inside—a sort of hissing scream—and something bulges and bites at Smith's hands through the crimson silk cover. Smith ignores the biting, just as if it's an annoying wasp. Whatever it is, it's furiously angry, and must be heavy, because Smith pants as he staggers up the castle steps and disappears inside.

It takes me a while to push through the crowd. By the time I get into the castle, everyone's gone. Smith must have carried the cage, and whatever's inside it, down to the red rooms.

I jiggle the handle of the door to the dungeons. It's firmly locked. Why am I *always* shut out of anything interesting?

Then again, if Father and the mysterious visitor are down there—and hopefully Foggy is too—there's no one to stop me going back to the library and climbing the ladder again.

I tiptoe along the corridor into the hall, push open the library door... and walk into a mountain.

Only it isn't a mountain, it's Smith, sweat pouring down his face, dragging the ladder. He grabs my arm and pulls me back into the hall.

'No, Mim.'

'But... but what's going on? What were you doing in there?'

'It's nowt to do with you.' Smith lets me go and looks at me sternly.

I duck under his arm and dash through the door.

The chain that Smith made hangs from the metal ring in the ceiling. And dangling from a hook at the end of the chain is the silk-covered cage, jerking and swinging, about ten feet off the floor.

'Satisfied, Mim?'

I hate it when Smith acts disappointed in me. But it's *his* fault just as much as it's mine, refusing to tell me stuff.

'What is it?' I whisper. 'What's up there?'

At the sound of our voices, the cage becomes still. It hangs silently, twirling slightly in the draught from the door, as if it's listening.

Smith sighs. 'Want the truth, Mim?'

''Course I do!'

'Then let's step back outside.'

I follow him into the hall. 'Well? What is it?'

'Truth is, Mim—I don't know. Orders were to string it up there out of harm's way. And unlike you, I don't poke my nose in where it's not wanted.'

I kick the floor with the toe of my shoe. It's so unfair! If people just *told* me stuff, I wouldn't have to try so hard to find out. It's not my fault I've got an Enquiring Mind.

Foggy bustles along the corridor towards the library, looking important.

'I hope,' she sniffs, 'you have not been in there.' Without waiting for an answer, she tugs my dress straight. 'Put on your crown. His Majesty has asked me to bring you to the throne room to meet his guest.'

*Yes!* I skip with excitement.

Smith looks at me strangely—almost as if he feels sorry for me.

'What?' I mumble, out of the corner of my mouth.

But Smith only shakes his head.

I set off after Foggy. Halfway along the corridor, I turn. Smith's still standing outside the library.

'Good luck, Mim,' he calls. Then he mutters something else. It sounds an awful lot like: *you're going to need it.*

# THE VISITOR

In the throne room, Father stands by the window, deep in conversation with the tall, red-cloaked figure, whose back is to us. A pair of white hands flash back and forth. They have long, sharp fingernails like talons, painted blood-red.

There's something different about the room. Something missing. I drag my eyes away from the cloaked figure to a pale space on the wall.

My ocean picture's gone. What has Father done with it?

Foggy pushes me forward with a jerk and I nearly fall over my heels.

'Don't forget to curtsy,' she hisses.

Father looks up and sees us. I bend my knees awkwardly. He lays a hand on the figure's arm and mutters something. Then he beckons me towards him.

'Come, Jemima,' he says. 'Meet our honoured guest.'

I stumble up the red carpet, Foggy at my heels. The red-cloaked figure goes on looking out of the window.

When I'm only a few feet away, Father says: 'Madame Marionette, may I have the, ah... pleasure of introducing my daughter, Her Royal Highness, Princess Jemima.'

The figure turns and lowers her red hood, revealing a beautiful white face with shocking crimson lips, and red hair falling in a silken sheet to her waist. She is dressed all in scarlet, except for the fur stoles hanging round her neck. I blink—they're made of the skins of little animals *and the heads are still on.* On her feet she wears scaly shoes which look like they're made from the skins of snakes.

'Jemima.' Her voice is low and accented. She holds out a white hand, her red nails like five tiny daggers. Rings with red stones cluster over every finger. She smiles, a sharp smile which doesn't reach her eyes. 'I am Madame Tomazine Marionette. How do you do?'

I take her hand. It's like touching an icicle.

A sound—between a gasp and a groan—makes me turn. Foggy's turned as white as mist. She sways as if she's about to topple over. Madame Marionette's lips twitch.

'Sister dear,' she says. 'Will you not welcome me? It has been a long, long time.'

I stare from one to the other—from Madame Marionette's beautiful white face and tumbling red hair to Foggy's pink nose and wispy, lank bun. They look like they're from different planets.

'You!' Foggy takes big gulps of air. 'What... what are *you* doing here?'

'Simple.' Madame Marionette smiles at Father, who blushes. 'His Majesty was in need of a new governess for Jemima. And so he wrote, in his wisdom, to *moi.*'

'A governess?' Foggy and I ask together.

'It is what I do.' Madame Marionette smiles in a modest way.

'What—' Foggy swallows so hard that I can hear her, 'what happened to your husband, the *Compte*?'

Madame Marionette's mouth turns down. She pulls a crimson silk handkerchief from her pocket and covers her eyes.

'Poor Philippe is dead. Like His Majesty, I am widowed. I suffer alone.'

She dabs at her eyes with the handkerchief and flutters her eyelashes at Father, who stares as if he's hypnotized.

'And so now,' Madame Marionette gives a brave little smile, 'I earn a pathetic living by educating *les petites filles*—leetle girls—to become princesses.'

She walks right round me, staring at me from top to toe. Her scent is exotic and heavy, like it's hiding something unpleasant.

'Hmm,' she says. 'Hmmmmmm.'

Then Madame pokes my arm with her fingernail. It's like being pricked by a needle.

'Ow!' I say. 'Stoppit!'

'What do you think, Madame Marionette?' Father asks, ignoring me. 'Is there hope?'

Madame's smile sends him twirling his moustache in a frenzy.

'There is always hope,' she replies. 'Even when the child is as clumsy and... unfortunate as this one. I see such girls as my greatest challenge. You have here a rough *leetle* stone. I will shape her and polish her until she shines... like gold.'

Then she pokes me again.

'There is grace hiding under this homely exterior.' She gives a grim smile. 'It only requires *moi*—governess *extraordinaire*—to make her bloom.'

Father steps forward.

'Madame Marionette, I place my trust in you. If anyone can transform Jemima into the perfect princess, it's you!'

Madame Marionette gives a girlish giggle. 'Oh, Your Majesty! Such praise!' She waves a hand about in front of her face as if to calm her blushes.

A choking sound comes from behind me.

'Sister? Is something wrong?' asks my new governess.

'You... *you!*' Foggy's spectacles are misted up and her long nose quivers with rage. She grabs my shoulder and pulls me to her. 'Princess Jemima is *my* pupil, d'you hear?'

'And look at her!' Madame Marionette smirks. 'Plain and grubby and *completement* without style. She is hardly a credit to you.'

I stamp my foot. 'Stop talking about me as if I'm not here!'

Father glares at me. 'Sssst, Jemima! This type of behaviour is precisely why I called on Madame Marionette. Fogarty has failed you. You will attend lessons in the royal arts with Madame each day from nine until five. And we shall see what changes that brings about.'

'But Father, I don't want—'

I'm interrupted by Foggy.

'And what am *I* to do?' Her nose is extra pink and her eyes watery.

70

'You?' Father waves a hand. 'Oh, you can clean. And cook. And,' he stares hard at her, 'perform your *other* important duties.'

Foggy looks at Madame Marionette as if she'd like to strangle her, then she turns on her heel and squeaks out of the room.

Father addresses me. 'You may leave too, Jemima. I have much to discuss with Madame Marionette.' And he twirls his moustache again.

'But I—'

'Ssssst! Now leave.'

I'm almost at the door when Madame Marionette catches up with me.

'I will see you at nine o'clock *sharp* tomorrow morning, in my rooms. You will learn to be a credit to His Majesty, and to me,' she bends down and whispers, 'because if not, leetle girl, you will be sorry.'

Her breath smells of onions.

# THE CAGE

I toss and turn under my thin, scratchy blanket. My breath makes angry shapes in the air. I punch my pillow. How *dare* Madame Marionette poke me and prod me! How *dare* she call me clumsy and 'homely'! The idea of spending every day in the red dungeon with her makes me want to scream or run away, or both.

*Why* do I have to become a princess? Why can't Father just leave me alone, like he has for my whole life so far?

The familiar squeak of boots along the corridor. I jump out of bed and tiptoe to the door just in time to see Foggy's billowing grey cloak disappearing into the hall. Is she going to the Outside again? Could this be what Father meant when he talked about her 'other important duties'?

A dim glow creeps through the crack in the cupboard door. The alchemy book's still where I left it, behind the pillows. And there it'll stay, since I can't read it. Why won't it open? My list of questions is getting longer and longer.

But answers don't just appear. You have to discover them. You have to *do* something. I sit on the edge of my bed and think. Is there a question I can find the answer to, right now, while Foggy's out of the way?

*What's inside the silk-covered cage hanging from the ceiling in the library?*

My heart begins to thud. Dare I creep into the library in pitch darkness and find out? Whatever's inside the cage scared Madame Marionette's men silly. Not only scared them but *attacked* them. And when Smith carried the cage from the cart, he got attacked too. But if the cage is still safely hanging from the library ceiling, then whatever's inside can't get *me*—can it?

*Do it, Mim,* I tell myself sternly. *Be brave.*

I pull out the brooch from my pyjama pocket. Somehow, I feel safer when I have it, as if Smith's with me. Before I can change my mind, I wrap the blanket round my shoulders and hurry out of my room and along the silent corridor. I tiptoe into the hall with the three doors and listen outside the door to the dungeons. Hopefully Madame Marionette's sound asleep.

But someone—or something—is awake.

A low, growling sound seems to crawl from under the door to the dungeons, into my ears. Maybe Madame Marionette snores? Only it doesn't sound like a snore—it sounds more like the snarl of a wild animal. I may have an Enquiring Mind, but no way am I going to find out what *that* is. Holding my breath, I tiptoe towards the library, and press my ear to the door. I'll have to be stealthy. I need to make sure that the cage is still safely hanging from the ceiling before I dare to talk to whatever's inside it. I push open the door.

A loud creak echoes round the room.

My fingers grab the door before it can creak any more, and I slip inside the shadowy library. The cage hangs from the chain in the ceiling, the red cloth still covering it. Whatever's inside must be asleep. Dare I wake it?

Holding my brooch tightly, I creep over until I'm standing right underneath the cage. It turns gently, high above my head, in the draught from the door. I clear my throat loudly.

'Ahem!'

For a moment there's silence. Then something shuffles. The red cloth shivers.

'Hello?' I whisper.

There's no reply.

'I won't hurt you,' I whisper again. 'I just want to talk to you. Can you talk?'

The cage begins to swing from side to side high above my head, as if something inside it is turning around.

Then a voice whispers: 'Yesss.'

I jump. Somehow, I didn't think what's inside would *really* speak. I take a deep breath.

'My name's Mim,' I say. 'Do you have a name?'

The cage slows until it's hanging still. Then the voice speaks again. 'My name is Sssky.'

'Sky? That's a strange name.'

The hiss whispers round the library. 'No more ssstrange than *Mim*.'

I stare at the dim shape above me. 'What are you? You're not a... a snake?'

The cage begins to sway violently.

'A sssnake? You should be punished for your insssolence!'

I take a step back.

'Sorry,' I reply. 'Only, I can't see you. And you're hissing like a snake. Are you an animal or a human?'

'I am a prince.'

'A prince?'

'Must you repeat everything I sssay?'

'No—I'm just... well, surprised.'

'Surprised that a prince should be locked in a cage? That makes two of usss!'

'You sound very angry.'

'Angry? I am *furiousss!* How would *you* feel, in my situation?'

I try to imagine what it must be like to be locked in a cage and hung above the ground.

'Why are you in here?' I ask. 'Is it—is it something to do with Madame Marionette?'

The hissing becomes ear-splitting and the cage sways faster and faster. It creaks and squeaks.

'Don't!' I whisper. 'She'll hear us!'

The cage slowly swings to a halt, turning gently. Then Sky speaks a bit more quietly, as if through gritted teeth.

'She captured me. Took away my freedom. Locked me in thisss cage, so small I can't even ssstand. Calls me her "leetle pet".'

'Doesn't she let you out—ever?'

'Oh, yesss,' hisses Sky. 'Every night, she gets that odiousss little man—'

'Hercules?'

'—to unlock the cage. And then she makesss me *dance* for her.'

'I bet she pokes you with her fingernails!'

The reply is a long, furious hiss.

'Can't you run away?'

Sky laughs sarcastically. 'Run away? With my ankle chained to thisss cage? And that vile creature sssnapping at my heels?'

'What creature?'

Sky doesn't reply. He seems to be thinking. Then he says: 'What are you?'

'I'm... well, I'm a girl.'

'A human?'

'Yes.'

'Are you a ssservant girl?'

'No. I'm the King's daughter.'

'You are... a princesss?'

'Yes, worse luck. I *hate* being one.'

'Hate it? But being the child of a king is the bessst thing in all the world!'

'That's what *you* think! Try having a father who doesn't love you—who says you've got to wear stupid clothes and shoes and a horrible crown for the *rest of your life*—who makes you have lessons with Madame Marionette...'

'Poor little princesss,' hisses Sky. 'So *very* sssad. Try being *me*. Stuck in here!'

'Okay,' I admit. 'It may not be as bad as that. But it's pretty bad.'

76

'Hah!' scoffs Sky. Then his voice turns softer. 'So tell me, fine princesss—what brought you here, to ssspeak with me?'

'I have an Enquiring Mind,' I tell him. 'And you are the answer to one of my questions.'

'Quessstions?'

I'm tempted to ask *him* if he has to repeat everything I say, but I'd better not infuriate Sky any more.

'I've got a long list of them. Only, no one will give me the answers.'

'What quessstions?'

'I want to know the truth about the Outsiders. Foggy says—'

'Foggy? You talk to the missst?'

'No! Foggy is—was—my governess.'

'What liesss did this "Foggy" tell you?'

'She told me that the Outsiders are murderers.'

Another sharp hiss. 'Murderersss? What elssse?'

'She said there are creatures called Wings, and that their king is a savage.'

'That king,' hisses Sky coldly, 'isss my *Father*!' The cage swings dangerously again.

For a moment I say nothing, my mind boggling. I'm standing just ten feet below an Outsider! A real, live Wing. Then I remember what I've just said.

'Sorry.' I swallow. 'I'm sure your father's very nice.' I'm not sure at all, but this isn't the moment to say it, so I rush on. 'And Foggy says there are Outsiders in the sea, too. Half human, half fish. That they kill sailors and steal their treasure.'

'That, at least, isss a fact,' says Sky.

'So it's true, then. The Outside *is* dangerous.'

'Foolish girl! Never listen to the opinions of othersss. Make up your own mind.'

'How can I make up my own mind when I've never been there? The only way I can decide things is by listening and learning. So *please*, tell me.'

'Why should I?' Sky's voice becomes a smidgeon more friendly. 'Unlesss...'

'Unless what?'

'Unlesss we barter.'

'What do you mean?'

'If I give you answers to your quessstionsss, what will you give to me in return?'

'I-I don't know.' All I have is my golden brooch. And my lead crown. Sky surely won't want the crown. And no way will I give him my brooch, not even to find out about the Outside.

'I do not want your *thingsss*.'

Can he hear my thoughts?

'What can I give you, then?' I ask.

'I need your help.'

'What do you want me to do?'

'Firssst, you must ssswear that you will help me. Do you ssswear?'

I hesitate. 'I-I can't. Because there are so many things I'm not allowed to do. Or that I can't do because I'm not strong enough or tall enough.'

'Then will you ssswear to do all in your power to help me?'

78

Can I swear this? I do want to help Sky. And I *so* want the answers to my questions. I take a deep breath. 'All right, I swear. So, what do I have to do?'

'All in good time. Firssst, I will tell you the truth about the Outside.'

I shiver with excitement.

The cage begins to sway from side to side, only gently this time, like a lullaby. When Sky speaks again, his voice is full of sadness and longing.

'There are no chains on the Outside. No cagesss. Only air... and light... and freedom...'

A terrible howling comes from the dungeons; a screaming, a yowling, a snarling and a growling. Every hair on my head feels like it's standing up on end.

'Wh-what's that?' I whisper.

'It's that creature...' hisses Sky.

'What is it? It sounds like a werewolf!' I read about them in *Werewolves: Their Types and Habits.* 'Does Madame Marionette keep a werewolf as a pet?'

'Go!' hisses Sky. 'Get out before she sets the creature on usss!'

I don't need telling again. I stumble for the door, tripping over my blanket, which has fallen off my shoulders, and pelt across the hall and along the corridor to my bedroom. Inside, I drag the chair over until it's wedged under the handle. *No werewolf's going to get me!* Then I huddle in my bed and shiver until dawn.

# THE FIRST LESSON

**I** wake with a start to the sound of the bell tolling nine. It's Christmas Eve, and all I've got to look forward to is my first lesson with Madame Marionette. There are only moments to throw on my dress, shoes and crown and race along the corridor and down the stone steps to the dungeons. No time to slip into the library and make sure Sky is okay.

Outside Madame's room, I listen. There's no howling or shrieking or growling. Even if the creature I heard last night *is* a werewolf, werewolves only come out at night, and this is morning. I knock.

No answer. Maybe Madame is in her dressing-room and hasn't heard me. I knock again, louder. Then I push open the door and walk into the red, half-dark room.

And freeze.

Eyes stare at me from every corner. A monkey, dressed in a red coat, perches on a red chair clutching a banana. Underneath the chair a snake coils, its jaws open ready to strike. A tiger crouches by the fireplace, its yellow eyes fixed on me. A grizzly bear rears up on hind legs. Something growls, deep and harsh. In slow motion, I back towards the door.

'*Arrêtez!*'

Madame Marionette steps out of the shadows. She wears a cape made of rusty red feathers, and pointy red shoes. A fox's head hangs around her neck, its dull brush tail falling over her shoulder. Her brooch seems to be made of coiled human hair. She smiles her cruel smile and waves her long, sharp fingernails at the animals.

'My leetle collection,' she says. 'Look, if you wish.'

And then I see that all the animals are dead, stuffed. I walk among them, my knees trembling. A puma crouches like a black shadow. A tarantula spider with thick, hairy legs sits on a table. Rows of dead butterflies, their bright wings stiff and dusty, are pinned in lines on the red walls. On the mantelpiece sits a row of birds' eggs, each with a tiny hole—someone has sucked out the baby birds before they can be hatched. Stuffed nightingales are mounted on twigs, their beaks open—only they will never sing again.

'My leetle pets,' says Madame Marionette. I feel sick.

'Pets? But they aren't alive!'

'I like to 'ave dead things about me.'

A fat handbag made of crocodile skin gapes open on the table. Something in the room smells metallic and hot, like blood.

I take a step backwards, and Madame Marionette points at me with a red fingernail.

'*Stop!* And stand still.' She walks over to me and bends down so that our faces are on a level. 'You will learn, Jemima, to obey me. Or—like these creatures—you will suffer the consequences.'

'What d'you mean by that?' My voice sounds braver than I feel.

'When creatures do not obey me, I become... bored.' She waves a hand at the stuffed animals. '*Pouf!* They cannot bore me now.'

I shiver. Is this what she plans to do to Sky, if he bores her? I must warn him—tell him to dance for her and keep her entertained, however angry he feels. Then another horrible thought occurs to me. She can't have *me* stuffed, can she? Father would never allow it. Would he?

'*Attention!*' snaps Madame Marionette. 'We shall now commence our lessons. Starting with *déportement.*'

Is that even a French word? Something about the way Madame speaks feels sort of *wrong*, only I can't work out what it is.

She reaches into her crocodile-skin handbag, pulls out a thick red book and hands it to me. It's heavy as lead. I turn it over to look at the title. Maybe it's about something interesting. But the title reads, in curly letters:

*The Education and
Instruction of Princesses*

Before I can open it, Madame points her sharp fingernail at my head.

'Take off your crown. Now, balance the book upon your 'ead.'

'What?'

'Are you deaf?' Madame raises her voice. 'BALANCE THIS BOOK UPON YOUR 'EAD.'

The book's even heavier than the crown. It slips off my curls immediately. I just manage to catch it as it falls.

'AGAIN!'

The book teeters on the top of my head. I stand as still as I can, my neck stretched up, and try not to breathe.

Madame Marionette points at my feet. 'Now, walk.'

In slow motion, I take a step forward. It's hard enough walking in the high-heeled shoes. This is impossible. The book see-saws.

'Straighten the back! Chin up! Shoulders down!' snaps Madame Marionette. 'A princess does not slouch. She walks with her 'ead held HIGH.'

I stop and glare at her. The book slides off my head.

'You can't order me about!'

Madame's eyes narrow. 'Watch me, leetle girl.'

'I'll tell Father.'

'*I'll tell Father!*' Madame Marionette imitates my voice. 'All your father wants is a perfect princess, and he doesn't care how that is achieved. He's paid me a very large fee to teach you. And teach you I will.'

'But Father can't afford to pay—'

'Can't he? We shall see,' says Madame Marionette, with an unpleasant smile. 'Book on 'ead! *Allez-oop!*'

I grit my teeth and try. But my hair's slippery and it's impossible to keep the book on it. When it falls off for the twentieth time, Madame pokes the back of my neck. Her fingernails prick like little daggers.

*That does it.*

'Don't—you—*ever*—poke—me—again!' I hiss.

I make for the door. But instead of following me, Madame shouts: 'Groucho! Here, boy!'

From the room next door, an enormous dog slinks in— bigger than me, with long, matted hair and a jewelled red collar. A growl rattles in its chest and it bares needle-sharp teeth. *This* must be the creature Sky talked about. It steals past me until it bars the door. Slivers of saliva drip from its pink tongue and pool on the floor. Its breath smells like raw meat.

'Groucho wants you to stay, don't you, leetle boy?' Madame Marionette smiles.

Groucho raises his nose and gives an ear-splitting howl, just like the one I heard last night.

'Poor Groucho, he is tired.' Madame points at the floor. 'Lie down, boy!'

The dog slowly eases down to lie in front of the door. His yellow eyes never leave me.

'And now we shall try once more. Book on 'ead! Stand straight! Walk forward!'

I do. But I've never hated anyone so much. And inside my head, words churn around. *I'll tell Smith. He'll help me. Or Foggy. She hates Madame Marionette. She'll stop this.*

Because if this is the way my life's going to be, and no one makes it stop, there'll be nothing else for it. I'll have to run away to the Outside.

Only if I do that, I'll never see Smith again.

Over and over I walk, the book teetering on my head. My back aches. My head pounds. If I so much as move towards the door, Groucho raises his head and shows his needle-sharp teeth in a snarl. Surely it must be lunchtime?

Then, as if in answer to my prayers, there's a sharp knock at the door. Groucho growls.

'Who is it?' says Madame.

'Your sister.' Foggy sniffs from the other side of the door.

'One moment.' Madame smiles a slow, cruel smile and turns to me. 'Give me the book.' I hand it over thankfully.

Madame delves into the crocodile-skin handbag and pulls out a bloody package. Groucho's ears immediately perk up. He licks his lips.

'Good boy, Groucho,' Madame whispers. 'Here's your reward.'

She wafts the package under Groucho's nose and draws him away from the door and into the bedroom. He leaves a trail of foul-smelling saliva behind him.

'Let her in,' she calls over her shoulder to me.

I open the door. Foggy stands there, white as a sheet apart from her pink nose which quivers with rage.

'Foggy, she's *horrible*,' I hiss. 'She's making me—'

But Foggy ignores me. Her eyes are fixed on her sister. Madame Marionette stares back. Her red lips twist into a nasty smile.

Then she turns to me and pushes me—hard—towards the door.

'You may go, Jemima,' she says. 'But you will return in thirty minutes sharp, when we shall be studying *élocution*.'

'E-Electrocution?' Is she planning to shock me into behaving?

'Stupid leetle girl,' sneers Madame. '*ÉL-O-CU-TION*. The study of 'ow to speak like a princess.'

Then Foggy steps inside and Madame shuts the door firmly in my face.

# THE ROW

**I** crouch down with my ear pressed to the keyhole. I don't like to eavesdrop, but it seems like the only way to get answers in a castle of secrets.

At first there's silence, apart from the squeak of Foggy's shoes.

Then she hisses: 'Why have you come here?'

Madame Marionette laughs softly.

'I have to make a living, sister.'

She's dropped the French accent.

'But why *here*?' says Foggy. 'We swore never to speak or see one another again.'

'Promises,' says Madame Marionette, 'are made to be broken.'

'So you think you can barge in here after all these years and take my job?'

'That's the idea, yes,' says Madame, with a sneer in her voice.

Foggy's voice quivers with fury. 'Ever since the Day of the Catastrophic Curse, when the Queen died, I've been like a mother to that child. I've lavished her with tenderness and care—'

Tenderness and care? I press my fingers to my mouth to stop myself laughing out loud.

'—I've educated her to the very best of my ability—'

'And what a pig's breakfast you've made of it,' says Madame Marionette. 'Her father, the King, is ashamed of her!'

I clench my fists.

Foggy carries on as if Madame hasn't spoken. '—and I've done all this out of loyalty to His Majesty—'

'Loyalty?' Madame's voice is low and taunting. 'I don't think so. More like a *crush*. Does my poor, plain sister *lurve* the handsome King? Does she? Does she?'

Foggy gasps. I can just imagine how steamed up her glasses must be, and how pink her nose. But before she can speak, Madame Marionette goes on.

'What chance do you think you stand with the King? Why would he pay attention to *you*, when *I* am here? Already, he's falling under my spell.'

'W-what?'

Madame laughs nastily. 'I flirt. I smile. I flatter. It will only be a matter of time before—*Pouf!*—he falls in love with me.'

Foggy yelps. 'You... you *fake!*'

'And just what is that supposed to mean?'

'Ever since you married the *Compte*, you've paraded around with your airs and graces and your fake French accent. You're no more French than—than—fish and chips! You're a phoney, a liar, a deceiver—'

'A deceiver?' Madame Marionette's voice takes on an icy tone. 'Oh, sister dear. I think *you* know far more about deception than I.'

There's a long silence. Why isn't Foggy arguing? She *always* argues.

Footsteps squeak over the floor, back and forth. Then they stop abruptly.

'So that's your plan, is it?' Foggy gives a loud sniff. 'To come here and sneak your way into His Majesty's heart, just to spite me?'

Madame laughs softly. 'Watch and learn, sister. Watch as I wind the King around my little finger. Watch as I turn his pathetic daughter into a princess. Watch him pay me his fortune to do so.'

'What fortune?' snaps Foggy. 'His Majesty has no fortune any more.'

'He sold the very last painting,' says Madame. 'Which was just enough to pay for my services.'

So *that's* what happened to my special painting, the painting of the ocean. Father's sold it—to pay Madame.

'But that painting was worth thousands of pounds!'

'I am worth it,' Madame says.

'*That,*' growls Foggy, 'is a matter of opinion!'

'Unlike you, dear sister, I know what the King needs,' says Madame Marionette. 'First, he needs the perfect daughter. Not an odd, wild little savage who makes him a laughing stock.'

A savage? My fingernails press so hard into my palms they leave white marks.

'Second, he needs a loving wife. Which is where I come in.'

Foggy makes a choking sound.

'And third, in order to have these things he needs gold. Lots of lovely gold. And there's only one way to get it. Which is where *you* come in.'

'I-I don't know what you mean!' splutters Foggy. I press my ear harder to the keyhole.

'What a bad memory you have, sister! I know all about your night-time visits to the Outside.'

There's a silence.

'How... how d'you know about—?'

'Oh, the King and I are like *that*,' Madame clicks her fingers. 'He's told me everything. I know all about the old man. I know about the gold.'

My ears prick up. Gold?

'There *is* no gold,' Foggy mutters.

'But there will be,' says Madame.

'That's where you're wrong,' says Foggy. 'The old man's tried—and failed—for eleven years. There will be no gold.'

What old man? And what has he been trying to do? This is all getting stranger and stranger.

'He will succeed, this time,' says Madame Marionette coldly. 'And now, I have work to do. You may leave.'

'I certainly will!' hisses Foggy. 'I'm going straight to His Majesty to tell him everything—about what a fake you are, a schemer—about how you only want to marry him for the gold. You'll be out of here before the end of the day!'

Madame Marionette gives a low laugh. 'Oh, you won't be doing that, sister.'

'How will you stop me?'

'Like this...'

Madame's high heels click over the floor towards Foggy. Is she going to set Groucho on her? Her voice becomes menacing.

'If you so much as open your mouth to the King,' she whispers, 'I will tell him your *special little secret*. About what happened on the Day of the Catastrophic Curse. About... Jemima.'

I stop breathing. A secret? About *me*?

'You... you wouldn't.'

'Wouldn't I?'

'To think,' whispers Foggy, 'that I trusted you once. I told you everything. And now, you threaten to betray me.'

'Things change, sister.'

'No—*you* changed. After you went off with the *Compte*, all you cared about was luxury and gold.'

'True.' Madame gives a low laugh. 'Anyhow, we have a deal, yes? I'll keep your secret—if you keep mine.'

It sounds as if Foggy's grinding her teeth.

'Goodbye, sister dear,' calls Madame. 'Groucho will see you to the door.'

A distant growl makes me jump to my feet and pelt up the steps and back to my room. My head's bursting with even more questions. Who is this old man? What did Foggy do on Curse Day that is such a big secret?

And what's it got to do with *me*?

# ÉLOCUTION

'*É*l-o-cu-tion, leetle girl,' says Madame Marionette, 'is the practice of speaking clearly and *correctement*.'

I long to say, *Why don't you drop that fake French accent and speak properly yourself?*—but I dare not let Madame know that I overheard her and Foggy. So I press my mouth shut and try to listen to her instructions.

'Repeat after me,' intones Madame Marionette. 'I saw a kitten eating chicken in the kitchen.'

'I saw a kitchen eating kitten in the—'

'Wrong!' Madame prods me with her long fingernail. 'Again!'

'I saw a chicken eating kitchen in the—'

'Stupid leetle girl. You will say it correctly, because I am becoming... *bored*.' She flicks a glance at the stuffed animals. They stare at me with cold dead eyes.

I close my eyes and concentrate. 'I saw a... kitten... eating... chicken... in the... kitchen.'

'Faster!'

'I saw a kitten eating chicken in the kitchen.'

'Faster!'

'I-saw-a-kitten-eating-chicken-in-the-kitchen!'

'Better. Now, repeat—Fred fed Ted bread, and Ted fed Fred bread.'

Now I know why they're called tongue-twisters. My tongue's twisted into a knot and my lips keep getting in the way. But that's only the beginning. Madame has dozens more terrible tongue-twisters to torment me with.

*Seven slick slimy snakes slowly sliding southwards.*

*The big black bug bit the big black bear, but the big black bear bit the big black bug back.*

I thought the longer ones would be the hardest, but they're not:

*Thin sticks, thick bricks.*

*Eleven benevolent elephants.*

It's impossible! The harder I try, the worse it gets. By the time I've practised a hundred times, it feels like steam's pouring out of my ears, and my mouth's full of tangled wool and loose teeth. Each time I muddle the words, Madame prods me with her sharp fingernail, until my legs and arms are red and sore. Inside, a smouldering rage grows and grows until it's all I can do not to scream. The only way I can stop myself is by making a list in my head of the things that make me happy.

*Smith.*

*My brooch.*

*The library.*

Except thinking about the library makes me think of Sky and my promise to help him. Is he good, or bad? Anyone would be furious if they were locked in a tiny

93

cage—but maybe he's always that way. And how can I help him escape, if I'm banned from the library and Foggy has her beady eye on me?

The bell tolls five times.

'*Finis.*' Madame Marionette gives my elbow a final prod and pushes me towards the door. 'Go. You will return in one hour.'

I rub my arm. 'But... it's five o'clock! Lesson time is over!'

'It is *I* who decide lesson times,' Madame replies. 'If you were a better student, it might be different. As it is, we shall be working until midnight—or later, if you are as slow as you 'ave been so far. Now go!'

'But it's Christmas Eve!'

'So?' Madame shrugs.

'At midnight it'll be Christmas Day!'

'And how do you usually spend Christmas Day?'

I stare at the floor. The truth is, we never do anything. Christmas Day is just the same as all the others. But I'm not going to tell Madame that.

'It's not fair!'

'What has "fair" to do with it?' Madame narrows her eyes. 'You should be grateful that I am prepared to devote so much precious time to your education. Because in seven days, on New Year's Eve, you will be examined.'

'What?'

'There will be a New Year's Eve ball in the throne room. And at this ball you will demonstrate to your father all that you have learnt from *moi*. You will walk gracefully, and talk clearly and politely, and demonstrate the manners of a princess. And you will dance.'

'Dance?' My heart sinks.

'Tonight we shall rehearse.'

I stare helplessly at my feet.

'I can't dance!' I whisper.

Madame glares at me. '*Can't?* If there is one thing in this world which *really* bores me, it is a child who won't try.'

'But I—'

'*Silence!* Now go.'

I stumble out of the room.

I ought to eat something, but I can't force it down. And anyway, I've got to stay out of Foggy's way—she's sniffing and muttering darkly under her breath in her room, clearly in a terrible mood after her row with Madame. It's bad enough having pricked, stinging arms and legs from all the poking and prodding, without being moaned and grumped at by Foggy.

Should I run over to the forge and tell Smith what Madame's up to? He's the only person who'll believe me. But if Foggy catches me with Smith in her present mood, she'll tell Father and I'll be banned from seeing him.

I stand outside the door to the library, thoughts whirling in my head. Dare I go in and see Sky?

*You'd better*, says a voice in my head, which is probably the voice of my Enquiring Mind. *It's the only way to find out the truth about the Outside.*

So I push the door open and step inside.

The covered cage hangs high above me in the dusky light. I shut the door quietly and creep over to the bookcases.

Then I silently pile the heaviest books under the door handle.

I tiptoe across the room until I'm standing right underneath the cage. I cup my fingers around my mouth and whisper.

'Prince Sky! Are you there?'

There's a sharp shuffling and the cage rocks.

'Naturally I am here,' comes a hiss. 'Where elssse would I be?'

'Look,' I say. 'I've got less than an hour, and then I have to be with Madame Marionette until midnight. You promised to answer my questions. I want you to tell me about the old man.'

'Old man?' Sky sounds suspicious.

'The old man who lives on the Outside.'

There's a long, furious silence. Then Sky hisses.

'Cheat! Liar and cheat!'

'What? I'm not!'

'You said you have never been to the Outssside!'

'I haven't! I overheard Madame Marionette talking to Foggy about an old man. But I don't know who he is or what he's up to. I only know it's something to do with making gold.'

'Gold?' Sky sounds excited. 'He hasss gold?'

'No—at least, I don't think so. But who is he? And what's he trying to do?'

The cage turns slowly in the air. Sky seems to be thinking.

'I will tell you,' he says at last. 'But remember that you ssswore to do all in your power to assist me.'

'I remember. And I will.'

'Then I will answer your quessstion. The old man is an alchemissst.'

My mouth drops open. *Alchemist*. I've never heard the word spoken before, but I've read a word very like it: the alchemy book is still hidden at the back of my wardrobe. My heart begins to beat fast.

'What exactly is an alchemist?'

'An alchemist is a mixture of a scientist and a magician. Hisss work is to transform lead into gold.'

I remember what Smith said, about Curse Day, and about the gold crown being turned into lead.

'So it's sort of the opposite?'

'Opposssite of what?'

'Of what happened on Curse Day.'

'Yesss, if you like.'

'So what *did* happen on Curse Day? Why did the crown turn to lead? Why did my mother die—and Smith's father? And why is it called Curse Day, anyway?'

'Because there was a curse, ssstupid girl!'

'I *know* that! But who was cursed, and why?'

'Sssit, and I will tell you what I know.'

So I sit down under the cage and listen.

# THE CURSE

'**I**t was eleven yearsss ago, on the winter solstice,' Sky whispers. 'And there was no wall around Galena.'

I nod. 'So people could go Outside whenever they wanted?'

'Yesss. There was free passage. And your father and his queen wore golden crowns upon their heads and sat on golden thrones. The Queen had jussst given birth to a baby girl.'

'That was me! The winter solstice is my birthday.'

'On the Outside, my father, King Wing, reigned in the air, while the Mer Queen reigned in the ocean.'

'The Mer Queen?'

'Queen of the ocean people, the tailed onesss.'

'Oh, I *wish* I could see the Mers!'

Sky hisses. 'Be careful what you wish for, human. Your father wishes now that he had never ssseen a Mer.'

'What happened?'

'Before I tell you, you must understand the nature of the Mersss. The ocean is their country. Humans travelling on the ocean must obey the Mer Law. And the Mer Law states that all the cargo on the ocean is rightfully theirsss. Humans sailing on the ocean do so at their own risssk.'

'Foggy told me that the Mers sing to the sailors and wreck their ships.'

'That is their nature. But your father wasss greedy. And on the night before the solstice, he was awaiting a ship full of precious cargo from the countries across the ocean—gold jewellery for the Queen, embroidered cloth for his wardrobe, and a golden cradle for hisss newborn child.'

'For me!'

'The night was stormy. The wavesss like mountains. The King's ship was approaching the shore, tossed and tired, when the Mers ssstruck. The ship was surrounded. Then the Mers sang—a terrible song that hypnotized the sailors so their strength seeped away and they lay senselesss upon the decks. The ship foundered on sharp rocks and sssank into the ocean. And the Mers swam down and stole the jewellery and the cloth and the cradle, and cut off the drowned sailors' beards for lining their nesssts, and left their bodies on the rocks for the sharksss to devour.'

I shiver and wrap my arms around my chest.

'Wh-what happened then?'

'The King was furious. He sent his men down to the ocean with netsss. Their ears were bound with cloth so that the Mer songs would not enchant them. And all day the men dragged the netsss in the ocean until, at dawn, there was a great tumbling and threshing and screaming.'

'They caught one of the Mers?'

'Worssse. They caught the Mer Queen herself. She was strong and muscular, but she could not escape the net. They dragged her to the ssshore and chained her. And once on the shore, her Mers were powerless to help her. She bucked and bit and screamed, but the King's men carried her into Galena.'

I have a very bad feeling. 'What did they do?'

'They brought her to the wooden platform outside the forge. They forced her neck into the executioner's block and bound her eyesss. And then...' Sky's voice dies away.

I shut my eyes. They must have made Smith's father do it. And Smith must have seen it. No wonder he refuses to execute anyone.

'And before the Mer Queen's head wasss parted from her body, she shook back her white hair and screamed at the executioner—for the Queen was the only Mer who could ssspeak—"*I curse you, killer!*" Then she turned to the King with hatred in her eyes. "*But most of all, I curse YOU—and I curse all that is dear to you.*"'

Sky's words seem to echo round the library.

'And that wasss the beginning of the war with the Outside. The Mers swore vengeance on the humans. And the King ordered the Wall to be built around Galena, and he never ssset foot Outside again.'

'But why build a wall? Can the Mers get out of the ocean?'

'No. But a few timesss a year the tide was so high that the waves beat against the castle and flooded the streets of Galena. The King feared the Mers would surge into Galena with the tide.'

'So Smith's dad died? And my mother?'

'Yesss. The moment after the Mer Queen died, the executioner dropped down dead. And the King went running to his queen. She, too, wasss dead.'

'And the baby—me?' I whisper. 'Wasn't I cursed too?'

'How should I know?' says Sky. 'But every piece of your father's gold wasss changed, that day, to lead.'

A heavy weight plummets into my stomach. I blink away tears. If the Mer Queen cursed everything dearest to my father, then why wasn't *I* cursed?

There can only be one answer, and I know it already. I wasn't dear to him. He didn't love me, and never has. It's not that I *want* to be cursed. But not being loved is just as bad—or worse—than a curse.

I swallow, hard. 'How do you know all this, Sky?'

'My father sssaw it all. And now, it is time for you to keep your promise to me. We will make a plan for my essscape.'

'But how? I can't get you down.'

'Ssspeak to your father. Tell him to free me. Fathers will do anything for their children.'

'Not my father,' I say quietly. 'He doesn't love me. And anyway, Madame Marionette has him twisted round her finger. She says she's going to be his wife, as soon as the old man makes gold. That's all my father cares about—gold.'

The cage spins wildly in circles, the chain clanking and groaning and Sky hissing fit to bust.

'Stoppit!' I whisper. 'She'll hear you.'

'I don't care if ssshe hears me. I will *not* stay in this contraption! I will *not* be her "leetle pet".'

Then I remember Madame's words, and the room full of stuffed animals.

'Sky—stop! You mustn't annoy her, whatever you do.'

'I will do as I please. I am the son of King Wing!'

'But you don't understand!'

'Underssstand what?'

'Madame Marionette kills her—her pets if they bore her or disobey her. And then she has them stuffed.'

There's a silence. The cage swings to a standstill. When Sky speaks again, it's in a very different voice.

'Help me,' he whispers.

'I'll try, I swear,' I whisper back. 'I'll think and think about it and maybe an answer will come. Meanwhile, whatever you do, don't annoy Madame Marionette.'

Outside, the bell tolls six.

'I have to go now. I'll come back just as soon as I can.'

'*No!*' Sky hisses. 'Leave now—and don't come back until you have a plan!'

'But what if I—'

'Do you imagine you are *helping* me, sssneaking in and out of here? She only needs to discover you here and I will be… killed—and—and ssstuffed.'

He's right. But how can I possibly help Sky? The cage is too high and too heavy to get down. And even if I *could*, I have no key to unlock it—and he says he's chained to the cage as well.

But I've promised him. And nothing is impossible—after all, I've solved three secrets already: I've solved the secret of what's hanging in the cage in the library, I've discovered

102

why my mother died, and I've found out who lives on the Outside. There's an answer to everything—there *has* to be—if I just keep looking for it.

'I'll be back, Sky. I promise. Just as soon as I've thought of a way.'

There's no reply. A low, sad, snuffling sound comes from the cage. It sounds like Sky is crying.

# THE BALL

**A** week later, on New Year's Eve, Foggy and I stand outside the throne room, waiting for the ball to begin. My scalp tingles from Foggy's hair-brushing and my ears ache from her grumbling. The leaden crown pinches my forehead and squashes my ears.

It's been the worst week *ever*.

Madame Marionette forced me to balance books on my head, to recite tongue-twisters and to talk in a lah-di-dah way. I had to learn etiquette (a posh word for manners): *take small mouthfuls, don't gobble, chew thirty times before swallowing, NEVER speak with your mouth full!!!* I had to practise the royal wave: *don't flap your 'ands like a duck, don't smile with your mouth open, keep those crooked teeth hidden!* But the worst lessons of all were the dancing lessons. Madame poked the backs of my legs with her fingernails until they were red raw. She made me practise the steps over and over until my toes blistered and wept.

At night, I've been too exhausted to even think about my questions. It's all I can do to struggle out of my uncomfortable clothes and high-heeled shoes and fall into bed. There hasn't been a single minute to visit Smith or to come up with a plan to help Sky escape. One night I heard Foggy's footsteps squeaking along the corridor and returning a short time later. She must have been visiting the old man—the alchemist. Maybe the strange shapes under her cloak were objects that turned to lead on Curse Day. Maybe she was taking them to the alchemist for him to change them back into gold. The alchemy book still glows at the back of my wardrobe, as if it's trying to tell me something important, but I'm too tired to find out what that is.

From inside the throne room comes a haunting single note—the same sound that Hercules, the puny driver, played on the horn when Madame Marionette arrived in Galena. I shiver with nerves. If I don't pass this examination, who knows what tortures she will have in store for me? Foggy glowers beside me. Instead of her usual black dress and scuffed boots, she wears a long, moth-eaten velvet gown. Her lank hair escapes from a tight bun. Worst of all, she's got make-up on. Her lipstick is sort of mud-coloured and she's drawn big black circles round her eyes, like a panda. She's obviously trying to compete with Madame Marionette for Father's attention.

'Let the Princess enter!' It's Father's voice.

Foggy pushes me inside.

The throne room is full of people. There's Father of course, looking even more stylish than usual, in silken breeches and an embroidered waistcoat, his moustache curled into corkscrews. Beside him stands Madame Marionette, her hand resting on his arm, just as if she's already his queen.

She wears a brilliant-red dress, plunging down at the front, with a necklace of rubies. Madame smiles up at Father, fluttering her eyelashes. Sprawled on the floor by the fire lies Groucho. He raises his head and growls at me, deep in his throat.

In the centre of the room a long table is laid with goblets and plates. People stand about dressed in their best, uncomfortable and whispering. Hercules, Jason and Atlas huddle together in a corner, well away from Groucho. Hercules, wearing a horrible yellow suit, wipes at the mouthpiece of his horn. Jason, almost bursting out of his black satin outfit, holds a violin. Atlas, in green velvet, has a drum. I see all this in a rush, before my eyes fall on Smith.

He stands alone by the wall, his beetly brows drawn together. I've never seen him wearing anything other than his sooty vest and trousers. Tonight he's unrecognizable in a clean white shirt, midnight blue trousers and a pair of shiny shoes. He shifts from foot to foot as if they're too small for him. The strangest thing is that Smith's here at all. He tries to smile when he sees me, then he winces and shuffles again.

A low murmur of 'Your Royal Highness' ripples round the room. Then everyone except Madame and Father (and Foggy, who's glaring at Madame) bows and curtsies. This is horrible. If only I could turn and run out of the door, out of the castle, out of Galena to the Outside—Mers or no Mers.

'Come, Jemima.' Father tears his eyes away from Madame. 'This is your opportunity to demonstrate the skills Madame Marionette has graciously taught you. If you pass—and I expect you to, or there will be *very bad consequences*—you will prove that even the most unpromising material can be shaped into something perfect.'

'Even the dullest lead,' says Madame Marionette, 'can be transformed—*Pouf!*—into gold.'

Foggy mutters under her breath, behind me.

'And now,' announces Father, 'let the ball commence. Jemima, you will begin by greeting your guests.'

I do my very best. I walk around the room with my head held high, just as if I had a book on it. I don't stumble in my heels. I wave and smile, keeping my mouth shut. Then Father orders us to sit at the table.

Madame Marionette takes the seat to his right, with a Cheshire-cat grin. Foggy sidles up to sit on Father's other side, but he waves her away as if she's an annoying fly, and makes me sit there, so she glares at *me* instead. If only I was sitting next to Smith, then I could tell him about Madame's horrible lessons and about meeting Sky. But Father makes him sit far away at the bottom of the table.

I pick up my goblet. Madame stares at me like a cat watching a mouse. I sip my water without slurping, and when the food arrives—soup, bread and cheese—I remember which utensils to use. I'm careful not to speak with my mouth full and I chew thirty times before swallowing (that isn't difficult—I feel sick with fear). Groucho watches my every move, his saliva making puddles on the floor.

The meal seems never-ending. Surely I've passed, so far? If I can just keep going, maybe Father will tell Madame Marionette to ease up on my lessons and let me go back to visiting Smith. And maybe Smith can help me find a way to set Sky free.

Father taps his wine glass with a spoon. Silence falls over the table.

'And now for the most important test of all,' he says. 'Jemima will demonstrate her dancing.' He waves to Hercules, Jason and Atlas.

'Take it away, boys,' orders Hercules.

'Yus, chief,' mutter Jason and Atlas. They pick up their instruments and begin to play a gloomy dirge, with a lot of wrong notes.

I can't get up. After all my rehearsing—all the aching, the prodding and poking, and all Madame's cruel, critical remarks—I still can't dance. My cheeks burn and icy shivers pass up and down my spine. How can I stand up and make an idiot of myself in front of all these people?

*I can't. I just can't.* I glance down the table at Smith.

*Go on, Mim,* he mouths. I shake my head and stare down at my feet. They stay still, as frozen as the rest of me.

'Jemima!' Father's voice is irritated. He nods at the table, and everyone begins to clap in time to the music. My hands grip the side of the chair.

Madame Marionette stands up. 'Jemima is shy, I think.'

Is she going to let me off? I fix my eyes on her imploringly, and Groucho gives another growl.

'Are you shy, leetle girl?' She has never spoken so softly to me. It must be because Father's here. 'Perhaps you need... a partner.'

She points her red-nailed finger at Smith.

'You!'

Hope lights up my insides like sunshine. Smith's so much taller than me that if he takes hold of me, he'll lift me off the ground. Then I'll look as if I'm dancing. My legs begin to work again and I stand up and totter towards him.

But Madame jerks her head in the direction of the door. Smith turns and leaves the room, leaving me standing alone in the middle of it. All the eyes bore into me as the music plays on.

At last, heavy footsteps approach the throne room and stop outside. At a signal from Madame, the music dies away. Hercules drops his horn and scurries across the room to open the door.

Through the doorway staggers Smith.

And in his arms is the covered cage from the library.

# THE DANCE

Smith lumbers into the room, almost losing his balance as the cage, still covered in its crimson cloth, jerks about in his arms. Sky must be desperately trying to escape. The music dies away.

Smith lurches across the floor towards Madame Marionette and sets the cage down at her feet, panting and rubbing his hands where the cage has bitten into them. Groucho raises his head, gives an ear-splitting howl and creeps across the floor towards the cage. The cage becomes very still. Madame points her finger at Smith.

'Remove the cover, executioner!'

Smith flashes Madame a look of intense dislike. Then he steps forward, takes a corner of the crimson silk cloth and, in a great sweep, pulls it from the cage. Groucho sneaks closer, eyes narrowed, ears flat.

The cage is made of ornamental metal, painted rusty red. A padlock secures its door. Inside, a hunched black shape crouches, rock still. I peer at it. Is this Sky? A terrible thought flashes through my mind. Maybe Sky's been taken away and stuffed, and this... whatever it is... has been put in the cage in his place. Then a hiss echoes round the throne room. It *is* Sky.

Hearing the hiss, Groucho howls again and launches himself at the cage, yelping and snarling, his spit frothing the floor. The dark shape of Sky flattens itself against the bars, away from the hound. Madame Marionette steps forward and seizes Groucho's collar.

'Down, boy!' She smacks him across the ears. Groucho whines and slobbers but lies down. He never takes his eyes from Sky. Father comes over to join Madame, keeping a safe distance from Groucho.

'So this is your secret pet, Tomazine?'

'*Oui*,' says Madame. 'He is the son of King Wing. Like his father, he is haughty and stubborn.'

'A prince... Why do you keep him in a cage? And why did you ask me to have it hung from the library ceiling?'

'To keep him from prying eyes. And to teach him humility. He is—how you say?—too big for his boots.'

'The Wings are indeed haughty creatures.' Father hesitates, glancing from Sky's hunched figure to Madame's triumphant face. Just for a minute, he looks as if he might argue with her. Then he nods quickly. 'Yes. Of course he must be taught a lesson.'

Madame burrows in the pocket of her red dress and pulls out a rusty key. She tosses it at Smith, who catches it in one large hand.

'Free him,' she orders.

Anger and pity scurry across Smith's face like clouds. He can never bear to see anything suffer. He bends to the cage door, fits the key into the padlock, turns it and unhooks the padlock. The door swings open.

The hunched shape stays where it is. In the flickering candlelight, I make out a long metal chain on Sky's ankle, the other end attached to the bars of the cage. Then the cage begins to shake. Sky is shivering. If only I could call out to him—tell him I'm here, that Smith won't let anything terrible happen to him. But if I do, Madame will know that I've secretly visited Sky in the library.

Madame steps forward, her dark eyes full of triumph.

'Leave the room, executioner.'

Smith glares at her. But he turns and leaves the room. Every atom in my body wants to follow him.

Holding Groucho back by his red collar, Madame walks up to the open cage.

'Come, my leetle pet,' she whispers. 'Come out and play.'

Sky doesn't move. Keeping her back to Father, Madame bends, laughing softly to herself, and prods at Sky's hunched shape with her finger. Sky gives a sharp hiss, leaps away and flattens himself against the bars again. Groucho howls, a melancholy yowl which echoes round the room.

Father touches Madame's shoulder.

'Is the creature... quite safe, Tomazine?'

'Safe?' Madame gives a high, gleeful laugh. 'Oh, no. But what would life be without a leetle danger, eh?'

Father steps backwards. Madame, her eyes glinting, prods at Sky again. All of a sudden, he stumbles out of the cage, trips over his ankle chain and sprawls in a black heap on the floor. My eyes nearly burst out of my head, trying to make him out. He seems nothing but a mess of dark, gleaming feathers.

'Get up, boy!' orders Madame.

A curved wing untangles itself. Then another. A boy—about the same height as me—stands before us, his keen, dark eyes alight with hatred, his black skin gleaming in the candlelight. A sharp nose—like a beak—curves above an angry slash of a mouth. Everything else about him is bird: black feathers erupt in a plume from his head, more feathers cover his body and legs. Instead of hands and arms, there are strong-looking wings.

I remember the swarm of bird-creatures dive-bombing the library. Those were the Wings. And this is the son of their king.

'Your partner, leetle girl,' says Madame Marionette. She pushes me towards Sky, and signals to Hercules, Jason and Atlas.

As they begin to play, I grab a handful of black wing feathers. Sky's dark eyes flash with fury.

'How *dare* you touch me!' he hisses, under the music.

'It's me, Sky,' I whisper. 'Mim.'

'Traitor!' Sky's spittle wets my face.

'What? I'm not!'

'You promisssed to help me.' Sky glances at Madame and lowers his voice even more. 'I kept my side of the bargain. You lied to me.'

'I didn't!' I whisper. 'You've got to trust me. Give me time.'

113

'Trussst you?' hisses Sky. 'What have you done to earn my trust?'

The musicians are playing some kind of waltz, and everyone is watching us expectantly.

'Now, *dance!*' orders Madame.

My feet are rooted to the floor. Sky stands statue-still, glaring at me. Madame comes close, her onion-breath tickling my ears.

'Stubborn, eh?' she whispers. 'Perhaps Groucho can persuade you.'

Groucho strains at his leash, his yellow eyes fixed on us. Suddenly, he lunges forward and snaps at my ankle. I jump out of reach. Too late—a drop of blood snakes down my foot to the floor. Sky's wing trembles in my hand. I turn imploringly to Father, but he's gazing at Madame Marionette.

'We've *got* to dance,' I whisper to Sky, under cover of the music.

I try to remember the steps Madame taught me, but my mind has gone blank.

'How can I?' Sky hisses. 'With my ankle chained to that cage!'

'You've got to try!' I whisper desperately. 'If you don't, she might—'

But Sky's eyes are fixed on Groucho.

I screw up my face and concentrate on my feet. The first steps of the dance come to me and I begin to shuffle through them, pulling Sky with me, his ankle chain clanking behind him, dragging the cage. He limps and hisses at me with every step.

'Just follow me,' I whisper to Sky. 'It's going to be all right.'

Only it isn't.

# AN ANNOUNCEMENT

**S**omehow, our feet get tangled together in Sky's ankle chain. I try to untangle them, but it only makes it worse. Sky howls and hisses.

'Traitor, I sssay! Traitor!!!'

'I'm sorry! I'm sorry!' I whisper. 'Help me with the chain—'

I trip over Sky's feathered legs and our heads bang together. Sky screams in fury, his black wings flaring. He leaps into the air, but the heavy chain twisted round our ankles pulls him down. He hisses and flaps like a panicked bat, his wing tips making a hurricane.

'Please—please stop, Sky!'

He drags me, the cage bucking and crashing behind us, across the room towards the fire. I kick out to free myself, but my foot catches a burning coal, singeing Groucho's fur and setting him yelping. Sky drags me over to the table and we fall together on it, legs entangled, sending goblets of water and wine splashing over the floor. My elbow lands in a bowl of soup. Slivers of cheese stick to my hair. And still Sky flails and fights, and hisses terrible words at me.

We stumble round the room again, dragging the cage behind us, to where Hercules, Jason and Atlas scrape and blow at their instruments, eyes wide with fear. As Sky and I come near, they drop their instruments and back into a corner. Madame screams at me, Father shouts orders at the men, and everything is pandemonium.

'STOP!!!' roars a deep voice.

Smith is back, filling the doorway. He strides over to me and throws off Sky's chain from my legs.

'You've got to help us, Smith!' I whisper, under cover of the rattling chain. 'Madame captured him—Sky—and took him away from his father. I've promised him I'll help him to escape.'

'Oh, aye?' Smith glances at Sky, who has cowered away at the sound of Smith's voice, his wings covering his head. Smith squeezes my shoulder. Then he reaches out and touches Sky's wing. Sky jumps as if Smith's given him an electric shock. His wings flap and flail, but his legs are still tangled in the chain.

'Quietly, bonny boy.' Smith leans towards Sky and holds out his hand. Sky hisses and bites, and drops of blood seep from Smith's hand. But Smith ignores them and bends down to Sky, whispering in his ear. Sky stops hissing. Then Smith kneels beside him and gently strokes his feathered head, just as if Sky was a tame blackbird. Sky bends his head and slowly folds his wings.

At last I have a chance to look around me. My insides flip with horror. Broken plates litter the floor; bread and cheese is trodden into the red carpet; soup drips slimily from the table. The fire is gone out and ash lies scattered over the floor. Father and Foggy stand silent and open-mouthed. Hercules, Jason and Atlas cower in a corner, the horn buckled, the violin smashed, the skin of the drum torn in a great jagged slash.

Madame Marionette stalks across the ruined room to join us. She glares at Smith, whose hand still rests on Sky's bowed head.

'Leave him, executioner!' Her cheeks flame livid red and her dark eyes flash sparks of fury. 'He is mine.'

Smith glances up at her and slowly gets to his feet. 'A man should be called by the job he does,' he says evenly. 'I'm a blacksmith. And as for you, ma'am, what gives you the right to claim ownership of this boy?'

'The boy is mine,' repeats Madame. 'And you will obey me. Get out of this room, now!'

'I will not.'

'What? Do you know to whom you are speaking?'

'You're nowt to me, ma'am.'

'Nothing to you, am I? We shall see about that.' She sidles up to Father and grabs his arm. 'Tell him, now. Tell them all.'

Father draws himself up and twirls his moustache.

'This *was* to be a very special occasion. A new year. A new start.' He looks at me coldly. 'I am ashamed of you, Jemima. Your behaviour has been unforgivable. But this sorry situation has shown me, once and for all, that only one person can bring me pride, comfort and hope.' He takes Madame's hand, brings it to his lips and kisses it.

118

Foggy gives a strangled cry and sways, her face grey.

'Therefore, I have great pleasure in announcing,' Father says, 'that Madame Marionette and I are to be married.'

'Provided, of course,' Madame Marionette flutters her eyelashes at Father, 'that *certain conditions* are fulfilled. Isn't that right, sister dear?'

Foggy drops to the floor in a dead faint. Gasps flutter around the room but I barely hear them. Father and Madame are to marry. Madame Marionette will be my stepmother. And I'll be stuck with her and Groucho and her horrible lessons for the rest of my life.

Smith hurries across the room to where Foggy's lying, her velvet dress spread around her on the floor.

'Leave 'er!' commands Madame Marionette. But Smith ignores her. He kneels beside Foggy and gently fans her white face. Madame grabs me by the shoulder.

'So, Jemima. You have failed your examination.'

'It was the chain—'

'FAILED!' Madame turns to Father and smiles at him, though her smile doesn't reach her eyes. 'But fear not, beloved. I am not defeated. We shall redouble our efforts.'

She bends down and whispers in my ear.

'Leetle girl, you will pay dearly for this. You 'ave humiliated me in front of everyone—you and that wicked boy.' She glances at Smith, who's helping a tearful Foggy to her feet. 'And as for *you*, executioner, leave my sister alone.'

'Mebbe you should take your own advice,' retorts Smith.

'You will be punished for your insolence!'

'Oh aye?' Smith half carries Foggy to the door. They disappear through it and the door creaks shut.

Madame turns to Father. 'That man is a very bad influence on Jemima. Leetle wonder that she has behaved the way she has.'

Father nods. 'I've thought so for some time.'

'He isn't!' I shout. 'He's—'

'Ssst!' Father clicks his fingers. 'You will have no more to do with Samuel Smith. I forbid you to speak to him or to visit him at the forge.'

'But he's my best friend—'

'Silence! You will obey me.' Father turns his back on me and begins ordering people to clean up the mess.

My heart pounds and my eyes fill with tears. Not seeing Smith is the worst punishment of all. Then Madame stalks over to Sky, who is curled in a feathery ball, just as Smith left him.

'And as for *you*...' She prods him with her finger and he gives a sharp hiss. She leans down and whispers, so that Father can't hear her. 'You *bore* me.'

'No!' I shout.

Sky's body begins to shake. Madame pokes him again and again, until he shuffles back inside his cage, dragging his ankle chain. Madame jerks her head at the musicians, and Hercules cautiously approaches the cage, his eyes darting nervously at Sky.

'Lock it,' says Madame.

'Yus, Madame.' Hercules grabs the padlock, inserts the key, and turns it with a click.

Madame flicks a glance at Father, to make sure he isn't listening. He's still busy ordering the cleaning-up. She leans down until her face is close to the hunched figure in the cage. I strain to hear her words.

'Tonight, at midnight, my men will come for you,' she whispers. 'They will pluck out your precious tail feathers, one by one, so painfully that you will wish yourself *dead*.'

Sky gives a terrible cry. I cover my ears.

'You will wish yourself dead...' Madame repeats. 'And then... why, *then* your wish will come true. Won't it, Hercules?'

'Ho yus,' Hercules grins and makes a sign as if cutting his own throat.

But Madame hasn't finished.

'Your insides will be torn out. You will be stuffed with sawdust, mounted in your cage and you will take your place alongside the other leetle pets in my collection. And you will never see your father again.'

I can't bear it.

'No!' I burst out. 'It's not his fault! Punish *me* instead.'

Madame turns to me. 'Oh, don't you worry,' she whispers. 'You *will* be punished—first thing tomorrow. Groucho will see to that, won't you, leetle boy?' At her words, Groucho crawls towards me on his belly, growling softly, his hot, meat-smelling breath in my face.

And at last, I know what I have to do.

# THE MIDNIGHT HOUR

I lie in bed, counting the minutes. At midnight, Madame will send Hercules and his men to kill Sky. I won't let that happen. But first I've got to wait until Foggy's safely asleep—she's been shuffling around in her room for ages. And there are plenty more obstacles in my way. I have to get out of the castle, without alerting Madame and Groucho. Then I must somehow get past the sentry on the Great Wall. And when I've done that, I've got to persuade Smith to help me.

Heavy snores echo along the corridor. Hopefully Foggy's taken her sleeping potion. I jump out of bed, wincing as my feet hit the stone floor before I push them into my slippers. In my pyjama pocket, my fingers find the golden brooch.

'You'll keep me safe,' I whisper to it.

Out in the corridor, I scurry past Foggy's door, to the hall. Outside the door leading down to to the dungeons, my heart begins to bash around in my chest. Is Madame awake and listening? Is she with Hercules, planning what they'll do to Sky? I feel my way to the front door, grab the handle and push.

It doesn't open.

I grope around for the key. Surely my fingers must be missing it in the dark? But no. The key has gone and the door is firmly locked. Madame must have guessed that I'd try to see Smith and has locked me in. Tears prick my eyes. Any time now, Hercules and his men will come to torture and kill Sky. I blink away the tears and tell myself to think. *Think.*

Can I save Sky by myself, without Smith's help? Impossible. Not only is Sky locked in the cage and hoisted high above the library, but he's chained to the bars of the cage by his ankle. And even if by some miracle I got him down, unlocked the cage and broke the chain, there's no way we could escape the castle, since the front door's locked and the windows are all too small to climb out of. Sky is doomed.

I have to see him. Keep him company. No way will I leave him alone in the dark, counting the minutes until midnight and his death. I hesitate outside the library door. I'm probably the last person—apart from Madame and her men—Sky wants to see. He'll still be furious with me—after all, if it hadn't been for me, this wouldn't be happening to him. And he already thinks I'm a traitor for not keeping my promise to help him escape.

Ideas pinball round my head. *Maybe I can hide in the cupboard... then, when Hercules and his men come, I can jump on them and...* But how can one small girl overcome three men? Impossible.

I press my ear to the library door. Someone's moving around inside. Is it Sky, desperately trying to escape? But the sound's too near the door. I almost groan out loud. Hercules and his men must be here already. I look around for something to use as a weapon. Beside the front door is an umbrella stand, and inside it are three large umbrellas. I pull out the biggest and pointiest.

My knees shake, and my tummy feels like it's twisted into a knot, and I've stopped breathing. But I made a promise to Sky, that I'd do everything in my power to help him—and I'm going to keep it. I wrench open the door and leap into the room, the umbrella held above my head like a spear.

The cage is on the floor in the middle of the library, a dark figure standing beside it.

'Leave him alone!' I point my umbrella at the figure.

'Expecting rain, Mim?' Smith's dreadlocks spring in all directions from his head as if he's just got up. A warm feeling steals through me, like ice melting.

'What are *you* doing here?' I say.

'Might ask you the same question.'

'I came to try to help Sky. But how did you get in?'

'Through the front door, of course.'

'But it's locked!'

Smith delves in the pocket of his trousers and pulls out the key.

'Why did you lock it behind you? I was trying to get out to see you—'

'There're three men out there who'll be coming for the boy any minute. And I've work to do.' Smith nods at the cage.

'You mean,' I say, 'you've come to save Sky?'

'Aye. If I can.' Then his face grows serious. 'Make yourself scarce, Mim. Get back to your room.'

'No way! I'm going to help you!'

'If that woman finds out you've helped the boy escape, there'll be hell to pay. Your life won't be worth living, that I know. Go!'

'And what about *you*? What'll they do to you?'

Smith grunts. 'Can't execute meself, can I?'

'I promised Sky I'd help him. And I'm not going to let him down.'

Smith sighs. 'I'm not going to argue with you, Mim. Time's running out.'

A sarcastic voice from inside the cage hisses: 'Then when you've *quite* finished wasssting it...'

Smith gives me a wink. 'Beg pardon, Your Highness.'

'It must be almost midnight!' I say. 'We've got to get him out of here before Hercules and the others arrive.'

'Yesss—hurry up!' hisses Sky.

Smith bends to the cage. 'Stay quiet, boy. And still as you can. I'm going to lift you and carry you to the forge.'

'Get a move on! They'll come as sssoon as they hear the midnight bell.'

Smith grins. 'That's exactly what I'm counting on.'

'What do you mean?' asks Sky suspiciously.

'It's my job to ring the midnight bell.' Smith tosses the key to me. 'Mim, lass, mebbe it's best you're here after all. You'll be the lookout. Open the front door and make sure they're not about.'

I catch the key and, still holding the umbrella, tiptoe out into the hall. I can't help smiling—Smith always makes things better. Behind me, he grunts as he heaves Sky's cage from the floor. There's no sound from the dungeons. I slip the key into the lock, turn it, and open the front door. A gust of chill air sweeps around my feet. I peer around the castle courtyard and scan the path beneath the Great Wall, but no one seems to be lurking there. I open the door as wide as I can and turn to where Smith waits, his arms straining around the cage.

'The coast's clear,' I whisper, knowing he can't see around it.

Smith's already breathing heavily. He moves awkwardly towards the door. It's going to be a tight fit for both him and the cage.

'Careful!'

I hold my breath. Slowly, he inches through, his knuckles scraping the door frame. Finally, Smith and the cage are at the top of the steps, and I slip round behind him to shut the door.

'Lock it,' he tells me. 'That woman and her hound will be after us once she finds the boy missing. It'll hold her back a while.'

I'm just pulling the key from the lock when a noise from the steps makes me swivel round. Smith—unable to see around the cage—has stumbled off the top step. I watch in horror as, still clutching the cage, he topples down into the courtyard.

# ESCAPE

**S**mith sprawls on the cobbles like a beached whale, Sky hissing and the cage juddering in his arms. I dash down the steps and crouch beside him.

'Smith?' He gives a low groan.

'What'sss happening? What'sss happening?' Sky rattles the bars in a panic.

'Hush, Sky! Smith tripped on the steps. Smith, are you all right?'

Smith shakes his great head groggily.

'Aye, lass. I'll survive.' He struggles to his knees and stands up shakily. Sky rattles the bars again.

'Stay *still*!' I tell him, and with much hissing, he obeys.

I scan the silent courtyard. There's no sign of Hercules and his men. Smith hefts up the cage again and begins to stagger over the cobbles towards the forge. In the shadow of the Great Wall, I grab his arm.

'The sentry!' I whisper.

On the top of the Wall, the sentry's torch dances. Any minute, he'll spot us, and then the game will be up.

'Stay here,' I hiss. 'I'll distract the sentry, while you get to the forge.' I've no idea how to do this, but I just have to trust that an idea will come. Smith grunts and steps back into the shadows.

I march up to the Gate. The sentry's torch flickers down over the Wall.

'Who goes there?'

I cup my hands around my mouth and call up.

'It's me. Princess Jemima.'

'Your Royal Highness? You shouldn't be out at night.'

'I-I need your help.'

'With what, Your Royal Highness?'

'I want... I need...' Then my mouth seems to work of its own accord. 'I want you to open the Gate. I want to go Outside.'

'That is forbidden, Your Royal Highness.'

'Then... then I'll break through the Gate!' I brandish the umbrella. 'I have a weapon!'

I stride to the Gate and begin to bash it with the umbrella.

The sentry drops his loudspeaker and climbs down the ladder, the flames from his torch lighting up the rungs.

'Go, Smith!' I hiss. Behind me, Smith staggers off towards the forge. I carry on hitting the Gate. The sentry jumps down from the ladder and snatches the umbrella from my hands.

'What's got into you, Your Royal Highness? The Outside is strictly forbidden.'

I give a weak nod. 'I know.'

'Then I'll have no choice but to tell His Majesty about this.'

I hang my head.

'Now, be off with you, back to the castle. And don't let me see you here again.'

I don't need a second telling. As soon as the sentry turns to climb up the ladder, I hurry off. Not, of course, back to the castle but towards the forge. I only hope that the noise I made hasn't woken Madame—or Groucho. I pull my icy fingers up into my pyjama sleeves. Soon I'll be in the warmth of the forge and can thaw out by the furnace.

But Smith and the cage aren't inside the forge—they're out on the wooden platform. Then I realize why: the cage is too wide to get through the door. Smith is on his knees beside the cage, the crimson cloth thrown back, sawing at the padlock with a hacksaw.

'Hurry, Smith! It must be almost midnight—and that's really loud!'

'Can't be helped,' Smith grunts. 'And anyroad, they're used to me making a racket at all hours.' Sweat pours down his face and spatters his trousers. Inside the cage Sky crouches, his dark eyes fixed on the hacksaw as if willing it to free him. With a snap, the padlock breaks. Smith tosses it aside and the cage swings open. Sky leaps towards the door, hissing.

'Wait!' I whisper. 'Your ankle chain! You're still chained to the cage!'

Sky mutters something rude, but stands still while Smith reaches inside and grabs the chain.

'Hold it taut,' he tells me, and begins sawing at it.

'Oh, hurry!' I whisper.

'Patience, Mim,' mutters Smith, his huge arm tense above the blade.

Sky and I stare as it scrapes back and forth, back and forth. My fingers ache from holding the chain straight. The trouble with waiting for things to happen is that your mind speeds up. Is it midnight yet? Is Madame awake? Has she been to the library and discovered Sky is gone? What will Father do when the sentry tells him I tried to go Outside? Even more worrying, what'll they do to Smith for helping Sky escape?

Great drops of sweat pool on the platform. The hacksaw is only halfway through the chain when lights flash on in the castle. The night is split by a terrible howling and Madame's voice screams for Hercules.

'She's awake—she's found out!' I whisper, my spine turned to ice. The chain trembles in my fingers.

'Hold *still*,' grunts Smith.

'Fassster-fassster-fassster!' hisses Sky.

Smith speaks to Sky in a low, urgent voice.

'Boy,' he says. 'You must take Mim with you.'

Sky is silent, his dark eyes wide.

'What?' I gasp. 'What do you mean?'

'Your life won't be worth a shrug once they find out about this. It's the least he can do for you.' He turns to Sky. 'Take her to the Outside. Fly her to the old man.' His hands work frantically with the hacksaw, to and fro, to and fro...

I find my voice. 'No, Smith—I'm not leaving you!'

130

'You have to, Mim!'

I turn to Sky. 'Can't you carry Smith, too?'

'Of courssse not!' hisses Sky.

Shouting echoes from the castle courtyard. It sounds as if Hercules and his men are trying to beat down the front door of the castle. All the while Groucho howls, a keening, unearthly sound.

The hacksaw blade cuts through the chain and it rattles to the ground. Smith sits back on his heels, gasping. Sky flails out of the cage and staggers dizzily over the platform, shaking his metal-ringed ankle as if he can't quite believe the chain is gone. Then his wings spread wide, gleaming in the moonlight. A strange cry seems to come from deep inside his body. And as if in answer, a cloud of Wings swoops down over the forge. The largest of them all, with a man's haughty face, calls Sky's name. His voice holds all the pain and loss and joy in the world. Then the Wing turns and soars upwards, until he and the others are a distant cloud in the night sky.

Sky gazes after them. 'Father!' he whispers.

'Quick, Mim!' pants Smith. 'Get on the boy's back.'

'But—what about you?'

'I'm big enough and ugly enough to look out for meself,' says Smith. 'Now be off!'

I throw my arms round him as far as they'll go and hug him with all my strength. Then I turn to get on Sky's back.

But Sky isn't there.

With a wild cry, he spirals up, up—over the Great Wall and into the night sky, wheeling and cartwheeling and swooping. The Wings are already far away, flying in the direction of the mountain I saw from the library. Sky streaks after them. They swarm across the stars until they disappear from view.

'Sky!' I whisper. But I know it's impossible.

Sky isn't coming back.

# IN HIDING

The sentry's torch flickers over the Great Wall as Groucho's howls echo closer and closer, along with Madame's shrieking and the angry voices of Hercules and his men.

Smith shoves Sky's empty cage off the platform out of sight. He grabs my arm and pulls me into the forge. Footsteps clatter over the cobbles towards us.

Smith wrenches open the door of the store cupboard. Its three broad shelves are full of pickled eggs and bottles of cider and bags of flour. Smith sweeps aside a line of jars on the top shelf and swings me up onto it. The cupboard door slams shut. The mattress creaks and loud snores rumble around the forge.

The larder smells of vinegar and old cheese. Something walks over my arm and I almost scream. I *hate* spiders. There's a tiny crack in the cupboard door, where a knot of wood used to be. I can see through it, just a little bit.

'Open up!' Madame's voice screams.

The forge door shakes. Jason and Atlas must be thumping on it. Smith's snores become even more mountainous. Outside the door, Groucho gives a single howl.

'Break down the door, Hercules!'

'Yus, Madame.'

I stuff my fist between my chattering teeth. The door collapses with a crash. Bodies tumble into the room, along with muttered swearing from Hercules and his men, and whines and growls from Groucho. Smith sits up in bed and gives a gigantic yawn.

'Get up, man!' snaps Madame. ''Ave you been drinking?'

'No, ma'am.' Smith gives another ear-cracking yawn. 'Just sleeping the sleep of the innocent.'

'Innocent? I think not.' Madame's heels click around the forge, followed by the *tap-tap-tap* of Groucho's claws.

'Where is he?'

'Who, ma'am?'

'Who do you think?' Madame's voice rises. 'The boy. My leetle pet. Where have you hidden him?'

'There's no boy here.'

'Hercules, Jason, Atlas—search. Groucho, leetle one, smell the boy out.'

I wriggle soundlessly to the very back of the shelf. Meanwhile the workbench crashes over. Groucho's heavy breath comes closer and closer. His claws scratch at the cupboard door.

'Enough!' Smith's deep voice cuts through Groucho's panting. 'The boy is gone.'

'Gone?' Madame's voice is dangerously low. 'Prove it.'

I lean forward and peer through the knothole. Smith steps over what's left of his front door and out onto the platform, closely followed by Madame, Hercules and his men, and the slavering Groucho. He leans over the edge of the platform and drags up the empty metal cage, its door hanging open.

A shriek rends the air.

'My leetle pet! My boy! Gone!' Madame turns her fury on Smith. 'And did he haul *himself* down from the ceiling? Did he carry his own cage here? Did he gnaw through the bars and chains with his teeth?'

'No, ma'am,' says Smith. 'I freed him.'

'Then you will pay in blood,' snarls Madame. 'Hercules—'

Groucho snarls. Jason and Atlas close in on either side of Smith. Hercules pulls something from under his cloak. He raises his arm and the blade of a knife flashes silver in the moonlight. Smith is three times bigger than Hercules and could easily disarm him. But he doesn't move.

I wriggle to the edge of the shelf, shove the door open and drop down to the floor. It's higher than I thought and my knees buckle as I hit the tiles. Then I run, full-pelt, at Hercules, grabbing his arm.

'Don't you touch him!'

Hercules swivels to face me, his thin face twisted with cruelty.

'You!' Madame's eyes are black shadows in her white face. 'I might have known it.'

'Leave Smith alone! It was all my idea—'

Madame drags Groucho by the collar towards Smith. 'Guard him, leetle boy. Hercules—don't let the blockhead move until we're safely back at the castle. Jason, Atlas—take the brat and follow me.'

Jason and Atlas each grab one of my arms. Smith steps

towards me—and Groucho lunges at him, sinking his sharp white teeth into Smith's wrist. Smith swears.

'Naughty, naughty!' chastises Hercules with a grin, returning the knife to his pocket. 'Now, boys—you 'eard wot Madame said. Take the brat and follow 'er.'

'Yus, chief.' Jason and Atlas hoist me off my feet and set off after Madame. Her heels clatter towards the castle, her red gown billowing over the cobbles.

Inside the castle, Madame heads straight for the throne room, Jason and Atlas dragging me between them. She yanks the door open, shouting for Father, who appears, dishevelled and cross in his silk dressing-gown. Jason and Atlas deposit me on the red carpet in front of him.

'What's this, Tomazine?'

'I am *en détresse*. This—this *child* is the very devil.'

'What has Jemima done now?' Father glares at me.

'Not only 'as she failed her examination and humiliated us both, she 'as conspired with the executioner to steal my pet—the Wing boy—and free him from his cage. He is *gone*—gone for ever!'

Madame pulls out a crimson handkerchief and dabs her eyes, giving gasping little sobs. Father pats her hand.

'Beloved Tomazine... calm yourself. The boy is only an Outsider.'

Madame swells with fury.

'Only an Outsider? He's only the most valuable Outsider of all, the son of King Wing. Even stuffed, he would be worth a fortune!'

I scramble to my feet. Jason grabs my arm but I shake it free.

'And that's *why*, Father—why I did it! She was going to stuff—'

'Sssst!' Father glares at me. 'Is this how you repay Madame Marionette for all her work on your behalf? You are an ungrateful girl and will be punished.'

Madame points at me with her long, sharp nailed finger.

'What can you expect of a child born on the Day of the Catastrophic Curse? Just because she's your daughter, she thinks she can get away with anything she wants. Look at what she did at the ball. This is all thanks to my sister's laxness...' Madame gives another little sob, '...and yours.'

'Mine?' Father's mouth falls open.

'I think, perhaps, you are not the man I hoped for. I would be unwilling to marry a man with a daughter such as this—'

A tiny flicker of hope lights my heart. Maybe Madame is going to break up with Father and leave. Father twirls his moustache frantically.

'But... but, Tomazine, my beloved—'

'You tolerate too much! Look at the situation with the old man. Year after year, you've watched him fail to come up with the gold. You should 'ave put your foot down long ago.' Madame draws herself up, her eyes flashing. 'A strong woman such as *moi* needs a strong man—not a mouse!'

Father looks more like a goldfish, opening and shutting his mouth. If only he'd stand up to Madame. If only he wasn't so bewitched by her.

'Don't you love me?' whispers Madame. 'Don't you want to marry me?'

'More than anything!' gasps Father.

'Then prove it. Leave this unfortunate child to me, and focus on persuading the old man to make gold.'

'But he fails! He always fails!'

'Then give him an ultimatum.'

*What's an ultimatum?* Father looks confused too.

'An ultimatum?'

'Send my sister to him at first light and tell him...' Madame glances at me and lowers her voice so I can't hear. Father nods.

'Yes! Yes, Tomazine. It will be done, I promise.'

Madame narrows her eyes. 'And here is my ultimatum to *you*.'

'To... to me?'

'If the old man fails, you will lose not only your hope of gold. You will lose *me*—for ever.'

Father turns white. Madame smiles and caresses his cheek. Her long nails leave crimson tracks over his skin. She turns to Jason and Atlas.

'Take the girl to her room.'

She bends to whisper in my ear.

'You will be sorry for what you 'ave done, brat. So sorry, you will wish you had never been born. Now, get out!'

And Jason and Atlas drag me from the room.

# THROUGH THE GATE

I pace up and down my bedroom for hours. What will Madame do to Smith and me in the morning, for helping Sky escape? Outside the window, snow falls softly, the black cobbles already turning white. What might have happened if Sky had carried me with him to the Outside? I look up at the dusky, empty sky. Maybe... maybe Sky has told his father about how we helped him. Maybe he and King Wing are planning to help *us*, right now...

*Don't be daft, Mim.*

Why should the Wings care about Smith and me? Sky is free now, back with his father and his tribe. He probably forgot we ever existed as soon as his wings hit the sky.

A dim glow creeps over the floor. It comes from the cupboard, where the alchemy book is still pushed behind the old pillows. If I ever get into the library again—which is unlikely—I'll put it back on the shelf and try to forget all about it. Maybe Foggy was right all along. Maybe my Enquiring Mind only causes trouble.

It's the first day of a brand new year. A bleak new year, more like. If Madame gets her way, the old man—whoever he is—will finally turn lead into gold. Then Madame will marry Father and I'll be stuck in the dungeons with her and Groucho every day, forced to dance and learn etiquette and deportment for the rest of my life. Even worse, I'll be banned for ever from seeing Smith...

I pull out my golden brooch from my pyjama pocket. It seems to warm my cold fingers and fill me with courage.

I won't just wait here. There *must* be a way for Smith and me to escape Madame. I'll sneak out and see Smith, right now, before daylight. He'll know what to do. I just hope he's alone, and that Hercules and Groucho have gone back to bed.

But what about the sentry? There's no way he'll let me past—especially after I attacked the Gate with my umbrella.

Then I have an idea.

Silently, I slip out of my room and along the corridor to Foggy's bedroom. I press my ear to her door. A huge snore bellows through the keyhole. *Good*. Foggy's still asleep, thanks to her sleeping potion. And if she's slept right through the sound of Hercules and his men battering down the castle door, she won't wake up now. Holding my breath, I turn the handle and push open the door.

It's dark inside the room, except for a sliver of moonlight between the not-quite-meeting curtains. It falls on Foggy's ancient clock—its hands showing four-thirty—and on a thin, snoring hump in the bed. An empty glass sits on Foggy's bedside table, along with the bottle of sleeping potion. I slip inside. Foggy mutters—something about babies—and turns over, burying her nose in the pillow.

140

On the back of the open door hangs Foggy's long grey cloak, its folds shifting in the draught. Silently, I reach up and pull it from its hook. Then I tiptoe out of the room and gently close the door.

My heart's beating hard as I push my arms into the sleeves, draw the cloak close around me and pull the hood down over my head. It smells dank and musty, like Foggy. But it covers me from head to toe. Never have I been so thankful that Foggy and I are the same height.

Along the dark corridor and into the hall I run, the cloak sweeping behind me like a bride's train. I slip past the door down to the dungeons, through the broken front door, down the icy steps and across the courtyard. The Great Wall rears up in front of me. I only have to get past the sentry again, and run along the inside of the Wall to the forge. Then Smith and I can make a plan.

'WHO GOES THERE?'

The sentry's voice booms down the loudspeaker. The torchlight glimmers, lighting up whirling snowflakes.

I clear my throat, give a big sniff and put on my best Foggy voice.

'It is I, Miss Fogarty,' I call.

'Right, miss.'

*He believed me!* The torchlight flickers away. I'm just about to turn right and run on towards the forge, when the Gate creaks. I glance up. The sentry's turning the winch. He must think Foggy wants to go Outside.

For a moment I stand frozen, my eyes fixed on the Gate as it slowly creaks open. A smell of salt and freedom whirls in with the snowflakes and seems to dance around my body, saying, *Come with me.* It feels like something's tugging at my heart with a string, first one way, then the other. This is my one chance, not only to escape Madame and Father and Foggy and Groucho, but to go to the Outside for the very first time. But how can I leave Smith?

I can't. *I won't.*

The Gate is half open now. Through it, a stretch of wide, wet sand leads down to an endless mass of moving water. The ocean.

I've *got* to look, just for a moment. My feet creep closer to the Gate, and closer still, my eyes greedy to see everything, until I'm standing at the threshold.

A million stars twinkle and a huge yellow moon hangs low on the horizon, heavy enough to sink into the ocean. There's the tower that I saw from the library window. Its light rakes over the ocean, flickering over the waves, which hump and move like strange, slow animals. I can't help remembering Foggy's warning about the Mers, and Sky's story about the Mer Queen: her hatred for humans, and her curses. The ocean looks empty... yet somehow it feels full of watching eyes.

An icy wind slips through the open Gate and sucks at Foggy's cloak, making it billow around me like a grey sail. I stick out my tongue and taste the salt of the ocean. The swish and froth of the waves fills my ears.

Then, another sound begins.

Thin and ghostly, a chorus of unearthly voices seems to drift out of the ocean towards me and wrap itself around me.

'You all right down there, Miss Fogarty?'

The sentry's voice comes from a long way away.

I lick my lips and try to concentrate on being Foggy.

'Yes... yes, I'm all right.'

'I need to close the Gate, Miss Fogarty.'

High above me, the winch creaks. I must duck back inside before the Gate shuts. I've got to see Smith... Only my eyelids are sort of heavy, as if lead weights are dragging them closed. It's as if the ghostly singing's gone right inside my body and drained all the strength from me.

Fear jitters in my tummy. My fingers creep into my pyjama pocket to find my golden brooch. And then, just as if the ghostly voices have taken hold of my feet, they walk me right through the closing Gate and into the Outside.

I've never felt so small. There are no narrow streets out here, no walls, no *edges*. Only the black, jagged mountain breaks up the emptiness in the distance, its head wrapped in cloud. A boat lies on its side under the Great Wall, attached by a long rope. But there's no time to look. My slippers stumble across the flat, cold, white sand towards the ocean, and the singing.

The wind grows fiercer. I pull Foggy's cloak tight around me. The water is close now, folding over in a frothy mass, pouring towards me over the sand then sucking back on itself, like it's breathing in. The singing is louder now, filling up my head, pulling me in.

Water swirls and froths up to my ankles. It's like walking in icicles. My slippers are pale fish under the surface. Yet still my feet march in, kicking up splashes and tangling in cold green ropes of slippery stuff. The hem of Foggy's cloak is heavy and claggy as the water grasps hold of it.

Now the water's up to my knees. The waves rise in great humps. A bigger one catches me, slapping ice against my chest. But it's like I've been hypnotized. The ghostly singing has taken over my body. I try to blink myself awake. But I wade further in, sucked and smacked by the water and the foam. I'm out of my depth, yet my feet still run through the water as if they can keep me afloat. I pinch my nose to stop the water going in and clamp my mouth tight shut. I don't know how to swim.

*I'm going to drown.*

Then come the hands.

Ghostly, silvery-white hands reaching out to me.

I try to grab them, only there's no strength left in my arms, and the hands slip away. Then they're back, running over me with chill fingers. The fingers slip around my brooch. A sharp tug, as it's almost jerked from my pocket. These hands aren't here to help, but to steal.

Or worse.

A black wave rolls towards me like a mountain, towering higher and higher, blocking out the sky. With a thunderous roar, it crashes down on my head and the world turns dark.

Foggy's cloak swirls around my throat, gagging me. My mouth fills with freezing water as the white hands grab and poke and search and I'm dragged down, down, into the blackness. My ears echo with the boom of the ocean and it's in my eyes and my nose, and it's filling up my chest...

And then it has me and I'm lost in icy darkness.

# RESCUE

*K*ick those clever legs of yours.

Am I dreaming? My eyes are locked shut but something's got hold of my arms, pulling at them. Is it the ghostly hands again? I try to shake them off, but my arms are too weak.

*Oh, come on—kick! Don't leave it all to me.*

I open my mouth to say I can't move my legs, but the ocean fills it up and I cough and splutter. An impatient sigh gusts against my skin.

*Kick! Or I'll have to leave you to drown.*

With the last bit of strength I have, I give a feeble kick. At least my feet seem to be mine again. My legs tangle in Foggy's cloak. I kick again, and they come free.

*Better. Keep going.*

The ocean washes and slaps, but it seems a bit calmer. The hands holding me are strong. Someone's breathing in my ear.

*Grab hold of that rock.*

I force my eyes open. Right in front of me is a black, slippery-looking rock. I reach out and try to grasp it, my fingers sliding from the surface. There's a grunt and someone tries to push me up onto the rock. I can't get a handhold and I slip back into the icy water.

*Try harder.*

Water swirls as my body is lifted upwards, then drops back again. This seems to go on for a long time and there's lots of breathless cursing and muttering. Then, at last, I'm lying flat on my front on the rock, sodden and streaming with water, and freezing.

*Don't just lie there like a stupid jellyfish!*

The voice is below me now, coming from the water. With a huge effort, I raise my head from the rock and begin choking again. Then, when the choking passes, I shake my wet head and roll over into a sitting position. My fingers are blue and my whole body aches.

*Ever thought of saying 'Thank you'?*

I turn to face the ocean. It's still dark and heaving, but less so than before. The light from the tower—which seems much stronger and brighter now—rakes over the water, over a mass of wet, white hair and beneath it, a silvery, blue-white face. Then the light moves on, and there's only a ghostly paleness in the water, staring up at me.

'Well?' The voice is impatient.

'Thanks. For saving me.' I push the sopping hair out of my eyes.

'Hmmmph. I should have let you drown.'

'I mean it! Thank you. I-I'm just a bit shocked, and... well...'

'Are you a human?'

'Yes... yes, of course I am!'

'I thought as much. What were you doing in the ocean at five in the morning?'

*What was I doing in the ocean?* 'It's a long story.' I begin to shiver violently and my teeth chatter together.

'Wring out your cloak. Then wrap it round you.'

Before I do, my fingers find the shape of my brooch, still safe in my pyjama pocket. Feeling a bit better, I manage to squeeze the water out of Foggy's cloak and wrap it tightly round my body like a bandage. I'm still wearing my slippers, but they're soggy as sponges. I pull them off and squeeze them too. The beam of light sweeps round again, lighting up the girl in the water. Her eyes are the palest grey and she looks sort of familiar. *She* doesn't seem to be shivering, though her white dress is sopping wet.

I hold out my hand to help her out of the water. Her eyebrows cross together.

'What are you doing?' she says coldly.

'Helping you out. You must be frozen too.'

There's a long, uncomfortable silence, as the beam of light travels off over the ocean. There's no sign of the Mers. It's as if they never were.

The girl ignores my hand, so, feeling a bit stupid, I put it down.

'Ring the bell.' The girl's voice is colder still.

'The bell?'

She gives an impatient sigh. '*Humans*. The stupidest things.'

'Aren't *you* a human, then? Are you an Outsider?'

'That depends on how you define "Outsider".'

She doesn't say anything further. And what does she mean, '*Ring the bell*'? Why would there be a bell out here, on a rock in the middle of the ocean? I turn round to look.

I'm sitting on the rocks that the white tower is built on. Its bulk rears up above me, as big as the library tower, or bigger. Near the top, under the turning beam of light, is a circle of windows. Halfway up is a single port-hole window, with strange objects hung from the wall around it. And at the bottom, a little way from where I'm sitting, is a wooden door. Hanging on one side of it, a rusty metal bell pull sways in the wind.

I turn back to the girl. Why is she in the ocean? Why did she refuse my hand to help her out? There must be only one reason.

'Are you a Mer?'

The girl's eyebrows cross again.

'*No. I. Am. Not.*' Her voice sounds strangled.

I probably should have shut up then. But the trouble with having an Enquiring Mind is that it's always at work, *especially* in times like these.

'Why don't you get out of the water, then?'

'*Why*,' the girl's voice grates, 'don't you mind your own business?'

'I just want to understand who you are. You rescued me... *very kindly*... from drowning. And I thought—because of the singing—'

'The singing?'

'I heard them—the Mers. Their singing sort of pulled me into the ocean. I know how they sing to wreck ships.'

'If you know that,' the girl's voice is cold as the water, 'then it's all the more disgusting that you accuse me of being one of *them*.'

'I wasn't accusing you. I was asking you.'

'What's the difference?'

'It's called curiosity.'

'That's not what I'd call it.'

My teeth are beginning to chatter again, but my Enquiring Mind won't let go. 'It'd be easy to prove.'

'Prove what?'

'That you're not a Mer. You could just come and sit up here with me...'

The water below me boils and threshes, as if it's as angry as the girl.

'How *dare* you!' she spits. 'I rescue your pathetic human body from certain death—and this is the way you repay me!'

'I'm sorry—I didn't mean—'

'Sorry?' The light rakes over us both again and the girl's face blazes with scorn. 'Never—*never*—will you be as sorry as me!'

She somersaults into the water and disappears beneath the surface. But not before something slaps the water hard, creating a wave and soaking me through again from head to toe. I gaze at the empty, swirling water, my mouth wide open.

Because of the last bit of her I saw.

A scaly fish's tail.

# THE LIGHTHOUSE

I stare and stare into the water, willing the girl to come back. But she doesn't, and when the light beam returns, the ocean is empty. But the memory of her fish tail sticks in my mind. *Was* the girl a Mer? And if so, why did she get so angry when I asked? And why did she lie and say she wasn't?

Shivering, I wring out Foggy's cloak again, wrap it around me and think about what to do next. One thing's for sure: I can't sit here any longer. I'm freezing and wet and at this rate I'll become an icicle. I stand up, cast one last look at the empty water, and turn back towards the tower. If there's a bell, someone must live inside.

The bell pull is brown and red with rust. Smith told me how metal rusts when it gets wet, especially when there's salt in the water. Will I ever see Smith again? The warm forge seems a world away from this cold rocky island in the ocean. My eyes prick with tears.

*Stoppit, Mim.*

I *will* see Smith again. And if there's someone living in the tower, then there'll be warmth and maybe even

151

something hot to drink. I reach out and tug at the bell pull. High above me, inside the tower, there's a distant crashing sound. Any minute, someone will look out of the window, wondering who's here at this time of night.

But what if they're asleep?

I tug the bell pull again, harder this time.

Another far-off crash. But no one comes.

I press my ear to the rough wood of the door. But it's impossible to hear anything, what with the whistling of the wind and the roar of the ocean. I tug Foggy's hood down over my head, turn my back to the door and sit on the cold stone doorstep. I don't know if the saltiness rolling down my cheeks is the salty ocean or my tears.

All of a sudden, there's a new sound behind me: a ratchety-scratchety-creaky sound—like the sound of the winch turned by the sentry to open the Gate. I jump to my feet and stare at the door. Slowly... very slowly... it opens.

'Hello?' I call.

There's no reply.

My fingers find my brooch and hold it tight. Straightaway I feel braver, as if Smith's here with me. I walk through the doorway, my heart hammering. No sooner am I inside than the ratchety-scratchety-creaky sound begins again and the door slowly shuts behind me, leaving me in pitch darkness.

The good thing about this is that it's warmer out of the wind and the cold. The bad thing is that I can't see a thing.

'H-hello?' My voice sounds thin and quavery in the darkness.

I stretch out my hands in front of me. They hit something hard and solid. A wall. I shuffle cautiously round. What if there are invisible steps here, down to a cellar—or a trapdoor? What if I fall headlong and break my neck? I inch my feet forward.

The stone floor seems solid. My toes hit something hard. An up-step. And another, above that. I spread my arms out wide. They find a curving wall. A spiral staircase.

I hesitate. I don't like the idea of climbing in pitch blackness towards who-knows-what. Then I jerk with fear as a harsh, scraping sound begins, just above my head.

'Who's there?' I whisper.

Another scrape; a flash, a sizzling sound and a bitter smell in my nostrils. High on the wall above me a candle flickers and burns. There's no sign of the person who lit it.

Shadows dance on the circular walls leading up and round and out of sight. But my eyes keep going back to the candle. How did it burst into flame of its own accord? I take a few steps upwards until my eyes are level with it. A matchbox and a pair of metal pincers sit beside it. The pincers are attached to a long metal chain strung along the wall. A device for lighting candles! My Enquiring Mind longs to discover exactly how it works; but it's more important to climb the spiral staircase and find out who—or what—is at the top.

A metal handrail circles upwards. I grab it and, hitching up Foggy's wet cloak, I climb, my ears alert. The stairs go round and round, up and up. Just as I run out of light from the candle below, there's a scrape and a flash, and another candle burns above me, lighting the way.

I have a new thought. What if no one lives here at all? What if everything runs automatically, just like the door and the candles? I don't know how I feel about this. If the tower's empty, there'll be no warmth or food or drink. But if someone *is* living here, they might be angry or dangerous. Or both. Dizzy from climbing, I turn another spiral.

On my left is a closed door.

I knock. Nothing happens, so I turn the handle. The door opens into a small room, perfectly round, which smells faintly of fish. There's a mattress on the floor, and a port-hole window. Moonlight floods through it, glinting on all kinds of odd things: several long, thin wooden sticks with wire attached, and little hooks tied to the end of the wire; a metal trumpet—like the loudspeaker the sentry shouts through; and lots of green wire netting. This must be some sort of storeroom. Beside the window is a thick, black metal tube on a stand, one end pointing up at the stars. Could it... could it be a real telescope? I run across the room and squint through its magic eye. All I can see is fuzz and fog. I look out of the window instead.

I'm about halfway up the tower. There's the Great Wall surrounding Galena across the water, and, in the distance, the dark mountain. Outside the tower window hang more strange things: wooden wheels and pulleys gleam in the moonlight, buckets of all shapes and sizes—some half full of water—dangle from hooks in the wall. I feel surer and surer that *someone* lives here. And if they do, I'd better find them.

The stairs seem to go on for ever. I stop for breath beside another port-hole window. A few steps further up is a closed door. The strangest smell seeps out from under it: a sharp, burning smell—a smell which seems to whisper *hurry* or *urgent*. Someone—or something—shuffles about behind the door. There's a muttering, and a sort of blopping and sizzling, then a long, drawn-out hiss.

Suddenly, I remember Sky. Could it possibly be *him* inside? Could this be where the Wings live? The hissing gets louder and sharper. If it *is* Sky, he sounds extremely angry. I press my ear to the door.

The smell is disgusting now, so bad that I have to pinch my nose. The muttering reaches a crescendo. Footsteps pound towards the door. I step back in case Sky comes flying out. Then the door is wrenched open, there's a flash of white light and something warm and heavy tumbles through the door, knocking me down and squashing all the breath out of my lungs.

# THE STRANGER

**S**omeone breathes very fast next to my ear and grips Foggy's cloak so tightly it almost strangles me.

'Gerroff!' I gasp.

Foggy's hood has fallen over my eyes. The air is full of smoke and bitter fumes and strange croaking sounds. Whoever's tangled up with me pulls away, coughing hard, and stumbles down the stairs towards the port-hole window. There's a creak and a groan as it's flung open, and fresh, cold air floods in. The smoke gradually clears and whoever-it-is stops being a muzzy shadow and becomes a solid, real person: the hairiest man I've ever seen.

A ginger-and-white beard tumbles down his chest, almost to his stomach. Curls corkscrew from his head in all directions. Violet eyes almost disappear under fat, ginger eyebrows. White hairs curl out of his nostrils, and even out of his ears. A pair of ancient spectacles hangs off one ear. With shaking hands, he pushes them back onto his nose.

'Miss Fogarty,' he growls. 'Back already?'

This must be the old man Foggy visits at dead of night. Should I pretend to be her, until I find out whether he's friendly or fearsome?

Without waiting for an answer, the hairy man pushes past me, muttering something under his breath that sounds like *darn frogs*. The smoke is clearing, though the smell—like rotten eggs—still burns my eyes. I follow him in.

The room, like the one below it, is completely round, like the library, except for two things: from waist-level up, there are windows, so you can look out any time you want to; and below the windows, the walls are lined with shelves—only there isn't a single book in them. The upper shelves are filled with bottles of coloured liquids and jars full of powders, all lined up neatly and labelled. I long to read the labels and find out what they are. On the bottom shelf is a collection of metal tongs, spoons and ladles. Above this is a shelf of strange glass beakers with long necks and curved handles, weighing scales, test tubes, droppers, pots and flasks.

Wherever I look, there's something interesting. A rickety ladder goes up to a sort of trapdoor in the ceiling. A clanking, clockworky sort of sound comes from up there. That must be where the light is. By the windows a huge chalkboard stands on an easel, its surface covered with scribbled diagrams, letters and numbers. A dark-blue curtain hangs over an alcove beside it. And right in the middle of the room stands a huge brick furnace—taller than me and even bigger than Smith's furnace—its hearth full of glowing coals. A rocking chair is pulled up in front of it. A washing line hangs above the furnace, with a pair of holey yellow socks pegged to it. Beside it lies a poker and a pair of bellows and on top of it an old kettle bubbles and hisses, steam pouring from its spout. So *that's* where the hissing came from!

The hairy man seems to have forgotten me. He's bent over a fat cooking pot beside the furnace, waving away the black smoke pouring from it. Whatever's inside bloops and bubbles and smells so bad I pinch my nose again. An oily green liquid spreads across the floor, steaming.

I open my mouth to speak, but gasp instead when something cold and damp lands on my arm. A frog gazes up at me, its mottled throat trembling into a croak. With shaking fingers, I brush it off. It tumbles to the floor and hops away on long, green legs.

The hairy man turns, his brow wrinkled as if he's trying to remember who I am.

'What's the matter, Miss Fogarty?'

I point at the frog. 'A frog—it landed on me.'

The hairy man picks up another frog from the seeping mess on the floor and sets it down on a small table by the rocking chair.

'Plenty more where that came from.'

'But how—why—?'

'Consider yourself lucky, Miss Fogarty, that today it's only frogs. Last week it was snakes. Week before that, tarantulas.' Then he seems to remember something. 'What brings you back so soon? I'm sure it's not the pleasure of my company.'

Should I go on pretending to be Foggy? He seems harmless. I make my decision and slowly pull off the cloak. The hairy man blinks once, twice. Then he takes a step backwards, narrowly missing a couple more frogs.

'I'm not Fog—I mean, Miss Fogarty.'

'Who *are* you, then?'

'My name's Mim.'

The hairy man frowns. 'Why are you wearing pyjamas?'

'I-I was in bed, only I couldn't sleep because Father's going to marry Madame Marionette and she's a *monster*—and I made a plan to see Smith so we could escape—and I, er, borrowed Foggy's cloak to get past the sentry—only he opened the Gate and the Mers sang at me—and I ended up in the ocean and the Mer girl rescued me and—'

He holds up his hand.

'Slow down, if you please! You are making no sense at all.' He pushes his spectacles up his nose and absent-mindedly picks up another frog and places it on the rocking-chair. 'You say you know Miss Fogarty?'

'She's my—I mean, she *was* my governess.'

He stares at me. 'What did you say your name is?'

'Mim.' My hand strays to my pocket and circles my brooch.

'Short for?'

'Jemima.'

The hairy man's expression changes. He bends into a deep bow.

'Your Royal Highness.'

'Oh please—don't! I hate being a princess.'

'Does your father, the King, know you are here?'

'No.'

'Then go back! Quick! Before he comes after you.'

'He won't come after me. He won't go Outside. And anyway, I-I think I've run away.' *Please don't make me go back there.*

'Run away?'

'It's a long story.'

'I've no time for long stories. Or short ones, for that matter. Now, be off with you. There's work to be done, and no time to be lost.' He picks up a cloth and removes the hissing kettle from the furnace. Then he turns back to the gooey mess on the floor. 'Dross,' he mutters. 'Nothing but dross.'

He bustles over to the chalkboard, wipes out a long string of letters and symbols with his sleeve, and scribbles furiously, with much squeaking.

'Um... could I dry out, first?'

'What?' The hairy man turns to look at me, and his eyes soften. 'Very well. But be quick about it.' Then he returns to his scribbling.

I watch him for a few moments, then tiptoe over to the furnace and drape Foggy's cloak over the washing line. The heat warms my cold cheeks and my pyjamas steam gently. If I close my eyes, I could almost be back in the forge with Smith... Only there's no time to daydream. Keeping one eye on the hairy man, who's completely engrossed in his work at the chalkboard, I head for the shelves. On the top shelf, a line of jars and bottles is neatly labelled in alphabetical order, just like the books in the library. But these are words I've never read before:

*Aqua Fortis*
*Black Antimony*
*Cinnabar*
*Green Vitriol*
*Hartshorn*
*Sal Ammoniac*
*Saltpetre*

I'm just about to pick up *Green Vitriol* when there's a tremendous crash. It seems to come from outside the door. The hairy man growls, throws down his chalk and leaves the room. I tiptoe after him.

Above the door hang two cymbals, the sort that musicians play in orchestras. They're attached to a long piece of wire which disappears down the spiral staircase. The wire gives a jerk and the cymbals crash together. I cover my ears. The hairy man hurries over to the port-hole window and leans out. Then he mutters in an irritated sort of way.

'What is it?' I ask.

'Still here, are you?' He crosses to a wooden wheel mounted on the wall. 'It's *her*.'

'Not... not Madame Marionette?'

'Miss Fogarty.' He turns the wheel, and the ratchety-scratchety-creaky sound begins—the sound I heard when the door opened. 'Come to take you back, has she?'

'No!'

Footsteps echo on the stone stairs. I grab the hairy man's sleeve.

'She mustn't know I'm here! Help me—please?'

Behind his spectacles, the old man's violet eyes are surrounded by deep crinkles and creases. It's like he's looking right into my heart.

The footsteps squeak closer and closer. I can hear Foggy sniffing.

The hairy man strides across the room and pulls aside the blue curtain. Then he jerks his head at me. I scurry across the room and duck behind the curtain. It falls closed in front of my face.

I'm in a tiny alcove, with nothing in it but some kind of seat with a wooden cover over it. The air smells damp and musty. It must be the toilet. Cautiously, I lower myself to sit on the wooden cover. Foggy's complaining voice drifts up the stairs.

Then I remember: Foggy's cloak is still draped on the line above the furnace. And it's too late to get it back.

# THE ULTIMATUM

'This is most unexpected, Miss Fogarty. It's been barely five days.'

Inside the alcove, my knees shake. Any minute, Foggy's going to spot her cloak hanging by the furnace, and the game will be up.

'I beg your pardon?' Foggy's voice is irritable.

'Remove your earplugs,' says the hairy man.

'Oh. Yes.' There's a pause. 'I risk my life every time I make this crossing.' She grumbles on. 'I was woken from a *very* deep sleep to come here at this ungodly hour. And on top of that, I'm frozen to the bone because my cloak has gone missing—'

'What have you there?' interrupts the hairy man.

Something clatters onto the floor.

'Lead pipes. They almost sank the boat.' Foggy sniffs. 'I assume that there is no progress—as usual?'

'There is progress,' says the hairy man. 'I've reached the stage of frogs, which is a very important phase of the Work.'

Foggy gives an impatient sigh. 'Frogs?'

'When frogs appear, the transformation is near.'

'You said that when the chameleons came.'

'And I was correct. The Work proceeds at its own pace, Miss Fogarty.'

'Then when can we expect to see gold?'

'Gold?' He sounds flustered. 'Ah.'

'I thought as much. That *mess* on the floor tells me all I need to know. All His Majesty needs to know. You are *still* not focusing on the gold.'

There's a silence. Then the hairy man says, in a low voice: 'You know why.'

'That girl,' says Foggy contemptuously.

'My granddaughter has a name. Miranda.'

'Since the Day of the Catastrophic Curse, you have put that girl before your duty to the King.'

'Love must come before duty,' mutters the hairy man.

'*Love*,' says Foggy, with a sniff. 'For a child with a tail.'

'For a child *cursed* with a tail. A child doomed, since the day she was born, to live in the ocean. Only think, Miss Fogarty, of Miranda's life—unable to climb these stairs to be with me. Forced to live among the Mers, who hate her. Surely you can understand why I must make it my priority, for the rest of my days, to break the curse on her?'

Then I understand. The girl who rescued me must be Miranda, the hairy man's granddaughter. So she *was* telling the truth about not being a Mer girl. She's a human, just like me. Another person suffering from a curse.

'The rest of your days?' Foggy sniffs. 'You had better make haste, then.'

'I may be old,' says the hairy man. 'But I have years in me yet, God willing.'

'You misunderstand me,' says Foggy. 'Your days are numbered.'

'What?'

'I bring an ultimatum from His Majesty.'

'An ultimatum?'

'You have twenty-four hours to transform lead into gold. If you fail, you will be arrested at first light tomorrow, taken to Galena—and executed.'

I almost gasp out loud. Surely Father wouldn't do this. But Madame Marionette can make him do anything, even sentence an innocent old man to death. Will they force Smith to execute him?

Foggy's footsteps squeak towards the furnace. I'm surprised she can't hear my heart beating, it's thudding so hard in my chest. Any minute now, she's going to notice her cloak. Then she says:

'I shall return, as His Majesty ordered, at first light tomorrow. And if there is no gold...' The silence she leaves feels menacing.

Foggy's footsteps squeak towards the door and echo down the spiral staircase. What happened? How did she miss seeing the cloak? I count to thirty, just to make sure she's really gone, then I twitch open the curtain. The only clothes hanging on the line over the furnace are the two yellow socks. Foggy's cloak has disappeared.

The hairy man sits in the rocking chair, his head bent. I go over and touch his arm. Then I see it. Foggy's cloak.

Stuffed under the cushions of the rocking chair. He must have spotted it and hidden it just before she arrived.

'Thank you,' I whisper. 'For hiding her cloak. And for not giving me away.'

He pulls a handkerchief from his pocket and blows his nose very hard.

'Twenty-four hours,' he says. 'Impossible.'

'You can do it!' I try to sound positive. But if he's failed to turn lead into gold for eleven years—how can he possibly do it in a single day? He looks as if he's thinking the same thing.

'All I've achieved so far is dross.'

'What *is* dross, exactly?'

He waves his hand at the mess on the floor. 'This. And Slow Henry isn't helping.'

'Slow Henry?'

I look round the room. Maybe Slow Henry's his assistant. But the hairy man nods at the big brick furnace.

'That's... Slow Henry?'

'He's supposed to heat slowly and steadily—hence his name. But lately he's been heating too fast, which is what causes the smoke and fumes. And possibly the frogs.' He gets to his feet, pushes his spectacles up his nose and gives a faint smile. 'Now that I've introduced you to Slow Henry, I'd better introduce myself.' He holds out a veined hand. 'Trismegistus MacWhisker, at your service. Mac, for short.'

His name sounds like one of Madame's tongue-twisters. I try to say it to myself, only my tongue gets mixed up with my teeth. Luckily, MacWhisker doesn't notice. He's down on the floor, scooping up the gloopy slime with his hands and slopping it into a bucket.

'Mr, er... Mac?'

'Yes?'

'Why do you have to do it—change lead into gold—for Father? Why you?'

MacWhisker gives a heavy sigh. 'Because I am the only alchemist alive.'

*Alchemist.* My mind flashes back to my bedroom cupboard and to the alchemy book hidden there. The book that refused to open.

'So what exactly do you have to do, to change lead into gold?'

MacWhisker sighs again. 'You ask a lot of questions.'

'I have an Enquiring Mind.'

The ghost of a smile drifts across his face. 'That makes two of us. Every scientist in the world is inquisitive. Curious.'

It's like the sun has come out inside me. Could *I* be a scientist one day? Then I remember Foggy.

'Foggy says curiosity kills cats.'

'If cats die from curiosity, they die in pursuit of truth. What nobler reason can there be for dying?'

'So... ' I speak without thinking, 'If you get executed in twenty-four hours, will it have been worth it?'

MacWhisker snorts. 'Enquiring Minds ask the questions lesser minds hesitate over. But at this particular moment, I'd prefer not to debate the merits of death.'

'Sorry.' I glance at what's left of the dross on the floor. 'What will you do?'

'Clear it up.'

'No—I mean, what will you do about Father's ultimatum?'

'I shall redouble my efforts.'

'To change the lead into gold?'

'Not exactly.'

'What, then?'

'I shall redouble my efforts to break the curse on my grand-daughter. And if, as a by-product, lead is transformed into gold, then so be it. The Work, you see, may accomplish both.'

'What do you mean?'

'Let us return to your question. What is alchemy? Alchemy is the art of Transformation. Its goal is to set right what is wrong; to change what is inferior or imperfect into something worthy and beautiful. If the alchemist does the Work correctly, then yes—lead will be transformed into gold. But, far more importantly, curses will be reversed.'

'You mean... the Mer girl... I mean, Miranda... will get her legs back?'

'Precisely.'

I think of my mother, and Smith's father. 'And... and people who've been cursed and died? Will they come back to life?'

MacWhisker shakes his head. 'Not even alchemy can return what is dead to life. Only curses on the living can be reversed by the Work.'

'What is the Work?'

MacWhisker's eyes almost disappear under his ginger brows. 'It would take a lifetime—or more—to answer your question. We have only twenty-four hours.'

'We?'

'Well, you're here. You might as well make yourself useful.'

*He's letting me stay.* I roll up my pyjama sleeves.

'What can I do?'

'You may round up the frogs.'

'Oh... right.' I look around the room. Frogs hop among the glass bottles on the shelves, croak from the toilet alcove. One sits on the rocking chair, dozing in the heat, looking remarkably like a little green man. 'Er... how?'

MacWhisker goes to the window, retrieves another bucket, and hands it to me. 'Collect them in this.'

I'm not keen on frogs. They're not exactly slimy, but they're cold and wriggly and their long legs keep jumping them off in different directions. But after the first couple, I sort of get used to it.

'Can I ask you more questions, Mr Mac?'

MacWhisker grunts. 'You may ask me one question for every five frogs you collect.'

*Four.* I drop another frog into the bucket and look at MacWhisker.

'I met Miranda, you know.'

'Did you? She usually keeps herself to herself.'

'She saved me from the Mers.'

MacWhisker raises his gingery eyebrows. 'Did she, indeed?' He pauses. 'Miranda has a good heart, though she keeps it well-hidden.'

I scoop up a frog from the rocking chair. 'That's five! So here's my first question. How did Miranda's legs get cursed?'

# MIRANDA'S CURSE

'It was eleven years ago, on the Day of the Catastrophic Curse,' MacWhisker tells me. 'I was Keeper of the Library.'

'The library?' I pause, a frog wriggling in my hand. 'Which library?'

'The library in the castle, of course.'

'You mean—you lived in the castle? You looked after all the books in the library?' Excitement fizzes through me.

MacWhisker wags a bony finger at me.

'One question every five frogs. Besides, I haven't finished answering your first one.'

I press my lips together. So many questions want to tumble out. But I carefully drop the frog into the bucket. *Two...*

'I had a daughter then. She was expecting a baby. On the Day of the Catastrophic Curse, she gave birth to Miranda.'

'I was born that day, too.'

'A bad day to be born.' MacWhisker sighs. 'Miranda was such a delicious baby, with ten little toes like jelly babies—and she seemed so happy to be here.'

*The Miranda I met was one big frown,* I almost tell him. But instead I concentrate on picking up frogs. *Three...*

'After her baby was born, my daughter slept. I lay Miranda in a little box lined with an old shawl and went to the library to read. I was in the middle of a fascinating book when I heard shouting outside. Your father's men had the Mer Queen in a net. She was spitting and screaming. They had taken her from her country, the ocean, and from her people.'

'I know what happened,' I say. 'She cursed Father, and all he held dear. And then they executed—um...'

'Correct.' MacWhisker swallows. 'I hurried back to make sure that my daughter and Miranda were all right. My daughter was still asleep. I ran into the little room where Miranda lay. You can imagine my relief when I found her still sleeping, her tiny thumb in her mouth. I picked her up, the shawl fell from her body, and... then I saw it.'

'The tail?'

He nods. 'She too—an innocent baby—had been cursed.'

'But why Miranda? I thought the Mer Queen only cursed Father and all he held dear.'

'She cursed the executioner too. Who knows how many others were cursed?'

I pop two more frogs into the bucket.

'What happened to your daughter?'

MacWhisker sighs. 'She ran away from Galena. When she saw Miranda's tail, she said she couldn't live with a cursed child. We've never seen her since.'

'Oh.' I can't help feeling sorry for Miranda. A mother who didn't want her, and a fish's tail. I look round for more frogs, so I can ask another question. I scoop up three from the shelves, and two more from a cushion on the rocking-chair.

'How did you end up here? And why didn't you bring your books with you?"

'Your father ordered me to leave Galena. He couldn't bear the sight of Miranda's tail, because it reminded him of the Mer Queen and what she'd done. I packed up as much of my laboratory equipment as I could load into a cart, along with Miranda, and took them away. I planned to return later for my books. The only habitable place was the lighthouse. It was a deserted wreck. Renovating it took many months.'

He nods at the trapdoor above the rickety ladder, where the clanking sound comes from.

'I got the light working, with paraffin and clockwork— the Mers fear strong light. And I set up this laboratory. But when I returned for my books, your father had built a high wall around Galena and I wasn't permitted to enter.'

'So... so what did you do? About Miranda's tail?' I forget for a moment that I'm not allowed another question yet. MacWhisker doesn't seem to notice.

'I kept her in a bucket at first,' he says. 'But as she grew bigger, she couldn't stay cooped up in the lighthouse. So I carried her down to the ocean and put her in the water.'

'At least she could swim about.'

MacWhisker nods. 'Only I hadn't allowed for the Mers. They hate humans because your father beheaded their queen. So far, they've never dared to actually harm her.'

'Why not, if they hate humans so much?'

'Because they know I'm an alchemist, and they're afraid of me. Luckily for Miranda, they think my powers are greater than they are. In actual fact—' he sighs, '—I can do nothing against them. But they make Miranda's life miserable enough.'

'No wonder she's so cross.' I pick up another frog and drop it into the bucket.

'It breaks my heart to see her suffering. But what can I do? I swore to devote every day of my life to finding a way to overturn the curse on her tail. Year after year I've tried... but the more I fail, the angrier she becomes. Lately, she will scarcely speak to me.'

His eyes look far away.

'The trouble is, I'm working alone and in the dark. If only the fire hadn't destroyed all my books...'

'The fire? What fire?'

'The fire in the library. Miss Fogarty told me that it must have been started by a candle, the night I left Galena. It swept through the library, burning everything.' He shakes his head. 'All that knowledge... gone for ever.'

'But... but—' I try to make sense of what he's just said. 'But there's never been a fire!'

'What do you mean?'

'Foggy must have been fibbing! The library's just as it was when you lived there. The books are on the shelves, as you left them! I've been reading them—all the ones I can reach, that is.'

MacWhisker is motionless, his face pale. 'My books... my books are safe?'

I nod, my mind spinning. Why would Foggy lie to MacWhisker about a fire destroying the library? Why wouldn't she want him to have his books? It doesn't make any sense at all.

MacWhisker stumbles over to the rocking chair and drops down into it, muttering to himself. I put down the bucket of frogs and cover it with a plate to stop them escaping. Then I go and sit on the hearth rug at MacWhisker's feet. His hands are shaking, and he keeps taking off his spectacles and rubbing them. I reach out and touch his arm.

'Mr Mac?'

He jumps. 'What? What is it? My books—'

'I found a book... a book about alchemy. At least, I think it is. It wouldn't let me open it.'

MacWhisker stares as if he's seen a ghost. 'You have it? *The Three Impossibles?* Where is it?' He peers at my pyjamas as if I might be concealing the book under them.

'It's in my bedroom at the castle. I hid it in my cupboard.'

'Oh.' His shoulders slump.

'What's so special about it?'

'*The Three Impossibles* contains all the knowledge about the Work—all the instructions I need to complete it.'

'But don't you remember what it says? I remember *everything* from the books I've read.'

'*The Three Impossibles* is no ordinary book. It only allows you to turn a page once you've completed the Work on the previous page.'

I frown. 'It wouldn't let me open it, let alone read it!'

'Only an alchemist can open it. It won't open for anyone else—not even an alchemist's apprentice.'

I can't sit still any longer.

'We've only got until tomorrow.' I jump to my feet and pace up and down, narrowly missing a couple more frogs. 'Do you think you could do the Work by then, if you had the book?'

'If I did, there is a minuscule chance. But I don't have it.'

'Then I'll do it. I'll sneak back into the castle and get *The Three Impossibles*!'

MacWhisker stares at me. 'But how?'

'If I wear Foggy's cloak, they'll think I'm her and let me in.'

MacWhisker frowns. 'No. Miss Fogarty's only just gone back. The sentry will be suspicious if you turn up soon after.'

I glance at the windows. There's a pale gleaming on the horizon. 'What's the time?'

MacWhisker pulls an old-fashioned watch from his pocket. 'It's seven o'clock.'

'The sentries change over at eight o'clock. The new sentry won't know about Foggy's trip. If I can sneak into my room without anyone spotting me, I can get *The Three Impossibles* and bring it to you. Now, get up, Mr Mac—I need Foggy's cloak.'

MacWhisker gets slowly to his feet and I pull out Foggy's cloak from under the cushions. He looks bewildered.

'But—why would you do this for me? Why would you go back there if you hate it so much?'

'Because you didn't give me away to Foggy. Because you mustn't be executed. Because it's not fair that Miranda has a tail.' I take a deep breath. 'And because—because I like you, Mr Mac.'

MacWhisker's eyes are watery.

'That is extremely kind. And please, no more "Mr Mac". We're friends now.'

'OK, Mr—I mean, Mac.'

'But I have to ask something else of you.'

'What?'

'Promise me that you won't tell Miranda about the ultimatum.'

'But why? If she knows, she can help us!'

'If she knows, she will give up all hope.' He pulls out his handkerchief and blows his nose hard. 'Do you promise?'

'OK,' I say. 'I promise. But... will you do something for me, too?'

'What's that, Mim?'

My name sounds odd in Mac's voice instead of Smith's, but I like it very much. He watches me as I wrap Foggy's cloak around my shoulders, shivering at its dampness.

'I want you to let me be your apprentice,' I cover my head with the hood. 'I want to learn the Work and become a scientist, like you. I promise I'll do what you tell me to. And—and I'll really try not to ask too many questions.'

'I see.' Mac seems to be thinking deeply.

Then a smile peeps out from under his beard, sending his violet eyes sparkling.

'Mim,' he says, 'we have a deal.'

# THE BOAT

I pick up the bucket of frogs.

'Shall I tip them into the ocean on my way out?'

'Dear me, no!' says Mac. 'Frogs live in fresh water. They will die if you put them into the sea.'

'What shall I do with them, then?'

'You could take them back to the castle with you.'

Then I remember something. 'But—how will I get back to shore?'

'By boat. Miss Fogarty always rows herself here and back in it.'

'But it'll be on the shore, where she left it.'

'Miranda will get it for you.'

'Will she?' Miranda was angry enough last time she had to help me. If I ask for help again, she's likely to blow a gasket. But Mac isn't listening. He's bustling around his laboratory, humming to himself.

Suddenly my shoulders feel heavy, as if a great weight's pressing down on them. I've got to bring *The Three Impossibles* back. If I don't, Mac will be executed tomorrow, and Miranda will never get her legs back. I shiver, draw the cloak tighter round my body, and make for the stairs.

Outside, the sky's a world of clouds: pink and orange, streaked with blue. Miranda sits alone on the rock, her white-blonde hair and pale skin ghostly in the early morning light. In her white dress, with her tail hidden in the water, she looks like a normal girl. Two bobbing heads close in on her and a pair of thin white arms reaches towards her.

'Get away!' She gives a sharp cry. But the arms grab her and pull her in. Suddenly the water is a thrashing whirlpool. Tails whip and flash. The two Mers turn and swim off, their mocking laughter echoing over the waves. Miranda, her hair in wet clumps, hauls herself back onto the rock, choking.

'Are you all right?' I stumble over the rocks to her.

'Do I look all right?'

The frogs are trying to crawl out of their bucket, so I pull off Foggy's cloak, fold it and place it over the rim.

'Oh, it's *you*.' Miranda scowls. 'I thought it was *her* again, for a minute.'

'You mean Foggy?'

'The gloomy, sniffing one who never speaks to me. How do you know her name?'

'She was my governess, at the castle.'

'The castle? You live in a castle?'

I nod, reluctantly. 'I used to.'

'Are you... a princess?'

'Yes.'

Miranda stares at me. 'I suppose you have all sorts of fine things.'

'Not exactly. We don't have fine things any more. Not since Curse Day.' I reach into my pocket and pull out my brooch. 'This is the only fine thing I have.'

Miranda gazes at the brooch greedily. 'Is that... gold?'

I nod again.

'I s'pose that's why you've come to see him—my grandfather?' Miranda jerks her head at the lighthouse. 'To make him turn lead into gold? Just like *she* does.'

'No! I—'

'Well, I wouldn't count on it. I've waited all my life for him to overturn the curse on my tail, and look at *me*.' She flips her scaly wet tail, spraying my face with water, and lowers her voice to a whisper. 'Even the Mers think he's clever enough to do it. That's why they never go further than teasing and bullying me. They're afraid of his powers.'

She glances up at the lighthouse.

'If they only knew the truth! He's worse than useless, living up there in his tower, thinking he can solve every problem with his brain. If I had proper legs, I'd climb up to that laboratory of his and have a go myself...' Her face falls. '...except, if I had legs, I wouldn't need to.'

I wipe my wet face with a corner of the cloak. 'He's going to do it. And I'm going to help him.'

'You?' says Miranda. 'How?'

'Well, first of all I'm going back to the castle to get an important book. And I need your help.'

Miranda glares at me. 'What use can *I* be to you? A poor half fish, half human?'

'Well, you can bring me the boat, for a start.'

'What will you give me?' Quick as a flash, she reaches towards my brooch. I grab it and hold on tight.

'I won't give you anything! Don't you want to help your grandfather? Don't you want your curse to be overturned? Don't you want to walk and dance?'

'Don't *ever* talk to me about walking or dancing!' Miranda swallows hard, as if she's trying to push down her fury. She scans the ocean. The Mers have gone. In a flash, she dives into the water and swims towards the shore.

I uncover the bucket. The frogs stare up at me with their bulbous eyes.

'Maybe she's right,' I tell them. 'Maybe it *is* all impossible. But I've got to try. And even if it all fails, at least you'll be OK.'

While I wait for Miranda, my mind jumps about like one of the frogs, trying to come up with a plan. If I'm going to live in the lighthouse and be Mac's apprentice, I'll never see Smith again. Which is also impossible. So it's not only the book I need to bring back with me.

Miranda swims up, tugging the boat by its rope.

'Here.' She swipes her sopping hair from her face and reaches up a pale, wet hand with the rope. I grab it and pull the boat towards the rock.

'Thanks.' I gingerly lower one foot into the boat. It rocks crazily and I almost fall in.

Miranda smirks, but she sets her hands on the boat to hold it steady. Clutching the bucket of frogs, I step in.

Boats are tricky things. They sort of slip about on the water and swerve with every move you make. I stand as still as I can until it stops rocking, then I shuffle until I'm sitting on the seat in the middle.

Lying in the bottom are two long pieces of wood, a bit like wooden spoons, and a rough bucket. Quickly, I turn the bucket upside down so that it covers the bucket of frogs. Then, trying to move as little as possible, I shrug on Foggy's cloak and pull its hood down over my face.

'What do I do now?'

'Use the oars, dummy.'

It's all very well for her. I've never been in a boat before, far less a boat on a moving ocean. I pick up the two pieces of wood—the oars. Do I have to somehow stand up in the shaky boat and paddle with one of them?

'Fit them in the rowlocks.'

Miranda points at two u-shaped metal hooks on each side of the boat. Carefully, I slot an oar into each one.

'Now hold the oars and dip them into the water.'

I pull hard and the boat moves backwards. I dip the oars into the water again. Suddenly one flies up, hitting my chest, and I'm lying on my back at the bottom of the boat, the buckets knocked over. Frogs hop over me, croaking.

Miranda laughs. 'You caught a crab!'

'Where?' I look around, expecting to see a big crab crawling among the frogs. Miranda laughs even louder.

'Not a real crab! It's called catching a crab when you miss the water with the oars.'

Gritting my teeth, I sit up. One of the oars is floating away and I lean over the side of the boat to grab it. A thin white hand—not Miranda's—shoots out of the water, towards my pyjama pocket and the brooch. A cold feeling shivers inside me and I slap it away. The boat swerves and rocks wildly.

When it settles, I pick up the frogs one by one, return them to the bucket and cover it again.

This time the rowing goes better. I get into a good rhythm and soon I'm halfway between the lighthouse and the shore. The sea rocks me gently, slap-slapping against the boat.

Then the singing begins.

It starts with a low hum. I look for Miranda, thinking it must be her. But Miranda is nowhere to be seen. The humming gets louder and louder. It's as if the ocean itself is singing.

It's the Mers again.

There are no words, only a wave of haunted, chilling sound which seems to wrap around my throat like a noose. I can't hold on to the oars. Through half-closed eyes, I watch as they slip out of the rowlocks and drift away.

The ocean is full of bobbing heads—twenty or thirty of them, their white, corpse-like faces turned up at me, their mouths opening as they sing, revealing sharp rows of fish teeth.

I have... to... stay... awake...

Only I can't.

My eyes fall shut as the bobbing heads close in around the boat.

# THE PLAN

'ake *up!*'

Someone slaps my face. But it's as if my eyelids are glued shut. My fingers find my brooch and hold on tight. No way are the Mers getting it.

Another slap. '*Wake up!!*'

It's Miranda's voice. I shake my head. It's like I've got cotton wool instead of a brain.

'Stick your fingers in your ears.'

'Wha—?'

'Stick them in your ears. *Now!*'

Groggy, my arms as heavy as lead, I shove my fingers into my ears. I still can't open my eyes.

The boat begins to move forward in jerky tugs. Every few moments it rocks wildly and there are distant shrieks. Water splashes over my face and body. But at least I can't hear the singing any more. I grit my teeth and focus on blocking out every bit of sound.

After what feels like a lifetime, there's a sort of grinding beneath the boat. Then it stops, and my eyes slowly open.

I'm lying on my back at the bottom of the boat, which seems to be tilted to one side. Above me, the sky is bright and clear. Cautiously, I pull my fingers out of my ears and sit up.

The boat lies on the sand outside the Great Wall, the oars laid neatly beside me. How did it get here? I screw up my eyes against the sharp morning light and stare out at the ocean.

Swimming towards the lighthouse, as if for her life, Miranda's pale head dips and splashes. All around her, like a flock of angry sea-crows, the Mers shove her and push her and tug at her hair.

*Go, Miranda*, I whisper, willing her to reach the rocks before the Mers hurt her badly. I only breathe out when she hauls herself up onto the rock, clumsy as a seal, and swings her tail out of the water. Then I lift my hand in a wave. She doesn't return it.

I sigh. Miranda may be angry and hard, but she's just saved my life for the second time. And I know how it feels to be trapped and alone. I jump out of the boat and, with all my strength, haul it up the beach so it'll be safe from the tide. I pick up the bucket of frogs, wrap the cloak tightly around me and walk over the sand until I'm standing in the shadow of the Great Wall. So much has happened since I slipped through the Gate for the first time, only a few hours ago. The sentry—a different one from the one who let me past that time—stares down at me, and his voice booms through the loudspeaker.

'You all right there, Miss Fogarty?'

I pray he's only just noticed me, and hasn't seen what happened with the Mers. I put on my best Foggy voice, keeping my head down.

'Perfectly fine,' I sniff. 'Hurry up, man, and open the Gate!'

'Yes, miss.'

I breathe a sigh of relief as the Gate slowly creaks open. Then I slip inside, my knees still trembling. The first part of my plan has succeeded. Now for the second.

I clear my throat, give another loud sniff, and call up to the sentry.

'I shall need to go out again shortly. Orders of the King.'

'Very well, miss.'

The streets of Galena are empty. There's no sign of Madame or Hercules and his men. As far as they know, I'm still in bed—though it seems like a hundred years since I walked out of the Gate. Madame will be waiting for me in the dungeons, planning a horrible punishment for me, for helping Sky escape.

Holding the bucket of frogs, I run across the courtyard to the castle door, which still shows signs of being battered by Hercules and his men. Gingerly, I push it open and I tiptoe into the hall, my ears straining and my mind full of what ifs.

*What if Madame hears me?*

*What if Foggy catches me returning to my room?*

*What if they've already discovered I'm gone?*

I scurry up the corridor past Foggy's door and slip into my room. My heart leaps about in my chest just like the frogs in the bucket.

Everything's exactly as I left it. A faint light glows from under the cupboard door. *The Three Impossibles* is still there!

I dip a finger into the jug of water beside the basin. Luckily it's not iced up. I pour the water into the bucket of frogs, and they splash around happily. Then I carry the bucket over to the cupboard and push it into the darkest corner.

'Stay here,' I whisper. 'And don't let Madame find you.' They croak, as if they understand.

Then I pull out *The Three Impossibles*, still wrapped in my princess dress. I hurry to my bed, roll up the dress and shove it under the blanket. I push the high-heeled shoes in at the bottom and place the lead crown on the pillow. Then I drag the blanket right up over it all, so it looks like I'm asleep in bed.

The second part of my plan is complete. But Part Three will be the hardest of all. Rolling Foggy's cloak into a bundle, I tuck it under my arm, along with *The Three Impossibles*, and tiptoe along the corridor, across the hall and through the front door, across the courtyard and past the Gate towards the forge.

There's no sign of Smith outside the forge. I edge past the executioner's block. Tomorrow morning, Mac could be kneeling here, his arms tied behind him, his neck on the block.

*Stoppit*, I tell myself firmly. I must remember what Smith always says: *'The future doesn't exist, Mim. Now is all that counts.'*

I push open the forge door as quietly as I can. Smith, his wrist bandaged, is working the bellows at the furnace.

'Smith?'

He turns.

'Mim! What are you—'

I grab his arm, words tumbling out of my mouth. 'Smith-please-listen-and-don't-say-anything-'cos-this-is-important-and-I've-been-thinking-and-thinking-and-I've-got-a-plan—'

'Whoah, Mim. Slow down.'

I take a breath. 'I've been to the Outside.'

Smith's beetly eyebrows almost hit his hair.

'And I've met the old man—Mac.'

'Trismegistus MacWhisker?'

'Yes. And Madame's made Father give him an ultimatum.'

'An ultimatum?'

'He's got to change lead into gold by first light tomorrow—or else he'll be executed.'

'Executed?' Smith's face is suddenly drained of colour.

'Yes! So we've got to help him. And you have to come with me.' I tug at his sleeve.

'Hold on, Mim. Come where with you?'

'To the lighthouse.' I pull out *The Three Impossibles*. 'Mac needs this book to do the Work. And I'm going to help him. Be his apprentice.'

'That's all very well, Mim.' Smith says, slowly. 'Trismegistus MacWhisker is a good man. And it's true, your life won't be worth living with that woman here. But why me?'

'Because—because...'

I want to say, *because I'd miss you too much*, but Smith would be embarrassed. So instead I say:

'Because *your* life won't be worth living either, if you have to execute Mac.'

Smith looks grave. 'But I won't execute him. I'm a blacksmith, not an executioner. I make things. I don't—I *won't*—destroy 'em.'

'They'll make you! And even if you refuse, they'll get Hercules and his men to do it.'

'Let them try.'

I stamp my foot. 'Smith, *listen* to me! You've got to come to the lighthouse. Mac needs you. He's not strong—but you are. You can look after the furnace. And—and anyway—'

'Yes, Mim?'

My hand finds the brooch in my pocket and I squeeze it hard.

'I won't leave you here. You're my best friend in the world. I-I love you, you see.'

Smith clears his throat with a harrumphing sound, just like I knew he would. Under his muscles, Smith's heart is soft as butter. He won't actually say he cares about me, I know that. He made me the brooch. That's his way.

'Let's go, Smith! Madame'll soon find out I'm gone and she'll—'

'How, Mim?' says Smith. 'There's no way the sentry'll open the Gate for us.' But he picks up a bucket and pours a stream of water over the coals in the furnace, setting up a furious hissing. So he *is* going to come with me.

'He will if he thinks we're Foggy.'

Smith stares at me as I pull out Foggy's cloak.

'Here. Put this on. Pull the hood down over your eyes.'

The cloak is so big and billowing, it just covers Smith's huge body. Except for his thick legs, which stick out under it like a pair of tree trunks.

'You've got to bend your knees! And now, give me a leg up.'

I climb up Smith, using his bended knee as a foothold. It's like climbing a great oak tree.

'This is a daft plan, Mim,' he grunts, as I settle into his arms. 'Even if they *were* to believe me to be Miss Fogarty, you're sticking out like a big lump.'

'Foggy's always carrying stuff under her cloak—taking lead objects to Mac. Now, let's go!'

Muttering under his breath, Smith lurches forward.

All I can see is the ground under our feet. The stone floor of the forge... the wooden planks of the platform... the cobbles of the street. Smith's heart pounds like a huge bass drum in my ear. At last, he stops.

'What now?' he whispers. 'We're at the Gate.'

I clear my throat, part Foggy's cloak a little bit, give a loud sniff, and shout.

'Open the Gate, sentry!'

'Yes, Miss Fogarty.' The winch begins to turn, with a creak.

Part Three of my plan is working! I shake all over with excitement and nerves. I can hardly believe that everything's going so smoothly.

Only then, the turning of the winch stops abruptly and Smith mutters something.

'What's the matter?' I whisper. Smith's hands tighten around me.

And a voice, sharp and angry, cuts through the air.

# KIDNAPPED!

**M**y heart drops to the soles of my feet. I know that voice only too well.

'SAMUEL SMITH! What are you doing in my cloak?'

'Morning, Miss Fogarty.'

'Well?'

'I, er... found it.'

'Found it?' The silence is full of Foggy's thinking. 'When last I saw that cloak, it was hanging on the back of my bedroom door. Then it disappeared. How exactly have *you* laid your hands on it?'

Smith is silent.

A finger prods at me through the cloak. 'And what's that you're carrying?'

'Nowt of interest, Miss Fogarty. And now, if you'll excuse me, I need to get back to the forge.'

He turns and begins to walk away. I clench *The Three Impossibles* tightly to my chest. If I don't breathe, maybe we'll get away with it.

'Not so fast, Samuel Smith!'

Smith sighs.

Foggy's footsteps squeak round until her voice is right in front of us.

'Show me what you're hiding—or I'll raise the alarm.'

'With respect, Miss Fogarty, it's none of your business.'

'None of my business?' Foggy's voice is high and furious. 'You're wearing *my* cloak—pretending to be *me*!' She gives a long, wet sniff. 'If you won't show me what you're hiding, I'll find out for myself!'

Her fingers scrabble at the cloak.

'*Run, Smith!*' I hiss.

But Foggy holds on. As Smith moves, the cloak is pulled open—leaving me for all to see, clutching *The Three Impossibles*.

For a moment, Foggy simply stares. Then she screams.

'KIDNAP! KIDNAP! Sound the alarm!'

The sentry shouts down from the Wall.

'What is it, miss?'

'SOUND THE ALARM!!! This man is trying to kidnap Her Royal Highness!'

'Yes, miss—right away, miss!'

The booming of an enormous gong echoes round the walls. It sears into my head so I can't think straight. Smith seems frozen too. Then, out of the castle runs Madame, with Groucho straining at his lead, followed by Hercules, Jason and Atlas. Groucho adds his keening howl to the booming of the gong, along with Madame's and Foggy's shrieks and the three men's shouts.

Smith seems to come to his senses. Holding me tightly, he stumbles towards the forge. Madame, wearing a crimson dressing gown, her red hair in disarray, points her finger at Smith and me and lets Groucho off his leash.

'Kidnapper!' she screams. 'Get him, leetle boy!'

Groucho's hot, meaty breath is on my face and his needle-sharp teeth are bared as he leaps up at Smith, trying to grab me. Smith jerks me out of reach.

'Smith, put me down!' I hiss. Any minute he's going to get badly bitten. But Smith ignores me.

Madame, Hercules, and his men, trailed by a panting Foggy, catch up with us. Madame grabs Groucho's lead, pulling him back.

'Let her go, executioner.' Madame's voice is cold as an icicle. 'Or face the consequences.'

Smith grips me tighter still.

'Hercules,' says Madame. 'Show him.'

'Yus, Madame. C'mon, boys.'

Hercules, with Jason and Atlas on either side, draws out his gleaming knife and advances towards Smith and me. Slowly, Smith lowers me to the ground.

'Get out of here, Mim,' he mutters. 'Now.'

*I'm not going anywhere.* This is all my fault.

I stand in front of Smith. No way is Hercules going to stab him.

'Get out of the way, leetle brat,' hisses Madame.

'No!' I do my best to stop my voice from shaking.

'Seize her,' Madame orders Jason and Atlas. They close in on me, one on either side.

And then everything goes crazy. Smith gives me a massive shove and I fall sprawling on the ground. Groucho snaps and growls at Smith, and Hercules raises his arm, the knife glittering. With all my strength, I kick at Hercules' legs. He howls with pain and the knife clatters to the ground. Then Atlas snatches the cloak and throws it over my head and someone tugs it tight about my arms.

I kick and struggle but it's useless. *The Three Impossibles* and I are bundled up in Foggy's cloak like a parcel, and dragged to lie at Madame's feet. I can hear Smith panting as he fights, and Groucho howling and snarling, and the men swearing. Then Smith gives a huge groan and everything seems to still.

'Now.' Madame's voice is steel. 'Chain him.'

Footsteps march over the wooden platform and there's a creak as the forge door opens. Then a heavy, rolling clanking sound. Smith groans again.

'Let this be a lesson to you, executioner,' Madame says. 'Kidnapping is a very serious offence. His Majesty will be grateful to have his leetle brat safely restored to him. Very grateful indeed.'

Rough hands unfasten the cloak. Madame stands over me, her face a mask of triumph. Beside her, Foggy looks furious. Smith, a livid gash on his cheek, is chained to the executioner's block by his ankle, his hands chained and padlocked too. Before I can move towards him, Foggy steps forward and points a quivering finger at *The Three Impossibles*. Her face is white as ash.

'What are you doing with that book?'

'N-nothing.' I hug it closer to my chest.

Madame stares at *The Three Impossibles*.

'What is this book, sister?'

'It's nothing.' Foggy flushes. 'Just... one of the old man's books.'

'*The Three Impossibles*...' Madame squints at the title. '*A Book of Alchemy*. If I am not mistaken, isn't alchemy the art of changing lead into gold? Such a book would be worth... a king's ransom.'

Foggy splutters and turns to me. 'Give it to me! I'll take it to His Majesty, right now!'

Madame slips between us. 'I think not, sister dear. *I'll* take it. With this book in my possession, I need not depend on the old man for gold.'

I take a step backwards, but Madame's too quick for me. She snatches hold of the book, grazing my arm with her long fingernails, and tugs hard. I hold on as tightly as I can, but then Foggy dashes in and grabs the other corner of the book. I don't stand a chance against the two of them.

*The Three Impossibles* seems to leap out of my fingers as the sisters face one another in a tug of war.

'Give... it... to... me...' Madame grunts, yanking the book.

'No chance,' spits Foggy, tugging back.

And then the sky turns black, full of beating wings.

# FLIGHT

I jerk my head up to look.

Twenty or thirty Wings swoop above our heads. Before we can move, they're down on us like a hailstorm. Hercules draws his knife and stabs wildly at them, but they twist and turn like acrobats in the air, the blade barely grazing their feathers. Groucho snarls and howls, leaping after the Wings, but they dive-bomb him until he skitters away, whining.

Foggy and Madame drop *The Three Impossibles* and cover their heads with their arms. I pull the hood of the cloak over my head to protect myself, but the Wings don't seem to be attacking me. It's Madame Marionette they're after. She shrieks for Hercules, her red fingernails flying, her hair pulled into a tangle. But Hercules is backed against the wall of the forge, covering his face, and Jason and Atlas lie curled into balls on the ground.

Then, as one, the Wings abandon Madame and fly around me in a black, hissing cloud. Their wings beat around my head. I sink to my knees, trembling all over. Are they going to kill me? I squeeze my eyes tight shut and my fingers find my brooch. The air stills and an uneasy silence falls.

'Ssstand up, human.'

The voice is familiar. I open my eyes. The Wings surround me and Smith in a feathered circle, staring at us with beady, inquisitive eyes. Madame hobbles away towards the castle like a tatty red scarecrow, dragging a whining Groucho behind her, with Foggy in their wake. There's no sign of Hercules and his men.

'I said, ssstand up.'

'Sky? Is that you?'

The Wing who spoke to me has Sky's lean, proud face and coal-black eyes. Only he's much taller and older than Sky.

'For the third and lassst time—ssstand up!'

I stumble to my feet. 'Wh-who are you? And where's Sky?'

The Wing's face hardens.

'We do not speak of Sssky.'

The Wings shift and murmur behind him, their voices like wind in the trees.

'What has he—?'

'We are here to avenge him.' The Wing's eyes are stern. 'And to sssettle his debt.'

'His debt?'

The Wing jerks his head at me impatiently. 'Climb on my back.'

I glance over at Smith, the gash on his face weeping blood, his hands and ankle chained.

'But what about Smith? Can't you—'

The Wing shakes his head. 'Impossible. We cannot break chainsss.'

'I won't just leave him!'

'You mussst, if you value your life.'

'No!' Tears fill my eyes.

'Mim, bonny girl.' It's Smith. 'Go. Take the book and go with King Wing.'

'But I—'

Smith raises his voice a little. '*Go*, Mim. It's your only chance.' He turns to King Wing. 'Take her to the lighthouse. And—who knows—if the old man makes gold, all may yet be well.'

The tears leak from my eyes and roll down my cheeks. Smith's still speaking.

'I'll be with you. Here.' He taps his chest. 'Never forget that.'

My fingers find the brooch in my pocket. It seems to glow there like a little fire.

'Make haste, human.' The Wings fidget behind King Wing, their eyes fixed on Madame's distant figure.

I hurry over to where *The Three Impossibles* lies, scuffed and dusty. As I pick it up, it seems to glimmer a little more brightly.

I tuck it under my arm, pull the cloak around myself and climb up onto King Wing's back. His feathers are warm, as if touched by the sun. I bury my cold hands in them, looking for something to hold on to.

'My neck,' Wing says, as if he's heard my thought. I put one arm around his neck, the other gripping the book. 'Lean into me.'

I press my body down against his feathered back. Then his great wings spread wide and he leaps into the air, followed by all the others. The beating of thirty pairs of wings whirlwinds about my ears, swirling my hair about and making me gasp, as, in perfect formation, we rise up above the forge.

I stare down at Smith, chained and bloody, and more tears wet the air. 'I'll be back! I promise, Smith. I'll be back.'

'Godspeed, Mim.' Smith's great head droops.

Then we're high above Galena, high above the Great Wall, high above the sentry, open-mouthed and gawping. The air is icy, but King Wing's feathers are warm. Up here, the wind's stronger. Every now and then an especially strong gust buffets his body and he adjusts his flight. Now we're flying over the empty sand. There's the rowing boat, where I left it. King Wing glides down over the ocean. I can almost touch the waves. Then he soars up until the ocean is a blue haze. Miranda and the Mers are nowhere to be seen, and it's only a few moments before the lighthouse is below us. King Wing's body tilts alarmingly as he banks, then plummets towards the rocks. The other Wings sweep above us, as King Wing lands right outside the door. I scramble off his back.

'Thank you.' I try to get my windswept hair out of my eyes.

'The debt isss paid.' King Wing's stern, proud face is so much like Sky's. He spreads his great wings again.

'Wait! Can I ask you a question?'

King Wing inclines his feathered head.

'Why did you rescue me? What's the debt? And where is Sky?'

'Three questionsss.'

'Y-yes. I have an Enquiring Mind, you see.'

King Wing stares out at the ocean, thinking, then he nods to himself.

'Sky has outcassst himself from our tribe.'

'Why?'

'He is ashamed. You sssaved him from the clutches of the evil woman—'

'Madame Marionette?'

'*She* isss not worthy of a name.' King Wing spits on the rock at his feet. 'You sssaved my son, and he abandoned you. Wings are honourable beingsss. We do not abandon those who help usss.'

'I don't think he meant to. I think he forgot about me, because he was free...' I can't blame Sky for what he did. He'd been so desperate and afraid.

'I believe thisss, too,' says King Wing. 'But Sky is proud. Too proud. He cannot forgive himssself for abandoning you. And so he has left us, and insssists on living alone, without communication.' He bows his feathered head. 'Which hasss broken his grandmother's heart... and my own.'

Before I can say anything else, he spreads his wings—they must be at least six feet across—and leaps into the air to join the others. They form the shape of an arrow in the sky, their black wings beating in unison. The arrow flies, straight and true, towards the mountain topped with its dusty grey cloud. I watch until the arrow's swallowed up in the cloud and the Wings are gone.

But King Wing's words are still here, inside my head, and I can't make them go away.

*We do not abandon those who help usss.*

I left Smith. Abandoned him. But if I'd stayed with him, Mac wouldn't get the book. Without *The Three Impossibles*, the curse on Miranda's tail will never be broken. And if Mac doesn't change lead into gold by sunrise tomorrow, he'll die—because even if Smith refuses to execute him, Hercules will do it instead.

I reach inside my pocket and pull out the brooch. My name sparkles in the morning light. I cup it in my hand.

'I'll come back for you, Smith,' I whisper. 'I swear.'

Then I walk to the lighthouse and ring the bell.

# THE BOOK

**M**ac is waiting at the door as I pant up the final steps to the laboratory.

'You have it? *The Three Impossibles?*'

Words tumble out as I tell the story.

'Smith and I tried to escape with it—only Foggy saw us and sounded the alarm—and Hercules and his men attacked Smith and chained him up—and Madame and Foggy fought over the book—and then King Wing swooped down and got me out—'

Mac's shoulders slump and he suddenly looks very old.

'You didn't get it.'

Silently, I draw out *The Three Impossibles* from the folds of Foggy's cloak and hand it to him. As he takes it in his gnarled hands, it seems to tremble.

'Thank you, Mim,' he whispers, his lined face lit by the book's glow. 'You have proved yourself a worthy apprentice.'

Mac's words seem to curl around my heart like a warm blanket, and my ears tingle with pride.

Cradling *The Three Impossibles* as if it's a baby, Mac hurries into the laboratory. I follow him, pulling off Foggy's cloak and draping it over the rocking chair. Mac's been busy: he's cleared up all the dross, and Slow Henry's full of fresh coal, the bellows and poker ready beside him.

A pair of bulbous eyes peers out at me from the folds of Foggy's cloak.

'A frog! I thought I'd got them all.'

'Hush!' says Mac. He stares at *The Three Impossibles*. Why doesn't he try to open it? Another, scary thought occurs to me.

'Foggy and Madame know about *The Three Impossibles*, and what it does. They're going to tell Father about King Wing taking me away. Do you think they'll come after me?'

Mac glances up at me with unseeing eyes. 'I doubt it. Too scared of the Wings. No one'll come until...' He stops.

'Until what?'

'Until the ultimatum runs out.'

'But that's tomorrow, at sunrise!'

He says nothing. I wander around the laboratory. I can't keep still.

'And what will we do about Smith? They've chained him up...'

I pick up the glass bottle labelled *Green Vitriol* from the shelf and remove its stopper, then choke as sharp, burning fumes go up my nose.

'Put that down!' Mac says sharply. 'The bottles are laid out in a very particular way and must not be disturbed.'

'Sorry. But Smith—'

'Hush, Mim! And come here.'

I go and stand beside him. *The Three Impossibles* glows and trembles in his hands. Light floods our faces and hands as it slowly opens to the first page. Illuminated words seem to throb, they're so bright. Blue... red... silver... gold—like stained-glass windows in a church.

'It's... it's—' I can't find words to describe what I am seeing.

Mac nods.

The light from the page is so bright it hurts my eyes. But somehow Mac begins to read, his voice unsteady. As he speaks each line, it lights up in gold.

### ALCHEMIST, SEEKER OF THE THREE IMPOSSIBLES: WATER, AIR AND FIRE.

*After one Impossible, the elixir is formed.*

*After two Impossibles, health is restored.*

*After three Impossibles, the phoenix flies, curses are lifted and lead becomes gold.*

This is *so* exciting. What's an elixir? What's a phoenix? And what *are* the Three Impossibles? Every bit of me itches to find out. I reach over to turn the page.

And leap back, clutching my hand.

'It zapped me!'

Mac peers at me over the top of his spectacles.

'Sometimes not knowing is just as important as knowing. Even an Enquiring Mind must learn patience.'

'But there's no time! And how can we do the Work if we don't know what the Three Impossibles are?'

He puts his finger to his lips. 'Wait. Have faith. The book will show us what we need to know.'

I stuff my fingers in my mouth to stop myself asking anything else. We both stare at the book. Nothing happens.

'What time is it?' I need to know how long we have left.

Mac nods towards his pocket watch, lying on the table. Eleven o'clock.

My mind calculates. Sunrise in midwinter is around eight o'clock. That means we have only twenty-one hours until the ultimatum runs out. If we don't sleep, that is. Twenty-one hours to complete the Three Impossibles.

No wonder that's what they're called.

Maybe if I stop watching the book, it'll open quicker.

I walk over to the rocking chair. The frog gazes up at me.

'You need a name,' I tell it. 'I'll call you Samuel, after Smith.'

The frog croaks, and his wide mouth seems to grin at me.

'You must be lonely without your friends. And you need some fresh water.'

There's enough cold water inside the kettle. I take a bowl from the shelves and pour in the water, then nudge Samuel until he climbs onto the edge. He sits for a moment, grinning up at me. He seems a particularly intelligent frog. Then he jumps into the dish with a splash and swims round in enthusiastic circles.

'Maybe you're a lucky frog. Maybe—'

'Come here, Mim!' Mac's voice is urgent. He points to the book.

'What is it?'

The page is turning.

We almost bang our heads together as we peer down at the new page. I screw up my eyes against the bright light, to read the words.

## THE FIRST IMPOSSIBLE: WATER

*In the egg, collect tears...*

'The egg?'

Mac nods at the furnace. 'Look inside Slow Henry.'

Above Slow Henry's hearth is a little door. I pull it open. It seems to be some kind of oven. A white oval object, like an ostrich egg, sits inside. I reach in and pull it out. It's warm and smooth in my hands.

'Open it,' says Mac.

I peer at the egg. A thin line divides the top from the bottom, just like when you cut the top off a boiled egg. Carefully, I lift off the top half. Inside, the egg is empty. I carry it over to Mac.

'What is it?' I ask him.

'The egg is the most precious piece of alchemical equipment. And the strongest. Within it, the elixir will be made.'

'What's an elixir?'

'You will discover that, in time.'

I stare at the page.

*In the egg, collect tears...*

'Collecting tears is easy! I can do it right now!' I hold the open egg under my chin.

'What are you doing, Mim?'

'Shhh! Let me concentrate.'

I think about Father, and how he doesn't love me. I think of Smith, and how he gave me my brooch; how he was willing to risk his life for me; how I left him, gashed by Hercules' knife, chained up and alone. I think of the look on Smith's sad, tired face when I flew away on King Wing's back...

Tears trickle down my cheeks and drip from my chin into the egg. Soon, there's a little pool of them at the bottom. Only I can't seem to stop crying.

Mac pats my shoulder.

'There, there, Mim,' he says in his gruff voice. 'I was so caught up with *The Three Impossibles*, I didn't think about all you've been through to get it for me.'

'No,' I sob, 'it's Smith. I left him, you see. He's all alone.'
*Stop crying, Mim.*

I squeeze my eyes closed and do my best to swallow my tears. After a bit, I take a deep breath and hold out the egg. 'There. A collection of tears. Now what do we do with them?'

Mac looks sad.

'Oh, Mim. These are precious tears. But we must wait...'

'Wait?'

Mac says nothing. He just nods at *The Three Impossibles*.

Suddenly I'm angry. 'It's all very well talking about waiting, and patience, and faith. What about the ultimatum? What about Smith? What about Miranda's tail?'

Mac taps the book. Did I read the words wrong? I look at them again.

## THE FIRST IMPOSSIBLE: WATER

*In the egg, collect tears...*

'I don't get it!' I say. 'I've collected tears—look!'

I shove the egg under Mac's nose.

Then, as if blown by an invisible wind, the page turns.

I stare at the words on the next page and my heart drops into my feet.

*...from the ocean.*

# THE FIRST IMPOSSIBLE

**W**e stare at the page. How can you possibly collect tears from the ocean?

'What does it mean?' I dare not try to turn the next page, in case I get zapped again. But surely there must be more—some sort of explanation, a list of instructions.

Only there isn't. *The Three Impossibles* stays stubbornly open at those three words.

I run to the window and gaze out at the ocean. All that water... and whose tears? My mind whirls.

'Maybe it's the Mers! Maybe it's *their* tears we've got to collect.'

'Mers never cry.' Mac joins me at the window. 'Even when their queen was executed, all they thought of was revenge.'

'Then who? What? How?'

But Mac has moved to the chalkboard. He scribbles numbers and symbols, muttering to himself.

'If $H_2O$ meets *sodium chloride*... hydroxyl ions...'

'What are you doing?'

'Calculating.'

The chalk squeaks across the board. I think of Miranda's words about her grandfather.

*He's worse than useless... living up there in his tower, thinking he can solve every problem with his brain.*

As I stare down at the rocks below, Miranda swims up—as if thinking about her has conjured her. She grasps a rock and hauls herself onto it, her tail flailing under her white dress, her face—as usual—like a thundercloud. All around her, the water swirls and slaps against the rocks.

The First Impossible is all about water. That much is clear. Maybe... just maybe...

'I think—I think I'll go out and see Miranda. Is that okay?'

Mac grunts and scratches on. But Samuel gives me a slow, froggy wink. I take that as a yes.

Miranda is wringing out her salty wet hair as if she wishes it was someone's neck.

'Miranda,' I say, moving near her. 'Is it true that the Mers never cry?'

'Never ever. Didn't you know, Mers are heartless? Literally. Their chests are empty.'

I glance down at the grinning Mer faces and shiver. No wonder they act like robots, attacking ships and people. I go on thinking.

'What about fish? Do *they* cry?'

Miranda laughs. 'Those cold-blooded creatures? 'Course they don't!'

'Seals? Octopuses? Dolphins? Turtles?'

'Nope.' Miranda stares at me. 'Why this sudden interest in crying?'

'Because the book says we've got to collect tears from the ocean.'

'But that's impossible!'

'It's some kind of a riddle. And I'm trying to think how to solve it.'

'*Think!*' Miranda's mouth twists in a sneer. 'I was right— you are just as bad as him. He's been thinking for eleven years, and where has it got us?' She flicks her tail and I get an eyeful of water. 'Looks like it'll be another eleven years before the curse is broken—or maybe even twenty-two years, since you're *both* so keen on thinking.'

'It won't be years at all, because of the—'

I stop. Mac made me promise not to tell Miranda about the ultimatum. Luckily, she's not listening. She slides into the water, glaring at the Mers as if daring them to come near. I keep thinking.

'The clue is about something—or someone—who lives in water. I know it is.'

Miranda slaps her hand at the water swirling around the rocks.

'Shut up about water. I hate it! It's cold and wet and full of Mers. I want to be dry! I want to wear dry clothes, like you. I want to walk about on dry land.'

I stare at Miranda's cross, pale face. What if it's *her* tears we need to collect?

'Miranda... do *you* ever cry?'

Miranda glowers at me.

'Didn't you hear what I just said? My life's all wet. No way will I add to it by *crying*.' She glances at the Mers and lowers her voice. 'Besides, if they get even a whiff of weakness, they'll torment me even more.'

'Crying isn't weak.'

'Says *you*.'

My mind's concentrating hard now. A germ of an idea comes to me.

'Did I ever tell you about my life—in the castle?'

'No.' She glares at me. 'And you'd better not.'

This isn't looking promising. But I can think of only one way to make Miranda cry—and that's to tell her about all the things she longs to do herself.

I sit down nearer her on a rock.

'I hated my life there just as much as you hate *your* life.'

Miranda plays with a strand of seaweed, but I can tell she's listening.

'They wanted me to behave like a princess.'

'So? You *are* a princess.'

'They made me wear a long silk dress.'

'Was it dry?'

'Of course it was dry!'

'Lucky you, then.' Miranda frowns.

'I had to wear high-heeled shoes too, and a crown. And I had to learn electro—er, elocution and deportment.'

'Is that so?' Miranda's voice is dangerously low. She swims over to lean on the rock at my feet. I move away a little. There's no telling what she's likely to do when I say the next thing. I take a deep breath.

'They made me learn to dance, too.'

Miranda's eyes are like daggers. 'I *warned* you. *Never* talk to me about dancing!'

Her tail whips around in the water in a dangerous sort of way. But I've got to go on. From the top window of the lighthouse floats the sound of chanting. What's Mac up to?

I get to my feet and stumble over the rocks until I'm out of Miranda's reach. Then I begin to dance the steps Madame taught me. Or what I can remember of them. I jump about, my arms flailing around. Miranda's eyes are fixed on my feet. Her face turns from frozen white to crimson. She glares at me as if she's about to explode.

'Think you're so clever, don't you? Teasing and torment-ing me about all the things I can't do! You're no better than *them*.' She jerks her head at the Mers.

I dance away from her: now on tiptoe, pirouetting over the rocks; now lifting my back leg in a clumsy *arabesque*. Down in the water, Miranda spits and seethes. Suddenly, she hauls herself out of the water, her tail glittering wet.

'How dare you mock me! I *hate* you! I should've left you to *drown*.'

This is hopeless. She's only going to get madder and madder. I stop dancing.

Then something hard hits me on the head and bounces onto the rocks. I pick it up. It's a piece of chalk.

'Why's Mac throwing chalk out of the window?' I ask.

Miranda taps her head, still glaring. 'Because he's daft, that's why.'

Mac's voice drifts down.

'It *should* be working... *Why* won't it work?'

Despair weaves round my heart. 'He's trying. Trying to break the curse on your tail.'

'And he's failed—again!' Miranda swishes her tail, her face like a black cloud. 'How much longer am I s'posed to believe in him? How much longer do I keep hoping he'll do it?'

'Not much longer,' I mutter.

'What? What do you mean?'

I glance up at the lighthouse window. Teasing Miranda was bad enough. But now I'm going to have to do something terrible, something I never dreamt I'd do.

'Miranda, I need to tell you something. About your grandfather.'

'What?'

'I promised him I wouldn't. And I've never broken a promise in my life.'

'What promise?' Miranda looks uncertain.

'My father's given your grandfather an ultimatum.'

'What's an ultimatum?'

'A deadline. To change lead into gold.'

Miranda smiles. 'At last! Maybe he'll get a move on now.'

'You don't understand.'

'Understand what?'

'He's got to do it by sunrise tomorrow.'

'But that's impossible!'

'And if he fails... they're going to kill him.'

Miranda stares up at me. Then she turns her face up to the lighthouse, with its buckets and fishing rods and odd

214

devices. Up in the top window, Mac's hairy face appears, gazing down at us. He looks old and sad and alone.

'Kill him?' Miranda blinks hard. 'They can't do that. He's... he's my grandfather.'

I hate doing this, but I have to.

'They will, Miranda. They'll come for him and take him to Galena—just like they did with the Mer Queen—and they'll tie up his hands and make him lay his head on the executioner's block, and they'll—'

'No!' Miranda covers her ears. 'I won't let them!'

'There's nothing you or I can do.' *I'm sorry. I'm so sorry...*

Mac's voice floats down from the window.

'Miranda, my child. I'm still trying. So close now...' His frail voice trails away.

Miranda drops her head. A sound comes out of her, halfway between a groan and a sigh. She mutters something, her voice so choked up that I have to lean down to hear.

'I l-love him, you see. I do, even though I grouse about him.'

'I know.' I reach out and take her cold, wet hand in mine. 'And he loves *you*, with all his heart.'

Tears fall from Miranda's eyes, dripping down into the water. Silvery tears, like mercury, each one floating on the surface like a tiny fish. I drop Miranda's hand and slip my own hands into the water, to catch the tears before they dissolve and disappear. They twitch like minnows, darting back and forth through my fingers.

'Catch them!' I cry. 'They're the First Impossible!'

Miranda stares at the tears. Then she too plunges her hands into the water.

'Careful—or we'll lose them!'

Slowly, Miranda's hands circle the shimmering tears. Then she whispers, so as not to frighten them. 'I'll protect them—you lift them out.'

Holding my breath, I float my hands under the tears until they're resting in my palms. They glisten in the sunlight like moving pearls.

'Be quick,' whispers Miranda, 'or they'll escape.' Her face looks softer and clearer, as if the tears have washed it clean.

Holding the precious tears, I set off towards the lighthouse. In the doorway, I turn.

'Thanks, Miranda.'

Miranda's voice follows me up the spiral stairs to the laboratory: 'Good luck.'

# THE SECOND IMPOSSIBLE

'I've got them!' I run into the laboratory, my hands tightly cupped around the precious tears.

Mac's still staring out of the window.

'I beg your pardon?'

'I've got the tears from the ocean! They're Miranda's.'

'Miranda's? Surely not...'

The tears wiggle in my palms like silver tadpoles. There's a loud croak from the rocking chair. Samuel the frog stares greedily at my cupped hands, his long tongue darting.

'Quick, where shall I put them?'

Mac crosses the room to Slow Henry. He opens the oven door and pulls out the egg, lifting the lid. Hardly daring to breathe, I open my fingers and drop the tears inside. They skitter around as if looking for a way to escape. Mac gives a deep sigh.

'You did it, Mim. You did it! The First Impossible.'

'But now what do we do?'

Mac drops to his knees in front of Slow Henry and strikes a match.

'We heat the tears.'

He holds the match inside Slow Henry, among the coals. A flame seeps along a piece of kindling.

'The egg, if you please.'

Mac closes the egg and places it carefully inside the oven. The flame burns blue, then gold. Slow Henry shifts and trembles, just as if he's breathing in and out. Mac polishes his spectacles.

'The Work has begun.'

I sort of shiver inside. Samuel jumps down from the rocking chair and crawls up to Slow Henry, his eyes fixed on the egg. He croaks again, and I scoop him up.

'Don't you even dare, Samuel! Not unless you want to be boiled alive.' Then I notice something. 'Mac—the book! The page is turning!'

The book glows. We stare down at the new page. Mac reads out the words:

## THE SECOND IMPOSSIBLE: AIR

*From the air, collect...*

To distract myself from waiting for the page to turn, I scratch Samuel's head. His grin gets even wider. Beside me, Slow Henry heats up. There's a rattling sound as the egg wobbles inside him. Mac hurries over.

'Steady, Slow Henry. Behave yourself.'

Samuel croaks loudly.

'What is it, Samuel?'

Samuel's long tongue curls towards the book. It glows, brighter than ever, and the page turns. I read:

*...a flash of light.*

Mac stares at the page over my shoulder. 'Ah.'

'This really *is* impossible.' A sort of greyness fills my heart, like ash.

'Ever heard of Alexander the Great?'

'Who?'

'King of Ancient Greece. He said: "There is nothing impossible to him who will try." Sometimes, things *seem* impossible—until you look at them in a different way.'

He wanders over to the chalkboard. Soon the air's filled with the sound of scratching and squeaking.

*Look at things in a different way.* The clues must be there—just like they were for the First Impossible. That was all about water, and the clue was in the ocean. This one is about air, so maybe the clue's in the sky. I hurry to the window and gaze out. The sky seems to stretch on for ever, heavy with clouds. However can we collect a flash of light from it?

'Maybe... maybe we've got to, I don't know—fly to the sun, or something?'

'Hush, Mim.' Mac scribbles on.

'Or lightning!' For a moment excitement fizzles through me, until I remember. 'Only we can't *make* lightning happen. We'd have to wait for a thunderstorm. And that could take months.'

I tell my Enquiring Mind to concentrate.

*From the air, collect a flash of light.*

All of a sudden, I seem to hear Sky's words, when he was telling me about the Outside. What was it he said?

*There are no chains on the Outside. No cagesss. Only air...
and light... and freedom...*

Air... and light. I stare at the jagged black mountain,
rearing up beyond Galena, its peak covered in a bank of
dark cloud. A tiny sliver of hope glints inside me.

'Mac—I've got an idea!'

Mac pauses. 'What's that, Mim?'

'Who lives in the air? The Wings do! Maybe they can
help us find the answer... maybe Sky...'

My voice dies away. Of course Sky won't help me. He
didn't last time. But his father might.

'The Wings?' Mac's face is grave. 'They are proud, fierce
creatures—why should they agree to help us?'

'King Wing saved me from Madame Marionette and
her men. And who else can fly in the air?'

'Hmmm...' Mac says. 'It's a small possibility. But it's all
we have.'

He goes to a cupboard and pulls out an ancient rucksack.

'Black Mountain is cold, and steep. We will need provisions.'

'We?' Mac doesn't look like he could climb a mountain.
'Um... don't you have to keep an eye on Slow Henry?'

He gives a rueful smile. 'So I do,' he says. 'And you will
get on much better without me.'

A shiver of excitement trembles between my shoulder
blades.

'I'll ask Miranda to get the rowing boat.' And I run,
helter-skelter, down the spiral staircase to the door.

I push it, but it stays firmly closed. What's going on?

Has Mac accidentally locked it, using one of his devices? I push harder, and it opens just a crack. Something—or someone—is sitting against the door and blocking it.

'Miranda?'

The only reply is a strangled sob.

'Miranda—it's me, Mim! Let me open the door.'

There's a shuffling, and after a few moments, the door creaks open.

It's almost high tide. An icy wind blows the waves into peaks. Miranda half sits, half lies on the rock, her tail flapping up and down... up and down. Water seeps over the rock towards her.

'Miranda? What's the matter?'

'They've come to get me.' Miranda's voice is flat. I follow her gaze.

Just under the surface of the water, hundreds of white jellyfish bob, their tentacles floating around them like streamers.

Only they aren't jellyfish.

The white blobs are the faces of the Mers and the tentacles are their long white arms. A mouth full of sharp fish-teeth gapes and a pale, grasping hand breaks the surface of the water. Miranda cowers back.

'What's going on? What are they doing?' I ask her.

Miranda's face is white as stone. 'I told you. They've come for me.'

'But why?'

'They saw me cry. And they heard what you said about the ultimatum. They know that tomorrow, my grandfather will... will...' She swallows. 'They've never dared to really hurt me up to now, because of him. Now they know he's going to d-die, so they're waiting to get me.'

I stare over the ocean towards Galena. Below the Gate, the rowing boat bobs. And beyond the walled town, Black Mountain rears up, its head in heavy cloud.

'Miranda, I've got to climb Black Mountain. I'm going to ask the Wings to help us with the next clue.'

'The Wings won't help you.'

'They have to! Anyhow, I'm going to try. Only, I need the rowing boat.'

Miranda shudders. 'If you think I'm getting into the water with *them*...'

'What shall I do, then?'

There's a long silence. Then Miranda says: 'There is a way.'

'What is it? I can't swim—and anyway...'

I glance at the Mers and they stare back at me like white corpses.

'There's a rock path under the water.'

'You mean, I could *walk* to the shore?'

'If it's an especially low tide, and if the ocean's calm. And if you hurry—you'll only have about ten minutes to get across.'

I take a deep breath. 'When's low tide?'

'In six hours' time.'

'But that's at six this evening. We'll waste six precious hours! And anyway, it'll be dark... and cold. Even if I get across the path to the shore, I'll have to climb Black Mountain at night.'

222

Miranda shrugs, her eyes fixed on the white bobbing heads of the Mers.

Suddenly I feel very tired. I didn't sleep all night, and when you're tired everything feels much harder.

'All right,' I say, 'I'll do it. I'll wait.' I don't have any other choice. I've got to get to Black Mountain. I turn back to the lighthouse.

'Mim!'

I stop. Miranda's never called me by my name before. 'Yes?'

'There's something else.'

'What?'

'Even at low tide, the water never completely clears the path.'

The Mers bare their teeth and unearthly laughter hovers over the water.

I swallow. 'So they could still...'

Miranda nods quietly.

The Mers' laughter whips around us like an icy wind.

# THE PATH

'Wake up, Mim.' Mac shakes my shoulder. 'It's half past five.'

At first, I'd refused to go to bed in the daytime—my mind kept going round and round, planning the expedition—but Mac insisted, saying I hadn't slept last night, and I'd need all my strength for the climb up Black Mountain. No sooner did I lie down on the mattress in the little round room with the port-hole window—along with the telescope, the loudspeaker and the wooden sticks (which Mac says are fishing rods)—than my eyes dropped shut.

Outside, it's already dark. The light travels over the black ocean, round and round. I try not to think of the hundreds of Mers lurking beneath the surface.

Up in the laboratory, Mac hands me the rucksack.

'Hot tea, though it won't stay hot for long. I've wrapped the bottle in a towel. And there's water for your climb, and fish-paste sandwiches.'

I nod my thanks, trying not to make a face about the sandwiches, and hurry over to the rocking chair, where

Samuel sits in his favourite spot, on Foggy's cloak. I push him off gently and shrug myself into the cloak.

Mac frowns. 'You'll get frostbite if you wear that up Black Mountain.'

'I haven't got anything else.'

Mac crosses to a cupboard. He pulls out jumpers, scarves, trousers, gloves, boots. 'Here—choose from these. I'm taller than you, but you can roll up the legs and sleeves.'

The clothes smell old and fusty. I choose a thick, much-darned jumper and a pair of heavy trousers, which immediately fall down. I thread a frayed silk tie through the belt loops and fasten it in a knot at the front. I push my precious brooch deep into one of the pockets. Then I pick up a pair of thick leather boots—I hope they're waterproof—which look many sizes too big for me.

'You'll need socks, lots of pairs.'

I pull on some woolly purple ones, which smell faintly of mackerel, and then add another two pairs on top. A stripy scarf and thick fur gloves complete the outfit. Mac inspects me.

'You'll do.' He picks up a little glass jar with a stopper from a shelf. 'Put this in your rucksack.'

'What's it for?'

'To collect the flash of light, of course. Now, be off—the tide'll be at its lowest in ten minutes.'

I hesitate. This is all very well, but how am I going to find my way across a black rocky path, half covered in seaweed and water, in pitch darkness? I place the glass bottle carefully in the rucksack, go over to where

Slow Henry trembles and sighs, and pick up a box of matches.

'Can I take these?'

'Why, pray, do you need matches?'

'To see where I'm going.'

Mac grins. 'We can do better than that.'

He picks up a hammer from a shelf, then, puffing and panting, he climbs the rickety ladder up to the light. The mechanism which turns the light clicks and rattles invisibly.

*CLANG!!!!* There's the sound of metal hitting metal, and the clicking and rattling stops. I run to the window. The light is stopped. It shines directly down onto the rock path, lighting it up all the way to the shore.

'Genius!'

'I wouldn't go that far. But it should be of help. And the Mers fear the light. They're less likely to try anything if it's shining on the path.' He hands me the rucksack. 'Now, hurry—or you'll miss your opportunity.'

The rucksack seems to be croaking. I peer inside. A pair of shiny round eyes stares back.

'Samuel! You can't come with me!' I grab him and put him back onto the rocking chair. 'Stay right here. And don't you dare go near the oven.'

Samuel grins and his long tongue flicks, as if he's sticking it out at me.

'Look after Samuel, won't you? He's got his eye on the egg.'

'Will do. Now, go!'

I hesitate. Then I run across to Mac and throw my arms around his neck.

'Goodbye, Mac! I'll see you soon... I hope.' I plant a kiss on the side of his crooked nose.

Mac harrumphs a bit and straightens his glasses, but I can tell he's pleased.

'So you're really going to do it?'

Miranda sits with her back against the lighthouse. Now the tide is low, there's more space between her and the water, but she still looks uneasy. The rock path to the shore lies before us, lit up by the light. It looks like a magic road, the gleaming water slipping gently over the rocks, almost as if the moon was shining on it. But there is no moon. The sky is a mass of thick cloud and there's a strange stillness in the air, as if it's waiting for something to happen. I turn back to Miranda.

'I have to. It's our only chance.'

Miranda nods in the direction of the ocean. 'Watch out for the Mers. They'll try all their wiles. I hope you've got nothing valuable on you—they smell out precious things.'

My brooch seems to burn inside the pocket of Mac's trousers. No way am I leaving it behind. It's kept me safe so far, and maybe it will protect me from the Mers.

'They won't come near the path,' I say, hoping Mac is right. 'They're scared of the light.'

'I wouldn't count on it.'

I stare at the water as it slips and swirls. There's only blackness, which seems to go down for ever.

'See? They've gone.' My voice sounds braver than I feel.

'Don't you believe it. They'll be waiting for you. Be careful, Mim.'

I shiver. Then I shift the rucksack into a more comfortable position on my back and take a deep breath.

'See you later then.'

'I hope so.' Miranda doesn't sound hopeful.

I step onto the path. The tide may be at its lowest, but an inch or so of water slides over its surface. Lucky the boots have thick, stout soles. On either side of the path, the water sloshes gently.

'Mim?'

I turn. Miranda raises a pale hand. 'Good luck.'

I nod. Then, remembering the way the Mers sang at me and took away my strength, I tie my stripy scarf tightly over my ears. Why didn't I think to make some earplugs out of candlewax, like Foggy? But it's too late now. I begin to walk. It's not so very far to the shore and there should be almost ten minutes until... but I won't think about that. If only I knew how to swim, it wouldn't be so scary. The rock beneath the water is uneven; sharp with barnacles and slippery with seaweed. I must watch every step.

A splash right beside my feet sends me trembling. But it's only a fish, its scales flashing silver in the light.

Another splash.

Maybe the fish are attracted by the light.

I'm already almost halfway across. A few hundred yards ahead of me, the Great Wall looms. The rowing boat lies on the sand, waiting for the tide. I just have to keep going, and I'll soon be safe on dry land.

*You can do this. You can.*

Is the water a little deeper? Waves slide in over the rocky path. An especially strong one swirls water almost to the tops of my boots.

I'd better hurry up.

Just as I think this, everything goes black. The path disappears beneath me. I swivel round and stare up at the lighthouse.

The light's gone out.

I blink. What happened?

A figure appears at the laboratory window, waving frantically at me. I loosen my scarf from my ears.

Mac's voice, magnified by the loudspeaker, booms over the water.

'MIM, THE PARAFFIN RAN OUT!... RUN FOR YOUR LIFE!!!'

# THE MERS ATTACK

**R**unning is out of the question. I can't see a thing. Even my feet have disappeared. I've no idea where the path is. And now the splashing is everywhere, all around me, as if the fish are fighting in the water.

Only it isn't fish.

Hundreds of ghostly, bobbing heads surround me. Bony white hands thrash the water into a whirlpool, and chilling laughter echoes over the waves. Miranda's words echo through my mind.

*They'll be waiting for you.*

My fingers fumble to pull the scarf around my ears again. Where's the path?

A faint light shines in the distance. It must be the sentry on top of the Great Wall. If I head towards it... I stumble forwards, my boots sliding on the seaweed. My breath comes in gasps, half from trying to stay upright and half from terror. It mists round my face in an icy cloud.

Then, as suddenly as it began, the splashing stops. Blank, empty eyes stare up at me hungrily. Mouths silently open and shut, sharp with fish teeth. *They're singing*. I knot the scarf more tightly over my ears.

A white hand darts out and grabs my ankle. I kick hard, and it falls back into the water. More hands reach towards my feet, thin bony knuckles clenching and unclenching.

They must be after my brooch. Thank goodness it's safe inside Mac's trouser pockets. As the hands snatch at my legs, I jump high in the air, praying I'll land back on the rocky path. I stumble forwards, kicking wildly. But there are too many hands. They bring me down, grazing my knee on a barnacle-encrusted rock. The hands are all over me now, grabbing at my clothes, my arms, my hair...

My rucksack.

Suddenly, I know what I must do. I wriggle my arms out of the straps. I unzip it, pull out the glass bottle and shove it into my pocket. With my last ounce of strength, I throw the rucksack into the water.

Just in time. The white hands snatch and tug, and the rucksack jerks away, down into the water, surrounded by bobbing white heads. There's a rending, a tearing, a ripping. A towel and a packet of fish-paste sandwiches float for a split-second, before the white hands fight for them and they disappear beneath the surface. The singing mouths sink with them.

I crawl along the rock path, feeling my way forward towards the light on the Great Wall and the sound of the waves on the shore ahead, praying that the path won't disappear under my hands and knees. The icy water soaks through my heavy trousers and gloves. All I care about is that I'm moving: towards Galena and the rowing boat and the sand.

Towards safety.

Dark clouds scud across the moon as I crouch and shiver under the Great Wall.

I long to shout so Mac and Miranda know I'm safe, but I can't: the sentry's on guard somewhere above me, coughing in the evening cold. Across the dark water, the lighthouse is a faint white shape, the top window dimly lit. Is Mac still trying to find some paraffin? Or is he with Miranda on the rock, staring over at the shore and worrying about me? Maybe he's got his telescope trained on me right now. I stick my thumbs up just in case.

A cold wind whips my wet hair round my face. There's no sign of the Mers, or of what was inside my rucksack. I'd give anything for a sip of the hot tea, or even the fish-paste sandwiches—or better still, for the heat and friendliness of Smith's forge, just behind the Great Wall. Except Smith's in chains. My fingers creep into my pocket and find my brooch.

*I'll see you soon, Smith. I will.*

The wind whirls over the empty beach. The grey, heavy clouds look full of something—snow, or rain.

The darkest cloud of all hovers over the top of Black Mountain, a long walk away. It looks hard and forbidding, as if it's daring me to go near. I push myself to my feet, my boots squelching, and set off over the scrubby grass towards it.

# BLACK MOUNTAIN

I'm almost at the top of Black Mountain when the storm strikes.

I must have climbed for hours. If it hadn't been for the moon, appearing and disappearing behind the scudding dark clouds, I'd never have been able to do it. As it is, I have to stop every time it disappears, because it's pitch black and I can't see anything. The narrow, icy path, carved out of the rock, winds round Black Mountain like a necklace, spiralling up and up until it disappears into the cloud at the top. The Wings have chosen the most unfriendly, barren place in the world to live.

I've never, of course, been up a mountain: the higher I climb, the dimmer the ocean, the lighthouse and Galena become. The one good thing about climbing a mountain in the dark is that you can't look down—or rather, you can't see much if you do. I discovered I didn't like heights when I climbed the ladder in the library, and this is a million times worse.

Not only is it dark, but it's harder to breathe, as if there's less air up here. Every now and then a rumbling sound echoes over the mountain and the rock beneath my feet seems to shake. Is there going to be a thunderstorm? I scan the heavy sky, hoping against hope for a flash of lightning, but it remains black and cloud-ridden. The path grows narrower and narrower until I have to walk heel to toe, as if I'm on a tightrope. To make matters worse, there's nothing to hold on to, except the wall of jagged, slippery rock.

It's getting colder. An icy wind gusts at me, threatening to blow me off the path. I flatten my back to the rock wall.

Then the snow begins.

At first it's only a few uncertain flakes, spiralling down. I stick out my thirsty tongue to catch them. But soon the world turns white. Whiteness pelts my face, blowing into my eyes and my open mouth. Whiteness lodges in my neck and my ears. I can't see anything except the rocky wall at my side. I will have to stop, and wait it out. I'd feel safer sitting down, so I grab a spindly, leafless sapling growing in a crevice in the rock, and pray it won't snap off. Then I lower myself to crouch on the narrow path, dangling my legs over the edge. I shut my eyes tight and wait.

After what feels like an hour, but is probably just a few minutes, the wind seems to double in strength like a giant fan, blowing icy air right into my face. I open my eyes. The snow's stopped falling and a dark shape hovers in the air before me.

I rub my eyes. The shape is a bird, its grey wings pumping so it hovers motionless in the air. It stares at me with one dark eye. The other is covered by an eye patch. Its face is human. The face of an old woman.

A Wing!

'What bringsss you here, human?'

'I h-have to see K-King W-Wing.' My teeth are chattering, so I can barely speak. I brush a pile of snow off my lap. My legs are too cold to stand.

'That isss forbidden,' says the Wing. 'Return to your own kind.'

'I c-can't. I n-need his help.'

'What makesss you think King Wing will help you?'

'He h-helped me once b-before.' I rub my fingers together, hoping they don't have frostbite. 'B-because of P-prince Sky.'

At the mention of Sky, the Wing's expression changes.

'Ssso you are *that* human.'

She wheels around and flies off, banking in the dizzy air. My heart feels numb, only not from the cold. Have I climbed all this way for nothing? Long minutes pass. Then, a grey speck appears in the sky and glides down until it's floating above my head. She's back.

'You will come with me.'

'H-how?' There's nowhere for her to land on the wall of rock.

The Wing suddenly drops like a stone until she's hovering in mid-air below me, her grey wings almost grazing the sheer rock wall.

'You mussst jump onto my back,' her voice hisses up at me.

'W-what?'

'You mussst jump!'

I stare at the pumping wings and the feathered back below me. 'I-I don't think I c-can.'

'You mussst.'

There's no feeling left in my feet. I haul them up onto the ledge and reach up to grab the sapling. A shower of icy snow goes down my neck. Slowly I pull myself up to a standing position, my eyes pulled like magnets to the black void beneath. My knees almost give way. There's nothing—apart from a hovering Wing—between me and the ground, hundreds of feet below.

'Make haste. My wingsss tire.'

*I can't do it.* What if I miss, and plummet through the air into oblivion?

Then I think of Mac, and Miranda. All their hopes are pinned on me. My fingers find the shape of my brooch in my pocket. I calculate exactly how far I need to jump in order to land on the feathery back.

I leap.

For a few seconds it's like I'm suspended in mid-air, then I drop like a stone, spreading my arms and legs as wide as I can. With a soft flump, I land on the Wing's back, just as if I'd jumped into a feathery cushion. But her feathers are slippery. Already I'm sliding off. I grab a handful of feathers and the old Wing hisses angrily at me.

'Be very careful, human, lessst I drop you.'

'S-sorry.' I grip the Wing's neck, just as I did King Wing's when he saved me. Suddenly we're no longer hovering in mid-air, but soaring up, heading straight for the dingy grey cloud at the top of Black Mountain. Then we're inside the cloud and there's nothing to be seen but damp mist. The Wing flies on, straight up, until we burst through the cloud. Her grey wings stop flapping and we float down onto a ridge above a huge dish-shaped crater.

I slip off the old Wing's back. She stalks off, limping, before I can thank her.

It's too dark to see much. A black wall lines the top of the ridge and the only living thing is an ancient gnarled tree, its bare white branches gleaming in the darkness like a skeleton.

Another deep rumble makes my head jerk up. But the sound seems to come from deep in the crater below me. A plume of black smoke swirls out of the crater, along with a fine, ashy dust which makes my eyes burn and my throat feel tight. A shiver runs down my spine as I remember the book I read from cover to cover in bed, by candlelight: *Volcanoes.*

As another rumble echoes around the crater, the moon appears. The black wall isn't a wall at all—it's dozens of Wings, huddled together round the edges of the crater, staring at me with dark, fierce eyes. King Wing steps from among them, his thin face haughty in the moonlight.

'Why have you come, human?'

I bend in an awkward bow. 'Your Majesty, I'm here because I need help.'

'Why ssshould I help you further? The debt for my ssson is paid. There isss no further obligation.'

I think hard. He's right. He owes me nothing. But I've got to try.

'Because of Mac—er, Mr MacWhisker. He has a grand-daughter, you see—her name's Miranda. And she's been cursed with a tail.'

'Cursssed? By whom?'

'By the Mer Queen.'

King Wing stares at me, down his proud, beak-like nose.

'And what isss that to do with me?'

'Miranda can't live with Mr MacWhisker, because of her tail. And he loves her—just the way you love Sky...'

A low hissing comes from the ranks of Wings, as if in warning, but I carry on.

'Anyhow—Mr MacWhisker's got to change lead into gold by sunrise, or he'll be executed. Unless...'

'Unlesss what?'

'Unless you can help us. We need a special ingredient.'

'Ingredient?' King Wing narrows his eyes, his head on one side.

I pull the glass bottle from my pocket. 'A... a flash of light.'

A gasp rises from the Wings. They shrink back, hissing.

Suddenly, King Wing laughs. 'The human isss joking.'

'No, I'm not! I mean it—every word.'

'Then you are a fool.' King Wing turns and stalks off towards his people.

'But—'

The wall of black feathers parts and King Wing is gone.

# SKY RETURNS

**S**omething screws up inside my heart, like crumpled paper. But I won't give up. Not after all I've been through to get here. I step towards the line of Wings.

'Won't one of you help me? Tell me how to get a flash of light?'

But the Wings turn their faces away. A whispering hiss echoes around the crater.

'Go now, human.' It's the female Wing with the eye patch. 'Humans are humans. Wings are Wingsss. Our natures are different.'

'No! I won't give up! Not until I've asked each and every one of them.'

The hissing is louder, like a nest full of snakes.

'Take my advice and don't wassste your time. We owe you nothing now.'

I ignore her, and shout above the hissing: 'Surely one of you will help me?'

Not one steps forward.

The old Wing limps towards me.

'Listen to me, human. There is a difference between bravery and foolishnesss. And there is only one way to get a flash of light—'

'What is it? Please tell me!'

She stares at me with her one good eye. 'Lightning.'

I gaze up at the sky. 'I can't wait for a thunderstorm!'

'Not *that* kind of lightning.' The old Wing jerks her grey head at the crater below. 'Lightning from the mountain.'

Then I remember. All those nights when I sat up in bed by candlelight, reading *Volcanoes*.

Volcanic lightning.

It's all to do with electricity and ice particles and ash, when a volcano erupts. It's rare, but some volcanoes create bolts of lightning, just like the ones during a thunderstorm.

'You mean—Black Mountain is an active volcano? Is it... is it going to erupt?'

'Vol Cano? Er-upt? Your human language makes no sense.' The old Wing stares down into the smoke-filled crater. 'Each night, the Mountain breathes fire and ash. Each night, the lightning forks above it in the air. No Wing with any sense would fly over the Mountain then.'

She turns to the assembled Wings.

'Who among you is prepared to scorch their feathersss for an old man and a girl with a tail?'

The Wings shake their heads. The hissing rises almost to a scream.

'There. You have your ansssswer.' She spreads her grey wings. 'Return to your own kind, human. It will soon be time.'

The Wings flap into the air above me, blowing my hair into my eyes. They hover like a mass of cinders above Black Mountain before flying away in a black cloud. I watch them until they disappear over the horizon.

I sit with my back against the skeleton tree above the rumbling crater. Who cares if it's about to erupt? Nothing matters, now I've failed. I can't bear to think of Mac's and Miranda's faces when I tell them that the Second Impossible has proved to be just that—impossible. Hopeless tears make my cold cheeks colder, so I wipe them away. But more tears follow, and more. I stare at the little glass bottle in my frozen hands.

After a while I have the strange feeling that someone—or something—is watching me. I look around. There's no sign of any living creature. The rumbling sound gets louder, and a thicker cloud of smoke and ash billows from the crater.

'Princesss.'

The voice comes from above me. I scramble up, my legs almost giving way from having sat so long on the cold ground. Staring down at me from the branches of the skeleton tree is Sky.

I hardly recognize him. He looks so different to the Sky I last saw—the Sky who was angry and proud and determined to escape. His shoulders are hunched. His black feathers are dull, and his eyes are too.

'Why are you here, Princesss?' His voice is weary.

'I came to ask your father for help. He told me he'd paid off his obligation to me for helping you escape. He won't do anything more.'

Sky stares at the ground, so I carry on.

'And then the old one with the eye patch—'

'My grandmother.'

'She said that no Wing would agree to help me. And they wouldn't. Not one.'

Sky spreads his black, tattered wings and glides down to join me. Close up, he's thinner even than he was in Madame Marionette's clutches.

'What wasss it you wanted?'

I show him the glass bottle.

'I have to collect a flash of light. From the lightning in the Mountain.'

Sky draws back. 'The lightning?'

'Sky...' I take a deep breath. 'Could you—would you—help me? You're my only chance.'

There's a long silence. Sky stares at the ground again. Then he says: 'The lightning isss dangerous, Princesss.'

I keep trying. 'I know you're brave enough.'

'Brave?' Sky's head jerks up. 'Was I brave, that night? When you helped me essscape, and I abandoned you? When I took my freedom and left you to that woman's mercy? Was that the action of a brave prince?'

'Madame was going to kill you and tear out your feathers and stuff you. I don't blame you for escaping when you got the chance.'

'But *I* do. I blame myssself.' Sky shakes his head dully. 'From that day, I've lived alone, away from my father, and my tribe. I am no longer worthy of the title "prince".'

'But your father loves you! He—'

'I don't dessserve his love.' He gazes at the horizon where the Wings disappeared.

'You mean—you're just going to, to—give up?' Am I talking to Sky, or to myself?

Sky doesn't reply.

Suddenly, I feel exhausted. Maybe... maybe he's right. Maybe it's time to stop trying to do impossible things. I want to comfort him, but I can't think of anything to say. I shove the glass bottle into my pocket and blink hard to stop tears falling.

'I've got to go back to the lighthouse. I've failed, but I have to face them. And I need to be with Mac before they take him away. Good luck, Sky.'

I walk to where the path down Black Mountain begins. It looks narrower than ever, and icy. I step down onto it.

'Wait, Princesss!'

I turn.

Sky stares at me. 'Get on my back. I will fly you.'

'Thanks. That's kind of you. The path is so icy—'

'You misundersssstand.' Sky raises his head. There's a tiny sparkle in his eyes, a glimpse of the old, proud Sky.

'Get on my back. I will fly you...' he swallows, '...to get your lightning.'

# CATCHING
# LIGHTNING

**I** scramble onto Sky's warm, feathery back and circle my arms round his neck. His heart beats through my body, strong and fast. Immediately, he spreads his wide black wings and leaps into the air.

Up, up, up we fly. The crater of Black Mountain grows smaller and smaller below us. Ash drifts far beneath our feet, a grey misty shadow. The night air is deliciously cold, like ice cream. I breathe in as much of it as I can.

'So lovely!' I can't help shouting.

Sky turns his head slightly.

'This is nothing. I will ssshow you more.'

He wheels, his wings diagonal, in a circle. Then he spins through the dark air, over and over, until I no longer know which way is earth and which is sky. Then he flies straight up, turns sharply, and we plummet towards the crater of Black Mountain in a loop-the-loop.

I clutch his warm feathers and scream with excitement. My tummy's upside down and inside out and I've never felt so free.

A harsher rumble seems to shake Black Mountain below us. A great hot sigh billows out from deep inside it.

Sky's face darkens. 'It's almost lightning time, Princesss. Have your bottle ready.'

Gripping Sky's back with my legs, I pull the glass bottle from my pocket and take out the stopper.

Suddenly, Sky wavers and slows until he's floating, motionless over Black Mountain. Has he changed his mind? Is he too scared, after all?

Then I look down.

A cloud of Wings hover beneath us like a black wall. Their dark wings beat together, wing tip to wing tip. Their hissing echoes in my ears. King Wing and Sky's grandmother swoop up to hover directly in front of us.

'It is as you feared,' King Wing addresses Sky's grandmother. 'The human has tricked him into helping her.'

'Aye,' says the old Wing. 'Never trussst a human.'

'I-I've done no such thing!' I stammer.

'How dare you, human!' King Wing's dark eyes are full of fury. 'What power have you over my ssson, that he risks destruction?'

'He... We...' My tongue feels as twisted as it did with Madame's riddles.

Then Sky speaks.

'The human has no power over me, Father. I choose to do thisss.'

King Wing frowns. 'Then you are more foolisssh than I supposed. You will abandon this half-witted scheme immediately and return with usss!'

Sky stares back at him. 'I will not.'

His grandmother, her grey wings beating, moves closer. 'Sky, beware! Think of your feathersss!'

Sky's shuddering vibrates through me. But he goes on staring at his father.

'Father, I did wrong. I abandoned thisss human.'

The Wings are silent, the only sound from them is the beating of their wings.

'I gained my freedom, but I lost something even more preciousss.'

King Wing stares at him. 'What did you lose, Sky?'

'I lost my ssself respect.' Sky bows his head.

No one says anything for a long time. King Wing looks deep into Sky's eyes.

'Then go, my son. Do what you mussst. I will not stop you.'

'Thank you, Father.' Sky's voice trembles.

'Look out for him, human,' King Wing mutters. A single tear creeps down his fierce face. He jerks his head at the assembled Wings below us and they part to reveal the gaping crater, with its swirling cloud of ash.

Sparks of red and gold shoot from the crater, just as if Black Mountain is a massive firework. The Wings form into the shape of an arrow behind King Wing and Sky's grandmother, and the arrow flies towards the dark horizon once more.

Sky looks, one last time, at the distant Wings. Then he says, in a voice more like his own: 'Head down, Princesss. We go on the flight of our lives!'

A great roar echoes out from Black Mountain. Dark smoke billows from the crater and flames flare up at us. Sky's wings beat harder, propelling us into the scorching air above. Sweat runs down my cheeks and down my back.

Sky's body vibrates, like a purring cat, but a glimpse of his face shows he's shuddering and shaking.

'When the lightning ssstrikes, I must dodge it,' he whispers, his voice a croak. 'And you must catch what you can. Keep your head right down.'

I lay my head on his hot feathers. Every breath burns my throat and my lips are blistered. This is what a chicken must feel like, roasting on a spit. Sky pants, his wings working like bellows.

My brooch seems to burn in my pocket.

*Keep us safe*, I whisper to it.

'Are you ready?' Sky's voice is hoarse.

'Ready!' My voice sounds braver than I feel.

'Brace yoursssself.'

I hug Sky's feathered back, though the heat of it is unbearable.

The darkness flashes into light as a great fork of lightning sparks right beside us. I blink, dazzled. Everywhere I look, bolts of lightning flash and fork. There's no telling where the next bolt will strike. Sky darts through the air, turning on a sixpence, back and forth as if he and the lightning are performing a terrible dance together. Then the biggest bolt of lightning sizzles right at us.

'*Now!*' Sky yells. I hold the little bottle out as far as I can reach. The world flashes white. Whiter than clouds, whiter than snow. I squeeze my eyes shut. The cinder smell of burning fills my nose. Did I catch something? Or did I miss? There's no way of telling. Blindly, I squish the stopper closed and push it back into my pocket.

The burning smell is coming from Sky's wings. Flames eat at his feathers. Sky gives a terrible cry and cartwheels down towards the crater.

'Sky? Are you—' Frantically, I slap at the burning feathers. There's no answer.

We plunge down. Every few moments, Sky gives a feeble flap of his smoking wings, but his eyes are half closed. I grip his back with my legs and shout in his ear.

'Sky! Wake up!'

Sky groans and, making a huge effort, flaps his wings once more. For a few seconds we rise, floating in the smoke and ash. I clutch my hot brooch. *Help us... please... get us out of here.* Then, as if in answer to my prayer, a gust of icy wind gathers us in its grasp and hurls us away from Black Mountain.

'You did it, Sky!' I whisper.

But Sky's eyes fall shut again. We barrel down through the black air, turning and spiralling. The world turns thick and white and cold as we drop into a bank of snow clouds, and I can no longer tell if we're upside down or right side up.

The dark ocean's below us. We dive towards the lighthouse and the rocks. If Sky doesn't wake up, we'll smash into them.

'Sky! *Please—*!'

Sky's wings flail, like a clockwork toy winding down. With a moan of pain, he stretches them wide, his feathers smouldering. It's just enough. With the air under his wings, our headlong fall becomes a glide. The ocean comes up to meet us, less quickly than before but still too fast.

*SPLASH!!!!*

Water hits us like a fierce slap and I'm thrown off Sky's back. I sink under the surface, my eyes and ears and mouth full of water, pedalling with my legs, my arms flailing, my lungs bursting. Just as I think I'm going to drown, my face breaks through the surface and I take great, thankful gulps of air. Wiping my stinging eyes and choking, I look around for Sky.

A few yards away, a mass of feathers lies flat and lifeless on the black water.

'Sky!' I choke, frantically trying to keep afloat.

But the feathers don't move.

# SAVING SKY

I'm sinking again. Cold fingers grab my arms.

*The Mers.*

I kick out at them.

'Stoppit!'—a familiar voice in my ear. I'm yanked through the water at great speed and pushed up onto the rocks. I sit there like a drowned rat, spluttering and shocked. Then, unable to speak, I point a shaking finger at the feathers in the water. But Miranda's already swimming towards them, her tail flapping and splashing. Drawn by the commotion, white bobbing heads move towards Miranda and Sky, closing in.

'Miranda, watch out!' I find my voice. Then, everything's chaos as Miranda splashes and fights, and the water stains dark with blood.

The Mers are going to kill them. If I could swim, I'd dive in and help. But I can't.

Then I remember Mac's words: *the Mers fear the light...*

I hardly dare pull the glass bottle from my pocket. Did I catch a flash of lightning? What if I missed, and the bottle's empty?

But it isn't.

Light flashes and darts and sizzles inside the glass bottle, so I have to screw up my eyes to look at it. I push the stopper in hard and shout to Miranda.

'Catch!'

Then I throw the bottle as hard as I can in her direction.

She's heard me. Her arm reaches up above the splashing Mers and she catches the bottle. Miranda turns her face aside as the light flashes over the threshing water. There's a sudden, unearthly cry and the Mers scatter and dive.

Miranda, her forehead bleeding from a cut, grabs Sky's feathers with her free hand and drags him slowly, slowly to the rocks. Shading her eyes, she hands me the flashing bottle and I push it into my pocket.

Getting Sky out of the water is hard. His feathers are waterlogged and it takes a few attempts to haul him onto the rocks. He lies face down, his fine feathers burned and singed, his eyes shut. Down in the water, Miranda, panting, wipes the blood from her forehead.

I shake Sky's shoulder.

'Sky! Wake up!'

He doesn't move. Surely he can't be... And if he *is*, it's all my fault. Tears fall, dripping over Sky's lifeless body.

I shake him again. 'He *can't* be dead! He can't be.'

'Wait! Look—' Miranda points. Sky's back rises and falls with one small, frail breath.

'He's still alive!'

'Only just,' says Miranda.

'What'll we do?'

'Get Grandfather. He'll know.'

I run to the lighthouse door and almost bump into Mac.

'Mim!' His eyes light up. 'You're safe...'

Breathlessly, I tell him about Sky.

He takes one look at the huddled mass of feathers and shakes his head. 'Did you get the light?'

I nod impatiently. 'Yes—but we've got to do something about—'

Mac holds out his hand. 'Give it to me, if you please.'

'But Sky—'

'Quickly. Give me the bottle.'

I pull the bottle from my pocket, shading my eyes against the dazzling light from it, and pass it to Mac, who quickly takes it and covers it with his palms.

'Now, come with me.' He makes for the stairs.

'No! You go up and see to the Work. I'm not leaving Sky.'

He turns, his face stern. 'Do as I say. Quickly.'

I look at Miranda. She nods at me.

'Do what he says, Mim. I'll stay with Sky.'

With a last, reluctant look at Sky, I hurry up the spiral staircase after Mac. His breath comes in wheezy gasps.

'Just in time!' He hurries over to Slow Henry, who's trembling and vibrating. The coals inside are white-hot. Heat seems to sizzle in the air. Out of the corner of my eye I glimpse Samuel, gazing at me from the rocking chair. Holding the bottle tightly in his hands so that no light escapes, Mac nods at Slow Henry.

'Quick, Mim—pour some water onto the coals.'

I pick up the kettle and dribble water into the furnace. There's a loud hiss and a splutter.

'Slow Henry's playing up again,' mutters Mac. 'Heating too fast.'

'Never mind Slow Henry! What about Sky?'

Mac pulls on his big leather gloves, bends over Slow Henry and peers at the coals.

'It's time.' He throws me a pair of gloves. 'Put these on and come here, if you please. This part of the Work needs two people.'

My face feels as hot as the furnace and I clench my fists. As if he knows this, Mac turns to me.

'Have faith,' he says. 'And remember your promise to me.'

'My promise?'

'When you asked to be my apprentice. You promised to do what I told you, and not to ask too many questions.'

'But—'

'Put on the gloves and come over here.'

Reluctantly, I join him.

'Take these tongs and remove the egg from the oven.'

I pick up the tongs and open Slow Henry's oven door. A blast of heat bellows out, making my already-blistered face sting. The egg sits, white-hot, in the centre of the oven. I open the tongs, grip the egg and carefully pull it out.

'Good. Now hold it steady while I lift the lid.'

Shading his eyes, Mac carefully places the glass bottle on the hearth. Then he uses another pair of tongs to lift the top half of the egg.

'That's the elixir.'

A strange smell swirls out of the egg. Honey... buttercups... freshly baked bread... I peer inside. Miranda's tears are gone. In their place is a thick golden fluid, like an egg yolk.

Mac picks up the glass bottle, his eyes squeezed almost shut against its light, and holds it upside down over the egg. Inside the bottle, the light makes a buzzing sound, like a bee trapped in a jar. Mac pulls out the stopper and the light tumbles into the egg.

The elixir crackles and sizzles and fizzes, like water poured into hot fat, and acrid smoke billows around our heads. The smell makes my eyes stream and my nose run.

'Shall we close the lid?'

'Not yet.' Mac hurries to the shelves and picks up a glass dropper. He dips it into the elixir, withdrawing a single drop, and holds it up to the light. It's silver-blue-violet-white-gold, brighter than a peacock's tail.

'Now we can close the lid and return the egg to the oven.'

The egg shivers and trembles in the spitting flames. Mac pours more water onto the coals, producing more hissing.

'Behave yourself, Henry. Slow and steady.' But he looks worried.

'Now, what about Sky—?' I jump up and down with impatience.

Mac hands me the glass dropper with the elixir inside. 'Take this to the boy, Mim. Make him drink it.'

'Aren't you coming too?'

'I must watch Slow Henry. If he overheats now, it'll be disastrous for the Work.'

I almost snatch the glass dropper from him, and pelt down the stairs.

# THE ELIXIR

Sky lies where we left him, face down and still. Miranda has hauled herself up onto the rock beside him.

'How is he?'

Miranda looks pale and worried. 'Bad.'

I drop to my knees beside Sky. In the moonlight, his face is the colour of clay and his eyes are shut. Every few moments, his chest takes a desperate, rattling breath. Then there's a long, horrible wait until the next.

'What's that?' Miranda gazes at the glass dropper.

'It's a drop of the elixir.' I bend down and whisper in Sky's ear. 'Sky! You have to drink this.'

There's no reply. Sky's lips are blue.

'He can't drink it,' says Miranda. 'He's too far gone.'

'Then we must roll him over and drop it into his mouth.'

We grab handfuls of feathers and tug, but Sky gives a terrible moan and doesn't move. His body is heavy as lead.

'We need help.' Miranda looks up at the lighthouse. 'I'll call Grandfather.'

'But he has to look after—'

'GRANDFATHER!' she shouts, ignoring me. 'COME QUICK! YOU'VE GOT TO HELP US!'

Footsteps echo on the staircase. Mac, still wearing his gloves, hurries towards us.

'What is it? Has he drunk it?'

'No!' I say. 'He's unconscious. And we can't turn him over.'

Mac's knees crack as he kneels beside us.

'Miranda—take his head. Mim, his leg.' He grabs Sky's shoulder and arm. 'Ready?'

Together, we heave at Sky's body and he groans again.

'Again!' grunts Mac.

'He's moving!' gasps Miranda. And he is. His body flops over onto its back, his wings spreading around him. Mac pulls Sky's mouth open.

'Quick, Mim, the dropper.'

My hand shaking, I position the dropper between Sky's blue lips and squeeze. The single drop of elixir hangs over his open mouth.

Then, unbearably slowly, it falls onto his tongue.

Sky lies face up, his eyes closed, his skin like wax. There's no breath. Has Mac got it wrong again? Did I waste precious time up in the laboratory—time when I could have helped Sky stay alive?

I bend to him, my tears dripping onto his face. 'Sky, come back! Please—'

'Patience.' It's Mac's voice at my shoulder. 'Give it time.'

I glare at him. 'But we *have* no time! Can't you see, he's—'

Then Miranda grabs my arm. 'Look, Mim—look!'

She points at Sky's wings. The dull, smouldering feathers are no longer so flat and dead-looking. They glisten and gleam with a black, strong sheen. A tiny speck of colour flushes Sky's grey cheeks. Then his chest rises and falls, rises and falls.

'He's alive! He's breathing!' I hold my hand above his mouth and feel the warm breath on it. Sky's eyelids tremble and his dark eyes open. His wings tremble too, folding and unfolding as if trying to fly. Then he shakes his head and slowly sits up, rubbing his beaky nose.

'What happened?' he asks.

Mac stares back at him as if he can hardly believe what he sees.

'The Two Impossibles,' he mutters.

'What?' says Miranda.

Mac nods to himself. '*After One Impossible, the elixir is formed. After Two Impossibles, health is restored.*'

I clap my hands. 'It worked! It worked!'

Mac smiles. 'Thanks to you, Mim. And, of course, to Sky.'

I throw my arms around Sky's neck. 'You're a hero, Sky! You completed the Second Impossible!'

But Sky's staring at Black Mountain, a longing in his eyes.

'I mussst go back,' he says. 'My father will be waiting for me. He'll fear that I failed.'

He gets to his feet, his great black wings spread wide.

'Goodbye, Sky,' I say. 'And thank you.'

'Goodbye,' he replies, but I can tell he's not really with us any more. Then he's in the air, his wings beating like bellows. Without a backward glance, he flies like an arrow through the darkness towards Black Mountain.

Mac pats my shoulder. 'He's a Wing... that's his nature.'

'I know,' I sigh.

Miranda harrumphs. 'Would someone like to tell me what's been going on?'

When I tell her about our flight over Black Mountain, her eyes open wide.

'You and the bird boy did this? Risked your lives, for us?'

'Well, it was Sky, really,' I say, embarrassed. I turn to Mac, who's still gazing after Sky, a faraway look in his eyes. It won't be long before sunrise. And we still have another Impossible to complete.

I take a deep breath. 'What must we do next?'

Before Mac can answer, Miranda grabs my hand and points up at the lighthouse.

'What's that?'

Black smoke is pouring out of the laboratory windows. An ominous vibration echoes down the stairs. Mac's face changes.

'Slow Henry! He's overheating—'

He dashes for the lighthouse. The staircase is full of smoke. We pound up the stairs, coughing and choking. Halfway up, Mac stops, clutching his chest, tears rolling down his cheeks.

'Stay there, Mac! I'll see to it!' I brush past him and race up the final steps, holding my arm in front of my mouth against the fumes.

At the door of the laboratory, I pause, gasping for breath. Smoke billows towards the open window. Samuel croaks loudly, a wild, frightened sound. In the centre of the room, Slow Henry rumbles and vibrates, the oven door gaping open. Inside, the white-hot egg wobbles, ablaze.

I've got to cool Slow Henry down. Where's the kettle?

Half blinded by the smoke, I stumble across the laboratory, grab it and aim its spout over Slow Henry's raging coals.

Nothing comes out.

Slow Henry hisses, louder than a host of Wings, rocking and trembling. I look round for a bucket.

'Mim—get back!' It's Mac, leaning against the door post, tears streaming down his soot-striped cheeks.

'We've got to—' Surely there's *something* I can do.

A sound like thunder rumbles out of Slow Henry. He wobbles violently from side to side. A screaming sound seems to come from the egg, like a seagull mewling. I take a step towards it.

Then a heavy weight lands on me and knocks me to the floor. Winded, I try to raise my head, but something shoves it down.

'It's too late, Mim!' Mac's voice hisses in my ear. 'Don't move!'

And then, with a gigantic roar, Slow Henry explodes.

# EXPLOSION

The explosion echoes round the laboratory, along with the sound of splintering glass. My ears ring. Black dots dance in front of my eyes. Smoke burns my lungs and I cough and cough. Somewhere in the distance, Samuel croaks. When I've stopped choking, I stagger to my feet and peer through the thick smoke.

The laboratory is ruined. All the windows are shattered and the shelves hang jagged from the walls. A huge hole in the ceiling is half blocked by the cracked light, which must have fallen into it. Glass vessels splinter the floor. The small table beside the rocking chair where Mac kept *The Three Impossibles* is collapsed and smashed. The rocking chair itself has lost one rocker and leans at an angle. There's no sign of *The Three Impossibles*. And Slow Henry is no more. All that's left of him is a mangled mountain of bricks and rubble.

Mac lies face down on the floor, just the way Sky did, except that his breath comes fast—too fast. I throw myself down beside him and shake his shoulder.

'Mac! Are you all right?'

A groan is the only reply.

'Can you get up? Let me help you.'

'Too late... the Work... the Third Impossible...'

A huge lump swells on his forehead. His leg is twisted at an odd angle.

'Hold on, Mac. Don't try to move.'

I jump to my feet and dash over to what remains of Slow Henry. Somewhere underneath will be the egg. A drop of the elixir will heal Mac, just the way it healed Sky. I scrabble in the smoke and dark among the mess of hot, broken bricks and pottery, hardly noticing my burning fingers and the glass splinters in my knees. If only I could see better. Behind me, Mac groans again.

The egg must be here somewhere. It must.

Unless... I hardly dare think it. What if the egg shattered into tiny pieces when Slow Henry exploded? What if the elixir spilt or evaporated?

*Stoppit, Mim. Concentrate on looking.*

My fingers—scratched and stinging from hot coals and slivers of glass— grope and fumble, tossing aside fragments of wood, scraping and rummaging in the muddle, until they fall on something smooth... and egg-shaped.

'I've got it! The egg!'

There's no reply.

The egg lies miraculously upright, propped against a piece of hot brick, its lid hanging open. It's too dark to see the elixir inside. Carefully, I cup it in my hands and carry it over to the window. A faint voice shouts from the darkness below.

'Grandfather... Mim... are you all right? What's happened?'

I call down. 'I'm okay, Miranda, only your grandfather's hurt. But I've got the elixir, so he can be healed—'

'Quick, make him drink it!' Miranda's voice is anxious.

Streaks of pink lighten the distant horizon. It's almost sunrise. The open egg sits in my palm. My throat feels tight, too tight to speak. I lift the egg higher, to catch the dim light. Surely it's there...

But it isn't.

The egg is empty. The elixir is gone.

'Mim!' It's Miranda again. 'Hurry up and do it! They're coming!'

A wavering light moves slowly across the water towards the lighthouse. The rowing boat, with three figures inside it, wallows in the waves. I screw up my eyes to make them out. Hercules crouches at the front of the boat, swinging a large lantern and staring down into the water. Jason and Atlas bend to the oars. All around the boat, hundreds of Mers bob, keeping well clear of the light.

My legs shake so hard I can hardly get across the room. I kneel down beside Mac and take his cold, veiny hand in mine. His eyes tremble open.

'It's sunrise, Mac. They're coming for you. What shall we do?'

Mac mutters something and I lower my ear to his mouth. 'What did you say?'

'It's all over for me, Mim...' His voice fades.

'No! Never say that. There must be something—'

'Only one person... can complete the Work...' Suddenly he grips my hand tight. 'And that's you.'

I shake my head. 'I can't.'

'Add... the Third Impossible... then heat the elixir in the... furnace...' His eyelids close.

'But I don't know what the Third Impossible *is*.' Bitter tears leak from my eyes and dribble down onto the blue veins of his hand. 'Slow Henry's destroyed. The book's disappeared.' I hold out the empty egg. 'And the elixir's gone.'

Mac whispers on, as if I haven't spoken. 'You'll know... when the Work is complete... because the phoenix will fly...'

'The phoenix?'

'The bird of fire... rises from the ashes...' Mac's breath wheezes as he struggles to speak. What is he talking about?

'Think, Mim, think. Solve the last... Impossible. Use that... Enquiring... Mind of yours.'

He must be delirious. What can I possibly do now?

Footsteps clatter up the stairs towards us. Mac grips my hand harder.

'Quick, Mim... hide...'

'No way! I'm not leaving you.'

'*No*, Mim.' His eyes close. 'It all depends... on you, now. If you... care for me...'

'I do! You know I do!' My shoulders shake.

'Then make... yourself... scarce...' His voice drifts away.

Voices echo up the stairs, harsh and sharp. A fist bangs on the laboratory door.

'Open up, old man! Time's up! Show us the gold!'

Slowly, I let go of Mac's hand. I pick up the empty egg, shove it into my pocket and stumble to my feet, his words burning through my mind.

*Solve the last Impossible. Use that Enquiring Mind of yours...*

Can I rebuild Slow Henry? Of course not. And even if I could, the elixir is gone. And there's no book to guide me.

'Open up, I say!' The hammering on the door gets louder. I back towards the curtained-off toilet.

*Think, Mim, think.*

The door shudders. Jason and Atlas must be battering it with their shoulders.

I duck behind the curtain and sit on the toilet, all scrunched up. Then, with a splintering crash, the door breaks open.

# SAMUEL SAVES THE DAY

There's a long silence. Hercules and his men must be taking in the ruined laboratory.

'Fink we've got our answer, boys.' Hercules says at last. 'No gold.'

Jason mutters. 'Me back aches wiv all that rowing... and what for? For nuffink.'

'Not to mention keepin' all them Mers at bay,' says Atlas.

'More to the point,' says Hercules, 'Madame's not goin' to be 'appy.'

Footsteps echo across the floor and stop.

''Ere, what's this?'

'It's the old man. Done for, by the looks of 'im.'

'Shall we leave 'im? No point dragging 'im back wiv us if he's dead.'

'Wait!' says Hercules. ''E's still breathin'.'

'Only just, though.' A wily tone comes into Atlas's voice. 'Maybe we could finish 'im off. No need to take 'im back, then.'

I clench my fists. Let them *dare* do anything to Mac. I'll be out of here and on them before they get a chance.

'Nah,' says Hercules. 'We'll be good boys and follow orders. Besides... I likes a good hexecution.'

Jason and Atlas laugh.

'We'll never get 'im down the stairs, though,' says Jason.

'What we need,' says Atlas, 'is some sort of a stretcher. There was a fishin' net in that storeroom downstairs.'

Footsteps echo down the stairs, and return.

'Just the job,' says Hercules. 'You take 'is legs, Jase, Attie, grab 'is arms. I'll take 'is head.'

*Please be careful with him. Please don't hurt him.*

Mac groans again as they shuffle and complain.

''E's pretty heavy for an old 'un.'

'Mind 'is head...'

The voices echo down the stairs. I pull aside the curtain, my mind running in circles like a dog chasing its tail. Without the elixir and Slow Henry and *The Three Impossibles*, how can I possibly solve the last Impossible and complete the Work? Mac must have been feverish. And yet...

*He believes I can do it. He's relying on me.*

What did he whisper? Something about adding the final Impossible... and heating the elixir...

A croak comes from the broken rocking chair. Foggy's cloak's still draped over it, and the sound comes from underneath. I pull it back.

'Samuel! You're safe.'

Samuel's eyes gleam up at me. I reach out to pick him up and he climbs awkwardly into my hand. I scratch his head and his grin seems to widen.

Then I stop breathing.

Samuel must have been squatting on them: two torn fragments of paper lying on the rocking chair, their edges charred. Gold and blue paint sparkles from the words written on them.

Pages from *The Three Impossibles*.

I snatch up the fragments of paper and run over to the window. In the early light, I read the first, which has a single word:

## IMPOSSIBLE

Then I read the second, which looks like another part of the same page:

> *To create gold,*
> *you must destroy gold.*

What does this mean? I stare out of the window. It sounds— from all the mumbling and cursing—as if Hercules, Jason and Atlas are still carrying Mac down the stairs. There's no sign of Miranda.

'What shall we do, Samuel? It's a clue, but it makes no sense at all!'

Carefully, I tuck the papers into my pocket and my fingers brush the smooth shape of the egg.

'If only we had the elixir,' I whisper. 'Then we could save Mac.'

Samuel stares at me hard, almost as if he's understood what I said.

Suddenly, his long tongue darts out. On the very tip of it, a tiny drop shimmers and trembles.

The elixir.

For a long moment I just stare, as if my eyes are stuck to it. Then I come to my senses and grab it. Samuel's tongue disappears inside his wide mouth and one eye closes in a wink. My hand shaking, I lower him to sit on the hearth, and slowly open my fist.

The elixir rolls around in my palm like a golden pearl. Holding my breath tight, I pull the egg out of my pocket and carefully tip the drop of elixir inside. My heart thuds with relief. Samuel winks again and gives a froggy grin.

Voices drift up from below.

'Careful now, Attie. Get 'is legs in first—'

I watch out the window as Hercules, Jason and Atlas bundle Mac from the fishing net stretcher into the rowing boat. Miranda peers at them from behind a large rock, her brows drawn furiously together.

*I've got to get to Mac.* I've got to make him drink the elixir. But how? If Hercules and his men see me, they'll take *me* prisoner too...

Suddenly, I know what to do.

I pick up Samuel and put him safely back on the rocking chair. Then I throw on Foggy's cloak, pulling the hood down over my face. There's only one way to save Mac.

But I'll have to take a massive risk.

''Oo goes there?'

Hercules' voice is sharp.

'It's that governess... Fogarty,' mutters Jason.

'*Miss* Fogarty, if you please!' I say, giving my best Foggy sniff.

Hercules steps forward. 'What're *you* doin' 'ere?'

'I've come on the orders of His Majesty, of course. To find out if the old man made gold.'

'Didn't see yer upstairs...' mumbles Atlas. 'Where was you hidin'?'

'Such insolence!' I hope they can't see my knees shaking under Foggy's cloak. 'For your information, I was in the toilet. Not that it's any of *your* business...'

The men look at one another.

'And now,' I say, as firmly as I can, 'I suggest we stop wasting valuable time. The old man has failed in his task. We must take him back to Galena for his execution.'

Hercules doesn't move. 'I don't get it,' he says. 'Last time I saw you, after them Wings carried off the little Princess, you said you'd never go Outside again, not for nuffink.'

I take a deep breath. What would Foggy say?

'After a sensible period of reflection, I decided that duty must come before fear.'

'Let's go,' hisses Jason to Hercules. 'We've still got to get across that there water.' He casts a nervous glance at the ocean. 'An' I don't trust them Mers.'

'Not to mention them Wings...' Atlas stares up at the lightening sky.

But Hercules doesn't budge.

'Speakin' of crossin' the water,' he stares hard at me. ''Ow exactly did *you* get here? Swim, did yer?'

Even my mind can't get me out of this one. I open my mouth but nothing comes out. My heart thunders like a hundred drums. Then a voice behind me speaks.

'I helped her.'

And Miranda shuffles, on her bottom, out from behind the lighthouse, her scaly tail scraping on the rock.

# CROSSING THE WATER

**H**ercules, Jason and Atlas step backwards towards the boat.

'It's one o' them Mers,' hisses Jason.

Hercules grabs the lantern and waves it menacingly towards Miranda.

'Stay back, you—or else.'

Miranda ignores him. 'You wanted to know how Miss Fogarty got here. She rowed over in the boat, and asked me to take it back to the shore for you. Didn't you, Miss Fogarty?'

'Um, yes,' I sniff.

But the three men aren't listening to me.

'A talkin' Mer,' mutters Hercules.

'An' it's just a young 'un,' whispers Jason.

'Are you finking what I'm finking?' Atlas lowers his voice.

''Ow it'd look, in Madame's collection...' says Jason.

'Stuffed,' adds Atlas.

'Good finking, boys. It'd be just the replacement for that Wing boy wot escaped. An' it'd make up for tellin' Madame there's no gold.' Hercules grins. 'She'll be very, very pleased wiv us...'

Miranda's face is a pale shadow in the early morning light. She doesn't know what they're talking about. I flap my arms silently at her.

*Get into the ocean, Miranda.*

Miranda's gaze flickers over the water. The Mers, with their white corpse faces and skinny tentacle arms, close in around the lighthouse. They stare at Mac in the rowing boat and evil laughter floats over the waves. Miranda backs away over the rocks. The three men creep towards her, fake smiles on their faces.

''Ere, little Mer,' Hercules says. 'Come to Uncle Hercules.'

'We ain't goin' to hurt yer,' says Jason.

'Not much, anyhow,' mutters Atlas.

Hercules gives a nasty laugh. He rummages in his pocket and draws out his knife. Its blade glitters in the moonlight. But Atlas grabs his arm.

'We don't want no marks on the creature, chief!' he hisses. 'Better use the net.'

Hercules nods reluctantly. Each man takes a section of the fishing net and they move slowly towards Miranda.

'Get away from me!' she spits, her back up against the lighthouse. It makes me bristle to watch. Every atom in me longs to throw off Foggy's cloak and help Miranda. But if Hercules and his men recognize me, I won't stand a chance of giving Mac the elixir.

'Ready, boys?' whispers Hercules. Jason and Atlas nod. 'Now!'

The three men fling the fishing net over Miranda and pull it tight around her flailing arms. They bundle her into the rowing boat alongside Mac and jump in beside her. Hercules picks up the lantern.

'Let's go.' He waves it threateningly at the Mers. Then he turns to me. 'You comin', or what?'

'O-Of course.' I wrap Foggy's cloak more tightly around myself.

'Get a move on, then.'

I step into the back of the rocking boat and sit down between Mac and Miranda. Mac's eyes are closed. Miranda's are wide open, staring up at me. Wrapped in the net, she looks like a hooked fish.

'What were they talking about, putting me in a collection?' she hisses. 'And who's this Madame?'

A weak sound comes from Mac's lips. His eyes open. 'Miranda... what are you... doing here?'

'Hush!' I whisper. I glance up at the three men. Hercules is busy waving the lantern, scouring the ocean for the Mers. Jason and Atlas row, their breath fogging the air.

'Drink the elixir, Mac,' I whisper. 'There's only one drop left. Open your mouth.'

Mac raises a trembling hand. 'No, Mim.'

'But you've got to! Without you, we can't solve the last Impossible!'

'Without the elixir—' Mac tries to raise himself '—you can do nothing.'

Jason looks back over his shoulder. 'What's 'e sayin'?'

I put on my best Foggy voice. 'He's feverish. Row faster, man!'

Jason curses under his breath but returns to his job.

'Grandfather,' Miranda's voice hisses from the net. 'Drink the elixir. Now!'

Mac shakes his head stubbornly, clutching his chest.

'You... need the elixir...' he whispers hoarsely, '...for Miranda's tail.'

'Never mind my tail, Grandfather.' Miranda's eyes are full of tears. 'I'd rather have you.'

Mac's violet eyes soften. 'I've waited... so long... to hear you say that.'

I blink my eyes hard. If only *I* had a grandfather who cared about me the way Mac does about Miranda.

Miranda turns to me. 'Give him the elixir. I'll take my chances.'

But Mac pushes the egg away. He clamps his lips together and his eyes fall shut.

'It's no good, Miranda,' I whisper. 'I can't force him to.'

Miranda glares at me, her face white. 'He might die.'

I swallow. 'I know. But unless we complete the Work and turn lead into gold, they're going to execute him anyway. Maybe... maybe he'll hang on... maybe we can work out the Third Impossible... maybe we can turn lead into gold...'

Miranda frowns. 'That's a lot of maybes, Mim.'

'I know.' My mind turns and tumbles. 'But it's all I've got.'

'Wot's all that whisperin'?' Hercules calls from the front of the boat. 'Speak up if you got somefing useful to say!'

'N-nothing,' I give a big Foggy sniff. 'Can't you row any faster?'

Atlas and Jason mutter, glaring at me. 'Don't know why we brought 'er wiv us,' says Jason.

'Should 'ave left her at the light 'ouse,' says Atlas.

'Nah.' Hercules shakes his head. 'We need 'er.'

What does he mean by this? But there's no time to find out. We're almost there. The rowing boat is in shallow water now and the Great Wall looms in front of us. The Mers hang back, their eyes fixed on the lantern.

''Op out, you two, an' pull the boat in,' orders Hercules.

Jason and Atlas roll up their trouser legs and splash into the water, grumbling about the cold. The bottom of the boat scrapes over the sand.

Hercules waves the lantern and signals to the sentry. The Gate creaks open.

'Jase, carry the Mer. Me an' Attie'll take the old man.'

Jason grabs a struggling, kicking Miranda and hoists her over his shoulder.

'Ouch! It's bitin' me!'

''Urry up, then, and get it inside.'

I follow as Jason carries Miranda through the Gate and dumps her, still bundled in the net, on the ground. The Gate closes behind us.

'Right, boys,' says Hercules. 'You carry the old man to the King. I'll take the Mer down ter the dungeons and present it ter Madame.'

Jason and Atlas look at one another.

'You mean, you get the jammy job?' says Jason.

'While we got to tell the King there's no gold?' says Atlas.

''E ain't goin' to be 'appy,' Jason says. ''E's been crabby for days.'

'Wot wiv them Wings carryin' off the Princess,' says Atlas.

Quickly, I turn to the forge. 'I must see the blacksmith about the old man's execution.'

'Not so fast.' Hercules grabs my arm. 'You got to go wiv Jase and Attie.'

'What do they need *me* for?' My heart thuds. I *must* get to the forge and see Smith.

'For backup,' says Hercules, hefting up a scratching, biting Miranda. 'In case the King don't believe my boys about there bein' no gold.'

'But—'

'Get a move on,' snaps Hercules.

Jason and Atlas carry Mac towards the throne room. And I have no choice but to follow.

'Enter.'

Father's voice is irritable. I pray he's alone. He never takes any notice of Foggy, so with any luck I can skulk at the back of the room. But if Madame's with him, she's bound to smell a rat. I slink in behind Jason and Atlas, clutching my brooch for courage.

Father is alone. I keep my head down under Foggy's hood and press my back against the wall. Jason and Atlas dump Mac on the red carpet.

'What's this?' Father frowns.

Jason nudges Atlas.

Atlas nudges Jason back, harder.

'Well?' snaps Father.

'Yer Majesty.' Jason steps reluctantly forward. 'It's the old man from the light 'ouse. The al... alchem-thingy.'

'Alchemist, dopey!' Atlas hisses in a hoarse whisper.

'I can see who it is!' Father says. 'Why is he lying there like that? Is he ill?'

Atlas bows. "'E's 'ad a bit of a haccident, Yer Majesty.'

'And the gold?'

Jason and Atlas look at one another.

'It... ain't here,' mutters Jason at last.

'Speak up, man!'

'There ain't no gold, Yer Majesty. The old man failed.'

There's a long silence. Father's face twitches.

'Failed?'

'Yessir,' whispers Atlas. He turns to me. 'Ain't that so, Miss Fogarty?'

I nod, and sniff loudly. Father glares at me.

'I trusted you, Fogarty, to make it clear to Trismegistus MacWhisker that this was his last chance. That he would face execution if he failed.'

I hang my head. 'I'm sorry, Your Majesty.'

Father paces up and down, tugging at his moustache.

'Eleven years, I've waited. Eleven years wasted! And now I have no option but to order his execution.'

I take a deep breath. 'Your Majesty, couldn't you show him mercy?'

'Mercy, Fogarty?' Father growls. 'What mercy was shown to *me* on the Day of the Catastrophic Curse? I lost my queen and my gold, that day, and I've suffered ever since.' He turns to Jason and Atlas. 'Take the old man to the forge and make preparations for his execution. And tell Samuel Smith, by my order, to be ready to behead him in one hour.'

# FIRING UP THE FURNACE

I follow Jason and Atlas as they carry Mac up the steps to the platform outside the forge. The executioner's block waits, the axe gleaming in the cold early light. The forge looks different—sort of still. Where are the leaping shadows on the walls and the golden light of the furnace?

With much grunting and cursing, Jason and Atlas lay Mac down on the wooden platform.

'Can't—can't you make him more comfortable?' I ask. He looks so cold and alone.

Jason smirks. 'Comfortable! That's a larf, ain't it, Attie?'

'Not much point in bein' *comfortable*,' says Atlas. 'Not when 'is 'ead's comin' off in an hour!'

'C'mon,' says Jason. 'Better get them chairs out for the spectators.'

'What spectators?' I ask.

'Can't 'ave a good hexecution wivout a audience. Reckon it'll be packed. When was yer last one?'

'Eleven years ago,' I sniff like Foggy. 'On Curse—er, the Day of the Catastrophic Curse.'

Hercules swaggers up, his face wreathed in smiles.

278

'All right, boys?'

Jason and Atlas stare at him stonily. 'You look very pleased wiv yerself, chief,' says Jason.

'It's turnin' out to be a good day,' Hercules grins. 'Not only am I in Madame's good books, but I gets me a hexecution on top! Bag me a front-row seat, boys. I've gotta make somefink for that Mer.'

'So Madame liked 'er new pet?' says Atlas.

'Ho, yus!' Hercules draws himself up and puts on Madame's accent. '"Oh, 'Ercules, what 'ave we 'ere? A talkin' fish! Never 'ave I seen such a creature. It will be my pet *extraordinaire*. It must be dressed and displayed for all to marvel at."'

'Huh,' says Jason. 'An' did yer mention to Madame about the old man?'

'Yeah,' says Atlas. 'Did yer tell 'er there's goin' ter be no gold, after all?'

Hercules avoids their eyes. 'Mebbe. But that's between me and Madame.'

He gives Mac's body a kick.

'Still alive, are yer, old man?'

Mac groans.

'Well, you'd better stay that way.' Hercules runs his fingers over the axe blade. 'No point in hexecuting a dead man.' Then he points at me.

'Make yerself useful,' he says. 'An' tell the hexecutioner to sharpen up this 'ere axe. I got work ter do.' He leaps down from the platform. 'Boys, make sure them chairs are in straight lines.'

Jason and Atlas make faces at Hercules' disappearing

back. If only I could pull off Foggy's cloak and wrap Mac in it, or at least place it under his head for a pillow. But Smith will know what to do. I knock loudly on the door of the forge. When no one answers, I push open the patched-up door and step inside.

The forge is dark and still and very cold. The furnace is out. Ash is strewn over the floor. The air smells damp and sad.

Smith sits on the mattress, his great shoulders hunched, his head dropped to his chest. Round his ankle is a fat chain. His hands are chained and padlocked too.

'Smith?'

His head jerks up.

'Oh.' His face falls. 'Miss Fogarty. For a second there, I thought...'

I pull off Foggy's cloak. Smith's eyebrows jump up. Then he rubs at his dull eyes with his chained fists.

'Is that really you, Mim?'

I run across the space between us and throw my arms around him as far as they can go, which isn't far. I bury my face in his vest. Smith smells the way he always does: of sweat, hot tea and home.

'Oh, Smith!' I whisper. 'I said I'd come back, but I didn't know how!'

'Mim, bonny girl!' Smith stares as if he's still trying to believe it's me. 'Are you all right?'

I nod. 'I've so much to tell you! But there's no time to waste.'

'How d'you mean?'

'You've got to execute Mac—Hercules told me to tell you to go out and sharpen the axe.'

Smith frowns and shakes his head. 'I'm not executing anybody.'

'You won't have to—not if we complete The Third Impossible!'

'What are you blethering about, Mim?' Smith turns to stare at me. 'You're making no sense.'

'Impossibles don't make sense,' I say. 'That's why they're called Impossibles.' I turn to the furnace. 'We've got to fire this up—as quick as we can.'

Smith raises his chained and padlocked hands. 'No can do, Mim.'

I glance at the workbench, where Smith's hacksaw lies. Can I use it to cut the chain, the way he did to free Sky? *No.* I'm not strong like Smith, and besides, we don't have time.

I hurry over to the hook where Smith keeps his old apron. I wrap it round my middle.

'All right, I'll do it. What must I do first?'

'Sweep out the ash. Then fill the furnace with coal.' He gives a heavy sigh.

'Are you... are you OK, Smith?' I grab a broom and begin sweeping ash from the furnace.

'Aye.' Smith sighs again, then adds gruffly: 'Thought I wouldn't see you again, Mim.'

I pull out my brooch. 'If it wasn't for this, I don't know what I'd have done. It was like having you with me. It kept me safe. And it helped me to be brave.'

'Get on with that sweeping,' Smith wipes at his eye with his arm. 'Darn coal dust...'

I turn back to the sweeping, so as not to embarrass him. Soon I've filled a bucket with ash and the furnace is clean. I grab handfuls of coal and pile them up in the hearth. Then I pick up a box of matches.

'Shall I light it?'

'Yes. Carefully, now.'

I strike the match. A flame creeps along the paper in the furnace and sparks on the kindling.

'Use the bellows.'

I point them into the mouth of the furnace and squeeze them with all my strength. A wheezing rush of air sends the flames leaping and crackling.

'That's better.' Smith sounds a bit more like himself. 'So, what's this Third Impossible?'

'It's the last part of the Work. The Work that'll overturn curses and change lead into gold.' I take off the gloves, wipe my hands on a ragged cloth and pull out the egg from my pocket. 'This is all that's left of the elixir. Mac says we've got to heat it up in the furnace.'

By the light of the flames, I carefully lift the lid and show Smith the single drop of elixir. His dark eyes widen. Carefully, I replace the egg in my pocket and pull out the torn pieces of paper from the book.

'These are the only clues left, after the—'

The door shudders. Someone's banging hard on it.

'Open up!'

'Get behind the door.' Smith strides over to the door, the chain on his ankle rattling behind him. Using both hands, he jerks the door open.

'You ready to do the hexecution?' It's Jason's voice.

Smith brandishes his chained hands. 'Nope.'

'Ho yus, you are.' A key jangles and Smith's padlock and chains drop to the ground. Smith rubs his wrists.

'Now, get a move on,' says Jason.

'Can't execute a man with a blunt axe,' says Smith. 'I'll need my sharpening stone.'

''Urry up an' get it, then.'

'I'll get it—in my own good time.' Smith shuts the door in Jason's face. His ankle chain clatters as he ambles to the workbench.

'Smith—d'you think you'll be able to stall them until I've worked out the Third Impossible? And look after Mac?'

'I'll try my best, Mim.' Smith picks up the sharpening stone from his workbench. 'Watch the furnace.'

I nod. I'm not going to make the same mistake we made with Slow Henry.

'When it's hot as it can get, use the tongs to put the egg in the coals,' he tells me.

'And then what?' I falter. 'I wish I had a plan.' I pull out the two torn scraps of paper. 'All I've got are these... but I've no idea what they mean.'

'Sometimes it's okay not to have a plan,' says Smith. 'Sometimes, you've just got to do the next right thing.'

'I-I wish you could be here...'

'You're an alchemist's apprentice.' Smith walks to the door. 'It's your job now, Mim.'

The door closes firmly behind him.

# THE ALCHEMIST'S
# APPRENTICE

I hurry to the window, raise the worn curtain a little and peep out. A semi-circle of seats is set up around the platform. A crowd has gathered, muttering and pointing at Mac's still body lying on the platform, beside the executioner's block and the gleaming axe. Smith kneels beside Mac, feeling his pulse. Then, dragging his chain, he moves to the block and begins to slowly sharpen the axe. In the front row of seats, Father sits silent and alone, wrapped against the cold in a thick cloak, an empty seat beside him. Where is Madame Marionette? And what's happened to Miranda? I can't help remembering Miranda's stricken face as Hercules carried her away.

Foggy, her hair piled in a scraggy bun and wearing too much lipstick, elbows her way through the crowd and plonks herself down in the empty seat next to Father. He purses his lips, clicks his fingers at her and glares. If a look could kill, Foggy would be a pile of dust. She leaps off the seat and backs away, sniffing, to a place a few rows back.

The flames roar in the furnace behind me, sending shadows dancing round the forge. When will it be hot enough to put the egg into the furnace? I pull out the fragments of paper from my pocket and look at them again.

*To create gold,*
*you must destroy gold.*

If only the next page of the book hadn't been destroyed in the explosion. If only Mac wasn't lying unconscious out on the platform—if only he was here, with me. Between us we could surely work out the meaning. His words, and Smith's, run round and round in my mind.

*Only one person... can complete the Work... And that's you.*

*Sometimes, you've just got to do the next right thing.*

*You're an alchemist's apprentice. It's your job now, Mim.*

Everything depends on me.

I force myself to concentrate.

*Destroy gold.* But there *is* no gold to destroy... and if there *was* gold, we wouldn't need to do the Work. Is this Third and last Impossible just that—a riddle no one can solve?

The words become misty before my eyes. I squeeze them tight shut.

*Don't cry, Mim.*

The forge is boiling hot. Sweat's running down my face and my hands are damp. I stare into the scorching flames. Surely it must be time?

I reach inside my pocket and take out the egg. Carefully, I balance it on the workbench. Then I pull on Smith's massive leather gloves. They're at least three sizes too big, which makes it hard to manipulate the metal tongs, even using both hands.

I manage to grip the egg in the tongs and lift it towards the fiercest part of the furnace. Hungry flames lick around it. My face burns, but I mustn't look away. I've got to keep the egg upright. If it topples over, the lid will come off and the last drop of elixir will slip into the flames and be gone for ever.

Gritting my teeth, I lower the egg right into the centre of the flames and set it down among the blazing coals. Not daring to breathe, I release the tongs. The egg sits safely among the coals, surrounded by crackling flames. Now I've got to wait until it becomes white-hot.

The sound of a beating drum comes from outside. What's going on? I get to my feet and run to the window.

A procession makes its way slowly down the street towards the forge. Jason and Atlas march in front, dressed in black. Jason plays the horn and Atlas beats the drum in a dirge which makes the hair on my head tingle. Behind them rattles Madame's red carriage—driven by Hercules, dressed in a scarlet uniform with gold frogging, and flicking a leather whip. The horses toss their proud heads and trot in time to the beat, their hooves echoing over the cobbles. Behind this carriage, a line of smaller carts clatter towards the forge, each covered by a ruby-red silk cloth.

As the carriages draw to a halt, Father jumps to his feet, running his fingers through his hair. Hercules opens the carriage door with a flourish. Groucho jumps out of the carriage first, a red bandana tied around his mangy neck, his yellow eyes scouring the crowd.

I glance over my shoulder to check on the furnace. The flames crackle, strong and fierce, around the egg. How long will I have to wait for it to get white-hot? And what then? I swallow my worry and try to remember Mac's words about being patient and having faith.

I turn back to the window, just in time to see Madame Marionette step out of the carriage, helped by a smirking Hercules.

She has never looked more beautiful, or more deadly. Her long, curved nails are the colour of blood, matching perfectly her tumbling red curls, her bold scarlet lips and her crimson silk gown. I shiver, in spite of the heat.

Father bows so low that his sleeves brush the cobbles. Then he takes Madame's hand and kisses it. Foggy's face is like a thundercloud about to burst.

I turn to check on the furnace. The egg looks exactly the same. I grab Smith's heavy leather bellows and point them into the flames. With all my strength, I force them shut. With a creak and a groan, a stream of air sends the coals glowing red and the fire licking around the egg. Then I put the bellows down and edge closer to the window. Father's speaking to Madame. As silently as possible, I push it open a bit so I can hear.

'Beloved Tomazine,' Father takes Madame's arm. 'Allow me to escort you to the front. Unless of course, you prefer to sit further back. I would not want your fine gown spattered with blood.'

Madame laughs, a high, unpleasant sound. 'Since I wear red,' she says, 'a leetle blood will not be a problem.'

She jerks Groucho's lead as he slavers over Father's shiny shoes. Father takes a hasty step back and clicks his fingers at Jason, who falls on his knees to wipe the trail of spittle away with his sleeve.

At a signal from Hercules, Atlas beats the drum again, only this time it's an urgent drum roll, like a warning. Father, preening himself and twirling his moustache, climbs the steps to stand on the platform beside the executioner's block. Smith tests the sharpened axe with his thumb, a faint smile curling at the corner of his mouth. Father signals Atlas to stop playing. In the echoing silence, he raises his voice and addresses the crowd.

'Citizens of Galena. We are gathered here this morning,' he announces, 'to witness the execution of Trismegistus MacWhisker. I ordered him to perform his duty, to transform lead into gold. Yet he has refused to do so. I trust that this will serve as a lesson to you all. Defy your king, and you will pay for it—with your life.'

''Ere, 'ere,' says Hercules. He nudges Jason and Atlas and they mutter ''Ere, 'ere,' too. The crowd is silent.

'It is time.' Father holds his hand up. 'Samuel Smith—is the axe sharpened?'

Smith bows his great head. 'Aye, Your Majesty.' The faint smile is still there.

'Then,' says Father, 'let the execution commence!'

# THE THIRD IMPOSSIBLE

The drum rolls again. My heart drums even faster. I run to the furnace, almost tripping over the bellows, and throw myself down in front of it. The egg sits in the flames, unchanged.

*What can I do?*

The egg isn't ready—and even if it *was*, I have no idea what to do next, not without instructions. A sob wrenches from my chest. I pull off Smith's gloves and run back again to the window. I squeeze my eyes shut, tighten my fingers around my brooch and whisper a prayer. Maybe it will somehow find a way to Mac. Maybe...

'Wait!'

Madame's heels click-clack as she walks slowly up to the platform and turns to the crowd. She points a red fingernail at Atlas, who gawps and drops his drumsticks with a clatter.

'Before the execution begins, I 'ave a leetle announcement of my own.'

'An announcement, Tomazine?' says Father.

Madame smiles. 'As some of you may know, I am a collector. I 'ave in my collection the most exotic and wonderful creatures from around the world. But never—never before 'ave I owned a creature like this.'

She signals to Hercules. He, in turn, jerks his head at Jason and Atlas, and they follow him to the first of the covered carts. The crowd turns, whispering, to watch them.

'Reveal the creature,' orders Madame. The three men pull back the red silk cover.

The crowd gasps.

I hardly recognize Miranda. She sits on a sort of wooden throne, her hands tied together with rope, a rough blindfold over her eyes. Her hair is a golden river flowing over her white shoulders. She wears a blood-red dress. A ramshackle rail with a crimson curtain has been set up around the lower half of her body, hiding her tail from sight. And tilted over her head is a crown—the lead crown that I left on my bed when I escaped.

'Beloved, who is this?' Father stares at Miranda.

Madame ignores him. She nods at Hercules, who climbs up onto the cart beside Miranda.

'Now, Madame?' he asks.

'Now,' she commands.

With a flourish, Hercules pulls back the crimson curtain. Another gasp from the crowd echoes round the street. Miranda's tail glitters silver in the sunlight.

Father is suddenly whiter than a ghost. He backs unsteadily away.

'Is that... a Mer?'

Behind him, Foggy sways as if she's going to faint, her face pale as the moon.

'Hercules—the knife!' Madame orders. My mouth goes dry as dust. Is Madame going to have Miranda killed, so she can be stuffed and added to her collection? Hercules raises his arm, the knife's blade flashing silver. Then he swipes with his knife at the blindfold. It falls to the ground. Miranda stares about with furious, flashing eyes. Then she sees Mac and goes statue-still.

'Grandfather!'

The crowd gasps again, Father loudest of all. But Mac doesn't move. Miranda tugs savagely at the rope around her wrists.

'Grandfather—get up!'

Madame laughs. 'Not only is it a Mer. It is the only talking Mer left in the world. And it is mine, all mine.' She signals to Hercules, who draws the curtain back around Miranda's tail. 'From now on, anyone who wishes to see the creature's tail must pay.'

Father says in a weak voice: 'I will have no Mers in Galena. Not after the Day of the Catastrophic Curse. Remove it immediately!'

Madame laughs again. 'Remove it, you say? Your wish, *mon cher*, is my command. But I 'ave to tell you this—when the Mer goes, so will I.'

'W-what?' Father says. 'But, Tomazine—our marriage—'

'What marriage?' Madame's lips twist in a spiteful smile. 'Don't you remember my ultimatum?'

'I-I don't recall—'

'I told you very clearly—"if the old man doesn't deliver gold, you will lose me".'

Father opens and shuts his mouth like a goldfish.

Miranda, her eyes fixed on Mac, bites at the rope around her wrists. Tears pour down her cheeks. Madame smiles again.

'It is lucky that the creature has fallen into my hands. I shall exhibit her around the world. She will make my fortune. But first,' she glances coldly at Mac, 'we have an execution to carry out.'

'Grandfather!' Miranda's eyes are full of terror. 'Wake up! Don't let them—'

Madame laughs. 'How unfortunate that this hopeless old man—this so-called alchemist—is the creature's grandfather. But how fortunate for *her* that I am willing to take her into my care after his death.'

She turns to Smith. 'Executioner, perform your duty.'

Smith folds his arms.

'Are you deaf, man? I said, perform your duty!'

'No, ma'am.'

'What?' Madame narrows her eyes. 'I hope I misheard you.'

'You heard me correctly,' says Smith quietly. 'I don't destroy life. Never have, never will.'

*I knew Smith wouldn't do it.* My knees feel like jelly with relief, and I stumble back to the furnace. I peer into the centre of the flames. The egg is a white-hot globe.

It's time.

But time for what?

I pull out the scraps of paper and hold them, one in each hand. In my right hand, the riddle:

292

> *To create gold,*
> *you must destroy gold.*

And in my left hand, the single word:

## *IMPOSSIBLE*

I clench my fists to stop myself throwing the papers into the furnace. For the first time in my life, my Enquiring Mind is completely blank.

Madame's voice, harsh and furious, drifts in through the open window.

'Another fool disobeys you, Your Majesty. First, the old man. Now your own executioner.'

Then Father's voice. 'Samuel Smith! I command you to do your duty.'

Smith's deep voice says:

'Sir, I will not.'

'There's no making him,' Father sounds irritable. 'After all, he can't execute himself!'

*Keep stalling, Smith.* I stare at the paper in my left hand.

## *IMPOSSIBLE*

What did Mac say, about looking at impossible things in a different way?

A spit and a crackle from the furnace sends a hot spark shooting out. A tiny black burn mark appears on the paper in my left hand, between the letters I and M. The word seems to shiver before my eyes, as if it's trying to tell me something.

Then I see it.

Instead of IMPOSSIBLE, it now says:

## *I'M POSSIBLE*

Could it be telling me that the Third Impossible *is* possible, after all?

Outside the window, Madame's voice rises.

'No making him, is there? We shall see.' Her voice is thin and cruel. 'Executioner, you *will* behead the old man, clean and sweet. If you choose not to, you condemn him to a death far more painful and drawn-out...'

A terrible snarl rends the air, followed by a horrifying howl.

'...because Groucho will tear the old man apart, slowly, limb from limb. Won't you, leetle boy?'

'*No!*' screams Miranda from her throne.

'No!' My own whisper echoes Miranda's. Clutching the papers, I rush to the window.

Father's head is buried in his hands. On her wooden throne, Miranda's face is drained of colour. She gives another long, terrible cry, as if someone's wrenching out her heart. Madame Marionette begins to unleash Groucho. His sharp teeth are bared. His yellow eyes fix on Mac's unmoving body.

'WAIT!'

It's Smith, his face pale and very, very still. 'Hold back the dog. I'll do it.'

Madame's lips part in a cruel smile. She yanks Groucho back.

'A sensible decision, executioner.' She turns to Atlas. 'Sound the drum, and let the execution take place.'

The drumbeat begins, menacing and slow. Smith glances at the forge window, sees me watching, and shakes his head. Then he slowly bends and picks up the gleaming axe.

I can't bear it. I pull out my brooch and hold it tightly in my hand, its letters spelling out my name in gold...

*Gold.*

I gasp. The scrap of paper in my right hand trembles, the words shifting before my eyes.

> *To create gold,*
> *you must destroy gold.*

I run to the furnace. My hands shake so hard I can hardly get Smith's gloves on. The tongs shake too. I bite down on my lip to try to keep them steady. Slowly, I move them into the heart of the furnace where the egg sits, whiter than white. Holding my breath, I use the tongs to lift the lid. Inside, the last drop of elixir glitters.

*It's now or never.*

I move the tongs to pick up my brooch. My name— MIM—glows pure gold in the light from the leaping flames. It's my best, my most precious possession—it kept me safe when I almost drowned in the ocean, when the Mers tried to get me, when I climbed Black Mountain in the snow. It's the one thing that helps me be brave.

Shielding my face from the searing heat, I drop my brooch inside the white-hot egg and close the lid.

There's a flash, and a sudden, terrible cracking sound.

I stare at the egg, or what's left of it. It's broken into a hundred pieces. There's no sign of the elixir—only a small pile of white-grey ash among the flames.

My brooch is gone for ever. And the Three Impossibles have been nothing but a stupid riddle, a cruel joke.

# THE END OF THE TAIL

**O**ut on the platform, Smith stands over Mac, the axe trembling in his huge hands. Madame holds back a snarling Groucho, his lead straining. I stumble to the door and yank it open.

'*STOP!!!*' I scream.

A sea of faces stare, and a hubbub of voices shout at me. I glimpse Miranda's stricken face, Foggy's horrified one and Father's bewildered expression. Then I scramble over to where Smith's axe is poised above Mac and throw myself down on top of him, just the way he threw himself over me to save me from the explosion in the lighthouse.

'Mim—what the devil are you doing?' Smith lowers his axe.

'So, leetle brat, you are back.' It's Madame's cold voice, whispering in my ear. 'Will you never learn to keep your nose out of my business?'

'Leave Mac alone!' I shout.

Madame laughs. 'The old man is doomed. And once he is gone, his granddaughter will be mine. Now step aside and let the execution take place.'

'I won't!'

'Won't?' Madame's white face is next to mine, her smile evil. 'Then I'll 'ave to—accidentally, of course—lose my grip on Groucho's lead...'

'You wouldn't dare.'

'Watch me, leetle girl.'

Groucho's yellow eyes bore into mine, just inches from my face. His sharp teeth snap, dripping saliva. His meaty breath is hot on my face.

I squeeze my eyes shut. *She's really going to do it. This is the end.*

'WAIT!!!'

It's Smith. My eyes jerk open to look at him.

The axe has dropped to the ground. Smith stands stock-still, his arm outstretched, pointing at something with a shaking hand. Everyone—even Madame—turns to see what it is. I stumble to my feet.

Miranda still sits on her wooden throne, her hands tied. But on her head, the lead crown—the crown Smith's father made—shimmers and glows...

*...in the purest gold.*

The crowd gasps. Then, out of the forge door flies a bird. Not a Wing—this bird is about the size of a peacock. Its head and breast are covered in golden feathers and its eyes are as blue as sapphires. It swoops down to perch on the executioner's block, opens its bill and gives a long, melodious cry—a cry of joy and sorrow and hope. Then it spreads its wings and flies up and over the Great Wall.

Something moves, down by my feet. Mac raises himself on one elbow to stare at the bird as it flaps over the Gate.

'The phoenix,' he whispers. His voice is deeper, and somehow younger.

'Mac!' I grab his hand. It's surprisingly warm and strong.

'Help me up, Mim.'

I hold on to his arm as he slowly gets to his feet. Spots of colour flush his veiny cheeks and his violet eyes sparkle.

'Oh, Mac—are you recovered?'

'Remember the first page of *The Three Impossibles*?' he whispers. 'When the phoenix flies, the Work is complete.'

I fling my arms around him. He is warm and solid and I can feel his heart beating strongly in his chest.

Suddenly, Miranda's voice calls out.

'Grandfather... Grandfather!'

Mac turns to look.

Slowly, Miranda bends to the crimson curtain. With her bound hands, she clumsily tugs it open. I gasp. Her silvery tail is gone, and in its place is...

...a pair of thin, white legs.

Miranda stares at them as if she can't quite trust what she's seeing. Then she bends and touches each leg, her eyes full of wonder. A smile such as I've never seen before spreads slowly over her face and her eyes shine.

She stands up, wobbling a little, and takes an unsteady step forward. But Mac is faster. He leaps from the platform like a much younger man, his face pouring with tears, and runs to the cart, his arms spread open. He and Miranda gaze at one another for a long moment. Then Miranda laughs and jumps into the air, her new legs flailing, down into his arms. They hug and hug.

Mac raises his head and looks at me.

'Dear Mim,' he whispers. 'You did it!'

'You mean—'

'You completed the Work! You solved the Third Impossible. But how?'

'I—it said I had to destroy gold to create gold. And the only piece of gold to destroy was my brooch...'

Before I can say any more, Miranda runs—yes, runs!—over to me. She flings her bound arms round my neck.

'Oh, Mim!' she whispers. 'I can walk—just like you!'

Madame Marionette pushes through the crowd towards us. Her eyes are fixed on Miranda's head. 'Hercules!'

'Yus, Madame?'

'Give me that crown!'

'Wotever you say, Madame.' Hercules lifts the gold crown from Miranda's head and passes it over to Madame. She cradles the crown in her hands, her cruel face bathed in its warm golden light.

'Gold...' she breathes. 'Real gold. So you did it, old man, after all.' She lifts the crown and puts it on her head.

Foggy, her nose bright red, points a quivering finger at Mac.

'How did you do it, Trismegistus MacWhisker? How did you turn lead into gold, without *The Three Impossibles*?'

Her face drops and she slaps her hand over her mouth.

I step forward. 'What did you say, Foggy?'

'Miss Fogarty!' But a blush spreads over her face.

'All these years,' I say slowly, 'on Father's orders, you've been bringing Mac lead objects to change into gold. And from the very start, you could have given him *The Three Impossibles*, so he could succeed. Why did you hide it?'

'I-I don't know what you mean.'

'Why did you move *The Three Impossibles* to the highest shelf in the library? And why did you lie to Mac? Why did you tell him his books had been destroyed in a fire?'

'Fogarty?' Father glares at Foggy. 'Is Jemima right? Have you been deliberately preventing Trismegistus MacWhisker from carrying out his work?'

'Yes, sister,' smiles Madame Marionette. 'Isn't it time you told His Majesty the truth?'

Foggy turns on her.

'The truth? Maybe *you* should tell him the truth! About why *you* came here. Why you pretended to l-love him. All *you* care about is gold and power! Everything's always been about *you*! You always treated me like I was invisible... and then you went off and married the *Compte*, and put on that fake French accent, while I...'

Her mouth opens and closes as if she's run out of words. Father's face is white and still.

'Oh dear,' Madame smiles unpleasantly. 'It is sad that my very own sister should be so jealous of me. But it is a burden I must bear.' She adjusts the crown on her red hair. Then she smiles over at Father. 'I shall wear this at our wedding, beloved.'

Father stares at her. 'What do you mean, Tomazine?'

Madame flutters her eyelashes. 'The old man has succeeded in turning lead into gold. He's met the conditions of our ultimatum. The wedding can go ahead, as planned.' She casts a cold look at Foggy. 'And when we are married, I see no reason why my sister should be needed in the castle. Perhaps it is time to let her go.'

Father's face is white and cold. 'Married, Tomazine? I think not.'

'What?... What do you mean?'

'I have been a fool,' says Father. A shocked murmur whispers through the crowd. 'Blinded by the flattery of a wicked woman. Fogarty is right. You pretended to care for me—pretended you wanted to be my wife—when all you really cared about was the gold.' He holds out his hand. 'Give me the crown, Tomazine.'

'*Pardon?*' Madame frowns.

'You heard me. The crown. Hand it over.'

'What if I won't?'

There's the sound of a chain dragging along the ground. Smith stands behind Father, his huge body casting a shadow over Madame.

'Best hand it over, ma'am, and be off.' He gestures at the waiting carts. 'Lucky you've already done your packing.'

Two red spots of colour appear on Madame Marionette's white cheeks. She tosses the crown at Father.

'How *dare* you accuse *moi* of pretending, of deceiving you. What I have done has been as nothing compared with *her.*' She jerks her head at Foggy.

302

'I-I don't know what you mean.' Foggy's face is beet-root red.

'Don't you, sister?' says Madame. 'Then perhaps it is time for me to tell the King what *really* happened on the Day of the Catastrophic Curse.'

Foggy turns and begins to push her way through the crowd. But Smith follows her and grabs her arm.

'Not so fast, Miss Fogarty.' He marches her back to Madame Marionette. 'Seems we have a mystery here. Mebbe you—and your sister here—can help us clear it up...'

'She's lying!' whispers Foggy. 'There *is* no mystery.'

'There is!' I say. 'I overheard you both when you were arguing. Madame Marionette said she knew all about your secret. And she said the secret was about *me.*'

Madame Marionette's lips part in a cruel smile.

'The brat is right.' She yanks Groucho's lead so that he's standing between her and Foggy. 'And if my sister won't tell you, then I will...'

Foggy glares at her. Then she pulls off her spectacles and polishes them frantically. 'I only did it because—because I... loved him.' She glances at Father and blushes again.

'Did what, Fogarty?' says Father. 'I command you to tell me.'

Foggy gives a big sigh. She looks at Mac, at Miranda and finally at me.

'Very well.' She sniffs and pushes up her spectacles with a shaking hand. 'I will.'

# WHAT REALLY HAPPENED ON CURSE DAY

'Life was very different in Galena before the Day of the Catastrophic Curse,' Foggy begins. 'The castle was full of exquisite objects—expensive paintings, fine furniture, and gold everywhere, as befits a king's home.'

Miranda's eyes are wide. 'Were there beautiful clothes and jewels? Were there balls and banquets?'

Foggy nods. 'The Queen loved such things.'

'Ah yes,' says Father, a faraway look in his eye. 'The dancing we had! How perfect everything was...'

'*He* lived here, then,' Foggy jerks her head at Mac, 'as Keeper of the Library, along with his daughter. Both she and the Queen were expecting babies, and both gave birth on the same day—the Day of the Catastrophic Curse. I was to be nursemaid to the baby Princess—such a great honour to serve Their Majesties...'

'Get on with it, Fogarty,' snaps Father.

'Yes, Your Majesty.' Foggy blushes. 'After the Mer Queen made her curse, and the Queen died, I went running to the

304

nursery to make sure the new baby was safe. And that was when I discovered...'

'Discovered what?' I whisper.

'Patience, Jemima!' Foggy takes off her spectacles again and polishes them. Then she perches them on her long nose. 'The little Princess was crying softly in her cradle. I picked her up to soothe her. Then her blanket slipped off, and...'

'And? And?' I jump up and down.

'Interrupting will not help me tell the story!' Foggy pulls out her handkerchief and blows her nose with a honk.

'Hurry *up*, then,' I say.

'Yes, sister dear—get a move on!' says Madame Marionette. Foggy's face is a thundercloud, but she goes on.

'As the blanket fell away, a terrible thing was revealed. The baby's legs were gone. And in their place was... a fish's tail.'

I gasp, and look at Miranda. Her mouth is open too. Father stares at Foggy, his face the colour of cold porridge.

'But... but I haven't got a fish's tail!' I say. 'Only Miranda—'

'Sssst!' says Father. 'Let Fogarty tell her story.'

'Thank you, Your Majesty,' Foggy lowers her eyes. 'I was horrified, as you can imagine. I knew how Your Majesty loves things to be perfect. How would you feel to have a daughter with a fish's tail, like one of those dreadful Mers? How could you live with such a terrible reminder of the Mer Queen's curse, after the death of your own beloved queen? So I made a plan...'

'What did you do?' Father's face is very still.

'I-I carried the baby to Trismegistus MacWhisker's rooms. Luckily, *he* wasn't there—he was in the library with his nose stuck in a book, as usual. His baby granddaughter lay in a box, wearing a rough nappy and covered with an old shawl. As quickly and quietly as I could, I swapped the babies' clothes. Then I lay the Princess in the box and covered her tail with the shawl. I carried the other baby, dressed in fine silk, back to the nursery. And I placed her in the royal cradle.'

There's a long, long silence. I'm surprised I can't hear all our minds whirring and thinking.

'You mean...' Four of us speak at once—Miranda, me, Father and Mac.

'Yes.' Madame Marionette points at Miranda with her red-nailed finger. '*She* is the real daughter of His Majesty.' Then she turns to me. 'And this leetle brat is—'

'My granddaughter?' Mac and I stare at one another.

'I tried and tried to teach Jemima to behave like a young lady,' Foggy goes on, 'but it was impossible. She was clumsy and wayward and inquisitive and far too fond of books. Not princess material at all.'

'And that,' smirks Madame Marionette, 'was where I came in.'

Smith steps forward and grabs her by the arm. 'But *this*, ma'am, is where you leave.'

Madame Marionette wrenches her arm free. 'Oh, don't worry, executioner. I'm going.'

She stalks to her carriage, dragging a whimpering Groucho behind her. Hercules flings open the door for her, while

Jason and Atlas hurry to the other carts. Hercules leaps into the driver's seat and signals to the sentry to open the Gate.

'Good riddance!' Foggy shouts, as the procession clatters over the cobbles and disappears through the Gate into the Outside.

Father and Miranda smile at one another. They look so alike, with their tall, thin bodies, their grey eyes and their blonde hair—no wonder Miranda reminded me of someone when I met her.

'You are the very image of your mother,' says Father. 'And of me. It's like looking in a mirror.'

I swallow, and look at Mac. He looks back at me in a sorrowful way. He must be so disappointed to discover that I'm his granddaughter. I'm not pretty or graceful like Miranda. And of course, there's my Enquiring Mind...

'Mim?' he says in his gruff voice. 'I'm so sorry...'

'Sorry?' I whisper. 'What for?'

He's going to tell me he's sorry, but he doesn't want me for a granddaughter.

'I'm sorry that you've found out the truth. You've been brought up as a king's daughter. A princess. How does it feel to know you're the granddaughter of an old man with no gold, no luxuries, and only a ruined lighthouse for a laboratory?'

'How does it feel?' I say slowly. 'It feels... wonderful.'

Mac's eyes go all watery.

'But what about you, Mac?' I ask. 'You had a beautiful girl for a granddaughter. A girl who loved you very much. And now... well, now you've just got me.'

307

Mac suddenly laughs. 'You'll do me just fine. And besides, I doubt that Miranda will stop loving me, just as I'll never stop loving her.'

'Of course I'll never stop loving you!' says Miranda. 'That would be impossible! And I'll never forget how you tried and tried to overturn the curse on my legs, even when I was horrible to you.'

'So,' says Mac, 'I get two granddaughters for the price of one!'

Then he holds out his arms and I run into them.

'Dearest Mim,' he whispers, his whiskers tickling my ears. 'Do you have any idea how special you are?'

'Me? Special?'

'Don't you see? Without you and that Enquiring Mind of yours, none of this would have happened. Thanks to you, Miranda has her legs—and she can dance and dress up in fine things, just as she's always wanted to. His Majesty has his real daughter back, and his gold. And as for me—I have the most marvellous granddaughter. Not only that, but an apprentice who loves alchemy just as much as I do!'

And then he hugs me all over again.

'Miss Fogarty.' Father's voice is stern.

Foggy jumps, then drops into a curtsy, her boots squeaking. Her nose turns pink. 'Y-yes, Your Majesty?'

'You did a terrible wrong, in exchanging my daughter for Trismegistus MacWhisker's granddaughter.'

Foggy hangs her head. 'I know, Your Majesty.'

'But you... well, you had your reasons.' Father flushes. 'So you are pardoned, I suppose.'

Father turns to Mac.

'Trismegistus MacWhisker, you cared for my daughter for eleven years. You worked tirelessly trying to restore her legs, and you risked your life to do so.' He bows low. 'I thank you, from the bottom of my heart.'

Mac pulls out his handkerchief and blows his nose loudly.

'Samuel Smith,' Father continues.

Smith's great head jerks up in surprise.

'I misjudged you. You are a man of honour, like your father before you. Your loyalty and your honesty are unmatched. I give you my word that I will do all in my power to reward you.'

Smith nods gruffly.

Then Father turns to me. There's kindness in his grey eyes for the very first time. 'I've been blind to many things in the past eleven years. And now, because of your courage—and that wonderfully Enquiring Mind of yours—my eyes are opened. There will be no more secrets here.'

I give an embarrassed nod.

'I'm a vain man, Jemima. And all too susceptible to flattery. I only wanted flawless, perfect things around me. I spent too much time looking at the outsides of things—and people. And I was determined to make *you* into a perfect princess. Which is why I paid that woman to be your tutor.'

Foggy gives a loud, indignant sniff.

'But I've learnt an important lesson—a lesson I'd have thought impossible a few short weeks ago.' He holds up the crown. 'Gold is a fine, fine thing. But the best place to find it isn't in castles, or in jewellery, or even in crowns—but in the heart. And you, Jemima,' he smiles, 'or rather, *Mim MacWhisker*... have a heart of pure gold.'

My face burns. Mac takes my hand on one side, and Smith on the other.

# AFTERWARDS

*B*ONGHHHHHH...

The tolling of the bell echoes round the stone walls of my bedroom. It's the twenty-first of March—the spring solstice. There are two beds in the room now. In the other one, Miranda stretches and yawns and smiles. I haven't seen her frown for weeks. She swings her legs out of bed and wriggles her feet into her new slippers. A fire crackles in the fireplace, and a jug of hot water, for washing, boils above the flames.

'Hurry up, Mim!' Miranda throws on her new silk dressing gown and grabs her silver hairbrush. Every morning, she brushes her long, golden hair one hundred times.

I jump out of bed and run over to the window in my bare feet. The forge windows are filled with dancing light from the flames. There's Smith, tolling the bell. The executioner's block and the axe are gone. Father—I mean, the King—ordered them to be taken away and thrown into the ocean. I wonder what the Mers made of them?

There's a knock on the door, and Foggy bustles in, her arms full of clothes. She's stopped wearing black, since she confessed what she did on Curse Day. She's still just as snarky, though. Today she's wearing a bright-green dress which makes her look like a giant pea, with eyeshadow to match.

'Make haste, Your Royal Highness,' she sniffs. 'We mustn't keep His Majesty waiting, on this of all days.'

She tosses my patched trousers and baggy jumper at me. Then, she places a long, golden dress on Miranda's bed.

'Ninety-nine... one hundred.' Miranda puts down the hairbrush and hurries over to her bed. 'Oh...' She runs her fingers over the fabric of the dress. 'Real silk. And studded with diamonds.'

Foggy almost smiles, then remembers she's Foggy and stops. She pulls open a satin bag and draws out a pair of high-heeled shoes sewn with golden thread, even higher than the ones I had to wear.

Miranda gasps. 'So beautiful. I wonder if I can dance in them?' She sits on the bed and puts one on, turning her foot this way and that.

I grin. 'I'm sure you can. I'm just glad *I* won't have to!'

The bell tolls again.

Foggy frowns. 'His Majesty is waiting in the throne room. Stop distracting Miss Miranda.' She glares at the wash basin, where Samuel's swimming round and round. 'And kindly remove that frog from the wash basin, Jemima.'

'Mim,' I correct her, out of habit, popping Samuel into my pocket. 'Can I go and see Smith?'

'Absolutely not,' snaps Foggy. 'You'll see Samuel Smith at the coronation. Now, follow Miss Miranda's good example, if you please, and brush that bird's-nest hair.'

Gold chandeliers hang from the ceiling of the throne room; heavy silk curtains threaded with gold billow to the floor; thick rugs cover the floor, so deep your feet disappear in them. Golden statues are dotted about on plinths, and each of the mirrors has a gleaming golden frame. The King sits on his gold throne, dressed in gold from head to foot. On the table beside him, the glittering crown rests on a plump red-velvet cushion. Rows of seats are set out, most of them full. I run, in spite of Foggy's tutting, to sit between Mac and Smith in the front row.

Miranda enters the room. With her long hair brushed to silk, her shimmering golden dress and her high golden heels, she floats, graceful as a dancer, to stand before the throne.

The King gets to his feet. His face is light and open, as if the sun's shining on it. He lifts the crown from its red cushion and holds it high over Miranda's head, before setting it down on her golden hair. 'Arise, Princess Miranda!'

'Wow,' I whisper to Mac. 'Doesn't she look beautiful?'

He exchanges a smile, over my head, with Smith. 'Don't you wish you were a princess, now?'

I shake my head violently. 'No way! In fact...'

'What, Mim?'

'N-nothing.'

I won't tell Mac that I miss the lighthouse. After all, the King has told Mac he is welcome to use the dungeons for his laboratory. He has his library back, and all his beloved books. And of course, Miranda lives here now.

But Smith's deep voice interrupts my thoughts. 'Spit it out, Mim.'

'It's just...' I twist my fingers together. 'I just wondered...'

'Let me guess,' says Mac. 'You wondered if we could go back to live in the lighthouse. Is that right?'

I nod. 'I know we can't. After all, it's ruined, since the explosion. And it was dangerous enough going back to get Samuel, what with the Mers hating humans so much.' I gently pull Samuel out of my pocket, and he stares up at me with his bulbous eyes. 'And anyway—I never want to lose Smith again, or Miranda, or the library... so I know it's impossible, really.'

'Is it?' says Mac.

'What d'you mean?'

Mac and Smith exchange glances again.

'That Enquiring Mind of yours solved The Three Impossibles, didn't it?' Mac says. 'Haven't you learnt *anything* from that, Mim MacWhisker?'

'I-I don't understand...'

'Sometimes, as I told you, all you need to do is look at impossible things in a new way.'

I look at him, remembering the spark from the furnace: *I'M POSSIBLE.*

'Maybe,' says Mac, 'it *is* possible to have it all.'

His ginger whiskers have grown so long that I can't see his mouth at all, but I can tell he's smiling by the way his violet eyes sparkle. My heart leaps with hope.

'You mean—we can go back to live in the lighthouse? And come here whenever we want to? But how?'

'You'd better come back every day, bonny lass,' says Smith, in his deep voice. 'If we're going to go to all the trouble of building a bridge.'

'A bridge?'

'An iron bridge, Mim.' Smith grins, his dark eyes alight with excitement. 'Stretching over the ocean between Galena and the lighthouse. Made by you and me, in the forge...'

'...and designed by me,' says Mac.

He pulls out a notebook and a pencil and licks the point.

'Now all I have to do is calculate the dimensions...'

I look at Smith over Mac's busy head, and his eye closes in a wink.

'Hear that, Samuel?' I whisper, scratching his head. 'We're going home.'

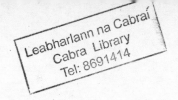
# ACKNOWLEDGEMENTS

Writing a novel is about attempting to turn the impossible into the possible. And I'm so grateful to the following people, who helped turn *The Three Impossibles* into a book:

First, my wonderful agent, Silvia Molteni, who believes in my writing and has championed it tirelessly from the beginning.

To the team at Pushkin Press; Rory Williamson, Poppy Stimpson and Elise Jackson; Tilda Johnson for her meticulous copy-editing; Thy Bui, whose cover designs make my heart sing; and above all to my fabulous editor, Sarah Odedina, who always helps me to find the true thread of the story and diplomatically reminds me to remove all the kitchen sinks I've thrown in.

I'd like to thank Michael Rosen for allowing me to use his father's wise words in the epigraph.

And finally, to two special people: Satya Robyn, whose wisdom, patience and compassionate understanding are always there; and to my dear friend Charlotte Gaskell, who listens to me sounding off about the invariable ups and downs of writing and laughs at my terrible jokes.

## More from Susie Bower

# INSPIRED
## MIGRANT WOMEN IN IRELAND
### (Vol: 1)
## DIVERSE VOICES & PERCEPTIONS

## EDITED BY
## CAROL AZAMS

**SKYLINE PUBLISHERS**

WWW.SKYLINEBUREAU.COM

Skyline Publishers is a registered Irish publishing company
(CRO: 542943)

# FIRST PUBLISHED BY SKYLINE PUBLISHERS

Dublin – Republic of Ireland, 2018
Email: Skylinepublishers@yahoo.com
Website: www.skylineBureau.com/publishing

British Library Cataloguing in Publication Data
A catalogue record for this book is available from the British Library

**Copyright © 2018 – Carol Azams**

Views expressed in this book are solely of the individual contributing writers and do not in any way reflect the views of the editor or publisher and editors. The publisher and editors hereby disclaim any responsibilities associated with them.

ISBN: 978-0-9955349-8-8

**Printed in the United Kingdom - 2018**

# Contents

## Dedication:

*This book is dedicated to migrant women all over the world.*

*May your host country bring you peace & fulfilment.*

# Acknowledgements

I am super excited to introduce you to all the amazing women who have contributed to making this book (Inspired Migrant Women in Ireland – Vol:1) a reality. I personally know some of them known for quite some time now and others I haven't even met until I started the process of this publication. There are many migrant women living in Ireland than we have featured inside this one book, and I tried my humble best to reach out to a greater number of them, expectedly, not all heeded my call to participate but at the same time, so many of them put their names forward in the first instance, they just weren't enthusiastic enough to follow through and had to drop out mid-way—I thank them all for their initial interest. I hope they can take part in the next volume.

As a Publisher and writer and fellow-migrant woman, I have nurtured the idea of using my expertise and years of experience in the publishing industry to offer my services as a way to encourage and empower more women to become published authors in order so their voices could be heard more in public …this I have achieved with this book and I hope that it becomes a source of reference and inspiration to others in some way and form.

I am particularly thankful to the following 51 women for following this through with boldness and courage as they step forward to lend their voices to what I personally call 'a new movement of women' motivated by a shared desire to have a civilized discussion around issues that affect us all in society. I also look forward to seeing some of them go from here to writing and publishing their own books in the near future.

Ladies, it has been a long journey of many months and now we have a finished product in our hands, I sincerely express my heartfelt gratitude to all of you for given your voice to this call. I am very proud of all of you. I like to wish you all, and myself—peace and fulfilment in our adopted and host country, Ireland.

# 🖐 Thank you ... 🖐

*Giovanna Rampazzo, Elena Cristofanon, Princess Pamela Toyin Akinjobi, Ava Collopy, Franca Olivera, Asia Kuzma, Anca Lupu, Ada Christine Eloji, Anna Stanuch, Claudia O'Riodan, Yemi Adenuga, L.O.D, Erika Pena, Evangeline Ngozi Omini, Frida Maurimootoo, Paola Maggiorott, Marlene Smith-Torriani, Shireen Sanders, Gloria Manyangu, Patricia Guerra, Annie Waithira Burke, Miren Samper, Deborah Onyema, Esmeralda Usiahon, Nicole Stapff, Isabella Gabacz, Elizabeth Allauigan, Ema-Amarie Idowu, Heloisa Generoso Callagy, Elena Pelendritou, Angela Sylva, Ini Usanga, Angelina Marra, Catherine Kayya Murphy, Monica Walsh, Kasia Forest, Ediones Diniz, Amaka Okonkwo, Monica Manzzi Barlocco, Marluce Lima, Thandeka Ndzondza, Ogbeyalu Okoye, Raquel Murillo Diestro, Maksuda Akhter, Ritu Gupta, Zeina Roz, Vanessa Kennedy, Matilda Chongwa, Katherin Henderson, Esther Ewulonu, Jane Beatrice Ejim.*

# INTRODUCTION

## Welcome to Inspired Migrant Women in Ireland Book.

*This brief introduction acts as a guide and provides explanation for you—the reader to a better understanding of how the book is structured so you can navigate well and enjoy your reading.*

*This book was provided as a platform to profile the contributions of the contributing writers to society, while showcasing their personalities to Irish public at the same time. It is structured in the manner that allows them to express their thoughts about what is like to be living in Ireland, and more importantly for them to share their differing viewpoints about some of the hot topics that are causes of concern for Irish residents.*

*The women were presented with six of the same questions and asked to sincerely answer all of them if they can, with an option to pick and mix a minimum of four. Their responses are based on which questions that they choose to address, these are then presented in essay style format. You will find each question as you read along and enjoy the flow of the messages therein, which I hope that you find to be useful and entertaining.* **Happy Reading!**

CAROL AZAMS (EDITOR & CEO)
SKYLINE PUBLISHERS

# *Giovanna Rampazzo*

*"If I could change something in Ireland, it would be free health care to be available to all residents."*

*M*y name is Giovanna Rampazzo. I am Italian. Since January 2017, I have been working in the Graduate Research office of DIT. I have been living in Dublin since 2001. I moved to Dublin mainly because I wanted to have a better life and was frustrated with the limited prospects of Italy's stagnant job market and with the extreme difficulty of conducting further studies without any family support. In Ireland, thanks to the economic boom, I could easily find work and return to education. Here I had the opportunity to work and study and over the years I completed an HND, a BA, an MPhil and also a PhD. I did it all supporting myself completely, with some assistance from VEC grants which covered my fees.

I love seafood, especially octopus and squid, my favourite Irish dish is seafood chowder. I do not miss Italy, but I enjoy going there on holidays once a year. I sometimes miss the friends and relatives that I still have over there. There are many things that I love about Ireland and specifically Dublin.

I love that Dublin is very cosmopolitan, there are people from everywhere in the world and it's great to constantly meet people of different nationalities and cultural backgrounds. For this reason, I never felt like an outsider. Dublin is very vibrant and there's a wide choice of concerts, shows, cultural events to go to. Of course, I love the fact that it's much easier to find work here, and to receive a fair wage, than in many other countries. I also love that there are grants and opportunities for mature students to return to educational pursuits.

*What are some of the most challenges faced by migrant women in Ireland? (b) What advice would you give to young and upcoming migrants women?*

Personally, I don't find life in Ireland challenging because I am a migrant. Being from a country that is a part of the European Union made my life easier, but I know that many non-EU citizens struggle to get a working visa or to have their qualifications recognised to work in Ireland. I found Dublin very welcoming and it's easier for me to live here rather than in Italy. The only challenging thing is that healthcare is private in Ireland and if you don't qualify for a medical card routine GP visits and medicines can cost a lot. It is useful for women moving to Ireland to bring over a supply of medicines they routinely need (e.g. the pill, allergy medicines) to avoid having to spend a lot of money just on prescriptions.

I would advise women coming to Ireland to take advantage of the educational opportunities available in the country, in terms of grants, free courses, and flexible study programmes.

*There is a worldwide momentum for gender pay-gap, do you think that women have suddenly started to speak up in demand of effective change, or do you think that men have only started to pay more attention and listening more to women?*

I think that gender pay-gap is a worldwide problem that has been highlighted in the past year thanks to the uproar generated by the **#MeToo** movement, which has helped address gender inequalities and forced men to face the fact that women are being discriminated against in many ways. I don't believe men would admit that it is true or do anything to address the problem otherwise. According to recent statistics, women are paid about 14% less than men in Ireland, so action is needed to change policies and guarantee equal wages to women working in Ireland.

*Do you think that Ireland has done more to protect the rights of women? If you answered yes, in your opinion —why are there so many stories about domestic violence? If you answered no, then what do you think Ireland should do more to protect women?*

I believe that Ireland needs to do much more to protect the rights of women. Frequent news reports about the Tuam babies, Magdalene laundries survivors, rapists being given ridiculously lenient sentences, and the fight for reproductive rights, all demonstrates that women are still treated unfairly. Policies should change to guarantee women equal protection and rights.

*What has been a defining moment in your life/career or business since living in Ireland? (b) If you could have breakfast with any three Irish women, who would you choose and why?*

The most defining moment in my life in Ireland was to be awarded a doctorate from DIT in 2017. I would like to have breakfast with Christina Noble. I think she is an extraordinary woman because, in spite of the hardship she had to endure throughout her life, she was successful in setting up a foundation to help children in need in Vietnam.

*The government recently launched 'Project Ireland 2040', which the Taoiseach said is a document about building a republic of opportunity. Have you seen this document, if so do you think that in its mapping there is provision to create an enabling space for migrant women to be heard and lead? (b) The Prime Minister is the son of a migrant father from India, does this alone give you the slightest hope for the future of the children of migrants in this country, and why? (c) If you have the power to change anything in Ireland, what will that be?*

Project Ireland 2040 looks like a very ambitious project and I hope that it will achieve at least some of its outcome in terms of wellbeing, equality and opportunity for people in Ireland. Of course, the project would be very beneficial for migrant women in terms of granting equality and inclusion. I do not think that being the son of an immigrant makes the Taoiseach more sympathetic to the plight of migrants. Significantly, in 2008 he proposed to deport unemployed migrants to their countries of origin and warned bout cultural differences that might prevent migrants from integrating into Irish society.

*If I could change something in Ireland*, it would be free healthcare to be available to all residents.

# *Elena Cristofanon*

*"A big step forward is the legalization of abortion, on which Irish people voted at the May 2018 referendum."*

*M*y name is Elena Cristofanon, I moved to Ireland four years ago from my beautiful country, Italy. I graduated in Art History in the perfect city to do so, Rome, the place of my heart, where I lived for almost ten years and that I left in tears. After what it may seem a complicated journey, I established myself as a photo editor, graphic and web designer in Dublin. Becoming a freelance it seemed what made more sense to me, as I wanted to work cultivating all my interests at the same time. I have no chance to get bored with my job as it varies from day to day. It gives me the opportunity to meet many people from different backgrounds, which make every job a new adventure.

Being self-employed also gives me the flexibility to travel a lot and, basically, whenever I want to; which is awesome as I love travelling, discovering new places and cultures and at the same time immersing myself in different realities and, of course, taking photographs – one of my passion. I consider my experience in Ireland my third life. I was born in the North of Italy, grew up in a small village in Piedmont where I lived for 19 years. I moved to Rome – to my second life, to study at La Sapienza, not because there was not a closer University to my hometown, but because when I visited Rome for a holiday and just felt like I belonged there; that Rome was my place to be. When I moved there, I think I spent about a year to get used to what it seemed to be a different culture. Yes, it obviously was my own country, but there were plenty of differences between my village and the capital city. First of all, the size: 5,000 people against 5 million. Then, funny enough, the language. In Rome, they do not speak a dialect, like in many other cities and towns of Italy, but they do use a huge number of idioms and expressions and have a peculiar sense of humour that to a girl from the North sounded like a new code to learn. And I loved it. I enjoyed every single day I spent there, with beauty hidden in every corner of the city, a lively cultural life, with over 50 cinemas to choose from, and plenty of delicious food… In short, my paradise.

When I moved to Dublin it was kind of the same at the beginning: a new code to learn (much more difficult, though), new people to meet every day, new discoveries etc. I really enjoyed the experience for the first three months, when I was living every day as a tourist. But then decided to stay and not going back as I had planned, things got complicated. I looked at everything from a different perspective, not care-free anymore. And I started missing a lot of things about Italy. First, being able to communicate with anybody in any context. To me, to echo Karl Jasper, home is where I understand, and I am understood. I didn't feel at home. That's very frustrating and the more time passes the worse it gets as I still feel I cannot express myself in all the shades I am able to communicate in, using my mother tongue.

I also miss the Italian architecture. Don't think it is silly. Environment affects people, their behaviour and their mood. I miss the gorgeous, warmth facades of Roman buildings. I miss the atmosphere of sunsets in spring; I miss understanding people at a glance; I miss inexpensive fresh vegetables in the markets; I miss the sense of surprise of a rainy morning; I miss home. On the one hand, there are various aspects of Ireland that I like a lot and that I will miss when I decide to embrace my fourth life in the next country. Above all, the kindness of people, the respect that in general Irish people show to other human beings, no matter who they are and where they come from. At least, this is my personal experience.

*What are some of the most challenges faced by migrant women in Ireland? (b) What advice would you give to young and upcoming migrants women?*

I didn't feel I had to face particular challenges as a migrant woman in Ireland. Generally speaking, I feel that Irish people respect women probably more than in Italy or in Southern Europe in general. I've never felt discriminated or treated differently by Irish people because I am a woman, which in reverse, it happens every now and then in Italy, where sexism is part of our culture, even on an unconscious level. Which is obviously heritage of hundreds of years of a male-dominated culture, but that was increased by the last 20 years of very sexist cultural politics, run with any means, especially mass media.

*Do you think that Ireland has done more to protect the rights of women? If you answered yes, in your opinion —why are there so many stories about domestic violence? If you answered no, then what do you think Ireland should do more to protect women?*

I think Ireland is a very safe country to move to for young women, who can enjoy an enriching experience abroad without big risks. On the other hand, I'm aware that in Ireland there is a plague of domestic violence and mistreated women. But, as far as I know, that affects a particular segment of the population, troubled also with drugs and alcohol problems, whose scale, by the way, shocked and still shocks me. There is for sure room for improvement regarding women's condition in Ireland - like anywhere else in the world. But, in my opinion, a big step forward is the legalization of abortion, on which Irish people voted at the May 2018 referendum. However, something that would affect positively not just women but all the people living in Ireland is a structured plan of building a huge number of decent houses. Ireland has done great with its economic politics, drastically reducing the taxation for big companies. As a result, thousands of people have come to live here seeking jobs, making Ireland a multicultural country, but increasing the demand for houses so badly that now finding a decent room in a decent shared house is an absolute nightmare, in terms of prices and living conditions. I won't even mention the utopia of finding a non-shared apartment without spending a whole salary on it.

*What has been a defining moment in your life/career or business since living in Ireland?*

Despite the tough housing situation, Ireland gives a lot of opportunities to develop studies and careers. I could establish myself as a self-employed very easily and quite quickly and that changed my life. Another real turning point for my professional life was meeting Francesca La Morgia (Assistant Professor in Clinical Speech and Language Studies in Trinity College Dublin and coordinator of the Irish Research Network in Childhood Bilingualism and Multilingualism) and begun to be part of her organization Mother Tongues, which aims to raise awareness of the benefits and challenges associated with bilingualism. Mother Tongues provides advice and support for parents, education professionals, health care professionals, businesses and for anyone working in multilingual environments.

When I found out about Mother Tongues I really wanted to join them in some way, but I was nor a linguist neither a speech therapist or anything like that, so I was really just tempting my fortune when I emailed Francesca. Little did I know that my design skills were something that she was really looking for at that moment. So, it began my adventure with Mother Tongues, where I could meet a group of incredible women (almost all of them from abroad) who shared their various experiences with me, making me feel better and part of a community. Little by little, we built the project of a Mother Tongues Festival. Dr La Morgia thought that I could be the right person to take care of it and so, with great joy, I became the Festival Manager. The Festival's first edition took place on the 24th February 2018 and it was a resounding success with over 300 people attending, 22 workshops and performances in over 10 different languages; featured on the TV news and in the main Irish newspapers. Our festival allowed people to connect through language, and diversity did not represent a barrier, but rather a reason to get together and celebrate. What I experienced that day, the good vibes, the atmosphere of the community gave me hope – more than anything else - for the future of children of migrants living in Ireland.

*If you have the power to change anything in Ireland, what will that be?*

**If I had the power to change something in Ireland**, I would build enough houses to satisfy the demand, in order to decrease the crazy rents that currently people have to pay.

# *Princess Pamela Akinjobi*

*"One thing evident from the prevalence and patterning of domestic violence is that it has no boundaries and can happen to women across all groups, religion, race, and ethnicity"*

*I* am Princess Pamela Olutoyin Akinjobi, a Journalist, Author and TV Presenter. I am a double Princess in a rare occurrence. I was born into royalty, from a Royal kingdom family in Ogun state Nigeria, and I am married to Prince Ogunwusi from a prominent Royal Kingdom and current ruling house in Osun State, Nigeria. I am in my 50s and can be regarded as an accomplished Executive with working experience of over thirty years in different fields. I started my working career as a hotelier/caterer in the Hotel Industry in the mid 80's and moved on to the corporate world in the 90's after training as a bilingual secretary. I have worked for reputable companies both on full time, part time and freelance capacities in Ireland, UK, Nigeria and a few other countries. I have toed significant paths including Community Development, Administration, Workshop Facilitation, Journalism, Public relations, International relations, Print and Broadcast Media. I am currently a columnist with Metro Eireann Newspaper, run an online TV and manage a media outfit, Echoes International, which is an organisation with a mission to project and promote professionals that are sources of creativity and value to their society. We also report from the diverse section of the migrant and host communities, issues that are often ignored but are important and beneficial to their development and growth. As a media consultant, I strive to bridge gaps of multicultural understanding between migrants and their host communities. With a passion for diversity I have reported diverse range of issues within the migrant communities within and outside the shores of Ireland.

In 2004 I was the only African woman invited by renowned Irish publisher Sarah Webb, to contribute to 'Travelling Light', a book compiling articles by Ireland's top women writers. The book was published to help raise funds for a hospital in Uganda. After that, I personally researched and interviewed women from different African countries living in Ireland, to stimulate and inform debate on their migration experiences, and in 2005 I documented their stories in 'Her story', (a book that shares true life migration experiences of African women living in Ireland). 'Her story', published by the African women's network (Akidwa), created significant immigration waves in Ireland, changing commonly held stereotypical assumptions about African women. This precipitated former President of Ireland Mary McAleese to host me with members of the African Women's Network for discussion and deliberation on issues concerning African women in Ireland and the need for their inclusion in policy making. I have championed so many causes including helping to reshape the migrant communities for effective integration and inclusion process through my media and Public relations work. I interact and work with women across the world, including participating at the United Nations. I also make significant contribution as a Research Writer/Producer to various local, international and governmental bodies, as well as non-governmental and women organisations. In addition, I am involved in different charities including my own personal effort, 'Pamela Royal Foundation', born out of the desire to help those in dire need. I am a founding member and Director of Women Writers in Ireland Network (WINNI), established by University College Dublin in 2007. Women writers, like women activists, have always done significant amount of heavy intellectual work that needs a lifting so part of the aim of the network was to demonstrate the importance of women writers to the literary world, and to bring them the critical attention they deserve. Contributions of women writers often receive scant attention and go unrecognised and the idea of setting up the network was to empower women writers and keep them represented on the shelf space. WINNI Network was well managed for several years but became silent after the recession set in and funding was no longer available for its activities.

I have lived in Ireland for about 20 years and the beautiful scenery of the country and natural unspoilt environment resonates with my nature. To be realistic, I can no longer stand the scorching sun back home, so I prefer the colder climate even though the country has one of the oddest changing weather systems. I love Ireland as the most welcoming city in Europe. The wonderful national parks, enormous castles, green hills and peaceful valleys are some of the delight I am enjoying. I'm not sure if I have a particular favourite food, but I do have a few good Nigerian dishes that tickles my fancy. I would say I love natural healthy drink made from fruits and herbal extracts. I've been a health freak since I rediscovered the simple rules of healthy eating. I miss experiencing my culture in the real sense of it, the hustling and bustling drama that ensures daily on the streets, visits from family and friends, exclusive parties, communal settings, festivals, fashion, clothes and many others. Nigeria is a country you can call 'one big drama' or soap opera that unfolds on a daily basis because one can watch interesting TV series just sitting on the balcony of a house. These and many other things make Nigeria exceptional without equal.

*What are some of the most challenges faced by migrant women in Ireland? (b) What advice would you give to young and upcoming migrants women?*

Gender and migration remain a critical issue especially for women who are not socially and economically empowered. One thing evident from the prevalence and patterning of domestic violence is that it has no boundaries and can happen to women across all groups, religion, race, and ethnicity. For migrant women, there are key issues which have significant impact and prevent them from bringing such issues into the mainstream. Some factors include migrant women facing dual problem of racism from the wider society and rejection from their own communities if they report abuse. In addition, cultural differences and lack of understanding are significant barriers to migrant women seeking help and protection. Despite the so-called feminisation in migration, the narratives of women have gained far less attention.

In Ireland, migrant women need to be engaged more in the job market because there are no clear methods in Ireland taken to increase their engagement in the job market, thus a high percentage of the skills and experience of these women don't match what they do. Expensive childcare, coping with managing the home, husband and children also poses difficulties for some. And for the undocumented, legal status, immobility that accompanies lack of documentation, racism and other factors are key issues affecting many. For other women not in this category, competition with other workers, gender related discrimination are added risks. Therefore, for a smooth transition, it is advisable for women who wish to migrate to have a thorough understanding of the immigration laws of the country they wish to migrate, and this includes laws on taxes, housing, banking, attaining citizenship etc.

*What has been a defining moment in your life/career or business since living in Ireland? (b) If you could have breakfast with any three Irish women, who would you choose and why?*

For me, one of my defining moments of my life was when I wrote my first novel in my late teens in the early 80's. The excitement was deep, and even though I didn't get my work published then, it triggered something that has come with me this far and remained a part of my subconsciousness. Another defining moment was when I began to write, edit and produce content for print media. I published my first article in a prominent magazine in the early 90's back home in Nigeria. My captivating titles and writing style drew readers to my column and I was swept by the various manners of their reactions in writing which were published by the editor of the magazine. That experience defined my writing path. Decades later came yet another defining experience which encouraged me from my very first day with Metro Eireann in year 2000. It was a big leap into the real world and that spurred me to further my Journalism career. I can also recall the adrenaline that shot through me when I picked up a professional video camera for the very first time to film and make a documentary on women writers in Ireland, when I started a talk show in Ireland in 2007 and when I produced my first online TV News. All those tasks sparked the defining moment that has continued to set a tone for my career in life.

If I could have breakfast with any woman in Ireland, I would choose former Irish President Mary McAleese again. Her public persona was charming and the experience with her was great. I would also like to dine with Mary Robinson, the first female President of the Republic of Ireland. Both women are synonymous with improving the lives of women. My third preference would be Sinead Burke, the inspirational public speaker, broadcaster, blogger and school teacher.

*The government recently launched a 'Project Ireland 2040', which the Taoiseach said is a document about building a republic of opportunity. Have you seen this document, if so do you think that in its mapping there is provision to create an enabling space for migrant women to be heard and lead? (b) The Prime Minister is the son of a migrant father from India, does this alone give you the slightest hope for the future of the children of migrants in this country, and why?*

We cannot predict the future as things are, but if Project Ireland 2040 fulfils its objectives of making Ireland a better country for everyone, and guiding Ireland's development in the right direction for the next 22 years, then the country's situation will no doubt be favourable in all ramifications for all citizens, migrant women inclusive. No one can categorically have clear cut answers on issues to do with immigrants especially as perceptions about them keep changing. However, Rotimi Adebari's election as a Mayor and Prime Minister Leo Varadkar of Asian parentage has given many migrants reasons to feel optimistic because these men have proved possible what minorities could only imagine before. So, we continue to ask, will Leo Varadkar be the first and last 'son of an immigrant' Prime Minister? Only time will tell.

# Ava Collopy
### Living, Working, and Protesting in Ireland
*"Now, I understand that people may get concerned about immigrants taking over jobs when Ireland typically doesn't have a lot of jobs."*

*I* almost always say, "I'm from Oregon, in the U.S." rather than saying, "I'm from the U.S." because there are many things the U.S. government does without the vote or consent of its people, whereas the state of Oregon better represents my values. And since becoming an English as a Second Language Teacher I try to remember to always say "the U.S." rather than "America", and do not refer to myself as an "American." This is out of respect for some of my fellow teachers and students, who are also from the Americas and thus also identify strongly as "Americans". To clear up the confusion I always add, "It's the state north of California" because most people haven't heard of Oregon but will have heard of Los Angeles and San Francisco. When there's confusion I can add things like, near Seattle, near where grunge music was invented, or near where Starbucks originated, and this always clears up the confusion about the whereabouts of my home state. It's no worries though; I've met people in the U.S. who thought Oregon was next to Minnesota (in the centre of the country). I smiled and politely corrected them that it's on the Pacific Coast. I have been in Ireland for over five years and have stayed for two main reasons:

1. I am of Irish heritage and always wanted to visit. Collopy is a County Limerick name, and Ava is Irish as well. In Irish my name is Aoibhe Ní Cholpa (pronounced ee'fa nee hholpuh). The Ní in traditional Irish culture indicates that I am a "daughter of", whereas Ó Colpa would mean "a son or grandson of", though after the British invasion, when Irish names were Anglicized, our family name was changed to O'Collopy and helped to denote that our family was Irish-Catholic and not Protestant like the English after the Reformation.

2. College, as it turns out, is drastically less expensive here than it is in the U.S., yet some colleges will take federal student loans from the U.S. There's really no sense in staying in the U.S. for college when European degrees are often better quality for less money. I have had many classmates who came here from the U.S. and took out loans to pay for tuition, rent, and everything else and they came out with far less debt than they would have had by staying in the U.S. Additionally, they had a great, international experience.

For the most part I haven't missed the U.S., I have missed Oregon terribly, and the West Coast generally. For financial reasons I haven't been back even once; it's a lot of money to go clear to the other side of the North American continent and there are no direct flights to the Portland International Airport. I think the closest flight is the Aer Lingus direct to San Francisco, which is a good 636 miles (1,023 km) from Portland. I miss everything about Oregon; the people, the gorgeous scenery—ranging from rain-soaked forests on the west side to deserts on the east side, how completely unique it is, how political yet laidback it is—all of it. But, as the saying goes, "money doesn't grow on trees." Oregon and Ireland actually have a lot in common and I don't just mean in terms of cold, rainy, and wildly unpredictable weathers. There are parts of Dublin that reminds me of Portland, especially a couple of eclectic streets in Temple Bar Square that are bursting with local, underground artisans and their work, and small, excellent indie cafés. And when I spent the day in Galway with a friend of mine I was surprised at how much it was, like a little Irish Portland. This isn't entirely surprising given that a great many people in Oregon are of Irish heritage; most of the Caucasians in Oregon are of Irish, German, Swedish, or Scottish heritage (I'm all four of those).

*What are some of the most challenges faced by migrant women in Ireland? (b) What advice would you give to young and upcoming migrants women?*

I was recently at a Trade Union rally which was ostensibly for one issue, but the people gathered brought up several issues, which helped me to know more about what is going on for immigrants, refugees, and asylum seekers in Ireland that, as an immigrant from a "Schedule 1" country, I wouldn't normally be made aware off, especially as the popular news media here normally ignores the issues faced by these demographic groups.

Anyway, while waiting at the Garden of Remembrance for that rally to start, some very active activists were handing out papers and flyers with more information about different issues faced by immigrants to Ireland, and other issues such as the ongoing genocide of Palestinian people by people in power in Israel (a country supported by the U.S. without the vote of the people). I became aware that asylum seekers are being denied access to jobs. Now, I understand that people may get concerned about immigrants taking over jobs when Ireland typically doesn't have a lot of jobs. However, immigrants, especially non-native English speakers, typically take the jobs that non-immigrants think they're too good for, such as janitorial work, au pair, or making sandwiches and coffee at small shops. My take is that if a country can't afford to let immigrants, refugees, and asylum seekers have jobs then why let them enter your country in the first place? To look good politically but then not take proper care of these people? It costs the government money to provide things like emergency housing or emergency health coverage for all legal residents in Ireland will be treated at hospital in an emergency, this costs the Irish citizens who pay taxes; these people also want to work and pay taxes back into the system, thus taking away any burden from Irish citizens. It makes no logical sense to deny them access to jobs when they genuinely want to pay back into the system and have the self-respect and dignity that comes with being able to do so—which is the same thing that Irish immigrants wanted when they entered other countries.

Many of the people in Ireland are quite welcoming to immigrants while others, especially those from rural parts of Ireland, can be extremely narrow-minded towards "foreigners". I know one Irish couple from County Dublin who moved to a village next to Mullingar, in the middle of the country, and they and their children were treated very badly because they were outsiders. This seems wildly hypocritical given that Ireland has traditionally been a land of emigrants; people have been leaving Ireland for places like the U.S., Canada, Australia, and even Argentina for centuries. Yet some people around here can't seem to wrap their minds around the idea of emigrants from other parts of the world immigrating to Ireland. They will simply have to get used to sights like children with very dark skin walking to school in the same Catholic school uniforms that Irish children also wear. As we go ever forwards with time people need to accept change. That is why there are so many marches, protests, and demonstrations in Dublin city centre and elsewhere in the country.

Anyway, while waiting at the Garden of Remembrance for that rally to start, some very active activists were handing out papers and flyers with more information about different issues faced by immigrants to Ireland, and other issues such as the ongoing genocide of Palestinian people by people in power in Israel (a country supported by the U.S. without the vote of the people). I became aware that asylum seekers are being denied access to jobs. Now, I understand that people may get concerned about immigrants taking over jobs when Ireland typically doesn't have a lot of jobs. However, immigrants, especially non-native English speakers, typically take the jobs that non-immigrants think they're too good for, such as janitorial work, au pair, or making sandwiches and coffee at small shops.

My take is that if a country can't afford to let immigrants, refugees, and asylum seekers have jobs then why let them enter your country in the first place? To look good politically but then not take proper care of these people? It costs the government money to provide things like emergency housing or emergency health coverage for all legal residents in Ireland will be treated at hospital in an emergency, this costs the Irish citizens who pay taxes; these people also want to work and pay taxes back into the system, thus taking away any burden from Irish citizens. It makes no logical sense to deny them access to jobs when they genuinely want to pay back into the system and have the self-respect and dignity that comes with being able to do so—which is the same thing that Irish immigrants wanted when they entered other countries. Many of the people in Ireland are quite welcoming to immigrants while others, especially those from rural parts of Ireland, can be extremely narrow-minded towards "foreigners". I know one Irish couple from County Dublin who moved to a village next to Mullingar, in the middle of the country, and they and their children were treated very badly because they were outsiders. This seems wildly hypocritical given that Ireland has traditionally been a land of emigrants; people have been leaving Ireland for places like the U.S., Canada, Australia, and even Argentina for centuries. Yet some people around here can't seem to wrap their minds around the idea of emigrants from other parts of the world immigrating to Ireland. They will simply have to get used to sights like children with very dark skin walking to school in the same Catholic school uniforms that Irish children also wear. As we go ever forwards with time people need to accept change. That is why there are so many marches, protests, and demonstrations in Dublin city centre and elsewhere in the country. The Irish, though kind people generally, have a serious problem with not speaking up or with burying and forgetting problems. Too often people are silent and complacent, or afraid. No one will deliver your rights and social justice to you, you must stand up and claim them, or fight for them. It's usually best to get involved with non-profit organizations or unions so you won't have to stand alone.

*There is a worldwide momentum for gender pay-gap, do you think that women have suddenly started to speak up in demand of effective change, or do you think that men have only started to pay more attention and listening more to women?*

Around the world women do not get equal representation in government or business, little girls are married to middle-aged men (child brides; common in parts of Africa and the Middle East—even though youth pregnancy and childbirth are extremely dangerous), girls have their genitals ritualistically mutilated so they won't enjoy sex and will be completely subservient pieces of property for their future husbands (FGM; Female Genital Mutilation, common in parts of Africa and elsewhere), women may be imprisoned for being raped as it may be seen as premarital or extramarital sex while the rapists, suffer no ill consequences (this has happened in recent years in Saudi Arabia for example), girls do not have equal access to education, women on the whole do not get equal pay for equal work even in the most developed countries, "domestic violence" is often disregarded as a private family matter or a woman's fault, and in places where abortion is illegal the same amount of women and girls seek abortions but they often die from unsafe, illegal abortions. The World Health Organization has shown photos of young women who have been disembowelled and died from unsafe, illegal abortions. For me, two things about this and all the other abuses against women stand out most of all:

1.  Every government's complete disregard for women and lack of willingness to change things so that women and girls are actually treated with basic human dignity and compassion.

2.  How much and how often it's older women that enforce these horrific abuses on girls and other women.

There are actually many compassionate men out there who care deeply about improving things for women. For example, one of my fellow ESL teachers, who's married to an immigrant woman from Ukraine and recently became a father, is involved with the Social Democrats to promote the "Yes" vote in the upcoming referendum. There are many men who genuinely have hatred for any women who stand up for their rights, but there are also plenty of women who pass on the generations of abuse and oppression to other women and to girls. There are many men who are actively fighting against injustices against women. And I think more would be active in this fight, alongside their sisters, if they were invited in more. It is quite understandable that a great many women, after perhaps being gang-raped, denied equal wages for equal work, and forced to flee her home country to get an abortion to save her life, might grow to hate men. However, this "us and them" paradigm is ultimately inaccurate and unhelpful. We could get more support for women's human rights issues if we engaged and encouraged all the good men who believe in treating women like human beings to join in the fight for gender equality instead of blaming all men for the crimes committed by some of them. A part of it is simply educating them on the issues. Many men may take it for granted that of course women will get paid the same as them for the same work and simply don't know that any inequality is happening. Men do have a tendency to go along with a kind of "tunnel vision" that can prevent them from seeing a whole and complete picture of things. Or it may just not occur to them to look for the information. For example, my thesis supervisor in college was very much a Feminist, completely believed in equality between the sexes, but was surprised when I told him that abortion rights were in no way a guarantee in the U.S. just because it was a post-Roe versus Wade U.S.; religious and political conservatives in many (if not all) states kept trying to pass laws to limit access to safe, legal abortion further and further every year, and they seemed to be winning too, since most liberals were being complacent and not fighting for women's rights. He had no idea that that was happening. Some women like to keep espousing the myth that it is men and only men that keep oppressing women. This is absolutely not true. Women are very much complacent in the abuse of women, and many women are quite active in abusing other women. You can call this "Stockholm Syndrome": identifying with your abductors/abusers, and then even helping them. Setting men up as the only enemy is not an accurate picture of things, and it is very likely turning away a lot of men who would be allies in women's fight for rights if they weren't told that they're basically horrible people who are guilty of abusing women even when they themselves have not taken an active part in the injustices against women.

All of that being said I think the global push for equal pay for equal work is a fantastic point to pick on because it means admitting that women and our contributions are equal and that we do contribute a great deal to society; we aren't just at our jobs to look pretty or decorate the office, we actually contribute an incredible amount of work to society as do our brothers—that we're pretty and often do a little decorating around the office are just added benefits. I do think women have begun to speak up more about this and many other issues. I think the majority of women were quite aware but quite silent about all of the women's inequality and abuse issues throughout my entire life until just recently. Most people were quiet about issues of racial inequality, and other top social issues, until recently as well.

I've been greatly heartened to see that there have been many protests in the U.S. regarding lethal force being used by our police disproportionately against black people, that there have been walk-outs of public schools in regard to the rampant use and misuse of guns in the U.S., including many protests in several countries in regard to several different women's/gender inequality issues. I definitely think people are speaking up a lot more about the challenges in      society that we still need to fix. I think the majority of people were far too quiet about these issues throughout most of my life (from the 1980's to very recently.) And I think a lot of it is because of the younger Millennials. I don't think my generation, the non-digital native Millennials or older Millennials, or Generation X (the generation before mine), did enough to address social injustice issues. In fact, in the 1990's MTV had a campaign called Rock the Vote to try to motivate young people to vote. Young people just didn't care and didn't take any responsibility for maintaining their and others' civil rights. It isn't surprising then that we keep seeing political and religious conservatives trying to scale back civil rights in different Western countries, and sometimes succeeding at doing so. A freer society with more rights is not just something that you can take for granted, it's something that needs to be maintained. And sadly, it seems that the majority of the Baby Boomers, who were once very active in trying to change society and push things forwards, have become conservative with age and basically betrayed all the principles they had when they were younger. A lot of them now be-moan the way society is today and say things like, "Back when I was growing up we had family values" and forget that:

- They're the ones that changed the social and family structures in the first place, and; there were good reasons for why they changed things.

For example, hundreds of women died every year from unsafe, illegal abortions in the U.S. before Roe vs. Wade in the 1970's. Or that when they were children, in the1950's, in the U.S. black people were still segregated; they couldn't use public drinking fountains, swimming pools, or toilets that white people used. Also, they were protesting an unjust war and military draft for Viet Nam and Korea. I'm less familiar with the Baby Boomer activism in other countries but I know that generation worked hard to change things in several countries, not just the U.S. The Boomers started a social revolution but unfortunately never finished it. Now many of them like to hark back to imagined wonderful times and scale back human rights for this imaginary past instead of continuing forwards. That generation also has a complete disconnect from the economic realities faced by younger people today. They claim that young people don't have money and are in massive debt because of laziness because, "back in my day we worked while we were in college and paid our way through it", being completely oblivi-ous to the fact that the value of our money has gone down massively with inflation, wages have come nowhere even vaguely close to matching inflation, and the Boomers are the main people who ruined the West's once strong economy in the 1980's with their greed.

People need to understand that protesting injustice can never be a one-off event, it has to be a way of life. If you don't consistently tell those in power that you want justice, and explain what you mean by justice, they certainly won't bother troubling themselves to put in the extra effort to give you your legal rights. And people on the street protesting must always remember that it isn't for the government or anyone else to give you your rights—they are already yours! It's a matter of getting those in power to admit that they are your rights already and then make sure that laws follow this reality.

*Do you think that Ireland has done more to protect the rights of women? If you answered yes, in your opinion —why are there so many stories about domestic violence? If you answered no, then what do you think Ireland should do more to protect women?*

I don't think the Republic of Ireland (Éire) or any other country has done nearly enough to protect the rights of women and girls. That is why activists keep having to take to the streets. Around the 1900's women all over the West had to take to marching down the streets to protest having no voting rights. They were at times beaten or arrested for having the so-called audacity to claim that they were deserving of equal rights to men, who were supposedly their absolute superiors; of course, many women in that time did not protest and did not like the Feminists. Too many women and men—today act like "Feminism" is a dirty word and forget that no girl or woman today would have equal education, voting rights, or most of the jobs women hold today such as lawyer, banker, doctor, dentist, or CEO if it weren't for Feminism and Feminists. Though admittedly the trouble also is that some women these days think "Feminism" is synonymous with "man-hating". It is not. If you look up the definition of the word "Feminism" you'll see that it means "gender equality" and not "all men are scum". Now women and men are once again having to take to the streets to say that women deserve human rights. They're having to say that women have a right to not be gang-raped by men and then brag about it on social media as with a recent rape case in Spain. This is 2018 and we're still having to tell the world that women's bodies are not pieces of public property for men or the state to do with as they wish, without suffering any consequences. Until now, the Irish government treated pregnant women as worthless vessels whose lives don't matter. This is largely a hang-over from when Ireland was essentially a Catholic vassal rather than an actual nation-state, that if a pregnant woman in Ireland had a crisis pregnancy, a life-threatening miscarriage, or even cancer she is denied any health care that may harm her foetus in any way, even if not getting treatment will definitely kill her. I have some friends who are Catholic and are good people, but the Catholic Church in Ireland was quite horrific. For example, they used to have some-thing called the Magdalene Laundries. These were workhouses that unmarried girls and women who had had any sexual contact whether consensual or by rape—were sent to as punishment. They were basi-cally concentration camps where girls would often give birth while in agonizing pain. The nuns would not allow them any help, saying their pain was their penance. Among other things, this led to girls dying in labour, and massive graves full of dead newborn babies, as well as babies being sold on the black market to wealthy couples from the U.S. The last Magdalene Laundry was shut down as recently as the 1990's.

In 2012 Savita Halappanavar, a happily married Indian dentist liv-ing in County Galway, suffered a miscarriage and because of the Irish law that has now been recently repealed, she died because a doomed foetal heartbeat was deemed far more important than her heartbeat. No one in the Irish government suffered any negative consequences because of this. No one but her husband, family, friends, and the In-dian immigrant community in this country. Until now pregnant women all over Ireland, and their families were the only ones who had to worry that should they have any complications during their pregnancies they might wind up lying in a hospital bed, in agonizing pain for days, while doctors watch them die. At the school where I work there has been at least one pregnant teacher at all times the whole time I've worked there and this issue hits even harder when you're looking at your work-mates and thinking, "Wow, if she has any complications they'll murder her by not intervening with life-saving medical care because a foetal heartbeat is considered more of a human being than a full-grown woman."

Finally, Many of us, including most Irish government officials, though in no way taking a casual attitude towards human foetuses or abortion in general, believes that women own our own bodies and that preg-nant women are not vessels with no rights who deserve to die if they have complications during pregnancy and therefore joined forces and went for the Yes vote, which in essence means that women in Ireland will finally be treated as human beings for a change.

*The Prime Minister is the son of a migrant father from India, does this alone give you the slightest hope for the future of the children of migrants in this country, and why? (b) If you have the power to change anything in Ireland, what will that be?*

The idea of a Taoiseach (Prime Minister) having an immigrant par-ent might sound hopeful with regards to improving things for immi-grants, but Irish politicians, like most politicians elsewhere, have a ten-dency to maintain the status quo and care only to appease their sup-porters rather than do their job and represent the people. Most Taoi-seach's in my opinion have been quite self-serving and corrupt, like most politicians. At least Mr. Varadkar has supported the campaign to change the Irish Constitution and stop killing women with the 8th Amendment to the Irish Constitution. This at least this gives women more fully legal rights—and this is very much an immigrant women's issue since they can't necessarily travel to England for health care. But it is important to remember that Ireland, like the U.S., has still yet to have a woman leader of the country. Ireland has had two women presidents, but that role is mainly a figurehead and ceremonial posi-tion. Every Taoiseach I've seen has been an excellent representation of maintaining the status quo and this one is no exception. However, I think there is hope for the future of the children of immigrants to Ireland because the youth of the country is the hope; as Irish children grow up with classmates from places like Latvia, Lithuania, Ukraine, Nigeria, and India they will, as children do, simply adapt to this. Things are much better in Ireland now than they used to be. For example, an Irishman I know who was born in 1973 and raised in County Dublin once told me that the first time he saw a black person in real life was when he was 11. He saw one single black man while walking around Abbey and O'Connell streets. Now if you walk around Dublin the ethnicities are quite diverse, even outside the city centre. He himself was surprised when he was riding the LUAS one day in the past few years and saw a dark-skinned boy of about 12 or so in Irish uniforms, calling out to a classmate with a thick Dublin accent and using the local vernacular: "Ah yeah, she's a bleedin' madyoke so she is!" Things have changed here, and they continue changing going forward. No one can stop that. And regardless of what the government does, one thing that is quite distinctive about the Irish is their adaptability. It is a part of why my people always end up doing well for themselves wherever they go.

*When we went to the U.S. we were pariahs; diseased famine emigrants of the hated Catholic version of Christianity. In about a century we had a U.S. president in the White House.*

Older people in Ireland will find these changes very hard but the younger ones are growing up with the children of immigrants being part of the normal scenery of their daily lives. I have little to no faith in almost all of the current politicians but have a lot of faith in the youth of Ireland, and I think that others should as well.

*If I could change one thing in Ireland* it would be the part of the vast majority of those born and raised here that makes them act as if they're afraid to speak up; there is a complacency in them, a seeming fear of standing up for things they believe in, and a fear of drawing out into the open and dealing with longstanding problems and a general desire to bury problems that have been unearthed. For example, recently it was found that the government has not taken proper steps to ensure that women who are found to have the first stages of cervical cancer are actually informed in a timely fashion. Some women have only found out 18 months to three years after a doctor had discovered cervical cell abnormalities. Some of the Irish teachers I work with have said that this reminds them of something that happened around 1994; the Irish blood service took donations from a U.S. company and it turned out that the company had taken blood from prisoners in prison. This led to some teenagers who'd received blood transfusions finding out they had HIV/AIDS. Let's remember that back then this was even worse because there were little medicines to take and it wasn't nearly as effective as the antiretroviral drugs that exist today. I have been here for over five years and this was the first I'd heard of it. My Irish colleagues were saying the government just buried it, and they assumed it would do the same with the cervical cancer controversy. People must not tolerate this kind of behaviour anywhere. People are too complacent; they pretty much either complain about the government but go along with it or they emigrate—they get so frustrated with things like the government here that they essentially flee the country in the hopes of going someplace with a better government.

# *Franca Oliveira McManus*

*"Some migrant women fall into typical migrant worker jobs - like bar staff, kitchen or nannying because of a lack of confidence with English."*

My name is Franca Filomena Oliveira McManus. I was born in the picturesque county of Shropshire, England to an Italian mother and Irish-English father. I had a very happy childhood there. I grew up in a small market town called Bridgnorth which at the time was my whole world. I was very close to my Italian grandmother growing up, she lived with us and I spent a lot of time with her. I can still remember climbing into her lap for cuddles, sneaking into her bed after nightmares and the Italian lullaby she would sing to me... "Nunnarella" My childhood felt like I was neither here nor there. My mother and grandmother spoke Italian at home and we had Italian family living close by so even though I was born in England I was different from most kids. I remember hanging out with my friend in the evening after school one day, she was invited for tea and got served polenta, which in 2001 in a small countryside town was something extremely exotic and I think to her mind a little weird. "It's like porridge for dinner" she said.

I felt a little bit ashamed especially as it was one of my favourite suppers. In my second year at the University, my mother set her heart on moving back to Italy and so they bought a house in the south near where my mother was born. After less than a year my beloved grandmother (whose name was Filomena, I am so proud to have) suffered a stroke, and after a week passed away. I was waiting in a shop queue at the time, as soon as I got the phone call, before I even answered, I knew what had happened and my stomach flipped over. I booked my flight and moved there less than a week later, just left all my stuff and ran to comfort my mother. Although I had studied Law at University, I got a job as an ESL teacher and found my vocation. Teaching instantly clicked with me, I had always loved words and grew up in a bilingual household and I felt really at ease in the classroom.

After less than 2 years of me living in Italy I lost my mother to cancer. She deteriorated from a very strong woman whom I admired, someone who was full of life and fire, who had been beautiful all her life, into something painful to look at, bloated from the drugs, without hair, barely understanding what was going on. It was a terrible thing to happen to a 23-year-old girl. We had not been very close throughout my teens and now as an adult I always wonder if she is pleased at the person I'd become. I stayed on in Italy principally because my father was settled there, and he enjoyed the sunshine. Eventually - after my mother had been gone for about 4 years - he met a woman and they moved in together. Around that time, I chose to visit Dublin to do a CELTA course (it's a certificate in teacher training) and fell in love with the city. I had some friends already here from Italy and I spent a month doing the intensive course/enjoying the June sunshine. When I got back to Italy I decided to look for a permanent position in Dublin and got a job at SEDA college after a telephone interview - seemed like fate. I started in September 2015, managing to find an apartment sharing with another Italian girl in Ballsbridge. After a month of working, a handsome Brazilian happened into my classroom and the rest is history. We have been married for a year and we have an 8-month-old son who is going to grow up gorgeous and multilingual! My decision to settle here and leave my father is bittersweet. His relationship with the woman he moved in was tumultuous and ours suffered as a result, he just didn't want to listen to me anymore and it hurt me a lot because I spent my twenties taking care of him and we had always been close, I was his "baby". He actually passed away in April 2017 just after I had told him he was going to be a grandfather again. I miss him terribly and sometimes I get down when I think about how I lost so many people I loved in such a short period, but I just grit my teeth because sometimes you just need to get on with things and now I have Tomás, my little boy, I only want him to know happiness and it keeps me positive. I'm back teaching part time whilst taking care of my son, there's not much time for much else in the way of hobbies but I like to cook and read. When we get the chance we travel, mainly in Ireland and we both enjoy photography, though we are far from professional!

My favourite food is parmigiana di melanzane, which is fried aubergine layered with cheese, egg, mozzarella and parmesan. As delicious as it sounds. Every grandma has their own recipe or way of preparing it. It's rich tasting and saucy, the aubergines get so soft and sweet when they are cooked this way. I used to love it on a sandwich with crusty bread. A close second is rice, beans and farofa, which is cassava flour sprinkles/seasoning- I married a Brazilian and this is pretty much their staple food. Brazilian food is so tasty and so simple. I'd always thought it would be spicy, I don't know why. My favourite drink is a good red wine, especially if with cheese and olives, or a decent cup of coffee, which is sadly hard to find in Ireland! That's probably what I miss most about Italy, the coffee here always tastes burnt or too watery.

What I do like about Ireland is the people's attitude. They are so friendly, and Dublin is the perfect city, small enough to feel like a town. The people have a town mentality, they are never cold or standoffish like I've heard the people in London can be. I've had the best conversations with the taxi drivers. They always want to talk and swap opinions and know your life story. The Irish love to tell stories and the cab drivers have plenty. Go further into the countryside and the people are yet more kind and genuine. When I moved here I visited my dad's cousin in Monaghan and she has become a second mother to me. Her house feels like home and she is a wonderful woman, and I'm happy my son has something like a grandmother figure in her.

*What are some of the most challenges faced by migrant women in Ireland? (b) What advice would you give to young and upcoming migrants women?*

I think the biggest challenge is the language, and I'm an ESL teacher so I've seen first-hand how that can affect your ability to communicate. I've met women who are incredibly smart but have difficulty in putting their point across because they lack the language skills and as a result don't show their true potential to prospective employers. I think it hugely limits your opportunities here. Also, I feel like some migrant women fall into typical migrant worker jobs - like bar staff, kitchen or nannying – because of a lack of confidence with English and then they settle for what they are doing because they are still making better money than they would do at home. Also because of pressure to pay the rent. I'd like to tell them to have more faith in themselves, but also to try not to stick to the safety of their own kind but get out and meet other people with whom they don't share a common first language and practice their English, to try and integrate more. Dublin is such a multicultural city, so there are opportunities to meet all kinds of people, really expand your horizons, open your mind to other cultures, and that's a beautiful thing. Sadly, I think another challenge faced by migrants of both sexes is racial prejudice. I think it's unavoidable where there's a lack of understanding and a lack of education. For anyone affected by racist comments I could only suggest not to rise to the aggravation. Be the bigger person and move on.

*There is a worldwide momentum for gender pay-gap, do you think that women have suddenly started to speak up in demand of effective change, or do you think that men have only started to pay more attention and listening more to women?*

I think it must be a combination of both. Women have found a voice through social media, and there's solidarity in groups of people with the same objective. The Internet makes it easier to access information and share ideas otherwise some women wouldn't even notice that their male co-workers are earning more than them. They wouldn't question or second guess the situation and just take it for granted. These days we are finding a greater quantity of strong female role models in pop culture, speaking up about equality issues like the gender pay gap and slut shaming which definitely means girls are more focused on equality issues from a young age. Years ago, I think you'd have to move in the right circles and be particularly well-read to consider equality. My mother's generation simply accepted their lot. They were destined to be mothers, homemakers and wives. Even when feminism began to creep in in the seventies, feminists were seen as deviants, upsetting the status quo. Now every girl wants a career; in fact, I think my generation want it all, we want a successful career and the perfect family and most of us juggle everything pretty well. That's probably why the gender pay gap is particularly upsetting to women affected by it: we make sacrifices men don't have to just to be at work, to complete the presentation, to attend the meeting, and it's like a slap in the face when we receive less compensation for our hard work. I believe in the same way men are learning about less patriarchal societies and accepting different realities because of social media and feminism in pop culture. Whether or not they accept it is a different story, though I'd like to think they would accept that a discrepancy in pay between men and women is nothing if not completely unfair and doesn't have a place in 2018.

*Do you think that Ireland has done more to protect the rights of women? If you answered yes, in your opinion —why are there so many stories about domestic violence? If you answered no, then what do you think Ireland should do more to protect women?*

I think Ireland does what it can to protect women from domestic violence, through helplines, shelters, etc. Unfortunately, it's something that goes hand in hand with drinking which is a big part of the culture over here. I think a lot of women, especially those in long term relationships who feel a sense of loyalty to their husbands, are really prepared to make excuses for all kinds of bad behaviour. They would argue that it's not him, it's the drink. That he's not usually like this but the drink brings out the worst in him. I can't remember my father ever lifting his hand to my mother, but he did like to drink and sometimes it would bring out the worst in him. He would become belligerent, pick fights over nothing. My mother was a fiery tempered woman and there would be screaming matches. (That's probably why I felt so close to my grandmother growing up, she was like a safehouse when my parents were fighting.) I know my father cheated on my mother and she threw him out once but took him back. When she died they had been married for 46 years, and though they loved each other very much I think that their relationship had its ups and downs. Especially in a Catholic society there's the sentiment that you will do everything you can to make things work, even if it involves putting up with disrespect, infidelity, mental or physical abuse. About other women's rights in Ireland I can't fail to mention the current Yes/No debate raging as I write. It's something that is dividing families and ruining friendships. Rather than being swayed by propaganda I did my own research and learnt about Savita, the X case and Ann Lovett and think they were just three of the many women Ireland has let down with the 8th amendment. I think women deserve to be trusted and given the right to choose, and I think more freedom in application of the law is necessary in the circumstances where a medical abortion might save the mother's life, as with Savita's case. I know it wouldn't be a decision any woman would take lightly - like I said, they need to trust us.

*What has been a defining moment in your life/career or business since living in Ireland? (b) If you could have breakfast with any three Irish women, who would you choose and why?*

When I arrived in Dublin I was 29 years old, I'd been living with my dad for the last ten years or so and while I had never been financially dependent on him, it was the first time I had to handle my own money and manage a household. I spent the first couple of months eating

Tesco pizza and of course enjoying all the pubs Dublin has to offer! I was single throughout my twenties, apart from pining after a couple of unsuitable and really not that great Italian men, and actually didn't feel like I wanted a boyfriend. It was around that time that Marcelo, my husband, happened to turn up in one of my classes. It wasn't one of those love at first sight kind of situations, though in hindsight I probably fancied him a bit. When we ended up going for beer he kissed me, we started to see each other regularly and it just worked. So, Ireland brought me the love of my life, as cheesy as it sounds. He's my perfect complement because he's more responsible than me in some things and always thinking ahead whereas I live in the moment. He's my rock and lifts me up when I start to get down about things, he's always reminding me of all the good I have in my life. He makes me want to be a better person for him and for our son and is infinitely patient with me when I'm scatter-brained or faffing about when he wants to leave the house quickly. I love him to pieces and when I finish writing I'm going to give him a cuddle and tell him so!

If I could have breakfast with any woman in the ROI I would choose Ruth Negga, Rosie from Love/Hate and Tulip from the Preacher series. She was born in Ethiopia when her mother was working as a nurse out there and she lived there until she was four, then moved to Limerick. I think it'd be interesting to talk to her since she's mixed race, has a mixed background and I always wonder if she felt different growing up or if she ever suffered bullying or discrimination because of that. She's also beautiful and I love her style which reminds me of Audrey Hepburn in some way. I'd probably invite Saoirse Ronan along for breakfast too since she's local to Dublin and she'd probably have some gas stories about growing up here. I feel like she'd be easy to relate to and she must have a sense of humour - she got Ed Sheeran to tattoo "Galway Grill" on his arm. Rather than breakfast we could go out for drinks - I think we'd have a great time.

*The government recently launched 'Project Ireland 2040', which the Taoiseach said is a document about building a republic of opportunity. Have you seen this document, if so do you think that in its mapping there is provision to create an enabling space for migrant women to be heard and lead? (b) The Prime Minister is the son of a migrant father from India, does this alone give you the slightest hope for the future of the children of migrants in this country, and why? (c) If you have the power to change anything in Ireland, what will that be?*

I think one of the keys aims of Project Ireland 2040 is to spread economic growth across the country, to other cities like Cork, Limerick, Shannon and I think that will create opportunities for migrant workers, especially since so many of those coming to Ireland are skilled workers and they have greatly contributed to the country's economic growth. Hopefully this means there would be some provision for migrant women to influence the new Ireland.

The fact that Varadkar is the son of a migrant father is not the only thing that gives me hope for the future of children of migrants, like my son; I think that the new generation growing as it is, multicultural, means tolerance, acceptance of other cultures and religions and ideas. Multilingual and multicultural people. That's the ideal for Ireland and worldwide I think, the dream. It's an attractive ethos but I'm not sure how workable it might be.

**If I could change anything in Ireland** I think maybe an improved integration policy for the migrants. I think Ireland's future will continue to show patterns of migration and that it needs to move to accommodate and facilitate life for migrants.

# *Asia Kuzma*

*"There are drug free ways to get off drugs and there is a huge need to educate people on the real effects of drugs."*

Asia Kuzma is my name, I am from Poland originally. I left Poland and moved to Ireland in 2004 prior to Poland joining the EU and right before the big immigration of Polish into Ireland and England. I was young when I moved here. My journey was a very interesting and challenging one so far. It brought me through ups and downs in life, made me face problems and discovered solutions, but overall it helped me to become a much stronger and more confident person. Today I volunteer full time at the Church of Scientology & Community Centre in Dublin. I realise that many people need genuine help in life and I always wanted to help. Scientology helped me tremendously and I want to give the same back to others. I work with community groups as well as individuals who want to improve themselves or society. We run a series of humanitarian programmes – education on the effects of drugs and on human rights, environmental projects, clean-ups, volunteer initiatives. We also organise multi-cultural events, art competitions, family fun days and a lot more. All in addition to providing Scientology courses and services which offer knowledge and help in various areas of life – communication, relationships, motivation, spirituality and a lot more. This is the most fulfilling job I've ever been involved.

What I like most about Ireland is the spirit of the people. The Irish are actually similar to Polish people in many ways, for example like the Polish they are determined and don't give up easily. They also stand up for a cause and really care about each other. There is a strong sense of community in Ireland. And the passion for the arts in this country is fascinating. It ties in with the community spirit as people get together through the arts, they help each other through the arts which I find very uplifting. My country is rich in tradition and culture and I do miss the Polish tradition and culture here, and of course the food. I most definitely miss my favourite Polish foods.

*What are some of the most challenges faced by migrant women in Ireland? (b) What advice would you give to young and upcoming migrants women?*

One of the biggest challenges for migrant women (as well as men in fact) is to preserve their own cultural identity while integrating in the area they now call home. There is a lot of talk about "integration". For me the simplicity of this issue comes down to the fact that we are often faced with a lack of true knowledge about, and *understanding* of, the culture and character of the new place. It is often quite different than what one is familiar with or has grown up with at home. What helped me a lot in dealing with this issue is a principle which I learned in Scientology. It is called the ARC triangle and it stands for Affinity (A), Reality (R) and Communication (C). If you try this in life you will see that every time you raise one of those elements, the other two follows. Let's take the example of a young immigrant in a new country: Having moved to a new country you have to want to find out more about the people in the area —their likes and dislikes, what people consider good behaviour, what is acceptable to them and what's not, and the things they are proud of through good Communication. And when you discover this, you will find a lot of things you can agree with. This is how you increase your Reality about the place and the people. By so doing you will also find that you start liking the place and the people a lot more – your Affinity for them also grows and you will be more likely to talk to them and exchange ideas, which again is more Communication. By increasing these 3 elements – Affinity, Reality and Communication, you gain true understanding of your new environment – both the people and the surroundings and you can bring about true understanding about yourself, your own culture and habits. For me the success of an immigrant in a new country, depends on her ability to maintain her own identity, letting others know about and appreciate her own culture and background, while at the same time also learning about theirs and treating them in the same way as she expects them to treat her – with respect, understanding and appreciation. This is what the principle of the ARC triangle helped me understand and apply in life.

I would advise any young migrant woman to learn as much as she can about her new home, look for things she can agree with in her new country and learn to appreciate the people she now lives with. At the same time never cut ties with her own culture and traditions, preserve them, talk about them and let others learn about and appreciate them. If you want to make it, no matter where you are, you need to have a clear vision as to what you want to achieve, and you will make it. You have to believe in yourself, learn the skills you need and treat others around you as you want them to treat you – with understanding, respect and appreciation.

*There is a worldwide momentum for gender pay-gap, do you think that women have suddenly started to speak up in demand of effective change, or do you think that men have only started to pay more attention and listening more to women?*

The gender pay gap exists also in Poland and probably in every country in the world. I see it more like a development we are going through than an issue to fight against. What I mean by this, is that the role of the woman in the modern society is being redefined. Not so long ago, being mothers, wives, and taking care of the household were the main role women played, while the breadwinner of the family was traditionally the man. This has evolved over the years and today women are playing more roles in the society including all the above. The gender pay gap is an aspect of this change which hasn't been totally solved yet. I believe that through communication and bringing about understanding we can resolve this.

*Do you think that Ireland has done more to protect the rights of women? If you answered yes, in your opinion —why are there so many stories about domestic violence? If you answered no, then what do you think Ireland should do more to protect women?*

Not only women's rights but human rights in general are unfortunately still an issue in Ireland and in fact, the world over. We witness human rights abuses daily. They are sometimes concealed and sometimes unbelievably public. We hear about domestic violence in the public domain every day, but do we really know what goes on behind closed doors. No matter how many laws, regulations and restrictions we write, try to implement and enforce, there is only one solution I see to this problem and this is *education*. To me it is shocking that today, 70 years after the United Nations adopted the Universal Declaration of Human Rights, those rights are not taught in schools and young people grow up having no idea what their rights and the rights of others are. If you don't know the rules, how are you supposed to play the game, let alone be successful at it? I was always aware of human rights abuses, in Poland, in Ireland and other places I have lived. I always wanted to do something about it and be part of the solution.

Some years ago, I came across a very simple but powerful educational human rights campaign – Youth for Human Rights. It was started by a teacher and human rights activist from South Africa, Mary Shuttleworth. The campaign makes the 30 human rights easily understandable in the form of brochures and short videos – available to anyone. Today the programme is part of the work I do with the Church of Scientology & Community Centre of Dublin and is also part of my personal mission to make human rights a reality. Internationally, we have placed millions of these booklets in people's hands, over 80 million to date. Doing something effective about the problem made me feel good about it and gives me hope that we CAN change the situation by empowering people through knowledge.

*What has been a defining moment in your life/career or business since living in Ireland? (b) If you could have breakfast with any three Irish women, who would you choose and why?*

Although it wasn't always easy, I was doing pretty OK from the start in Ireland – I had a job and was making my living. However, I didn't feel that I had accomplished what I wanted as I had goals which seemed far away. I felt I needed to understand more about life in general and somehow be able to be more on top of things. This is when I came across Scientology courses on Middle Abbey Street years ago. At the time I didn't know that this was going to be a defining moment for me nor that it would change my life as it did. At first I was curious and probably a bit skeptical so decided to see for myself what could I get from this. The first course I did was called Overcoming Ups and Downs in Life. It gave me a lot of confidence as it confirmed a number of things I had observed already in life but didn't dare to face. It gave me information in very simple terms about who I could trust in life, what are the characteristics of people who would enhance my life as well as of those who would drain my energy. With this new viewpoint I became much less susceptible to negativity in my life. Then I did 2 more courses – Success Through Communication and Personal Values and Integrity. These simple yet powerful three short courses gave me enough understanding and information for me to start being the lead in my own life, the way I wanted it. I decided to start a business. Together with my partner at the time, who is my husband now, we opened a chiropractic clinic in Dublin. We started in a small room with only one staff member. I continued my training and did many courses regarding management and organisational basics, all based on the materials of L. Ron Hubbard – a writer and philosopher who founded Scientology.

These courses were different than anything I had done before as they taught me *practical* skills. It wasn't about the certificate but the application of the information. I went on applying what I learned on these courses and my business grew exponentially each year, expanding to 5 staff and half a floor two years after opening. Then the economic crisis hit and I continued to learn and apply the information. It was hard work, but during the crisis my business expanded 5 times and we moved into a new, and larger premises in Dublin city centre. Instead of a small room we were now renting an entire floor. We were doing something few others achieved – we basically grew through the Recession. The business is still there even though I turned it over to other people when I decided to move on in life and engage in volunteering. It is still expanding and servicing many with health problems.

I would love to have breakfast with Sabina Higgins, the wife of the President of Ireland, Michael D Higgins. I admire her for being so energetic, powerful, and yet calm. I admire her involvement and support of the arts and nature, and she is always there for her husband, her family, and the nation. Sabina is a role model, and she is setting a good example for others.

I would love to meet with former President of Ireland and former UN High Commissioner for Human Rights Mary Robinson. Her passion and work to promote human rights internationally is outstanding and impressive. Her actions have left a permanent mark in the history of Ireland and the world. She is a true leader.

Lastly, I would be curious to meet with Ali Hewson. Being the wife of Bono is a unique role in itself but she is much more than that – an activist, a businesswoman and inspiration not only for her husband but for many women in Ireland and around the world.

*The government recently launched 'Project Ireland 2040', which the Taoiseach said is a document about building a republic of opportunity. Have you seen this document, if so do you think that in its mapping there is provision to create an enabling space for migrant women to be heard and lead? (b) The Prime Minister is the son of a migrant father from India, does this alone give you the slightest hope for the future of the children of migrants in this country, and why? (c) If you have the power to change anything in Ireland, what will that be?*

I have heard about the project, I've even seen it but I'm not familiar with all the details it contains in order to make a comment. About the Taoiseach being the son of a migrant, I am certain that there are opportunities for anyone from any background, nationality or creed in Ireland. If one really wants to achieve something, and works hard to get it, with the right know-how, understanding of their environment and dedication – they will succeed.

If I had powers to change something in Ireland; The big problems many people want to solve in Ireland are homelessness and drug addiction. These problems are related and if I had the power to change anything in Ireland I will definitely start by education on the dangers of drugs on a large scale, parallel to building drugfree rehabilitation centres. Politicians take a lot of blame for not building enough housing but after talking to homeless people, people at risk, people who have been homeless and have made it out of the trap, as well as professionals who work in this area, I see that drug addiction among the homeless people is a major problem and an obstacle to overcome, on their way back into society. Even if there are more houses there will still be many difficulties to house and integrate homeless who are affected by substance abuse.

We have to tackle the issue with education and real drug rehabilitation. It is not true that a drug addict has to remain a drug addict. It is not true that drugs are safe to take. It is not true that people don't want to know about it. There are drug free ways to get off drugs and there is a huge need to educate people on the real effects of drugs. We have had an overwhelming response in South Dublin and nearby counties where we distributed over 75,000 booklets with information and education on drugs recently.

# *Anca Lupu*

*"Women in Ireland have much more support and protection than in other countries."*

*I* am Anca Lupu, originally from Romania. I have been living in Ireland for nearly 19 years. I am currently working as Development Manager with Citizens Information Service for Dublin North West. I am also the Honorary President of Romanian Community of Ireland, a voluntary charity supporting Romanians living in Ireland and organizing socio-cultural events for this community. I have been involved with RCI for the last 15 years developing and progressing the organisation's goals and activities.

My favourite food is fried fish fillets with polenta and garlic (traditional food from Romania). What I miss most about my country is being with my family, I also miss the hot weather. Ireland has beautiful scenery, I love the nature, its beaches, parks, rivers and gardens. I like the people and the cooldown approach to everything, a stress-free country.

*What are some of the most challenges faced by migrant women in Ireland? (b) What advice would you give to young and upcoming migrants women?*

I think that some of the challenges faced by migrant women in Ireland are most importantly, fitting in, adjusting to the various systems, and finding a job that they are qualified for. Parenting is another aspect to some of the challenges due to a different parenting culture in Ireland. Often women cannot work or are forced to work only part-time because they cannot afford to pay high rates for preschools and after-schools. Women also lack family support and lack of resources to provide for their families.

The best advice I would give to young and upcoming migrant women is for them to believe in themselves and their inner strength. To be open and to get out to meet people, get involved in their community, in the life of the school their children go to, in the local community, in their neighbourhood. To make Irish friends, find out more about Irish life and the people of this country.

*There is a worldwide momentum for gender pay-gap, do you think that women have suddenly started to speak up in demand of effective change, or do you think that men have only started to pay more attention and listening more to women?*

I think more and more women are aware of this and decide to put themselves in equal opportunities for employment.

*Do you think that Ireland has done more to protect the rights of women? If you answered yes, in your opinion —why are there so many stories about domestic violence? If you answered no, then what do you think Ireland should do more to protect women?*

Regardless of the statistics, I think that women need support in these situations. I also think that women in Ireland have much more support and protection than in other countries. I also know that many women in these situations do not have the confidence and the necessary support to end domestic violence so more campaigns and supports are needed to protect women and children and decrease/end domestic violence.

*What has been a defining moment in your life/career or business since living in Ireland? (b) If you could have breakfast with any three Irish women, who would you choose and why?*

The moment I decided to volunteer for an Irish NGO called Cairde. While volunteering there I learned about Ireland, its people, advocacy, policy, challenges migrants like me faced living in Ireland. Cairde gave me the confidence that there is support out there which motivated me to get involved in community work to support and give confidence to other people who were struggling. Cairde also gave me the opportunity to do training in community development which helped get my first full-time job in Ireland as a Community Development Worker. Since then I worked for other Irish NGOs from which I learned hugely and progressed in my career from a project worker to a manager and subsequently to a CEO.

**I would love to have breakfast with the following women:**

1. Mary Robinson, former first female President of Ireland, because she has an impressive career, human rights work and campaigns.

2. Miriam O'Callaghan, because I admire her straightforward personality, her political approach as a TV presenter and her

involvement in charity work.

3. Emily Logan, Chief Commissioner of IHREC, because of her warm but firm personality, her passion for the human rights and her determination to bring change.

*The government recently launched 'Project Ireland 2040', which the Taoiseach said is a document about building a republic of opportunity. Have you seen this document, if so do you think that in its mapping there is provision to create an enabling space for migrant women to be heard and lead? (b) The Prime Minister is the son of a migrant father from India, does this alone give you the slightest hope for the future of the children of migrants in this country, and why? (c) If you have the power to change anything in Ireland, what will that be?*

**No, I haven't seen it this document.**

• The issue of the Prime Minister being the son of a migrant father from India, I think hope comes from the inside, not from external factors. I have huge hope that migrant children will be involved in shaping the future of Ireland.

**If I have the power to change anything in Ireland, that will be:**

❖      To end Direct Provision.
❖      To employ more migrants in public jobs.
❖      To create more facilities for the youth in Ireland.

# *Ada Christine Eloji*

*"Each time women gathers togethers, the world heals a little bit more"*

*M*y names are Ada Christine Eloji. Born and raised in Nigeria. I am a naturalized Irish citizen and has lived in Ireland for over 15 years. I am an organiser and facilitator of women & community education and, the Author of a book titled, 'Forming a Relationship with Self: A practical guide for today's inspired woman' which was launched in November 2016. I am passionate about inspiring, empowerment and educational advancement for women and youths. I am a guidance counsellor and a qualified Adult and Further Education Tutor majored in community education, personal and professional development, facilitation, parenting and women studies. I am the founder of FAITH Family Initiative (FFI) Women's group, an organisation I started over

8 years ago, with an aim is inspire and empower women to become agent of positive change. The Organisation holds monthly support group meetings, outreach programmes and an annual women seminars/conferences known as The Inspired woman of Faith in Leadership (The IWIL) and World Taste of Food Diversity and Cultural Exhibition.

I am married with four lovely children, an award recipient from different sectors of the society including100 Most Influential Africans in Ireland and Northern Ireland 2011 and 2012. I'm an Ambassadorial Award winner for Champions for Women (2013), Pan African Lectures Community Service Award Ireland, 2015. Woman of Influence Award, Atlanta, 2016, Inspirational Woman of the Year IRARA Award in Ireland, 2018. I am Mentor, motivational speaker, a gospel music minister, a Christian counsellor and life & empowerment coach. I am a board member of Kildare Integration Network (KIN) and the Secretary of the Pastoral Council of African Catholic Family Community, Kildare and Leighlin Diocese. I hold a H.Dip in Business Management, BA(Hons) in Community Studies and Master's degree in Community Education, Equality and Social Activism. I am also trained in Family Therapy and Brief Encounter, and in suicide assist and behavioural/interactive management among others. Currently, I am studying MA/Post Graduate Diploma in Guidance Counselling at Maynooth University. I am passionate in helping women, youth and couples in developing their inner qualities to enable them face everyday challenges using spiritual discipline and positive thinking and living principles. I am a qualified Adult educational Guidance project worker and community education tutor and facilitator with years of experience working with individuals and groups in a formal, and education sectors in Ireland and abroad and undertakes one to one and group mentoring.

I am a Christian, a Mentor, mother, wife, sister, a friend and the agony Auntie. My mentoring and coaching stem from my encounter with this particular bible words taking from Habakkuk 2 vs 2-4. Lastly, I'm that kind of woman that has formed the habit of come rain or shine I always fling open my door and say loudly to my neighbours 'morning!' and tell anybody I come across how mornings bring it gifts, surprises and opportunities and how I look forward to a great day. Although, I have faced many challenges, but as a tough-minded optimist with positive dispositions, I have always come out victorious. My philosophy always is 'Never give Up.' I am motivated through strong faith in God. I love reading, writing, singing, cooking and meditation. On a good day, I spend time with my family or go on day trips with them. Listening to old school music brings out the girl in me. As one of the members of the Minister of the Eucharist and a Minister of the Word in my Parish community, I feel honoured to live, serve and be a part of a Christian community of Faithfuls, and in doing so spread, the gospel of love within and among the new Irish community and the Host community through my voluntary work.

My favourite food is anything that produces steam. Soups especially. All kinds of soup both African and Intercontinental. My drink is mainly warm water and green tea. I consider myself a non-alcoholic woman. I miss the sunny weather in my country, the organic foods and fruits and vegetables that abound in every corner. I miss my dearest and nearest like the close family yearly reunion with cousins, in laws, siblings, parents, grandparents, mates, nieces and nephews and close friends and so on. Our way of attending Mass is also different and the dance, songs and Homilies all bring nostalgic feeling of loss to me each time I imagine that.

*What are some of the most challenges faced by migrant women in Ireland? (b) What advice would you give to young and upcoming migrants women?*

Life is so different here in Europe. For example, you are always by yourself having been separated from your known family and support system. With such an added responsibility and added pressure in finding one's self, learning to rely on yourself and joggling with life's struggles can be exhausted. 21$^{st}$ century Irish migrant woman has robbed many migrant women of the idea what a woman is, from provider, carer, etc., being put in a subjected role where you are literally everywhere. Apart from barriers from proper integration, there is a lack of knowledge with getting information about various system of operations in Ireland, like housing, health services, access to education and all other aspects of Irish society. There are conditions and situations that affect migrant women and the way they see the world, or the way they behave. One of the situations is the socio-cultural belief system, and some of what the society requires of us as women or mothers, some which could lead to emotional disturbances. If I had people who motivated and encouraged me, it would have been better and easier, but I have personally found a way to survive. I have things that worked for me and decided to give out which I have in turn given other women a sense of purpose and meaning to their life. As the saying goes, 'only a fool learns from his mistakes.' As a migrant woman leader, I intend to reach out to as many women as I can to help them because I know that changing even just one woman's life is priceless, as she too will likely go on to create changes for others in need. I have been directly affected by these problems; (social, psychological, economic, cultural). I have always believed if I have a stone in my shoe, no one other me and those with similar stones in their shoes will know exactly how it feels, others may have read about stones, seen stones, or even had a similar experience with a pebble caught in a sandal. However, only myself and those who have them in their own shoes are experts on these situations because we have experienced it.

*There is a worldwide momentum for gender pay-gap, do you think that women have suddenly started to speak up in demand of effective change, or do you think that men have only started to pay more attention and listening more to women?*

There is need not only to engage women in education and personal development but more so to learn together on how to act collectively to bring social change in our communities, and it a better place to live. In Ireland for instance, women's community education emerged during the 1970s. The objective and purpose for this stems from communities that were experiencing unemployment, poverty and high anti-social activities among their children. Women based community education is a necessary investment for achieving gender equality, women empowerment as well as improving the well-being of women through literacy classes and courses.

Do you think that Ireland has done more to protect the rights of women? If you answered yes, in your opinion—why are there so many stories about domestic violence? If you answered no, then what do you think Ireland should do more to protect women?

As a woman, I have the right to be taken seriously. I have a right to make decision that affect my life and my future. I have a right to my reproductive organs as well as the right to equal distribution of power and status, including a right to every relationship within and between those wider forces that affect my life or the lives of other women. For instance, putting women at the centre of enquiry and examining women's status in the society and also improving the conditions of women's lives, seeing women as a subject of study and that which includes women, feminism and gender related issues. This is particularly important for migrant women because it allows for integration to take place and it puts them in a position of responsibility. It may also provide an opportunity to move out of their comfort zone, which is purely domestic functions in instances, to transition to independence through the work-force. It is therefore reasonable to think that women's performance and participation in education should bear in the direct way; on their global self-esteem and confidence.

What has been a defining moment in your life/career or business since living in Ireland? (b) If you could have breakfast with any three Irish women, who would you choose and why?

My defining moment in life will be my willingness to work with the most marginalised people which to me has been my defining character. I have worked in many sectors of Irish society, from being an outreach support with migrant families in Kildare County to a community youth worker with Catholic youth Care, to becoming a Project worker within the guidance services with Kildare/Wicklow Education and Training Board and onward to being on a tutor panel of KWETB within the Further Education and Training and working in homeless and disability services and also becoming the Chief Inspirational Officer of a women and family support group has put me in the position of becoming a vessel for positive change.

Any woman I could have breakfast with includes, Dr. Brid Connolly, Denise Croke, Agnes Patricia Michell and Donna Mae-Linton. I choose these women among many others because of the impact they have created in my life. I am motivated by women who spend their time to inspire, empower other women and their families. I am motivated by women around the world who in spite of all the hard-work they do or tough time they go through, still create time to be a mother, wife, friend, sister, helper, mentor and the same time go about contributing immensely towards work matters and community engagements. I am motivated by women who make things happen by finding ways to offer their services either voluntarily or professionally to other women and families in need in various capacities.

*The government recently launched 'Project Ireland 2040', which the Taoiseach said is a document about building a republic of opportunity. Have you seen this document, if so do you think that in its mapping there is provision to create an enabling space for migrant women to be heard and lead? (b) The Prime Minister is the son of a migrant father from India, does this alone give you the slightest hope for the future of the children of migrants in this country, and why? (c) If you have the power to change anything in Ireland, what will that be?*

When we look at women's movement globally, for instance, women of colour, black feminists in comparison to migrant women in Ireland, potentially, movements for migrants' women here in Ireland will take time but, in the meantime, more awareness raising, organising campaigns, and project which requires certain structures with more than one or two individuals are needed. Conversely, if you are in an existing organisation and wanted to raise a new issue, like gender inequality, the response may vary based on different ideology. In other to achieve a homogeneity of one cause, we need to acknowledge each other's uniqueness, differences, putting into consideration that every woman is fighting a just cause (oppression). On a final note, because women have been structured by society and our parents to accept gender role (sexist thinking), we have not stopped for once to ask questions or challenge why it has been so. For me, feminist paradigms have influenced my way of thinking and informing my feminist thought. As a woman of colour, a migrant woman, a visionary feminist educator, I advocate for education for all women in the world.

***If I had the power to change something in Ireland;*** Just as education is a basic human right and has been recognized as such since the 1948 adoption of the Universal Declaration on Human Rights, therefore, there is a need to engage ethnic minorities (migrant women) through community education. What has the system done towards education and acquisition of skills for migrant women. Is the approach taking to engage migrant women person-centred and friendly? If so is it effective, and to what extend has it been effective? Was there a research by any organisation or institution in Ireland to ascertain its effectiveness? Do migrant women and their families need one-to-one guidance in order to be motivated? Who are the motivators? What is their background and experiences with the other side of life? As a migrant woman learning in a foreign environment and aspiring to be heard, but are they being heard? I was told that women's education ends in kitchen but to me women's education begins from the moment a girl is born; she is told how to walk, talk, eat, dress and how not to behave. Therefore, the education of women has been, rather the process is lacking within migrant women's group who need to introduce praxis; theory and practice, activism, and conscious-raising. In the case of migrant women's groups here in Ireland, most of the groups are autonomous, some highly disconnected and others linked to religious owned affiliate, with Christian counselling, personal interest and power relation from the headquarters. Similarly, there is also a strong anti- feminist climate among migrant women because of their multi-religious believe system and traditional family system. As a result of these factors, there has been little or no change in the structure and also in forming a formidable and strong alliance. Again, there is little or no invested energy to challenge these structural social and cultural change on the part of the migrant women leaders, either by learning through the struggle of others or using their own personal experiential learning to challenge these structures.

My greatest desire is to be in a world where men, women and youth are inspired, empowered to live more fulfilled lives and transform their families and nations. A world where women will never to be treated as second class citizens and children will never die or abandoned. All these we can achieve by living peacefully together in harmony. I want to be remembered as a woman of many Gifts and Potentials, the greatest being my FAITH, in my own translation, 'for without Faith, it is difficult to achieve anything in life, nor will you be able to achieve your God given purpose, place and destiny in life. I feel honoured and excited indeed because, "Each time women gathers togethers, the world heals a little bit more. When a woman is inspired, the world does not remain the same, she automatically becomes an agent of positive change to herself, community and nations." - **Ada Christine.**

# *Anna Stanuch*

*"Somehow, the people who complain the most about it, are the ones who go on holidays abroad."*

Anna Stanuch is my name. I am originally from Poland. I came to Ireland in 2006 with my partner and our son who was one and a half years old. We came because we could. It had never happened before that a western country opened their job market to Eastern European people and we felt that it would be incredibly stupid not to go and see what life in another country is like. I think it's a misconception that Eastern Europeans came to Ireland mostly due to economic hardships in their native country. From what I see, the major factor was pure curiosity and a romantic vision we held about Ireland.

After we came, I started working as a waitress. It seemed logical because I had experience in this kind of work on American cruise ships and there was a massive demand for waiting for staff in Ireland back in 2006. I stayed in this occupation until 2014, when I finally decided to turn my life around. I took intensive English lessons, passed my IELTS and signed up for a number of different courses.

One of them was a course in digital marketing at DBS, which really got me hooked. After getting some experience as a freelancer, I landed myself a job that required a background in life science (I have a degree in biotechnology) and qualifications in digital marketing. Surprisingly, the employer didn't mind me having worked as a waitress for so long or that I had a scarce experience in marketing. Instead, they showered me with encouragement, positive feedback and provided good training, so I learnt everything I needed to do my job. I have been doing it for almost two years now and still really like it. My job title is online and marketing manager and it encompasses many tasks of preparing and sending mass e-mail campaigns to correspond with industry associations and maintaining our proprietary database of the life science industry. It is quite a lot, but I have full freedom of organizing my time and tasks. I cannot recall why I had stayed in the hospitality industry for so long, subjecting myself to the stress completely inadequate to the very low pay. It was probably a mixture of my poor English, the recession, and a lack of confidence. Even though my life as a waitress wasn't always cheerful and satisfying, I have never missed Poland. Ireland is a wonderful place to live. For a start, the kindness and relaxed attitude of Irish people makes up for any stressful situation you can encounter. Also, even if you are in a low pay job, you never feel really poor as many commodities are available relatively cheaply. Of course, the prices for accommodation are very high now, but somehow, the people who complain the most about it, are the ones who go on holidays abroad. So, it can't be all that bad. I don't live under a rock and can see the homelessness problem. However, I do believe that there is a way out of it.

The only thing I could potentially miss from Poland is the food. Fortunately, there is a Polish shop stacked with all sorts of wonderful products on almost every corner in Ireland, so there is nothing to miss. My husband, who is also Polish, is a chef and we have a traditional Polish dinner whenever we fancy one. I love all kinds of food from Mexican to Indian to Irish. I would die for good fish chowder! However, my absolute favourites are fermented foods, which are a staple in

Poland. We eat massive amounts of sauerkraut, fermented cucumbers (weirdly called pickles by English speakers), milk kefir, etc. A few years ago, I started a blog, fermetedfoodfreak.com, where I gathered traditional Polish recipes, a bit of general information about fermentation (my biotech background came in handy here) as well as some stories from my life back in Poland. Unfortunately, I don't blog anymore due to a lack of time, but I still run several social media profiles under the name Fermented Food Freak and pay for the blog's domain so it's all still there.

Irish peoples' attitude towards food amazes me. As open and adventurous as they are, they are strangely reluctant to adopt new tastes. When I worked as a waitress, it always annoyed me that eighty per cent of guests would either order a steak or some variation of fish and chips. I ran quite a few fermented food workshops and gave talks with tastings and, yes, there was a big interest, but very few people would actually add ferments to their diet.

*What are some of the most challenges faced by migrant women in Ireland? (b) What advice would you give to young and upcoming migrants women?*

I strongly believe that regularly leaving your comfort zone is the way to live life. And, the advice I would like to give to all immigrants is this – cancel your native TV subscription, learn English and go see people different than your own nationality. Join meet-ups that interest you, sign up for courses, and accept all invitations to parties that scare you. Also, don't let yourself be limited by gender stereotypes.

If you are a woman, don't believe that if your husband has a career, education, contacts, etc., it will somehow rub off on you or will give you credit in life. Go and actively create the life you want to live.

*There is a worldwide momentum for gender pay-gap, do you think that women have suddenly started to speak up in demand of effective change, or do you think that men have only started to pay more attention and listening more to women?*

I do not have much to say about the gender pay gap, because I have never had a job in the 'high tier' where this problem is the most visible. Similarly, I cannot recall a situation when I was overlooked for a promotion because I am a woman. However, I have been in out-of-work context situations when someone assumed my incompetence because of my gender. I found it hilarious at the time but can imagine that it would upset me deeply if I was in a position that it could seriously affect me. This is why I am so happy that more and more women speak up nowadays.

A much bigger issue for me has been people assuming that I'm incompetent because I'm not a native English speaker. I suppose that some people just have some sort of issue with their own accent or lack of education and choose to project it on immigrants. It is pretty sad, but it motivates me to work on my English. In general, I perceive Ireland to be a very inclusive country. However, this can be because I am an EU citizen and have never had to apply for a work visa. Also, Poland is culturally quite close to Ireland due to the same religion and an unfortunate past afflicted by oppressors. To be honest, I don't even feel like an 'immigrant woman' but rather an EU citizen who chose to live in Ireland. From what I can see and have experienced, Ireland is a country abundant in opportunities. There is always hope and there is always something good waiting behind every corner. I remember that I panicked when the recession happened because the hospitality industry became quite ruthless towards their employees. I quit my job in a hotel because I couldn't stand being bullied by an overwhelmed supervisor, sleeping four hours between my evening and morning shift, and being on-call on my days off. I was sure my family was doomed to poverty and prepared myself for the worst. However, I found out that Fáilte Ireland was running courses for hospitality workers. I joined and received an allowance that was pretty much the same as my wage in a hotel (which I find outrageous, by the way). I was then recommended for a job and everything went pretty smoothly. The story repeated itself years later when I had my course at DBS financed by the Springboard program. So, if you really want to, you will always find incentives to grow and enrich your life in Ireland. In all the courses that I undertook, there were always people from outside the EU participating as well. So, forgive me if I am wrong, but I have an impression that the state doesn't make too many obstacles for foreigners. Of course, I'm not talking about asylum seekers, whose situation is scandalous, and my heart is all for them being granted the right to employment.

During the big emigration wave from Eastern Europe in 2004-2006, a lot of people came to Ireland with children that had already started their school education. Most of them spoke very limited English due to the flaws in the Polish education system. I felt sorry for those kids, picturing the hard time they must have had to go through in an Irish school. But you know what? It all went perfectly well for them. They are now adults and most of them I know personally, did very well in their Leaving Cert exams and are now attending high demand university courses or have good jobs. Again, forgive me my ignorance, but I just cannot see how children of immigrants are worse off than native Irish children. There are probably other, more complicated factors, than being of a certain nationality that I simply have no idea about.

*The government recently launched 'Project Ireland 2040', which the Taoiseach said is a document about building a republic of opportunity. Have you seen this document, if so do you think that in its mapping there is provision to create an enabling space for migrant women to be heard and lead? (b) The Prime Minister is the son of a migrant father from India, does this alone give you the slightest hope for the future of the children of migrants in this country, and why? (c) If you have the power to change anything in Ireland, what will that be?*

Reading Project Ireland 2040 filled me with optimism, as it is a very heartfelt and well-intentioned document. However, I am also a bit sceptical. For example, it is easy to say that the state will aim for an equal access to childcare, but there are no plans for subsidizing it by the state, as far as I know. So, how is it going to be equal? This is a crucial issue for immigrant women, most of whom don't have an extended family here to help.

*If I could change anything in Ireland right now,* childcare arrangements would be the first thing. The current system forces parents to stay at home. In a sense, it is more beneficial for a baby to be at home with their mum or dad rather than in a full-time crèche, but, it should be a matter of choice for the parents rather than a necessity that makes people resentful. Besides that, if I was really powerful, I would implement a so-called Universal Basic Income. This is a concept that is currently being tested in Canada, Finland and other countries and I have my fingers crossed that it will be proved superior to the current social welfare systems in western countries. UBI guarantees that all residents are paid exactly the same amount of money monthly, regardless of their other income. So, there is no situation when an unemployed person has to turn down a job offer because it would make them worse off than to be on the dole due to costs like childcare, transportation, etc. I believe that Ireland will prove progressive enough to implement it at some point in the future.

To finish up, I would like to say that I am utterly happy to be here. I love the multicultural environment, the unpredictability of the weather, the perseverance of hope, the belief in luck, and the very long summer days. Wishing everyone a pot of gold at the end of the rainbow!

# *Claudia O'Riordan*

*"I just love Ireland so much that if someone hates it I just can't understand why."*

I am Claudia O'Riordan, from Mato Grosso in Brazil. I have been living in Dublin Ireland for 11 years. I had planned to stay in Ireland for a year only when I came because at the time I'd arrived with a student visa but I fell in love with the country and decided to stay here longer and now I am calling Ireland home. In 2013, I was diagnosed with MS (Multiple Scleroses) after already being here for 6 years, it was a huge shock, spending 3 and half months in Hospital here in Dublin and after transferred to a Rehabilitation in Donnybrook for 3 more months, it was a long journey into hospital but got lots of support from all the team of nurses, doctors and staff in Mater Hospital and my boyfriend (now my husband). It was a big challenge for me as a migrant having a long-term disease, but Ireland gave me and still gives me medical support. I do love my home country but there is something in Ireland that got my heart. Ireland is a special and magical place in my opinion. I just love Ireland so much that if someone hates it I just can't understand why. I love to discover the countryside travelling around to learn from the past in this stunning country. Even love my cup of tea at home, it's a precious time at home.

*What are some of the most challenges faced by migrant women in Ireland? (b) What advice would you give to young and upcoming migrants women?*

As migrants the most challenges at the beginning is usually the language, our accent sometimes can be a bit difficult to understand and vice versa for any us, it doesn't matter what gender. As a migrant woman I never had any issue in my 11 years living here. I always respected the country and the system, looked to be integrated into the Irish community through my involvement in voluntary work and events.

Since 2016 I have been doing voluntary work in Enable Ireland, and in 2017 started work with Casa Brasil Ireland (non-profit organization), it's a Brazilian and Irish community network, created by Brazilians. I worked there as an Event Coordinator, I am a Co-Founder and Co-Host of the YouTube channel - Travel Tips Ireland, where I am a Filmmaker and Location Planner. We've had over 50, 000 watched minutes across 20,000 views to date. I have never been discriminated against at work by an Irish person, always got respect even when they knew I was Brazillian. Ireland is a friendly place and very welcoming, I got the chance to work and integrate with my Irish colleagues.

I have been very lucky, Ireland gave me many chances that I'm proud of and grateful for, including a good job even as a migrant who don't speak the native language but one that only required my native language, after working on different types of casual work, although I now speak English in the workplace.

My advice for a young migrant is to get involved in the community through friendship, voluntary work in your neighbourhoods, discover Ireland, understand the country roots and try to mix with the Irish culture. All migrants especially from non-EU countries, should make time to look for more information about what we can be done while living in Ireland, a lot of us don't know that we have the right to register and vote in local elections, and help to do something significant in Ireland, especially we as women need to be more confident that we are just as good as the men. Ireland is realising that need to do more for us, so more women need to try to get engaged in politics and business, through which we can effectively fight for our rights.

*If you could have breakfast with any three Irish women, who would you choose and why?*

I would like a chance of meeting more woman in Ireland for breakfast. There are so many powerful women that it is hard to choose. However, I am not a person that is into politics but if I have a chance to invite a woman for a breakfast it would be Mary Lou McDonald, I think she's an inspirational strong woman who fights for her ideals no matter who comes against it. Another person would be Mary Robinson, first female president to hold the office in Ireland and working to strengthen women's leadership and encourage corporate social responsibility, she is an admirable person. A great example for us to believes that we can make a better life.

Lastly, I wouldn't miss a chance to have a breakfast with Katie Taylor, she is such a young and strong woman who fought for her dreams. She is an example that we can all fight for our dreams and conquer it if we believe in ourselves.

The Prime Minister is the son of a migrant father from India, does this alone give you the slightest hope for the future of the children of migrants in this country, and why?

Ireland is a country famous for its welcome to tourists and this also extends to migrants. Leo Varadkar being the son of an Indian immigrant and now in the role as Prime Minister is another great symbol of how Ireland welcomes immigrants, on top of that, he is from the gay community as well. It was only about fifteen years that people in Ireland were not allowed to be left-handed. So, this country has come a long way, and I'm proud to be living here, such a small country that receives us all. All of us as a people, if we want to be treated as equal, we must also respect the land and keep giving it our best.

# *Yemi Adenuga*

**"Don't focus on your colour or country of origin, rather focus on your abilities and the skills you have to make a difference."**

*I* am Oluwayemi (Yemi) Adenuga, originally from Nigeria and I have been living in Ireland since the year 2000. While I am a serial-Entrepreneur, I like to describe myself as a Personal and Business development Strategist. When people ask me what I do, I say: I build people.

**I am Group CEO of D-Dymensions communications (A holding company for my range of businesses).**
- Phoenix Institute of Training and Development
- MIB Academy
- Energy-N-Motion Publishing
- D-Dymensions Productions
- DY Relationship Clinic (DYRC)
- dMoTiVe TV

- N-MOTION Ensemble (Customized Shoes / Bags / Accessories)
- Motion Blazers (for the power dresser)
- Energ' body oils and Perfumes
- The Slippers Party

I am Founder/President:  SHEROES Global (Social Enterprise)
And Founder/Executive Festival Director:  Nigerian Carnival Ireland (NCI) (Social Enterprise)

My favourite foods are rice served with well fried stew with fish and fried plantain. I also love Seafood, and Chinese Chow mein. My favourite drinks are Water and tea. What I miss most about Nigeria is the communal spirit in the rural areas. Everyone looking out for their neighbour and becoming concerned if they don't see or hear from their neighbour in a day or two, pus the Sheer beauty of a whole village feeling responsible for raising every child in the village.

What I like most about Ireland is the honesty and genuine-heart with which people who believe in you use the power of 'word of mouth' to move you forward in what you do. When the Irish believe in what you do and trust you, they will recommend you to everyone they believe needs your product, service and expertise.

*What are some of the most challenges faced by migrant women in Ireland? (b) What advice would you give to young and upcoming migrants women?*

## Some of the Challenges faced by migrant women in Ireland:

•  **Stereotyping:** Many migrant women experience this on a daily basis. They are stereotyped because of their accent, marital status, skin colour, religious belief, dress sense, number of children they have etc.

•  **Employment**: It is hard enough to get a high positioned, good paying job as a woman, talk less of being a migrant woman. Securing a high level job can be even more difficult for a migrant woman, especially if there is a pre-conceived notion on the part of the employer about people from the migrant woman's place of origin. With 3 strikes against her (A migrant, a women, has an ascent), and a possible 4th strike (motherhood), She has to strive 3 times harder to prove she qualifies to get the job, and then work 4 times harder to prove she's great at the job to keep the job.

• **Integrating:** The experiences of migrant women to integrate are significantly shaped by the policies and practices of the state. Each woman's experience of integration and how they settle differs as it does not occur at a similar rate across all aspects of life. Some migrant women may be well settled in one dimension of their life (e.g. employment) but poorly integrated in other aspects (e.g. social inclusion) which could lead to isolation and impact on their self-esteem and mental health. To enhance better integration experience for the migrants, the issues of racism and discrimination have to be addressed.

• **Domestic violence**: An increasing number of migrant women, both married and single, suffer domestic violence in silence. In some cultures, it is an abomination for the woman to speak out about her domestic affairs in public, and in other cases, a woman could be bound by her religious belief to stay in a loveless and violent relationship.

• **Physical and mental health:** A large number of migrant women suffer from a poor state of mental health and a visit to some of the Psychiatric hospitals in Ireland will reveal this. Many experiences this as a result of bad relationships, depression, loneliness, struggle to raise difficult children alone, rejection, low self-confidence and self-esteem etc.

• **Not being taken seriously by the authorities:** It is rather disheartening that when migrant women from certain cultural backgrounds, who would ordinarily not have the courage to report an abusive situation, summon up the courage to report incessant issues of violence, harassment, discrimination and racism, they are sometimes not taken seriously by relevant authorities. The excuse is usually that the women don't press charges even when it is obvious that they have suffered some form of abuse, and so the authorities conclude that the women will sought out their domestic problems in 'their own way. (Then something terrible might happen).

• **Lack of self-confidence and courage to step out and be more**
A large number of migrant women fall into this category. Some lack the self-confidence (because of their limited spoken English and accent) to integrate in their local communities. Others who were perhaps qualified professionals

in their countries of origin, have reduced themselves to working menial jobs, simply because they are forced to re-qualify in Ireland for their profession and they may not have the drive to study all over again.

**My advice for young and upcoming migrant women:**
•   Before you begin to look at yourself as a migrant woman, first see yourself as YOU; a young, smart, intelligent and ambitious young woman who can do anything she sets her mind to. Don't focus on your colour or country of origin, rather focus on your abilities and the skills you have to make a difference in the lives of people around you, in a business environment, in your community and in the country of Ireland. While some see colour, accent and gender as a disadvantage, make it an advantage for yourself and tick the buttons for all the right places that see young women with the skills you possess.

•   The sky is no longer the limit, it is beyond it now. Reach for it, paint a big picture of where you would like to see yourself in 1 year, 3 years, 5 years and 10 years and place yourself in that picture each step of the way. Don't let anyone take the brush to paint the picture of your life for you. Paint it yourself.

•   Find yourself a solid mentor. Seek out that woman who exemplifies the kind of woman you aspire to be and connect with her. Make it clear to her what you want from her and let her guide you to being even bigger than she is.

•   Network with people from every work of life who are in your line of work. Go to events, attend functions that will keep you up to speed with current affairs that relate to things you do or want to do.

•   Choose your tribe wisely. Do not be one of those migrant women who feel that the only way to be successful is to disconnect from women who come from your country of origin and connect with only Irish women. It's not about the country they are from, it's about the person. Those you need in your tribe are honest, genuine, focused, result-oriented, goal-getting and driven women who want to succeed and are willing to help others along the way as they do, regardless of where they are from.

• Be proud of your heritage. While they might be negative stereotypes about your country of origin, don't let that stop you from being the change you want to see about your country. Let your actions bring positive attention to your country of origin, such that your country will be proud of you when she hears of you in diaspora.

•   Support other migrant women who are younger than you as you grow and climb the ladder of success, for as you look up to successful women ahead of you, other women will look up to you too. As a successful woman mentors you, pay it forward and mentor another woman.

•   LET YOUR MOUTH BE NICE, ALWAYS. If for any reason you are feeling low and have nothing positive to say at a given time, say nothing. Whenever you open your mouth to speak, make sure only positives words that uplift and motivate come out of it. It cost nothing but a kind heart to be nice.

*There is a worldwide momentum for gender pay-gap, do you think that women have suddenly started to speak up in demand of effective change, or do you think that men have only started to pay more attention and listening more to women?*

With an increased awareness of the existence of a percentage difference between the average earnings of males and females, gender pay gap was bound to gather momentum and become a global discuss. While the EU has a legislation to provide "equal pay for equal work" enshrined in its law, a gender gap still persists in every EU state due to the type of work women are involved in, which is comparatively lower paid than equivalent male roles. The EU average gender pay gap is 16.4%, which is above that of Ireland's (13.9%). This is, however, an increase from 12.6% in 2006, which reflects the fact that our pay gap figure is increasing. Civil society groups have also played a major role in amplifying the voices of women who demand effective change and also got men to pay attention. This has been done through the various awareness campaigns that include activities such as the Equal Pay day or the Equal pay for equal work, to increase the public attention received by the gender pay gap.

Gender pay gap has serious implications for a woman's lifetime earnings and her ability to support her family and to save for retirement. For these reasons and more, the issue matters, and while it has long been unlawful in the EU and US to discriminate with regards to employment decisions or to pay women less than men for doing the same job, these equality laws have failed to close the gap in earnings between men and women. Governments, as well as NGOs are still looking at new ways to drive the needed change. As part of measure to bring about the change, various groups in EU countries are now required by law to publish regular reports on the current state of gender pay differences. However, only firms with more than 250 employees are compelled to do so. Some of these companies produce numbers that don't add up and some only release the required data to avoid scrutiny, embarrassment and shame. An organisation that degrades the contrition of female staff errs on commercial and ethical grounds and this amount to exploitation, which demoralises staff and chase talents and assets away from an organisation. Very few claims are taken in Ireland in respect of equal pay issues and these might suggests that some complex social issues, e.g. role of men and women in the home, childcare cost, the glass ceiling and differences in the number of women in part-time employment, are results of the gender pay gap. There is no single method to regulate this issue, but while the issue gains momentum, it is expected that regulation will continue to increase. Women who find themselves in the gender pay gap need to begin to practically address the issue by gathering facts and getting the relevant information required to prove there is a gender pay gap in their workplace, in order to build an open and shut case.

*Do you think that Ireland has done more to protect the rights of women? If you answered yes, in your opinion —why are there so many stories about domestic violence? If you answered no, then what do you think Ireland should do more to protect women?*

I believe Ireland is doing well to protect the rights of women in general, but there is always room for more to be done. Though the country has traditionally been conservative, social norms in Ireland are changing, and it's now one of the best countries for women. The rise in the cases of domestic violence in Ireland is not as a result of the country not protecting the rights of women, but more about the mental and social state of mind of the people. People who are jealous, like to be in control, who derive pleasure from isolating their partner, enjoy forced sex and who hold very rigid gender roles, are likely to be violent if their partner triggers any of these anger buttons in them. The less self-confident and aggressive people become in a relationship, the more they are likely to become violent.

Domestic violence is a major cause of injury to women and hundreds of women end up at the doctor's office or emergency rooms every year. The violence is not perpetrated by a stranger but by a man who had previously professed love to the woman. That is not to say that men are not abused by women, for there are also increasing cases of women who abuse their men repeatedly. Abusers do not take advantage because the state is not caring for women or men. They take advantage because they feel the need to exert power and control their partner physically, verbally, emotionally and sexually, and this can happen to anyone regardless of culture, race, religion, class or gender. One of the pointers to the fact that Ireland is improving in its drive to protect the rights of women is the passing of the new domestic violence legislation in the Oireachtas earlier this year. This is a ground-breaking law that covers psychological abuse and the views of children. Ireland was brought a step closer to ratifying the Istanbul convention which aims to combat domestic violence, by the reforms included in the Domestic Violence Bill 2017. Coercive control (which is psychological abuse in an intimate relationship that causes fear of violence, or serious alarm or distress that has a substantial adverse impact on a person's day-to-day activities), will now be recognised as a criminal offence in Ireland as a result of the new legislation, and women can be confident about this. Among other things, this bill will further provide that Victims of domestic violence will be able to bring a friend, family member or support worker into court to support them during proceedings or they may give evidence by live television link to avoid the risk of intimidation. Safety orders will be available to people who are in intimate relationships but who are not cohabiting and the previous requirement for a relationship to be "committed" in order for a person to apply for a domestic violence order has been removed. The Bill also makes provision for a new criminal offence of forced marriage, and the repeal of the legislative provisions that enable people under the age of 18 to marry. There are also several domestic violence support organisations in Ireland like Women's Aid, Safe Ireland, COSC, Amen, DVAS, SONAS, as well as many women refuges that are readily available to support victims of domestic violence. What needs to be further done to ensure the success of the new legislation is for the Gardaí to receive training that enables them to thoroughly understand the legislation and be able to use provisions in it to offer vulnerable women the chance to apply for immediate protection when it is needed, with adequately resource for this measure to enable it work in practice.

*What has been a defining moment in your life/career or business since living in Ireland? (b) If you could have breakfast with any three Irish women, who would you choose and why?*

## A defining moment in my life/career or business since living in Ireland:

• When I left a well-paid job to start my own business in 2010, that was a defining moment for me. It was like leaving certainty for uncertainty. I have a very creative and innovative mind and I needed to create the trajectory for my ever expanding ideas to be born and thrive. While I wasn't sure what to expect, I didn't expect what I got. It was a struggle to get things off the ground and establish a presence, even with all the planning that had preceded the take off. At one stage, I questioned my decision to leave my 9 to 5 job, but I wasn't one to give up or give in, so I re-strategized and began to explore and access all resources available to me. Becoming an entrepreneur was challenging but very rewarding. Today, the rest, like they say, is history. We have expanded from one business idea to a group of businesses that cater to the needs of our diverse clients and we are glad to add 2 social enterprises that positively impact our community. For me, being a serial-entrepreneur is not just about making profits, but also about impacting lives positively and this is who I was born to be.

• When my daughter got married in 2016, I noticed a shift in me with regards to the way I started to respond to things, especially unpleasant things. I became even-more patience, smiled away negativity and would not speak if I had nothing good to say. To top it all, when my grandson was born, I made an even conscious effort to always leave people feeling better anytime they encountered me. These two major events in my life further gave me an advanced beautiful conscience to only live for the good.

**If I could have breakfast with 3 women in Ireland, they would be:**

Mary Robinson: She is a woman's woman who I would be honoured to seat at her feet and learn from her wealth of experience and wisdom. She is a wife and a mother, proof that a woman can be married and still achieve her goals. She proved to be a remarkably popular President, first female to hold this office, earning the praise of Brian Lenihan himself who, before his death said that she was a better President than he ever could have been. She exemplified diversity and inclusion long before the words became buzz words. She is an all-round professional as an academic, barrister, campaigner, political and global leader. She was the UN first High Commissioner to visit Tibet and was bold enough to criticise Ireland's immigrant policy in her time. As one of the 'ELDERS', her voice has been heard on many vital issues and she contributes her wisdom, independent leadership and integrity to tackle some of the world's toughest problems.

Sinéad Burke: This public speaker, primary school teacher, broadcaster, blogger and fashion obsessive, is many things but shy. She is Confidence personified, who, as an inspirational speaker, uses her experience as a "little person" to speak on confidence, carving out one's own career path, defying expectations, and becoming your best self. Having won the final Alternative Miss Ireland Little, Sinead uses her experience as a "little person" to her advantage and titles her blog after her character creation, Minnie Mélange. I would love to have her in my tribe.

Julie Sinnamon: Her drive to use her influence to bring more gender balance into the Irish entrepreneurial landscape is inspirational. She uses her position as CEO of Enterprise Ireland to encourage more women to become entrepreneurs and shines the spotlight on the women who are succeeding as entrepreneurs, creating better support networks for working mothers. Her enthusiasm to see more women become their own boss resonates with me. I would love to learn about her challenges in helping women become more, and how she manages these challenges.

*The government recently launched 'Project Ireland 2040', which the Taoiseach said is a document about building a republic of opportunity. Have you seen this document, if so do you think that in its mapping there is provision to create an enabling space for migrant women to be heard and lead? (b) The Prime Minister is the son of a migrant father from India, does this alone give you the slightest hope for the future of the children of migrants in this country, and why? (c) If you have the power to change anything in Ireland, what will that be?*

Yes, I have seen Project Ireland 2040. The vision of Project Ireland 2040 is to see an Ireland where there is enabling opportunities for everyone, with a priority for the wellbeing of all the people of Ireland, wherever they live and whatever their background. It hopes to have a more equal and balanced society in which we all share increasing prosperity, wherever we choose to live and work. It is my understand that the provisions in project 2040 cuts across all sectors of the Irish society and while the Project's provisions are not broken-down for specific groups, it is important that every group, including migrant women and various ethnic minority groups begin to familiarize themselves with the provisions of the project and speak up if there are any concerns regarding how they are represented within the project's mapping. This is an opportunity for migrant women to get more socially inclusive and ensure that that they are not left out in the plan for the future of Ireland. Migrant women need to unite, put forward, and vote for their own candidate in elections, so they have a voice at the decision making table. It is not enough for migrant women to seek their right from the outside, they must send representatives into offices of power to ensure their interests are always on the agenda when decisions are made. Nobody can fight a person's course better than them.

On the Prime Minister's Background as the son of a migrant and hope for children of migrants: Being the son of a migrant father was not a criterial for being elected to the various positions that eventually lead to the Prime Minister being the head of our Nation. He worked his way up the ladder and did not rely on his background to be an advantage, nor did he allow it to be a disadvantage. He simply followed his dream and worked hard to achieve his goal, an indication that anyone, regardless of background, who works hard enough to win the heart of the people and make a difference, can lead this nation. There is certainly hope for the children of migrants in this country as many migrant children are already representing Ireland in various fields all around the world. Only recently, 15 year old Rhasidat Adeleke won the 200m gold for Ireland at the European U18s Championships in Hungary. When she was interviewed, it was as an Irish Athlete, not as a migrant running for Ireland. The resilient Deborah Somorin, who had to struggle through life as a young girl on her own, has proved that Children of migrants who excel in what they do will certainly be celebrated proudly as Irish. Everyone loves to be associated with success, so does a nation. I am certain that children of migrants are smart and intelligent enough to do exploits in the country, if they do not just think of themselves as children of migrants, but as a brilliant individual who can achieve anything they want for themselves, and for their country.

***If I had the power to change anything in Ireland***, I would change the education system in secondary schools where students have to pick their leaving cert subjects when they are in their 3rd year, a time when majority of them have no idea what they want to do for a career. As an alternative, I would let the education system in secondary schools focus on making various options available to students from the minute they get into secondary school so that the subjects they study are relevant to their future chosen career. I will also change the point system of entry into higher institution and replace it with continuous assessment, underpinned by the study of subjects that are relevant to students' chosen career of interest. In addition, I will try to help people find their way back to God so Ireland can be a nation that loves God once again.

# *L.O.D*

*"I believe a vote by the men and women of Ireland was to right past wrongs and make women and their independence and freedom, a priority."*

*I* would prefer not to give my full name as we live in strange times, but my initials are L.O.D. I was born in the United States in the state of Massachusetts. I have lived in Ireland since June, 2013. I am an English Language Teacher, Life Coach, Online Content Creator, and Editor/Proof-reader.

It's difficult to choose a favourite food, but I have to say that anything my mother makes is always healthy, delicious, and filled with love. So, her food is my favourite. What I miss most about home is seeing my friends and family, sitting on any one of their decks and shooting the breeze, with or without libations.

*What are some of the most challenges faced by migrant women in Ireland? (b) What advice would you give to young and upcoming migrants women?*

The challenges of living in Ireland can be described in separate categories, (bear in mind that my experience is that of an Irish-Italian American, and my identity is now widely considered to be 'white'). The first category is Social Challenges. Social challenges include: making friends, dealing with people outside the home, and fitting-in to the neighbourhood.

Making friends: It seems that making friends is always difficult in adulthood so, I don't think that this is unique to Ireland. We take for granted forced social situations such as, school. Adult friends already have established circles of close friends with whom they have history so it's hard to 'break in' or be 'accepted'.

Dealing with people outside the home, or just basic social interactions for business or pleasure are different in Ireland. Most of the interactions are more pleasant than back home. People are super polite and friendly, they will talk to anyone and not look at you as if you have 10 heads if you strike up a conversation. Even if you bump into someone and it's your fault, they will say 'sorry'. However, sometimes getting things done such as setting up a bank account, getting that first job, and getting the PPS number and card needed for said job are processed at a snail's pace.

Fitting in to the neighbourhood is not super difficult if you look Irish, which I do, but takes some getting used to. That said, I live in a very diverse area with Irish people, Low-Income people, and Immigrants living all together. Don't get me wrong, there are ignorant and racist incidents in Ireland occasionally, but they are far more infrequent than when I lived in the states. All the 'incidents' that I have witnessed in my five years in this country, in my neighbourhood or elsewhere, could be counted on one hand. So, all in all the neighbourhood is friendly and safe. Kids still play outside in the streets in Ireland and for the most part people still know their neighbours at least by face and they are polite. It reminds me of my country in the 1980s and early 1990s. The other category is environmental challenges. We start with the weather...this is the most common topic of conversation and being from New England I am used to extreme heat and cold, so it's not a huge bother for me. I've learned that when it's sunny in Ireland, all bets are off! People literally cancel all plans and go out in the sun, parks are packed full of people in summer clothes, bare white extremities are prevalent, and everyone enjoys a 99c ice-cream just as if they were a kid again. For me the other environmental challenge is littering. This is a twofold challenge; firstly, the government doesn't seem to enforce strict enough penalties on those who do not properly dispose of rubbish.

The majority of the people, especially in the countryside, really respect nature and don't litter or dump household waste, but enough do and get away with it that illegal dumping sites exist around the country. Another issue is casual littering in parks and on the street. Clearly, some sectors of society don't care about or understand the consequences of throwing a crisp bag, sweet wrapper, or bottle on the ground. It's off-putting and easy to reduce through public campaigns to raise awareness and shaming. I know people don't like the idea of shaming others, but when they are dirtying the streets, parks, and any green space we have, people should be ashamed. The lack of picking up after one's dog is also an issue. I would like to see stricter fines and consequences for illegal dumping, littering, and not picking up dog poop. This country relies heavily on tourism, so it makes good business sense besides just being responsible and logical.

*There is a worldwide momentum for gender pay-gap, do you think that women have suddenly started to speak up in demand of effective change, or do you think that men have only started to pay more attention and listening more to women?*

In terms of the gender pay-gap, women have been talking about it for ages and only now are men and society really and truly listening. While some are still trying to deny its existence, (namely the anti-feminists and neo-fascists who are backing the orange president in my country), most educated and working people will acknowledge that it exists. Women have been talking about it in my country since the 1960s and figure of the Women's Movement, such as Gloria Allred and Gloria Steinem... through the courts and field studies, respectively, have drawn a lot of attention and documented its vast existence across many sectors of the workforce.

Here in Ireland, figured such as Joan Burton, Mary Robinson, and Mary McAleese have through politics and political success brought to light the plight of women in work and society. With the huge success for women in Ireland recently with the positive outcome of the referendum in favour of repealing the 8th Amendment to the Constitution. This amendment made the life of an unborn child equal to the life of a mother who is pregnant and resulted in the complete restriction of access to abortion, even in cases of rape and incest. The way the country came together in huge numbers to get out and vote and how their votes really mattered had a huge effect on me. It's wonderful to see democracy in action in its purest form. We have work to do all over the world in terms of achieving true equality in society, but Ireland has made a lot of strides recently and I see a lot of smart and interesting women representing political parties. Hopefully there will be more and more participating from all different backgrounds. It's also very heartening that the last referendum was on marriage equality and it passed.

*Do you think that Ireland has done more to protect the rights of women? If you answered yes, in your opinion —why are there so many stories about domestic violence? If you answered no, then what do you think Ireland should do more to protect women?*

Ireland has not done much in the past to protect women. My country has also done horrible things to women, as have many. I think Ireland knows it has given women a raw deal in the past and that systematic shaming and treating women as second-class citizens and its exposed and is trying to cope with this history. This was very clearly reflected in the rhetoric and arguments for and against the 8th Amendment. Ireland voted 'YES' to support women in making their own choices for themselves. This, I believe was a vote by the men and women of Ireland to right past wrongs and make women and their independence and freedom, a priority. I see a lot more value for women, families, and pregnant women in society when I am out and about and when people interact and talk about those issues/situations. Time will tell how things manifest themselves in the future.

*What has been a defining moment in your life/career or business since living in Ireland? (b) If you could have breakfast with any three women in Ireland, who would that be and why?*

A defining moment in my life/career in Ireland, was when I started the process of becoming a life coach. Realizing that discovering myself and my likes/dislikes, passions, and motivations. I was able to recommit myself to learning about myself and the world and solidify my understanding that "there is always more to learn". I am blessed to have a few very fulfilling jobs where I am able to teach others, learn from them, and help others, every day.

Three Irish women that I would love to have breakfast with are Catherine Zappone the TD, Mary Lou MacDonald TD, and former Tainste, Joan Burton. I would like to hear their differing views on the state of the country and how they think we can continue to make strides for the Irish people, and women in Ireland.

*The government recently launched 'Project Ireland 2040', which the Taoiseach said is a document about building a republic of opportunity. Have you seen this document, if so do you think that in its mapping there is provision to create an enabling space for migrant women to be heard and lead? (b) The Prime Minister is the son of a migrant father from India, does this alone give you the slightest hope for the future of the children of migrants in this country, and why? (c) If you have the power to change anything in Ireland, what will that be?*

"Project Ireland 2040", seems like a great and progressive proposal. I hope that it includes all women who reside in Ireland and is really helpful in making this country successful into the future. I would like to see some concern for the environment and alternative forms of energy, conservations, ecotourism. These are all important factors which will ensure that Irish people have a good standard of living and standing in the world. It's very hopeful in this country at the moment and people feel very positive. Being here at this time is quite special and feels important. The fact that the current Taoiseach is the son of an immigrant show that the country is becoming more progressive and modern yet keeping a lot of its traditional values and cultural charm.

# *Erika Pena*

*"It is not normal for anyone who has a college degree to work as a nanny or toilet cleaner in pubs and in hotels."*

My name is Erika Pena and I am from Lima, Peru. I have been living in Ireland for more than 16 years with family. Many things have happened since we arrived, initially it was just my husband and I and two of our children, they were aged 1 and 8 then. It was not easy for my family to settle down here, we had difficulty with renting a place to live, buying a car, attending healthcare, studying and much more. I was not allowed to work as my husband was a student. He was doing his PhD in Physics; it was terrible! It was difficult to get a job with my nationality as most companies required a work permit and it takes longer to process the permit. It was like a loop, every time that I applied for a job they also asked me for the work permitted which I didn't have. However, everything changed when my husband finished his postgraduate studies and the university offered him a job. At the time I also found a job as IT teacher in a college. Since then things have improved in many folds, the family grew too, now I have a large family as we have been blessed with more children. I have been very concerned about how to keep our Peruvian roots alive in my children and I threw myself into community activities with fellow Peruvians. My passion grew and I suddenly had an urge to promote our culture here in Ireland. My friend offered me an opportunity to become part of the first Facebook group dedicated to Peruvians living in Ireland. Then it was simply, "Peruanos en Irlanda" (Peruvians in Ireland/ Peruvian Irish community in Ireland). But it was an Irish lady who started it, thanks to her. However, this Irish lady was moving to Australia and she needed to pass the administration of the Facebook group to my Peruvian friend, who in turn invited me, together we did a lot of promotion to try and reach out to our community. At the time the group had only 20 members, today it has more than 1200 members in the Facebook group. I started by answering emails, helping people and organizing free events.

My initiative was to create a Peruvian Facebook fan page and help others with information and advice in Spanish. I was involved with the Peruvian's Independence Day celebration and with helping our honorary consul with some activities, including polling stations for Peruvian presidential in 2011 and 2016. I have been very active within my community and have gained a mix of experiences now. Eventually, we created our first website also called "Peruanos en Irlanda" from where people could access more help and information. I am always ready to help them. I have managed the Facebook group now for more than 6 years. The group of Peruvians I work with are is amazing; they have the same vision of helping others. I was nominated for a worldwide prize called "Peruanos en el Exterior" and I won a special recognition from my country. In 2017, I started a new adventure with "Casa Peru Ireland". I am a founder and Director of "Casa Peru Ireland" and work with a great group of Peruvians. As a non-profit organisation, Casa Peru Ireland work to promote Peruvian culture in Ireland encouraging social inclusion, integration and to play a part of our second home: Casa Peru Ireland is "Licenciatario" of Marca Peru in Ireland the first one and only one now. In 2018 we got our first Peruvian Embassy in Dublin, Ireland, as a Peruvian I am very proud to have official representation in Ireland.

I love Peruvian food but in Ireland it is difficult to get local ingredients. However, in 2016 "Peruanos in Ireland" with my direction produced a book called "Peruvian Home Cooking Book". In this book, we did a fusion with ingredients that you can be found in Ireland to cook Peruvian food. The more important objective was that all the money that we generated was for 2 Peruvian charities. We sent 7000 thousand euros to them, thanks to this project with the help of our Peruvian community. In 2018 Peru was recognised and has been part of Irish Food festivals "TourRoir".

I love Irish nature, it is amazing and safe to be here. I know the weather is not so amazing but in Ireland it is unlikely to have earthquakes or big natural disasters as it happens in other countries. Rain and more rain has been our main complaint and lack of sun. I have learnt through the years living in Ireland that if you are looking for the sun, just get on an airplane and fly away. It is close and easy to access but to feel safe with my children is something that it is more important.

*What are some of the most challenges faced by migrant women in Ireland? (b) What advice would you give to young and upcoming migrants women?*

The beginning is always hard, and not easy if you are a migrant. Your educational degrees and experiences from a country that is not part of Europe is worth nothing when you arrive here. It is harder when you have children and try to work and can't find employment. Very often you see a woman with a good level of English and sound education working odd jobs just because she is a migrant. It is not normal for anyone who has a college degree to work as a nanny or toilet cleaner in some pubs and in hotels. It is ok to do whatever menial jobs available to make ends meet if they're without any skills or qualifications, but it is different when being a migrant becomes the only barrier holding a woman from succeeding with life. We are not here just to do simple jobs, having something to do is great but getting a good unemployment is a big challenge.

My advice to a young migrant woman. Be yourself, don't let anyone put down just because you are from a different country or you have a different skin colour and you probably sound different because of your accent. Remember that all these traits are unique and tells about who you are, they are your identity so be proud of who you are. We can all achieve something if we put our minds to it. Be strong because you will have upside downs, be prepared to face challenges as they come. But don't ever forget why you came in the first place —to make a life better for yourself, to grow your skills and achieve so be not afraid to talk to people and ask for help when needed. Access the educational system here and use it to your advantage to improve your skills and acquire more knowledge, you can study and reinvent yourself if necessary.

*There is a worldwide momentum for gender pay-gap, do you think that women have suddenly started to speak up in demand of effective change, or do you think that men have only started to pay more attention and listening more to women?*

Although men remain over-represented in most roles of power and decision-making in Ireland, and a sexist. Sometimes hostile culture in the media also impedes women's advancement. But I think women are standing for themselves, and women organisations are using technology platforms to build and amplify the voice of the girl-child and women, businesses have also starting to prioritise the advancement of women in leadership and there is a wealth of research and reports available that documents good practice and good results, so there has been significant progress in Ireland. Social media is a great advantage for women's movements which has seen tremendous positive reaction. The under-valuing of work traditionally done by women combined with austerity policies applied to Ireland's social infrastructure had combined to put a brake on women's progress towards economic equality. However, progress is being made in areas such as women's representation on boards and in politics. Women and men are valued for their knowledge and expertise in their individual field, that is what is more important. It is also important that depending on women's workload some of us prioritise our family life than our professional life or study life, but it is the women's own choice.

*Do you think that Ireland has done more to protect the rights of women? If you answered yes, in your opinion — why are there so many stories about domestic violence? If you answered no, then what do you think Ireland should do more to protect women?*

Something that really surprises me in Ireland is all information about domestic violence or any kind of violence you never find in the news TV or radio; the only way to get this information is to be involved in those subjects. Progress has been made in different areas, still there are parts that must be handled stronger.

*The government recently launched 'Project Ireland 2040', which the Taoiseach said is a document about building a republic of opportunity. Have you seen this document, if so do you think that in its mapping there is provision to create an enabling space for migrant women to be heard and lead? (b) The Prime Minister is the son of a migrant father from India, does this alone give you the slightest hope for the future of the children of migrants in this country, and why? (c) If you have the power to change anything in Ireland, what will that be?*

Irish society has become more diverse and equal compared to how things were years ago. When a person decides to leave their own country to go and reside elsewhere, it is usually to make something better for their future so those who ended up living here says about a lot about the greatness of Ireland, and as a country with hopes and a lot of opportunities for study, career and family life. The multicultural element has now added to all of that and now, with the Prime Minister coming from a migrant background makes it more real those opportunities that anyone can make a success of their life here.

If I had the power, I would change the health service system in Ireland to focused more on mental health issues, it lacks support in this area for children and adults alike. I would also give more support in the divorce process and the adoption process, which currently takes a very long time to process. The way the rent situation is managed is unfair for families, that is something I'd definitely change for the better.

# *Evangeline Ngozi Omini*

*"Work hard, pray hard, be tough and focused in order to overcome the plans of those, especially fellow migrants who want to bring you down out of jealousy."*

*I* am Mrs Evangeline Ngozi Omini, originally from Nigeria. My husband and I migrated to Ireland in 1998. This means that we have been living in Ireland for 20 good years! At the moment, we are living with our wonderful Irish children who are also University students. Our sublime grown up children have gone to live independently. I am a lawyer by profession, but my main occupation is writing. I am a published author. I started writing officially since 1992 as a journalist (columnist) in the National Light Newspapers, Awka, Anambra State, Nigeria. I was as well a Secondary School Teacher from 1986 to 1994 in Nigeria. I taught English Language and Christian Religion in Amorka Girls' Secondary School, Nnobi Girls' Secondary School, Oraifite Girl's Secondary School, Ifite Ukpo Boys' Secondary School (All in Anambra State of Nigeria). In addition, I lived in Lagos as a freelance journalist and a business woman shortly before I left the country. Due to the limited number of pages for this project, I would like to refer our readers to some of my books where I wrote my background in details; and what led to migrating from my country to Ireland. The links are inserted at the page where some of my published works are listed in this book.

When we came to Ireland in 1998, my husband and I lived in a B & B accommodation in Dublin. Barley two weeks of seeking asylum, I was selected among thousands of refugees and asylum seekers to write a speech and deliver at the first Official Welcoming of Refugees in Ireland, on the 13th of January 1999. I was thrilled to see Former Taoiseach, Bertie Ahern as he gave his speech and Former Tánaiste Mary Harney who was also in attendance. Selecting me from thousands of asylum seekers and refugees gave me much confidence to continue reading and writing in my land of refuge. Thus, when my family was blessed with 2 lovely Irish children (a girl and a boy) in 1999 and 2001 respectively, at the popular Rotunda Maternity hospital, we were given permission to live and work in Ireland. However, it was not easy for me to cope with work and raising the children born here, as well as the ones who later joined us. It should be noted that being far away from home, there are no relations to help young migrant mothers in minding children. And lack of affordable crèches and playschools compounded their problems. As a result of the circumstances beyond my control, I did not look for employment. After three years of the role of a house wife, which was very difficult for an academic, I eventually started my own business where I was able to switch from one role to the other. My roles as a wife, a mother, a childminder, a student, a businesswoman, a pastor, a care worker, a writer and eventually a lawyer earned me the nick name; 'MULTI-TASK MOM'. I did not know where I got such inspiration and strength from. But God has been there for me throughout my entire struggles.

**Below is the summary of the multi-task that gave me the 'award':**

| To Date: | My Books include: |
| --- | --- |
| • Writer (Published Author)<br>• Lawyer<br>• CEO/Editor:Interglobal Resources Charity work<br>• Graduated with 2.1 in LLB Law in Maynooth University.<br>• Pursuing LLM and PhD in Law at the moment. | • 'God's Love Prevails': published in USA by Xlibris in 2013. https://www.amazon.com/Gods-Love-Prevails-EvangelineNgozichukwu/dp/1483672115 <br><br>• 'Longevity with Joy': published by Author House, UK in 2014. https://www.amazon.com/Longevity-Joy-EvangelineOmini/dp/1496993357 <br>• 'Law Essays Made Easy', (To be launched in December 2018).<br>• 'New Healthcare Textbook' (To be launched in December 2018).<br>• Articles on Immigration, Human Rights, Christianity. |
| Sept. 2013 – June 2014: | Studied Healthcare in Dublin and had Distinctions in all the 8 modules for Healthcare qualifications. |
| Feb. 2006 – June 2012: | Manager, Surf and Call Internet Café, Naas, Co. Kildare. Went to Bible College in Tallaght |
| Sept. 2002 – 2005: | Studied ICT in computer schools in Maynooth and Newbridge. (ECDL & JEB). |

My favourite food is jollof rice with moi moi and vegetables. My favourite drink: Water, (coffee, when I am writing or studying). What I miss most about my country is my loving family who are denied visas to visit me. What I like most about Ireland is peace and freedom to raise children, to write, and earn a living.

**What are some of the most challenges faced by migrant women in Ireland? (b) What advice would you give to young and upcoming migrants women?**

**Marginalisation:** Ireland has done well in providing for thousands of people who flee their homes including me and my family. We appreciate that, but the government needs to perfect this kind gesture so migrants will stop living in limbo. As can be seen from my profile; I am an asset to any country that engages me in the running of the country. This is because I have much skills and experience in various aspects of life. But there is no job for me in the government after 20 years of studies and hard work. This is why many migrant women are now leaving the country. Secondly, some migrant women who have worked so hard are not officially recognised in this country. This would have made the lazy ones whose slogan is that 'Ireland is a leveller' for all migrants to sit up and know that hard work pays.

**Affordable Childcare:** Last but not the least; affordable crèches are needed for young migrant mothers, as their relations are far away. I know this from experience.

My advice to the migrant women is, no matter the challenges you face, do not give up. Work hard, pray hard, be tough and focussed in order to overcome the plans of those, especially fellow migrants who want to bring you down out of jealousy, because one day justice will prevail. If you find your work stressful, prioritise. Also engage your children. Do not underestimate the abilities and skills of your children. They will learn and in turn start teaching you. If you have no children, seek help from friends and loved ones.

*There is a worldwide momentum for gender pay-gap, do you think that women have suddenly started to speak up in demand of effective change, or do you think that men have only started to pay more attention and listening more to women?*

I think that women are beginning to come up in this area as compared to 100 years ago when they were even denied suffrage. Looking at strong global political leaders like former Presidents of Ireland, Mary Robinson and Mary McAleese, Prime Minister Theresa May, and Chancellor Angela Merkel, former First Lady Michelle Obama, to mention but a few, there is hope for women.

*Do you think that Ireland has done more to protect the rights of women? If you answered yes, in your opinion —why are there so many stories about domestic violence? If you answered no, then what do you think Ireland should do more to protect women?*

To some extent, Ireland has succeeded in protecting the rights of women. For instance, 100 years ago, women were denied suffrage, but now women are allowed to vote and are even Presidents and political leaders in Ireland. However, more need to be done to include migrant women. Though **#metoo** movement has geared up and developing into making women to be heard more than before, migrant women voices should be heard. What we are crying for is simple: give us the opportunity to bring out our skills and talents. We are smart and intelligent people.

*What has been a defining moment in your life/career or business since living in Ireland? (b) If you could have breakfast with any three Irish women, who would you choose and why?*

## Defining moments in my life are as follows:

- The individual periods I had all my children, including my Irish children. I was always over the moon each period I had a new baby.

- When God called me in 1992 and told me to choose a place to live in and evangelise. Also, when I was chosen to represent thousands of asylum seekers and refugees in January 1999; the Official Welcoming of Refugees for the first time in Ireland, after my essay was selected for the occasion. (Photos are in my book on Migration).

- Furthermore, when Co. Kildare Council gave my family and me a beautiful house/home in 2003, I heaved a sigh of relief. I planted my favourite plants including apples and flowers in the lovely virgin garden. After living in this beautiful home for 15 years, I thank God and Ireland everyday.

- Finally, my defining moment is this year that even my youngest (17 year old) has gone to University. I have also finished my hundreds of pages book on immigration which I was asked by publishers to write since a year ago.

There are many women role models in Ireland. It will be lovely to have breakfast with all of them. But as I am limited to 3 of them, I go with the former President of Ireland, Mary Robinson, former President of Ireland, Mary McAleese and former Tánaiste Mary Harney. This is because they are role models, empowering other women. I will listen to their advice if I am given the opportunity to be around them.

*The government recently launched 'Project Ireland 2040', which the Taoiseach said is a document about building a republic of opportunity. Have you seen this document, if so do you think that in its mapping there is provision to create an enabling space for migrant women to be heard and lead? (b) The Prime Minister is the son of a migrant father from India, does this alone give you the slightest hope for the future of the children of migrants in this country, and why? (c) If you have the power to change anything in Ireland, what will that be?*

I believe that 'Project Ireland 2040' will be successful in many areas. The Prime Minister is very intelligent and being the son of a migrant father from India, will enable migrant women to showcase their abilities and business acumen for the betterment of Ireland. I strongly believe that there is a great hope for the future of the children of migrants in Ireland. Our hard work, including this book written by Migrant women will inspire our children to aim higher.

***If I was given the power to change anything in Ireland***, I would set up an ad hoc committee to look into the plights of migrants, especially migrant women whose human rights are being denied and who are being marginalised. I will invite the UN Women, UNIFEM, CARE International, The Duke and Duchess of Sussex and other women in Ireland like former Tánaiste Mary Harney, who have passion in empowering women. In addition, I will encourage small businesses by setting up ad hoc committees to identify the talented business men and women from every race and support them financially. This will help them to expand and employ our youths. Finally, I will tackle the housing problem by inviting investors to build housing estates in approved areas.

# *Frida Maurimootoo*

*Being on a student visa for more years than needed keeps you in a part time job which means that you have to be careful with your spending.*

*I* am originally from Mauritius, but I have South Indian blood running in my veins. My grandfather on my mother's side, was from Pondicherry the French department of Tamil Nadu. I work, studied, and live in Ireland since my arrival in 2004. I am currently employed by a Market Research company and conduct surveys. This is a freelance job that I chose to do because it gives me plenty of free time to get involved in activities that I am passionate about. I enjoy creating videos, blogging, crafting other thing, and I do a bit of social work as well. I am not affiliated with any organisation, but on an individual basis I volunteer with different Christian groups where possible.

Leaving my home country, my friends, family and my pets (two cats which I left with a friend), to discover a new world was hard. I hated what I did but at that time, Mauritius, was still not the proper "platform" for me to grow and achieve my goals. Ireland was a better option for that. Going back to college in Mauritius is not something that is very common for people over the age of 30, most adults there already have completed third level education, before reaching 25 years old. Ireland is different on that, which is good because I was able to study at third-level without facing prejudice as would have been the case back in Mauritius.

It's now fourteen years since I've lived on Irish soil, and despite the daily challenges, I blend well with the culture now. Besides, Irish people are cheerful, and the Irish humour is what put a smile on my face all the time. I still miss my country, my friends and family (I lost my pets) but I travel back for holidays every two years.

Being Mauritian, our main dish is rice and curry, but a variety of cultures is very much present in our traditional foods. The African, Indian, Chinese and Europeans who settled there have greatly influenced our foods and as a food lover, I enjoy all including different foods from around the world with a preference for more spicy ones.

*What are some of the most challenges faced by migrant women in Ireland? (b) What advice would you give to young and upcoming migrants women?*

One big challenge that we face as migrants in Ireland is the Immigration policy which is somehow rigid. It took me eight years to obtain a probationary extension visa, a scheme introduced a few years ago as a follow up of my student visa and another two years to obtain my permanent residency. The permanent residence visa is renewed every year for five years after which I will be eligible to apply for citizenship. Unfortunately, those who arrived a year later could not avail of the scheme, it no longer applied to them. Sadly, the rigid immigration laws have led some people to even become undocumented. The probationary extension visa offered to us was barely helpful because it was not recognised by employers as a right for holders of such a visa to work full time. This situation has had a huge impact on personal lives. Being on a student visa for more years than needed keeps you in a part time job which means that you have to be careful with your spending. It delays your progress, shatters your dreams and puts you under pressure constantly. As far as I know, the Justice Ministry is still working on its immigration policy to allow non-Eu migrants to live and work freely in Ireland. Hopefully they will come up with something beneficial for migrants left in this category. For this reason, my advice to young and upcoming migrants who finds themselves stuck not to depend entirely on the immigration system of the country that you migrate to, to achieve your goal. Success does not depend on the odds surrounding us, it depends on ourselves, on the action we take to reach our goals.

**We shouldn't ever stop ask questions like the followings:**
- Why was I born?
- What am I doing with my life?
- What am I passionate about?
- What makes me happy when I think about it?
- Am I heading in the right direction?
- What is it that puts a smile on my face and keeps me cheerful?

Also ask yourself what you want to be in life: a musician, painter, chef, doctor, lawyer, writer, fitness instructor, social worker, software engineer, plumber, electrician, motivational speaker, etc. Whatever comes to us as the answers, we are responsible to pave the way to make them happen and be successful. *"for where your treasure is, there your heart will be also." (Matthew 6:21).* We live only once and we have to make our lives worth living. It is a crime to allow external circumstances, other people or the system they implement to dictate the way we live our lives. If they do steal our dreams or purpose from us, then we can only blame ourselves. We are bound to pursue our dream or, if you prefer, our God given purpose, non-stop. "Where there is a will there's a way." Young and upcoming migrant women are responsible to find their way by all means possible.

Although experiences of life shape and build our personal

development and qualify us to face life, education plays an important part too. Educate yourself on the things that you are already passionate about and have knowledge about. Whether you enrol on a new course, opt for distance learning or choose to be autodidact, you have plenty of opportunities in front of you to choose. Study and equip yourself. If the immigration system of a country imposes too much restriction and pressure, and becomes unbearable to the point of breaking, tearing you down, and destroying your dreams then, your life experiences and knowledge gained through education will equip you to move on. If you find it hard to keep the good fight, you can still relocate. Bear in mind that the most important thing in life is to fulfil your purpose. That is the number one thing which should matter to us. Everything else is secondary. I haven't achieved my own life's goal but it is a continuous process. I can proudly say that I am fulfilling my God given purpose one step at a time, like taking part in writing this book is also a part it.

*There is a worldwide momentum for gender pay-gap, do you think that women have suddenly started to speak up in demand of effective change, or do you think that men have only started to pay more attention and listening more to women?*

*To the woman God said: ".... and you will desire to control your husband, but he will rule over you." Genesis 3:16*

Planet earth is a place where women live in a man's world and are ruled by them. It has been like that since creation and men (although not all of them) have taken advantage of their superior position to not just rule over but to mistreat women in every area of life including the workplace. Being paid less for doing the same job for gender reasons is unjustified particularly when the job is as equally challenging and stressful for both sexes. One man might be better than a woman at handling challenging and stressful situations at work, after all different people have different approach to dealing with everyday kinds of situations at work and in our lives, based on their perception and not on their gender.

Women are as strong in and sound in mind just as the men. We are now living in a revolutionary time where massive awakening is taking place around the world. Our eyes are opened to see through the veils and to realise that much harm has been done in the name of gender. The gender pay gap momentum is the appropriately in the right direction. Women should continue to speak up and keep doing it until change happens. We can then talk about equal opportunity.

*Do you think that Ireland has done more to protect the rights of women? If you answered yes, in your opinion —why are there so many stories about domestic violence? If you answered no, then what do you think Ireland should do more to protect women?*

I believe Ireland, like other countries in the world, has done its part in protecting the rights of women concerning domestic violence, but when dealing with human nature it is an impossible matter. In my opinion, each and every one is responsible of his or her life and to improve it. The government can only bring support.

*What has been a defining moment in your life/career or business since living in Ireland? (b) If you could have breakfast with any three Irish women, who would you choose and why?*

A defining moment in my life happened in December 2008, I was on the train while going back home from work and college when I had an epiphany. It was a sudden awakening, a memorable moment which will stay with me until the day I die because it was a turning point in my life. That was a personal revival, I became fully conscious of myself. It changed my perception of the world. I became fearless, less judgmental, less worried and more forgiving. I stopped following the crowd and comparing myself to others, I realised that life was not about worldly pursuits, but more of a spiritual journey on earth. I began to see through the veil, and as time went by I gradually understood more about our human nature. My identity as a human being was not questionable anymore. The plans I had for myself were not worth pursuing now because God had a better one. *"For I know the plans I have for you,* declares the Lord*, "plans to prosper you and not to harm you, plans to give you hope and a future." (Jeremiah 29:11).* From that moment on, I knew that my life would never be the same. I was lost but He found me, and so I can say like R. Kelly: "I believe I can fly."

If I could have breakfast with any woman in the Republic of Ireland, the first woman would be Sinead O'Connor. I choose Sinead O'Connor for her revolutionary mentally. Her difficult past life contributed a lot into shaping her into the woman that she is today. Sinead is not afraid to speak up her thoughts. She is one, I would learn a lot from and be inspired by.

The other two are my former creative media teachers - Clair Wilde, Orla Rapple and Lorraine Morrissey from Liberties College where I studied a diploma in Creative Media. My teachers were very supportive, and they helped to build my confidence. In the class I was at ease and as a migrant adult learner I never felt like I was too old to be in a class of young adults. Besides, they are very passionate about the subject they teach.

*The government recently launched 'Project Ireland 2040', which the Taoiseach said is a document about building a republic of opportunity. Have you seen this document, if so do you think that in its mapping there is provision to create an enabling space for migrant women to be heard and lead? (b) The Prime Minister is the son of a migrant father from India, does this alone give you the slightest hope for the future of the children of migrants in this country, and why? (c) If you have the power to change anything in Ireland, what will that be?*

Project Ireland 2040 is a long-term project. It is very attractive, unfortunately there is much fluff around it. I personally do not believe in long term project. In theory it sounds doable but nowadays nothing is stable, and everything is very unpredictable. In my opinion setting shorter goals is more achievable. it's difficult for me to give an accurate answer on weather Project Ireland 2040 creates a space for migrant women to be heard and lead, but migrant women are already active today, there are spaces available through NGOs such as New Communities Partnership, Akidwa, etc for us to be heard. Will migrant women be represented in parliament one day? I believe so, but we should allow time to do its job, in the meantime, we have to keep being active and bring our best contribution that we can to make Ireland a better place to live in.

Leo Varadkar on the other hand, was not elected by the public so again, it is difficult for me to give an opinion on the matter. We have to leave it to time which is going to change many things in Ireland.

*If I had the power to change anything* at all in Ireland it would certainly not be the system, like dealing with the symptom of a problem and not actually treating the disease from the root. I would rather reach out to people and talk to their heart because that is where every system is conceived and birth to begin with.

# *Paola Maggiorotto*

*"If we keep a positive approach and are willing to see challenges more as an opportunity believing in our ability to get over them, we can overcome any situation."*

*I* am Paola Maggiorotto, originally from Italy. The first time I came to Dublin was in 2006 for an English summer course. I felt in love with the city and its vibes and knew I would come back… and so I did, moving to Dublin in April 2010… it's been over 8 years now and counting! I am currently managing a team of IT Support engineers in online advertising, working for one of the multinational corporations in Dublin. I am also sitting in AkiDwA's Board of Directors.

My favourite food would be the same as for most of the Italians: pizza and pasta. Here in Ireland I miss the concept of gathering with people primarily around food and not alcohol. It took me a good while to get used to the Irish drinking culture... and after 8 years I am still not to be considered a good drinker by Irish standards. I also miss is the Italian summers... even if we also got quite good summers in Ireland in the last couple of years... and that has given us the opportunity to enjoy the good weather, like walking around in the evenings with a gelato or sitting in restaurants and pubs terraces until night-time chatting with friends. We all know outdoor life in Ireland can be a bit limited by the rain.

There are so many things I like about Ireland, but the most important one is its people. Irish people have been extremely welcoming to me and I feel very much at home here. I feel trusted because I have been given both volunteering and work opportunities, which have guided me through my personal and professional growth and supported me during hard times. Dublin is also a very international city and I feel like I've met the whole world here. When I look at my friends I can't help being amazed by the combination of different nationalities and cultures they are coming from and how my life has been enriched by them. I have learnt so many things just by being around them and they made my life a hundred times better.

*What are some of the most challenges faced by migrant women in Ireland? (b) What advice would you give to young and upcoming migrants women?*

I have to say I am in a very privileged position, being Italian and European. I have never experienced discrimination due to my origins and cultural background. Instead, I have always seen a lot of curiosity for my culture and country and often talked about Italy for hours with complete strangers. Having said that, I definitely experienced some challenges being a woman. I work in a team of Support engineers and in close contact with developer engineers, which are areas traditionally dominated by men. I did experience situations where I felt that my voice was not heard, and my opinion not listened to because I was not part of the main group and its stereotypical characters.

The advice I would give to young migrant women is to always believe in yourselves, in your skills and capabilities. There are many challenging situations in life, but if we keep a positive approach and are willing to see challenges more as an opportunity believing in our ability to get over them, we can overcome any situation. I would also advise them to look for a mentor, either in the workplace or personal environment. I found it is critical to have some go-to-people you can always turn to when you are facing challenges and to get trusted advice.

*There is a worldwide momentum for gender pay-gap, do you think that women have suddenly started to speak up in demand of effective change, or do you think that men have only started to pay more attention and listening more to women?*

I think it is a combination of both things, women have certainly started to speak up more and ask for what they deserve, but men have also become more aware of the situation in the workplace and have become more open to listen.

*Do you think that Ireland has done more to protect the rights of women? If you answered yes, in your opinion —why are there so many stories about domestic violence? If you answered no, then what do you think Ireland should do more to protect women?*

As part of the European Union and bonded to its regulations and principles, Ireland can definitely be considered a privileged country for the rights of women. There is certainly always an opportunity for improvement, like we saw with the 'Repeal the 8th Amendment' campaign and referendum on legal and safe abortion in Ireland, but in general and I feel like women are protected by the Irish Law. In general, I personally think that there is still a lot of work to do to change people's mindset, and men's in particular, around equal rights and opportunities for women. And I also think quite often the Catholic culture has negatively influenced any potential progress in this area.

*What has been a defining moment in your life/career or business since living in Ireland? (b) If you could have breakfast with any three Irish women, who would you choose and why?*

The defining moment in my career happened two years ago when I got my current role. At that time, I was going through a very difficult time, experiencing very low self-esteem and this job came to rescue me. My manager at the time never hesitated to offer her help guiding me through the initial onboarding and challenges. So, thanks to her help, I felt empowered to contribute my best to the team.

### Three Irish Women I would love have breakfast with:

I would love to have breakfast with former President of Ireland, Mary McAleese. She is one of the most inspiring women I've listened to and did a lot for the migrant and women communities in Ireland.

*The government recently launched 'Project Ireland 2040', which the Taoiseach said is a document about building a republic of opportunity. Have you seen this document, if so do you think that in its mapping there is provision to create an enabling space for migrant women to be heard and lead? (b) The Prime Minister is the son of a migrant father from India, does this alone give you the slightest hope for the future of the children of migrants in this country, and why? (c) If you have the power to change anything in Ireland, what will that be?*

No, I haven't seen this document. Having a Prime Minister who is the son of a migrant is definitely a milestone that we have achieved going towards integration and equality and I am proud of Irish people for trusting and empowering him in this role. The only thing I would change in Ireland is maybe... the weather and especially the wind, but we cannot have it all in life!

# *Marlene Smith*

*"I consider the Irish government very passive when it comes to protecting women."*

**M**y name is Marlene Smith-Torriani, married to a Brazilian guy. I'm from Lima-Peru and hold double citizenship since my ancestors on my mother's side were Italian. I've been an immigrant at different stages of my life. I started travelling since I was 3 years old when my family moved to Paraguay and lived there for 5 years. After that, we moved to Costa Rica where we lived for about 3 years. As an adult, I worked on cruise ships for five years travelling the world and meeting people from every single country around the globe. I've been living in Ireland altogether for about 4 years. Although I am a chef, I currently work as an ESL English Teacher in a very well-known language school.

I love eating, drinking and experiencing new culinary destinations. My favourite food is obviously Peruvian since it is very varied, rich and tasty (and the best culinary destination in the world for those reasons). My favourite drink is any cocktail with Pisco (Peruvian national drink) and I consider myself a wine lover, being Touriga National (Portugal) my favourite vine. What I miss the most about my country apart from my family and friends are the FRUITS, weather and of course the delicious food. However, Ireland has been very kind to me by treating me always with respect and kindness, and one of the things that I like the most about Ireland are their people.

*What are some of the most challenges faced by migrant women in Ireland? (b) What advice would you give to young and upcoming migrants women?*

To my mind, I haven't seen that many support groups oriented to migrant women (or at least I haven't been introduced to any of them). I guess one of the challenges might be the lack of support upon on arrival in the country, especially for women who are mothers and have to work. I don't have children myself, but some of my work colleagues are migrant mothers who are juggling financially with working full time and being a mother at the same time, and you can see how they are struggling since there isn't an effective financial support for working mums who are migrants.

If a young migrant woman asks me, I'll probably tell her to keep herself informed and look for support or contacts in order to get some sort of guidance before arriving in Ireland.

*There is a worldwide momentum for gender pay-gap, do you think that women have suddenly started to speak up in demand of effective change, or do you think that men have only started to pay more attention and listening more to women?*

Being very honest, I'm not very familiar with what is going on in Ireland regarding those matters. However, there is a movement going on worldwide demanding equality not only in payment but also in treatment. In my opinion, men are only realizing it now. and there is still a long way to go in that respect.

*Do you think that Ireland has done more to protect the rights of women? If you answered yes, in your opinion —why are there so many stories about domestic violence? If you answered no, then what do you think Ireland should do more to protect women?*

Honestly speaking, I consider the Irish government very passive when it comes to protecting women. You only need to have a look around in any street; the number of abused women is just insane (by men or other women), the authorities don't do much about it and we are reaching a point where people don't care anymore. Ireland should be more active by promoting campaigns, educating children at school and reinforcing laws.

*The government recently launched 'Project Ireland 2040', which the Taoiseach said is a document about building a republic of opportunity. Have you seen this document, if so do you think that in its mapping there is provision to create an enabling space for migrant women to be heard and lead? (b) The Prime Minister is the son of a migrant father from India, does this alone give you the slightest hope for the future of the children of migrants in this country, and why? (c) If you have the power to change anything in Ireland, what will that be?*

I haven't seen that document, but I would love to. On the one hand, it is encouraging that the son of an immigrant somehow knows about his parent's challenges and might understand what migrants have to face. On the other hand, that doesn't guarantee anything taking into account that he is the "son of a migrant", not the migrant himself. The reason is that the son of a migrant feels more Irish than from his parent's country and might not feel identified with the problems of migrants themselves.

***If I had the absolute power to do so***, it'll be the weather. I guess I would try also to give more opportunities to more people to start up new small businesses, create and enforce laws that control tenancy issues as housing has become a major problem and nobody seem to be doing anything about it. I'd create more awareness about important matters such as domestic violence.

# *Shireen Sanders*

*"The biggest challenge is raising our children in a different culture."*

*M*y name is Shireen Sanders from South Africa. I am in Ireland for 10 years and became an Irish citizen after 5 years. I have been unemployed for most of the 10 years in Ireland. This is not for a lack of trying but rather getting no responses to my applications. I am a skilled PA/Administrator and Event Manager. I am qualified as a teacher, but according to the rules in Ireland, I am required to learn the Irish language to be able to teach here. Secondly, I tried to have my teaching qualifications vetted in Ireland but was told that they do not carry out vetting for "black education." I qualified in 1980 under the apartheid system and my Teaching Qualification states "Department of Coloured Affairs". I am also a Certified Estate Agent but was told I need to study for further two years to if I was to practice as an Estate Agent in Ireland. I did the first year of this study and passed with a distinction. I was marked down in the finals and could only afford a remark for one of the subjects. The remark changed my results and I was awarded a distinction. I decided not to continue with the second year. I am not formally attached to any specific migrant group, but I always try to support migrant events and causes. I used to organise the Annual Braai for South Africans in Ireland. I arranged the Africa Day event for the African Embassies in 2013, I also organised the farewell event for the Kenyan Ambassador, Catherine Muigai Mwangi in 2014.

I am a Muslim and don't drink alcohol. I love seafood, a good lamb curry and the traditional South African Braai. I enjoy cooking and like entertaining my friends. I miss the weather, family, friends, family gatherings and celebrations, but most of all I miss not being seen as different. I'm thankful for the opportunity of being able to live in Ireland. I love how green and safe Ireland is. For me, Ireland has a soul and it will always be my soul home. Most of the Irish people that I have interacted with or friended are the most incredible people I know. Ireland like most countries of the world, has its unique problems towards migrant women and I really hope that this will change soon.

*What are some of the most challenges faced by migrant women in Ireland? (b) What advice would you give to young and upcoming migrants women?*

Some of the challenges faced by migrant women are discrimination, no support system, adapting to a new culture, holding onto home values and cultures. I've listed some of the main challenges but from my interaction with migrant friends, the biggest challenge is raising our children in a different culture. Parents try to instil home culture, religion and norms with their children but most times it creates confusion for the children who interact and live the Irish Culture. It is not a choice for them because they need to assimilate and adopt much more of the

Irish norms and culture. No one is wrong here, but we need to understand that we are raising Irish kids because we made this choice for them. We have to realise as women, that we are the mothers of society, the nurturers. To keep our children balanced we must shift our thinking to keep a balance that is a happy medium for all including our neighbours. Most settling-in problems can be solved by dispelling our fears and those of the Irish people by interacting socially to getting to know each other as fellow human beings with the same needs, i.e. a happy home, a safe environment for our families and the opportunities of having access to education and social supports. Moving to a new country is never easy but the benefits only become obvious at least after a couple of years. There are positives about living in Ireland, we have to focus on those positives and build our lives on this because the good outweighs the bad.

*There is a worldwide momentum for gender pay-gap, do you think that women have suddenly started to speak up in demand of effective change, or do you think that men have only started to pay more attention and listening more to women?*

The world has changed from a patriarchal society to one of equality of the sexes and human rights for all. This has happened mostly by women speaking up and demanding their rights as equal citizens and asking for gender balance.

*Do you think that Ireland has done more to protect the rights of women? If you answered yes, in your opinion —why are there so many stories about domestic violence? If you answered no, then what do you think Ireland should do more to protect women?*

Ireland is fairly good at protecting women's rights but the social system of having healthy adults on the dole coupled with the culture of drinking is a huge factor in domestic abuse. When breadwinner status is eroded you create other social problems stemming from boredom and a feeling of having no validation. The social supports should change to creating a work pool for the unemployed to receive these benefits. Just doling out cash to the unemployed is a recipe for disaster. It also creates social disunity by people who work, just to make ends meet and have little time for family life.

*What has been a defining moment in your life/career or business since living in Ireland? (b) If you could have breakfast with any three Irish women, who would you choose and why?*

**Unfortunately, I have not yet experienced that defining moment in my life.**

I would like to have tea with the following notable Irish women:

Emer Costello: A native of county louth, Emer is a supporter of immigrants and minority groups in Ireland. Emer Anne Costello is an Irish Labour Party politician who served as a Member of the European Parliament (MEP) for the Dublin constituency from 2012 to 2014, Lord Mayor of Dublin from 2009 to 2010 and a Dublin City Councillor for the North Inner City area from 2003 to 2012. Emer has observed international elections in Cambodia, South Africa and Bosnia and Herzgovina.

Panti Bliss (RORY O'NEILL): The LGBTQI activist and foremost Drag Queen. Panti is arguably the only Irish drag act to move from innuendo-filled entertainment routines to nationwide discourse. This outspoken drag queen became an icon through a 'series of accidents' which sparked a national debate and fed into the marriage referendum, as it was gathering pace then.

Julie Cinnamon: The woman who broke the glass ceiling in Government. Julie Sinnamon has been the CEO of Enterprise Ireland for over 3 years. She was the first woman to climb to the top position in the governmental agency supporting indigenous Irish companies.

*The government recently launched 'Project Ireland 2040', which the Taoiseach said is a document about building a republic of opportunity. Have you seen this document, if so do you think that in its mapping there is provision to create an enabling space for migrant women to be heard and lead? (b) The Prime Minister is the son of a migrant father from India, does this alone give you the slightest hope for the future of the children of migrants in this country, and why? (c) If you have the power to change anything in Ireland, what will that be?*

"Project Ireland 2040" sounds idealistic, if it happens it would be good for everyone including migrant women. Taking into consideration the present situation migrant women in Ireland find themselves. I am extremely sceptical about most of this transpiring by 2040. If there is hope for this wide-scale economic and social system of equality to happen, there is a lot that can be done currently and it is not happening. My personal view is that this is just politics talking to make it look like they're doing something positive. There are still too many areas where migrants and migrant women are discriminated against. For this to become reality we need a political voice and we need it now!

# *Miren Samper*

*"I believe in the importance of equality, equal rights to education, work, and the good thing is that the men seem to be paying more attention now than before."*

$M$y name is Miren Maialen Samper. I come from Donostia-San Sebastian in the Basque Country. My educational background is in languages, and I currently work in languages and communication in foreign languages. I first arrived in Dublin in 1999, then moved to Sao Paulo in Brazil at the end of 2002, and returned to Dublin in 2004. But, Ireland is my home now.

I hold a Masters degree in Sustainable Development from the Dublin Institute of Technology, and a Postgraduate Qualification in Community Interpreting from Dublin City University (DCU). I am part of Comhlámh Trade Justice Group, Dublin Community Growers, the Dublin Cycling Campaign, the Vegetarian Society of Ireland and also part of the cultural and dancing communities in Ireland. I enjoy travelling and Latin American dancing such as Forro, Zouk, Samba, and as well Bal Folk dancing. Dance is my passion. I'm a pianist, but I also have a love for street photography, and cycling. I have done some collaborative work with magazines such as Women News and the Local Planet on issues like language and learning about traditions of countries and sustainability. I was part of the Migrant Women Writers Collective and I am very proud now to be part of the Migrant Women in Writing project and book.

My favourite food is rice and my favourite drink is Guarana. I miss my family, my friends, the beaches of my home city Donostia-San Sebastian and I miss speaking in my mother tongue, Basque "Euskera". But, I love Ireland's landscape, the mountains, the lakes, beaches and small Islands.

*What are some of the most challenges faced by migrant women in Ireland? (b) What advice would you give to young and upcoming migrants women?*

Some of the practical challenges faced by migrant women in Ireland are: Language barriers, access to housing and affordable accommodation, access to the job market and recognition of qualifications. But, in addition, you also have to deal with emotional and mental health problems, loneliness and home sickness. My advice is to migrant women be active - find about free events from local cultural centres, local enterprise offices, clubs, universities, third level places, churches, community organisations, etc. I particularly like dancing, singing and language meetups. I would also recommend using apps such as meetup to help you socialise.

*There is a worldwide momentum for gender pay-gap, do you think that women have suddenly started to speak up in demand of effective change, or do you think that men have only started to pay more attention and listening more to women?*

Women around the world have been fighting for their rights for decades, not only in connection with the gender pay gap, but also on the many issues that have created differences between the opportunities for men in 'a man's world' compared with those for women. In general, these days, most of the efforts are more generally linked with inequality and that is what women continue to fight against. I believe in the importance of equality, equal rights to education, work, and what's more, the good thing is that the men seem to be paying more attention now than before. To be honest, I don't think that the gender pay gap is as big an issue in Ireland, or at least I am not aware of it. However, it was recently reported in the Irish Times that the gender pay gap is widening in Ireland. This information was acquired from the CSO. Source link: https://www.irishtimes.com/news/social-affairs/gender-pay-gap-is-widening-in-ireland-cso-figures-show-1.3260896

*Do you think that Ireland has done more to protect the rights of women? If you answered yes, in your opinion —why are there so many stories about domestic violence? If you answered no, then what do you think Ireland should do more to protect women?*

Ireland is not doing badly in terms of protecting women. There are many NGOs now such as Women's Aid as well as the Women Council of Ireland that are working to improve the rights of women in Ireland. I believe there are also legislations too specifically for protecting women. But, the country should do more to make information easily available for women about where to find help because there are too many women out there that are vulnerable and do not know their rights or how to get help. It is worse for migrant women in particular as some of them don't have their families here to support them. I believe in the importance the importance of civil society and activism through employing different techniques in fighting for the rights of women and empowering them. I understand this, having participated for many years in the World Social Forum WSF in Porto Alegre in Brazil as well in the WSF in Nairobi Kenya. For example, I took part and helped with an exhibition called Arpilleras by the Chilean artist Roberta Bacic in Dublin. The "Arpilleras" are three-dimensional hand appliqué textiles from Latin America which originated in a folk textile tradition from the Isla Negra region of Chile. Violeta Parra, a folk singer from Chile made Arpilleras in the 1960s depicting social issues and her concerns about war and other historical events. Arpilleras depict scenes from the lives of the women who made them. Artworks such as these convey experiences that are difficult or impossible to communicate in words and cross the barriers of language and culture to communicate with other people starkly and directly.

Through the medium of Arpilleras, stitched by women living in or on the margins of violent, repressive regimes, insights were given into the struggles they endured and their resilience and courage in resisting, surviving and striving to create a better present that might lead to a less violent future. Through the simple act of sewing, women - whether working individually, or as a group - bear witness to, resist and denounce the atrocities in this jurisdiction and beyond. Thus, their sewing, a traditional domestic activity, became a powerful act of resistance and a mechanism for spreading that message worldwide. This is a good example of the importance of using arts to promote women's rights and the State could look into creating more of these avenues to help women find their rights.

*(Roberta is based in Northern Ireland and has contributed to various workshops all around the country.)*

*What has been a defining moment in your life/career or business since living in Ireland? (b) If you could have breakfast with any three Irish women, who would you choose and why?*

A defining moment is an important moment, and I've had quite a few of them. A distinct one was when I achieved my qualifications of Master of Science in Sustainable Development as well as the Postgraduate Certificate in Community interpreting in Ireland. Another moment was meeting the President of Ireland at the Áras an Uachtaráinas part of the Comhlámh member's delegation a few years ago and more recently when my boyfriend of so many years Ger finally popped the 'question' - of course I replied in the affirmative, 'I do!' A proud moment! Back in March of this year, myself and 100 women cyclists celebrated the important historical role of bicycles for suffragettes and the emancipation of Women. The theme for the Dublin Cycling Campaign was entitled 'Freedom Machine'.

I am an active cyclist and have been taking part and helping the organisation of the Dublin Cycling campaign in St Patrick's Day Parade for the past few years. This year we developed the Freedom Machine concept and the Parade was coordinated by a team of artists as well as activists. We were, in total, 100 participants in the Dublin Cycling Campaign for the St. Patrick's Day Parade 2018.

'Freedom Machine' had a hundred women of all ages in suffragette costumes with their bicycles in the parade, with handcrafted replica period banners, sashes and placards, followed by a smaller group of their family, supporters and members of the Dublin Cycling Campaign on bicycles and cargo bikes. Many women cyclists would still claim those feelings of self-reliance and independence, but sadly in 2018 the number of female cyclists is dwindling, with three times more men than women choosing to cycle. As we paraded on our freedom machines, we were encouraging more women to enjoy leaving their homes and return freely and safely on their bicycles. The hashtags #Votail100 and #VotesforWomen helped to promote the role of the bicycle in women's emancipation. It felt great to be a part of something that big. Just like the American civil rights leader, Susan B Anthony, wrote in 1896, "I think that bicycle has done more to emancipate women than any one thing in the world."

We were joined in the parade by Senator Ivana Bacik (Chair of Votail100), Joanna Donnelly (Meteorologist) who are daily cyclists, and by other women who enjoy the freedom on their bicycles.

Another proud moment was the Dublin Photo-Marathon. This is a photography competition in which participants must take a series of photographs on predetermined topics in a set period of time. They have been run all over the world since the 1980's.

One of the assigned categories was Dublin in the Coming Times, and I was invited to take part –with other photographers to the inaugural Dublin Photo-Marathon which took place on a sunny Saturday on 28th May 2016. Many Dubliners from Italy, America, the Netherlands, and from Ballybough and Rathmines, also took part.

One of the photos I took was selected for publication in the Dublin City of Literature publication. https://www.dublincityofliterature.ie/wp-content/uploads/photo-marathon_final.pdf

I would love to have breakfast with the former President of Ireland Mary Robinson, I would also love to meet and share breakfast with Micheline Skeffington, and former Irish Times Journalist, and cystic fibrosis campaigner, Orla Tinsley

*The government recently launched 'Project Ireland 2040', which the Taoiseach said is a document about building a republic of opportunity. Have you seen this document, if so do you think that in its mapping there is provision to create an enabling space for migrant women to be heard and lead? (b) The Prime Minister is the son of a migrant father from India, does this alone give you the slightest hope for the future of the children of migrants in this country, and why? (c) If you have the power to change anything in Ireland, what will that be?*

I read the Project Ireland 2040. I believe it could be a great opportunity to create better access to resources for migrant women in Ireland. With regards to hope for the future, I believe there is hope for sure once children of migrants are educated here and they go through the Irish education system and learn the intricacies of the Irish systems in general and it'll soon no longer matter whether or not their parents are immigrants. The Ireland of the future is about promoting integration and opportunities for all, so the future is bright not only for the children of migrants but all children in this country.

*If I had the power to change anything in Ireland,* I would change the political system, for example, to allow the direct elections of city Mayors like in other cities. Also, I would implement a participatory budget as has been done in cities like Porto Alegre in Brazil.
If I had the opportunity, I would also promote multilingualism among all children, especially children of migrants born in Ireland.
I would also introduce more cycling lanes in Dublin and better infrastructures for cyclists.

# *Gloria Manyangu*

*"I would say the men pay attention to see what will happen when women get what they want."*

*I* am Gloria Manyangu, from Tanzania. I have only lived in Ireland a little over a year now and may not have as much experience to share like many others who have lived here longer than me but for the fact that an opportunity like this one that allows me to talk a bit about myself may not come so soon again. Any, I am a medical doctor, I came to Ireland to pursue a postgraduate training in Preventive Cardiology at NUIG. I can tell you that I miss my family already. I am happy that technology makes it easier to cope and I'm able to call them up to chat on the phone and stay close on social media.

It is hard to find a day without communicating with my friends and relatives. I would say that life makes more meaning having the people you love around you all the time. Back home in Tanzania, I come from a tight-knit family lineage and there is a high level of closeness with each other we used to visit each other's houses including our neighbourhoods around. In Ireland however, I can see that life is self-centred, everybody minds his or her business. I was amazed to find out that the neighbourhood is not as close as people make it out to be. I hardly see my neighbours and when I see them we hardly wave to each other. I am worried that one day I will meet my neighbours outside our own neighbourhood and they won't recognise me, and even if they do there might. simply be silence between us.

I like different types of foods, especially foods from my home. However, roasted banana is my favourite. I've come to like many things about Ireland in this short period of time that I have lived here. For example, the maternity services in this country are excellent and I have learnt many things that I will go back and impact the knowledge to my fellow care workers in Tanzania.

*What are some of the most challenges faced by migrant women in Ireland? (b) What advice would you give to young and upcoming migrants women?*

Ireland being a foreign land, it always feels lonely. Having stayed for a short period I feel a sense of loneliness, this kind of feelings I fear may cause depression and further isolation for anyone unless it is self-managed. The system in Ireland is structured to support independent life, that is so different from Tanzania where there is communalism-kind of life. For example, in Tanzania transport system is not into real time-schedule rather spontaneous leading to long waiting hours in the bus station where it creates room for socialising, leading to making new friends.

My advice to upcoming migrants; embrace the new culture but also practice your old culture.

*There is a worldwide momentum for gender pay-gap, do you think that women have suddenly started to speak up in demand of effective change, or do you think that men have only started to pay more attention and listening more to women?*

I would say the men pay attention to see what will happen when women get what they want. I have grown up to hear about women rights to education, women's rights to work and leadership. Although not to the same extent but over here I see women take part in education, work and leadership position. However, in Tanzania, there is still very low response to gender pay-gap. Gender inequality is a generational problem that will take a long time before its roots are fully uprooted. For example, in Tanzania when a student gets pregnant she is not allowed to continue with her studies after delivery while the boy who is the father continues to study, this is not only gender inequality to education, but it also creates a sense of punishment associated with pregnancy. I would say many pregnant women will hide the pregnancy because it is a symbol of shame, and when pregnancy is no longer hidden girls who are likely to lose their rights to education may opt for illegal abortion. In my opinion I think that men are yet to listen to the demands of women.

I came to Ireland on a scholarship, yet I was pregnant when I got here because it was hard for me to postpone the scholarship, due to existing policies in Tanzania, I had to choose between accepting the offer or postpone, which means the scholarship would be given to someone else and who may not be a woman again. Considering the value of the opportunity, I spoke to my husband and he advised that I accept it. I knew nobody in Ireland, so I stayed in hostels before I got a shared house to live with this lovely woman in her eighties, she was so amazing, especially at how she accepted me and not minding our cultural differences. I stayed with her during most of my pregnancy and while attending college at the same time and only moved into a new apartment near my due date for preparation of the arrival of my baby. My new landlord was another kind and lovely woman who works at the university where I study. So friendly, and she could walk to my house to collect her rent, something that I liked. I always looked forward to her visits. On my due date, I took a bus to the hospital, natural birth eluded me, and I ended up having a caesarean section. Everything went well, a friend from church came along to the theatre and I felt confident having her with me. The hard part was when I took my baby home from hospital. It was now just me and the baby lonely in the house, I could have suffered from postpartum depression due to the solitary lifestyle in this new culture. But for the fact that the public health nurses were very helpful and gave me so much encouragements during the first three months. I joined a mother's groups, breastfeeding group and baby sensory class which all together offer perfect support to women especially after delivery when there is a high risk of depression. Time flies and my baby is growing so well. Despite the independent and solitary lifestyle in Ireland, most people are friendly and are ready to help whenever they can.

*If you could have breakfast with any three Irish women, who would you choose and why?*

I have been here not so long, but I have met so many lovely women and I'd like to appreciate them all. Among them, the one that have made the most difference to my stay here and made it memorable, is Bridge Hurley, the 84 years old lady who accommodated me while pregnant, even after I moved out of her place we kept in touch. Then, there is my second landlord, Carmel King from NUIG. She is a kind and polite woman who accepted a mother and a baby into her new apartment regardless of the baby's noises. While in Galway I volunteered with Pernet CLG organization that has incredible women leadership. When I delivered, these women took care of me and they made me feel so much at home — far away from my real home. Lastly but not least is Hellen Freeburn, she is the Minister of the Presbyterian-Methodist United Church that I used to attend. She is one of the humble ministers I have come across. She mobilised a team from the church to mind me and my baby when we were in the hospital after my surgery. The team included Sarah, Vick, Rachel and Erica, they even came home to take care of us after I was discharged from hospital, they helped to prepare meals and cleaned my house while I was recovering. Finally, Joahan Walsh and the family from international office NUIG, I had run out of option when finding accommodation one week before the surgery when I found Johana's family and they made me realise the easier way through, and in a matter of two days I got my accommodation. These women are my family here in Ireland, they might not know how much their presence have touched my life, but I celebrate them all.

# *Patricia Guerra*

*"The pressure is driving both men and women to feel the right to speak up and fight for our own conditions and for men the obligation to not ignore this fact anymore."*

*I* am Patricia Guerra, I work as a Finance Engineer (ACCA). I come from Peru and living in Ireland for the past 9 years. I was born in Peru in the 80s in a small and not much known town located between the mountains and the forest, Huánuco, primaveral city with a sunny sky you can see throughout the year. I consider myself very lucky to have been born in such beautiful corner of the world, although problems of terrorism and violence was at its highest level in Peru at that time and as much as political and economic instability. Many families, including mine lost many loved ones in the unreasonable terrorism war. Certainly, this is something that has marked my whole life with the eagerness for justice, my family went through a most painful mourning brought about the loss of loved-ones. I still remember how my mother struggled even as she was enveloped with grief to give me the best childhood. A very strong and brave woman so was my granny; both were my strong tower and pillar of my life and I admire them very much. Growing up they showed me that no matter what we go through in life, I must believe that there is always light at the other end, and because that I have the determination to fight and achieve any goal that I can dream of.

My childhood was full of love from my family and my friends, I grew up in an environment of solidarity and gratitude. Peru was a poor country, so it was pretty clear to people from all those years ago that if you are privileged to be well-off economically than others, you owe it as an obligation to help other who are less fortunate. I move to Europe to continue my education, I got my Bachelor in Economics in Italy and a Masters in Management in France. I was eager for more experience and that drove me to Sweden continue in a further education where I received second Masters in International Business. Sweden was a cultural revelation for me, a society where respect from fellow human being is a must regardless of a person's economic status, a society where woman has the same opportunity as men and in some case more than men. I fell in love with their way of living, I tasted freedom in a safe environment and loved and admired the fact that I was there, a place every person is made to face justice if they committed a crime. I realized how different life can be when you lived in a developed world. After my graduation, I was contacted by an Irish company with a job opportunity in Dublin. It was supposed to be a 6 months experience. It was in the Summer of 2009 that I first arrived in Dublin. I was curious of this new experience, I felt lonely I had no friends and knew no one and certainly no family, I suddenly realised it was once again a new challenge that I must face.

However, it didn't take too long before I discovered the positive sides to Irish life, there was a good vibe and positive flow of energy around the city, people were kind and always wanted to have fun. Soon, I discovered a multicultural environment and lots of professional opportunities and most of all, I met the love of my life, my beloved partner Bernardo; a native of Italy and to whom I share all my dream and achievements. Now, he is my companion for life. I love this country and I am grateful too. It has offered me financial independence, personal development and good professional experience. I have been working for well-known corporations and moved from Industry to financial services and to Tech. I went back to study and qualified as a global chartered accountant, ACCA. While it is true that years are passing by and I am settling here, I do miss my family and my childhood friends, I still miss the food sometimes and the sun of my little town, I have these nostalgic memories where neighbourhood and families get together to spend a lot of time chatting, singing and dancing the way Peruvians enjoy life.

*What are some of the most challenges faced by migrant women in Ireland? (b) What advice would you give to young and upcoming migrants women?*

My personal experience in this country has been positive so far. It has been a good place to pursue my professional carrier, I feel that I have opportunities and I can follow my ambition as much as I would like to go both with my professional and personal life. However, it is also important to mention as well that there is a segment of marginalized migrant women that are suffering due to lack of opportunities, or those that are taking paid jobs far lower than what they are qualified for. Therefore, there should be provision of free English courses to help them to integrate more into society and reduce the isolation that a language barrier creates.

In general terms, I consider Dublin a decent, social and safe place to live. In relation to challenges of women, the country has serious issues that requires major attention still. First at all, reproductive rights and affordable childcare is a major concern for many women, not only migrant women. Ireland until recently doesn't provide health support for abortion and adoption is heavily dependent on financial capacity rather than family desires. It is also a known fact that a mother will need the support and help with a newborn, in a traditional family this comes along from relatives and grannies but for a migrant woman it becomes more difficult. Emotional and care support is poor it often carries the risk of leaving the mother in a lonely place. Furthermore, creches are excessively expensive and can cause financial distress for low-income families as well as put the woman in the situation of choosing to step back from a carrier or to postpone the maternity, it is worth to mention that Ireland has no legislation that forces employers to pay for maternity leave thus limiting the options for women. Safety is an unease topic for migrant woman, unfortunately degraded social class still shows racist behaviours towards foreigners. Gardaí' shortages doesn't help in reducing street attacks which makes it more difficult for us women to feel free and safe to walk around. This risk can be associated with the current housing crisis; rental price tends to be cheaper around degraded areas that at the same time are more financially accessible to new arrivals or the young and upcoming woman.

My advice to migrant women is that, communication for reproductive and maternity rights may be poor. Migrant women shouldn't be afraid to ask for help and contact some of the organisations that can provide a bit of guidance in such a situation. They should become informed and be aware of certain areas when looking for a place to live. In addition, it is worth considering the fact that Ireland is a hub of technical employment where opportunities arise for well-educated people. Third level education can be costly but it is also true that SAS, Solas and other Education boards offer further education, training courses and programs for job integration that are frequently free of charge. I would highly advise young migrant women to take advantage of these tool to enter the labour market or simply to improve their set of skills and consequently boost their financial position.

*There is a worldwide momentum for gender pay-gap, do you think that women have suddenly started to speak up in demand of effective change, or do you think that men have only started to pay more attention and listening more to women?*

I believe it is a consequence of globalization and internet that have given more visibility to women around the world, causing a sense of pressure to improve social responsibility from developed countries, as in Ireland as well as companies with higher ethical governance to respond proactively to the topic. This pressure is driving both men and women to feel the right to speak up and fight for our own conditions and for men the obligation to not ignore this fact anymore. Countries in Europe are legally bound by the EU commission to implement and reinforce equality legislation and reduce such imbalance. However, Ireland is still behind when compared to other countries. Iceland for example has now made it illegal for men to be paid more than women in the same job. Nevertheless, in my personal experience men with a set of skills close to mine have better opportunities and when performing the same kind of job are likely to earn at least €10,000 euro a year more than myself, it reinforced by statistics showing that woman earns 13% circa less per year than their counterpart male.

*Do you think that Ireland has done more to protect the rights of women? If you answered yes, in your opinion —why are there so many stories about domestic violence? If you answered no, then what do you think Ireland should do more to protect women?*

**There are many areas to consider about women's rights:** Concerning domestic violence, Ireland has legal and cultural imbalances to work on, when compared with other EU countries. I believe that justice appears not to be reinforced by strong regulation and this hold women up to denounce any type of violence, the belief that nothing is going to change stops women from looking for help. Economic dependencies caused by unequal opportunities as well as lower household budget left after childcare costs leave women in the condition to accept domestic abuse. Therefore, government should introduce powerful directives against any psychological and physical abuse, improve the availability, quality and reliability of support centres and where already in existence promote those nationwide because need to feel protected by the state. Government should promote gender equality by imposing transparent declaration from corporations and other organisation on their remunerations package, and consequently demand to reduce the gaps reported; indeed employer has a huge influence on the change. Additionally, as mentioned before poor provision from the government on childcare impact negatively too as women are constrained to stay away from the labour market for longer periods reducing their income per year. Furthermore, we need to create a culture that empowers women more, that boost confidence in all areas of life that enables them to embrace their own human right of being respected and confident to report domestic violence, and to discover and accept their intellectual capability of doing well in education and in jobs that are believed to traditionally related to men and excel in them. But this is not the responsibility of government only, community support is also important because change has to come from all of us. In my personal experience, some organization and employers are contributing to this awareness, in fact I volunteered in workshops to meet up with young girls and raise awareness on the availability of work placement in finance and technologies, guiding to undertake engineers education, enhancing self-esteem and influencing the fact that women can pursue any type of carrier even if traditionally believed to be done only by men.

It's been 19 long years since I have been living in Europe, and I have lived in different countries including Ireland. I can honestly say that I have in this period experienced racism in some ways, it can be that some people are still not used to diversity and they act in ignorance, in some other instance it really can be scary for some and therefore they avoid the unknown by leaving foreign people isolated, also in other realities they have the expectations that foreign women can only do low paid job because they are coming from a developing or third world country, and for me it has always been a struggle to let people know that their attitude is not acceptable because if not for anything else, we are created equal and have ambitions to achieve our goals in life no matter where we live.

*What has been a defining moment in your life/career or business since living in Ireland? (b) If you could have breakfast with any three Irish women, who would you choose and why?*

There was an interesting incident some months after I arrived in Ireland and started working with an Irish company. I had to present a project to a panel of professionals in my area, to say the least, I was shy and had no confident in my speaking ability but my manager who was Irish said something I will never forget "it doesn't matter that your English not perfect, you have good ideas and I just want you to bring them to the table." He added. "there are so many English natives here that can help you with things like spellings and corrections but none of them has the background that you have." Those words lifted my spirit instantly, my professional confidence soared and my love for this country increased automatically. It was the first time in 10 years living in Europe that I felt that much accepted, that moment also sealed my decision to stay around longer. It was just natural for my manager then to say those words, but it was more important for me to hear them; it was as if all my efforts were repaid in the belief that this was a country without prejudice and people were treated according to their actions rather than where they are from. I wish everyone, every employer, and all those in higher authority adopts this strategy and be completely genuine in their dealings with the general public including all migrants.

*The government recently launched 'Project Ireland 2040', which the Taoiseach said is a document about building a republic of opportunity. Have you seen this document, if so do you think that in its mapping there is provision to create an enabling space for migrant women to be heard and lead? (b) The Prime Minister is the son of a migrant father from India, does this alone give you the slightest hope for the future of the children of migrants in this country, and why? (c) If you have the power to change anything in Ireland, what will that be?*

From my understanding, Project Ireland 2040 aims to create a republic of opportunity by investing in infrastructure, housing, education and wellbeing. There are no clear indications of any investments for migrant women directly. However, if Ireland as a country is to grow and improve the quality of life of the population, it will impact positively on migrant women as well; investment on childcare provision, better access to education, housing regulation, security and legislation reinforcement will reduce the problems that women are suffering now. The truth is that I believe Ireland is kind to women migrants, my network is made up of women from other countries, but all have found in some ways in Ireland a place that they now call home. Ireland is a country of opportunities and gives space for growth to any personal or professional ambition. The society is open to diversity and we can be proud of an international culture that accepts us and allows for us to contribute and share the benefits of the country.

Ireland Primer Minister being the first leader from an ethnic minority background has indeed increased the hopes for the children of migrants. Just he said it himself in a speech that "it doesn't matter where are you coming from but rather where you want to go."

*If I could change anything in this country*, it would be to invest more in education and healthcare and make it available for the entire population for free. I would also redesign the welfare system; it would make more sense to invest on integration of the low social classes than give people free money.

# *Annie Waithira Burke*

*"Ireland needs better policies and legislation that will help women and will also combat the epidemic that is domestic violence."*

*I* am Annie Waithira Burke. Originally from Kenya and have lived in Ireland for over 10 years. I currently work at AkiDwA as the administrator. I am also a leader of the Young Migrant Women's Group. I would like to believe I am a lady of many talents and have a lot of strings to my bow. I am a therapist by trade as I love working with people face to face and looking after people and their wellbeing, working with persons on all levels in mind, body, and soul. I have been working in the hospitality sector for a long time working in hotels, restaurants, shops, spas, and reception. I am aspiring to go back to university so as to acquire my qualification in political science and law. I believe that having the opportunity to help communities and the people is my calling. Running for the local election in 2019 is my next step to a bigger dream. This would be a way to represent the underrepresented, using my voice to speak for those who cannot; a platform to make a change for many, as well as my children and their future.

My favourite food would be Ugali, nyama choma and kachumbari (maize flour made with water served with roasted meat and a salad made with coriander, tomatoes and onions with a touch of chilli. My favourite drink is African tea (loads of milk and water boiled over the hub then loose tea leaves added in with a bit of herbs called tangawizi).

I miss my family most of all and the sense of belonging and how close a community can be. Additionally, I miss how accessible and affordable groceries and convenience items were at home. I love Ireland. Céad Míle Fáilte – A country of one hundred thousand welcomes. My home and a place where I strongly believe my heart belongs. Ireland's nature from the beaches to the landscape is mesmerising and so beautiful. Not forgetting the people. Majority of the people are very warm, welcoming and caring. Ireland's culture and history are not too different from my home country so there is a lot of understanding and similarities that I did not experience a massive culture shock when I first moved here.

*What are some of the most challenges faced by migrant women in Ireland? (b) What advice would you give to young and upcoming migrants women?*

Challenges faced by migrant women in Ireland are plentiful. From my own personal experience and some of the challenges faced would be identity crisis, racism, segregation, cultural difference, access to jobs and services, language barriers, religion, stereotyping and lack of information.

My advice to the young and upcoming migrant women would be "equip yourself with as much information and knowledge as you possibly can. These will be your weapon in life no matter where you are in the world. Do not forget who you are in the process of trying to fit into the society. God made you unique for a reason. There is no one like you and you are the only one who can bring your 'Je ne sais quoi' flare, ideas, solutions, hopes and dreams to your own communities. Regardless of anything, always be true to yourself.

*There is a worldwide momentum for gender pay-gap, do you think that women have suddenly started to speak up in demand of effective change, or do you think that men have only started to pay more attention and listening more to women?*

Historically, we have seen women fight for the right to vote, study, work and equality in the workplace. My view is that women's rights movement and gender pay-gap movement started centuries ago. The reason why it's being addressed more now is that there are more women who are entering the workforce than ever before, we are seeing more of an understanding of the gender pay-gap and sexism in the workplace. I find that the women in the workplace are experiencing the indifference and are more knowledgeable and well informed than before. I also trust that we are more vocal, active and willing to fight for ourselves for a better life for ourselves, our daughters, grandchildren and future generations

*Do you think that Ireland has done more to protect the rights of women? If you answered yes, in your opinion —why are there so many stories about domestic violence? If you answered no, then what do you think Ireland should do more to protect women?*

In my opinion, Ireland is working hard and trying its best to protect the rights of women. I would have loved to see some of these changes years ago, but as we all know "even the greatest empires were not built in a day". It will take time. I am proud of Ireland as it has started taking steps toward protecting its women and the girl-child. But let's be honest we still have a very long way to go. Looking back at the history of Ireland, we as women have gone through the mills in regards to our safety, sexuality, our bodies, our looks and many more. Recently a great achievement for the country was when the yes vote won as the 8th amendment was repealed. As a woman being able to make my own decision and choices about my body and life without the state interfering was a relief. Also, the fact that women are now in decision making positions like in politics, boards and on roundtable meetings, meaning that women are being represented and their demands and voices are heard. It would be awesome to have an equal number of women and men, 50/50 in decision making. There is much work to be done but Ireland is heading in the right direction.

With domestic violence unfortunately not much has changed. There is a lot of misunderstanding, not enough information or maybe it's just ignorance, I don't know. There are many ways domestic violence happens; most people only know of the physical part of it. In my experience, some cases are not dealt with until it is so bad or worse until it becomes a tragedy. 'How is it ok to send a person back to the same house as his victim, or allow an abuser back into the community he has committed the crime?' These adds to the trauma, anguish, hurt, emotional distress and more pain to the woman. Yet her story will be scrutinised and end up being her word against his. The system has failed women for generations hence they do not trust that there is help for them or even a way out. The stigma associated with these as well makes it harder for people to come forward as they do not want anyone to know how bad things are behind their closed doors. I find that even neighbours, friend and families are afraid of getting involved. As some say, "humans wear blinkers if it's something that does not affect them directly." Ireland needs better policies and legislation that will help women and will also combat the epidemic that is domestic violence. We can start by educating our children, for them to know about the topic and understand how domestic violence is triggered, starts to affect and how to spot and stop it before it's a catastrophe.

Let us teach our future generations to protect themselves. If we give our children, the right tools and knowledge we are setting them up for success and a better tomorrow. Knowledge is power.

*What has been a defining moment in your life/career or business since living in Ireland? (b) If you could have breakfast with any three Irish women, who would you choose and why?*

My defining moment, unfortunately, was negative but I turned them to a positive and that has made me who I am today. These included discrimination, racism, segregation and sometimes physical assaults. Living in fear for years and always looking over your shoulder wasn't the way I imagined my life to be. My turning point was when my children who are Irish by the way (mixed race that is) where being discriminated against in school as well as at home up to the point where my daughter who was aged only 7 years at the time wanted to commit suicide. "Your skin is covered in poo that's why your skin in that colour" a comment made to my children at a playground and in school. It was unbearable, and my children didn't understand why others were mean and horrible considering these children were friends. "You look poor, homeless and disgusting like those kids on TV with big bellies," they'd say and laugh, or things like "Go back to where you came from". I used to ask them where is it that they wanted my children to return to, because they were Irish like any of them. I wanted to know why they hated my children so much, and quite frankly how did those other children themselves aged just about 6 and 7 years old, learn to speak such hateful words. But the worst of it all was when my children started receiving hate mail through the letter box, soiled with ants inside it and dog-poo with notes written "we hate u, wish you were dead." This is not the way we as grown-ups and little children should live. My children and I were constantly in fear. When walking, minding your own business only to get spat on for no reason and told you do not belong. My recent encounter where an older man walked into me at a time that I was unwell and in pain and on my way to the hospital; he took one look at me and called me stupid and spat on the floor and then walked off. These experiences or moments made me think 'enough is enough.' I went on to post my worries and concerns on a community page on Facebook, to my surprise I was not the only one going through these types of horrible experiences. So, I sat down with my children one day and discussed about how they were being affected and we then worked on a solution that to help my and the community at large. I turned this negative experience into something positive. I figured most of it was happening because there was a lack of knowledge, there were ignorance and misinformation. I started by creating a multicultural, diversity and integration day in my community. I used it to help educate the young ones but mostly as a platform to encourage, give confidence and pride to my own children—for them to love themselves and be proud of who they are. It was also a day for the community to celebrate our diversity, share food, show off traditional wears, and learn about all the cultures that are represented and with music and entertainment. The Intercultural Jam is now three years running and has been a great success. And because of that life is much better for me and my children, now they have friends and love with less fear. Now I believe what my mum always told me "God cannot give you a cross you cannot bear." From here we started doing modelling, self-difference classes, music and the arts to help boost our confidence and for my little ones to know how to stand up for themselves and be proud of their origin.

**I would love to have breakfast with the following women:**

1) Mary Therese Winifred Robinson was the 7th president of Ireland. Being the first woman to hold this position in Ireland she opened up a lot of opportunities for women across the board. She was known to be an advocate for change and well known for being a transformative figure. She has stood against big political parties and worn standing as an independent candidate when she ran for the presidency. What a woman and an inspiration for the future generations in Ireland and new Irish. Having breakfast with her would be a dream come true, she is a role model for me and as I ready to pursue my political career her

insight and advice would all I would love to have and possibly an autograph as well.

2) Katie Tylor, a boxer from a small town, Bray. She is an example of not quitting no matter what. I would have breakfast with her just to know how she gets the strength to keep going and be true to herself and still be loyal to her homeland. As a proud African-Irish lady, anytime Katie steps in the ring it's always a proud moment for me and my children. I would love to face and look at the world the way she does, as a fighter who wins against all odds. She is a true role model for the younger generation as my daughter looks up to her and aspires to be like her (going for what she believes in and working hard towards it). For this am grateful to have a lady like Katie appear on my television set.

3) Joanne O'Riordan is a Student and campaigner. Joanne was born without limbs and that hasn't stopped her. She has taken her disability and made it her weapon to fight and be the voice for people with disability. This lady's power to fight is something I've never seen before. Following her journey and reading her story brings tears to my eyes. I am in awe of her work, passion, and commitment. Having breakfast with her would be the icing on the cake for me.

*The government recently launched 'Project Ireland 2040', which the Taoiseach said is a document about building a republic of opportunity. Have you seen this document, if so do you think that in its mapping there is provision to create an enabling space for migrant women to be heard and lead? (b) The Prime Minister is the son of a migrant father from India, does this alone give you the slightest hope for the future of the children of migrants in this country, and why? (c) If you have the power to change anything in Ireland, what will that be?*

With regards to the launch of the "project Ireland 2040", I have read it but still trying to have a better understanding of it. There is so much information and strategies that the government is hoping to work on by 2040, and with this I can see progress toward a better Republic. In my opinion it is opening a gateway for the migrant women and that includes me as we, so it is a good start. I believe there is more that can be added to the plan to ensure security and provide more for women. One step at a time as Ireland is working towards a better to-morrow, to become an all-inclusive society for the Irish and migrant community.

For Ireland to have a Taoiseach who is of Indian descent has a positive impact on the society. It's a beacon of hope for the migrant community as we can see that they are willing to embrace change and progress, and of course someone of a different background who brings diverse ideas, experiences and vision.

*If I had the power to change anything* in Ireland it would be immigration, healthcare especially mental health, and mostly ending violence against women and the girlchild, and equality. Another would be creating a space for our youth to grow. I feel they are forgotten in our planning when it comes to the running and growth of the country. From ages 19-30, we need more platforms for their voices to be heard.

# *Deborah Onyema*

*"So many women who constantly fall victim of abuse are not taken very seriously."*

*M*y name is Deborah Onyema, (a.k.a. Debsandy). I come from the West African country of Nigeria, often referred as 'The Giant of Africa.' So much has been happening in Nigeria that has attracted a lot of negative publicity lately. Consequently, this title that very much befitted the status of Nigeria before has been put to disrepute by some, and for good reason too. The instability, restlessness and safety threats lately has shown Nigeria in a different light, rather than it was best known for in the not too distant past. However, Nigeria to me, remains my beloved country, in which I was born and brought up. That is the reason I miss it, though not terribly now, having lived in Ireland for 17 good years. But I miss the Nigerian communitarian style parenting and the sociol-cultural celebrations.

My favourite foods are mixed vegetables, cooked with either meat or fish and served with boiled rice. Being a typical Nigerian, I like Jollof-riced and fried chicken very much, or just plain white rice and stew. This also has to be Nigerian style-stew which we normally prepare with assorted meat, because without the assorted meat what you'll be eating will be just old hot sauce.

What I like most about Ireland is the Irish educational structure, child and vulnerable adult's poverty eradication programmes and support networks. Professionally, I am a Health Service Advisor. I am also an international Gospel Singer, and the founder of Debsandy Foundation & I-care Health & Wellness Campaign.

*What are some of the most challenges faced by migrant women in Ireland? (b) What advice would you give to young and upcoming migrants women?*

Migrant women living in Ireland would likely experience more difficulties with the welfare of their children. This only from my own experience and only my viewpoint, but I think that migrant women living in any other countries in the West away from family and friends would in many ways suffer economic independence also, but the upbringing of their children is an aspect many find difficult to cope with, because so many of us are used to different ways of bringing up children that are so different from how it is done here in Ireland. For this reason, some migrant families have found themselves in serious trouble with Irish Authorities.

My advice to the young migrant woman is simple; embrace all that is positive and empowering but do not lose your identity in the process.

*Do you think that Ireland has done more to protect the rights of women? If you answered yes, in your opinion —why are there so many stories about domestic violence? If you answered no, then what do you think Ireland should do more to protect women?*

Too many women are living in countries where their rights are non-existent and men in those countries see it as their right to abuse these women just as they like without fear of reproach. If we all lived in environments where no one can be held accountable, imagine what our world would be like, yet this is the same kind of situation millions of women find themselves, and often no one to speak for them, so if you try to compare Ireland to those countries, then we are right ahead. The way human right issues are handled may not be perfect, and there are so many women who constantly fall victim of abuse and not taken very seriously too, but Ireland is doing ok, although more still needs to be done. Domestic violence is quite rampant and Irish government can really do more to protect women.

*What has been a defining moment in your life/career or business since living in Ireland? (b) If you could have breakfast with any three Irish women, who would you choose and why?*

The defining moment of my life was when I launched the Debsandy Foundation and Icare Health Outreach. If I had the opportunity, I would love to have breakfast with the two former female presidents of Ireland, Mary Robinson, and Mary McAleese. The third Irish woman I'd like to have breakfast with is Ciara Dunlon.
Mary Robinson & Mary McAleese; both former Presidents of Ireland who championed human rights and humanitarian causes. Ciara Dunlon for her outstanding healthcare solutions for women with post-breast cancer surgery.

*The Prime Minister is the son of a migrant father from India, does this alone give you the slightest hope for the future of the children of migrants in this country, and why? (c) If you have the power to change anything in Ireland, what will that be?*

Leo Varadkar's tenure as Prime Minister will always serve as a reference point, and a source for reassurance to citizens from new communities that yes, we can become whatever we want, including aspiring to occupy principal political offices in Ireland.

# *Esmeralda Usiahon*

*"If we all stand in solidarity, the government can no longer ignore us, and then we can achieve much needed change."*

*M*y name is Esmeralda Usiahon (Lubbers). I am originally from Zaandam, The Netherlands. I moved to Ireland 15 years ago at the tender age of 18. It took me a while to get settled as a young immigrant, and I moved around Ireland a lot in the first 6 years of living here. I lived in Ennis, County Clare and Galway City before eventually moving to County Laois in 2007. I am a mother of 4 lovely children aged 8, 11, 13, and 14. I have worked in many jobs, from being a guest room cleaner to a hotel receptionist before I decided in taking a Fetac level 5 studies in Nursing, that was in 2008. After that, I got a job as a care assistant, a job I stayed in for several years before finally deciding to pursue an Honours degree in Applied Social Studies and Professional Social Care in 2015. I just finished the 3rd year and will hopefully go into the final year in September of this year. In addition to that, I am also currently employed as an assistant support worker for Nua Healthcare and have worked here since the past 19 months.

A few years ago, I got into the modelling and pageantry industry due to my children having an interest in it. Back then, however, I had no intention to pursue this because I felt that I was too 'fat', but the pageant director reassured me that no one was considered too fat to take part of the pageant and so I decided to go for it, and ended up winning my category, this was in 2015. I felt amazing especially when the crowd started cheering, it gave me a huge boost to my confidence. I also must mention that I have bad social anxiety before but going into pageantry has had a positive impact on my outlook towards social events. Since then I have been actively taking part in events like this, including photoshoots for charity events and more. Now, this has become a dream of mine in the future to empower women from all walks of life, to encourage them to feel confident in their skin.

Before I moved to Ireland, I was a child in the care of the state. The move to Ireland gave me a new lease of life and turned my life around for the better. I am happy to use my own experiences as a skill to help others, through the pageantry platform to inspire women who may be shy to talk openly about their past or who do not feel confident enough to make a positive change to their lives due to past experiences. This is my aim to share my personal story with people and to give them hope for the future.

It is hard for me to think about the food I miss most from my country. I suppose the Dutch traditional foods such as 'Hollandse Nieuwe Hering' which is raw herring and with raw onion bits, and 'zuur'-(gherkins). I also love 'gerookte paling' or smoked eel. I never ran across them in Ireland. Perhaps not so healthy, but there are snacks that we eat traditionally at football matches, such as bitterballen, frikandellen, kroketten etc. I can make bitterballen and kroketten myself, but time doesn't permit me, so I only prepare them occasionally. Things I miss most about my country is the bicycle. In Holland you don't really need a car, if you go a long distance, the public transportation system is there. It is advanced more than Ireland. No offence! But when you need to go anywhere locally, people always prefer the bikes. From dropping the kids off at school to grocery shopping, or just good old exercise, the bike is our holy grail. That is something I really miss about The Netherlands. It is a great way to stay fit and avoid excess weight and save money that way. Back to Ireland; what I love about Ireland is the beauty of the landscape, it is so beautiful. The mountains, how green it is, the clean air, Ireland is also very welcoming to tourists. It is very family oriented, something The Netherlands could learn from.

*What are some of the most challenges faced by migrant women in Ireland? (b) What advice would you give to young and upcoming migrants women?*

Thinking back to some of the challenges I faced as a young migrant moving to Ireland (not gender specific, however) is the lack of information that was available to me. I was just 18 years of age when I first arrived in Ireland, and had to rely on advice from people I barely knew, about entitlements, job searching, housing, medical care and so on. It was a very challenging time. When I applied for a FAS course in 2004 an employee acted very rudely towards me, saying that I was not entitled to take the course because I was foreign. However, I was aware of my rights, as my country is an EU-member state. I informed her that I was entitled to do the course, but she was adamant. This lady went on to ask how long since The Netherlands was part of the EU. I advised her that it was one of the founding members of the EU, and she was clearly shocked and still behaved rudely. I found this very upsetting, but it was quite eye-opening to how non-nationals were treated. But Ireland has moved beyond that period when people perceived us merely as the immigrants who came to take their jobs and were in the habit of frequently asking when we were going to return to our country of origin. I always replied that I had no intention of leaving Ireland as Ireland was my home, it still is. Some people found this hard to believe, and always had a stigma towards us. Many people don't even know they are doing it, and it is important for us to speak up about these things in order to force those doing to become aware of their own behaviour.

The best advice I can give to a migrant woman are the followings: Know your rights, research your entitlements, and don't give up hope on your future. Don't take no on face-value, many people cannot know for certain if the information they give you about something is accurate. The law changes constantly, and even if something is written in law, we can come together to challenge that law and the government will listen if enough people challenges a particular law together. That is the beauty of this country.

*There is a worldwide momentum for gender pay-gap, do you think that women have suddenly started to speak up in demand of effective change, or do you think that men have only started to pay more attention and listening more to women?*

I only became aware of the gender pay-gap in recent years due to the media talking about it. While I certainly believe that women became more vocal about the issue, I am yet to see improvement on the matter. I am a comment reader on social media, and while I certainly respect views on both sides, there are many women who accept this as a reality and believe that men deserve more for an equal job. I disagree with this. Take the secondary school teachers protests for example, while it is similar, it isn't based on a gender pay gap. It was about equal pay for equal jobs. That is what this should be about nationwide. In addition, in male-dominated jobs women feel intimidated to apply for such jobs, even though they are just as capable to do well in comparison to their male counterparts. Unfortunately, we see inequality everywhere we look, and again I am a fierce believer in talking openly about these issues so that people become aware. Now on the other side of the coin, the government is not taking enough action to tackle this problem. I believe that more women need to speak up about it, and if all of us stand in solidarity, the government can no longer ignore us, and then we can achieve much needed change.

*Do you think that Ireland has done more to protect the rights of women? If you answered yes, in your opinion —why are there so many stories about domestic violence? If you answered no, then what do you think Ireland should do more to protect women?*

I believe that Ireland has come a long way from history, it is still a patriarchy. In the constitution, women are seen as homemakers, taking care of the family, and were not allowed to work once they got married, it was their duty to stay at home to look after the children. Unfortunately, this mentality has embedded in society today, with women still believing that men are their superiors, that men are the head of the house. Women are afraid of the implications of leaving abusive relationships. Children are witnessing this, and it turns into a violent cycle. The Belfast rape trial illustrated that this problem not only starts with the perpetrators but the entire justice system. Male-dominated professions such as the An Gardai Siochana and the legal system are, in my opinion biased. Issues such as first-time offenders do not consider that women may have phoned on several occasions making complaints about an abuser, and far too often the perpetrators are not being taken into custody or are let off with a warning.

Every phone call should be taken seriously, but often, women are continued to be exposed to danger in their own homes. In addition to that, women's shelters rely on charitable contributions. The government should take steps in assuring that when a woman picks up the phone or walks into a gardai station fearing for her safety, that she is listened to and taken seriously. Many abuse victims are isolated from family and friends, and so it is not always possible for them to seek safety away from home. More women shelters should be opened to be able to cope with the rising numbers of women who are unsafe at home. The government should introduce new legislation to safeguard women, supporting them to make informed decisions and support them when they find the strength to leave their abusive partners. A system that records all phone-calls or visits made by a member of a household to the gardai, highlighting how many times they contact emergency services, and aiding those women who need the help in real time. This reduces the likelihood of women 'slipping through the net'.

*What has been a defining moment in your life/career or business since living in Ireland? (b) If you could have breakfast with any three Irish women, who would you choose and why?*

The year 2015 was a very big year for me on many levels. It was the year I was first introduced to the modelling world. Through this, I realized something about myself. I learned who I was as a person. For many years, from childhood until then, I lived to be a people's pleaser. I strived to be well liked amongst the people I knew. I was not myself. However, that year I got to know that many people did in fact not like me decided to move away from those who exerted control over me. I found this out through becoming involved in the modelling industry. Simple things as not being able to make it to church, my dress style changing, basically looking after myself caused people to move away from me. It was at this point that I became more determined than ever to do what I wanted to do the most. It was this year also that I decided to apply to go to college. At the start, I was extremely nervous because I didn't do well in secondary school. I felt that I would fail miserably. I'm the only person in my family to have attempted to get a degree. I had a difficult childhood, not many people who have been in care would ever dream of getting the opportunity to go to college. However, as I started, I soon realized that I had nothing to worry about. My grades were up there, I had so many boosts to my confidence, and I realized that all the excess baggage I was carrying were other people's opinion on my life's outlook. I had extremely low self-esteem before that year which transformed my life. In addition, when I started modelling, I believed that I was too fat, in addition to that I had social anxiety. However, the first pageant I was involved with had a great impact on my self-esteem. I started to believe in myself. Now 3 years later, and I am participating in more pageants as a hobby and never felt better about myself as a person. I can say that I am a confident woman, who has turned the table. Many women in my class, friends, and even total strangers come to me for advice regarding confidence, how to build up their self-esteem, and how to break into the modelling industry. I am going into my final year in college in September. I never could have dreamt of becoming a graduate, but it is just around the corner now.

There are many women in Ireland that inspire me, and I would like to have breakfast with if the opportunity ever presented itself. However, I will only mention one of them. I had the pleasure of meeting Vicki Mooney in 2015 at a casting call for her modelling agency V Plus Models. While we met in a formal way, since then I greatly admired her. She is an inspiration to me. She has battled through so much, from body shaming to domestic violence. However, she never gave up. She did not let the body shaming get to her, instead, she decided to set up a plus size modelling agency. She has empowered myself, and many other women that I know. I would love to have a meeting with her, to understand what it is that keeps her going in this tough business.

# *Nicole Stapff*

*"Over here I had just myself to do everything, and for a new mother that was very hard, at times, I felt overwhelmed."*

*M*y name is Nicole Stapff, I was born in Uruguay.

My family's background is German, Italian, Spain and Uruguayan. I am a Montessori Teacher, I graduated here in Ireland after studying 4 years of college in Killester College of Further Education and Saint Nicholas College of Ireland which is the only Montessori accredited college in the country to award students with a level 8, as mine.

I came to Ireland in 2003 to volunteer full-time for the Friends of the Elderly, an NGO that works to alleviate the loneliness and isolation among Elderly people. I loved my time volunteering for them, it was a liberating experience. I am also a single mother to a very handsome young man, aged 13, he is very excited about going into secondary school this September. He is my main priority for as long as I live.

I am a Biodanza Didactic facilitator for children and adults, and facilitates two weekly Biodanza classes, one in a Montessori school and also teach biodanza adults only class every week. Biodanza is a type of dance described as the "the dance of life", a dance that combines music and harmonious movements, which helps to create a sense of belonging among groups and integration within the community as it is inclusive of everyone and welcomes diversity and different cultural backgrounds. It originated from South America and embodies the philosophy of the Biocentric Principles which tells us about life itself.

My favourite drink is a Uruguayan drink known as "Mate". What I miss most (is) the "asado" Uruguayan BBQ, I miss the weather, sun and the beaches in my country. What I love about Ireland are the people, the greens around the countryside and the fact that I can live here and raise my child here. He was born in Dublin. I also like the fact that Dublin is becoming more multicultural and diverse.

*What are some of the most challenges faced by migrant women in Ireland? (b) What advice would you give to young and upcoming migrants women?*

For a start, I am a single mum living here as a single parent and not having my family around was the most difficult thing I have ever done especially at the beginning when my baby was born. In my country it is easier for a lone parent to manage and do things with the help of close family members. Over here I had just myself to do everything, and for a new mother that was very hard, at times, I felt overwhelmed. But thankfully, my mother was able to come and visit us later and she stayed for two months which was extremely helpful. I can imagine many migrant women going through this type of challenge because of the lack of family support system. A different kind of challenge that migrants are facing is straight out stereotyping. Some people are stereotypical because you look different, or have a different accent, but our differences are what makes this world so colourful and unique.

I remember an incident that happened around when my mother came to visit, I was still breastfeeding at the time. My mother has a Uruguayan passport and had needed to update her visa and I'd taken her. My baby started crying and I'd gone to breastfeed him in the car, the next I knew, an immigration police officer was banging at the door, he forced me to open it and ask me to come out of the way to come in to my own home. It was so abrupt, I panicked because I wasn't expecting anything like that, but he'd falsely assumed that I may be doing something illegal or worse hiding someone. When I told him that I was only breastfeeding my baby, he was so sorry and apologetic that he offered help if needed.

My advice would be to be careful not to mix with strangers or people they don't know.

*There is a worldwide momentum for gender pay-gap, do you think that women have suddenly started to speak up in demand of effective change, or do you think that men have only started to pay more attention and listening more to women?*

Women were able to speak up many decades ago, having said that, women from times before us viewed men as the 'high and mighty', and caretaker of the universe so even though they were aware of enormous pay gaps and protested, they were never taken as serious because men always have their way of making it out why they deserve more and better than women. The only difference now is that women have become so resilient and forceful in a way, and men are simply forced to listen because we have worked hard to earn our rights. Mutual respect is also at an increased level than ever before.

*Do you think that Ireland has done more to protect the rights of women? If you answered yes, in your opinion —why are there so many stories about domestic violence? If you answered no, then what do you think Ireland should do more to protect women?*

Ireland has made huge progress at some level with regards to protecting the rights of women, but there is still work to do in terms of protecting women and children from abusive ex-partners. Single parents who are homeless especially with young children needs protecting. It is very upsetting to see an Irish woman sleeping in a Garda station because she has nowhere to go. This happening this century is a disgrace and does not give a positive outlook of a country that defends women.

*What has been a defining moment in your life/career or business since living in Ireland? (b) If you could have breakfast with any three Irish women, who would you choose and why?*

One defining moment in my life in Ireland is when I received my BA (Hons) in Montessori Education considering that English is not my mother tongue, and having my son witness my huge achievement was extremely important.

One would be fond of meeting Mary Robinson because she visited Uruguay, Mary McAleese for advocating for gay people even though I am not gay myself but I'm aware of the discrimination that some of them suffer. Finally, Mary Black, I love her music, particularly the song called "only a women's heart" or "no frontiers".

# *Isabela Garbacz*

*"For migrant women we usually don't have other family members around, so dropping the kids off at grandma's is not an option."*

*I* am Isabela Garbacz, originally from Poland. I have been in Ireland since 2007. I'm a full-time mum, independent manager & team leader at Oriflame. I designed and run an online direct sales coaching program to give my team the best possible tools to grow. There is also a new project which I started quite recently, with creating special skin care products that is completely natural and without preservatives and synthetic ingredients. It is a new line for young teenagers that I plan to launch soon in the year. It was inspired by my 13 years old daughter, Aleksandra.

My all-time favourite food is beetroot salad and home-made oat cookies – absolutely to die for! I drink a lot of water, and just love to enjoy wine especially at weekends. I miss being around my family in

Poland and enjoying Polish summer and beautiful warm autumn. One thing that I like about Ireland is their hospitality towards strangers. I remember my first day in Ireland as a stranger, people I met in the streets kept smiling and said "Hi" as if they already knew me. They have a warm attitude towards strangers and that is something I appreciate.

*What are some of the most challenges faced by migrant women in Ireland? (b) What advice would you give to young and upcoming migrants women?*

The most obvious challenges faced by migrant women are the language barriers and cultural differences, but the biggest challenge is a balance between family and work. While it is a huge issue to choose between raising your children and going back to work, women in general don't get enough support in this matter here in Ireland. For migrant women it is even more complicated as we usually don't have other family members around, so dropping the kids off at grandma's is not an option for us, and the cost of childcare doesn't help either.

My advice to young and upcoming migrant women is that they should continue to dream big and not limit themselves at any point. If they strongly believe and work hard enough, everything will fall in place and at the right time.

*There is a worldwide momentum for gender pay-gap, do you think that women have suddenly started to speak up in demand of effective change, or do you think that men have only started to pay more attention and listening more to women?*

I believe both things are happening now, and they are strictly connected. But the truth is that women are speaking up more and even louder. We have become more visible, more important and there is no way that we are going to give up now, so people should better pay more attention and listen to us more often.

*Do you think that Ireland has done more to protect the rights of women? If you answered yes, in your opinion —why are there so many stories about domestic violence? If you answered no, then what do you think Ireland should do more to protect women?*

No. We cannot do ENOUGH when it comes to protecting and promoting the rights of women; this issue is beyond just a matter for migrant women. Women's rights everywhere are the rights of our children, that is why this matter should be a priority for every society and every government. I have personally met migrant women and Irish women who have really gone through a lot; suffered from physical violence to mental and financial abuse and there is one pattern that comes back each time – they don't get enough attention at the beginning of their problems. The attitude is usually as though their problems are "not big enough" at early stage, people who are the first point of contact for us like social workers, inspectors etc., often diminish the importance of first signs of domestic abuse and seem to follow the same template of assessment and that need to change. They must remember that every case is different and deal with them accordingly.

*Do you think that Ireland has done more to protect the rights of women? If you answered yes, in your opinion —why are there so many stories about domestic violence? If you answered no, then what do you think Ireland should do more to protect women?*

Defining moment in my life will be my son Leon's birth and everything else that came in the package because he had health issues, and facing those issues together as a family created a different point of view to life; it completely changed my attitude towards our future.

I'd like to have breakfast with Ruth Coppinger. She seems to be one of the few politicians out there who had not change her path since many years that she has been working and has continuously done her job well. I respect her for that.

# Elizabeth Allauigan

*"Stripping a person of the right to a freedom of conscience is to undermine his/her fundamental dignity as a person."*

*I* am Elizabeth Shirley Allauigan, a beautiful name from a beautiful country, the Philippines —Pearl of the Orient Seas. I am a critical care nurse, worked most of my years in the various critical care area and intensive care in the last 40 years of my life as a nurse. A sense of commitment and deep passion is the driving force that keeps me going for the purpose of service and care for every patient that I come in contact with is a cue of the suffering Christ. Having been involved with a lot of community organizations empowers me to do more to improve, guide and set a good example especially to the young generation which will create a big impact for them.

I specifically do not have a favourite food. I eat anything- almost everything that appears to my eyes to be good food. I do not drink nor smoke, simple as that. My main passion is traveling. I like to see the beautiful world that God has created for all of to enjoy.

What I miss from my own country? Put simple; it is more fun in the Philippines and the fact that there is no place like home, but of course there is nothing more important than family. I miss them, especially my mum and my siblings who are far away from me, but my mind is set for practicality- greener pastures which is why I see Ireland as my second home. What I like in Ireland... well experiencing five seasons in a day and how easy it is to travel to everywhere and enjoying life to the fullest.

*What are some of the most challenges faced by migrant women in Ireland? (b) What advice would you give to young and upcoming migrants women?*

1. Migrant women do not feel empowered to challenge discrimination and racism.
2. Women generally are in the high risk of emotional, physical and sexual exploitations
3. Most migrant women are facing precarious working condition
4. Chronic underpayment: where they are forced to work in low paid jobs.
5. Some women migrants experience stalking
6. Childcare is a huge issue as it is extremely expensive
7. Loss of identity coupled with non-acceptance of educational qualifications already attainment before coming here.
8. Many suffer anxiety over family separation and limited social networks.
9. Many struggles to access appropriate and affordable housing.

I have the following advice for all upcoming young migrant to seek practical advice and help from the Citizens Information Centre where they can get practical help if they have problems. They can seek the joint council for the welfare of immigrants, seek legal advice and assistance on all aspects of immigration and asylum law, and learn to stand and fight for what they believe in. 'Empower yourself and get to social media. Above all, believe in yourself that you can strive to change things if you put your mind to it.

*There is a worldwide momentum for gender pay-gap, do you think that women have suddenly started to speak up in demand of effective change, or do you think that men have only started to pay more attention and listening more to women?*

Wage differences do exist. It means that one employee earns more than another. They are not forbidden, not between men and women, neither between persons of different creeds and colours. Wages differences frequently occur because individuals with more work experience or performing highly qualified jobs make more than individuals who have hardly any education or are starters in the labour market. Women are more likely to achieve pay parity with their male colleagues when they mirror what men do- that is if they work full time and don't take time out to have children. I think in Ireland today men still dominate the workplace and are main decision makers in business and politics, while women are lagging when it comes to equal opportunities and income. While it is true that women are dominant in health and education the fact remain, that women face a great deal of barriers not experienced by men.

*Do you think that Ireland has done more to protect the rights of women? If you answered yes, in your opinion —why are there so many stories about domestic violence? If you answered no, then what do you think Ireland should do more to protect women?*

For women and men conscience is the reflection in their own heart and voice supported with faith and reason. Stripping a person of the right to a freedom of conscience is to undermine his/her fundamental dignity as a person. Every health care professional has their own responsibility to serve life. Recently I have read in a survey that Ireland has the second highest number of women avoiding places or situations for fear of being assaulted out of all EU countries. Yes, as a concerned citizen there should be an intensive measure to protect women's right here in Ireland. Everyone has the responsibility to help, whatever it takes. Ireland should act now before it is too late.

*What has been a defining moment in your life/career or business since living in Ireland? (b) If you could have breakfast with any three Irish women, who would you choose and why?*

Defining moments in my life enables me to hone my best talents to live life purposefully and be successful. My moments of success had allowed me to maximize my potential, uncover my own passions and become a better leader. For me the best moment in my life is the realization that I have met a lot of people along the way and with different cultural backgrounds serving them as a friend, a patient and letting them become a member of my family.

**I would be honoured to have breakfast with the following women:**

Eileen Creedon — She is a graduate from the University of Cork, she received her professional training at the incorporated Law Society of Ireland. She worked in a number of areas in offices which include civil litigation, state property and criminal prosecution work. In January of 2012, she was appointed as the first female Chief State Solicitor; at breakfast I would love to hear her experiences on how she is able to give the best defence to her clients.

Danni Barry – An elite group of female Michelin- starred chefs, and only the second female chef ever in Ireland to gain a star an accolade that she won. To have breakfast with her would be a great opportunity for me to ask about her secret for her dedication to excellence in her being a chef and in the business.

Phil Ni Sheaghdga – She is the General Secretary of the Irish Nurses and midwives organization - a lady who enjoys hillwalking, reading and travel during downtime. A keen promoter of the Irish language. A lead negotiator in all major industrial agendas. Having breakfast with her will surely be a promising one as she is a person with intense and firm decision. A lady you can count on that she will be there to fight for you no matter what it takes.

*The government recently launched 'Project Ireland 2040', which the Taoiseach said is a document about building a republic of opportunity. Have you seen this document, if so do you think that in its mapping there is provision to create an enabling space for migrant women to be heard and lead? (b) The Prime Minister is the son of a migrant father from India, does this alone give you the slightest hope for the future of the children of migrants in this country, and why? (c) If you have the power to change anything in Ireland, what will that be?*

Project Ireland 2040 is the governments overarching policy initiative to make Ireland a better country for everyone. A country that reflects the best of who we are and what we aspire to be in future. This project though emphasizes a lot of programmes that the government will have to be implement to better the wellbeing of all Irish people regardless of their background. Well, as a principled man I think Leo Varadkar can always look back to where his parent came from and know that whatever it takes, he is going to be the best for everyone living in Ireland. As an educated doctor and politician, I believe Leo will do all in his power to stand up to his words and bring about changes and improvement to the incoming generation of children here. His own self is a living testament of what he was before in trying to build a better future for Ireland.

**If I have the power to change anything in Ireland,** firstly, I would impose a change in the fees to education for those who want to study higher their education in order that they can change their perspectives in life. Secondly, I will declare a reduction in tax for all those working in the government service, then I will invest in high technologies which will guarantee human happiness and increase employment opportunities.

Finally, I don't have the power to impose the above changes but I have the power to change my own self and live my life in the best that I can, most especially so that in every person and every patient I come in contact with - will always be a cue of the suffering Christ as he has set the greatest example of love for each and everyone of us.

# *Ema Amarie-Idowu*

*"I believe in differences, they make us unique, giving that extra flavour, on the table of life. As you know variety is the spice of life!"*

*I* am Ema Amarie-Idowu, living in County Dublin. It seems like time has gone by so fast; it is amazing to say I have lived in Ireland going almost two decades with my immediate family. It was a challenge coming to Ireland in search of a better life and the journey has been well worth it because I have learnt and developed over time. I have come to better appreciate life in the sense that I had to make a life without the usual assistance of my extended family but instead gradually friends filled that role. Well, that is the most wonderful part of it all. It is a well-known fact that the world has gradually become smaller. People have travelled more, have become more exposed leading to a significant reduction in language and cultural barriers. Improving understanding and in turn, led to better integration. I will like to believe or hope that we the migrant women have shown significant impact wherever we dwell around the globe. Brought better awareness to our culture, our trials and tribulations.

Work and livelihood for me since coming to Ireland has been both challenging and interesting. My occupation has varied between self-employed, customer services, teaching, working with young people, public speaking and for a brief moment healthcare. Did I learn anything? Yes, I did! In each of these environments, I learnt the importance of people skills. As a reserve and quiet person, having a crack at self-employment opened up opportunities for me. I learnt the hard way to speak to people, to ask and to receive from people. I am still on the journey of personal development because I find that no matter how much I think I know, there are still more lessons to be learnt. It is a thing of joy to understand that wisdom sometimes comes with age, I strongly believe that time heals and teaches, we need experience, to feel life's disappointments as well as joys to understand ourselves and other people's experiences and feelings. Work is interesting, by this I mean I have so much diversity in skill set and knowledge that I have sometimes felt lost. When I take time to focus and organise myself things just seem to be alright again. My values and perspectives have changed over time due to various changes in working with different people and different environment

I love volunteering, I believe in giving back; it gives me the opportunity to learn new skills without obligations, a genuine purpose to be myself, to give of myself and generally feel free to choose my time and be valuable. Volunteering is a blessing both to the volunteer and the community because through volunteering, I get to release my talents. I seriously recommend and encourage that people take time to volunteer for them to be responsible for the formation and development of their community in whatever capacity they can and are willing to give. Volunteers shape the world eventually, they make the world what it is today and for the next generations. The amount of time and effort volunteers give for development cut across local, regional, national and global and it's open to everyone who is willing or has some time to spare for human and nature.

My favourite food; My tastes changed over time, I was not a big eater from the start, relying on sweets or very little food when I was a child, but now give me some rice any day and you got me. I love lasagne and pizza well done Italian style. It is OK to have some deserts. I love Baci Perugina and Ferrero Rocher chocolates as special treats and Pandoro at Christmas. What I miss about Nigeria, my country of origin, are many. First, I miss my childhood friends, families I haven't seen in a long while, organic foods, the craziness of people; by this I mean Nigerians are natural fun-loving, so every day has its own drama—I miss that. I won't be a party goer, but it is nice to see people who love parties and the news you hear from such gatherings can be anything from funny to disaster. Parties are good places to hear the latest news going on about town, sometimes I think people look for any opportunity to party to show wealth, whether real or not, the important thing is people are happy.

Secondly, the beaches, I love the beaches when we can visit them. I love seeing my dad do the dives into the seawater and the accompanying strong swimmers, people who can go into the deep. I love collecting seashells, then race with my siblings along the beaches and sometimes we get to ride horses, led by the horsemen or lads who tend to them. It is a different challenge when I get to do it, but I won't call myself a horse rider or anything close. We bring our picnic baskets filled with treats to the beach each time. I can say that I have visited most of the beaches in Lagos with family and some with friends.

Christmas has special meanings for us in Nigeria; it was always family as well as the community. Before the Christmas, I remember the preparations of Carols and songs. My family and I were in our local church choir. We start our rehearsals as early as August or September to prepare our songs for the church harvest and Christmas. I was also in my school's choir with the same choir Master so after rendering the school's Christmas carol and songs, I will still participate with my whole family at the church's in December, a week or two before Christmas day and on the Christmas day itself, 25th of December.

Normally what we do on Christmas day in Nigeria, we share food and gifts, we had festivities with women and children having a change of clothes, the famous Christmas wears, children dancing along the streets and are given gifts and money. We had masquerade dance, in colourful and real loud and powerful strides. It was always fun. For my family, Christmas day is a day of staying home to entertain guests with food, drinks and chats. My mum starts her day very early cooking all the various assortment of foods and drinks, she makes the best Chapman drink I know. Every year we will have jollof rice, fried rice, white rice and that special stew with lots of assorted meats and fish. Her goat meat pepper soup is super! After cooking she will dish some for us kids to bring to close neighbours as we wish them a 'Happy Christmas', it was such fun to hear our neighbour exclaim their delight at the gifts and some would give to us the children some money, some neighbours return the favour of food as well. The day after Christmas which is 'Boxing Day', we go out to the beach or visit nice places like Federal Palace hotel, theatre, picnics or just do our thing, in some cases, we also have other friends go out with us on a group outing. I love the beautiful chime of Christmas Carols, they are special.

I love Ireland. Ireland has been home for more than one and a half decades. We have settled in, become citizens and I treasure that a lot. My hope is to be of value as much as I received and to teach my children to make it home too. It is actually home to them, they have been here almost all of their lives and are happy. Christmas is also very special here in Ireland. Every Christmas is different for us. We have done different activities from Santa's treasure hunt to going abroad and still have fun. We have had family visits, Snow and without our Snow, to celebrating as a small family and everything in between, I have never had a bad Christmas. As much as I love Ireland, my wish is that Nigeria will emerge well too. My hope is to be in the position that can also give back to enhance and make life better for those who are looking after the place while a lot of us left. My hope is to be in the position to be able to collaborate with other powerful individuals and groups to bring about positive and sustainable changes to both Ireland, Nigeria, Africa and the world at large. I love people, so it hurts me to see people suffering. I crave to see people comforted, people at peace, people who love each other regardless of differences. I believe in differences, they make us unique, giving that extra flavour, on the table of life. As you know variety is the spice of life!

*What are some of the most challenges faced by migrant women in Ireland? (b) What advice would you give to young and upcoming migrants women?*

Some of the challenges experienced by migrant women in Ireland are so complex it is difficult to isolate a single issue as a cause. Some issues include language barriers, cultural differences, unemployment, discrimination, low self-esteem and low confidence. Within these are hidden symptoms of health and mental wellbeing, issues of a wide range such as mental health leading to depression. Most migrant women have left home for the first time to Ireland with no family or friends. In some situations, introverted personalities not used to have many friends or lacks confidence to approach strangers, live in isolation. From isolation comes other challenges so that these people start to lose confidence when they are not able to connect in the society. They experience exclusion and it is only a matter of time before they degenerate through various stages of mental health problems leading to depression. Isolation is not good for migrants. Humans need nice friendly places, good, clean homes, safe places to socialise and feel belonged. It is important that migrant women are involved in the society at different activities of interests to exist well among people especially when they have children. Children need to go to school, they need to engage in after-school activities to maintain a healthy life balance. Another big issue experienced by migrant women is lack of employment or lack of employable skills. This is to say that some women are perceived as not educated enough, or they are perceived as not educated in the English language and therefore have difficulty communicating in ordinary day's conversation. Since English is not their first language and the people around them do not understand their original dialect to help them sooner. This poses a barrier to getting jobs. Some women have very advanced education, but the barrier of not having enough experience hinders their entry into Irish work environment.

Cultural difference is an issue. We all have different belief and values. Getting to Ireland means you will struggle with your personal beliefs and that which exist in Ireland. The first barrier is to understand that there are differences, the next is a decision to adhere, avoid or accept this new way of living. Women and families are very challenged in this area. It takes time to understand, start believing and adjust to cultural differences. Within cultural differences are many underlying issues to name a few; are belief around religion, child upbringing, family values, money and interpersonal relationships. Discrimination is another element of worry for migrant women. Discrimination can be perceived as real or misunderstood, in either case, it is a thing of concern and a barrier in relating with people if you are not sure you are being treated differently because you are non-Irish. Again, this barrier can be overcome with time and good communication.

If I am to advise a young migrant woman, my advice is not going to be a one size fits all situation. I will like to know the person, their particular issues, how they view themselves, how they view their community and how they see the world. Analysing of their views will make it become clearer where they are coming from. An understanding of their perceptions will make it better to be able to guide them to see the bigger picture and see the opportunities around them in their new place where they call home.

*There is a worldwide momentum for gender pay-gap, do you think that women have suddenly started to speak up in demand of effective change, or do you think that men have only started to pay more attention and listening more to women?*

Gender pay-gap is being recognised as an issue, like many other issues in our communities. To fairly address this issue, I think an in-depth view of all main and surrounding circumstances are examined properly and that each individual conclusion is drawn within its own merits. I say this because as a woman and a migrant I struggled with the issue of how to get or be given the opportunity to work to earn a living. From my experience, there were issues around 'experience'. Where I would have experience, and be open to develop within the organisation, it did not seem to materialise in some situations, because the 'Irish' view of experience was probably different from mine, the idea to sell myself was not one I was used to. I also discovered that there are other issues that are not said, but you have to find out for yourself. Things are getting better now with the number of recruitment agencies and job training skill organisations springing up around the country. Another issue is time out of employment. in Ireland, one tends to lose all or most experience obtained previously, or should I call it an elimination factor? I bring this on because women tend to lose experience whenever they are out of the workforce, especially when they take time out to rear their children and look after their family. Whether this is fair is one question I believe when answered fairly, will resolve a lot of the issues surrounding gender pay-gap.

Fair play to gender differences. Consideration should be given to the capacity to perform not whether a man or woman is doing the work. All other factors in place, I think each circumstance should be handled fairly. Individuals should be selected based on what they bring to the organisation. I strongly suggest a transparent and fair process be adopted.

*Do you think that Ireland has done more to protect the rights of women? If you answered yes, in your opinion —why are there so many stories about domestic violence? If you answered no, then what do you think Ireland should do more to protect women?*

Ireland is a small country and is continuously developing new policies to meet the nation's needs and challenges. Legislation and policies are being reviewed and updated constantly, we have recently only updated the 8th amendment to the constitution after so many years. Whether it is correct or wrong is no longer what is at stake. The constitution and general rules and regulations continuously reflect the needs of the masses, so with this in mind, I think the rights of women in Ireland are being protected alongside other issues. The major right to vote and be voted for has opened up the gates for women to be properly represented. There are movements inviting women's equal participation in politics. A good search on the internet will give you the information needed to enter into politics as a woman or as a migrant woman. I am a believer that as much as one group want recognition for their effort and contributions, it should be properly spread so no one gets left behind. What I mean by this is, that decisions should be inclusive of men, women and children. It can be hard, but people should be treated fairly, regardless of gender, age or other differences otherwise even the strongest becomes vulnerable when they are not properly supported.

*What has been a defining moment in your life/career or business since living in Ireland? (b) If you could have breakfast with any three Irish women, who would you choose and why?*

Every day is a challenge. I have had some defining moments, but I will talk about one here. At the early stage following my arrival in Ireland, I thought I would gain employment soon, do some work, rear my family, live a quiet life and life should be fine. Things don't always happen the way we think or plan. But in place of gaining employment I came across an opportunity to work for myself with Network Marketing and my life changed forever. I saw the possibilities to earn an income doing what 'I love', work for myself, grow my income as I choose—like they tell you, etc. I went into Network Marketing, not making all the money, but what I found so much more invaluable was the personal development, the exposure, people skills development, the opportunity to go deep within myself to find out who I really am, and the confidence to know that I can do all things through Christ who strengthens me.

Breakfast with any woman any day is something I love to do, so it is hard to select just three women. I struggle with all the wonderful STARS in my life, but I will choose three. I have chosen these three women because of their strengths, belief and courage. They are hardworking people who have impacted the community in their own ways and I just love them.

Marion Fitzgerald. Marion ranks up there with women. She is a wonderful person, a wonderful wife, mother to her children and grandchild, a great woman in the community, a woman of courage, care and love for people, she is a networker! When I turned my life around, she was there with me and for me. She started me on a journey of self discovery and personal development, she believed in me, very supportive, my mentor. I will eat breakfast with Marion at any time or day, month or year. She has been a wonderful friend to me and my family.

Emma Brezing. She is humble, a lovely woman with a kind heart, friendly, down to earth and a woman of God. I will eat breakfast with Emma every day of the week if we had the chance. She is very supportive and loves people. She cares for her family and stands for what is right at all times. Emma is very creative, a brilliant teacher, she has developed such skills in music that only Emma can. Her style of teaching is so creative that I marvel at her skills. Emma is very hands on and will do what it takes to make a situation work well for people around her.

Elena Trower. In the time I have come to know Elena, she has shown to be hardworking, very supportive and a woman with a big heart for the community. She loves her family and believes in what is right regardless of the difficulties around her. Elena is very sensitive to people especially young people. An excellent cook, I will eat breakfast with Elena any day of the week. Elena has a lovely smile.

*The government recently launched 'Project Ireland 2040', which the Taoiseach said is a document about building a republic of opportunity. Have you seen this document, if so do you think that in its mapping there is provision to create an enabling space for migrant women to be heard and lead? (b) The Prime Minister is the son of a migrant father from India, does this alone give you the slightest hope for the future of the children of migrants in this country, and why? (c) If you have the power to change anything in Ireland, what will that be?*

This is a National strategy to enhance development. I am very pleased with the document and the strategy. Growth is inevitable considering current day Ireland, being strategically ready means the government is taking the initiative to plan the direction in which it's development will go with her citizens, rather than seat expecting someone else will do it or leave it hoping that things will happen of their own accord.

Following statistical trends and opportunities, we can improve our chances of survival by doing things effectively and differently. We can magnify a project or explore higher or lower for opportunities to accommodate future growth and development. I am proud of the Irish government for being so forward thinking, transparent, encouraging citizens to be part of the change, part of the plan and part of the development. The ten strategic outcomes with wellbeing, equality and opportunity give room for citizens to support in whatever capacity they can to build the nation. There are many women organisations gearing up to take advantage, to direct the affairs that concern women. As stated earlier, there are a number of vibrant organisations and groups empowering women and migrant women through seminars, workshops and a variety of means to participate in politics, balancing the ruling powers of the state. This creates opportunity for women to be heard, it gives women and migrant women the chance to influence policies addressing issues that affect them and their community. For a change I believe women are gradually taking their place to resolve issues that concerns us all. I may suggest that we hold this position with respect and compassion for all, that we thrive well rather than become power drunk, abuse our position and loose the opportunity. Hopefully women will hold themselves with pride and show true compassion for those they lead. The opportunities here in Ireland and within the project have no limits. It all depends on citizens to take charge and be responsible for what will happen to our community.

I believe that citizens are well able to make it work. The more we work together, the better the nation will progress. The more we let our voices be heard in a positive and constructive manner, the better people will listen. We, as citizens have a part to play to make Ireland a better place for all. Migrants have the power to lead and be led, the choice is in how we choose to exercise these powers giving consideration to those in authority at any time. To enjoy life well, we need to choose wisely, who governs us. We should exercise our rights by voting for our choice, what is right and beneficial for all, we should select people who show fairness and transparency, not a person or group who will favour only a particular group, neglecting all others.

I believe Ireland's focus should be balanced, as previously stated, it is important to look after the minority, the marginalised and vulnerable, but we should not neglect the strong, the go-getters, the few who go through the sleepless nights to make it work for the nation. We want the strong to be encouraged, to do more maybe even duplicate their efforts and release more of those talents to better enhance our communities. Whatever programmes are developed, it is my opinion to give everyone equal chances to explore and develop their talents without fear or hindrance. How this will be done is up to everyone - entrepreneurs, businesses, schools, government and the general population. In a nutshell, I am saying we need to be tolerant of people, protector of both the weak and the strong.

There is hope for the people of Ireland. This historical precedence of our current Taoiseach symbolises opportunity and hope for all citizens to aspire to the best of their abilities, to reach places that were some time ago unreachable. I have hope for myself, my children, migrants, hardworking citizens anyone who is willing to do something exceptional and kind will excel.

*If I had the power to change something in Ireland*, it will be to help people take advantage of opportunities with compassion and care. It will be to help people look around them, think outside the box - look to the skies and below the earth. Example there is lack of recreational facilities in the Balbriggan area, such as sports swimming pool etc, this creates the opportunity to explore or be a part of those who raise awareness of these issues and be the voice that helps to rectify the problems. Ireland stands on her own Acres of Diamond.

## *Heloisa Generoso Callagy*

**"Don't feel too shy to ask for help, there are people out there who are very nice and helpful. Befriend your neighbours, don't refuse an offer to go out for a cup of coffee together."**

My name is Heloisa Generoso Callagy, from Brazil, I have been living in Dublin since June of 2012. My initial decision to come to Ireland was for study, I wanted to further my knowledge of English. Although before coming to Ireland, I had already a Post Graduate degree in Business Administration, and Peoples Management. I'd also studied English language which I thought was good enough to allow me settle in, and then further my studies. I arrived in Ireland and discovered my level of English wasn't something close to how I would have wanted to describe it. Me understand of English was quite good, but for me to become a confident speaker I had to start all over again. I enrolled in an English school which I did part-time, I also worked at different jobs that were well below what I would normally accept as a job, like cleaning, nail technician, childminding, etc. I had to survive. But I've come a long way, now I am the Coordinator of Brazilian Open University in Dublin since October 2016. I am also studying a second degree in UNIGRAN. But the best part is meeting the love of my life, a very handsome Irish guy named Ian, we were introduced by a mutual friend; love at first sight it was, and now we are husband and wife. He has learnt a few phrases in Brazil, my parents were so pleased to meet him the first time we to visit Brazil. I like to think that my journey to Ireland has fulfilled its real purpose, that is to find my love, and now I'm here to stay for good. I find Irish people to be very polite, for example, how they always thank the bus drivers), I like the education system too.

May favourite food is feijoada (from Brazil), vegetable with chicken.

*What are some of the most challenges faced by migrant women in Ireland? (b) What advice would you give to young and upcoming migrants women?*

The difficulty in finding a job that matches one's qualifications is an issue here. It is very depressing, especially because there is not much you can do to change it. Another is the lack of English language, this has created a serious barrier for many migrant women, not being able to understand what the other person is saying to you and you on the other hand cannot communicate your thoughts back to the person you're meant to be having a conversation with, it is the worst feeling anyone has to endure. I'm glad that my English has greatly improved so I'm no longer burned like some.

My advice is more to all migrants arriving newly to Ireland. I'm sure that your first few weeks and months were just as you expected, but then the excitement wains and something else sets in, that something else is the small gap that you leave open before you start doing something and it is filled very quickly if you start to miss home and before you know what is going on, depression sets in. Please do not stay in isolation, it will lead you to suffer from mental distress. Reach out to people as much as you can especially if you are here alone. Don't feel too shy to ask for help, there are people out there who are very nice and helpful. Befriend your neighbours, don't refuse an offer to go out for a cup of coffee together. Socialise on social media and be active in your local community in general. Don't forget to use any opportunity you have to educate yourself, and then try to look for work. Finally, to you and upcoming migrant women, look after yourself and don't indulge in reckless lifestyles that will potentially ruin your future.

*There is a worldwide momentum for gender pay-gap, do you think that women have suddenly started to speak up in demand of effective change, or do you think that men have only started to pay more attention and listening more to women?*

Women are demanding for their rights of equal pay as the men in the same job capacity. If we can do the same kinds of work, then we deserve equal treatments, that is what is important. Men see and treat us as the weaker sex when there are big problems, you see that they really can't ignore women totally because they find they can't get everything done by themselves and we have continued to improve and strive to get to higher positions in societies.

However, I think it is fair to say that the men are equally listening now so there have been some clear changes. I believe that what you don't ask you don't get, so fair play on both sexes.

*Do you think that Ireland has done more to protect the rights of women? If you answered yes, in your opinion —why are there so many stories about domestic violence? If you answered no, then what do you think Ireland should do more to protect women?*

Ireland is trying in terms of dealing with human rights issues if you compare it to many countries. Always in every society, women and children are vulnerable so they must do much more to protect all the women and their children. One problem that is very noticeable is domestic violence. Because it happens inside the house people don't believe victims sometimes. Another issue is racism, some migrants including asylum seekers and refugees have very bad experiences of racism; people treat you differently because you do not look like them or speak like them and then these sometimes turn into verbal or physical attacks. I understand that the police have so far not had anyone prosecuted for racism. If people go about attacking others because they are anti-immigrants, such people need to be brought to court and judgement served, it is the only way to try and end racism.

*What has been a defining moment in your life/career or business since living in Ireland? (b) If you could have breakfast with any three Irish women, who would you choose and why?*

A defining moment for me since I came to Ireland, was finding my special man Ian Callagy, and getting married to him. Our wedding took place here in Dublin with my husband's family and my friends in attendance; it was special and simply beautiful! My family was absent because of the difficulties in flying everyone to Ireland, we couldn't possibly afford it, instead we went over there after the wedding. It was an obligation for me to bring my groom home to meet my family in Brazil. My parents, especially my dad was very pleased to meet their Irish son in-law. I'm so lucky because my in-laws are great and love me like a daughter and I in turn respect them so much. Ian and I both adore children, but we don't want one of our own. We talk so much about everything else about life, love, big plans, etc. I'm so glad I met him.

*What has been a defining moment in your life/career or business since living in Ireland? (b) If you could have breakfast with any three Irish women, who would you choose and why?*

My mother in-law is a great Irish woman, but I can share coffee with her whenever I want. So, it'll have to be Marian O'Callaghan on this occasion. She is a popular broadcaster with RTE. I was a guest on her programme 2 years ago.

*The government recently launched 'Project Ireland 2040', which the Taoiseach said is a document about building a republic of opportunity. Have you seen this document, if so do you think that in its mapping there is provision to create an enabling space for migrant women to be heard and lead? (b) The Prime Minister is the son of a migrant father from India, does this alone give you the slightest hope for the future of the children of migrants in this country, and why? (c) If you have the power to change anything in Ireland, what will that be?*

In my humble opinion, the fact that the Taoiseach is from a migrant background doesn't really matter. The future of every society lies with the youths and that is all Irish children, including those of migrant people who are born and brought up here and live in the country.

# *Elena Pelendritou*

**"As women, we multi-task but learning a new language can be daunting for a lot of them who would rather stay in the house and mind the children."**

I am Elena Pelendritou, originally from Cyprus. I had previously lived in Ireland but I'm on and off now between Cyprus, Ireland and other places since the last 4 years as my business takes me around the world. The weather in Cyprus is naturally super and that is what I miss most when I'm out of the country. My favourite food is steak-pie. The most part of why I like Ireland is that the country is becoming more multicultural than it ever was before. I find Irish people are charming, they always like to smile.

I am in full-time Entrepreneurship and Business Coach. I represent a billion dollars company, helping other people travel the world and make money at the same time. I'm the kind of woman who love to bring smile to people's faces and help to build leadership in women. I am a mother of 3 grown-up children, in fact I have been a single mother for 28 years yet managed to bring up my children on my own, with support of a few friends and families but I have never relied on a man. Needless to say that I've seen the other side of life, I wouldn't dare try to explain how difficult it was raising my children on my own in this confined space because it is a long story, however no matter what I did I'd have to always have it at the back of my mind and remind myself constantly that I have children who look up to me, I tried my very best and by the grace of God, today my children are successful. My eldest daughter got married recently, my second eldest child who has been visually impaired since age 9 and now aged 31 became a Paralympic Gold Medallist swimmer and World record holder at the age of 15 for my home country. My youngest son is a Professional tourist/ trainer and a Speaker just like me. Therefore, I always advice women, especially single mothers to look after themselves and focus more on their children. 'Don't give up just because you don't have a man in your life. It is important for to stay strong and positive, be a believer that tomorrow will be better and build self-confident to go out there and follow your dreams.' My motto is to believe that nothing is impossible in life and to stay positive always.

*What are some of the most challenges faced by migrant women in Ireland? (b) What advice would you give to young and upcoming migrants women?*

The most challenges faced by migrant women anywhere in the world I think first of all, is isolation. In Ireland, language isn't the worst barrier because not many people speak the native Irish even though it is the country's official language. But English has also proved to be what is stopping many migrants to go out and pursue their careers and find jobs, this is doubly hard for the women who, on top of everything else must take care of the household first and foremost before contemplating on taking time out to learn how to speak English. It might look simple enough to some and as women, we multi-task but learning a new language can be daunting for a lot of them who would rather stay in the house and mind the children.

*Do you think that Ireland has done more to protect the rights of women? If you answered yes, in your opinion —why are there so many stories about domestic violence? If you answered no, then what do you think Ireland should do more to protect women?*

Domestic violence in my opinion, always starts with money issues and dishonesty in relationships. Like anywhere else, it is happening in Ireland and I think there has been much talk about it, there is still so much more the government can do to protect women, for example introduce new legislations that are stricter — enough to scare the perpetrators, that will women confident to come forward to report such violence and abuse.

*What has been a defining moment in your life/career or business since living in Ireland? (b) If you could have breakfast with any three Irish women, who would you choose and why?*

A defining moment in my life was that special moment I got an idea to start a new business. I had been sulking for a long time after losing my job in the banking sector. What they say about 'one door closes and another opening; I had been working in a bank for over 15 years and it all came to me losing everything in just one day. To say the least that I was devastated. I really didn't think that I would ever be able to pick myself up and look for another job in a long time. But a new idea came to me after a while and it was like a Joke initially, but it saved me from total ruin. I decided to become self-employed, that was how I started a business in the tourism and hospitality sector. My business gave me freedom and fulfilment, and now it takes me around the world and I'm very happy and content.

I meet wonderful and interesting women from around the world all the time. When it comes down to whom I would like to share breakfast with, there are many on the list, and because I'm not always on ground it is more difficult to mention names, but I wouldn't miss an opportunity to share a lovely breakfast with the first female president of Ireland, Mary Robinson. She is great in doing her humanitarian work and she has also paved the way for other women to follow in her footsteps.

# *Angela Sylva*

*"Migrant women have challenges getting any financial support they to build a good business and sustain it."*

*M*y name is Angela de Sao Pedro Silva from Brazil. I was born in a small Village on the north side of State Bahia. I have been living in Ireland since 2006. I am a self-employed business woman and run my own fashion business called A2 in Boyle, County Roscommon where I am based. I love seafood and Japanese food. Accurately, I miss my family, but I'm used to saying that, 'home is where is your heart is' and my heart is here in Ireland, so this is my home now. I love the people in Ireland, the environment and much more.

*What are some of the most challenges faced by migrant women in Ireland? (b)*
*What advice would you give to young and upcoming migrants women?*

I have faced many challenges in Ireland, my biggest one to date still is the lack of financial support to keep to my business running. Many small businesses are struggling and many more have closed due to this same reason. My aim is to grow my business but needed financial support, after many years it is where it was in the beginning and I find it extremely hard to keep afloat. I feel so lost sometimes because it is even harder to secure a small loan to support the business to grow. This is a shared problem with many migrant women that I know, as they too have challenges getting any financial support to build a good business and sustain it.

*Do you think that Ireland has done more to protect the rights of women? If you*
*answered yes, in your opinion —why are there so many stories about domestic*
*violence? If you answered no, then what do you think Ireland should do more*
*to protect women?*

I think the justice system is too slow, consequently there are so many cases kept on hold in the court, and without the cases being processed women who have been caught up in domestic violence or abused and have taken the courage to speak up may never get justice. I think that women are not listened to enough and there are so many out there who need support from the system but they either don't trust the system or don't know precisely where to get help. Women need to be well assisted and Ireland owe them the responsibility to protection against all forms of abuse from predators, and more so to make rights of women happen by paying more attention to them. The main key is for them to LISTEN and take ACTION.

*What has been a defining moment in your life/career or business since living in*
*Ireland? (b) If you could have breakfast with any three Irish women, who would*
*you choose and why?*

My defining moment would be when I first started my business. I have done so much to improve myself and develop my business since and although my career in still a work in progress, but I'm proud to say that I have developed so much from when I first arrived in Ireland. I have ambition to be a more successful business woman and I know it can still happen one day — it is only a matter of time. Since been here I have gained a degree in IT, graduated in Fashion and Beauty School and I still have lofty plans and dreaming about good things coming to me and my business in the future.

I would love to have breakfast with the following two women: Mary Lou MacDonald, she is seen as a strong Irish Politician and a woman who has inspired many. My second choice is the owner of the Assents Model Agency.

# *Ini Usanga*

*"No matter how many times you get a no, keep striving until you get a yes. Integrate and be open minded"*

$M$y name is Iniobong Usanga, and my Country of origin is Nigeria.

I have been living in Ireland for almost 18 years and now an Irish citizen. I am a proud Philanthropist, Family Violence Expert, Social Entrepreneur and a human right advocate. I am very passionate about issues of social justice, reproductive rights, equality and fairness. I have over twenty years working experience in the community development sector and on women's economic empowerment issues. I am the founder of Love and Care for People, a Cork based NGO that provides support, information and other empowering services to migrant families particularly women, young people and children who are survivors, victims or at risk of family violence, the initiator of YouthsRule, an intercultural youth club that provides a safe space for young people to meet, make friends, develop life skills, access to employment and make positive contributions to the community. I initiated Ireland National Diversity Awards, Extraordinary African Women Achievement Awards; Africa Ireland Based Achievement Awards. Cork County Intercultural Festival, Sásta International Children Festival, African Art Exhibition Cork and Ireland Carnival are also initiatives I created to showcase diversity in Ireland and promote integration and social inclusion through the arts, songs and dances, music, food, culture and informal learning. Ireland International Women Awards and Nigeria Ireland Based Awards are also my initiatives. These initiatives are social enterprises which aims to promote and celebrate the achievements and contributions to society made by migrants in Ireland. I have received several local, Regional, National and International awards in recognition for my contribution the community development and human rights field. I am a member of Cork County Council Social Inclusion and Policy Committee; setting the bar high and inspiring other migrant women to engage in community development and take on leadership roles in society. Recently, I was elected to the Board of the National Women's Council of Ireland, and I am chairperson of All Ladies League-Ireland chapter, NIDOE coordinator Cork and also sit on the board of several organisations.

My favourite food is Fufu and Afang; a delicious delicacy from Southern Nigerian. Fufu is made from Cassava and Afang is a mild spicy and flavour rich vegetable. I miss close family relations, the different variety of dishes, and the fantastic sunny spells. Ireland is a peaceful country, I like that.

*What are some of the most challenges faced by migrant women in Ireland? (b) What advice would you give to young and upcoming migrants women?*

The problems migrant women face is multifaced; many are not familiar with how the system works in Ireland. Language is a barrier for some, access to proper information and support services for others, discrimination, access to justice, very low representation in Irish politics, cultural differences, accent, institutional factors, low/no education, lack of recognition of certificates from home countries, childcare, living alone, sexual exploitation, specific health care needs, gender, social capital the list goes on and on. However, these factors cannot stop a migrant woman from being ambitious, setting goals and achieving them. Those who need support to kick start their lives again can also achieve anything they set their minds to with the right support.

My advice to a young and upcoming migrant woman is, any dream/vision is achievable. If you can see it in your mind, you can make it happen! Believe in yourself; and know there are no barriers or limit to what you can achieve except the ones you have set for yourself. Take the necessary action you need in other to achieve your target. Ask for help if and when needed (don't be shy, embrace your fears but do not give up). Use your fear as a fuel and not as an excuse. No matter how many nos you get, keep striving until you get a yes. Integrate and be open minded. Embrace change. Live is like music, dance with it; use your own pace not someone else's. remove the labels and judgements and just dance with live.

*Do you think that Ireland has done more to protect the rights of women? If you answered yes, in your opinion —why are there so many stories about domestic violence? If you answered no, then what do you think Ireland should do more to protect women?*

In comparison to some Countries, Ireland has done a lot to protect the rights of women in general. In recent times, we have seen the advent of referendum that favour women. However, more can still be done is certain areas. Particularly in the areas of domestic violence. An Irish time article stated, "Ireland is falling short of its obligations under international law to protect the human rights of women affected by domestic violence". They also suggest that the UN Committee on Economic, Social and Cultural Rights has called on the Government to strengthen its response to domestic violence. Improvements can be clearly made in housing support for victims of Domestic violence, access to Justice, and perpetrators of domestic violence need to be accountable for their actions on their victims. Mental health support for ethnic minorities and migrants' women is another area that needs some life and action among others.

*What has been a defining moment in your life/career or business since living in Ireland? (b) If you could have breakfast with any three Irish women, who would you choose and why?*

The most defining moment for me was at Christmas 2013 when my team and I raised over 1800 euros to organise outings and present Christmas gifts for 120 children living in direct provision centres in Cork. That experience brought me to tears to see the joy and smiles on the faces of all the children. It goes to show kindness; compassion and a sprinkle of Love and Care for People play a major role in making our living experiences enjoyable. Together with unity we can do and achieve a lot.

I would love to have breakfast with Former Irish President, Mary Robinson who is campaigning for human rights causes around the world. Ann Nolan, for her role in re-shaping the banking industry in Ireland, and Norah Casey a philanthropist helping touch lives through her philanthropy.

# *Angelina Marra*

*"We have seen so much positive change and momentum.
Together we are moving forward."*

*M*y name is Angelina Marra, I'm a Canadian/Italian who calls Dublin home. Dublin is my good luck city, my friend and an unending adventure. I came to Dublin for a holiday 7 years ago and instantly felt this odd feeling of familiarity, a homecoming, a return to myself. In a sad and chaotic time, I returned (3 years later) with one small suitcase intending to stay for 2 weeks, and I never returned to Canada. I live centrally, with the heartbeat of the city close to me and each day I walk along the Liffey as I spill my heart out. I share my joys and my concerns, and the river runs past as a good listener, my constant friend. Dublin opened its arms to me and has bestowed opportunities that I did not know I deserved. I am currently completing a degree in digital marketing.

As career cabin crew my feet are never on the earth for long, but when they are they are grounded in Ireland. Each week as I fly home exhausted from early morning travels, I see the coast of my emerald island I am filled with the peace that only a homecoming can bring. I am rejuvenated by my city, Dublin.

I am fuelled by espresso, a passion for veganism (peace for all sentient beings) and the inspirations I call friends. I am a feminist. I encourage everyone to learn the true meaning of the word and to make friends with it, to find a comfort with it and to proclaim it proudly. People often ask me why I do not return to Canada, "Don't you miss it? they ask." I miss my grandmother and my dog, job security, and large modern houses but I am happy where I am, in my perfectly imperfect city. In Dublin, we are spoilt for choice in cultural events. At least weekly we walk to the theatre, take in a comedy or participate in a festival or party of some kind. In Ireland, people are friendly and happy to talk. In Dublin, I never feel alone. We are laid back and accepting.

*What are some of the most challenges faced by migrant women in Ireland? (b) What advice would you give to young and upcoming migrants women?*

Speaking from personal experience I found some subtle nuances difficult to learn and I am still learning. "Grand" for example. In Canada grand means very elaborate or stunning. Here it can mean several different things from "meh" to "ok" or "fine". I am fortunate as an English speaker to have migrated to an English-speaking country, but I am aware that there are slang and phrases that I do not fully comprehend, fortunately, my Irish friends explains things for me.

My advice to you young migrant woman would be; bring the best of your authentic self forward because that is more than enough. We need you, your perspective, your richness of character, your unique gifts. Leave behind the heavy shackles of the past that no longer serve you. This is your fresh start darling. The future is bright, and you are unlimited. So, be bold!

*There is a worldwide momentum for gender pay-gap, do you think that women have suddenly started to speak up in demand of effective change, or do you think that men have only started to pay more attention and listening more to women?*

Our time is now. We have reached a critical mass. Is it our access to unbiased and free information on social media? Is it how we have used modern tools such as Facebook to organize and support other women around the world? Are we simply fed up with being second-class citizens? Yes! It is all of these factors in a beautiful, powerful tsunami of collaboration. At times it is glaringly and depressingly obvious that women in Ireland have had to struggle for every small step forward we have made. Fortunately, this year we have seen so much positive change and momentum. Together we are moving forward and as a result, our sisters throughout the world will benefit from the shade of the trees of the seeds that were planted by the strong Irish women and those of us activists who call Ireland home.

*What has been a defining moment in your life/career or business since living in Ireland? (b) If you could have breakfast with any three Irish women, who would you choose and why?*

The defining moment of my life since I moved to Ireland has been enrolling in university in a field that I have always seen as being for people far more technically inclined than myself. I set my fears aside and jumped in and every day I am surprised at what I can achieve and how supportive the university is.

**It would be such a privilege for me to share breakfast with following women:**

I am especially inspired by one modern-day hero, Ruth Coppinger TD., a Solidarity-People Before Profits politician. (Ruth Coppinger Wikipedia 18 Sept 2018) Her FB post rallying like-minded women have been a beacon of hope in stormy political times this past year. Seeing her speak at various rallies inspired me to see that activists can work within the establishment to bring our causes forward.

To know that a logical, successful woman with a political position is hearing us, and takes the courageous step to empower our voices gives me great hope for positive political change.

From history, I must share with you my admiration for Lilian Bland. Like me, Lilian was a fly girl. The land was not vast enough to hold her, so Lilian took to explore the skies on the wings of her imagination and determination. Lilian Bland was an aviator, aeronautical engineer. "She lived an unconventional lifestyle for the period, smoking, wearing trousers, and practising martial arts."(Wikipedia) She became the first woman in Ireland to design, build and fly an aircraft. (http://www.lilianbland.ie)

**If you have the power to change anything in Ireland, what will that be?**

We have the power to move things forward in a progressive Ireland. I envision public health care for all of us living in Ireland including access to free visits and preventative health care measures. Affordable stable housing. permanent jobs with benefits and separation of church and state.

# *Catherine Kayya Murphy*

**"It is very easy for migrant women to fall into depression due to the lack of family support in various matters."**

*M*y name is Catherine Kayya Murphy, the vice chairperson of the Association of Tanzanians In Ireland (ATAI), a community of Tanzanian Diaspora in Ireland with the aim of helping each other out and also exploring options of investing and giving back to the motherland. Originally from Tanzania, now residing in Ireland for the past 8 years, I graduated from IT Carlow with a BA in Applied Humanities. My final undergraduate project is a thesis titled "Ethnic diversity of Television presenters in Ireland." The research evaluates the representation of the ethnic diversity as well as the attitudes of the people towards presenters from minority backgrounds on Irish television stations. Ireland today is different from that prior to the Celtic Tiger era and/or joining the EU, it is now a multicultural society.

The richness of the ethnic diversity is seen from the presence of the members of the new communities, recognition of Travellers as an ethnic group, the legalization of same-sex marriage and the current Taoiseach (Prime Minister) from a migrant background, Mr. Leo Varadkar.

I utilised Content analysis of Irish television stations as well as questionnaires as research methods which have facilitated in providing answers. Quota sampling was applied where participants from different ethnic groups present in Ireland were invited. The focus of my research is on presenters from BAVEM (Black, Asian and Visible Ethnic Minority) group who have previously hosted or are still hosting programmes on the six television channels operating in Ireland; RTE1, RTE2, TG4, and (TV3, 3e & be3, now Virgin 1, Virgin 2, & Virgin 3 respectively).

While still in education, I started interning with AKIDWA as a Young Migrant Women (YMW) leader with the role of coordinating programmes and sourcing out activities for the participants. Thereafter I moved to working with the Immigrant Council of Ireland as a Research and Integration Intern where I dealt with the anti-racism helpline, researching my own topic of Swahili speakers in Ireland, with the aim of promoting the language to be used for mobilisation of migrants on political participation in the coming elections. My achievements from working with the Immigrant council are representing the organisation during the Migrant and Refugee Women's Integration and Empowerment in Europe seminar – Rome, Italy and also delivering a presentation on Immigration and citizenship to Filipino Migrant Workers in Ireland. Working at the council eventually led to becoming a Yellow Flag school evaluator (under the Irish Travellers Movement) where I evaluate schools on their commitment to multiculturalism and inclusion for their students. I have enjoyed visiting different schools and seeing the work the students and teachers put towards embracing diversity that already exists in the school and how the students from these schools are very mindful and respectful of each other's cultures.

I have also worked with as an English/Swahili translator and participated in trainings that have aided in building my capacity i.e. Women for Election Conference, Migrant Leadership Academy and Democracy Camp coming up this October that will include migrants from all over Europe and America. I enjoy volunteering and activism for different causes close to my heart. Currently fundraising for "Their Lives Matter Halloween Gala" in aid of children's cancer services in Tanzania, coordinated with my local football club for donations of jerseys for Peace for Conservation organization in Tanzania who run an annual "sports for conservation" tournament as a way of raising awareness on elephant conservation and fighting against poaching around Serengeti.  The jerseys were worn by village teams who compete during the tournament. I was a youth advocate for ONE organization advocating against global extreme poverty and pressuring the Irish government to commit to 0.7% of overseas development aid.

My activism took me to Munich, Germany in 2015 together with other global ONE Youth ambassadors demonstrating against G7 leaders urging them to do more in combating global extreme poverty. I had the privilege of meeting with Andrew Doyle TD and Stephen Donnelly TD where we discussed on Ireland's position on the commitment to 0.7% of ODA. I was a community ambassador for FGM (Female Genital Mutilation) and was a contestant for Miss Centenary Ireland in 2016. I am a proud owner of Catitya shop, selling handmade products from small scale entrepreneurs in Tanzania to Ireland and the rest of the world. The shop developed from my passion of crafts and the desire to help small scale entrepreneurs in Tanzania who work hard in making beautiful first class products but never get the recognition they deserve due to the lack of market. In my spare time I enjoy crocheting and making accessories such as earrings and bracelets.

My favourite food is ugali (maize meal).  What I miss most in Tanzania are the local cuisine, the people and the lovely weather.  And what I love most about Ireland is the respect of people's views and the respect of rights of women and children and the overall adherence to ethics compared to my native country.

*What are some of the most challenges faced by migrant women in Ireland? (b) What advice would you give to young and upcoming migrants women?*

Lack of family support. It has been the biggest challenge of my life as a migrant woman. It is very easy for migrant women to fall into depression due to the lack of family support in various matters such as child care, socializing and consolidation in times of the difficulties we face. This lack of family support triggers the pursuit of one's dreams as you may have to put some things on hold until you are completely able to participate fully.

My advice for upcoming migrant women is to mingle out with people other than with only those from the same countries. They should not isolate themselves. Becoming active and participating in different community groups or religious centres such as churches can help eliminate the isolation and along the way you get to form relationships with people. I can testify to this as I have been so blessed to form relationships with people in the community, some of whom have become like family.

*What has been a defining moment in your life/career or business since living in Ireland? (b) If you could have breakfast with any three Irish women, who would you choose and why?*

Becoming a mother to two beautiful intelligent boys and completing my degree course are moments that I cherish dearly.

If I could have breakfast with any woman in the Republic of Ireland, it would be Mary McAleese, the 8th and the second female president of Ireland. She serves as an inspiration to women who have a passion for politics. She is also a fighter for women's rights and fights against misogyny. Recently during the "Voices of Faith" Conference in Rome she called for the church to end the virus of misogyny. The church systems expect women to do all the hard work but yet deny them a voice and visibility. Misogynism can manifest itself twice as much on migrant women than their white counterparts as a result of the existing racism in the society. And having an influential person such as Mary McAleese speaking against it will pave way for organizations working with migrant women to speak out and encourage migrants women to be on the same levels as other women.

Trish Scanlan is another amazing Irish woman I would love meet up for breakfast. This Irish paediatric oncologist founded Their Lives Matter (TML) charity in 2006 providing free treatment to children with cancer in Tanzania. She was awarded the inaugural alumni award for medicine by UCD in 20114 and a lifetime award for contributions to cancer prevention by the international Prevention Research Institution in 2018. Her devotion to helping these Tanzanian children who may come from poor backgrounds brings joy and hope to many Tanzanian families.

*The government recently launched 'Project Ireland 2040', which the Taoiseach said is a document about building a republic of opportunity. Have you seen this document, if so do you think that in its mapping there is provision to create an enabling space for migrant women to be heard and lead? (b) The Prime Minister is the son of a migrant father from India, does this alone give you the slightest hope for the future of the children of migrants in this country, and why? (c) If you have the power to change anything in Ireland, what will that be?*

On project Ireland 2040, I didn't hear about it until now, but I have therefore researched it to familiarize myself with the initiative. The project focuses on the wellbeing, equality and opportunity for all. Out of these three themes, ten promising outcomes are predicted to happen; (i) compact growth (ii)enhanced regional accessibility (iii) strengthened rural economies and communities (iv)sustainable mobility (v) enterprise, innovation and skills (vi) international connectivity (vii) Heritage (viii) Low carbon society (ix) Sustainable environmental management and (x) Quality childcare, education and health services. The project looks promising for the future as it covers key areas of concern crippling the population such as the housing crisis, unemployment, childcare costs and linking the rural areas not only with just Dublin but with each other. I applaud the government for taking this initiative. Sadly though, the project has not put diversity into consideration. There is no recognition of minority groups and their plight for equality at all. While it is true that even the minority groups will benefit from the plan, but it looks as though that we might end up being on the lower ladder due to the institutionalized racism that already exists. This may or may not be the case, but I do worry about our children's future if the sufferings of minorities are not addressed by the government in any way. And even though the Prime Minister is from a migrant background, this does not guarantee equality for migrants if the government does not prioritize migrants in its plans and policies.

*If I had the power to change something about Ireland*, I would make Ireland a country where everyone is treated equal regardless of their ethnicity. Ireland as we know it has a good reputation for being nice to visitors "Ireland of the Welcomes"; however, this is only one dimensional as only people from white background enjoy the welcomes while the others are made to feel like they are not welcomed. Having said that, I would like to acknowledge the generosity of Irish people who have loved, supported and embraced us. These amazing people have opened the doors for me and my family into their lives. I have been truly blessed with such kind-hearted people in my life and for that, I am forever grateful.

# *Monica Walsh*

*"Settling down in a new country takes time, migrant women may find the process boring and long, but they must try hard to not lose their sanity over it."*

I am Monica Walsh. I was born in Poland and living in Ireland since 2004 so it has been 14 years now in Ireland. I left Poland in my early 20's so I remember my childhood and school years there, but my first job and family life all started here in Ireland. I currently work as a teacher and model part-time.

Sadly, I've no close family left in Poland, all my family are in Tel-Aviv, Israel. I don't eat red meat, only chicken or fish occasionally. I like

Italian food. Ireland is my home now and I like everything about Ireland. This is where most of my dreams materialised, so I'd like to say that Ireland has been so good to me, it gave me more opportunities and the freedom to express myself.

*What are some of the most challenges faced by migrant women in Ireland? (b) What advice would you give to young and upcoming migrants women?*

There are challenges everywhere in the world and that includes Ireland. People generally go through difficult times at various times in life. I don't think there are any bigger challenges here in Ireland than in any other countries. Settling down in a new country takes time, migrant women may find the process boring and long, but they must try hard to not lose their sanity over it.

My advice to young and upcoming migrants women is; As a young and upcoming migrant woman, you have so many things that you want to accomplish, my advice is follow your dreams and make them happen, but to make them happen you need to work hard because it is never easy to accomplish something without the hard work put into it first. It doesn't matter which country you come from, Ireland is a great country to have your education and experience. I know many migrant women who also run their own businesses and are doing great and happy. I came to Ireland on my own and didn't know a single person and look at me now, winning international titles, getting invited for huge events, becoming an ambassador of Domestic Violence Foundation and now being published as an author by taking part in this book. If you believe in yourself, you can achieve anything that you put your mind to.

*There is a worldwide momentum for gender pay-gap, do you think that women have suddenly started to speak up in demand of effective change, or do you think that men have only started to pay more attention and listening more to women?*

There is a clear difference from time past and now, the truth is that women are raising their voices more and men are listening and paying more attention to us. There are so many successful and influential women playing important roles in our society today than they did before. Many women make the same amount of money as their men counterparts now and that on its own is empowering.

*Do you think that Ireland has done more to protect the rights of women? If you answered yes, in your opinion —why are there so many stories about domestic violence? If you answered no, then what do you think Ireland should do more to protect women?*

Domestic violence has been around for a very long time and still happening in many homes. I'm saddened by the prospects of not seeing a visible solution to end this menace in our society while abusers continue to perpetrate their ills without fear of repercussion. Those who suffer domestic abuse are afraid to speak out because of the way they are treated by the public as if women are liars who make these things up, so they're humiliated and sometimes ridiculed even when there are evidences. Even cases that manage to go through to the courts are also delayed unnecessarily while the situation grows to become worse. Many women are suffering in silence, therefore a lot more must be done to protect the rights of women.

*What has been a defining moment in your life/career or business since living in Ireland? (b) If you could have breakfast with any three Irish women, who would you choose and why?*

A defining moment for me was when I won an international beauty pageant, it changed my life and from that day my self-confident sored. Since then, I've had opportunities to meet so many amazing people. I have also been given the chance to work with talented people around the country and raise awareness about domestic violence. On the part of my career, it led me to start my own fashion blog as it was one of my passion.

**The three women I would have breakfast with are:**

1. Wife of the president of Ireland Sabina Higgins. She seems like a very interesting woman and I'd love to ask about her experience as First Lady.

2. The second woman is Rosana Davion. She won the biggest beauty pageant title of Miss World in 2003, which is great. Being in pageantry myself, I see her as an idol. I would like to thank to her, for bringing such honour to a small country like Ireland. I would love to find out more about her experience as Miss World.

3. The third woman is the Director of Women's Aid, the domestic violence organisation. I have personal questions that I would like to ask her, about their work as I can only imagine how hard and sad it can be, being one of the biggest organisations fighting to help women in domestic violence every single day.

*The Prime Minister is the son of a migrant father from India, does this alone give you the slightest hope for the future of the children of migrants in this country, and why? (c) If you have the power to change anything in Ireland, what will that be?*

I have to say yes, because for me I see it as a great success for Ireland and a big sign for a brighter future for all children of migrants. Leo Varadkar's role as Ireland's Prime Minister given his backgrounds shows that if you work hard enough, you can make your dreams come true.

Even if I had the power to change anything in Ireland, I wouldn't change much as I'm so in love with this country, people are so calm and nice all the time. Ireland is a country whereby you can be yourself and get on with your life quietly. If I did have the power though, I would change the weather to make sure the sun stays longer.

# Kasia Forest

*"I do admire those women who take a personal leadership and acknowledge both their successes as well as failure in order to learn from them and to improve instead of blaming others for their own incompetence."*

*I* am Kasia Forest. I was born in the town of Radomsko, in Poland where I grew up in and where I'm from originally. I'm an artist, a broadcast journalist and the founder and director of Hello Irlandia, a media brand located in Dublin. There, I started my art practice and self-development training. I completed my studies in 2009, where my interests focused around art therapy, stimulating imagination and the nature of the mind. These themes intertwine with each other and are reflected often in my work. I believe that an imagination allows me a sense of freedom. Creating art and, particularly the glass painting process which is a passion of mine and a source of inspiration for me. I think that creativity and the arts make a significant difference to people's health, well-being and success. It is important for me to live a meaningful life and to make time for creativity and relaxation. I am a fan of photography, entrepreneurship, and design.

When it comes to food I love smoothies and soups. Little can beat a delicious bowl of Polish homemade beetroot soup called Borscht. After 12 years abroad, I miss my family and friends in Poland, but Ireland is my home now. I love everything about this country. If you work hard in here, Ireland will give you an opportunity to spread your wings.

*What are some of the most challenges faced by migrant women in Ireland? (b) What advice would you give to young and upcoming migrants women?*

The Polish are the second-largest nationality in Ireland after Irish people, which makes us the biggest minority group here. Census 2017 results show that there are 122,515 Polish people living in Ireland. For the last 10 years Polish women have been migrating to Ireland more often than they did in the past, and in many cases on their own as single independent women looking for a chance to grow. Polish women look not only for a stable career path and financial independence outside Poland. They seek personal development first and a chance to live a fulfilled life. The most challenging is the lack of the Polish owned cafes, restaurants or maybe a Polish Institute which are indispensable when you live abroad, and you feel homesick. For ladies, in general, these type of places are important especially when they experience difficulties and need support.

For a young and upcoming migrant woman, I would suggest that you surround yourself with open-minded and successful people who can positively influence your life. I would recommend joining some networking events for migrant women in Ireland and getting involved in a community work. It is a great way to help others and empower the migrant community.

*There is a worldwide momentum for gender pay-gap, do you think that women have suddenly started to speak up in demand of effective change, or do you think that men have only started to pay more attention and listening more to women?*

In my experience, women are using their own powers more often than ever before. I am so fortunate to be a part of the Ladies Night Club, it's a monthly meetup for women entrepreneurs which have been tremendously helpful. When we meet, we create many memorable moments together and I often get the impression that women have started supporting each other more than they are competing against each other. Being part of a group and having its strong support, one can achieve much more than being on your own and minding your own business. There is a saying: United we stand! Owing to this fact, women feel stronger, they speak their authentic voices and are feel more assured in discussing their needs, including those related to their financial freedom. I think many women have been working hard to have their voices heard and be counted.

There are many smart women who saw opportunities and many other brave ones, who were able to catch them. To all those able women to so I pay my respects. I consciously do not want to call them "feminists", because this term, in my opinion, have been abused in the last few decades and today is commonly associated with angry and unhappy women who blame men, or any other social groups for every possible misery they experience. I believe in personal responsibility and personal ability, I believe in cause and effect – some call it karma but thanks to my own struggles that if you are committed to your goals and work hard you will achieve them. Women are perfectly capable of being strong without being aggressive, and of staying independent even when engaged in a romantic relationship as far as it has a character of partnership where both sides support and inspire each other. I do admire those women who take a personal leadership and acknowledge both their successes as well as failure in order to learn from them and to improve instead of blaming others for their own incompetence. It is those powerful women with integrity that have in many ways paved the way for my own personal realization - and they remain the best examples of success. I am enormously grateful to all of them for their bravery and determination in proving that aspiring, working hard and staying ethical in one's actions always leads to achievements regardless of your gender but with an utter respect for your own female qualities.

*What has been a defining moment in your life/career or business since living in Ireland? (b) If you could have breakfast with any three Irish women, who would you choose and why?*

There have been a lot of defining moments in my life because I am fortunate enough to keep meeting inspiring people over and over. It is thanks to them that I am who I am today. One of those significant moments was meeting Mick Hanley, who invited me to join the Dublin City FM radio station crew. It has changed a lot; it has been a truly empowering moment in my life. You can hear the Hello Irlandia broadcast journalists and myself every Thursday at 8:30 pm - we broadcast interchangeably in both languages, English and Polish. It is very important that the Polish community's voice can be loudly articulated here; as it is crucial that the assimilated non-native long-term residents have their own media. This is not about being stuck in an immigrant ghetto and not staying open - or grateful for that matter - to the native community, who accepted them in their own motherland. It is about the necessity of nurturing the minority's own native tongue and culture. I consider myself very lucky to be able to help my country mates feel at home here, in Ireland.

For my lucky breakfast, I would choose to have it with Maya Dunphy, an Irish journalist. I had the opportunity of meeting her at RTE during the shooting of the Dancing with the Stars. She was a partner of the professional Polish dancer, Robert Rowinski. She is an extremely intelligent and beautiful woman and I think it would be great to meet up with her and talk over coffee about what we have in common, i.e. journalism. But I am also very curious about what her thoughts are about dancing with Robert. There are plenty of other amazing women living in Ireland, whom I would like to meet, among all of those immigrant women who are a part of this book.

# *Ediones Diniz*

*"Women have learnt better strategies over the years in order to better negotiate better salaries."*

*M*y name is Ediones Diniz and I'm from Amazon-Brazil. I've been living in Ireland for the past 13 years. I work within a retail department the moment. I am a member of the Board of Management at my daughter's primary school, a member of the Mud Island community garden and the founder of Casa Brasil Ireland, a cultural integration project.

I love Italian cuisine – any Italian food with a beautiful pint of Guinness is just perfect. Do I miss home? Yes, of course. What I miss the most are the magical moments spent with my family. But I have Ireland – it is a place I've fallen in love with. Why did I fall in love with Ireland? That is easy to explain because for me, I haven't been around the world and don't know much about the rest of world, but it is a pleasure to live here. For one thing—I get to live in an English-speaking country, with good education and job opportunities, good shoes and an umbrella that makes my day a rainbow!

*What are some of the most challenges faced by migrant women in Ireland? (b) What advice would you give to young and upcoming migrants women?*

Many immigrant women are forced to work in low-paid jobs and the childcare is extremely expensive. This a major challenge for many women in general.

My advice to young and upcoming migrant women is that Ireland is a beautiful country, but like all other places it has its issues. But if you are brave enough, do come here and enjoy the rain. There are opportunities for migrant women to learn and grow if they are willing. They just must be determined.

*There is a worldwide momentum for gender pay-gap, do you think that women have suddenly started to speak up in demand of effective change, or do you think that men have only started to pay more attention and listening more to women?*

Women have learnt better strategies over the years in order to better negotiate better salaries. We must empower ourselves to fight for equal pay and fairer benefits and promotions. Women cannot wait for the so-called "trickle-down" effect to emerge out of nowhere. We must continue to demand for equality in all spheres of life.

*Do you think that Ireland has done more to protect the rights of women? If you answered yes, in your opinion —why are there so many stories about domestic violence? If you answered no, then what do you think Ireland should do more to protect women?*

No, not really. I don't think that much has changed. The system is failing to support women. The legislation is not strong enough for the protection of women. It is very difficult for many women to feel confident about reporting the full details of their abuse and without shame.

As well as better laws, we also need better support services for victims of domestic violence. Educating students in school about domestic violence as a crime may also help. I know that it is probably going to take a long time before we see things change. So, in all, I think Irish laws and support services should start taking violence domestic more seriously.

*What has been a defining moment in your life/career or business since living in Ireland? (b) If you could have breakfast with any three Irish women, who would you choose and why?*

For me, every single day in Ireland is defining. As I said earlier, I truly fell in love with Ireland. Everything here in Ireland makes me feel very fortunate – my family, my friends, my Sunday games in Croke Park, my Guinness, my trips all over of Ireland, my job. I even like the rainy days!

If I could have breakfast with any three Irish women, it will probably be with the followings:

Julie Sinnamon, the CEO of Enterprise Ireland. She is one of a few women who are using their influence to bring more gender balance into the Irish entrepreneurial landscape. Marian Keys as she is undoubtedly one of the most successful Irish writers of all time. Tarsila Kruse because she is one of the best illustrators in Ireland. She has illustrated a few children books in Irish language.

*The government recently launched 'Project Ireland 2040', which the Taoiseach said is a document about building a republic of opportunity. Have you seen this document, if so do you think that in its mapping there is provision to create an enabling space for migrant women to be heard and lead? (b) The Prime Minister is the son of a migrant father from India, does this alone give you the slightest hope for the future of the children of migrants in this country, and why? (c) If you have the power to change anything in Ireland, what will that be?*

Yes. I read the project 2040, but I couldn't find anything in particular about migrant women in Ireland but even then, I believe in Project 2040 as it could be great opportunity to create something better for migrant women in the future of this country. I agree that Ireland is changing, and our Prime Minister Leo Varadkar is a very good example of that. The Prime Minister a big inspiration for our sons and daughters even though he has lived all in Ireland his life. He also happens to be the youngest Prime Minister that Ireland has had to hold the position and that is an added reason for migrant families to hope for the best in our children's future.

**If I had the power to change anything in Ireland**, it will most probably be to create a more efficient, reliable and affordable health system, a better public transport not only for Dublin but for all of Ireland and build affordable houses for the people who are living in this country. I also think we need to reform our education system. Get rid of single-sex schools and remove the control of church in primary and secondary education altogether.

# *Amaka Okonkwo*

**"I want to see Ireland where African Diaspora are represented in leadership positions across all sectors"**

$M$y name is Amaka Mercy Okonkwo, Founder and coordinator at eDundalk.com. I am a social entrepreneur, community development consultant, Human right activist, public speaker, health care practitioner, a legal secretary, office administrator and Christ ambassador. I went to Trinity College Dublin (TCD) where I studied Racial and Ethnicity studies. I studied Equality studies at the National University of Ireland Maynooth (NUIM) and bagged a B.A in Development Studies at Kimmage Development Studies Centre Dublin (KDSC). By the time you are reading this piece, I would have completed a diploma programme in psychology and counselling. I have many other professional certificates which come to play whenever the experience is needed. I am a Fellow at the School for Social Entrepreneurs, Ireland (SSEI). Since 2014, I have been mentoring women entrepreneurs globally with Cherie Blair Foundation for women (UK) and have been awarded for my achievements. I have diverse and extensive experience working in the business, non-governmental organisations (NGOs), Charity, Voluntary and Public sectors. I sit on the Board of Louth Volunteer Centre, Ireland since 2013 where my main interest is to promote volunteering amongst migrant communities and African Diaspora in particular. I am very passionate about employment, entrepreneurship, volunteering, community development, women empowerment/leadership and family unification. Everything I do is directed towards those objectives. My work has taken me to different European countries where I participated in different projects. I was born in Nigeria but moved to Ireland in 2001. I have an amazing family.

**"I love to see everyone given equal opportunity irrespective of where they live and to see every family economically empowered."**

In 2012 at the hit of being unemployed, I initiated a platform called eDundalk and in 2014 the website - www.edundalk.com was launched by then Senator Mary Moran with the vision to see Ireland where African Diasporas are represented in leadership positions across all sectors. My mission is to promote employability, entrepreneurship, integration, community development and social inclusion. eDundalk aims to highlight and create awareness on employment/entrepreneurship challenges faced by African diasporas in Ireland. We also use the platform to highlight the positive economic contribution from the said target group to the Irish society which in most cases is not highlighted in the media. eDundalk provides information, mentoring, advertising, training and online marketplace to help our mentees and target group sell their finished unique products. Due to the direct impact of our work, the annual eDundalk International Networking Dinner was introduced in 2014 to draw people from all nooks and corners of the world to meet, network, connect and share inspiring stories, ideas and experience to help and support one another to succeed. This event was also initiated to bring our numerous clients and contacts under one roof for human/physical contact which the social media is fast taking away from our well being and society. The platform has inspired a lot of women to start up doing something for themselves. While some of our participants went back to education and self development programmes, others learnt new skills and more women became self aware. eDundalk networking event has helped to promote social inclusion, integration and mental well being. The event has helped a lot of our participants to move from point A -B. It has helped to reduce isolation and exclusion and has created a trusted platform where participants can learn practical tips to start their own business or pursue their career. We generate income through advertising, sponsorship, mentoring, presentation/training, newsletter publication and ticketed events. For some families who face employment/business issue, resulting to health and family breakdown, this event has become the magic pill! It has become one event that many people look forward to every year due to its originality, quality, inclusiveness and purpose-driven. The sixth edition is scheduled to take place on 16th, February 2019, in Dundalk. Since I joined the Louth volunteer centre as a board member in 2013, the number of volunteers from African background has increased tremendously because of the campaigns I championed to raise awareness on the benefits of volunteering among which is opportunity to access employment and self confidence.

In 2014, I was selected to join Cherry Blair Foundation for women (UK) as a mentor and since then I have mentored several women entrepreneurs from different parts of the world and who have been able to start up their own business. Since the launch of www.edundalk.com in 2014, nearly five million visitors from across the globe visited the website for various reasons between 2014 and 2018. Also in 2014, out of about seventy applicants (social entrepreneurs) from across Ireland to School for Social Entrepreneurs Ireland incubator programme, eDundalk was amongst twenty seven projects selected to participate on the programme. I was the only one from

African backgrounds in the whole process. In 2015, we rented an office space at Creative Spark business hub in Dundalk and held an open day that same year. We employed, through the help of Social Welfare & Protection Department, an Intern who completed his Masters degree in Entrepreneurship and Marketing from Dundalk Institute of Technology to work with us. Since then we have had over thirty people who have had work experience or volunteered with us in various categories. Unfortunately, this office space was forced to close down after few months due to lack of financial support. Also in 2015, eDundalk was a finalist at the Dundalk Chamber of Commerce Business Awards and in the same year, I was awarded at the Africa Day Awards Dublin by Metro Eireann – the longest established and the only multicultural newspaper in Ireland. Getting recognition from the Chamber of commerce in Ireland was my biggest achievement because such an award is hard to come by.

My favourite food is white soup (ofe nsala) served with freshly pounded yam. This choice is influenced by my marriage to Nteje man in Anambra state of Nigeria but do not tempt me with bitter leaf soup – Nnewi style! I sincerely miss the way Nigerians Praise and Worship God in Nigeria. I also miss the way I used to sit, eat and play with my siblings and relatives and laugh over everything. I miss the ever organic food. I miss my parents especially my mum who died few months after I moved to Ireland but due to travel documents, I was unable to go home for her funeral. She taught me how to give and love everyone without expecting a return. My dad was a complete gentleman who loved and sacrificed for his family.

I love everything about Ireland except that many Irish people are currently turning away from God and the priceless legacy and values Ireland is known for all over the world. Hopefully, there will be a turnaround one day. Irish weather, ironically, is the best thing I like about Ireland. I find the unpredictability of Irish weather so fascinating. Wisely, understanding and embracing Irish weather has helped me in associating and integrating fantastically well with indigenous Irish.

*What are some of the most challenges faced by migrant women in Ireland? (b)
What advice would you give to young and upcoming migrants women*

Employment and or starting your own business, I think, are the biggest challenges faced by the migrant women in Ireland. Most people migrate due to economic reasons. What benefit is it then if you cannot access the 'greener pasture' in your new country? I am speaking from experience and reason I was driven to start eDundalk. The amount of rejection I got from Irish employers initially got me thinking. With so many 'unsuccessful job application letters' I began to interview other migrant women and then I discovered that it was not just peculiar to me but many, especially those from African backgrounds. It was then I decided to go back to school not college! I started with FAS with Diploma in office administration and management. Though I made progress afterwards, many migrant women did not. I also discovered that unemployment has linked to health issues, such as depression and mental illness, family breakdown and anti-social behaviour from the young people, so I thought it wise to come up with a solution to tackle the societal issue. eDundalk became my solution! People getting employment in the areas where they are qualified for is the beauty of employment. In Dundalk for instance, if you look at the businesses or companies in the town including financial institutions and schools, you will not see a face of African migrant woman! We have over a thousand professional migrants living in Dundalk but few lucky ones have to travel all the way to Dublin, Athlone or elsewhere to work. It is my desire to walk in to any establishments in Dundalk and see qualified women from African backgrounds as part of the workforce. I want to see more of them starting and running their own business successfully. Majority of migrant women contributions to the Irish society and economy are not often celebrated or talked about in the media. I was invited to an event where I was practically the only person from African background but the photographer could not figure out why I was there, so he picked others sitting with me to take a group photograph for the media and I was left out! Starting Your Own Business can be quite daunting for migrant women from African backgrounds. There is lack of accurate supporting information and practical help available. You don't always get the same fair treatment as you would expect. Majority of women from African background living in Ireland are professionals in different fields. They are hardworking and resilient, but they are hardly involved in decisions that affect them. They are nowhere to be seen in any political offices, you can hardly see any in management positions, and promotion in workplaces is not common either. Migrant women need to be involved from planning to execution stages of projects that affect them. *"Women are not numbers but human beings "– Amaka Okonkwo*

My advice to young and upcoming migrant women is to invest in themselves. Personal development is very vital in pursuing your career. Be open-minded and accept people for who they are considering the content of their heart and not their skin colour. Be positive and always see any failure as a stepping stone to the next level. Never give up. Develop an ability to accommodate others, work hard, be aspired and inspire others. Never look down on anyone. Do not create class barriers because it breeds inequality and poverty. Keep pushing and never be comfortable in your comfy zone. Be always ready to step out! Share information among yourselves. If a door opens for you, find out how you can let others in as well. Always promote positive image and never run down anyone. Never work or do anything to be better than anyone else but yourself. Do not Hate, Love!

*There is a worldwide momentum for gender pay-gap, do you think that women have suddenly started to speak up in demand of effective change, or do you think that men have only started to pay more attention and listening more to women?*

I think it is a work in progress. Going by the Irish history, I think Ireland has improved a lot. I understood there was a time that women in Ireland were not allowed to work or vote. Today, all of that have changed. I am only concerned about how those who violate or abuse the rights of women are allowed back into the community without proper monitoring. Going by some of the stories we hear in the media, most offenders have been convicted in the past. This brings me back to one of my strongest reasons why I supported the No campaign during the Irish Abortion Referendum in May 2018. I argued that instead of free abortion, the government should invest on cracking down sex offenders/rapists/paedophiles and make them pay for their dehumanising actions against women. In fighting for the rights of women, the government should also fight for the rights of the unborn children and say no to free abortion. Special squad should be trained and equipped to tackle rape crisis and that will automatically reduce the number of "unwanted pregnancies" and indeed protect the rights of women. If only Ireland would critically understand that the abortion clinics would be highly patronised by natives, then in the future, a time will come when Ireland becomes highly populated by foreign born Irish nationals and their descendants who subsequently will grow up and take over the land. More women should be represented in the political ladder and management positions across all sectors. I want to see African women in the Dial. Equal Employment opportunity should be created for all, otherwise, more young women are most likely going to immigrate to other countries where their skills are in high demand while others may resolve to all forms of anti-social behaviour. Currently, many young women relocate to other countries for better employment opportunities after acquiring a third level education degree in Ireland. This is a loss to the nation.

*What has been a defining moment in your life/career or business since living in Ireland? (b) If you could have breakfast with any three Irish women, who would you choose and why?*

A major defining moment in my life since I moved to Ireland was in 2002 when I had my first child and officially became a mother! That was a climax for me as a woman. Subsequently my second and third children arrived in 2003 and 2004 respectively. The whole process changed my whole perspectives about life. My lifestyle and everything revolve around my family. I initiated eDundalk without a job and money, to me, that was a defining moment. Amidst uncertainty, I defied every odd and invented a very creative, innovative purpose-driven platform to tackle deep societal problem in my own little way. That job lost at that time became a turning point for me. I retraced my steps. I began to invest in myself. Currently, I think that if I did not lose my job at that time, I would have remained in my comfort zone. My unemployment status became a source of inspiration for me. It was at that same period that I gained admission to study a degree in Development Studies at Kimmage Development Study Centre, Dublin. This course has played a major role in my career progression and passion for what I do today. My active role in volunteering since 2003 to date cannot be overstated because it has helped to define my status, personality, network and contribution to the Irish society, my community and family. Being the first African entrepreneur to ever reach a finalist position at the Dundalk Chamber of commerce business awards in 2015 was an incredible experience for me. Africa Day Awards by Metro Eireann also boosted my confidence and aspirations. In 2017, I was invited to speak at Euroverge conference in Zurich where I spoke on leadership challenges and success of a woman of colour based on my work at eDundalk. I was on the panel of discussion at the World Village Festival Finland in May 2018 to share experience on the African women empowerment and community development. My divine connection with Fatima Usman, Josephine Atanga and Abel Ayodeji (African-Finish citizens) has made a huge impact in my work. When I look at the progress of my mentees in their various start-up businesses, I feel challenged and want to do more. It is inspiring! I can't complete this session without acknowledging the opportunity I had to work with two great African professionals in Ireland - Chinedu Onyejelem (editor and publisher of Metro Eireann newspapers) and Salome Mbugua (AkiDwA founder and president) who inspired me and were instrumental to my rise. As for women in Ireland I would want to have breakfast with, I believe every woman is as important to me as the other. It does not matter to me who I dine with, but I cherish any woman who is hardworking, resilient, purpose-driven and who does not pull down fellow women!

*The government recently launched 'Project Ireland 2040', which the Taoiseach said is a document about building a republic of opportunity. Have you seen this document, if so do you think that in its mapping there is provision to create an enabling space for migrant women to be heard and lead? (b) The Prime Minister is the son of a migrant father from India, does this alone give you the slightest hope for the future of the children of migrants in this country, and why? (c) If you have the power to change anything in Ireland, what will that be?*

I have learnt that there are things you don't beg for especially when it is your privilege. It will or may only take time but at that ripe time, it takes a natural occurrence. Having said that, we need to keep the awareness campaign going and invest in our personal development. I am an advocate of the Power of Identity. Knowing who you are and, being consistently committed and connected to the right people are very important. Keep doing the right thing that you are doing. The current Irish prime minister – Leo Varadkar, I would think have passion for politics and he followed the right path consistently and committed. He mingled with the right crowd and at the right time, the power was handed down to him! I think there are huge opportunities for migrants in Ireland in the future. I still see Ireland as a virgin! There is so much to explore in this country. All I am asking for is equal opportunity for all to participate and for people to be ready for the harvest time.

***If I have the power to change anything in Ireland,*** there would be many changes, not just one. First, I'd campaign to ensure every employer with a minimum of 10 staff have at least one qualified migrant of African descent working in their company. I will support more funding streams that are accessible to social entrepreneurs such as sole trading. I will promote diversity at workplace. I will definitely look into homelessness crisis in Ireland and invest in affordable housing scheme. I will pay attention to the elderly people and people with disability living in nursing homes and other public institutions to make sure they are given quality services.

Finally, I will practically beg Ireland to return to God! Irish people are very good and have great and compassionate heart. The people have invested so much in other nations and in people through missionary works and the social welfare systems. I think the people still hurt due to clerical abuse, but my prayer is that God heals every wounded and broken hearts/families. Let Ireland look up once again on God: The Almighty but see clerics as humans. St Patrick left a lingering legacy and we still celebrate him on St Patrick's day. I will re-introduce Christian religious studies in all primary and secondary school levels and make it compulsory in primary school level. Entrepreneurship will be introduced in all secondary schools as a subject. I will also pay good attention to young people and encourage them to get involved in politics. I will do everything possible to create and invest employment and entrepreneurship opportunities. I will make good use of brain gain of African Diaspora in Ireland and make sure that the they are well represented in leadership positions across all sectors in the country for maximum productivity. To all those who have supported me in different ways on my journey in Ireland, I say, THANK YOU!

*Carol, thank you for this great initiative. You are a good example of what a social entrepreneur is. Thank you to all my co-writers, my friends and amazing family. I love Ireland!*

# *Monica Manzzi Barlocco*

*"I believe that the level of English is a key issue why some Migrant Women in Ireland are facing hard times."*

$M$y name is Monica Manzzi Barlocco, I am originally from Montevideo, Uruguay. My grandparents were French and Italian who migrated to South America over a century ago. I came to Ireland 13 years ago. I have been aware since early stages that there is a big world to see, and I knew I was not going to live in my country all my life. One day when I was 6 years old I asked my mother if she could send me somewhere to start to learn how to speak English. How funny it turned out now because I ended up in Ireland, which English would become my new and most used language.

I love Ireland because Irish people are very polite, and I find them always happy and helpful. Since being in Ireland, I have learnt so much about multiculturalism and other things through the years, I have so much love for this country and I am very grateful and happy here.

*What are some of the most challenges faced by migrant women in Ireland? (b) What advice would you give to young and upcoming migrants women? What are some of the most challenges faced by migrant women in Ireland? (b) What advice would you give to young and upcoming migrants women?*

I believe that the level of English is a key issue why some Migrant Women in Ireland are facing hard times. Some of them that come to Ireland are very experienced in different roles while other ones have very little or no English at all and they find it difficult to adapt. But again, many migrant women especially single mothers who are qualified also have problems in getting jobs, this also depends of many factors, therefore there is a huge competition and then there is the issue of inequality and of pay-gap between women and men.

My advice for upcoming migrant women would be the following: It is important to first of all learn to understand and speak English as the language commonly spoken in Ireland, this will help them to integrate into the society. Secondly: Try to do something you are passionate about. We all know, the beginning of this journey is not an easy task. For some of us it could be easier or more difficult. Been part of a new culture and doing learning different ways of life and behaviour involves many challenges. It is important to integrate in the new culture but also important that we never forget where we are coming from because it is the essence of who we are and should be ambassadors of our own countries and cultures. I take pride in showing my culture and also learn from other cultures through participating in charity, fundraising, volunteer activities.

As soon as I came to Ireland, it did not take long before I got a job, and I started to work for a very prestigious company as a makeup artist. I believe I do have a creative side, and I started to explode straight away. After many years working for this company, my first baby Neisha came along, I decided afterwards to move on and explore other fields. I was looking for something that would let me work freelance and be able to spend more time with my daughter. I have always had a love of photography and liked the idea of making it my next career pursuit. And after I met my partner Konrad, who is a professional photographer and gave birth to my second daughter Janka, this became a reality.

Photography for me was always hobby, I was inspired by my mother. She used to be really detailed when taking pictures, I even remember laughing at her because she would make such an effort moving objects around to make the best family pictures. I convinced myself to enrol in a photography course, and I did so well at the beginner's level and then moved to complete more advance levels and before long, I became a professional photographer, and without realising it one day I saw my work published in newspapers and magazines. I have even won awards, and so far it is a sign which signals that I have become very good at my profession—photography! I believe if you do things with love and with passion and be consistent, you can become your best.

I have another side of me also which I have been exploring since I came to Ireland. This is helping people through charity, through fundraising events. I used part of my knowledge and working experience in organising events and I have made a few happen.

They were great personal achievements, believe me, been an altruist is one of the best things humans can do. Using my knowledge of makeup and once on holidays I organised in Uruguay the "Journey of Beauty and Health". I wanted to do this because my mother was fighting cancer at the time and in this process, she met many other women in the same situation, or even worse. I got help from another to makeup artist named Silvia, which I had the pleasure to meet in Ireland years before, and we both did makeovers and had chats about proving skincare treatments during chromotherapy and other treatments. When I contacted her for this, she was ready to help.

Some of the women were receiving treatment in a public hospital in Uruguay "Hospital Pereira Rosell". We wanted them to feel better, at least to make them about what they were going through momentarily! I never felt so happy, seen them smiling, having a "treat" and my mother feeling so proud of me. It was magic! But it didn't finish there, most of them had come from outside the capital, with very little resources, making it very expensive for their families to visit them. I thought about the importance of these families to be closer at such a hard time so on my return to Ireland I spoke to my friends Kevin and Aga who are artists, and they kindly donated some pieces of art in order to raffle them and fundraise money to enable me purchase 2 laptops to be used among the women in the hospital ward. To have a laptop is very common for people in developed countries like in Ireland but it is not so where I'm from so it was very much appreciated and a great achievement for me.

My next project involved me working with another Irish artist, Dominick was It was a multimedia project combining art, photography and testimonials of participating models titled "A Place to rest your Head". We planned to raise awareness of the female breast and male chest regarding breast cancer and other relevant issues. We had an amazing opening exhibition in the heart of Dublin, in which not only gathered some money from cards to donate to give to some charities. I also had the chance to read a poem that my mother wrote before she passed away. I believe everything we do is special and this was one of the most specials things I've done. I think everyone has to work actively and when we do changes happen.

A few years ago, representing my country in Miss Ethnic Ireland, an event organised by Ifrah Ahmed, I learned about Female Genital Mutilation. I was totally numb about this, I could not believe this kind of practice existed and was carried out to women. This was a great journey and without realising I became an activist for the cause. And eventually, thanks to Ifrah and other women this practice has become illegal in Ireland. There are so many causes out there that need to be addressed, it's important each of us show some concern with our knowledge and passion in order to make little changes that we want to see.

I have organised some cultural events showcasing my country. This is one of the other things that represents the person I am. I love photography, arts and I love culture. I remember one day after a world cup match and meeting many Uruguayan patriots in a Dublin pub, 'Mateada colectiva' or "Collective mateada' was born —an event I organised to gather friends and share homemade drink we call 'Yerba Mate'. It is a typical infusion from South America more especially Uruguay, Argentina and the south of Brasil but Uruguay is one of the countries who consume most in the World per capita. Yerba Mate has many nutrient properties, you must drink it with a metal straw and a term as it uses hot water. Most people in Dublin really don't know what it is as people would look at me in a very strange way if they saw me with a termo drinking it and I felt like it was needed for education and people would actually benefit from the many nutrients, so it was a great achievement for me to be able to organise this 'mateadas' in different parks, some of them with a huge attendance of over 100 people and all from different parts of the world. This is a drink we're so used at home and it is probably one of the things I miss the most about my country — drinking mate with friends and having long chats.

*Do you think that Ireland has done more to protect the rights of women? If you answered yes, in your opinion —why are there so many stories about domestic violence? If you answered no, then what do you think Ireland should do more to protect women?*

I don't see much violence here in Ireland against women, but I'm aware it does happen. I have seen more unfortunately incidents of racism around, incidents no one wants to see, but in general, I think Ireland is a safe country. Sometimes things happen when you are in the wrong place at the wrong time and you meet the wrong people. On a personal note I have to say that I feel safer here in Ireland than I did back in Uruguay. I can say this because I am coming from a country in which violence against women has become a terrible problem so bad that in some cases violent men now have tags in their ankles if they committed a reiterated violent episode, to control and prevent them from getting close to women. I don't see this here. I used to live in Dublin city centre a few years back, for more than 10 years. I remember a few episodes against women, but not many, most of them were committed by intoxicated persons and these was more isolated episodes.

Ireland has an increasing problem with homeless people, drugs and alcohol and a big part of the violence is generated in the streets. My first project as a photo-journalist allowed me to go into the streets of Dublin to try and understand the real story behind some homeless people. I noticed from most of my interviewers that the main problem was violence and abuse from some members of the family. The idea of the project was to give them a bridge to tell their stories and raise awareness of the pain behind this faces that we see every day. There is stigma and this need to change, people must be more open to realise their destiny. Sometimes things happen, and it is not our fault or due to our own negligence. To reduce violence there is a need for information, there is a need to educate and for governmental organisations to be able to detect some of these problems and be prepared to help. I believe that certain things are changing, and everyday women are gaining equality. It has not always been so in Ireland. Only 30 years ago divorce was implemented, the right to vote is quite modern as well and recently the decriminalisation of abortion. We are on the right path, we just need time and work harder to make our voices heard and to be able to make new changes.

If I have the opportunity to sit and have breakfast with important women in Ireland, it means that I would choose all of those who are actively working hard to make changes for the world to be a better one for all of us and for our next generations. There are too many that I admire!

# *Marluce Lima*

*"I have grown up so much in this Island, as an individual, professional, daughter, friend, and as a woman."*

*M*y name is Marluce Lima. I was born thirty years ago in Brazil, and was reborn here in Ireland in 2014, the place where I have come to love as a new home, new land and new mother. Before I left Brazil, I was working as a Financial Analyst. I am terrible with numbers, and I made my best to improve myself as a professional. But I was living a life that was not filling, I was not getting full job satisfaction as my soul yearned for more. I knew I had the potential to achieve more and when the opportunity came I did just that. I left my country and came to Dublin, with no English at all, just hope and faith to do something better with my life. But then I soon realized it was not going to be easy to navigate my desired goals. I discovered what was missing to make my life happier; it was poetry!

Before that, I'd worked as a Deli-assistant, Cleaner, Au-pair, Babysitter, Dog-sitter, Food preparations and, Barista. Eventually, I worked my way up to the position of a Manager in a coffee shop - that was something I did not think would happen, but it did, and I was over the moon! Becoming a manager came with more responsibilities than I thought, and I was so stressed. Consequently, it affected my regular flow and I wrote very little that I decided to quit but on a second thought I step back to the position as a Barista, because at this time my Visa had expired. My employer knew about it and he retained my service as he needed someone with the skill and experience. To cut a long story, the business did not go very well for too long either and the job ended, while I found myself a new as a Deliveroo, however that too did not last very long because I was already suffering the chronic pain in my legs— and here I am, still trying to make my dreams come true. I have grown up so much in this Island, as an individual, professional, daughter, friend, and as a woman, and I have met many good people and allowed myself to try new things. I got engaged in a project with a Brazilian friend (Karina Pereira), called "Brazilian Clowning Project" - it is about connecting elderly people with children in the same atmosphere to mediate by clowning. I provide workshops for the volunteers such as poetry and creative writing, and I also created a website called "Italics Poetry" in an attempt to gather together people who love writing but could do not find space, opportunity and courage to do it alone, so this is a collective platform to encourage writers to write and share their words to the world.

*What are some of the most challenges faced by migrant women in Ireland? (b) What advice would you give to young and upcoming migrants women?*

I usually experience health problems. It is not always easy as it is expensive going to the doctors and do the examining. In my country we used to do the smear test every year and here I could make it only in my first year, almost 5 years ago. Another point is about xenophobic or sexist attitude here, I don't really know what people think or the reasons that make them act in certain ways but when I was a manager, for example, I noticed at the beginning that some of the male customers found it hard to believe that I was really the manager. They would walk into the shop asking to talk to male staff instead talking to me. I thought it was something about me being a woman and or foreign or perhaps something about my English. Once I asked one of them, and he joked that perhaps they were afraid of beautiful women, which is absurd as well because I was hardworking to show people that I am not just a pretty face.

My advice to you, young migrant: Take care of your health to avoid any complications and the need to go to hospital. With any racism or prejudice that you might face: do not take it personally because sometimes, people might just be having a bad day. Make your day better than their opinion.

*There is a worldwide momentum for gender pay-gap, do you think that women have suddenly started to speak up in demand of effective change, or do you think that men have only started to pay more attention and listening more to women?*

The internet gave power everyone to spread their own opinions and find people who believe in the same words as them, people who agree with something and people who don't, and so on. which in at the same point is good but also dangerous if you keep yourself in a bubble. Disparity can be real, but we have to take in account other variants such as language, education, skills, training, experience, work hours etc., to understand it in general and its peculiarity and also the kind of industry or business. Models who are women for example tend to earn more than men. I have never met a woman in the exact same position with the exact same curriculum as the man working in the same company who has said to me she is paid less than her male counterpart. But in any case, if this was happening it would have had to be negotiated based on her rights as well under law. I know some men in Ireland who earn less money than the wife or girlfriend, stays more at home to look after their children and undertake domestic chores like cooking etc, something that was much more common for women before.

*Do you think that Ireland has done more to protect the rights of women? If you answered yes, in your opinion —why are there so many stories about domestic violence? If you answered no, then what do you think Ireland should do more to protect women?*

Ireland is doing well with campaigns about the protection and care for women and children, also for the men and elderly people same as I have seen folders, advertisements, videos and articles about mental health, alcoholism, abuse and domestic violence. Domestic violence is a deeply rooted problem in Ireland that concerns the society at large. There are domestic violence services located in towns across Ireland, the services are usually free and confidential, for example the organization called "Safe Ireland", where the President Michael D. Higgins is the Patron. The most important thing is about letting people who are victims know that they are not alone, that they can speak out in confidentiality and trust, and that they have protection and the concern of associations who are willing to understand and help with capacity to respond and change the scenario. Honestly, I believe that women have started to feel more encouraged to search for help and are stronger than ever, and we can point out from the victory for the Yes side in the Campaign of Repeal the 8th amendment that happened in May this year. I am happy to be here in this special period of on-going changes in Ireland.

*What has been a defining moment in your life/career or business since living in Ireland? (b) If you could have breakfast with any three Irish women, who would you choose and why?*

Every person I've met and every step that I have taken have been a part of my maturation. Each opportunity I took I grew as a professional and as an individual. Some Irish and European people I met had helped me to improve my English and my point of view about things in the world and my inner world, for example my punctuality and clarity in the way I speak. Brazilians I met here have become the most important people in my life, they were believers in my words and this trustworthy relationship was crucial for me to try and define the best and the hardest decisions in my life and become who I truly am - a writer. Living in Ireland has changed my whole world for good.

I would love to have a beautiful breakfast and a chat with: Emma Donoghue, she is a writer and author of books like, 'Room, The Wonder' and others. I love her style of writing and her stories.

Second woman would be Brigid of Kildare - she is considered a figure of legend and Ireland's only female Patron Saint, as well as the goddess of poetry. She was held up as a symbol of divine femininity and freed trafficked women.

My third choice is the actress Tara Flynn. I saw her for the first time when I was assisting an Irish photographer doing some photos and videos for a promotion for her show "Not a Funny Word" and then I went to watch her. I admire her voice, her intelligence and her true beauty.

*The government recently launched 'Project Ireland 2040', which the Taoiseach said is a document about building a republic of opportunity. Have you seen this document, if so do you think that in its mapping there is provision to create an enabling space for migrant women to be heard and lead? (b) The Prime Minister is the son of a migrant father from India, does this alone give you the slightest hope for the future of the children of migrants in this country, and why? (c) If you have the power to change anything in Ireland, what will that be?*

Ireland has opened their door to many people who want to come here, now Ireland has no option but to increase the options for us. We are bringing our culture, our experience, new ideas and increasing the workforce, labour, paying taxes as other Irish. Many of my friends have found opportunities in big companies, that probably wasn't something easy thing to happen for immigrants before. Dublin is becoming a cosmopolitan city and it is nice to be witnessing it; like the LUAS in O'Connell street, I see it is going to be a big change for Ireland and the Irish people and I believe that if the government is planning to receive more immigrants they really need to start this plan and development right now, especially in the matter of house and infrastructure. I believe anyone can reach the position of Prime Minister and President if they have the ability and qualities to be there no matter the racial backgrounds.

*If I had the power*, I would change the way the Irish deals with homeless and addicted people, including gambling. They need and should to be treated as a human being with their rights, protection and access to treatment and a better life, but they also have to have their duties as any other person. I would think about programs, activities, workshops to include them, to give them the opportunity to change their own lives. Living marginalized could not be an option anymore, and a right for a decent life for them in exchange of volunteer work, paid work or something that could make them feel part of society again.

# Thandeka Ndzondza

*"My experience and what I can bring to the table wasn't looked at. As a woman of colour you do have to work harder than everybody else."*

*M*y name is Thandeka Noluthando Ndzondza. I have previously been known as Thandeka Monds and Thandeka Saul. As human beings and more particularly for me as a woman I see that the things around me are constantly changing and our lives are full of all kinds of challenges, but it is important that we appreciate all the different changes that come to us at different stages in our lives no matter what they are.

I work as a Marketing Assistant in the retail sector and this comes with its own challenges—successes and days where you question everything and what is really going on with your life.

I am a mum of two boys and that on its own is challenging enough and it doesn't matter whether you're so busy, too tired to get up from the sofa or too sick to go to work, you just have to keep your head up and get on with being a mother, because at the end of the day, you know that there are people who look up to you for everything . and in my case, two boys that I have to feed and clothe, nurture and protect. But I won't change anything about that, I love my boys to bits (Ayanda who is 13 years old and 9 years old Vuyo). They have taught me and showed me love in more ways than I could fathom. They challenge my behaviour; my thinking and emotions everyday have and at the same also softened me in many ways and because of them I have become more compassionate compared to when I was growing up, they are my life!

I was born and raised in South Africa where I spent most of my childhood in the neighbourhood of Dube, in Soweto. It still is my favourite place in the whole world simply because it keeps a good reminder of one special human being who graced us with her presence on this earth - my grandmother! I have been living in Ireland for 15 years now and it's been a journey of which I'm still trying to navigate but thank God I have such adaptive personality which has very been helpful. I noticed that there are people who have a lot of misconceptions about me, people who know very little or next to nothing about me yet assume that they know enough to judge my lifestyle. But what they fail to understand is that Thandeka that I am now is a completely different person from the Thandeka they use to know back home. I don't really like to reveal too much about myself to people unless to those closest to me and I like to keep it that way. I am a caring and sensitive person who is outgoing and sociable, my friends can attest to it. I suppose these characteristics I got from my mum's side of the family — my mum precisely. I love to cook, listening to music, if for anything, the lyrics and beat behind the music gives meaning to life.

When it comes to what I miss about my home, the first thing that comes to my mind is the food, yes ...food. I miss native foods like mugodu aka tripe, amanqina, atchaar, amakipkip or skopaas, Kota, nik naks, ghost pops, and ultimately, my mum's cooking. I also miss family gatherings and speaking our language 24/7. One of the rituals that I observe each time I visit home, I went straight to my grand-mother's, then stop by at the local shop by spykos where we used to shop for the whole family, before heading off to my mum's house. I miss the smell of my grandmother's house especially her pink walls. I had a dog named Hypa, which my grandmother didn't particularly like at the time, but she tolerated it because she made me happy. But they're together now in heaven and I still miss them both.

*What are some of the most challenges faced by migrant women in Ireland? (b) What advice would you give to young and upcoming migrants women?*

Challenges faced by Migrant Women in Ireland - One of the first few things that always reminds me of being a foreigner and a migrant in Ireland was my name. The colour of my skin was an obvious factor although I was constantly reminded that I don't really look black be-cause my skin is a little bit light. People often pronounced my name wrongly and I had to correct each time. It was a real challenge for many same as it was for me at the time to pronounce and spell the authentic Irish names, so it got me thinking that in order to make it easier for people pronounce it and also for me to just get on with things, I decided to shorten my name.

The advice that I could give to the young upcoming migrant woman is; don't ever compromise on your name and always stand your ground no matter what. Learning a new culture and lifestyle doesn't necessarily mean that you must agree with everything or accept eve-rything in it. The best advice that I ever received when I was moving abroad was a simple one enough, that I should make sure to say 'hi' to someone new every day as such practice would help bring me out from my comfort zone, and guess what? I did, and it helped me    immensely to meet new people every time even though I was a black African girl in Ireland. I'm passing down same advice to upcoming migrant women and the young ladies; be polite to people as by so doing will bring you closer to people regardless of where you come from.

*There is a worldwide momentum for gender pay-gap, do you think that women have suddenly started to speak up in demand of effective change, or do you think that men have only started to pay more attention and listening more to women?*

What is happening in the world right now with women is that they have realized that 'WE' have a voice. The gender pay gap is something has always been on everyone's topic of conversation in secret but never addressed publicly. The women of today are empowered, educated and boldly challenge the system in more ways than you could think off. Of course, it is going to make the patriarchy system uncomfortable and shaken because why would they want to be taken down from the towers and empires that they have built.

**The real questions here though that really need to be re-examined are as follows:**

1. Who helped them get there?
2. Who encouraged them and gave them focus?
3. Who fed them and washed their clothes, making sure that they looked presentable in public?
4. Who listened to them when they had ideas that no one believed in yet were encouraged to follow them through?
5. Who comforted them and healed their wounds when they returned from wars?

I'm sure we all know the answers to the above questions. It was 'we' as the female species. But we have always been boxed into this one juxtaposition, now women have finally woken up to realize that there is more to life than just being a wife, mother and carer. Women have realized and recognized that we have more to offer hence it eventually came down to questioning of why do we get paid less for working at the jobs as our male counterpart?

To be honest, I haven't heard seen that many campaigns against domestic violence in the 15 years that I have lived in Ireland. I have come across posts on social media but have not seen people protesting publicly against domestic violence. Now bear with me on this one. I am going through a very nasty divorce, the first that I was told when I sought legal assistance was that I shouldn't worry about it because the law in this country always protects women. What they didn't say is that I will need the patience of a saint to get through the process. I have spoken to numerous women who went through the same situation and what I found out actually was the opposite. According to them, the law did not protect them, and they were subject to their circumstances like I was.

*What has been a defining moment in your life/career or business since living in Ireland? (b) If you could have breakfast with any three Irish women, who would you choose and why?*

I really didn't have groundbreaking careers in Ireland as I felt that as a woman of colour and of different dialect like myself would always have to prove that I'm worthy of that job or worthy of that interview. I found it difficult just to get the opportunity to have my CV looked at. I realised it was because of my name and my status. The first question that always came up during any application process was if I was eligible or legally allowed to work in Ireland, usually what followed were something of automatic disqualification process and my experience and what I could bring to the table wasn't considered. So, I do believe that as a woman of colour you have to work harder than everybody else. I haven't had my breakthrough yet, I know it's coming soon as I'm still in the process of navigating my way through life in Ireland.

The first woman I'd like to have breakfast with is Mary Robinson. Being the first woman in Ireland to be president I would love the opportunity to ask her some questions.

2. Mary Lou McDonald leader of the Sinn Fein party. Her fearlessness and approach to politics is refreshing and it's great to see a woman speaking her mind and truth as she sees fit.

3. Rachel Doyle - Managing Director of The Arboretum Garden Centre. In an industry that is dominated by men she excelled and is still succeeding and building her brand from the ground up. How she brought it to where it is and always taking different approaches and exposing her brand to different markets yet maintaining her loyal following. That to me is a true sign of success.

*The government recently launched 'Project Ireland 2040', which the Taoiseach said is a document about building a republic of opportunity. Have you seen this document, if so do you think that in its mapping there is provision to create an enabling space for migrant women to be heard and lead? (b) The Prime Minister is the son of a migrant father from India, does this alone give you the slightest hope for the future of the children of migrants in this country, and why? (c) If you have the power to change anything in Ireland, what will that be?*

No, I haven't heard about the new project Ireland and I don't like the fact that I haven't. I think Leo Varadkar becoming Taoiseach has shown that Ireland and Irish people are open to change. I think it says they're willing to be led by someone who wants what's best for the country and its people regardless of where their parents came from. It also tells the children of migrants like mine too, that it's ok to be different and stand your ground and your beliefs, and if you do what you can with pride and dignity, you can achieve anything.

**If I had the power to change** anything in Ireland it would be the weather because it took many years for me to adapt to Irish weather, sometimes it feels like I'm still in that process of adapting to it after 15 years living here. Besides, this country is beautiful, and you can see the full beauty more when it is sunny in drier season.

# *Ogbeyalu Udeala-Okoye*

*"Not being able to vote because of status is something that is robbing many migrants of their fundamental human rights."*

*M*y name is Ogbeyalu Udeala-Okoye, I am a naturalised Irish citizen, born in Nigeria and grew up in Nsukka, a small town in Enugu state in the University of Nigeria community. I have a BSc in accounting from the University of Nigeria and special qualification in forensic accounting from Chartered Accountants in Ireland. I also have a Masters degree in Financial Services from University College Dublin (UCD), a Post-graduate Risk and Financial Analysis from Dublin Business School and finally, a Professional qualification in Risk Management, Internal Audit and Compliance from the Chartered Accountants Ireland. I served as a ONE Campaign Youth Ambassador Ireland for two years. I was also selected as an Empower women champion 2016-2017 based on my work with migrant women. I was selected to be a mentor at Cherie Blair Foundation for women for two years where I mentored women in start-up businesses around the world.

I have been living in Ireland for 17 years now. My favourite food is fried plantain and yam, my favourite soup is our native egusi soup. What I miss about my country is the cultural and traditional activities called the 'New Yam Festival' in my hometown and the occasional get together with friends. What I love most about Ireland is their culture, how similar it is to our own culture and their stories and how far they have come. I enjoy very much being the Irish International Ireland Amnesty Ambassador. I run a programme during my spare time where I encourage migrant women and girls, and also in Nigeria the importance of STEM education and the need to empower themselves economically.

*What are some of the most challenges faced by migrant women in Ireland? (b) What advice would you give to young and upcoming migrants women?*

The changes faced by migrant women are many, from being foreign and misunderstood, to difficulty integrating and no voting rights, and cultural differences. The cost of childcare is a huge problem especially where families are separated geographically, and it is almost impossible to bring over adult children to join their parents in Ireland. This is a huge issue, and some spouses finding it extremely difficult to join either their wives or husbands based on immigration and other government regulations. The lack of provision of language classes also pose a serious barrier for migrant women and families whose first language or official language is not English. Another problem is delay in making a decision on asylum cases, currently asylum-seekers have to wait up to 5 years or more before they can know their faith and, in the meantime, not able to legally engage in paid employment or pursue a career. Also, being secluded from main society based on accent and treated differently is another major problem which needs to be tackled. Finally, not being able to vote because of their status is something that robbing many migrants of their fundamental human rights. Information is key. My main advice to a young migrant woman, is to join as many local organisations as possible to be well informed. Engage with your local TDs to enable them work for you. Engage with people in your community where you live and help to bring changes in the community. Take advantage of technology and get connected with other migrant women on social media to get information about many things, including where and how to access free language classes and other free training which may be available to you.

*There is a worldwide momentum for gender pay-gap, do you think that women have suddenly started to speak up in demand of effective change, or do you think that men have only started to pay more attention and listening more to women?*

Women have become more aware of their rights in recent years. With movements like women's March, #metoo movements, etc our voices are being heard far and wide than before. I'd like to think that steady progress has been recorded. The men have come to realise too that to bring positive change in the society, equality should be at the forefront of change. The women gave their voices and the men have now followed, that is why you can see men who are feminists, fighting for gender pay gap and equality for women.

*Do you think that Ireland has done more to protect the rights of women? If you answered yes, in your opinion —why are there so many stories about domestic violence? If you answered no, then what do you think Ireland should do more to protect women?*

Not being born in Ireland, I don't feel particularly competent to answer this question because I don't have all the facts and experiences of women dating as far back as the 70s for example. But, judging by what we have available to us in recent years I can say that a few laws on abortion and gay marriage restricted women from having a voice and a choice for long. Based on stories I have heard and some of the changes that we've witnessed, I can say that domestic violence is taken seriously here in this country and the police/gardai have done a great deal of work to ensure the safety of women going through such problems.

*What has been a defining moment in your life/career or business since living in Ireland? (b) If you could have breakfast with any three Irish women, who would you choose and why?*

My defining moment: Becoming a citizen of Ireland and being chosen as a 'ONE' campaign youth ambassador Ireland. This meant a great deal to me having grown up in Nigeria and being given another chance in a foreign country to represent its youth. It was a proud moment for me.

**Three women I would love to sit with and have breakfast are:**

Mary McAleese former President of Ireland because she represents everything a woman can be in Ireland, especially because I was here while she served her tenures as Irish female President.

Mary Robinson: Having broken the barrier for Mary McAleese and many other women to become the first female president of Ireland.

Kay McNulty, she is one of the world's first computer programmers. Donegal-born Kay McNulty Mauchly Antonelli (1921-2006), who was brought up in Pennsylvania, was one of six women selected in the 1940s by the US Army to work on the ENIAC, the first general-purpose electronic digital computer.

*The government recently launched 'Project Ireland 2040', which the Taoiseach said is a document about building a republic of opportunity. Have you seen this document, if so do you think that in its mapping there is provision to create an enabling space for migrant women to be heard and lead? (b) The Prime Minister is the son of a migrant father from India, does this alone give you the slightest hope for the future of the children of migrants in this country, and why? (c) If you have the power to change anything in Ireland, what will that be?*

Project Ireland 2040 is a plan for our social, economic and cultural development being a ten-year plan to invest in the infrastructure of Ireland, €1.4 billion will be spent enhancing amenities and heritage. Project Ireland 2040 aims to set out how Ireland will develop as the population grows by one million people over the next two decades. Planning for the future, it envisages the building of 500,000 new homes; a €2bn urban regeneration fund for the country's five main cities; three new hospitals to tackle waiting lists; a series of road upgrades and €22bn for climate change initiatives. I believe planning for the future would include everyone in Ireland including migrants. This project focuses on social, economic and cultural development. I would say yes!

The Prime Minister being the son of a migrant father shows that there are changes in Ireland that cannot be ignored or overlooked. Ireland is fast becoming a multicultural country and a lot of migrant children have settled to call Ireland their only home. These children will grow up engaging in Irish politics, public offices and become part of lawmakers in Ireland. Yes, change has definitely come to Ireland which we have to accept just like other changes taking place globally.

*If I had the power to change anything in Ireland,* that would be seeing more women engage in politics and decision making. I would also like to see favourable legislation and laws that favour more women, and having more youths involved in bringing change using their voices.

# *Raquel Murillo Diestro*

*"Be prepared to lose some things, some of them will hurt you because you have to unroot yourself a little, and that is painful."*

*M*y name is Raquel. Murillo and Diestro are my surnames. Murillo is the first surname of my father and Diestro of my mother. They go together. Not Murillo without Diestro or the opposite. So, my full name is Raquel Murillo Diestro. I am from Spain, and living in Ireland since 2002, although I went back to Spain from 2009 to 2016. I am 42 years old. I thought I would never ever get married, or have kids, believing that it was not for me, but I did. Luis is my husband and we've been married now for 19 years. The most revolutionary thing I have done is stay married …and have kids. We share our lives with three amazing daughters and three cats.

My job profile is a mix of things: First of all, I am a full-time mum of three amazing girls: Iris 11, Maya 8 and Luna 6 years old. I work full time as a permanent library assistant in Fingal. I've also written a book and designed a project called Nacimiento Feliz, focused on pregnancy, birth and the early years of motherhood. I am also a blogger at www.babog.org, and a Philosophy teacher registered by the Teaching Council. I volunteer from time to time with a patch we have adopted in our neighbourhood, cleaning the streets of our lovely city of Balbriggan, Co. Dublin. I have been volunteering all my life in different projects about education and health in Peru, Algeria and Spain, with the NGO Medicos del Mundo.

My favourite food is "croquetas" a mushy fried recipe from Spain and my favourite drink is a good red wine or a pint of Guinness.I miss my family and friends, and the feeling of belonging. I miss the food, the weather, and sunny days in Spain. In Spain there is real sun most of the time. You just know it is going to be sunny from morning to night. I miss the party, the people in the streets, the Terrazas (people enjoying drinks on tables along the streets). I miss the familiar feeling. About Ireland, I love its landscape. Those beaches, the colour of the sea, the valleys, the gardens, the little mountains, the cliffs—Nature is queen here in Ireland. The air is clean, and the abundant rain. There are fairies everywhere you look, or so it seems. So many places to hide. I love the history of Ireland, its ancient past and monuments, its music, folklore and language. Ireland is unique. The people are friendly, taxi drivers normally talk nonstop, I like the old ladies who talk to my daughters with a smiley face. I love how easy it is here to get a good job with family-friendly conditions. I like how families are protected in Ireland. I love the way it is a young country, plenty of kids and youngsters everywhere with plenty of creative energy.

*What are some of the most challenges faced by migrant women in Ireland? (b) What advice would you give to young and upcoming migrants women?*

The challenges faced by migrant women in Ireland would depend on their situation. Are they coming here alone, with a partner, with children, do they have qualifications, understands the language, or they came on the heels of a job offer. But the first challenge for many migrant women like me is the language. Not being an English speaker is a huge barrier. After learning about it, I keep the accent. The second challenge is the lack of support for us especially if you are a mum, the lack of family around can be very constraint and upsetting. Then, there is also the most common struggle which is trying to fit in and become productive part of the society. It is double the effort when they have children, because they need to integrate themselves and make sure that their children are settled as well.

My advice to young and upcoming migrant women is to be open, to be fearless, to be flexible, understanding and above all be patient. It always feels a bit out of place in the beginning, but in a matter of time you will gradually find your space. Be prepared to lose some things, some of them will hurt you because you have to unroot yourself a little, and that is painful. But you will gain knowledge, you will gain strength, you will adapt and ultimately gain courage and wisdom that will help you to blossom and become the best version of yourself.

*There is a worldwide momentum for gender pay-gap, do you think that women have suddenly started to speak up in demand of effective change, or do you think that men have only started to pay more attention and listening more to women?*

I think throughout the history of humanity women have spoken up on many occasions and have been listened. Men want equality too. It is fantastic for them as well. But sometimes it just seems like both women and men get these things all mixed up and make it out as if it is a battle of the sexes, but it is exactly the opposite. Women are being listened more than before because we are making so much noise, and the noise must become stronger and louder if we want to achieve a gender equal society. Women (and men) need to speak up. Nobody can listen if you don't talk. The key to change is to propose a better way to dealing with these issues.

*Do you think that Ireland has done more to protect the rights of women? If you answered yes, in your opinion —why are there so many stories about domestic violence? If you answered no, then what do you think Ireland should do more to protect women?*

Ireland have recently voted 'yes' in the abortion referendum to repeal the 8th amendment clause from their constitution which until now equates the right of the "unborn" to be equal to that of a pregnant woman and forbade women to have a termination under no circumstances. Only in the last few years they realised same outcomes with the marriage equality referendum as well. The weight of the Catholic Church is still massive in political decisions, but it seems the hour for change has come and Irish people are reviewing their constitution as we continue to witness the changes that are taking place gently and slowly. Human Rights issues are being giving more attention and the rights of women have become more asserted. In comparison to other countries, Ireland is on par, but matters of domestic violence plagues Irish women and sometimes their cries are not taken very seriously. The authorities are not exactly folding their arms and watching but more could be done to prevent women who have been physically, sexually, and emotionally abused when they eventually summon the courage to come to them to report abuse and seek protection.

*What has been a defining moment in your life/career or business since living in Ireland? (b) If you could have breakfast with any three Irish women, who would you choose and why?*

Becoming a mother for the first time — that was my defining moment. There are many Irish women that I admire. If I could I would travel to the past and have a tea and a never-ending conversation with Iris Murdoch... I love her work. Then I would take a long walk with Mairead Maguire so she can talk to me about the North. And, finally, I would chill out with Enya Brennan about all the fairies in her garden.

*The government recently launched 'Project Ireland 2040', which the Taoiseach said is a document about building a republic of opportunity. Have you seen this document, if so do you think that in its mapping there is provision to create an enabling space for migrant women to be heard and lead? (b) The Prime Minister is the son of a migrant father from India, does this alone give you the slightest hope for the future of the children of migrants in this country, and why? (c) If you have the power to change anything in Ireland, what will that be?*

I am not an expert and I haven't read all the documents, but I think Project Ireland 2040 is a fantastic way of organizing a better country for us all, but I cannot find specific measures about migrants or women, and not at all for migrant women.

That the Prime Minister is the son of a migrant gives me hope. Of course, I hope he recognizes the struggles we go through when we move to a different country.

*If I have the power to change something* in Ireland that will be the weather. I think it is easy to work, to advance, to share, to understand and to smile when the sun is shining.

# *Maksuda Akhter*

**"Don't suffer in silence. Speak about this issue once you are safe, because silence is the worst enemy when you are a victim."**

$M$y name is Maksuda Akhter and I am originally from Bangladesh where I grew up. I come from a medium sized family of 7 siblings. My family could be described as a medium or upper-class family and had many of what was then modern luxuries as lived in a four-story building in the middle of Dhaka, the capital city of Bangladesh. It was customary or normal to live in shared accommodation with extended family and relatives, this means that I lived in our four-story building with 40 other relatives. As a young teenager, situations meant or dictated that I should leave Bangladesh and move to Ireland where I would start a new life in a country and culture that was Alien to me.

Ireland was only starting to accept coloured and mixed races when I arrived, it seemed like the years prior to the time I arrived in Dublin it was unusual to see anything other than white skinned people. I did not find this to be a problem as such, as I felt I was accepted and made friends with school colleagues. It was obvious that I was a different colour and my English was poor even though I had previously attended private school in Bangladesh and studied English. It was my biggest challenge with my education, however I graduated from college and went on to work in NCB Stockbrokers as part of a team in the finance section. I enjoyed working there and it allowed me to integrate with the Irish working class. I went on to work with Microsoft and was in charge of a production line and was responsible for directing 30 people in the production and quality control of Microsoft electronic products. I have always been a very competitive and driven person and always look to better my position and improve my skills. I find my English and accent to be a stumbling block, this has further compounded by the fact that I am a woman and despite holding an Irish passport I feel like not been accepted as being Irish because to this day when I meet with new people, I'm asked questions like 'where are you from?' and followed by 'where are your parents from?' no matter the explanations I give that I am Irish.

I have been living in Ireland for 17 years now. I work as a Pilot, a model and as a part-time actress. I also see myself as social activist.
I have always been involved in Modelling and competing in pageants over the years and I have been successful in many competitions, and well known as a judge in the modelling circles. I also coach young girls on how to present themselves and prepare for competitions in a natural way. I am proud of my achievements in providing a nice home for my children, and to see them integrate and learn in the local Malahide National School. My son is a member of the local GAA club and enjoys training and competing with the team on weekends, while my daughter loves to sing and dance, she enjoys learning Irish dancing and ballet. I love being involved in professional photo shoots it is very rewarding to work on set, to then see the finished product

and realise that you are the one promoting them. I have enjoyed working with some of the top Photographers. I have also joined a political party as this is my next challenge to fit into the space.

My favourite foods are Bengali Traditional foods and that is what I miss most about my country, which I love very much. But I miss my family and relatives more. What I like most about Ireland is the beauty of nature everywhere and the people. Irish people are very generous and kind.

*What are some of the most challenges faced by migrant women in Ireland? (b) What advice would you give to young and upcoming migrants women?*

From my own personal experience, the lack understanding in the work environment, cultural gap and lack of communication skills are some of the things I found to be most challenging for migrant people coming to live and work here.

My advice to upcoming migrant women is for them to learn the local cultures and try to understand how society works. Come out from your own community and your comfort zone and familiarise yourself with the area where you live and establish yourself. Take time out to learn and understand what works in the society at large, you'll be ready and able to face any challenges better. Your first struggle might be to cope with the local social and working environment but when you have introduced yourself with your uniqueness, people will accept you and your journey will become smooth and easier with the time.

*There is a worldwide momentum for gender pay-gap, do you think that women have suddenly started to speak up in demand of effective change, or do you think that men have only started to pay more attention and listening more to women?*

I don't think women suddenly started to speak up, but I think it is all about new technology; the internet, and social media has been very effective in helping women to spread our words and awareness to the people everywhere. Women have been neglected and suppressed by prejudice for many generations, their mouth tied up with pieces of clothing, but again there have been very brave women among them who raise their voices and fought for their rights without fear. Although their voices may not have reached as far due to less technology in those periods. Whereas, when women protest now our voices goes further due to the benefits of new technology. Now we can even protest or fight for our rights in our homes without having to go out on the road in some cases. There is the saying that" if a baby doesn't cry, the mother wouldn't know the baby was hungry." Unlike in the past when women used to protest and most of it were ignored, now people are more concerned and awareness of these kinds of issues are reaching people's doorsteps faster, so at the same time, men have been forced to be concerned and pay attention to women's issues. So, More Voices, More Attention and More Reaction!

*Do you think that Ireland has done more to protect the rights of women? If you answered yes, in your opinion —why are there so many stories about domestic violence? If you answered no, then what do you think Ireland should do more to protect women?*

I think Ireland is far better than some countries and they are constantly developing their systems. We all know how badly women are treated in Third World countries. How poor women's rights and security issues regarding women are handled. We only have to check the internet to see the hard life women living in some of those countries are subjected to, they are abused both mentally and physically every day. So, Ireland is in a much better position, yet they need to put stricter laws against domestic Violence. Irish government and their social system should also do their best to help women to where we can no longer see such mistreatment of our fellow women in those countries around the globe.

I would advise women who face domestic violence; don't wait for the next day or next time. They should take the step the first time it happens and seek help immediately. There are few free services available for the victims of this unsocial activity regardless of which country you come from. Open your mouth and don't suffer in silence and speak about this issue once you are safe. Because silence is the worst enemy when you are a victim.

*What has been a defining moment in your life/career or business since living in Ireland? (b) If you could have breakfast with any three Irish women, who would you choose and why?*

A defining moment in my career was when I decided to stand up and do something with my life, and the people from my native community rose up and tried to break me. They tried that several times even with a propaganda against me. However, I took them on as much as my strength could allow and worked through it with double effort. As an immigrant woman it wasn't easy to establish my position among the already local established people where public acceptance is important. What I still believe is that my position and struggles are still in many ways better than thousands of women around the globe who are still fighting for their basic human rights, freedom and from mental and physical abuses. Most of them are not privileged to be educated and are living in places where poverty is killing their hopes. My competition was always with myself, and my focus has always been based on how I can make my next step stronger.

I am a single mother of two and always inspired by other single mothers. Their stories ignite me. They are real warriors. I would love to have breakfast with any one of them.

*The government recently launched 'Project Ireland 2040', which the Taoiseach said is a document about building a republic of opportunity. Have you seen this document, if so do you think that in its mapping there is provision to create an enabling space for migrant women to be heard and lead? (b) The Prime Minister is the son of a migrant father from India, does this alone give you the slightest hope for the future of the children of migrants in this country, and why? (c) If you have the power to change anything in Ireland, what will that be?*

I certainly think that in its mapping there is provision made to create an enabling space for migrant women to be heard and lead. I think it will open new doors for immigrants in terms of opportunities to work together for our communities. This shows that there are no boundaries to our aspirations and it proves that Ireland has becomes more diverse. Our Prime Minister is a big example of this.

# *Ritu Gupta*

*"I have managed myself well up to this point, but the story is much different now because at least I have enough English to mix with the public."*

My name is Ritu Gupta. I am Indian originally. I have been living in Ireland for the last 10 years. I run my own business as a self-employed entrepreneur. My line of business is in children's entertainment and I also work as an Event planner at kiddies.ie.

Being that I'm from India, I like authentic Indian food, I love chickpeas and naan bread most especially they are naturally my favourites although I also enjoy most Italian foods now. My favourite drinks are juices and smoothies. What I miss most about my home country first of all is my family. I miss understanding people around me, and I miss the different types of gatherings that takes place around the year with the people in the communities, people that knows me and I know them. In Ireland, there are many festivities taking place around the country too, there is always a small difference. Ireland is a small country and I love the natural & beautiful landscapes, and the people are so welcoming.

*What are some of the most challenges faced by migrant women in Ireland? (b) What advice would you give to young and upcoming migrants women?*

In India we communicate in our local Hindi dialect and not much of English. I found it difficult to talk to people when I first arrived in Ireland, it was the biggest challenge that I faced in this country. It was a big problem not having many people who could speak the same language as you, and worse still not understanding them so my level of interacting with anyone outside my house was very limited. However, I well managed myself up to this point, but the story is much different now because at least I have enough English language mix with the public.

 I am purely vegetarian; I do not eat fish or eggs and finding the types of appropriate vegetarian food was a dilemma initially, that was another challenge that I had to overcome personally. These were my own struggles, but others have their own experiences, including that fact that it is very hard to get a well-paid job in Ireland. But again, how can anyone be offered a paid job if they don't have even basic English, because communication is key in the workplace, so language barrier can be a big problem for many migrant women.

My advice to young and upcoming migrant women is simple. Don't be afraid of challenges, because they can be overcome.

*There is a worldwide momentum for gender pay-gap, do you think that women have suddenly started to speak up in demand of effective change, or do you think that men have only started to pay more attention and listening more to women?*

In my opinion, women everywhere are demanding effective change and the men have also stepped up their game and starting to consider women's requirements at every stage.

*Do you think that Ireland has done more to protect the rights of women? If you answered yes, in your opinion —why are there so many stories about domestic violence? If you answered no, then what do you think Ireland should do more to protect women?*

I think Ireland should take more steps to protect the rights of women. We hear about abuses of women and children too much in the news. To protect the rights of women, the country should create more job opportunities for women to become independent. Women also need more flexibility in their jobs. A project that in training women to stand for political office and become more involved in public life will also be very helpful and maybe reduce some cause effects that leads to the onset of abuse.

*What has been a defining moment in your life/career or business since living in Ireland?*

A defining moment for me was when my daughters were born in Ireland. They both just completed my life's purpose and brought so much happiness to our family. Career wise, it would be the first time that I received a five-star review from my clients. It meant so much at the time.

*The Prime Minister is the son of a migrant father from India, does this alone give you the slightest hope for the future of the children of migrants in this country, and why? (c) If you have the power to change anything in Ireland, what will that be?*

I don't think that the Prime Minister being the son of a migrant father of Indian heritage mean that he is expected to do something different for children of migrants in this country. Because he needs to follow the set rules of the government and carry out his job accordingly.

**If I had the power to change something in Ireland,** I will provide long stay visa for parents of migrants, so they can stay more with their families here.

# *Zeina Roz*

*"Always Run your Empire with Energy & a Sharp focus that will allow you to succeed at whatever you put your mind to."*

*I* like to see myself as an 'International' person for I was born in London but have done my fair share of travelling since I was young and lived in many cities around our beautiful world. My name is Zeina Roz "AKA Baby Zi" and I have been residing in Dublin, Ireland for four years.

I am the CEO of Entertainment Inc. One of my favourite dishes is pasta and my favourite drink at this stage is a Monkey Moo shake. It is very hard to pinpoint one thing that I miss the most about London, but if I had to it would be the West End Shows and the city vibe that London brings. I love Dublin, it is a compact city, people are really friendly and smiley, the history of Ireland is very interesting, to sum it up in one word; Ireland is a very welcoming city.

*What are some of the most challenges faced by migrant women in Ireland? (b) What advice would you give to young and upcoming migrants women?*

Dublin is becoming a cosmopolitan city, challenges faced by migrant women in Ireland is hard to say but I think all challenges that one faces is not really linked to being a migrant woman, but more of being a woman as a whole. Unfortunately, gender equality is unfair towards women everywhere in the world.

I strongly advise the young upcoming women to stand up for their beliefs and not let anyone change their path. I am a true believer of a quote that was once passed to me by my father: "Always Run your Empire with Energy & a Sharp focus that will allow you to succeed at whatever you put your mind to"

*There is a worldwide momentum for gender pay-gap, do you think that women have suddenly started to speak up in demand of effective change, or do you think that men have only started to pay more attention and listening more to women?*

Ireland is trying harder to protect the rights of women. In 2016 the United Nation spoke regarding the abuses and suffering of women in Ireland, but sadly, and to my knowledge, the matter has not been fully attended to till this day. But there are many none profit organisations and associations in Ireland advocating for such causes and they offer support for most women who finds themselves in an abusive situation and are looking for help.

*What has been a defining moment in your life/career or business since living in Ireland? (b) If you could have breakfast with any three Irish women, who would you choose and why?*

Since my mother passed away in 2013, I was struggling to find a place where I would settle as nothing really helped me to overcome the grief that I felt of losing a loved one. So, if I have to define one moment of my life it would be since I arrived in Ireland because I finally found Peace. It was the one thing that eluded me for long and I got it here, that is why Ireland is a place I call home.

If I had the opportunity to meet any women in the Republic of Ireland I would love to meet Julie Sinnamon " CEO of the Enterprise Ireland as she managed to nab the top Job and the surprised a few.

Breege o' Donoghue " Executive Director Penny / Primark, at 70 years of age, O' Donoghue serves as a member of the Labour Relation's Commission and a member of the foundation of the National University of Ireland, Maynooth, I admire her hard work and the good she has accomplished.

# *Vanessa Kennedy*

*"There is also a discrepancy between white woman and black woman in relation to pay and other opportunities and security in the workplace."*

*M*y name is Vanessa Kennedy, I was born in Rio de Janeiro, Brazil.

I´ve been in Ireland for almost 6 years. My family and my friends are what I miss the most, I try to visit Brazil every other year, my sister Caroline have been in Ireland many times to visit me and my parents also have visited twice. I also miss our cultural celebrations.

We have a very diverse cuisines and I always choose Brazilian food over any other cuisines. I can say that I am very lucky as I am married to an Irish husband, Andrew Kennedy who also loves Brazilian foods and knows how to cook my favorite dishes.

I work as a Trainee-Specialist in the Trust and Safety team for Accenture, my job consists of giving training to all new joiners with intern policies and update the agents with new information that might occur. I am also founder and director of two volunteer community projects in Ireland, Casa Brazil Ireland and Little Bees Dublin. our aim at Casa Brazil Ireland is to promote Brazilian culture in Ireland and integration between Irish and Brazilian community in a positive way. Our first event was back in 2016 with a production of a play that took part in the "Cultural Night" programme in Dublin, an event that happens every year promoted by the Irish government. We had promoted more than 20 events since then, including educational, cultural and gastronomic with a mix of the public including Irish, Brazilian and other nationalities. One of our highlights was the production of the play "The Serpent" in December of 2017. The play was directed by Nina Ni Mendes and performed by Irish actors that did a brilliant interpretation of one of the best playwriters from Brazil, Nelson Rodrigues. It was the first time his play was performed in Dublin and we had a lovely surprise with a message from his Grandson Sacha Rodrigues congratulating us for the work, we had two sessions completely booked out with the ilustre presence of members of the Brazilian Embassy in Ireland. I take great pride of this work and the importance of promoting such a rich and diverse Brazilian culture.

Little Bees Dublin is a personal community project that is very close to my heart, it all started in the summer of 2016 when I did my first visit in The Hatch Hall Direct Provision centre and I met families that were living in there. I had the opportunity of meet their children and they took my heart by storm. Since day one I felt I could try to do something to make their journey through the system of direct provision a little bit easier, especially for the children that exhibited so much energy. I got together with some close friends and we started to offer weekly activities to the children, we would do some arts and crafts, games, nursery rhymes and help out with homework. However, we could not carry on with it because of the internal policies of direct provision. But since 2016 I developed a lovely friendship with the mothers and children there, I could see the development, they are overcoming all the difficulties that the system imposes on them with so much bravery, faith and love. Every single time that I go to visit them I feel empowered, I feel like they give me much more than I ever gave to them. Since we stopped the weekly visits I started to do seasonal projects with them, again I got together with some close friends and we came up with some lovely Christmas gifts for everyone, these were new clothes, toys and also treats for the parents. We repeated the same at Easter time to play with them and delivery Chocolate Eggs, same during Halloween and others special days in the year. I also created a project called Hope in a Bag, that is going on to the second year now. With this project, I asked my friends and friends of friends to donate a New School Bag each with Stationary materials inside to give to the children, we were able to collect 25 new school bags with lunchboxes, water bottles and other stationary materials. It was a such a blessing.

*What are some of the most challenges faced by migrant women in Ireland? (b) What advice would you give to young and upcoming migrants women?*

There are different types of migrants in Ireland, and the types of visas they have affects directly on the quality of life for the woman who decide to come and live here. In my experience, when I arrived I had a student visa, a clear plan, a vast educational background, I also had a career in Brazil at that time. I came to Ireland to improve my skills as a professional and to learn more about different cultures for one year then go back to Brazil with better English and plenty of experience in my 'baggage.' I remember my first challenge was the language, my English was very basic, I had a plan to try and immerse in the Irish culture, but I found myself sharing a house with other Brazilians and speaking Portuguese most of the time. Although we tried many times to create rules in the house for everyone to only speak English, but it was hard as everyone had very basic English and as a result conversations did not get very far, but we did have fun with that practice. It is hard to engage with locals and form new friendships when you cannot communicate very well.

My first advice for the young woman is to try to be involved in community projects, charity or meet ups, to meet new people and socialise is always good when you are away from home. Second of all, sometimes charity work is the type of experience you will need to give the first kick to try to get a job here besides, working for a good cause is always worth it. Another challenge that migrant woman face in Ireland is that sometimes she works hard but forgets to look after her mental health. I have met many women who suffer with depression and anxiety and have low self-esteem. The best way to treat mental health is to look for professional help when possible, I would also advice everyone to take time to look after yourself.

Also, I see it happening a lot in Ireland with migrants that are overqualified doing jobs that they would never do in your home countries. there are two implications when this happens, first is if you have a goal to improve your English and although the job and the wage is not even close to your qualifications, then it makes sense because it's for a period and you are getting the main thing, which is to practice the language. But I´ve seen women being treated really bad in their jobs, working to the point of exhaustion and lowering their self-esteem close to zero and afraid to complain because of financial reasons or because they are just afraid, for those women I just want to let you know that this is not ok. Any type of abuse is wrong, please speak to someone, ask for help, don't let anyone make you feel any less.

I also have to talk about women who come to seek refugee in Ireland, these are strong women that are looking for better life for themselves and their children. I always get myself thinking of how the world is divided and how some people have privileges just to be born in certain places or to be of certain color. I am no different from those women who come to Ireland but cannot access visas and enter in the horrific system of Direct Provision. I had a privilege of come to Ireland legally with a visa, with money in my account to look after myself, and the right to work, study and to travel as I please. I had the right to stay or go and those woman from other countries, or from different social background arrive in Ireland and are "locked" in a system where she is stripped of her rights for many years even before she gets the same rights as I did from start. The same as a European woman would have more rights than I do. And in this cycle of privileges my heart simply goes on for those women at the bottom of the list but keep on fighting to find their way out.

To resume what I would say to a young migrant woman, it does not matter the type of visa you have. Look after yourself, and do not let anyone put you down, look after your other sisters in the same situation and engage to the community but don't forget your roots and always look for things to keep you happy.

*There is a worldwide momentum for gender pay-gap, do you think that women have suddenly started to speak up in demand of effective change, or do you think that men have only started to pay more attention and listening more to women?*

Women have not suddenly started to speak up, we have been speaking up about rights since a long time ago in different places and in different forms. Just to add a note to this matter, we cannot forget that there is also a discrepancy between white woman and black woman in relation to pay and other opportunities and security in the workplace. We cannot forget that while white women were talking about woman rights and gender pay-gap a long time ago, black women were still fighting slavery in many countries, that means they were fighting for fundamental rights. There is a different timeline for the white woman and another for the black woman in relation to this matter and as I black woman I thought it is important to address it. That been said, in relation to nowadays, social media has played a huge impact in our fights. It was not that easy before when organisations were local and tackling the problems of that very community and local laws, for example, The Suffragettes movement in the UK. Nowadays, the fight has gone taken a different turn with global demand and women can relate to other woman across the world and try to help. We have access to information and we use in our favor. Being a feminist is wide spread now and men are invited to join the fight and they are doing. We still have a long way to go, to fight a still very much sexist society and the gender pay gap has indeed started to drop but it is still far way from ideal, at least now we have acknowledged it and we are tackling this problem. I think we educate our girls and boys at home and in the schools they will grow up in the next generation with better ways to build an equal society, and also we have to tackle our laws to make it illegal.

*Do you think that Ireland has done more to protect the rights of women? If you answered yes, in your opinion —why are there so many stories about domestic violence? If you answered no, then what do you think Ireland should do more to protect women?*

I think that domestic violence has more to do with education about sexism at its base. I came from a country that unfortunately has one of biggest numbers of domestic and sexual violence against women, although we have specific laws to protect women such as" Maria da Penha" law created after the name of a Brazilian Biopharmacist who suffered years of abuse from her husband who ended up shooting shot her, making her paraplegic for life and after she came back from the hospital he still tried to electrocute her and case was in the court for 2 decades while he remained free, yet this was not considered a high crime, only after being highly criticized that the government created the law that not just punish the perpetrators of abuse but also offer protection to woman who feel threatened. It is a mechanism that works in relation to the law, now at least the abusers are being prosecuted with more severe charges, however, the number of domestic and sexual abuse incidents in Brazil is still very high.

In comparison with Ireland, I feel more safe living here. I know that it is not a perfect place and there are women that are going through domestic and sexual abuses. I feel that the laws here, particularly for sexual abusers are not severe enough. I did a diploma degree in Law Studies here in Dublin and was shocked with some of the cases where the abuser got out of the court free or just got some years of sentencing that definitely does not reflect the trauma he would have caused his victim.

Back to my first statement, we need to educate our children not be sexist. We must educate them at home, making them understand that any type of abuse is not ok, and the our boys—that they too can always look for help. We should educate the boys that is not ok to talk about woman like the way some men from the rugby team in Belfast did about the girl in the famous rape trial who were found not guilty, and if any man thought this is normal way to talk about woman or that this is the "way" boys talk it is just a joke then we need really think about what men think about woman, what this type of behave will lead then to do. No person has the right to talk about another human being as if they are nothing but object of sexualization. I believe we have much more to educate and change in the society when we tackle this issues from the very start and not wait until they escalate into bigger issues like domestic and sexual violence.

*What has been a defining moment in your life/career or business since living in Ireland? (b) If you could have breakfast with any three women in Ireland, who would that be and why?*

A defining moment in my career was when I completed a diploma degree in Law Studies in DBS, I was very proud of myself and I also could understand much more about Irish legislation, history and culture. It was enlightened more about its constitution and how it was created, the constitution says a lot about its people and to study it inside out was liberating. I already had a degree and a Masters degree but this was my first diploma in English. It opened up my confidence. Another defining moment was when I started to create projects to help others and when the first one was completed which I started with my closest friends, and now we're bigger and able to help more people along the way to get inspired to do more.
I am so grateful to be able to do it and to all the people that engage together with me to conquer it.

There are many great women in Ireland, one woman that is really inspiring is the former president of Ireland Mary Robinson, her work catches my attention because she was the first female president in Ireland and a commissioner of Human Rights, presiding the world conference against Racism, a topic that really matters specially for immigrants and black people. She also is an advocate for women's rights. I would love to have a breakfast with her and hear more about her ideologies.

Another woman that has caught my attention in a different area, is Katie Taylor. A professional Irish Boxer and many times winner. It is brilliant to see a woman to get her spotlight in a sport that usually is dominated by men. It is even more satisfying to see a woman as young as her to be so successful with it. It is not always easy for women to get the same attention, pay and sponsorships as the men but Kate Taylor managed to have the country supporting her. I would love to have breakfast with her and get know more about some of the difficulties she went through and how she managed to overcome them, her next challenges in the career and what advice she would give to young female boxers starting the career and why not some tips on how to throw a good punch. Would be a great fun.

*The government recently launched 'Project Ireland 2040', which the Taoiseach said is a document about building a republic of opportunity. Have you seen this document, if so do you think that in its mapping there is provision to create an enabling space for migrant women to be heard and lead? (b) The Prime Minister is the son of a migrant father from India, does this alone give you the slightest hope for the future of the children of migrants in this country, and why? (c) If you have the power to change anything in Ireland, what will that be?*

The number of people in Ireland is increasing every year, according with the "Project Ireland 2040" the population will increase to extra one million in the next 20 years, that means Ireland will need to sort out more ways to accommodate it people, as we can also see a house crisis going on right now. The plan is good and I hope that it happens and not just in paper.

The 10 strategic outcomes and planning around the themes of wellbeing, equality and opportunity is very exciting and while I am very optimist about the planning, at the moment we are all suffering with the high costs of running a household and this is biggest concern at the moment in Ireland. I am not sure how much of visibility the migrant woman will have in relation to this project, but I am sure the government have to take into account that the increase of the population is also part of the immigration and listen to the needs of those from those backgrounds, it is the way to understand the new community of Ireland and the changes in its society if they want to guarantee wellbeing, equality and opportunity as they state in the program.

The children of migrants are raised in Ireland, and in my views have the same opportunities as every Irish child. The public system of education is really broad, what is not equal is the opportunities related to social status. Children with access to more educational support, sports, language classes, and parents who value education or are educated themselves are at an advantage to children born in less-privileged or raised in hostile households. However, I see great potential in the children of migrant families, the majority of them speak more than one language and learn some more in school. I am obviously talking about the migrant people that arrived in Ireland with legally to work, study and others who have had easy access to rights. It is a completely different story for those people in the asylum process and are caught in the Direct Provision System, although the children will have access to education in the primary and secondary school, but almost impossible for those children to access university education, therefore limiting their hope for a better future than their parents had. This would be something that I would change in Ireland if I had the powers to so.

# *Matilda Chongwa*

*"The '#metoo' hashtag has also helped women express the myriad of sexual abuses that they have experienced and has helped to truly rattle the Hollywood elite."*

*M*y name is Matilda Chongwa, a multi-award-winning Social Advocate from Ireland. I have been in Ireland for four years. I studied People Management at the University of Reading, UK, then completed a programme on the Diabetes Pandemic at the University of Dundee, Scotland. I am the CEO/Founder of Sunrise Foundation International, we bring Irish doctors and volunteers to Nigeria and other African countries on an International Diabetes Project that provides awareness and free screening for High Blood Pressure and Diabetes. I also organize the Mr. and Miss Sunrise International pageant and the famous Mr/Miss Valentine Ireland pageant which raises significant funds for charities in Ireland. I'm a former director of Miss European Ireland and the brain behind the International Runway Achievers and Recognition Awards, an annual event in Ireland that recognises people in Pageantry, Fashion, Entertainment, Community and Social media. I am also the founder and director of the World Diabetes Fashion Show. In 2016, at a prestigious ceremony held in Germany I was awarded the title of Africa's Living Legend.

*What are some of the most challenges faced by migrant women in Ireland? (b) What advice would you give to young and upcoming migrants women?*

Too many challenges to mention so let me give you a few examples. In the 1980s no one wanted to come to Ireland, it was a poor country, an economic basket case and people only wanted to leave. In the 1990s we had an economic boom called The Celtic Tiger. Ever since this period Ireland has become a wealthy and desirable country and therein lies the problem, people want to gain status and this desire to gain status inevitably causes desperation. People will do anything to get here and stay here. The trafficking of people is a huge problem on a global scale. Looking no doubt to escape poverty and make a better living for themselves. Domestic slavery and sexual enslavement are plausible consequences of this illegal trafficking. The trafficking of women is especially pronounced. Such cautionary tales of horror such as unspeakable abuses, domestic imprisonment, forced prostitution, working in subhuman conditions for far less than a minimum wage, a death of a dream of a better life should stop this phenomenon but it does not. If it sounds too good to be true, if you are promised things that just seem never in your wildest dreams can these be true, chances are they are not true. So, it's important to know who it is that you are putting your hopes and trust of a better life into. Sadly, such sharks are abundant, feeding of the needy, that so desperately desire refuge etc. in fortress Europe. Despite all these, migrant women have to be positive about life, educate themselves, integrate well in the community and keep themselves busy rather than living on social welfare.

*There is a worldwide momentum for gender pay-gap, do you think that women have suddenly started to speak up in demand of effective change, or do you think that men have only started to pay more attention and listening more to women?*

**Yes, there is a momentum worldwide to address the gender pay gap for the followings:**

1. It is fuelled by the pre-existing injustice because of there being a global gender pay gap.
2. The phenomenon of a voice via social media that has been given to the previously voiceless that has forced the patriarchal elites into a position whereby they must listen.

Social media has inspired revolution e.g. The Arab Spring, the revolution in Kiev, Ukraine, indeed you could say the rising in Egypt Tahir Square, the various popular demonstrations in Syria and throughout the Arab World from the streets of Beirut, Tripoli to Aleppo was very much a surge fuelled by social media. I think social media is utterly powerful. The '#metoo' hashtag has also helped women express the myriad of sexual abuses that they have experienced and has helped to truly rattle the Hollywood elite. Have women finally decided to speak up? I think the courage to speak up was always there all you must do is look at women's history for e.g. The Suffragette Movement which helped grant women the right to vote. Women are now looking for equality and I hope that as the elite are being bombarded with this awakening they will be pressured to react in a more just and fair way.

*Do you think that Ireland has done more to protect the rights of women? If you answered yes, in your opinion —why are there so many stories about domestic violence? If you answered no, then what do you think Ireland should do more to protect women?*

I think Ireland is a caring society that does protects the rights of all its citizens including minorities. In relation to domestic violence issues like social inequality, our culture of drinking and drugs needs to be studied in view of domestic violence to see how this affects the phenomenon. I myself would like to study what the causes are of domestic violence in Ireland. I have read reports that it is not only men that are committing this crime.

*If you could have breakfast with any three Irish women, who would you choose and why?*

Two Irish women I would love to share breakfast with are; first would be Anne Clarke from Diabetes Ireland because we share the same vision. The second would be Anita Ryan because she is so business minded and always ready to help others to grow their own business.

*The Prime Minister is the son of a migrant father from India, does this alone give you the slightest hope for the future of the children of migrants in this country, and why? (c) If you have the power to change anything in Ireland, what will that be?*

I'd like to answer yes, first it is refreshing that we have an Irish Prime Minister with Indian heritage. I feel hopeful that Ireland has not followed the right-wing anti-immigrant wave that has enveloped us since the Brexit and migrant crisis, Ireland has a compassionate outlook towards immigrants because Irish history is that of oppression and colonialism, and the children of immigrants I think have every right to feel positive about their future in Ireland. This country is probably the friendliest and most welcoming of European nations to visit.

**If I had the power to change anything in Ireland;** I dream of having affordable housing whereby, like on the continent of Europe, people can rent their homes at affordable rates with security of tenure. At the moment we are stuck with high rents/mortgages and an ever-growing housing crisis. I would like a decent pension for everyone by the age of 60. The retiring age has been raised to 70 this is too high. If this trend persists people will have no time to embrace their old age before they die. Pension and old age poverty are a serious worry for me. Private pensions have been wiped out on the stock exchange. I would like a state pension that offered a decent and secure alternative for people. A pension fund that would be there for people at the end of their years. So far this is not guaranteed. I dream of Universal healthcare not just what has been described as a two-tiered health care system. In Ireland the lucky ones have private health insurance, others like the unemployed have a medical card and yet again others like employed people have no medical insurance at all i.e. because of non-affordability have no health coverage. Our healthcare system needs reform. Education in post-recession Ireland is expensive. I would wish to see a return to free universities and abolishing privatisation of education. Basically, make our high level of taxation count for something. I would like to see a universal minimum wage for everyone in Ireland. I heard Finland is giving that a trial and are gaining unexpected results and Scotland are thinking of rolling that out. Currently, one in six families in Ireland are families with two jobless parents. I would love to see affordable and accessible childcare because this really is destroying women's mental and emotional wellbeing. In Ireland childcare has been described as an extra mortgage. The role of the mother has an indisputable position in the development of the child. I would love to see mothers get 3 years paid leave from the time of the birth of their child. And because our winters are bad I would love to see people get 30 days annual leave. Currently, mothers only get 6 months paid leave.

Finally, I think we need to look at the ills of capitalism such as ageism, worker exploitation, and profit over people. Basically, Ireland should learn from good and bad examples alike, and let us avoid the nationalism such that fuelled Brexit, and the ghettoization of immigrants in France and Britain which has lead to serious social problems in these host countries.

# *Katherin Henderson*

*"If you move to another country, you have to adapt. Learn their culture, their expressions, how they are, what's allowed and what's not, then mixed it up with your beliefs and your own culture."*

*M*y name is Katherin Henderson. I come from a lovely country in South America called Peru, and to be more specific from the capital city, Lima. I have been living in Dublin for almost 4 years now and I love it. I'm sure you must be wondering why my name doesn't sound anything like Latin-American. My birth-name is Katherin Ana Salcedo Burga, when I moved to Ireland I noticed that it was a bit difficult for English speakers to pronounce and write my full name so, I changed it to my marital surname. It is easier for everybody.

I'm an Educational Psychologist validated by the HSE. I completed my Degree in Psychology back in Peru at the Women's University of the

Sacred Heart (UNIFE). I'm an active and registered member of the School of Psychology of Peru and The Psychological Society of Ireland. Because of my educational background I love to work with the youth community and groups at risk. I believe that if we want to see a positive change in our world, we need to start with the ones that can change future generations and help them.

I decided to bring my experience to an Irish setting, so I started with volunteering, to keep learning especially as I did not know how things worked in this part of the world. Because of a family member, I discovered Foroige, I love their mission and vision and when I met the Group's Leaders John and Jessica, I knew that was the place I wanted to be. I was very nervous in the beginning, but they made me feel at home, and helping the kids was so rewarding. Unfortunately, I was there for less than a year due to a difficult pregnancy and on Doctor's orders I was advised not to exert myself. I did everything the Doctor said, and our son Dominick was born safe and sound in August of 2016. My husband is Irish, and all my family nearby are Irish.... but I wanted my son to experience Latin/Peruvian culture to expand on what I teach him at home. So, I found the perfect group called 'Peruvians in Ireland'. We started attending their events and it was really nice to find other people who shared my culture. A couple of months later, a few members started an NGO called "Casa Peru" and it was a great opportunity to start volunteering again.

I come from a country were the cuisines are recognised around the world, therefore I love to eat. I know! That is not an excuse, but Peruvian food is simply delicious. Some of the things that I miss most are: Sunday lunches, every week gathering of the whole family to have BBQs or a buffet, with Peruvian main dishes like. 'lomo saltado', chancho a la caja china, Arroz con pollo y papa a la Huancaina, Causa', etc. and to make an evening more memorable, we of course always down it together with our local drinks such as Pisco Sour, Algarrobina, Chilcano, etc. Don't get me wrong, I love Ireland too. Not so much for the food but I love it. First of all, I love my family here. I know that some people just call them in-laws but let me tell you something... I won the lottery with them, they are amazing! There are no words to describe how much I love them. The second reason why I love Ireland is the weather. Yes, believe it or not, I love the weather here, probably because I love cold weather in general and that serenity that comes with it... it also helps that I love dancing under the rain, jumping in muddy puddles and playing with the snow.

*What are some of the most challenges faced by migrant women in Ireland?*
*(b) What advice would you give to young and upcoming migrants women?*
*no, then what do you think Ireland should do more to protect women?*

I think that a big challenge faced by migrant women is being so far away from home: and I'm not talking about the actual distance. I'm talking about your family, friends, a place that you know your way around, your culture, etc. and if you're a workaholic like me: your job too. When I arrived in Ireland four years ago, everything was so overwhelming. It's not just jumping on a plane and heading off to an adventure, it's also about going to a place when you are starting from zero and sometimes that can be very scary. I was lucky and I'm so grateful because my family stepped in and helped me so much and they still do it. Other challenges will be the difference of culture & different points of views. I believe that when you move to another country, you have to adapt. I am not saying become Irish altogether but learn their culture, their expressions, how they are, what's allowed and what's not. And then mixed it up with your beliefs and your own culture. You don't need to change the essence of who you are, you just need to understand other people and their ways.

My advice, if you are closed minded and don't like change, then moving to another country is not your thing. Being able to adapt, respectful, patient and friendly is key to being a successful migrant. And if you're a woman, being strong emotionally also plays its part. Now, don't get me wrong, I'm not saying that we are emotionally unstable, I'm looking at it from the side that society nowadays asks much more from a woman. we need to raise a family, work long hours, have everything done at home, etc. and balancing that is really hard, especially being far from your family and friends. So, if you move to Ireland alone, it is important that you seek friends, don't stay at home all alone by yourself, because then it gets harder to enjoy being in such a lovely country. Irish people, for the most part are really nice. But as with most places, there are lovely people and there are really despicable ones. Mostly though, they are kind, supportive and are always willing to give you the information you need. This goes especially for matters relating to migrating and the necessary paperwork. Trust me, I have being completing paperwork and more paperworks since I'v been here and they are really friendly, they respect you and they will help you in everything you need.

*There is a worldwide momentum for gender pay-gap, do you think that women have suddenly started to speak up in demand of effective change, or do you think that men have only started to pay more attention and listening more to women?*

Women have become more vocal in the last few years. I think we became tired of being underestimated. Everything started with 'we can do it and better' attitude, and since then women worldwide have more jobs and more equality. We used to be low profile and do our job, then go home and take care of our family, because that was the main reason why we were working: to be supportive. But societies have changed, we are speaking up and demanding an effective change in the business and political world. We just don't work because there is a salary anymore, we do it because it's a professional advantage, because we want to be more, to learn more and be successful in our careers and be in that world that was once dominated by men only.

I read the following quote in a newspaper not so long ago.
**"Less women workers, lower women's wages and fewer female business leaders is not just bad for women, it holds back economic growth, meaning lower living standards for all'** ...

And I couldn't agree more. The fact is that in many countries, there are fewer numbers of women working or working less hours. The worst part especially in Ireland, there is an even bigger disadvantage and that is if you have children, and I think this is because Ireland remains one of the most expensive countries for childcare. The financial constraints can be discouraging for the stay at home parent – often women - to return to work rather and to just stay at home. I'm talking from experience, because ignoring the benefits of my educational and work background with regards to raising a child. I'm staying at home to take care of our son as we don't want to spend big money in a creche costs because it makes no financial sense. So, that is something to consider when you want to have a family in Ireland.

*Do you think that Ireland has done more to protect the rights of women? If you answered yes, in your opinion —why are there so many stories about domestic violence? If you answered no, then what do you think Ireland should do more to protect women?*

As well, I think that because we said, 'enough is enough.' We are starting to speak more about being mistreated, reporting physical & sexual violence to the authorities. We are speaking up. I believed that in this point, the authorities in Ireland are a little bit behind. I think, they don't have a proper way to collate statistics because agencies are not interconnected. You see, I come from a country where the mentality is 'machista' a belief system that men are superior to women. And even though society is changing and improving, there is still a number of men that have this mentality and that is the root cause to a lot of the reported cases of violence.

If they put a good system in place and all government agencies being interconnected, a better job can be done from the moment that a person goes to the police up to the point of arrest. Definitely, it will help to have better statistics, and therefore, to know how big the problem is and to put a plan of action in place.

*What has been a defining moment in your life/career or business since living in Ireland? (b) If you could have breakfast with any three Irish women, who would you choose and why?*

I think a defining moment in my career was when I started volunteering for Foroige, I love the work that they do. I think, if there was more Youth Projects, we could continue aspiring for a better world. I know it sound cheesy. But working with people that want to change, wants to make a difference and they want to look forward and have a better future is amazing. For me, working with such marvellous people is a plus. They improved the experience and increased my knowledge about the Irish system. When I first arrived, I didn't know anything about the schools in Ireland, about their children. I didn't know about the systems that they have and much less about the crime or the work that the Gardai does. It was remarkable and fulfilling.

**If I could have breakfast with any woman in the Republic of Ireland? That's a tough question as I have so many, but in my top 3 list, it would have to be: -**

Dr. Nora Khaldi: I love her work, she is using a combination of AI and DNA analyses to discover new disease-beating functional ingredients in food that have various therapeutic qualities, including the management of chronic metabolic syndromes. I'm a nerd (even my husband calls me that sometimes) and I don't mind. I wear that label with pride. I enjoy reading, research and I admire the idea that there is a women innovating and helping others at the same time. Absolutely love it, it's really inspiring.

Ciara Donlon: I think her work at Theya Healthcare is amazing. As a women diagnose with breast cancer, when the doctor gives you the news there is nothing to think about and you say yes to surgery straight away. The big problem is the aftercare, not just physical, it's psychological as well. And believe it or not, having the right brassier is a self-assurance, even a confidence booster and all the better if it's also designed for the comfort to damaged post-surgery skin. I have a couple of them and are amazing for radiotherapy as well.

Mary Robinson: I love her work in Human Rights. Specially all her work for women. I admire that she was the first woman to do to accomplish so much: like being the first female President, the First female Chancellor of Trinity College, etc. Her work on humanitarian issues is vast and I would love to know more in dept about her work in The Elders.

*"When Nelson Mandela brought us together as Elders, he did so in the belief that together we are stronger, that change happens when people collectively take action to make our world a better place." – M.R*

*The government recently launched 'Project Ireland 2040', which the Taoiseach said is a document about building a republic of opportunity. Have you seen this document, if so do you think that in its mapping there is provision to create an enabling space for migrant women to be heard and lead? (b) The Prime Minister is the son of a migrant father from India, does this alone give you the slightest hope for the future of the children of migrants in this country, and why? (c) If you have the power to change anything in Ireland, what will that be?*

I think that when Project Ireland 2040 is complete, there will be a lot of opportunities for everyone, especially people that want to work and make Ireland a better place, regardless of which nationality or background they have. With this Project, the Government wants to spread equality around Ireland, not just Dublin or major cities. Once the objectives are met, it will mean more work, more opportunities, enterprise, housing, better childcare... helping all women around Ireland to be able to work and manage their time better. And that's important, especially for women like us that want our children to have a better chance and better place to grow & live in. And what gives me even more hope is the fact that the current Taoiseach is the son of a migrant father from India which means your ethnic background doesn't matter. What truly matters is who you are, your achievements and the change that you want to be. He could be your child, my child, someone else's child that has a parent from another country, or even both parents. So just knowing that fact alone gives me the hope that my son someday has the opportunity to grow up and aspire to be whoever he wants to be, without fear from prejudice, and be proud of his heritage and background at the same time and use it to help others.

***If I had the power to change anything in Ireland***, it would be housing development. We are at a point where that the average rent in Dublin is approaching €2000 per month, despite the fact that a vast majority are paying such high figures, banks are still reluctant to provide mortgages. If you do the simple maths: €2000 x 12months equates to €24,000 a year. Mortgages are usually for 30 years, so that gives you €720,000 over that period. Imagine what a lovely mortgage we could have. But between the banks reluctance to give mortgages and the lack of housing stock entering the market, many people are on the line of being homeless. I really don't understand how this is possible. It's also really hard to be in a country for such a short period of time, because you haven't had enough time to save up the required deposit your options are limited... you just keep paying rent and it is a vicious circle. I've heard of a lot of people returning to live with their parents, to afford them the opportunity of saving money. But that doesn't apply to everyone, especially if you have children and would be even harder if you are migrant family with no other relatives in the country.

# *Esther Ewulonu*

*"The lack of support and appreciation by one another is causing migrant women to compete against each other and dragging down the other instead of standing by each other or simply be a helping hand."*

*M*y full name is Esther Ewulonu. I have been living in Ireland for 16 years. My occupation is in Human Resource Management Administration. I'm the author of the book 'Building a Family of Greatness', published by Skyline Publishers in 2017.

My favourite food is 'White Soup' known as Nsala soup. My favourite drink is water  and African Palm wine.What I miss most about my country is the fresh organic food from the farms, such like the Ugu vegetable and Ugu flower leaf that people in my area uses in making a special soup called "okpoko", good for treating high blood pressure as it is usually cooked without adding salt.

I also miss our cultural integration, freedom of business as it easier to set up a small business (kiosk) right in the front of your residential home, selling grocery products. Usually small but it empowers and helps the housewife to earn some personal money. What I like most about our host country - Ireland, is their advanced development in infrastructure, security, education and health management etc.

*What are some of the most challenges faced by migrant women in Ireland? (b) What advice would you give to young and upcoming migrants women?*

One of the most challenges faced by migrant women I believe is citizenship empowerment: As Irish law implies; if one is not documented by law, it bridges women success of advancement like in the labour market from being fully employed to earn a living. It also deters people not only from other good things like education, integration and some other incentives or the right to participate in certain things like political empowerment programmes. Another challenge is culture shock: Many migrant women find it difficult to comprehend with the Irish culture, like the Irish religion, language/ accent, integration, mixing in the society with other Irish women, and socialise the Irish way. Family issues are also challenge factors for migrant women: In my African culture for example, women take care of the children, mostly men will be out to get the jobs while the woman stay at home to take care of the kids, but in this process use it as an advantage to punish women. Some men are not good at helping out domestically and this ties down women from advancing in their careers, forgetting that most migrant women here have no relatives to help them out and the cost of hiring a baby sitter is at all-time high. There are other challenge factors also, like relationship issue/marriage issue; some young and single migrant women face so many challenges here before they can even be legally documented, as a result, men use them and dump them with children. Many single mothers due to wrong marriage or contract marriage and some women end up in wrong marriages which sometimes lead to domestic violence. Then, there is the financial issues; many migrant women are financially handicapped, and as a result, it bridges their career advancement, some end up in doing menial jobs to earn a living even though they are professionals, but the labour market has failed to recognize them even after retraining here. Competition is another issue: The lack of support and appreciation by one another is causing migrant women to compete against each other and dragging down the other instead of standing by each other or simply be a helping hand. Some Irish/European Law also pose a big challenge for migrant women trying to secure professional jobs with the only exception in the healthcare sector. This affects not only migrant women, it affects the men too. Most of migrant people are highly educated, unfortunately they can't find the jobs that matches their professional qualifications and that can be very depressing.

My advice to a young migrant woman is to be well skilled and educated and try to gain experienced in her chosen careers. Live within the laws and be properly documented. Work towards becoming self-employed because in my opinion, that is better than working for someone else. Identify your talent, remain focused and have faith in God because with God everything is possible.

*There is a worldwide momentum for gender pay-gap, do you think that women have suddenly started to speak up in demand of effective change, or do you think that men have only started to pay more attention and listening more to women?*

Gender pay gap issue has been around for long. Women have not suddenly started talking about men getting higher pay for doing the same job. This was started with research and analysis, evaluating wages and incentives in the labour market long ago. But men have been given authority over women in all aspects of life right from the beginning of time and being leader of the family. Society has it that men are more responsible with the financial responsibilities in the family, and for this reason they should earn higher salaries. Even in a family where a woman is enumerated higher than a man, I mean for example, where a woman earns €50,000 per anum and the man receives €30,000, the woman is more inclined to pocket the money for her own upkeep and demand excessively from the man as he is the head of the family. Some women will only use their money when the man is no longer able to help. In my opinion, I think that in some cases men are treated as tin-gods just because they do not exactly go on maternity leave or excuses to take the children to hospital appointments or have minor sicknesses like monthly period that often keeps some out of work for some days.

Men are seen to be always there to turn the company around with their smart ideas and brilliant knowledge and bring in the profits, that is why they get paid higher than women. But, this issue is not new to men either, I feel it is also affecting them because these women are their wives and daughters whom they expect to bring home good wages. This issue has been overemphasized, analysed and evaluated and many have come to the notion that women are gender discriminated on same job pay by men. This equal pay thing for the same job has started as early as in 1957 according to the Treaty of Rome 1957, article 119 which treats the principle of equal pay for equal work, to express anti-discriminatory law in the UK. The first British legislation was the equal pay Act 1970, Amended by the Equal Pay Amendment Regulations 1983. Even primitive age, women were subjected to glass ceiling effect, putting them in a job position where they cannot achieve their career expectation at work, doing the lower jobs like typist, nursing and cleaning so that they can go home in time to take care of their families, children and cook for their husbands while the bigger job positions are left for men as a giant tool of success for an organization. (Jill Rubery 1992 stated why women jobs are undervalued than that of the men.)

*Do you think that Ireland has done more to protect the rights of women? If you answered yes, in your opinion —why are there so many stories about domestic violence? If you answered no, then what do you think Ireland should do more to protect women?*

Ireland has done enough to protect women in the society and they have brought the issue of women's right to be debated about in schools, religion and in the employment sector. There are legislations guiding women from domestic violence. Family issues are sometimes left for family members to deal with especially in the homes of most migrant people and the police are not allowed to intrude unless where matters have become very serious and need to be investigated, in some case where the man or woman involved who is the bone of contention needs protection orders or restraining/removal orders to prevent the perpetrators from having further contact with the victim of the abuse. This legislation of Protection against Violence Act was first enacted by Australia, and other European countries like Germany and Ireland adopted it. It gives a Judge power to protect women from violence and meet their needs (The Book of "Building Family of Greatness"), 2017 by Esther Ewulonu, Domestic Violence, page 134 to 135. There is a helpline for domestic violence at so many public buildings in Ireland, for example in health centres where the report on domestic violence can be logged. A report can also be made through word of mouth where you see something is wrong and you report to the right department.

There is also a sexual harassment bill, where women who have been abused or raped can log their case. The employment law is there; workers who have been bullied, harassed or humiliated logged their case for investigation (The Ombudsman). Some departments in Ireland offer quality education on domestic violence, creating awareness for such issue for people to look out for signs of domestic violence on people. ("The Book of Building Family of Greatness"), Signs of domestic violence, page133 to page 134. Domestic violence is a worldwide issue, it does not happen only in Ireland. It also happens to men.

*What has been a defining moment in your life/career or business since living in Ireland? (b) If you could have breakfast with any three Irish women, who would you choose and why?*

A defining moment in my life since I came to Ireland is the quality opportunity I have been given to raise my children. With the help of facilities and the advanced infrastructure here has given me the opportunity to take care and manage my family on my own without the need to hire a house help like we are used to in my country. It is my greatest achievement so far, (Building Family of Greatness). Another defining moment is the opportunity to work with the local authority here in Kildare County Council years back as an admin officer, it gave me an opportunity of growth and exposure to management/making corporate life, and also, the opportunity to advance my career/retraining and live my life in peace. Another defining moment of my life here was when I had the opportunity of being documented legally. I have made friends with people from other nationalities as I can see myself now as a diverse person.

I would love to have breakfast with Brida, an Irish woman who was my supervisor in school, she is lovely who helped me to integrate
Well with the Irish culture.

*The government recently launched 'Project Ireland 2040', which the Taoiseach said is a document about building a republic of opportunity. Have you seen this document, if so do you think that in its mapping there is provision to create an enabling space for migrant women to be heard and lead? (b) The Prime Minister is the son of a migrant father from India, does this alone give you the slightest hope for the future of the children of migrants in this country, and why? (c) If you have the power to change anything in Ireland, what will that be?*

I don't really know much about project Ireland 2040 but with the little research I have made, I think it is a government project aimed for economic/ rural development and for population management in future. I don't see where it is directly connected with migrant women. However, any developmental project in Ireland which is meant to benefit its citizens must be enjoyed by all who are legally resident in the country either through employment, education or where our voices can be heard. There is no special legislation for migrant women here and even in other European countries and elsewhere, as soon as one becomes an Irish citizen, that person is automatically covered by Irish law. An adage says that when you are in Rome, you behave like a Roman. It is left to us as migrant women to figure out how to reach some departments to get what we want.

# *Jane Beatrice Ejim*

*"Being an immigrant means you can bring your distinct experience and perspective to situations, which can help to bring about the changes we all desire in our society."*

*I* am Jane Beatrice Ifeanyi Ejim (a.k.a. Jane Ovbude). I am a motivational speaker and Author of the book, Halo Life book of poetry. I am a student of the Bachelor of Business Marketing in IT Tralee, Kerry Ireland. I am from Umuahia, Abia State, Nigeria. I live in County Kerry, Ireland. In Nigeria I studied Accounting and Finance, worked in Contact Marketing as marketing coordinator in sales and promotion. I also did Personal Buying and Selling. In Ireland, I trained in Community Development, to become an Accounting Technician. I started and managed a retail shop for three years and I am now back to studying. My hubbies and interest in creative writing. My writing is predominantly on human interaction and Social cultural behaviour. I also fancy writing about human interactions with nature.

In 2006, I started a writer's group in Kerry called Tralee Diverse Writers Group. I am a member of Kerry Women Writer's Group;

member of Toastmasters International, Tralee branch and have been involved in many community groups in both Kerry and the rest of Ireland. I have published four books including works in poetry, short story and non-fiction. I have contributed to four other books including two Kerry Anthologies, 'Behind the Faces' by Tralee International Resource Centre (TIRC), and 'Close to the Next Moment' by Judy Randolph who is a New York-based author). I contribute occasionally to local radio stations - Radio Kerry, also Magazines and journals for international human rights organisations, Red Cross, UNICEF, Amnesty International, etc. I have presented the popular 'Sunshine Africa Show' on Diversity Community Radio (DCR) Ireland, found and produced by the initiator of this book, Carol Azams.

What I miss most about Nigeria is my native Nigerian food. I eat green, and I love nature. Nigeria has so much naturally grown wild fruits, exotic nuts, shrubs and herbs, and wild / naturally grown vegetables, so much variety of food prepared with natural healthy and spicy ingredients and so much variety to choose from. My favourite are: Ugba garnished with Stockfish or Garden Eggs as a delicacy, and then Garri served with any soup, (mainly okazi soup or ofe akwukwo (okro soup made with spinach). With the availability of African and Asian ethnic shops in Ireland I still try to maintain cooking Nigerian food. I grew up with homemade food which entails a lot of cooking though, but I enjoy cooking, and glad that my children can cook as there is less natural food in the Irish market. I miss natural drinks like pure naturally produced Palm wine and sobo drinks which I cannot get in Ireland. Natural palm wine straight from a palm tree is something you cannot carry with you or have a close alternative without preservatives. But for the Sobo drink, I'm able to use the dry flowers to make the drink at home. However, living in Kerry made me discover Dingle. Dingle is a town with proud natural food tradition. Dingle in particular has developed a reputation with its own beer (Tom Crean's), and also local farm produce. Another thing I miss much about Nigeria is the pressure-free lifestyle. There is less pressure to get around with daily life. The lackadaisical attitude to life in general by the majority does however results in general less structured Political, Cultural and Coherent Religious Framework. One might argue on the one side that having a loose structure paralyses a lot of activities in a society and the economy as a whole, as there is no one art of systematic unified body of knowledge to be sustained in the long run. This in one way makes the argument logical, yet on the other hand, there is less pressure and therefore better mental health enjoyed by members of the Nigerian society. I therefore always return home to have "a breath of fresh air" from daily pressure and routine of life pursuits for perfection and endless constant correction of some costly mistakes made in those pursuits which do impact on people's sense of peace and mental health.

In Ireland, what I like most is the communal effort to put value on life, and constant effort to sell these values to everyone politically, socially and religiously. This is something to treasure about Irish culture. The people of Ireland also make so much effort to preserve local treasures, values, social system and settings. All these keep me happy in Ireland because; Ireland as a nation, is a community that values people's contribution towards saving lives, and towards any overall community welfare in general. Any effort made by an individual to create and make an impact positively to the life of others, and also towards preserving cultural artefacts, are always treasured, valued and rewarded

*What are some of the most challenges faced by migrant women in Ireland? (b) What advice would you give to young and upcoming migrants women?*

Migrant women can be placed in two separate blocks, and could be viewed from different lenses, depending on what angle you are viewing from. The first block is the migrant women who came from their own country to live in Ireland (The first generation migrant /immigrant). The second block is the children and grandchildren of the first generation migrants (The second and third generation migrant women). Within the first block you are categorised as either, migrant, immigrant, refugee, asylum seeker, visitor, tourist or student (any of these set of category defines you the same person at different times in the same country in different ways).

While within the second block, you are usually a citizen or waiting for some document to be financed: Thus you get questions like, you are a citizen? But where are you originally from (this is not peculiar to Ireland, I could say it happens in most part of the world, my home town/country not excluded).

**Institutionalised Racist Streaming:** Institutionalised words that distinguish people creates barriers and boundaries for people in a society and this affects either positively but most other times negatively on how people define and see themselves and their identity. For example, in some official forms which ask applicants to fill their place of birth or state of origin, the same form could ask for 'state of origin' and 'nationality'. It's easy for me to state my place of birth or state of origin as Nigeria, and nationality as Irish because I was born in Nigeria and now live in Ireland as an Irish citizen.  My daughter who was born here in Ireland will hesitate to write down Nigeria as her state of origin even though she knows that her parents are Nigerians, because she grew up here and knows Ireland as her state of origin and not Nigeria. This is the same with the other Irish citizen children whose parents are from other countries originally. But these different kinds of criteria hampers people's confidence even as they become adults and leaves them with questions about their real identity in the country they are born in, work and live in. So, the category in which a migrant fall can determine the challenges they have, and it depends on what lenses we use to look at it. I am saying lenses again because, how people are classified officially are different from how ordinary person in the street sees and behaves towards them.

**The different lenses that we use to view migrant women can be based on any one of the following:**

1) Which continent have they come from?
2) Which race do they belong to?

3) What is their skin colour compared to the skin colour of people where they live.

4)  Do they fit in as diplomats, migrant workers, immigrants, asylum seekers or refugees? All of these have different political connotations and social labelling, cultural stereotypes and affect women in different ways.

5)  Are they First, Second or Third generation migrant woman.

**Gender social spacing:** There is a gender- social-interaction gab that I notice in Ireland, (which is not in Nigeria). In third level institution, male and female students seem less likely not to socialise together in Ireland. This is also evident in the work place. This could be because of the following reasons: -

Firstly, Irish historic association with the church and secondly the single-gender school, and finally the culture of grouping, and being sensitive to what others say. These affected how the boys interact with the girls in the society. If then there is a culture of boys only, and girls only, it might affect employment decision making, depending on who makes the top decision on a job recruitment panel.  If women in general faces this gender gap issue that widens the gap of social interaction for them, it will in turn have a negative impact on their opportunities as immigrants, both to have fewer social group to interact with and also lessen their opportunity to get their desired type of job. Again, the cultural clash for the younger immigrant child is living in between these two social interaction cultural differences and norms. For a second and third generation young immigrant securing a job is another huge employment problem. Ireland has a documented policy of balance equality in job opportunity for all. The existing informal network, (which is usually a universal problem) does not exist for second generation immigrant.  At first time job seeking, getting a job through connection of parents and grandparent and family links, do exist in most societies, Ireland is not an exception, with an estimated 70% of jobs filled without advertisement. This then becomes a challenge for the second and third generation young immigrant as they get set to launch into the labour market. When the refugees are dispersed, when of the criteria used is to allocate them evenly to all cities and town in Ireland, but then when the refugee families settle in and gets set to seek for employment, they have less opportunity to get jobs in smaller cities and towns than the non-immigrants.

Career Choice grouping: Grouping people according to nationality and career choices in the national census results in labelling. This has a profound impact on the choice of courses, work and careers that migrant women find themselves pursuing. The majority of individuals tend to follow societal expectations of them depending on the group they have been classified into. The effect of not following societal expectation, is the fear of ostracization (for some), from one's own internal community or close family, this may limits people's ability to reach their full potential.

**Casual comments and behaviour:** Furthermore, the use of casual but confusing and sometimes offensive comments by everyday people in the street is not documented. It is either being neglected or not noticed. For example, my daughter who has lived all her life in Kerry still comes across people who have the habit of asking , if she liked living here in Ireland.  If I was the one who got asked these types of questions, at least I have somewhere else to compare Ireland to, which is Nigeria.  But when the same question is directed to her, she does not have anywhere else to make that comparison.  On one of many incidents, someone made a comment about her having a good command of the English, my daughter didn't understand what the person meant, and her comment that day was that old people 'are so weird,'  I do get this said to me many times, as a 'nice gesture' I assume, but meaning I am expected in the first place not to have a good command of English. These comments are made casually, but it's necessary we pay attention to them because they shape people's experiences and affect their relationship with other people.

Another example is, on the street, people hesitate to ask you for direction or correction if they are lost based on the look, even if you are more knowledge than who they presume might know better.

One other of those informal behaviour towards the immigrants, is the selection of word like, ' emm do you—understand what I mean, how can I explain it for you to understand', and so many others .

Lastly forwardness to correct and direct: there is this internal block to understand what the immigrant is saying, replacing it with constant correction of what he or she thinks that you should say. This makes communication uninteresting and most times annoying. Amongst the young ones, I have noticed the immigrant teenagers withdrawing from their peers because of internal and informal competition of who is better or smarter based on race.

For young girls to excel, they must first see themselves as human being in that definition of human being regardless of how the society defines them, and this must be reflected on how the society sees, defines and treats first generation migrants who needs to be fully integrated in the real sense of it, without fear of meeting obstacles in things like admission into schools and job searches. For the first generation immigrants, this ignorance maybe understandable, but for the younger ones brought up and raised in the same society, same in the same cultural and social setting, it may not make sense to them, but rather cause tension, division and widens the gap of integration.

Having said all this, a young migrant woman who wants to excel needs to open her mind to see everything, hear everything, go everywhere they can; meet and face challenges, but at the same time make their own conclusions and draw boundaries, by listening to their own voices. If she has a heart and mind that yearns for a particular career and study, then nothing should stop her from achieving it. Lastly, everyone is different in their own way. Being an immigrant means you can bring your distinct experience and perspective to situations, which can help to bring about the changes we all desire in our society. Migrant men have held top positions in Ireland, but migrant women have yet to do so.

*There is a worldwide momentum for gender pay-gap, do you think that women have suddenly started to speak up in demand of effective change, or do you think that men have only started to pay more attention and listening more to women?*

To be heard, you have to firstly speak up, but to make a notable difference you have to be at the helm of affairs or be heard by somebody in the highest authority. The first woman TD was Constance Markievicz, elected in 1918 to the 1st Dáil Éireann. After 100 years, just under a quarter (22.2 %,) of TDs in Dáil Éireann were women (114 women ) in 2016', according to Central Statistics Office, it means that women are making progress politically in Ireland but slowly . Ireland has not experienced the leadership of a Female Taoiseach since its institution in 1922, and why? Women making a difference started by women getting to the top position of being TDS, Presidents, and Ministers, including Company Directors and Entrepreneurs. On issues concerning women it takes women bringing men on board, and at the same time women being key decision makers, for those changes to take place.

With regards to the gender pay-gap in Ireland, the Central Statistic of 2016 in Ireland stated thus: That in 2014 on the average, women were paid 14 per cent less than men compare to a 12 per cent in 2012. The latest data from the Central Statistics Office, shows that pay differences are widening. The figures are based on gross hourly earnings, so, despite improvements in other areas of gender equality in Ireland, this gap has been growing." According to the Irish times (2018 ) the CSO figures show that more than 55 per cent of all women aged 25-34 years had a third-level qualification in 2016, compared to 43 per cent of men in the same age group. So, women have made strides in education, but that is not translating into earning power.' I believe there is an hour-gap rather than pay gap which makes it look like a deliberate discrimination against women, in Ireland, which in my opinion it is not.

**There is a pay gap (based on gross hours earned) due to the following reason:**
1)  The number of women versus men who chooses to stay at home
2)  The different job types taken up by the different genders
3)  The difference in hours put to work by women versus men

4)     The possibility of women working outside home, town or home country compared to men (migration/immigration)

5)     Principal economic factors – more men aged 15 and above are more likely to make money earlier than women and therefore keep those job longer, while women either pursue higher education or branch out to have babies.

On gender equality in Ireland, the CSO statistics of 2017 shows that Ireland was eighth highest in the EU on the Gender Equality Index of 2015 with a score of 69.5, where it indicates total inequality and 100 indicates gender equality. This was above the EU average of 66.2 (https://www.cso.ie/en/releasesandpublications).

Personally, I think that Ireland has a strong system of equality in place for both men and women, migrant and Irish nationals with the exception of the institutionalised record streaming. It impacts negatively on women by the interpretation or meaning given to those names especially by those who sits in authority. Which also comes into play when deciding who gets what.

*Do you think that Ireland has done more to protect the rights of women? If you answered yes, in your opinion —why are there so many stories about domestic violence? If you answered no, then what do you think Ireland should do more to protect women?*

Ireland as a state has done much to protect women's right. The latest abortion referendum has been a long fight for the right of women, finally many thinks that the yes vote reflects the voice of the majority of the women. Examining who brings change to Ireland and who needs protection, needs to be explored more. The general protection comes from the constitution, but it is the community and human rights organisations and voluntary groups like, Amnesty International, The Voice Ireland, Social Justice Ireland, to mention but few, that push for changes through the leaders and political parties. I believe that they are therefore the change makers and the voices that protect and not the constitution, and they in turn needs more protection also. So, less power and less funding for these groups mean less protection for women. This is because research suggests that there are more women in community groups and voluntary non-paid jobs than men. Again, Ireland has done well politically but there is a cultural norm that need to shift. But until we highlight the cultural vices, we will not have a solution to those problems.

Followings are examples of some cultural vices that lead to domestic violence against women:

1)   Culture changes but very slowly. The culture of women not to speak out or speak out and be the 'odd' or 'the guilty one' is still very much prevailing in Ireland. This allows for continues domestic violence.

2)   Women's nature to protect and nurture: It is in women's nature to nurture men and protect their weak points. This makes women vulnerable to these men who capitalise on our nature and use it against us, rather than loving and caring in return.

3)   Emotional involvement and fear of losing what you have: Everyone likes to hold onto what they value and treasure. In my opinion, women get more emotionally involved in anybody they have sexual relationship with than men do, so while it means love for a woman to be in sexual relationship with a man, it might not really mean love or emotional involvement to the same extent for a man. Knowing who loves you and who you really love is naturally harder for women to decide than it is for men.

4)   Training, love, protection and control: Are women and men taught the difference between love and control before going into a relationship? While it is in the nature of women to love and nurture, men have it in them to protect and control, so, until men are taught the differences between love and control, domestic violence may not be easily curtailed.

5)   Parents role in their children's life: Children are bound to copy the behaviours of their parents. So for example, if a mother happens to be the type that accept and tolerates abuse in a home, a daughters will most likely convince herself that it is the best thing to do when and if it happens to her.

The same point applies to the man, if a young man sees his father beat and molest his mother/ wife at home, he could grow up believing it is hard to control himself from abusing a women even if he disapproves of this behaviour (on the positive side however, it could be a reason for him to be more protective and loving to women). Attitudes of people in every community have to improve with unspoken values and prevailing cultures passed on from generation to generation, which changes gradually and very slowly over time and it requires more women to make changes through the home, school, community groups, rather than state laws.

*What has been a defining moment in your life/career or business since living in Ireland? (b) If you could have breakfast with any three Irish women, who would you choose and why?*

The first defining moment for me was starting up my own business in Kerry, 'African Ethnic Shop' (Afro-Euro Fresh food store), although the business is no longer in existence. I went to one of the banks to ask for a loan, to start this business with my then loan officer after having a chat with me and going through my documents, he was forced then to reveal to me, that based on his training and information on the system from the central office, that I did not qualify for a loan because of my country of origin, (Nigeria). However, in his kindness, he said 'but I will make an exception and recommend you for this loan.' I was given the Business loan from the bank. I was also advised by a Kerry business owner to go for three or six month's 50% credit from a supplier, I managed to negotiate up to 80% credit for six months. This made me believe that even if institutionalised discriminating policies and laws do exist and undermines immigrants' contribution to the economy, one can still succeed through persistence only if they keep trying. Sometimes the gender is a help rather than a deterrent. In my opinion, there are lots of men out there who are willing to assist and help a person simply because that person is a woman.

Secondly, when Father Padraig O'Fiannachta an outstanding Irish scholar and traditional publisher published my second book, 'Triad of poetry and stories' it was a turning point for me in my writing career. Another time I went to the University of Maynooth in Kildare, with him for a Christmas Carol Service, the level of honour showered on him by his former colleagues (where he studied, and taught for 35 years), was stunning .The memory will stay with me even though he is gone. Thirdly, Dr Rayna selected my book 'Halo Life, book of poetry' for his PhD drama directing project. When they presented the drama based on the book in Killarney library on 17th May 2016, I embraced the fact that creative writing chose me, and since then I have continued to obey the call of creative writing.

If I get the opportunity, I would love to have breakfast with Mary McAleese, former president of Ireland. She is focused, fearless, articulate, and a very simple and elegant lady and leader.
I would also love to dine with Mary Lou McDonald, current Sinn Fein party leader. Mary McDonald is sound, fearless, articulate, and humane and does not bend the truth. I see her as somebody who works for the good of others even though her party remains a controversial one in Ireland. She also has a very pleasant voice.
Meeting Caroline Casey in an event was breath taking for me. She is enthusiastic, always on the go, doesn't see boundaries but open doors, she speaks for the inclusion of others, and a cup of coffee with her would be, heaven on earth.

*The government recently launched 'Project Ireland 2040', which the Taoiseach said is a document about building a republic of opportunity. Have you seen this document, if so do you think that in its mapping there is provision to create an enabling space for migrant women to be heard and lead? (b) The Prime Minister is the son of a migrant father from India, does this alone give you the slightest hope for the future of the children of migrants in this country, and why? (c) If you have the power to change anything in Ireland, what will that be?*

I have seen the draft, but I am yet to make full sense of it. On a general note, national constitutions and policies accommodate certain types of immigrants and do evaluate their true financial and cultural contribution. There is a blanket label of immigrants as takers rather than givers. Economist through academic journals do however highlight the value of the contribution of immigrants to a society... 'The Economics of Immigration' By GEORGE J. BORJAS University of California at San Diego.

Democratic states including Ireland, make effort to protect the right of immigrants to exist in the state, but existence is not the same as living. Having said that an ordinary person regarded as a refugee, migrant worker or immigrant do not have the same protection or right as an external investor whose defined interest is solely to invest or create job in the state, this is also the same as taking the resources of a society by way of exchange. Though they both give-and-take but are not regarded as such.

*If I could change anything in Ireland,* it would be the educational system. I think that the educational system should separate and clarify the role of the parents and that of the teachers, especially at primary and secondary level. The system teaches children right but not responsibilities to the parents and the society. The school system interferes on how parents should discharge their duty and responsibilities to their children on areas where they should not. The state as a system cannot play the role of parents in the life of the children through the teachers. Therefore, there should be clear boundaries and roles of parents and teachers to the children. There should be genuine unity of purpose also, and that purpose should be not to punish the child but to assist the child become a better person so that we will have better parents and leaders of tomorrow.

Lastly, most parents are afraid not to hurt their children's feelings and thereby not raising children that should value and appreciate the effort of their political leaders, parents and teachers to create a better society for all.

# About the Editor & Initiator

## Serial Entrepreneur
## (Publisher/Writer/Broadcaster)
### *Carol Azams*

The Idea of this book is the brainchild of fellow-migrant woman Carol Azams, a business woman and community organizer, who is originally from Nigeria and Irish by citizenship. She is the owner of Skyline Publishers, and herself a published author of over 8 titles, ranging from Young Adult novels to a series of non-fiction books including her soon to be released new offering that is all about Ireland, containing brief information about nearly everything that you need to know in a flash about Ireland.

The upcoming book is titled, **'The Emerald Isle: Ireland's Information made Simple.' Its foreword is written by the Irish Prime Minister Leo Varadkar TD**, who commends Carol's effort in putting together such a useful book. It took her over 2 years to fully assemble it. "I am very proud of it—I call it my gift to all Irish around the world." Carol is also the founder of Ireland's popular multicultural festival (Ireland's Festival of Nations) which started in 2016 through Diversity & Multicultural Initiative, a voluntary organization that she formed in the same year. She is a known media personality among Ireland's new communities, with many years of experience as a Radio Broadcaster, researcher, with fine interview techniques & sound-editing skills. She works the mixer so well that she considers herself 'a walking Radio Station.'

A few years ago, she started an online media platform known as Diversity Radio & Diversity TV—better known as Ireland's multicultural station. Earlier in the year, Diversity Radio was granted on-air broadcast license by the Broadcasting Authority of Ireland (BAI), unfortunately, the service could not take-off because it lacks financial strength expected to be fully operational. However, the process of a new temporary license for the new year is ongoing as Carol look forward to continuing with her team.

Carol Azams is a highly creative, energetic, hardworking and enthusiastic individual. As a Social Entrepreneur, she is open to new opportunities that will help her business to grow, and as a community organiser—she is always looking for something new and worthwhile to involve herself. Carol has been in Ireland with her family for more than 15 years. She is a married mother of 5 amazing children aged between 28 and 16 years.

# Notes

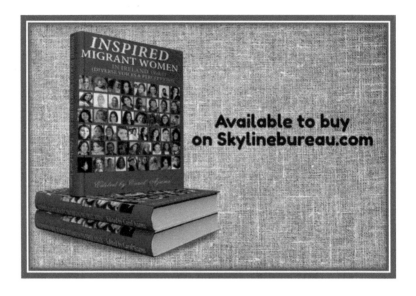

Lightning Source UK Ltd.
Milton Keynes UK
UKHW020642170219
337352UK00008B/53/P

9 780995 534988